Real loss is only possible when you love something more than you love yourself.

Someday We'll Be Together

Chapter one

After being handed lengthy prison sentences for the murders of the wealthy Arab Sheik Abdullah Hussein, and the corrupt British Foreign Minister Sir Geoffrey Fitzgerald, Dee Dee and her two friends were taken directly to HMP Holloway. Built in the 1850's, and once home to the suffragettes, the prison had also detained Ruth Ellis - a name synonymous with Holloway and still echoing to this day. Charged with the murder of her on-off lover David Blakely on Easter Sunday 1955, Ellis's enduring notoriety hinges on the fact that the Welsh born nightclub hostess unwillingly became the very last woman to be executed in the United Kingdom. The approach to the stark Victorian building conjured visions of a once brutal regime to all that entered those sinister gates.

Under Dee Dee's strict instructions, the three, housed in separate cells, kept their heads down and became model prisoners until eventually their obedience was rewarded and the close friends were reunited. Although after their very first night together in almost a year, Dee Dee and Maizie confessed they would rather share a cell with a criminally insane serial killer, than spend another night with their hapless friend Trisha who had kept them awake half the night with her now trademark nonsensical ramblings.

'All ar was tryna say Dee,' Trisha said, whilst brushing her teeth in the stainless steel corner sink, 'is that,' she gargled and spat before continuing, 'don't knock me tuna and peanut butter cookies til ya'v tried em. Ar flogged a load of em at me nan's old folks ome, ar got two quid a piece for em off the coffin dodgers ar did. Mind you ar coulda shit on a biscuit and they woulda paid for it the senile old sods.'

'Trisha!' Maizie said, holding her head. 'I aint slept a bleedin wink wiv you chattin shit all night, woss a matter wiv you? Don't you sleep for fuck sake?'

'Ar fink iss me nerves,' Trisha confessed, 'ar still aint got used to this place, it freaks me right out. I ad to stay awake in me last cell coz that fruit loop they stuck me wiv told me she bashed er own muvva's ed in with a nammer coz of er snorin. Well, me ex Gavin told me ar sound like ar'm garglin nuts and bolts when ar'm asleep so ar fought there's no friggin way ar'm kippin wiv that nut nut in the same room. You awake Dee?'

Dee Dee lifted her head from her pillow and glared bleary eyed at Trisha. 'Ar swear Trish if I ad a nammer right now ar'd cave your fuckin ed in meself. You aint shut the fuck up all pissin night, me ed's proper bangin wiv all your shite.'

Trisha dried her face, shrugging off her friends harsh remarks, and set about rearranging the cells limited furniture. 'Be nice if we ad bean bags wunnit?' she said, dragging a chest of drawers across the floor making a shrill squeaking noise that penetrated deep into Dee Dee's already throbbing head.

'TRISHA!' she barked, hurling a pillow in Trisha's direction. 'WHAT THE FUCK ARE YOU DOIN?'

'Feng Shooey,' Trisha said, turning the chairs to face the window. 'Ar read a pamphlet on it at the doctors once when ar was waitin to av me gromits done. Anyway, they reckon if ya furniture's all fucked up, all ya positive energy's goin out the winda, and if ya leave ya karzi seat up it goes daan there an'all. Iss proper intrestin stuff ar tell ya. Next time ar go for a smear or summink, ar'll pick one up for ya.'

'Don't bovver!' Dee Dee said. 'I aint interested in that shit, iss all bollocks if you ask me.' She kicked their one and only chair across the cell and then proceeded to stub a big toe on

the leg of her bunk. 'Arrrrrgh fuck it!' she cursed, 'fuck, fuck that urts!'
Trisha folded her arms and gave her friend a knowing look. 'See!' she said smugly, 'you've upset the feng shooey and now look woss appened.'
Dee Dee made a grab for her friend, but it was only Maizie's timely intervention that saved Trisha from an impromptu beating.
'Dee leave er!' Maizie said, restraining her enraged cell mate. 'It aint werf it mate, a'rll av a word with the guvna later see if she can av er moved to the psycho wing or summink. Let them ed cases put up wiv er.'
'Oh don't be like that,' Trisha moaned. 'We're mates aint we. Ar tell ya what Dee, you can ave mar bacon this mawnin ow bout that ay?' She held out a reconciliatory hand. 'Alright you can av me fried slice an'all, ar can't say fairer than that can ar Maizie.'
'Just stay out of er way till she calms daan will ya,' Maizie told her, pushing Trisha aside. 'You do it all the bleedin time dontcha.'
'What?' Trisha said, unaware of any wrong doing. 'She's always like this in the mawnin, aintcha Dee, you sure you're gettin enough vitamins? Me muvva used to tell me that if...'
'SHUT UP!' Maizie then yelled, clenching a fist herself. 'We don't bloody care what ya muvva, or yer auntie, or ya bleedin step bruvva's sister's cousin's fuckin nan said. ALRIGHT!'
Trisha took a step back looking down her nose at her two friends. 'If you ask me you two need to get an early night or summink, coz you're ratty as fuck when you ain ad no sleep aint'cha.'
Maizie could feel her blood pressure elevating. 'The only pissin reason we ain ad no sleep is coz some RETARD kept us up arf the night CHATTIN SHIT!'
It was now Dee Dee's turn to physically restrain Maizie, although a huge part of her wanted to let her go and assist with the beating.

'Ar'm goin for brecky,' Trisha said, hearing the neighboring cells being unlocked, 'you two comin or what?'
A burley prison officer opened the observation hatch before jangling her keys and opening the cell door.
'Mawnin!' Trisha said cheerfully, slipping by her and heading for the mess hall.
'What's the matter with you two?' the officer asked Dee Dee and Maizie, who were both white with rage and physically shaking. 'You look like shit, if you're having trouble sleeping, go see the doc she'll give you something for it. Now get a move on. I said NOW!'
'Whateva!' Maizie barked, barging past the officer, her nerves well and truly frayed.
'Trouble sleepin!' Dee Dee scoffed, following her friend. 'Listen to me geeza bird,' she said, pausing at the door, 'unless that dyke doc of yours has got a sawn off shoota, a nine mill or a friggin baseball bat, she aint no use to me. You got that?' Trisha had once again riled her soul and cell mates to intolerable levels, straining the now fragile fibres of their friendship to near breaking point, and all this with unwitting ease.
'Watch it Dawson,' the officer warned, receiving a defiant shoulder barge from the irate inmate. 'You three can always be separated again, one word from me that's all it takes.'
'Oh yes please!' Dee Dee called over her shoulder, clasping her hands in prayer.
Bemused by her remark the officer went about her duty, content just this once to let the insubordination slide.
'Dee they got bubble!' Trisha told her friend from within the queue, 'wiv onion gravy an'all.'
'Sweet,' Dee Dee replied, still miffed as she took a tray and joined Maizie at the rear.
'Double bubble love!' Trisha said, passing her tray across the counter whilst stood behind a huge twenty eight stone fellow prisoner. 'Mawnin,' she said, attempting to strike up a conversation, and reaching to tap at her rounded shoulder.

'What?' the woman snarled, looking round. 'What d'you say?'

'Ar said mawnin,' Trisha reiterated. 'Listen, I ope you don't mind me sayin but ar couldn't elp noticin you're carrying a coupla'v extra paands raand ya back end aint'cha. Now ar know iss none of mar business but ar reckon if ya cut down on ya carbs the weight'd drop off you in no time. Me auntie Joan cut out the pasta, pizza and pancakes and the paands fell off er, she looks like a bleedin racing snake now ar tell ya. Give it a go ay, you aint got nuffing to lose av ya?'

'You takin the piss!' the woman said, turning to face Trisha. 'Coz if you are, ar'll break your fuckin neck!'

Dee Dee and Maizie, being some way back in the queue, hadn't noticed the altercation and chatted amongst themselves. The woman that Trisha had inadvertently aggrieved was a category A lifer, Kathy Bennett, serving time for the multiple murders and mutilations of five Malaysian businessmen during a botched robbery in the mid nineties. Slightly unhinged with rage issues and acute schizophrenia, Kathy had bullied, beaten and bribed her way to the position of top dog at Holloway, a position that had remained unchallenged for some twelve years.

'You know ar could give ya summink for them black eds an'all,' Trisha said, eyeing Kathy's neglected complexion, 'toof paste and vinegar, me cousin Shelly swears by it.'

Kathy took a moment to process Trisha's insane behavior, having never met anyone brave enough to criticize her outward appearance. 'See you!' she snarled, setting her tray down, 'ar'm gonna teach you some fuckin manners, and believe me you fuckwit, it aint gonna be pleasant.'

Trisha flinched, unable to retreat through the shuffling queue.

'Bennett!' a passing prison officer barked, 'move it or you'll spend another night in the hole!'

Kathy growled under her breath, lowering her hand and taking her tray. 'Can I av a drop more gravy love?' Trisha asked, offering her tray back across the counter whilst keeping a watchful eye on the simmering Kathy. 'Ar'll ava a buttered bap to mop it up an'all.' She then reached out for an empty plastic mug to be filled at the tea urn in the corner of the mess hall. 'Oh shit, shit!' she cried, as the tray, heavily weighted on one side slipped from her hand. 'Bugger it!' she added, scrambling to retrieve it in a blind panic, but she could only watch in horror as her plate of hot bubble and squeak fell to the linoleum floor with the ladle and a half of steaming gravy splattering the tights of the peeved prisoner in front.

'FUCK, WHAT THE...!' Kathy shrieked, flinging her own tray to the floor and shaking her legs. 'Jesus, you burnt the fuck out of me you stupid bitch!'

Many of the surrounding inmates backed away, wanting no part in the ensuing melee, having witnessed Kathy's violent retribution on many occasions.

Kathy snatched at Trisha's slender neck dragging her face toward hers with glaring eyes, steadily increasing the pressure until she was unable to cry for help. 'You're gonna get daan there you slag and lick that shit off mar legs d'you ear me. And then ar'm gonna beat the fuck outta ya for muggin me right off you stupid little twat!'

'OY LUMPY!' Dee Dee called from the back of the queue. 'GET YOUR FUCKIN ANDS OFF ER!'

Kathy looked up, stunned at first that anybody would dare intervene. 'Which wunna you slags said that?' she asked, with the petrified Trisha still hanging from her hand. 'Come on, who was it ay?'

'Me, you fat ore!' Dee Dee said, stepping forward. 'Now let er go before ar get proper pissed off, and believe me you really don't want that to appen.'

Kathy raised a smile assuming the pretty Essex girl was high on contraband vodka, which was readily available to the inmates at a price - injected into citrus fruits and smuggled in amongst food parcels, the illicit liquor was traded amongst the girls for cigarettes, chocolate and in some cases sexual favors.

'Ar'v erda you,' she sneered, 'you're that Dee Dee Dawson tart aincha. Not so fuckin high and mighty now are ya. You done a coupla two bob murders and fink you can come in ear an av it large. Well listen to me you gobby bitch, do yaself a favor, turn araand and piss off back to ya cell before you get a taste of what's comin to this cunt.'

Dee Dee pushed several inmates aside approaching the hulking harridan. 'Ar tell ya what,' she said menacingly, 'ar'm gonna give you the same choice, drop mar mate and do one, or you'll get a taste of mar right hand you lardy twat!'

Those around them gasped at Dee Dee's blatant audacity, some relishing the thought of a riotous brawl that would give them the opportunity to even a few scores with the thuggish prison guards who would surely rush to quell the disturbance.

Kathy released Trisha's throat and watched her drop to her knees massaging her reddened neck and gasping for breath. 'Thas right sweetheart,' she said, stooping to snarl in Trisha's face, 'get down there and lick mar fuckin legs clean. Go on you piece a shit.'

Dee Dee snatched an aluminum ladle from a startled kitchen assistant and raised it above her head. 'Step the fuck away from er right now!' she snapped, with Maizie standing steadfast behind her, although a little apprehensive.

Kathy, whilst smirking contemptuously, raised a foot pushing Trisha to the floor and grabbed a steel tray from the counter. 'Ar'm gonna enjoy this,' she said through yellowing teeth, whilst flicking her lank hair from her eyes. 'Ar run this poxy gaff and every slag in it, and that includes you ya ponce, d'you ear me.'

'BENNETT!' the returning officer yelled, catching sight of her wielding the tray. Dee Dee quickly handed the ladle to Maizie who slipped it back onto the counter unseen.

'Piss off screw!' Kathy growled, without taking her eyes off Dee Dee.

'Bennett put it down right now,' Kathy was told once again by the approaching officer, who flicked the catch releasing a can of Mace from her utility belt. 'I will spray you if I have to, you know that,' she added, taking her radio from her shoulder strap and calling for assistance.

'Ar told you to piss off did'n I!' Kathy said, shaking the tray in the officer's direction, 'go on, jog on like a good little girl or you'll get some an'all.'

'Bennett, I'm warning you, put it down. NOW!' the officer insisted, taking aim. 'Or believe me I will be forced to spray you, and you've had a taste of this before haven't you.'

'You aint got the bollocks,' Kathy laughed. 'You dumb dyke, look atcha, dressed up like Johnny fuckin Bravo. Who d'you fink you are, tellin me what to do, AY? Now fuck off outta mar face before ar tear you a new arse ole.' Kathy swung the tray wildly at the steadfast officer who side stepped the onslaught and emptied half her can of incapacitating Mace into her aggressor's eyes.

'Arrrrrrggghhhh! You fuckin fuck!' Kathy screeched, dropping her tray and covering her face. 'YOU BITCH, YOU DYKE BITCH. AR'LL FUCKIN KILL YA!'

Unable to see through streaming eyes, Kathy began lashing out with her feet and fists catching one or two bystanders in the process. By this time five more officers had stormed the mess hall, breaking up the gathered crowd and grabbing Kathy's flaying limbs, with two of them receiving crushing blows to the face from her clenched fists.

'GET OFFA ME!' she screamed. 'GET THE FUCK OFFA ME YOU BASTARDS, AR'LL KILL THE FUCKIN LOTTA YA!'

Eventually, with more reinforcements arriving, Kathy was wrestled to the ground and subdued. Her arms and legs were bound with cable ties to prevent further injury, and she was then dragged squirming by six prison officers across the polished mess hall floor to the elevator that led to the basement level, and the solitary confinement cells.

'YOU'RE DEAD DAWSON!' she screamed, her eyes blood shot. 'DEAD, D'YOU EAR ME, AR'M GONNA CUTCHOO IN ARF YOU SLAAAAAAAAG!'
Dee Dee stooped and helped the now sobbing Trisha to her feet. 'You alright mate?' she asked, examining her friend's throat. 'Did she urtcha?'
Trisha stood shaking with her head bowed.
'Come ear,' Dee Dee said with her arms outstretched, 'come on mate.'
Trisha paused for a second before hugging her friend as tightly as she possibly could, finding some comfort in the closeness but still trembling and slowly going completely to pieces.
'Shhhhh, shh shh. Oy calm daan, iss alright,' Dee Dee told her reassuringly, 'Trish mate, iss alright ar promise.'
Maizie assisted by rubbing Trisha's back whilst keeping a watchful eye on the poised prisoners around them.
'D, D, Dee mate,' Trisha stammered, with her face buried in Dee Dee's shoulder, 'ar wanna go ome, ar wanna go ome. Please mate, ar wanna go ome.'
'Shhh ar know, ar know ya do,' Dee Dee said, choked at Trisha's heart felt plea. 'Ar know mate, ar'm sorry ar got you into this shit, ar really am.'
'Come on Trisha mate,' Maizie said, taking another plate of bubble and squeak from the counter, 'get this daan ya, you'll feel a lot better, onest.'
'Ar can't, ar can't do this anymore!' Trisha said, breaking away and sprinting back towards their cell.
'TRISH MATE!' Maizie called after her, 'TRISHA!'
'Leave er,' Dee Dee said, taking the plate from Maizie, 'she's just shook up thas all, she'll get over it.'
'She won't Dee,' Maizie replied, shuffling along behind Dee Dee. 'She aint gonna be able to do anuvva ten to fifteen years of this, ar know that. She aint like us, she puts on a brave face but she's fragile as fuck, aint she.'
Dee Dee said nothing, knowing full well that Maizie was right; Trisha was a sensitive girl with moments of sporadic

madness that would surely land her in hot water again and again during her stay at Holloway, and the next time she might not get off quite so lightly.

Meanwhile, Trisha had slammed the cell door closed behind her and leapt into her bunk, pulling the sheets up over her head.

During breakfast, one of the involved prison guards, a gaunt emaciated sixty-something approached Dee Dee and Maizie's table. 'I'm watching you Dawson,' she said, toying with her night stick, 'I run a tight ship here and I don't want it rocked by the likes of you. D'you hear me? Bennett might be a bastard, but she keeps the other girls in line, so my advice to you girl is to keep your mouth shut, your head down and get in line with the rest of them.'

'In line!' Dee Dee said, gripping her fork tightly. 'Is that what you call it. Well ar'm tellin you summink mate, she aint keepin me and mar mates in line thas for sure. She's obviously got you lickin er arse, so you can tell er from me she can go fuck erself. Now jog on will ya, ar'm eatin.'

The officer was indeed on Kathy's payroll, seeing to it that her reign of fear and intimidation went unhindered, and warning her in advance of any cell inspection so that her stash of narcotics and alcohol could be distributed amongst her willing minions for safe keeping.

'Now you listen to me!' the officer said, rapping her stick on the table.

'No!' Dee Dee said, grabbing the officer's wrist. 'You listen to me. Whateva you come ear to say, save ya breff, coz it ain appnin, alright!'

Dee Dee's aggressive stance suddenly had the aging guard rattled, feeling altogether uneasy and thinking twice about her approach.

'Well, just watch it!' she said, pulling away, 'that's all I'm saying.'

'Save it will ya,' Maizie said, sipping her tea, 'we aint listnin!'

The officer left, humiliated somewhat. 'What are you looking at?' she then yelled at a sheepish young inmate in

an attempt to reassert herself. 'Eat your damn breakfast then get back to your cell. ALL OF YOU!'
'They aint gonna keep that ed case locked up forever Dee,' Maizie told her friend, with Bennett in mind. 'We'll av to watch er, she's the kinda bitch that'll stick you in the back and fink nuffing of it.'
'Yeah ar know,' Dee Dee agreed, having tangled with the likes of Kathy in the past. 'She's probly got a few Labradors araand er an'all.' She was referring to Kathy's subservient followers on the wing, each at her beck and call at the click of her bloated, smoke stained fingers.
'We can't fight em all though Dee, can we?' Maizie added, as they sat among the hundred or so women, wondering how many of them were loyal to the Holloway hard nut.
'We don't av to,' Dee Dee told Maizie, returning the stares of several on the adjacent table. 'If we take out the big lump this lot'll roll over, you'll see.'
'I ope you're right mate,' Maizie said, eyeing a particularly aggressive tattooed bunch of shaven headed bull dykes. 'Uvverwise them rug muncha's are gonna eat us alive, ar swear ar can feel em undressin me wiv their eyes the dirty bitch's, they gimme the proper eebie jeebies they do.'
'Listen!' Dee Dee said, slamming the palm of her hand on the table and turning a few heads in the process. 'You aint gonna get lezz'd up ya doughnut, coz we aint gonna lose, d'you ear me? Don't you worry abaat that fat bitch, ar'v met er type before, all maaf and no knickers. Believe me, she gives it all the biggun, but ar reckon when it comes to a proper row she aint got the arse ole for it. Yeah she can use a blade or a nammer, but any cunt can do that can't they. You get er in a bare knuckle barney mate and she'll crumble, ar betcha.'

That afternoon Trisha refused to leave the safety and sanctuary of their cell to visit the exercise yard, stating to the guards that she was sick and needed to rest.

Dee Dee and Maizie paced the green tarmac marked out for netball and hockey, as a cold North Easterly blew the leaves from an avenue of Poplar trees growing outside the perimeter fence into their faces.

'Bet you wish you was sittin at ome by ya pool, don'tcha Dee,' Maizie said, blowing into her hands. 'Me and Enrique are normally ollidayin in the Maldives abaat now.'

'Speakin of Enrique,' Dee Dee said quizzically, 'where the fuck is e and why ain e bin to see ya?'

'Oh er,' Maizie replied, knowing that Enrique, her lover and F1 driver, had taken her incarceration badly, to the point of never visiting the UK, not even to take part in the British Grand prix at Silverstone, for fear of tarnishing his good name. 'Ar know e'z busy,' Maizie continued, 'e'll turn up when e gets time, you'll see.'

'Listen, e'z got all the bleedin time in the world ya daft cow,' Dee Dee said, confronting her friend. 'They aint got no Grand Prix at the moment, even ar know that, so where is e ay?'

'Alright, alright!' Maizie stormed, taking an envelope from her pocket. 'If ya must know e'z dumped me. E couldn't andle the fact that ar got meself banged up when we ad our ole lives togevva planned out. There, now ya know, you appy now?'

Dee Dee stood speechless for a moment. 'Oh,' she eventually said, taking the envelope from Maizie's hand, 'you never said nuffing did ya. Ar fought you bin a bit moody the last coupla days, are just put it daan to ya mumfleys or summink.' Dee Dee opened the letter and took a moment to read Enrique's pathetic attempt at letting her friend down gently. 'Prick!' she sneered. 'Spineless twat!' she later added, shoving the letter back into Maizie's hand. 'You wanna bin that, coz that nob aint werf cryin over believe me. If e couldn't come visit ya to tell ya face to face, then e'z some sorta c...'

'Yeah alright Dee!' Maizie said, stopping Dee Dee in mid sentence. 'Ya right, but it still urts mate. Ar loved im, just like you loved Travis. What the fuck went wrong, tell me ay? We ad everyfing we ever wanted, now look at the free of us banged up wiv fuck all to show for it. Trisha, the poor cow's, goin raand the bleedin bend in ear, and we won't be far behind er at this rate.'

'Yeah alright, alright ar'm sorry,' Dee Dee said, putting a hand on Maizie's shoulder, racked with guilt at having led the three of them to a life behind bars, and a miserable one at that.

Usually Dee Dee could figure a way out of the most difficult and challenging of situations, but at that moment in time she was all out of answers. 'Come on mate,' she said, kicking at the crisp autumn leaves and desperate to lift the mood, 'ar give you a game of table tennis, it's fuckin freezin out ear anyway.'

'Yeah alright Dee,' Maizie sighed, tucking the note back into her pocket, 'looks like iss gonna piss daan soon an'all.'

The two girls spent the remainder of the day working up a sweat in the games room, an altogether brief but welcome and much needed distraction.

'Four free!' Maizie yelled, retrieving the ping pong ball from beneath the sofa, 'you're goin daan Dee.'

'You reckon!' Dee Dee said, returning a blistering serve. 'Cop that bitch!' she cursed. She eventually cruised to victory in a thrilling ten eight tournament, leaving the pair of them sitting breathless at the side, grinning at each other having shed their earlier anxieties.

'We aint done that in ages av we,' Maizie said, wiping her sodden hair from her face. 'Ar'm proper fucked now though, ar didn't realize ow out of shape ar was. Blimey ar used to be able to go for hours over the community center.'

After their shower and a hearty evening meal, Dee Dee and Maizie returned to their cell for lockdown.

'Trish mate, ar brought ya some spag boll,' Maizie said, setting a plate down beside Trisha's bunk. Trisha hadn't surfaced from beneath her covers the entire day. 'Trisha, come on mate, you must be Ank Marvin.'

Dee Dee lifted the corner of Trisha's sheet and peered beneath. 'Trish come on, iss alright mate, they locked that fat fuck up in solitary this mawnin. Come on, eat this while iss ot.'

Trisha was indeed famished but her nerves were well and truly rattled. 'I aint comin out,' she told her friends, pulling the sheet tight around her neck.

'Oh alright then,' Maizie said, winking at Dee Dee, 'ar'll av to eat this roobub crumble meself then.'

'What!' Trisha said, poking her head out. 'You never said nuffing abaat roobub, thas mar favrit that is.'

'Yeah we know,' Dee Dee told her, 'and cold custard, wiv the skin on an'all, just the way you like it. Now scoff ya spag boll, then you can av yer afters alright.'

Trisha tossed her sheets to the foot of her bunk and sat bolt upright forking huge balls or twisted pasta into her mouth. Dee Dee and Maizie watched their friend devour a mound of spaghetti Bolognese topped with stinking parmesan, before tucking into her rhubarb crumble with hardly a breath in between.

'Ar got ya wunna these an'all,' Dee Dee told her, tossing a large Spanish orange onto her bunk, 'ar blagged em off a coupla tarts on the pool table earlier.'

'No fanks Dee,' Trisha said, licking custard from her chin and turning her nose up, 'ar don't really do fruit mate, not since me auntie Rose swolla'd a peach pip and nearly choked to deff on the bleedin fing, if me uncle Teddy never got er from behind and shook the shit out of er she'da bin a gonna ar tell ya.'

'You'll like this one,' Maizie said, taking one for herself and squeezing the juice through a hole into her mouth. 'Vodka an orange, niiiiice!'

'What!' Trisha said bemused. 'What you on abaat vodka?'

Dee Dee took a cup from Trisha's bedside, punctured the orange with her nail and squeezed out the spirit laced juice. 'Just get this daan ya neck,' she said, handing it to her.

'Corrrr bleedin ell Dee, thas strong as fuck that is!' Trisha said wincing. 'Jesus ar tell ya what mate, ar wouldn't mind growin summa these buggers meself.'

Dee Dee decided under the circumstances to let her traumatized friend believe that it was in fact Mother Nature that had provided the oranges alcoholic content, instead of the inmates smuggling relatives.

'Yeah me an'all,' Maizie laughed, 'ar'd av an ole bloomin orchard of em me.'

The combination of a filling meal, a large vodka and orange and her friends at her side went some way to allay Trisha's fears, but not entirely. 'Ar don't like it ear Dee mate,' she said, tearing open the orange and ripping out the innards with her teeth. 'It scares the shit outta me.'

'Look!' Dee Dee told her, while mutilating her own orange. 'As long as we stick togevva we'll be alright believe me. If them fuckers out there fink we're proper nut jobs they'll leave us alone, ar promise ya.'

'Well she aint got nuffing to worry abaat then has she Dee,' Maizie laughed, 'she's as mad as a boxa frogs aint she.'

'I ad a frog once!' Trisha told her friends, who were both seated on her bunk.

'Oh shit,' Maizie said, wondering what proverbial can of worms she had just opened.

'Ar called im Tyrone after im offa Corrie, ar dunno why e just ad that look abaat him.'

Although Dee Dee shared Maizie's exasperations, on that occasion she was content to let her friend waffle with a free rein.

'E could narf jump ar tell ya!' Trisha continued, mimicking her amphibious pet with her hand. 'Ar used to find im all over the ouse ar did, in me nicker drawer, me coat pocket, e even done a spin cycle wiv me double duvet in the bleedin washing machine the silly little sod.'

'What, and e survived?' Maizie asked, unwittingly drawn in.

'Yeah proper ard e was,' Trisha replied, 'ar say was coz e fucked imself in the end when e tried to back stroke in the deep fat fryer, ar didn't bury im though, ar give im to the dog coz we'd run out of pigs ears. You member mar black pug Denzil don'tcha, e used to make a right racket chewin them poxy fings on the patio. Ar do miss Tyrone wiv iz funny little face and wonky legs, not me frog, im offa Corrie, e aint bin in it for ages as e the funny little fella, always looks like e'z just licked a bleedin battry if you ask me.'

Dee Dee and Maizie had both failed to grasp the relevance, if there were any at all, to Trisha's twisting and, as many would agree, twisted tale.

'I ope they bring im back,' Trisha added, licking the peel dry. 'Flippin ell this is proper goin to my ed ar tell ya,' that being their first alcoholic drink in quite some time, 'got any more?'

'Eeya av mine!' Maizie said, handing over her orange. 'Ar reckon you need it more than me.'

'Oooh fanks!' Trisha replied, tucking in greedily. 'Nom, nom, nom!' she laughed, with juice trickling down her chin. 'Shame we ain up West, ar could get right on it now ar tell ya.'

'Ar know what ya mean,' Dee Dee agreed, missing their raucous nights out; slamming countless tequilas, guzzling Grey Goose and coming home in the early hours with either a boozed up boy on their arm, or a burger and a busted heel.

'We ad a laugh dint we,' Maizie said, reminiscing. 'Member when you broke ya big toe on that traffic cone Dee, flippin ell, ar pissed meself laughin.'

'Yeah!' Dee Dee snapped, recalling the unfortunate event. 'Ar was gonna hoof the flippin fing up in the air but some funny fucker ad stuck the poxy fing over a concrete bleedin bollard, fucked up me Jimmy Choos and busted me toe to bits. Good job ar was absolutely ammered on Absinth at the time, ar dint feel a fing till the next mawnin. But ar tell ya what it urt like fuck then believe me, member I ad to go to Benidorm with that dirty great boot fing on.'

'Not arf!' Trisha giggled, now inebriated somewhat. 'When you stacked it daan the stairs at Stansted ar was laughin so much ar farted and folla'd fru in me fishnet frillies. Ar proper bunged up the bog, dint I, flushing the flippin fings daan the karzi. I ad to go commando dint I.'

The girls sat chatting well into the small hours, with Trisha occasionally breaking into spontaneous song waking the neighboring inmates in the process.

'Trisha, shut the fuck up will ya!' Maizie said, attempting to cover her friend's mouth with her hand.

'Ar'm alright, ar'm alright!' Trisha slurred. 'I O SILVER LIIININ, ANY WHERE WE GO LA LA LA, CHEER UP SLEEEEPY JEAAAAN, OH WHAT CAN IT MEAN LA LA LAAAAAAAA!'

Footsteps could then be heard approaching and the tell tale jangling of keys.

'Shit now look what ya gone and done!' Maizie said, covering Trisha's face with her pillow.

'Alright Miss!' she said, as a prison officer burst in. 'If ya come to collect the ironin iss at the end of the bed there, oh and try not to burn the fuck outta me crutchless crusties next time ay.'

'What's all that noise!' the officer barked. 'It's half bloody four in the morning, and you're keeping the other prisoners awake.'

Trisha tried to mumble the words, 'piss off ya ponce,' under the pillow, but her attempts were stifled by her friend's firm hand.

'What was that?' the irate officer asked. 'What did you say?'

'Nothing Miss,' Dee Dee laughed. 'Goodnight. Don't let the door it yer arse on the way out will ya.'

'Watch it!' the officer said, pointing her stick at the girls. 'If I ear another peep out of you three there'll be trouble believe me. Now get to sleep, all of you!'

Maizie had to all but suffocate Trisha to keep her quiet as the officer left, slamming the door behind her.

'Stuck up twat!' Trisha eventually said, breaking free in a sweat. 'Who does she fink she is, ar'll kick er fuckin arse. OY AR SAID AR'LL...'

'Shut it will ya!' Dee Dee said, undressing. 'Get some bleedin kip will ya, them bitches'll be wakin us up in a coupla'v ours.'
'Yeah Trish ar'm knackered mate,' Maizie told her, 'thas enough karaoke mate, go to bleedin sleep.'
'But I aint tired!' Trisha said, flinging her arms about the bunk. 'Ar bin in bed all day. WOAAAAAOW LIVIN ON A PRAAAAAYER TAKE MY AND AN AR'LL MAKE IT AR SWEAAAAAR, WOAAAAAOW LIVIN ON A...'
'Trisha for fuck sake!' Dee Dee said, beating her with her pillow. 'Thas enough!'
'OK, OK!' Trisha said, defending herself. 'Ar'll shut up ar promise.'
'Good!' Dee Dee and Maizie both said, climbing into their bunks.
Trisha settled down closing her eyes and letting out a contented sigh. 'SWEEEEEET CAROLIIIIIIIINE, OH OH OHHHHHHH!' she then yelled at the top of her voice.
Which was followed by a resounding, 'SHUT THE FUCK UUUUUUP!' from many on the wing, equally unimpressed with her vexing vocal range.
'TRISHAAAAAAAA!' Dee Dee and Maizie screamed.

The following morning Maizie woke followed by Dee, the pair of them stretching their backs and yawning while their friend lay in her bunk snoring loudly.
'Look at er,' Maizie said, wanting to slip her hands around Trisha's throat and squeeze the life out of her. 'Ar've ardly slept again Dee, me eyes are angin out me ed.'
'Ar know the feelin mate, believe me,' Dee Dee croaked, donning her prison issue trousers and vest. 'Look at this shit,' she said, tugging at her clothes. 'Ar've seen pissed up tramps wearin better clobber than this.' Dee Dee shoved her sleeping friend, 'Oy silly bollocks, get the fuck up will ya, the screws'll be openin up in a minute.'
'Ohhhh me ed!' Trisha whined, opening one eye. 'Get me a cuppa tea Dee mate please.'

'You're avin a laugh aintcha,' Dee Dee scoffed. 'After what you put us fru last night, get up and get yer own friggin tea and while yer at it, get me and er one an'all. Iss the least you can bleedin do.'

'Yeah two sugars,' Maizie said, pulling the covers off Trisha. 'Come on ya lazy cow, get yer arse in gear.'

'I aint goin out there!' Trisha said, tugging at the sheets. 'Carn ar stay in again.'

'No ya can't!' Dee Dee snapped. 'You're comin wiv us, we gotta show them bitches that we aint scared of no one, d'you ear me. Now get up!'

'Oh flippin ell,' Trisha moaned, dragging herself begrudgingly from her bunk, 'but Deeee.'

'But nuffing!' Dee Dee growled. 'You're comin and thas that, alright!'

Without warning Trisha then dropped her knickers and lowered her bottom down onto the cold stainless steel pan in the corner of their cell. 'Jesus ar'll end up wiv pissin piles if I av to do me business on this fing much longer, pass the bog roll will ya Maize mate.'

'Get it yaself,' Maizie said, heading out the door with Dee Dee in tow. 'And flush that flippin fing will ya, ar don't wanna find a floater starin at me when ar lift the lid later do I.'

'Oh Dee pass the bum roll,' Trisha begged, 'the turtles ed's out already mate.'

'Like Maizie said Trish,' Dee Dee laughed, 'you can get it yaself, and don't forget to spray that freshner gear when ya done ya smelly cow.'

'Dee, Dee ang on mate!' Trisha cried. 'Deeee please mate, ar can't reach it, DEEEEEEEEEE!'

Dee Dee and Maizie savored the moment with a broad smile walking to the mess hall picturing their stricken friend on the pan.

The pair were already seated with their fried breakfast at hand when Trisha arrived looking altogether flustered. 'Fanks alot!' she said angrily, 'I ad to pucker up me bum ole and mince across the cell for the bog roll cozza you two, that was bang out of order that was.'

'Oh shut up, you ad it comin,' Dee Dee told her, spooning beans into her mouth. 'Get ya brecky, sit daan and stop bleedin whingin will ya.'

Trisha took her place in the queue paying close attention to the inmate in front of her, not wanting a repeat of the previous day's performance. 'Mawnin,' she said sheepishly.

'Oh morning!' the girl replied, stepping aside and giving up her place in the queue.

'Iss alright mate you crack on,' Trisha insisted, 'ar can wait.'

The girl, knowing that Trisha was part of Dee Dee's firm, smiled and left in a hurry to join the rear of the snaking queue leaving Trisha bemused. 'Ooh er!' she said, taking a sly sniff of her armpits. 'Weird!'

'Yes love what can I get you?' the caterer asked, rolling up her starched white sleeves. 'We've got bubble and squeak on special today with a lovely drop of gravy.' The specials menu often consisted of the previous days leftovers.

'Er no fanks,' Trisha said, giving it a wide berth. 'Ar'll just av the corn flakes an a cuppa rosy cheers, ooh ang on!' she added, eyeing the fried selection on display. 'Gissa coupla slices of black puddin an'all will ya, to dip in.'

'Dip in!' the woman said, scooping two slices of the dried blood delicacy onto a small plate. 'Dip in what?'

'Me tea of course,' Trisha smiled, placing it on her tray and shuffling along leaving the caterer perplexed.

'There's some proper weirdos in ear ar tell ya,' Trisha said, setting her tray down and sitting with her friends, whilst giving the girl at the back of the queue a sideways glance.

'You're tellin me!' Dee Dee said, looking her in the eye. 'What the fuck!' she then gasped, seeing Trisha dunk a biscuit shaped slice of black pudding into her mug of tea.

'What?' Trisha said, taking a bite. 'Don't tell me you aint tried it, corr blimey iss lovely, go on get involved!' she said, thrusting the dripping pudding under Dee Dee's nose.

'Get that shit away from me!' Dee Dee barked, pushing Trisha's hand away, 'you aint right d'you know that!'

'Jesus Trish!' Maizie said, screwing up her face, 'you're an animal mate ar swear it.'

'No, no ar'm not,' Trisha said in her defence, 'ar see this programme once abaat the first world war, apparently our boys used to av it before they went over the top as a last treat in case they never made it, or was it a chocolate digestive, ar can't remember. Anyway, it tastes pukka, you two wanna give it a go.' She then proceeded to spoon milk sodden cornflakes into her mouth at the same time.

Maizie pushed her tray away in disgust having suddenly lost her appetite. 'You not eatin that bacon?' Trisha asked, snatching it from her plate.

'If you dip that in ya tea ar swear it,' Dee Dee warned her, waving her fork in Trisha's face.

'Don't be daft Dee,' Trisha laughed, 'thas just sick that is!' She then left her friends gobsmacked when dunking the streaky bacon into her cereal bowl and licking off the milk.

'Oh leave off!' Dee Dee said, gagging and setting her own fork down.

'If ya not eatin that,' Trisha said, with her fork hovering over Dee Dee's sausage.

'You dare!' Dee Dee snapped. 'Ar swear Trish, ar'll chuck mar guts up all over ya!'

'D'you wanna nuvva cuppa?' Maizie later said, collecting their trays.

'Yeah go on mate, cheers,' Dee Dee replied, handing over her mug.

'Ar'll av one an'all,' Trisha said, draining her mug and spooning out the congealed lumps from the bottom, drawing attention with the resounding rattle. 'Mmmm, thas the best bit that is,' she added.

'Sick fuck!' Maizie said grimacing.

While the three of them relaxed with a second, and then a third mug of tea, a middle aged Asian inmate approached their table, dropped a folded piece of paper beside Dee Dee's hand, and hastily left.

'Woss this?' Dee Dee called after her. 'OY YOU!' she yelled, but the woman vanished into a crowd of milling prisoners.

'Woss that Dee?' Maizie asked, leaning across the table.

'Ar dunno,' Dee Dee said, unfolding the neatly written note.

'Gym, two o'clock, be there!' she read out. 'Woss that all abaat?'

'Who's it from Dee?' Trisha asked, craning her neck to see. 'It aint that big bird Bennett is it?'

'No you doughnut, she's banged up aint she,' Dee Dee told her. 'And it don't say, there's no bleedin name on it.' She scanned the crowd to see if they were being watched by any chance, but saw nothing untoward.

'You aint goin are ya Dee?' Maizie asked, fearing a trap of sorts.

'Yeah we are,' Dee Dee replied defensively, 'ar wanna know what the fuck this is all abaat. Don't worry though we'll be proper tooled up, ar nicked a couple pools balls from the table last night.'

'Oooh yeah pukka!' Trisha said, punching the palm of her left hand. 'Ar could stick em in me stockins and smack em raand the ed if they get larey. A'RM THE FUCKIN DADDY!' she yelled, mimicking a line from the iconic nineteen seventies prison cult classic, Scum.

'Mummy,' Maizie said, nudging Trisha.

'What?' Trisha said, losing her train of thought.

'Mummy,' Maizie said again. 'Itta be "ar'm the mummy" wunnit. You got tits so you can't be the daddy, can ya, ya soppy cow.'

'Shut it you melt!' Dee Dee said dismissively. 'All ar know is we aint walkin in there like mugs wivout a tool, so get yer game faces on girls, coz if fings go tits up in there we gotta stick togevva and fight like fuck, alright.'

'Yeah alright Dee,' Maizie said tentatively, 'if we av to.'

Trisha then covertly slipped a prison issue plastic spoon into her pocket.

'What ya doin?' Dee Dee asked, looking beneath the table.
'Gettin tooled up!' Trisha said, gripping the spoon. 'Them fuckers aint takin us wivout a fight, thas for sure.'
'Jesus,' Dee Dee sighed, realizing her friend was going to be of very little use if things did in fact turn ugly in the prison gymnasium that afternoon. 'OK mate,' she told her with a smirk, 'you just watch what ya doin wiv that fing won'tcha.'
'Yeah,' Maizie laughed, also catching a glimpse of Trisha's pointless makeshift weapon. 'You'll av some buggers eye out wiv it if ya not careful!'
'Thas the plan,' Trisha told them with a determined look. 'Apparently it aint what ya got, iss ow ya use it that counts. Enrique should know all abaat that ay Maizie, bein ung like a soddin goldfish.'
Dee Dee kicked out at Trisha's shins under the table and glared at her. 'Shut it you dozy mare,' she growled under her breath.
'OW, flippin ell Dee!' Trisha cried. 'What was that for, everyone knows Enrique's less than gifted in the traazer department.'
Maizie hung her head with a lump in her throat. 'It wern iz fault,' she mumbled.
'TRISHA!' Dee Dee snapped, slapping her friends arm. 'They aint togevva no more for fuck sake, give it a rest will ya.'
Trisha took a second or two for the news to sink in. 'Shit Maize, you never said mate, did ya dump im coz of iz tiny todger? Ar don't blame ya though, ar mean, woss the good of a chipolata when you've been used to a frankfurter, there aint no comparison is there. Iss like askin for a french stick an gettin a flippin finger roll ain it.'
Dee Dee tried in vain to get Trisha's attention to silence her, but her friend in all her naivety rambled on.
'Ar bet e olds iz dick in four fingers and pisses over free of em,' she laughed, now in full flow.
'SHUT UP, SHUT UP WILL YA!' Maizie suddenly yelled, turning every head in the mess hall. 'JUST SHUT THE FUCK UP!'

'What?' Trisha said, stunned by her friend's outburst and unaware of her own insensitivity. 'Wossup?'
'If you must know, e dumped me,' Maizie said angrily. 'You appy now are ya?' Maizie kicked her chair back scraping the legs across the polished floor and stormed from the table.
'MAIZE, MAIZE OLD UP!' Dee Dee called after her. 'MAIZIE MATE!'
'Woss up wiv er?' Trisha asked, shrugging her shoulders.
Dee Dee gave her yet another of her cold hard stares. 'Flippin eck Trisha, you av gotta be the most...'
'Ang on a minute Dee!' Trisha said, halting Dee Dee's impending abuse. 'No one told me racin boy dumped er did they, ar spoze you knew all abaat it dint'cha. Yeah ar bet ya did, well ar'm ya mate an'all ya know, you coulda said summink, ar feel a proper twat now ar do.'
'Er, yeah well,' Dee Dee replied, seeing Trisha's point somewhat, 'ar fergot din I.'
'Well it aint mar fault then is it,' Trisha said, holding up her hands. 'Don't worry though Dee, ar'll make it up to her. She'll be alright, ar give er a minute to calm daan then ar'll offer er wunna me coconut cremes, iss amazin ow many beatins ar've swerved wiv a biscuit or two.'
'You sure!' Dee Dee said, not sharing Trisha's optimism. 'Ar don't fink so somehow. She's got the right ravin ump ar can tell, ar'd give er more than a minute if ar was you.'
'Naaaah!' Trisha laughed. 'You watch, ar work me magic and she'll be eatin out me hand you'll see.'
Dee Dee and Trisha eventually found Maizie outside in the exercise yard, sitting alone on a concrete step staring into space.
'Alright mate!' Trisha said chirpily, but was then dragged back by Dee Dee.
'Leave er will ya!' she snapped.
'Iss alright Dee,' Trisha said, with her pockets bulging, 'ar got an olive tree.'

'A what?' Dee Dee said. 'You mean branch don'tcha,' she added, figuring her friend was bearing a gift of reconciliation, or an olive branch as the saying goes.

'No mate, ar got the ole fuckin tree!' Trisha said, emptying her pockets onto Maizie's lap; the contents containing chocolate bars of all varieties, crisps, toffee sticks, licorice pipes and her favorite retro sweet - popping candy.

'Flippin eck Trish,' Maizie gasped, 'where d'ya get this lot.'

'The tuck shop, Trisha told her, taking out a final finger of fudge. 'Ar bin savin up the dough they give us for sewin them poxy mail bags, ain I.'

'Cheers mate,' Maizie said, forgetting their earlier altercation. 'Thas proper nice of ya.'

Even Dee Dee had to admit Trisha's gesture went a long way to healing the rift between them. 'Thas pukka that is mate,' she said, patting Trisha's back.

Maizie shared her tasty treats with her two best friends and the three sat ridiculing a group of pigeons fighting over a licorice boot lace.

'So er,' Trisha finally said, her teeth partially gummed with toffee, 'as e got a little nob then?'

Maizie and Dee Dee both looked at Trisha in abject amazement.

'YEAH!' Maizie then laughed. 'As it appens e as!'

The three of then burst out laughing, mimicking Enrique's tiny appendage with a wiggling little finger, their frivolity going some way to mending her broken heart.

'Thas about the size of it!' Maizie chuckled, popping a jelly bean into her mouth.

Trisha sat holding her head after downing a handful of popping candy. 'Shit me ed's gonna burst, elp!' she cried, clenching her eyes tight shut. Maizie laughed, tipping the remainder of the bag into the palm of Trisha's hand.

'No, no, no!' Trisha said, shaking her buzzing head. 'Ar can't, ar can't!'

'Dare ya, dare ya, dare ya!' her friends chanted. 'Dare ya!'

Trisha finally relented and filled her mouth with the exploding candy. 'Shit, shit, shit elp me!' she yelled, rocking back and forth.
Dee Dee and Maizie were in complete hysterics at this point, sharing a second bag between them.
'Blimey this takes me back!' Maizie said, wincing with every pop.
Having devoured the entire sugary feast the girls huddled together watching a family of squirrels on the other side of the fence burying acorns amid the leaf litter in preparation for the long winter ahead, each of them with thoughts of freedom running through their minds.
'Ar be the wrong side of forty by the time ar get out of ear,' Maizie said solemnly. 'Thas me Magaloof days over then ar spoze.'
'Oh ar dunno,' Dee Dee laughed, 'wiv a bitta lippy and mascara ar reckon we could still blag it.'
'You're avin a laugh aint'cha,' Trisha said, jostling her breasts, 'me tits are already goin saaf, ava look!'
'Oh shuttup,' Maizie told her. 'You got the best lils out the free of us, and you know it ya lucky bitch, mine look like ar bin breast feedin a buncha pissed up Brummy brickies ar tell ya.' They then sat comparing breasts and varying degrees of sag for a while, ridiculing one another as friends often do.
'Oy come on!' Dee Dee eventually said, checking her watch. 'Iss arf one, we gotta get goin.'
Returning to their cell each of them armed themselves as best they could in readiness for a possible ambush in the gymnasium; Dee Dee with her pool balls and sock, Trisha with her plastic spoon and hairbrush for backup and Maizie packing a wooden leg broken from their chair concealed within her sleeve.
'Ready!' Dee Dee said, opening the door.
'Yeah fuck it!' Maizie said aggressively. 'Less do this shit.'
The gymnasium was a short walk from their cell and on most days overrun with posing pent up prisoners pumping iron in spandex vest tops and lycra shorts, but on this

occasion the tell-tale clinking of steel weights could not be heard on their approach.
'You alright?' Dee Dee asked her friends, gripping the sock tightly in her pocket. 'Member what ar said, stick togevva, and if it kicks off go nuts and urt as many of em as ya can, alright!'
Opening the door gingerly Dee Dee entered the seemingly deserted gym. Breathing a sigh of relief she turned to her friends to inform them the coast was clear and to stand down, but was immediately bowled over by a raging Trisha barging past her, spoon in hand.
'WHO FUCKIN WANT'S IT AY, COME ON COCK SUCKER'S!' she screamed at the top of her voice. 'COME ON AR'LL CUT THE FUCKIN LOTTA YA'Z!'
'What the fuck?' Dee Dee said, finding herself flat on the floor.
'What ya doin?' Maizie asked, helping Dee Dee to her feet.
'Goin nuts like you said!' Trisha replied, poised for any eventuality.
'YOU TWAT!' Dee Dee growled, lunging at her. 'Ar said IF it kicks off. IF IF IF YOU SOPPY BITCH!' Taking the sock from her pocket she swung it above her head.
'ANG ON DEE!' Maizie cried, grabbing it before it was brought down onto Trisha's harebrained skull. 'YOU'LL BLEEDIN KILL ER WIV THAT FING!'
'AND!' Dee Dee said, wrestling Maizie for possession of the sling-like weapon. 'She's got it comin to er!'
'Dee chill mate,' Trisha squealed, only making matters worse. 'We gotta stick togevva, member!'
'The only stick your gunna get you dopey cow,' Dee Dee raged, 'is the stick ar'm gunna beat yer flippin ed in wiv after ar belt ya wiv this. Maizie let go of me will ya, ar'v ad enough!'
Suddenly a voice from the back of the hall called out. 'Ahem. Good afternoon Ladies.'

Startled, the three squabbling friends turned to see quite possibly the last person they would expect to find in a women's prison.

'Fuckin ell!' Dee Dee gasped. 'Mr Amilton, what the bleedin ell you doin ear?'

'Bloody Nora!' Maizie added, equally stunned. 'What the fuck?'

'Alright Mr H!' Trisha said nonchalantly, as if it were an everyday occurrence. 'Ow's it goin geez?'

'Yes, yes it's going great thank you,' Clive Hamilton, the Prime Minister's nephew and close friend of the girls, replied.

Crossing the gymnasium Dee Dee and Maizie looked at one another bemused.

'Ar don't get it,' Dee Dee said quizzically, 'ar mean iss nice to see ya Mr H, but visitin times are between ten and arf eleven so woss this all abaat then?'

'Please, take a seat.' Clive said, ushering them to a bench beside him. 'Firstly,' he added, 'I must apologise for the rather clandestine nature of this meeting.'

'The what?' Trisha asked, lost from the off. 'Woss e on abaat Dee?'

'E means dodgy,' Dee Dee snapped, 'now shut up and listen will ya.'

'Ow's Crystal Mr H?' Maizie asked, clasping her hands together. 'Is she out of ospital?'

Having been rescued by the girls from their Somali captives, the Hamiltons and their gravely ill daughter, Crystal, had spent several agonizing months in a UK hospital where the child endured hour after hour of intense surgery, with a team of eleven working tirelessly around the clock to save her life, which at times had hung in the balance.

'Yes, yes she is, thank God,' Clive said grinning. 'She's at home convalescing, and doing remarkably well I might add, considering. And I must tell you she talks about you three all the time.' He reached inside his jacket. 'Here,' he said,

handing Dee Dee a folded piece of A4 paper, 'she insisted I give you this.'
Maizie and Trisha craned their necks as Dee Dee opened the gift on her lap.
'Look Dee!' Trisha squealed. 'Iss us free!'
'Ahhhhh,' Maizie sighed, 'thas lovely that it, tell er fanks won't ya.'
Crystal had drawn the three friends from memory using crayons, glitter and coloured tissue paper; capturing each of them remarkably well considering her age.
'Thas gotta be you Trish,' Maizie laughed, pointing out a hapless expression.
'Yeah whateva,' Trisha smiled. 'Ahhh, iss beautiful ain it Dee.'
Dee Dee sat with a tight knotted lump in her throat. 'Yeah, yeah it is,' she eventually said. 'We can ang it up in our cell can't we.'
'Yeah course,' Maizie agreed, 'itta proper brighten up the place wunnit.'
Dee Dee folded it lovingly and set it beside her. 'Make sure you tell er fanks from all of us won't ya,' she insisted. 'Tell Crystal we love it, yeah.'
'Yes, yes of course I will,' Clive said, looking across at the prison officer waiting in the wings before sitting opposite the girls. 'But er, hopefully,' he added, lowering his voice, 'you'll be able to tell her yourselves, which is why I'm here.'
'You coulda stuck it in the post couldn't ya,' Dee Dee said, interrupting the visitor. 'Ow d'you get in ear anyway?'
'Let's just say I pulled a few strings, so to speak,' Clive told them. 'Having family and friends in high places really does have its benefits.'
'So what ar ya doin in ear Mr H?' Trisha asked, twitching impatiently. 'Ar mean by the time we get out Crystal woulda forgot all abaat us won't she, we got a shit load more bird to do ya know.'

'She's right,' Maizie added, 'iss proper nice of er to fink abaat us an all that, but she's got er ole life ahead of er now. Just tell er we fink abaat er a lot an'all, don't we Dee.'
'Yeah course,' Dee Dee said, reminiscing with some fondness. 'Ar'm just glad she's alright thas all.'
'My wife and I,' Clive told them, leaning a little closer, 'have been campaigning tirelessly on your behalf ever since the three of you were sentenced and subsequently imprisoned.'
'Av ya,' Maizie asked, 'oh cheers!'
'Shut it will ya!' Dee Dee snapped, scowling and eager to hear more. 'Go on,' she said, folding her arms across her lap. 'Woja mean campaignin?'
'Well,' Clive continued, 'Sarah and I have written dozens of letters to the home office asking that your case be looked at in more detail, and to convene a court of appeal.'
'Appeal!' Dee Dee scoffed. 'You're avin a laugh aint'cha, we aint eligible, so they say for anuvva five years. So iss proper nice of you and all that, but ar gotta say ar fink ya wastin ya time Mr Amilton. Tell the Misses fanks though won't ya, from all of us.' Picking up Crystal's picture, Dee Dee got up to leave. 'We better go, come on you two.'
'Wait!' Clive said, raising a hand. 'Please hear me out. Granted it did seem like a tall order when we first began, what with the weight of evidence stacked against you, but we stuck at it. After what you girls went through for us and our daughter, it was the least we could do.'
'And!' Maizie said, listening intently. 'Av we got an appeal fingy or what?'
'Please, let me finish,' Clive said, silencing her with a raised finger. 'We both know what Sir Geoffrey did to your friend Travis, and how he left you to perish in that god forsaken land. But convincing my uncle, who I might add considered the Foreign Minister a close personal friend, was indeed a mammoth task. But eventually he bowed to pressure and agreed to look into Sir Geoffrey's affairs. And believe you me he was utterly devastated, to say the least, at the level of corruption unearthed involving such a high ranking

member of his own cabinet. And he is consequently keen to keep a lid on the entire affair.'

'Ar bet e fuckin is,' Dee Dee snarled, smelling a rat. 'No offense Mr H, but mar geeza's rottin in the ground in that shit ole of a country, and your bleedin uncle wants to sweep it under iz grubby little carpet. Thas proper choice that is, if you ask me e'z as bent as the rest of em. Come on you two, iss shepherd's pie today and ar'm starvin.'

'Ohh yeah nice,' Trisha chirped, leaping to her feet. 'I ope they got ice cream.'

'Yeah, wiv apple pie,' Dee Dee told her.

'Fuck that!' Trisha said, turning her nose up. 'Ar want it on me shepherds, iss gotta be strawberry though, so ar can mix it all in.'

Dee Dee and Maizie took a second or two to process Trisha's outlandish culinary request.

'You aint right, d'you know that,' Maizie said, having instantly lost whatever appetite she may have had. 'You gotta see someone mate, ar'm tellin ya, you need elp, seriously.'

'What?' Trisha said, heading for the door. 'It all goes daan the same way dunnit?'

'Ladies please!' Clive said, retrieving a file from his briefcase. 'Please, please hear me out. I'm sure you'll find what I have to say of great importance to you.'

'Ang on Dee!' Maizie said, tugging her friend's arm. 'Less just ear what e'z gotta say ay, we aint got nuffing to lose av we. And I aint that ungry now anyway, fanks to silly nuts there.'

'Yeah, me neeva,' Dee Dee agreed, returning to the bench. 'Trisha get yer arse back ear.'

'Ohhhh Deeee!' Trisha moaned, with one hand on the door. 'Last time we was late there was nuffing left, member, if ar never ad that cheese and ham toastie under me pilla ar'da gone to bed ungry.'

'That was mar toastie you feevin bitch!' Maizie stormed, starting after her friend. 'Ar knew you nicked it, ar turned

me back for two bleedin minutes, two minutes and you ad it away dint'cha!'
'What, what?' Trisha said flinching. 'I, I only done it for you mate onest, you are gettin a bit of a gut on ya, aint she Dee, tell er mate!'
'YOU WHAT?' Maizie raged. 'YOU SAYIN AR'M FAT!'
'Well, yeah,' Trisha said eyeing Maizie up and down, who indeed had piled on several pounds since her incarceration.
'She's right Maizie,' Dee Dee agreed, 'ar bin watchin you stuffin ya face day in and day out, and goin up for seconds an'all, ya greedy mare. And don't fink I aint noticed ya bungin bourbon biscuits in ya bedside cabnit eeva. You gotta knock that shit on the ed ar tell ya mate, you're gettin a proper builders crack you are.'
Clive stood bemused, having lost his train of thought completely.
'No ar bleedin aint!' Maizie shrieked, looking over her shoulder at her bottom. 'Shut up Dee, don't say that.'
'Ladies, ladies please,' Clive cried with his hands in the air. 'Please, I don't have much time!'
'Oh yeah sorry Mr H,' Maizie said, eager for the attention to be deflected from her. 'Sorry, what was ya sayin?'
Trisha reluctantly returned to the bench and sat beside her friends. 'Iss alright for you,' she sneered at Maizie, 'you got enough blubber to keep ya goin for a coupla days aint'cha.'
'Trishaaaaa!' Maizie snapped, shoving an elbow into her friend's side. 'Leave it out will ya!'
Clive buried his head in his hands. 'Maizie, Trisha,' he moaned, 'will you please just listen to what I have to say.'
'Yeah Trish,' Dee Dee added, growing tired of the bickering, 'leave lumpy alone will ya.'
'LUMPY!' Maizie cried. 'Thas it, I ain eatin jack shit no more, ar'm tellin ya!'
'Oooh, can I av ya biscuits?' Trisha asked, bobbing on the bench beside her. 'And that boxa bakewell tarts you got stashed in ya knicker drawer, don't fink I aint seen em.'

'Oy!' Maizie barked. 'What you doin goin fru mar knickers, eh?'
'Yeah Trish,' Dee Dee asked also, 'what you bin up to? Ar fought you said she weren't your type.'
'She aint,' Trisha admitted, as Clive shook his head in abject despair. 'But them Nazi nut jobs upstairs av been flickin their beans over er since she got ear.'
'DO WHAT?' Maizie yelled. 'You mean them psycho skin'eds wanna get in mar knickers!'
'Well they already are,' Trisha confessed, 'sort of.'
'SORT OF!' Maizie stormed. 'Woja mean SORT OF?'
'Yeah come on Trish,' Dee Dee insisted, 'what you gone and done?'
'Well,' Trisha said sheepishly, fearing the impending backlash and inching away, 'it aint mar fault, they frettened to bash me ed in if ar didn't get em.'
'Get what?' Maizie asked, the penny not having yet dropped.
'Ya knickers,' Trisha replied, edging further away. 'Ar'v ad to nick em arf a dozen pairs of yours so they can sniff ya gusset. You got loads though mate aint'cha, and ar never took ya new ones ar promise.'
'YOU DONE WHAT?' Maizie raged, leaping to her feet and raising a fist. 'YOU FEEVIN BITCH!'
Clive immediately stepped between them. 'Maizie please my dear, please will you sit down and hear me out.'
'Ar'm gonna slap the shit outta you Trisha, ar mean it!' Maizie cried, reaching over Clive's shoulder. 'Come ear!'
'Sorry mate,' Trisha pleaded, 'they made me do it, onest, ar won't do it again, ar promise. Ar promise ya mate!'
The prison officer approached them wielding her night stick. 'Break it up, break it up!' she said aggressively.
'It's OK!' Clive told her, raising a hand whilst restraining Maizie. 'It's just friendly banter that's all.'
'Friendly!' Maizie said seething. 'She aint no friend of mine ar tell ya!'

Dee Dee stood up to intervene. 'Maizie, she said sorry didn't she,' she said separating them, 'now leave er alone, ar'll sort the skin'eds out, believe me we won't get any more grief from them freaks.'
'Right, so that's that then,' Clive said, heaving a sigh of relief. 'Now can we please get on?'
'Hmmmm,' Maizie growled, retaking her seat, 'just don't talk to me Trisha, ar mean it ar'm proper pissed off wiv you.'
'Yeah but,' Trisha said, tugging at her sleeve.
'AR SAID!' Maizie yelled, yanking her arm away. 'DON'T TALK TO ME!'
Trisha hung her head. 'Ar said ar'm sorry,' she mumbled.
'Come on then Mr H,' Dee Dee said, checking the clock above the basketball hoop. 'Get on wiv it.'
'At last,' Clive said, opening the file in front of him. 'Now where were we?'
'Your flippin uncle,' Dee Dee said angrily, 'e'z shittin a brick ain e, if the papers find out abaat that fucker Fitzroy and what e done it'll blow the government's arse right out the water wunnit?'
'Well,' Clive said, clearing his throat, 'I'll agree it would be a tad embarrassing, but that's why I'm here to broker a deal, so to speak. If each of you would agree to, shall we say forget the whole Fitzroy incident and sign these gagging orders I have here, then you could be free in as little as a matter of weeks.'
'Weeks!' Maizie said, sitting upright. 'You mean we're gettin aat!'
'Yes, yes indeed you are,' Clive replied, taking a fountain pen from his breast pocket. 'Along with certain conditions of course.'
'Dee we're gettin aat mate!' Maizie shrieked, jostling her friend. 'Ar can't believe it!'
Dee Dee though hadn't taken the news with quite the same degree of enthusiasm.
'Woss a matter Dee?' Maizie asked. 'Dinchu ear im, e said they're gonna let us aat.'

'I erd im,' Dee Dee growled. 'An ar don't like it one bit, you know what you can do wiv that gaggin order don'tcha.'
'Dee mate,' Trisha said, hopping to her feet, 'woss up wiv ya, e said we can get aat if we sign them papers, so less sign em ay!'
Dee Dee in her entire life had never bowed to pressure of any kind, and with the death of her lover still haunting her sleepless nights, even a governmental pardon would not sway her. 'Ar'd rarva do me bird,' she told the PM's nephew. 'Fanks all the same.'
'Deeee!' Maizie whined. 'You aint serious are ya, we got anuvva ten years at least mate.'
'Yeah Dee,' Trisha added, rallying behind Maizie, 'you might be able to do it standin on yer ed, but we can't can we Maize. Besides all that, evry bugger in ear want's to kill me.'
'Ar know the feelin,' Maizie said, still peeved at having her underwear defiled by her fellow inmates.
'You two go,' Dee Dee told her friends. 'Ar see ya when ar get out.'
Clive raised the papers in his hand. 'I'm afraid it's all three of you, or none at all,' he told them. 'And it's non-negotiable.'
'What?' Dee Dee snapped. 'What difference does it make?'
'It's one of the conditions of your release I'm afraid,' Clive informed her. 'Unless I leave here with three signatures then there will be no question of you leaving this place in the near future. I'm sorry but it's the best I could do under the circumstances.'
'We'll go to the papers,' Dee Dee said, puffing out her chest defiantly. 'Tell em everyfing.'
'You are convicted murderers,' Clive reminded them. 'Who would believe you? Granted, on your eventual release you could tell all and stir up a hornets nest but I'd think very carefully if I were you. Do you think Deborah that your friends are cut out for a lengthy stay behind bars? You may possess the required backbone to survive in this environment, but think of Maizie and Trisha and how they would fare over the coming years.'

Dee Dee looked her friends in the eye, each of them vulnerable in their own way.

'Please Dee,' Trisha said doe-eyed. 'Please mate.'

'E'z right Dee,' Maizie added, applying a little emotional pressure. 'You might av the balls for this gaff, but me and Trish are scared shitless.'

Dee Dee paced the gymnasium kicking at the polished parquet flooring and searching her soul. To give in and sign would mean trashing Travis's memory and the spontaneous connection they had each experienced.

'Dee mate,' Maizie said, approaching her friend and taking her hand. 'Ar know what ya finkin, you don't wanna let im down, but e'z gone Dee, ar know it urts ya, ar really do, but me and Trish are still ear and we need ya, more now than we ever av.'

'FUCK!' Dee Dee cursed, kicking a stool across the floor. 'FUCK, FUCK, FUUUUUCK!'

'Steady Dawson!' the guard warned.

'Whateva!' Dee Dee snarled, returning to Clive. 'Alright, alright you got me,' she said, snatching the pen and papers. 'Ar'm gonna sign this fing, but ar'm doin it for me mates, thas all, an ar wonnit in writin that we're definitely gettin out, OK!'

'Yes, yes of course,' Clive said, retrieving further documentation from his briefcase, 'I think you'll find everything is in order here.'

'It better be,' Dee Dee said, scrawling her signature with pursed lips across the bottom of the first page, before handing the pen to Maizie.

'Fanks Dee,' Maizie told her.

'Yeah fanks mate,' Trisha reiterated. 'Ar'll split er bakewell tarts wiv ya if ya like.'

'OY!' Maizie barked. 'You stay outta mar drawers, d'you ear me!'

'Yeah alright, alright!' Trisha said, flinching once again. 'God Maizie, you can be so touchy at times, d'you know that.'

'Ar'll show you touchy!' Maizie said, glaring. 'If ar catch you wiv your grubby little hands in mar knickers ar swear ar'll beat the shit out of ya.'
'OK, OK,' Trisha said, with her hands in the air. 'Ar promise ar won't touch em no more.' After a moment or two of silence while Maizie signed her order Trisha piped up. 'You better av arf that bottle of ome made voddy ar got off the skin'ed's then ar spoze.'
'Whyyyyy?' Maizie asked, contemplating an unsavory reply.
'Well coz,' Trisha said sheepishly, 'ar swapped it for your peek-a-boo bra and Little Miss Naughty nightie.'
'You done what?' Maizie said, in abject disbelief. 'Tell me you're windin me up Trish, tell me or so elp me ar'm gonna...'
'Shut it you two will ya!' Dee Dee said, shaking her head. 'You're doin mar nut in.'
'But Deeeee!' Maizie protested.
'But shut the fuck up,' Dee Dee replied angrily. 'Ar tell ya when ar get out ar'm goin ome to Marbella and ar don't wanna see eeva of you'z for a coupla mumfs at least, d'you ear me!'
'Er I'm afraid that won't be possible,' Clive informed her. 'Like I said there are certain condition attached to your release and the first being that you three remain in the UK for a minimum of five years.'
'Do what?' Dee Dee cried. 'What the fuck for?'
'Well,' Clive continued apprehensively, 'that leads me to the second condition.'
'Go on,' Dee Dee said, 'ar'm listnin.'
'Each of you,' Clive said, scanning his documents, 'must take lawful employment and, of course, cease all criminal activities.'
'Lawful!' Dee Dee scoffed. 'You're avin a laugh aint'cha, we tried that once, it was shite, so if you fink ar'm gonna work mar tits off for a coupla quid an hour stackin shitty shelves or summink, you can fink again geez.'

'Well I'm afraid it isn't quite that simple,' Clive explained. 'Each of you will be required to help out at a charitable organization.'

'Charity!' Maizie shrieked. 'Oh flippin ell, what we gotta do that for?'

'I'm sorry,' Clive said resolutely, 'like I said it's one of the terms of your acquittal. Here are a list of deserving charities that would be only too glad to have you onboard.'

Trisha snatched the list from him. 'Oooh, I ope they got the edgehog trust on it, ar'd love to elp knit their little blankets ar would.'

'Great,' Dee Dee sighed, with zero enthusiasm. 'Ar told you ar'd rarva do me bird.'

'Oh come on Dee,' Maizie said, peering over Dee Dee's shoulder, 'it can't be that bad can it?'

'That's the spirit,' Clive said, rubbing his hands together. 'Crystal will be thrilled to see you on your release.'

'Ohhhhhh,' Trisha moaned. 'No flippin edgehog charity on ear, they ain even got nuffing for the squirrels, the poor little fuckers.'

'I'm sure there are plenty of worthwhile organizations there,' Clive told her. 'Now if you'll excuse me I really should be getting along. I'll be in touch in a day or so with the final arrangements. It was great seeing you three again, it truly was.'

'Yeah, you an'all,' Trisha replied, with her head buried in the paperwork. 'Oooh ang on look!' she shrieked, prodding the list. 'They got the R, S, P, C animal whatsit, thatta do for me. D'you two fancy it?'

'No ar bleedin don't!' Dee Dee snapped. 'I aint spendin the next five friggin years up to me neck in mangey mutts and flea bitten ferrets, gimme that!' Dee Dee snatched the list from Trisha, nodding to acknowledge Clive's parting wave.

'Seeya!' Maizie said, raising a hand before joining her friend. 'We gotta go straight then av we Dee?' she asked.

'Looks like it dunnit,' Dee Dee replied begrudgingly, running a finger down the list.

'Woja fancy?' Maizie asked, craning her neck.
'None of it,' Dee Dee said, 'an ar tell ya summink, I aint shakin no poxy tin in the high street poncin for nobody, so they can jog right on if thas what they got in mind.'
'Me neeva,' Maizie agreed. 'You never know if they're kosha do ya, so ar don't give em fuck all me.'
'Oh ar do,' Trisha chirped, 'ar do all the telly ones an'all. Ar give free paand a mumf to the skinny Africans, a coupla quid to Green peas, a fiver to the edgehogs coz they're me favrit, oh an ar'v adopted two elephants, a panda an a buncha meerkats.'
'Mug!' Dee Dee smirked, thrusting the list into Maizie's hand and heading for the door. 'You decide Maizie,' she told her friend, growing increasingly frustrated at having played her part in the cover up of a ministerial scandal. 'Ar can't be arsed.'
Trisha and Maizie followed Dee Dee to the mess hall and took their place in the queue.
'Ar knew it!' Trisha moaned. 'No bleedin pie left. OY!' she yelled over the counter. 'Aint'cha got no more bleedin pie?'
'No sorry love,' was the caterer's reply, 'your mates just had the last of it.'
Dee Dee and Maizie waved their steaming shepherd's pie under Trisha's nose with a broad smile. 'You snooze ya lose,' Maizie laughed. 'Call it Karma if ya like.'
'Oh flippin ell,' Trisha sulked, 'carn I av summa yours, ar don't fancy the spam fritters.'
'No you bleedin can't,' Maizie said, snatching her plate away. She then caught sight of the skin heads that Trisha had been supplying her lingerie to, each of them leering at her lustfully. 'Jog on over there wiv ya dyke mates,' she told Trisha, 'ar'm sure they'll share their shit wiv ya.'
'Ar can't,' Trisha replied, ducking out of view of the thuggish group. 'Ar still owe em ya silky suzzies.' The lecherous lesbians had indeed threatened Trisha with grievous bodily harm if she failed to deliver Maizie's suspenders before the day was out. 'Ar don't suppose there's any chance...?'

'No there flippin aint!' Maizie snapped. 'So eat the fuckin fritters and lump it.'
'Arm gettin sicka this,' Dee Dee said, setting her tray down and approaching the group.
Maizie and Trisha huddled together at the counter out of harms way and watched their friend stoop and confront the Neo-Nazi's.
'You listen to me you fuckin freaks,' she snarled, 'ar'm only gonna tell you this once so you better listen good.'
Dee Dee's reputation had preceded her and even though she was heavily outnumbered not one of the butch bullies would dare make the first move and retaliate, although collectively they could surely overpower her.
'See mar mates over there,' she added, each of the girls looked over their shoulders at Dee Dee's friends who both looked down at their feet so as not to make eye contact.
'Well, from now on you don't,' Dee Dee warned them. 'You don't look at em and you don't talk to em, d'you ear me?'
The group averted their eyes but said nothing, each wanting another to stand up to the Essex hard nut.
'Ar said d'you ear me!' Dee Dee said again, to which she received a mumbled acknowledgement. 'Coz if I ear different ar'm gonna come for evry wunna you'z, ar'll av ya on yer own or all togevva ar don't give a flyin fuck. Ar'll urt ya and ar'll urt ya bad, so stay the fuck away, alright!' Dee Dee plucked a plate of shepherd's pie from the tray of one of the stunned girls. 'You ain eatin that ar ya,' she said glaring at her. 'Ar didn't fink so,' she added when the girl remained tight lipped.
'Flippin ell Dee,' Maizie said, on her return. 'Woja say to em?'
'Ar just fronted the freaks and told em how it is,' Dee Dee told her friends, then thrust the plate of pie into Trisha's hand. 'Eeya, eat this and stop bleedin whining will ya.'
'Oooh ta,' Trisha said grinning, 'can I av ice cream an'all?'
'NO!' Dee Dee and Maizie both insisted, heading for an empty table.

'FANKS!' Trisha called across to the skin heads, but received no response.
'Miserable gits,' she said, setting her tray down beside her friends.
During dinner Maizie thumbed the list Clive had given them, while Trisha devoured her dinner as though it were her last meal.
'Turn it in will ya,' Dee Dee said, looking down her nose at her gluttonous friend.
'What?' Trisha replied, spooning the last into her already crammed mouth. 'Iss wunna me favrits.'
'Eeya av mine,' Maizie told her, pushing her plate across the table. 'I ain ungry no more.'
'Oooh fanks,' Trisha squealed, plucking a morsel of mash from her lap and popping it back into her mouth. 'Iss mar lucky day ain it, ar we still on for the bakewell tarts?'
'Don't push ya luck,' Maizie sneered, turning a page. 'Eeya Dee, what abaat a mental elf charity, ar'd love to do summink for them poor bleedas. It says ear all we gotta do is make tea and stuff and elp wiv the day to day runnin of the centre, that don't sound too bad does it?'
'Yeah whateva,' Dee Dee said, momentarily mesmerized by Trisha's furious feasting.
'You not eatin that?' Trisha said, reaching for Dee Dee's plate.
'Touch mar grub an ar'll break your arm,' Dee Dee warned her. 'Ar mean it an'all.'
Maizie shook her head at her friend's apparent stupidity. 'You won't bleedin learn will ya Trish, go and get a spam fritter if ya still ungry.'
'Sod that!' Trisha said, scraping her plate clean. 'Ar'd rarva chew me own tits than eat them flippin fings ar tell ya. Me nan used to cook em for us on a Friday, as a treat she used to say, some bleedin treat they were, they ad so many whiskers in em from er scabby chin that ar used to cough a bleedin fur ball up arf hour later.'

'Oh behave!' Dee Dee said, sliding her plate away and slapping Trisha's reaching hand. 'Leave it you greedy bitch!' she added, having witnessed enough for one day.
'Thas that then Dee,' Maizie said, shuffling the papers. 'We'll elp the mental mob yeah?'
'If ya say so,' Dee Dee agreed. 'Ar'm tellin ya though, ar don't mind makin em a cuppa, but I aint wipin no dribblin chins or shitty arses, d'you ear me.'
'It aint like that Dee,' Maizie said naively, 'issa doddle mate.'

Later, back in the cell, Dee Dee and Maizie sat mulling over Clive's surprise visit and their prospect of freedom, while Trisha stood at the window gazing out at a cloud she thought resembled the head of Kermit the frog.
'Gonzo was mar favrit,' she said wistfully.
'What?' Maizie asked, looking up.
'Gonzo,' Trisha said again, 'and iz little rat mate.'
'What are you on abaat?' Dee Dee asked, but Trisha turned her back and scanned the stormy skies, standing on tip toes and clinging to the steel bars. 'Ahhhh, that one looks like ma auntie Reenie smokin er pipe, god rest er soul, oh and that one looks like Arry wossizface from One Direction, ar prefer the little blonde one meself, e looks more like a girl.'
'Trishaaaa!' Maizie said, tossing a pillow at her. 'Ar carn ear meself fink wiv you chattin shit, shut up will ya.'
'Yeah, yeah, yeah alright,' Trisha said, returning to her bunk and tipping her pillow from its case. 'Ar better start packin ar spoze,' she said, filling it with her belongings. 'D'ya fink ar'll be able to take me bedside cabnit?' she asked. 'Ar made it in woodwork did'n I, and you did tell me the warden said it was the nuts.'
'No, she said it was shit,' Dee Dee confessed, without a thought for her friend's feelings, 'ar was just tryna make ya feel better thas all. Look at it, the drawer don't fit, the door don't bleedin close, and if you put an apple on it it rolls daan the back. So she's right, it is shit.'

Trisha looked down at her handy work which was indeed a sorry sight, but it was hers nether the less. 'Me nan'd like it,' she told Dee Dee, 'she could keep er umbugs and suduko mags in it.'
'You sure itta take the weight,' Maizie laughed, ridiculing the crude plywood box with its uneven splintered legs and heavy runs in the flaking varnish.
'Thatta be an antique one day,' Trisha said proudly.
'It already is,' Dee Dee laughed. 'The poxy fing looks a faasand years old already.'
'Shutuuup!' Trisha cried, attempting to open the crooked drawer but tearing off the knob in the process. 'It ain't that bad.'
'Well, you aint takin it anyway,' Dee Dee said. 'In fact, you aint takin any of your shit.'
'Ohhhh why not,' Trisha moaned, slipping a warped clay vase she'd made in pottery class into the pillow case. 'Ar can't leave this lot behind can I, iss priceless.'
'Priceless my arse,' Dee Dee sneered. 'Issa pile of shit thas what it is.'
'Ar got an idea Trish,' Maizie said, intervening. 'Why don't ya leave if for the next poor cow they stick in ear, ar'm sure they'd really appreciate it.'
'Ya fink so!' Trisha said, looking lovingly at her tilted table.
'Oh yeah,' Maizie said tongue in cheek, 'they're gonna fink they've ad it right off ar'm tellin ya, like when we was in Barcelona and they upgraded us for showin the bellboy our baps.'
'Yeah, ar spoze ya right,' Trisha agreed. 'Ar'd love to see their faces though when they come in and see it.'
'Yeah, so would I,' Dee Dee laughed, 'they're gonna fink they won the bleedin lottery findin that pile of... ar mean that little lot. Ar'd be proper made up if it was me ar tell ya!'
'Yeah,' Trisha sighed. 'You are right ar spoze, shall ar leave em me vase an'all then?'
'If you can bare to part wiv it Trish,' Maizie smirked. 'Thatta be real nice of ya.'

'Iss better to give than receive ain it,' Trisha told her friends, placing the crooked vase back on the window sill. 'Ar better leave em a note though, tell em not to put any water in it coz iss got an ole in the bottom.'

'Priceless!' Dee Dee scoffed.

'Ar fink so,' Trisha agreed, 'issa one off ain it, like the Mona Leeza or...'

'That leanin tower fing,' Maizie laughed.

'Oh shutuuup!' Trisha said, cottoning on to their mocking jibes. 'Thas a pukka vase that is.'

'It ain a pissin vase!' Dee Dee said, throwing her hands in the air. 'Ow can it be if iss got a bloody ole in it!'

Trisha soon ignored her friends' sarcastic remarks and took out the sewing project that had occupied her recent evenings. 'Ar'm defintly takin this and nuffing's gonna stop me,' she said defiantly. 'Issa comfort blanky for our Jade's newborn, good ain it, ar designed it meself.'

Dee Dee and Maizie gave the tiny blanket a sideways glance and were both immediately stunned at the presence of what appeared to be purple swastikas that Trisha had naively embroidered around the edge and centre amongst a hundred or so yellow daffodils.

'D'ya fink little Troy's gonna like it?' she asked, holding it across her chest.

'Yeah course e will,' Dee Dee said, biting her lip, 'if e grows up to be a flippin fascist that is.'

Trisha looked bemused as her two friends fell about laughing. 'What?' she said, looking her cotton gift up and down. 'Ar don't see what the problem is.'

'No, you probly don't!' Maizie said, nudging Dee Dee. 'Ar can just see the little bugger now at the muvvas and toddlers group, dribblin on iz little Nazi blanket.'

'NAZI!' Trisha cried. 'What you on abaat?'

'Never mind,' Maizie chuckled, 'ar'm sure e'll love it.'

'Yeah,' Trisha agreed, 'thas what ar fink, ar done one in pink as well just in case she ad a girl.'

That night the girls tossed and turned in their bunks, finding it hard to sleep with only one thought on their minds, freedom.
'TRISHAAAA!' Dee Dee suddenly yelled. 'Get your flippin feet back under the covers, they're chuckin up summink chronic. Ar fought ar told you to put that powder in ya plimpsoles.'
'Ar run out,' Trisha said, snatching her rancid feet back beneath the sheets. 'Me muvva's spozed to bring some up on er next visit, that and me cod liver oil fingeys, ar bin takin em for me joints ya see, arferitis runs in me famly so ya can't be too careful can ya. Ar said ya can't be too careful, anyway me auntie Barb, the poor cow, gets it proper bad she does. Ar said me auntie Barb gets it bad, er ands are proper fucked up they are, er old fella aint complainin though, e reckons she gives im the best Thomas the tank e'z ever ad, the saucy sod says e can't wait for er to get a dose of it daan under coz e'z pissed off pokin er parmesan Panini (ar fink e means er noo noo the dirty git). Ar said e'z a dirty git. OY YOU TWO! Dee you awake? Maizie mate are you listnin? Oh thas just bloody marvlus that is, ar might as well be talkin to meself.'
'Trisha,' Dee Dee said sleepily, 'shut the fuck up!'

CHAPTER TWO

'Anuvva day, anuvva dump,' Trisha said, rising the following morning before her friends, and squatting on the pan swinging her legs and breaking wind which echoed around the stainless rim.

'Fuckin ell Trisha!' Dee Dee cursed, burying her head beneath her sheets. 'At least open the pissin wina if ya gonna let one go ya dirty bitch.'

'Sorry mate,' Trisha said straining. 'Ar dunno what was in that blinkin pie yesterday but iss bunged me up good and proper.'

'Oh thas just bloody great that is,' Maizie protested, covering her face too. 'Why dint'cha wait and use the karzi daan the hall, you do this evry bloody mawnin you do.'

Trisha was about to reply when suddenly a tiny brown mouse crawled beneath their cell door and ran directly toward her.

'ARRRRRRGH!' she shrieked, pulling her knees up around her ears and resting her feet on the steel rim. 'SHIT, SHIT, ISS A SHITTIN MAAASE, DEEEE ISSA MAAASE FOR FUCK SAKE. QUICK GET IT WILL YA!'

Dee Dee and Maizie both sat bolt upright in their bunks. 'WHERE, WHERE?' Dee Dee cried. 'YOU SURE?'

'Yeah, iss gone under me poxy bed!' Trisha said trembling. 'Get it will ya!'

'You get it!' Maizie said, backing against the wall.

'Ar can't!' Trisha replied, looking around the base of the pan. 'Iss massive!'

The tiny rodent ran out from beneath Trisha's bunk and sat twitching, its nose beside one of her Barbie bedroom slippers.

'THERE, GET IT DEE, URRY UP, GET THE LITTLE FUCKER,' Trisha squealed, curling into a tight ball.

Without hesitation Dee Dee snatched Trisha's prized clay vase from the window sill and hurled it across the room.

'NO, NO, NO DEEEE!' Trisha shrieked with her hands in the air, seeing her cherished pottery possession strike the inquisitive creature across its bobbing head, killing it instantly before shattering into a dozen or more pieces before her eyes.
'Deeeeee me vaaase!' Trisha whined. 'Oh bleedin ell, now look at it.'
The three sat for a moment staring at the lifeless mouse's corpse, still in shock at its intrusion.
'Ahhhhhhh,' Trisha eventually said. 'Poor little bleeda.'
'Poor little bleeda!' Dee Dee snapped. 'You was the one screamin "get it Dee, get the little fucker" a minute ago. Now what, ar spoze ya feel sorry for it do ya?'
'Well yeah,' Trisha confessed. 'E looks like a gerbil I ad when are was seven, ar kept im in me dolls ouse and taught im to roll a malteaser fru a maze made out of macaroni.'
'What are you on abaat?' Dee Dee asked, shaking her head in disbelief.
'Well, if you adn't squished it Dee,' Trisha said, flushing the lavatory. 'Ar got arf a bag of bon bons under me pilla, ar coulda trained im up.'
'Trained im up!' Dee Dee raged. 'Listen you dozy mare, this aint the green friggin mile, and that aint Mr fuckin Jingles. Issa dirty orrible mouse and now issa dead dirty orrible mouse. OK!'
'You didn't av to break me vase though Dee,' Trisha sulked, 'the warden said it was...'
'Shit!' Dee Dee said, preempting her friend. 'Ar lied abaat that an'all, she said it was the biggest pile of shite she'd ever seen. There, now ya know.'
Side stepping the deceased rodent Trisha sat on her bunk cradling the shattered remains of her vase. 'Antiques of the future, thas what the pottry lady said,' she mumbled under her breath. 'Ar was proper proud of it ar was.'
'Never mind mate,' Maize said, hopping out of bed and joining her. 'You can make anuvva one can't ya, ar mean

you've obviously got the gift.' Maizie's remarks were tinged with a modicum of guilt seeing her friend so distraught.

'Yeah ar could, easy peasy,' Trisha said, attempting to piece together her creation. 'Ar wanna make a pottry orse next time, ar reckon ar'd be good at them.'

'Go for it,' Maizie urged her.

'Yeah go on!' Dee Dee added, with a little less feeling. 'You could flog em on ya web site WonkeyDonkey.com.'

'Deeee!' Maizie said, frowning at her friend. 'She as got a talent for it, aint she?'

'Alright, if ya say so,' Dee Dee reluctantly agreed, stepping out of bed, picking up the dead mouse and flushing it down the toilet. 'She's so obviously the next Michelangelo or summink, aint she.'

'Oh e'z mar favrit, ar love iz stuff,' Trisha smiled.

'What?' Dee Dee asked, surprised. 'What the bleedin ell d'you know abaat Renaissance art?'

'Ay?' Trisha replied, bemused. 'Ar'm on abaat the Ninja turtles. Donatello didn't do it for me, and Raphael looked like a proper wrongen, woja reckon Maizie?' But before Maizie could reply Trisha was off again. 'Ar'm gonna get me a pottry wheel when ar get out, dig up a bitta mud from me garden and crack on wiv it, ar could do a bust of you if ya like Dee, you could stick it on ya telly cabnit.'

'No fanks,' Dee Dee said, turning away. 'Ar don't want your shit in my ouse.'

'Oh but Deeeee,' Trisha pleaded, 'no one else'll model for me.'

'Ar'm not surprised!' Dee Dee laughed. 'Who the fuck'd be that stupid.'

'Ar'll model for ya mate,' Maizie said, adopting the good cop approach. 'Ar need summink to wedge me back door open.'

'Ooooh er!' Dee Dee laughed. 'Really!'

'Will ya!' Trisha shrieked, tossing the fragments of vase into the bin. 'Oh nice one mate, when ar get me dirt ar let ya know, you won't be disappointed ar promise ya.' Trisha then

began massaging the sides of Maizie's face tugging at her skin and prodding her cheek bones.
'Get off, what ya doin?' Maizie said, pulling away.
'Gettin the feel of me subject,' Trisha told her. 'Thas what the Pottry lady told us.'
'Yeah, well ar know what you're like,' Maizie replied, referring to Trisha's blatant bisexuality. 'Ar don't mind you makin me a pottry door stop fingy, but you aint coppin a feel an'all ya dirty bitch.'
'No, no, it aint like that!' Trisha said, defending her art resolutely. 'Anyway, you aint mar type.'
'Wod'you mean by that?' Maizie asked abruptly. 'Woss wrong wiv me then, ay?'
'Well,' Trisha said, not meaning to offend. 'You got flat feet, a pigeon chest, a pointy nose, oh and yer eyes are too close togevva.'
'DO WHAT?' Maizie cried, leaping to her feet and checking herself in the mirror. 'There aint nuffing wrong wiv me eyes, is there Dee?'
'Well,' Dee Dee said, hesitating for a second or two. 'You av got a bit of a beak on ya, and ar can defintly see what ya mean abaat the eyes Trish. Proper shifty lookin aint they?'
'Sod off you two!' Maizie snapped, examining herself closer still 'You're windin me up, aint'cha?'

Later that afternoon, while Trisha was attending another of her pottery classes, Dee Dee and Maizie, to pass the time, joined a short handed netball team who were trailing ten four at half time.
'Flippin ell Dee,' Maizie said, blowing hard whilst bent double with her hands on her knees after only a few minutes of play. 'Ar'm bollocks'd mate ar tell ya, ar can't remember the last time ar done anyfing like this.'
'You just feed me the ball,' Dee Dee told her, hardly breaking a sweat. 'Thas all you gotta do, ar do the rest.'
A tall heavy-set Nigerian then strolled by, shoulder barging Dee Dee in the process. 'Hear me now bitch!' she said,

smacking her lips. 'You'z gettin beat today by me and me bredrin yeah, we'z gonna wipe de court wid ya sorry white asses. So why don't you'z just give up now and craaaal back to ya cells now den, naar mean?'

'Get fucked!' was Dee Dee's immediate response, never one to succumb to intimidation. 'You aint winning fuck all, not today. And call me bitch again and ar'm gonna ram that ball daan your poxy froat. Now piss off, ya don't scare me ya slag, naar mean?'

The Nigerian, Dianabasi Obi, squared up to Dee Dee thrusting her chest out and flinging her arms out to the side. 'You tink you can take me girl,' she said, nose to nose with Dee Dee. 'Tink again, dat shit aint gonna happen yeah, you'z score one point against me, I'z cut you real bad, naar mean. Bitch!'

'Ar told you not to call me bitch!' Dee Dee said, shoving the girl away, snatching the ball from Maizie and bouncing it into the Nigerians face, causing a trickle of blood to immediately appear from her broad nose.

'SHIT! YOU FUCKIN BITCH!' the girl screamed, lashing out wildly. 'I'Z KILL YA FOR DAT, I'Z SWEAR DOWN BLUD!'

'OY BREAK IT UP, BREAK IT UP!' a nearby prison officer yelled, wading in with her night stick. 'I said break it up or you'll both spend a night in the hole d'you hear me. Stand down Dawson and you Obi. I SAID STAND THE FUCK DOWN THE PAIR OF YOU!'

Dee Dee and Obi backed away, staring one another down all the time.

Dianabasi Obi was a thirty five year old category A prisoner, serving a double life sentence for the murders of her eleven month old twin boys during a heroin fueled row with her live-in lover. At the time the story enraged the British public, the vast majority of them calling for the death penalty to be restored for all child killers; such was the infants' catalogue of injuries that several members of the jury left the courtroom unable to stomach the harrowing forensic photographs.

'Now!' the officer said, slipping her stick back into her belt. 'I suggest you both get on with your game in an orderly manner, or I'll be having a word with the warden.'
'You alright Dee?' Maizie asked, eyeing the hulking opposition with some trepidation. 'Why don't we sit the rest of the game out, ay?'
'No way!' Dee Dee insisted. 'I aint lettin that cunt fink she's got the better of me, no fuckin way!'
'Oh shit, ear goes,' Maizie said to herself as play resumed.
During the following fifteen minutes Dee Dee and Obi battled for possession of the ball, grunting and cursing one another out of earshot of the watchful guards. At one point Dee Dee was poised to shoot when Obi plunged an elbow hard into her midriff taking the wind completely out of her.
'Fuuuuck, you bitch!' Dee Dee snarled, hunched over and clutching her side unable to take a full breath.
Obi smacked her lips once again looking down on Dee Dee with contempt. 'You aint nutting compared to me,' she sneered. 'And you know dat.'
Dee Dee straightened her back wincing. 'Wanna bet,' she said, her ribs now badly bruised.
'Dee, less go mate,' Maizie urged her friend. 'This shit's gettin out of and.'
'I aint goin nowhere,' Dee Dee said, rallying her breathless squad rallied around her for a team talk. 'Right you lot, listen!' she told them, still reeling from the crushing blow. 'We gotta take them shit eds out of the game, d'you ear me, ar mean hit em ard and win every tackle whatever it takes. They're muggin me off and I aint avin it. Any wunna you'z that aint up for this can piss off now, this is war and iss a war we carn afford to lose coz them fuckers won't let us forget it, you mark mar words. I aint bein nobody's bitch and ar mean nobody's. So hit em and hit em fuckin ard, yeah!'
Dee Dee's rallying call to arms brought a renewed sense of belief into the underdog team as point by point they began to close the gap, but not without altercation, several from

both teams sustaining cuts and bruises from violent clashes at either goal end.

Dee Dee at one point managed to avert Obi's goal attempt by stamping down hard on the back of her knee, bringing her crashing to the tarmac with a thud.

Maizie, although exhausted and dripping with sweat, had Dee Dee's back at all times warning her of every impending assault.

'DEE TO YOU MATE!' Maizie cried, with a blistering long pass over Obi's head.

'Nice one!' Dee Dee said, wasting no time in netting the ball and staring Obi down. 'Eat mar shit!' she told her, running back to her own end to her delighted team mates.

Obi began shoving each and every one of her own players, cursing them for their lack of effort. 'Tree points, we are tree points clear!' she growled. 'We must not allow dem to score, you hear me. I SAID YOU HEAR ME!' Her players nodded, backed away from her and turned to face the opposition.

'You know what to do Maize,' Dee Dee told her friend.

'The Dee Dee special,' Maizie replied, bouncing the ball at her feet.

'You know that shit,' Dee Dee said, attacking Obi's goal with gritted teeth.

Maizie made three dummy passes to fool their opponents, flicked the ball across to a ginger team mate, side stepped the furious Nigerian before receiving the ball and tossing it to the waiting Dee Dee.

'YES!' she shrieked, delighted with her efforts. But suddenly she found herself flat on the floor in excruciating pain, having been struck between the shoulder blades with Obi's clenched fist. And to add insult to injury, she was then spat on by the aggressive team captain.

'Pig!' Obi snarled, looking down on Maizie. 'Stay down or I will break you in half.'

'You fuckin slag!' Dee Dee yelled, sprinting the length of the court to her floored friend, having just leveled the score.

'You touch er again and ar'll fuckin kill ya, you got that you piece of shit?'

Obi again lunged at Dee Dee but was dragged away by her team mates, seeing several officers approaching. 'DO NOT TOUCH ME!' she yelled lashing out. 'I WILL CUT YOU I SWEAR ON MY LIFE!'

With two minutes of play remaining Dee Dee helped her injured friend to her feet. 'Sit yaself daan,' she told her, seeing the pain etched on Maizie's face. 'Go on, ar be alright.'

'You sure Dee,' Maizie groaned, arching her back. 'Ar don't wanna leave ya wiv that bitch.'

'Just sit the fuck daan will ya,' Dee Dee insisted, wanting her friend out of further harm's way. 'Ar told ya, she don't scare me.'

Maizie reluctantly hobbled to the sideline and lowered herself slowly onto a wooden bench, cringing in doing so.

Now, with just over ninety seconds of the game to be played, Obi screamed at her players to push hard before receiving a blistering pass into Dee Dee's goal mouth.

'NO FUCK YA!' Dee Dee cried from a distance. She could only watch as a smiling Obi took aim and lobbed a near inch perfect shot.

'Shit!' Dee Dee cursed, clenching her fists over her eyes momentarily before darting back. But as the ball bounced twice on the steel rim, time seemed to stand still for Dee Dee and her team, until with an agonizing sigh of relief from herself and her fellow players, it fell to the side into the hands of Dee Dee's wing attacker Sharon.

Obi shoved two of her own players to the ground in an attempt to retrieve the ball, but the frightened girl quickly ferried it to her team mates down the line.

'GET HER, GET HER NOW!' Obi yelled, pushing her way through the mass of bodies.

'OVER EAR!' Dee Dee cried with her hands in the air at Obi's goal end. But her goal defender took a crunching tackle to the shins, went down and was dispossessed of the ball.

'SHIT, TAKE IT BACK!' Dee Dee screamed at the top of her voice. 'TAKE IT BACK FOR FUCK SAKE!' Her wing attacker then intercepted a bouncing pass destined for Obi's hands, and tossed it to the smallest member of their team who in turn, with Obi bearing down on her passed it on.
'NOW, NOW!' Dee Dee barked, with her arms outstretched. 'NOW YA MELT!'
Obi signaled for her girls to flank Dee Dee, but on seeing the gutsy Essex convict many of them chose to hang back allowing her to take possession of the ball. And with just enough time to smile at the seething Obi she lobbed a perfect shot through the hoop without touching the sides. The final whistle then blew and Dee Dee's entire team erupted with a deafening and jubilant cheer.
Dianabasi Obi had been beaten for the first time since her incarceration and she was far from happy about it. 'FOUL, THAT WAS A FOUL!' she stormed, attempting to overturn the victory, but even her own players were having none of it.
'You lose,' Dee Dee said, flicking Obi a finger, which incensed her further. 'Deal wiv it, bitch!' Dee Dee added with a broad smile.
Obi ran toward Dee Dee with her fists tightly clenched while the prison officers' backs were turned, both teams gasped and retreated, but Dee Dee stood her ground till the last before leaping into the air and butting the bridge of Obi's already bruised nose, shattering the brittle bone with ease. Obi fell to the ground reeling and clutching her bloodied face, but the fight as far as Dee Dee was concerned was far from over. With her team mates, and that of Obi for that matter, gathered around to shield her, Dee Dee dropped to her knees and grabbed the Nigerian by her slender neck hoisting her head from the ground.
'You wanna fuck wiv me, you slag,' she growled raising a fist, 'well fuck you!' She landed a battering blow to the side of the groaning Obi's face, fracturing her eye socket instantly. 'Thas for mar mate,' she snarled menacingly, before raising

her fist higher still. 'And this one,' she added, putting every fibre into a sledgehammer blow to the jaw dislodging three of Obi's teeth and splitting her lip wide open, 'thas for them kids you orrible no good murderin cunt!'

Obi lay unconscious spewing blood as Dee Dee first spat in her face with utter contempt, then let her head fall to the blood spattered tarmac.

'Quick, the screws!' a team-mate said, tapping Dee Dee's shoulder. Dee Dee leapt to her feet and mingled with her fellow players with her head down.

'She fell on er face miss,' one girl told the officer. 'Twice!'

The astonished prison officer first radioed for assistance then, and only then, checked Obi for a pulse. Being a mother herself, and along with every parent in the country, she had been appalled by Obi's crimes, therefor with a wry smile she was content to believe the girl and look for no possible assailant.

'It happens,' she told the surrounding girls. 'She should learn to be more careful, shouldn't she.'

While Obi's battered body was stretchered off to the infirmary, Dee Dee sat with her friend nursing her own wounds.

'She ad it comin dint she Dee,' Maizie said, pleased as punch that her murdered babies had been avenged in some small way.

'She deserves a shit load more,' Dee Dee replied, then looking up she found herself surrounded by between thirty and forty inmates, each jostling to shake her hand.

'Respect yeah,' one woman said with a tear in her eye. 'And god bless them littluns,' she kissed her hand before raising it toward the heavens.

'Yeah doll,' another said, clinging tightly to Dee Dee's hand. 'You done what everyone in ear has wanted to do since that piece of shit arrived. We got kids at ome d'ya know what ar mean, good on ya girl, good on ya.'

Dee Dee found herself overwhelmed by the show of appreciation for her actions. 'If the screws weren't araand,' she told them, 'ar reckon ar coulda quite easily frottled the fucker to deff.'

Hailed a heroine by her fellow prisoners Dee Dee was soon showered with gifts as a mark of respect; half a litre of gin concealed in a plastic lemonade bottle, soap and toiletries to better the prison's meager supplies and several cartons of cigarettes that, if not smoked, doubled as currency within the aging institution.

'Ar'm well proud of ya mate,' Maizie told her battle weary friend. 'Ar don't fink ar coulda stood up to er like you did.'

'That bitch is a bully and a crack ore,' Dee Dee said, acknowledging the prison officers' smiles. 'And bullies only fight them that can't defend emselves.'

'Like er poor kiddies,' Maizie said, with her hand on her heart. 'I ate to fink what them poor little bleedas went fru.'

'Don't remind me,' Dee Dee said, hanging her head. 'The more ar fink abaat it the more ar wanna put er daan like the mangey mutt that she is.'

Eventually making their way back inside to tumultuous applause, Dee Dee and Maizie were both then stopped part way along the corridor by the warden, a sour faced fifty something in a grey flannel suit.

'I've been watching you Dawson,' she said, through pursed and wrinkled lips. 'And I'll have you know that you are rapidly making your way to the top of my shit list, and that my girl is a very dangerous place to be.' She clenched a clipboard tightly under her arm and glared over her horn rimmed spectacles. 'You too young lady,' she said, wagging a bony finger at Maizie. 'And that goes for that half-witted friend of yours. Where is that damn girl anyway?'

'Pottry class,' Dee Dee told her, unfazed by the warden's warning. 'Gawd knows why, she aint got a bleedin clue what she's doin.'

'You're telling me,' the warden said grimacing. 'I have several of her ridiculous pieces in my office. I foolishly told the wretch that she has a rare talent, and now the moron brings me her cretinous creations day after bloody day. I have a gravy boat with no handle, four pointless pepper pots - I say pointless because there's no way of getting the damn pepper into them, a crooked crockery set with what I'm sure looks to me like swastikas on it for god sake, and a hideous blasted bust of myself that the damn girl assures me will be worth a small fortune in years to come.'

'Yeah, thas abaat right,' Maizie laughed. 'Iss yer own fault, you shoulda told er she was shit in the first place, serves ya bleedin right if you ask me.'

Trisha's shrill voice could then be heard reverberating along the narrow hallway. 'WARDEN, WARDEN AR DONE IT!'

'Oh god no,' the warden gasped. 'What now for heaven's sake?'

Trisha skipped toward them cradling her latest hand-crafted monstrosity. 'Eeyar!' she said, proudly handing the warden a life size replica of her recently deceased West Highland Terrier, whose death had devastated the prison head beyond belief.

Bobby had been the warden's sole companion for many years, never leaving her side, his cashmere rug and sterling silver bowl remained as a constant reminder beneath her desk months after his cremation, the remains of which were encased in a polished mahogany box with a brass engraved plaque.

'What, what is it?' the startled warden asked, looking it over with disdain. 'Is it a badger?'

'No ya dumb arse!' Trisha said, shoving the warden bodily. 'Iss Bobby ain it.'

The statuette bore absolutely no resemblance to the warden's faithful companion. In fact, it bore no resemblance to any living creature roaming God's green earth; more like a menacing mythical beast with huge protruding teeth, deep set staring eyes with a semi hypnotic gaze, four gangly legs of varying length which made it impossible to stand on an even surface and a slit halfway down its back.

'Issa money box!' Trisha pointed out, beside herself with excitement. 'D'ya like it, ar know ya little mutt snuffed it, so ar made it for ya to remember im by. If ya look on its arse ar'v signed it an'all, iss probly werf a few quid now but ar reckon in an undred years time the British Museum'll be trippin over their dicks to get their ands on it, nart ar mean.'

Dee Dee and Maizie both turned away covering their mouths to muffle their hysterical laughter.

'Well?' Trisha said, awaiting the warden's response. 'Ar can see yer overcome wiv emotion an all that, ar'v obviously captured im to a tee ain I?'

'I, I,' the warden stammered, with the pottery pooch in her hands. 'I don't know what to say.'

'Oh thas alright,' Trisha said, exuding modesty. 'Ya don't av to fank me, onestly mate, it was nuffing, it just comes natral to me, the pottry lady says ar've only just begun to tap mar true potential.'

With her top lip quivering the warden raised the statue above her head and hurled it with venom down onto the prison floor. 'YOU! YOU BEASTLY GIRL!' she cried, physically shaking and grabbing Trisha by the collar. 'HOW COULD YOU? HOW ON EARTH COULD YOU?'

'What, what?' Trisha squealed, astonished at her reaction. 'Ar fought ya'd like it, ar see a picture on ya desk an ar done it from memry.'

'MEMORY!' the warden raged, 'I don't know what blasted picture you were looking at, but I'm damn sure it wasn't my Bobby. I, I should throw your miserable carcass in the hole for this... THIS OUTRAGE!'

Dee Dee felt it time to intervene. 'Miss, Miss!' she said, attempting to separate the two of them. 'Please don't chuck er in the ole Miss, she didn't mean nuffing by it onest, she's just shit at pottry thas all, iss not er fault.'

'No I aint!' Trisha argued. 'Ar got a gold star for me porclin pigs ar did.'

'Shut the fuck up will ya!' Dee Dee snapped, fearing her friend was only making matters worse. 'When av you ever seen a poxy pig wiv webbed feet, ay?'

The warden tore a sheet of paper from her clipboard and shook it in Trisha's face. 'It seems you imbeciles have some friends in high places,' she said, referring to a letter from the Prime Minister's office. 'Well let me tell you this, another stunt like this and the three of you will rot in the hole. I'll see to it personally. I don't care if Her Majesty the damn Queen herself pardons you. Now get the hell out of my sight!' The warden shoved Trisha away, sparing her a trip to solitary. 'I SAID GET THE HELL OUT OF MY SIGHT YOU, YOU EVIL WRETCH YOU!'

Dee Dee and Maizie dragged their bemused friend back toward their cell leaving the warden distraught and hyperventilating.

'Come on you!' Maizie said, shaking her head at Trisha. 'What are you like?'

'Ar can't believe it,' Trisha said, eyeing the shattered remains. 'Ar bin workin on that for weeks I av.'

'It was shit, get over it,' Dee Dee said, bundling her friend through the door.

'She's right Trish,' Maizie added, 'you better give that pissin pottry up or we won't be goin, you erd er.'

Trisha flung herself onto her bunk and buried her head beneath her pillow. 'Ungrateful bitch!' she mumbled, still reeling from the warden's scathing attack. 'If she finks she's gettin the Bobby bedpan she can go fuck erself.'

'Shutuuuuup!' Dee Dee said, throwing her own pillow at her whinging cellmate.

'Yeah turn it in will ya,' Maizie barked. 'You give er that bed pan and we aint never gettin out of ear, d'you ear me!'

'Alright, alright!' Trisha snapped, furious at the constant barracking. 'Ar'm gonna put it on ebay and you'z two aint gettin a bean you wait and see.'

Trisha's four legged pee pot, with a tail for a handle and her own interpretation of the warden's dearly departed Westie's face at the opposite end, would hardly cause a ripple among the fine art collectors trawling the online auction rooms, let alone the ferocious bidding frenzy that she unwittingly envisaged.

'Dawson!' a guard then said, tapping at the door with her stick. 'You got a visitor.'

'Ay, who is it?' Dee Dee asked, not expecting any visitors at that time.

'How the hell do I know,' the officer replied arrogantly. 'Shift ya backside and go see for yaself.'

Dee Dee mouthed the word 'Twat' as the officer left.

Trisha emerged from beneath her pillow. 'Who is it Dee?' she asked, hopping from her bunk. 'Can ar come?'

'No!' Dee Dee said abruptly. 'You aint leavin this cell for the rest of the day d'you ear me, you've caused enough bleedin bovva for one day.'

'Ohhhhh Deeeeee but,' Trisha moaned, 'ar won't do nuffing ar promise.'

'Ar said no!' Dee Dee said resolutely. 'Maizie keep an eye on er, if she goes anywhere near that door kick er bleedin arse, d'you ear me.'

'Yeah alright Dee,' Maizie said, dragging Trisha back. 'Iss for yer own good Trish mate onest,' she told her. 'Ar tell ya what, why don'tcha finish ya jigsaw, iss comin along proper nice ain it.'

'D'ya fink so?' Trisha smiled, as Dee Dee left for her visitation. 'Ar lost a few of the bits but ar cut new ones out of a rice crispy box.'

Trisha's attempt to patch together a forty segment representation of Vincent Van Gogh's priceless sunflowers painting had failed miserably; the majority of the pieces had either been mislaid, cello-taped into place or completely remodeled to fit, giving the masterpiece an entirely abstract appearance. 'We ad a loada these dandelions in our garden in Manor Park,' she said, retrieving her plywood board from beneath her bed complete with tape and scissors.

Maizie settled down on her bunk with her titillating copy of 'Fifty Shades' to whet her appetite.

'Oh bugger!' Trisha then cursed, breaking Maizie's concentration. 'Ar'v only ended up wiv five bleedin corners ain I.'

Maizie donned her headphones and turned up her music to drown out Trisha's constant cries of frustration.

Dee Dee at that point was stood open mouthed in the visitors' centre. 'What the fuck?' she said, seeing West Ham Terry sat at a table dressed from head to toe in red and white, the colors of his beloved team's bitter North London rivals Arsenal. 'Tel, woss goin on geez?'

'Shut up for fuck sake!' Terry said, beckoning her over with a theatrical wink. 'Me name aint Tel, nart ar mean?' He looked furtively over his shoulder at the pacing guards. 'Ar'm still on the bleedin run ain I.'

'Yeah, ar know but,' Dee Dee said, looking him up and down, 'you're a gooner mate, sort it out!'

'Look!' Terry replied, pulling his woolly hat down over his ears. 'There's a mefod in me madness. No bugger's gonna recognize me dressed in this shit are they, ar don't like it believe me, ar reckon ar'm gonna end up wiv some poxy gooner rash or summink. Anyway iss a lot better than gettin me collar felt ar tell ya Dee, ar mean look at me, ar'm far too good lookin to do bird ain I. Ar'll av arf a dozen faggots angin out me bullet ole the minute ar set foot in the nick. So thas why ar'm deep under cover, nart ar mean?'

'Oh mate,' Dee Dee laughed, 'ar'd love to see you trussed up by the Pentonville pooftas ar really would.'

'Oh shut up Dee,' Terry protested, cringing at the thought. 'I aint no batty boy ya know, ar'm West Am Tel for fuck sake. Ar'm a face ain I.'

'They reckon it only urts the first time.' Dee Dee teased. 'After a coupla weeks you won't feel a flippin fing, and ya won't av any trouble droppin a log neeva.'

'No, don't say that,' Terry said, clenching his buttocks tight. 'Ar fink ar'd rarva top meself.'

Terry then leaned across the table and lowered his voice. 'Listen forget all that shit coz it aint gonna appen, the reason ar took a chance to come see ya is ar know this naughty little firm that reckon they can bust you'z girls out of ear. They got JCBs and all sorts of shit, all you'z gotta do in return is a coupla blags for em, Beckham's gaff and a few of them other poncy premiership players. Wod'ya reckon?'

Dee Dee thought the proposition over for a moment or two, weighing up the pros and cons. 'What if we get caught?' she asked Terry. 'We'll get shit loadsa time added onto our sentence and mate, if you saw how bonkers Trisha's goin in ear, you'd know that there's no way she'd survive. Besides we ad a visit from Mr Amilton, you know, the geeza we busted outta Somalia. Anyway, im and iz misses av been campaignin since we was banged up, and e'z gonna get us released in a week or two.'

'AY!' Terry gasped. 'They're lettin you out?'

'Yeah, result ay?' Dee Dee smiled. 'Maizie aint avin it too easy in ear neeva, so it's not before time ar tell ya.'

'Fuckin ell Dee!' Terry said, looking over his shoulder again. 'Thas pukka mate, we can do them blags and keep all the shit for ourselves. Oh yes mate, the old firm'll be back in business.'

'Fraid not Tel,' Dee Dee said, bursting her friend's bubble. 'We gotta go straight when we get out, and get a fuckin job an'all.'

'Shut uuuuup!' Terry laughed, sensing a wind up. 'You're avin a fuckin laugh aint'cha, you go straight, leave it out.'

'Iss true,' Dee Dee reiterated. 'Ar gotta give it a go Tell, for the uvver two, they're proper up for it.'

'What abaat you?' Terry asked. 'Don't tell me you're lookin forward to knockin ya bollocks out for a coupla'v undred quid a week. That aint you Dee, you're better than that shit all day long, and you know it.'

'Yeah ar do,' Dee Dee replied abruptly. 'But if ar didn't agree to it none of us woulda got out, so thas it, ar made me mind up, and you know me Tel, ar'm a stubborn cunt when ar wanna be.'

'Yeah, don't ar know it,' Terry agreed. 'Well, if you're sure mate,' he added. 'Least you'll be out, thas the main fing, we can av a coupla beers now and again can't we, but ar gotta keep me ed daan coz that prick Pritcher's still gunnin for me.'

DI Pritcher had sworn to apprehend Terry for his part in the foreign minister's murder, and had his men scour the streets and badger all his known associates, but as yet to no avail; which ate away at him causing him to hit the whiskey bottle harder than ever before.

Suddenly a voice from across the room called out, 'TELL, TELL MATE!'

'Shit,' Terry said, glancing over to see an old acquaintance from the Upton Park Terraces visiting his pregnant girlfriend. 'Ar gotta go Dee.'

'TELL MATE, ISS ME!' the man yelled again. 'JIMMY. TEL GEEZ, WHAT THE FUCK AR YOU WEARIN, DON'T TELL ME YOU GONE ROGUE ON US MATE. NOT WEST AM TEL, FOR FUCK SAKE!'

Terry got up from the table, pulled his scarf up around his cheeks and turned to leave. 'Ar dunno what ya talkin abaat fella,' he said, scurrying to the door, 'me names not Tel, now piss off!'

The visitor sat scratching his head for a moment until his irate girlfriend leaned across the table and slapped his face.

'Oy you dick, you come to see me din'tcha,' she said angrily. 'D'you bring mar fags or what?'

On leaving, Terry passed by a fellow Gunners fan also on a visitation.

'Up the Gunners!' the fan said, raising a fist in salute.

'Get fucked!' Terry growled, replying with a finger. 'I ope they get stuffed in Europe and the Ammers kick the shit out of em on Saturday.'

'What, ay?' the visitor gasped. 'Oh ar get it, nice one yeah,' he said assuming a wind up. 'GOOOOOOONERS GOOOOOOOOONERS!' he chanted.

'Melt,' Terry mouthed, turning his face away from the waiting guards and ducking out the door, where he then acknowledged the cat calls from several lusty inmates starved of male attention. 'Alright girls!' he said, puffing out his chest and sucking in his beer belly as best he could. 'Listen ar'd love to stick araand and slip you'z all a lenf, but these places proper freak me out, nart ar mean. But er, look me up when ya get out yeah. West Am Tel, everyone knows me, ar'm a proper face I am.'

Hearing this and looking him up and down, confused by his club allegiance, the girls suddenly changed their opinion of him fearing some kind of mental disorder had befallen him.

'Retard!' one of them said, watching him leave.

Dee Dee left the visitors' centre and returned to her cell, passing many of the prison's criminal elite who each in turn stepped aside as a mark of respect. Whilst Terry had delusions of grandeur, Dee Dee was the real deal, earning every one of her stripes the hard way.

'Who was it Dee?' Maizie immediately asked, removing her headphones on her return.

'West Am Tel, ar fink,' Dee Dee said, closing the door behind her.

'Woss e doin ear?' Maizie said, leaping to her feet. 'E'z on the run ain e, and woja mean ya fink, was it im or not?'

'Never mind,' Dee Dee said, dropping onto her bunk. 'Some firm wants to bust us out of ear, but ar told im we ain intrested. E laughed iz cock off when ar told im we was goin straight.'

'YEAH, AR DONE IT!' Trisha then shrieked, triumphantly. 'Wod'ya reckon?' She proudly displayed her pathetic puzzle, which would surely have had the eighteenth century Dutch impressionist turning in his grave. With copious amounts of tape, a little gum and a helping hand from her nail scissors, the replica Van Gogh in its mutilated state looked a sorry sight. 'Ar fink itta look better in a frame,' she told her friends, offering it to the wall. 'Woda you fink?'

'Itta look even better in a bleedin wheelie bin more like,' Dee Dee laughed. 'Trisha mate, you aint got an artistic bone in ya body av ya, why don'tchu just accept it and do us all a bloody favour.'
'Maizie tell er!' Trisha whinged. 'You like it don'tcha?'
'Er'm,' Maizie said, followed by an extended silence and a confused expression. 'Is it up the right way?' she eventually asked, seeing a segment of sky in the bottom left corner.
'Ar fink so,' Trisha said, checking for herself. 'Ar lost the box so I aint got a clue what iss supposed to look like.'
'Er, like a buncha bleedin flowers maybe,' Dee Dee said, stating the obvious. 'Not a pile a shite.'
'Well ar like it,' Trisha said, setting it down on the toilet cistern. 'The paintin lady said you av to av an artistic eye to appreciate it, so you'z two wouldn't understand.'
'Artistic eye my arse,' Dee Dee laughed. 'You gotta av a fuckin lobotomy to understand that shit, look at it for gawd sake.'
After defending her creativity to the hilt Trisha slipped into her pajama's and settled down for the night, as did her friends.
'I aint never comin back in ear,' Maizie said, after several minutes of silence. 'Never ar tell ya, this is bollocks this is.'
'Hmmmmm,' Dee Dee replied. To her the risks went with the territory, there had been no silver spoon to silence her newborn cries, and the school of hard knocks had dealt her and her kin some decisive blows over the years, but she was still standing, unbroken. Her Grandfather had served twelve years for his part in the Tate and Lyle payroll heist in the late fifties, at its time the most daring of raids making headlines the length and breadth of the country and even had a mention in The House of Lords.
'Ar kept me ed daan and done me bird,' her Grandfather had told her on numerous occasions, a mantra that had stayed with her throughout her life.
During her Grandfather's time the prison system was archaic to say the least, they were there to be punished for

their crimes, and punished they were each and every day. There were no televisions, games facilities or wireless internet to pass the time of day, just a white line daubed on a slate grey yard to be adhered to at all costs, stray from it and the full force of the totalitarian regime was brought to bear on you.

Solitary in those days meant being manacled to the wall of a six by six rat infested niche, in complete darkness with only the guard's urine laced water for sustenance; a far cry from the present day prisoner's pampered existence.

'Ar wanna Pina Colada when ar get aat,' Trisha piped up. 'An a large chicken shish.'

'Oooh, naah ya talkin!' Maizie said, licking her lips. 'Ar'll av a pint a larger, free yager bombs an a bacon double cheeseburger. What abaat you Dee?'

'What, ay?' Dee Dee said, deep in thought. 'Oh, me yeah, ar'll av a large JD and coke, no ice. As many flamin Sambucas as ar can fro daan me neck, an extra large deep pan Hawaiian wiv pepperoni and Jalapeno's, stuffed crust of course, tayter wedges, oh and don't forget the garlic bread.'

'Corrrrrr luuuvly,' Maizie said, longing for their fast food favorites. 'Ar'm gonna stuff meself stupid I am. Fuck the calories, ay?'

'Yeah,' Trisha agreed. 'Fuck em, who wants to be a size ten super bimbo anyway, gimmie a pukka pie, a pasty an a pickled egg thas what ar say.'

The girls lay lovingly listing the culinary classics they had yearned for since they were imprisoned.

'Walnut whips and Wham bars!' Trisha squealed, positively salivating at the thought of them.

'Tikka Masala,' Dee Dee said, getting in the swing of things. 'Mushroom rice, Bombay tayters an a pint a Cobra, and no ar don't want the friggin dessert menu!'

'Ar'll av it!' Maizie laughed. 'Ar want sticky toffee puddin, profiteroles, cookie dough ice cream, steamin ot custard an a cherry on top, mmmmmm.'

Each of them eventually drifted off to sleep with rumbling stomachs, to dream of all things edible. Trisha's of course being the most bizarre of fantasies, marshmallow mountains, french fry forests and a candy castle surrounded by a mojito moat.

The following morning Dee Dee and her friends were woken abruptly at six fifteen sharp by the sound of marching boots, jangling keys and raised voices.
'EVERYBODY OUT!' an officer yelled. 'CELL SEARCH. ALL OUT, ALL OUT!'
'Shit, what the fuck!' Dee Dee said, bleary eyed. 'Fuck iss the screws.'
Random cell searches were every inmates worst nightmare, many of them concealing contraband of one sort or another.
'YOU THREE, OUT!' another prison officer barked, rapping her stick on their cell door. 'NOW!'
Dee Dee's two friends had rolled over in an attempt to ignore the intrusion. 'Oy, get up will ya!' Dee Dee said, sliding from her bunk. 'And you Trish, come on!'
'Oh leave off Dee,' Trisha replied, from beneath her covers. 'Tell em to piss off will ya.'
'Trisha!' Dee Dee snapped through gritted teeth. 'We gotta play everyfing by the book, so get up or ar'll give you such a bleedin slap.'
Trisha and Maizie reluctantly hauled themselves from their bunks and trudged out into the corridor, tugging at their tangled hair to join their neighboring inmates.
Two officers were assigned to search each cell from top to bottom while the apprehensive occupants tapped their feet and crossed their fingers outside.
'We're alright,' Dee Dee told her friends. 'We aint got nuffing to ide.'
'Well, actually...' Trisha said, biting at a nail.
'Wod'you mean, well bloody actually?' Dee Dee snarled. 'What you gone and done Trisha?'
'Ar got a dooby under me mattress,' Trisha admitted.

'A what?' Maizie asked.
'A joint,' Trisha told her with a guilty expression. 'Ar swapped it for a Curly Wurly in metalwork, an ar was gonna trade it with the Baker sisters for some Vaseline. These dungarees ar chaffin mar bum cheeks summink chronic.'
'You stupid bitch!' Dee Dee growled. 'You'll get ten days in the ole if they find it.'
'Trisha!' Maizie said in abject disbelief. 'Ar don't bloody believe you!'
'Shit, they won't chuck me in the ole will they Dee?' Trisha said, immediately seeing the error of her ways. 'Ar can't go daan there mate, ar want me chicken shish.'
'You can kiss goodbye to that,' Dee Dee scoffed. 'Looks like me and Maizie'll be gettin out on our own.'
'Oh don't say that Deeee,' Trisha whined. 'Dee, ya can't leave me mate, please ar won't be able to cope on me own, you know that.'
Maizie shoved Trisha. 'We should leave you in ear to rot you soppy cow!' she said angrily.
Trisha lowered her head with a quivering lip. 'Ya can't leave me,' she sobbed, 'ar'm wunna the firm ain I.'
'Stop cryin ya dumb fuck!' Dee Dee said, thrusting an elbow in Trisha's side. 'Wiv a bitta luck these retards won't find it.'
But at that precise moment one of the officers emerged holding the marijuana laced cigarette proudly between thumb and forefinger.
'Well well well, what do we have here then?' she said sarcastically.
'Issa pork pie you melt!' Dee Dee scoffed defiantly. 'Wodya fink it is?'
Dee Dee's impertinence immediately enraged the officer. 'Funny,' she said, holding the joint to her nose. 'It doesn't smell like a pork pie, it smells like ten days in the hole to me Dawson. Now whose is it then, ay?'
Trisha slowly raised her hand.
'Iss mine!' Dee Dee admitted, swatting Trisha's hand down. 'Just a bitta personal thas all.'

The officer's smile widened further. 'You're not on the streets now Dawson,' she said, taking a zip lock bag from her top pocket and slipping the evidence inside. 'You know the rules. Warden's office, now!'
'But miss!' Trisha said, raising her hand once more.
'Shut it!' Dee Dee growled. 'Ar've already told er iss mine, alright!'
Maizie's heart sank. 'Shit Dee, what we gonna do?' she asked. 'We can't go wivout ya.'
'Don't you worry abaat me,' Dee Dee told them. 'If you got a chance of gettin out, you go and don't look back d'you ear me.'
'Move it Dawson!' an officer said, tugging at Dee Dee's arm.
'Yeah, yeah whateva,' Dee Dee replied, heading off along the corridor flanked by two guards.
'Trisha!' Maizie snapped. 'Now look what ya'v gone and done, she's proper fucked now she is.'
'Ar'm sorry,' Trisha said, wiping her nose and pleading her case. 'Ar didn't fink mate, ar was gonna get shot of it today, onest ar was.'
'Well iss too bleedin late now, ain it,' Maizie said, storming back into their ransacked cell. 'OY AINT'CHA GONNA TIDY THIS SHIT UP!' she yelled at the departing officers. 'LOOKA THE BLEEDIN STATE OF IT!'
The unfazed officers moved on to the neighboring cells, leaving the carnage in their wake.
'Ar'm really sorry Maize,' Trisha said, trailing behind. 'Praps ar should go tell the warden it was mar spliff, wod'ya reckon?'
'Ar reckon you should sit daan and shut the fuck up!' Maizie snapped, 'uvverwise you'll av Dee Dee to deal wiv, as well as the screws.'
'Yeah but,' Trisha said, dropping onto her bunk, 'ar can't let Dee take the shit for me can I, ay Maize. Maizie can I?'
Maizie turned her back on Trisha for fear of lashing out in anger. 'Gimme a minute to calm daan Trish,' she told her friend. 'Coz right naah ar wanna ring your bloody neck.'

'Alright mate,' Trisha said, staring at her jigsaw, tilting her head to make sense of the jumbled pieces.

Dee Dee was led to the second floor where the warden's office was situated,
'Move it Dawson!' an officer said, prodding Dee Dee's back with her stick. 'We aint got all flippin day.'
'Listen!' Dee Dee barked, spinning round. 'If you don't want that stick rammed up your shitty little arse, ar suggest you get it the fuck away from me!'
The officer immediately holstered her stick and led the way.
'Wait here,' she eventually told Dee Dee, knocking on the warden's door.
'IN!' the warden yelled, looking up from her notes.
'It's Dawson miss,' one of the officers said, entering and standing to attention. 'We found this in her cell this morning during the search.' She produced Exhibit A from her pocket and slipped it onto the warden's desk, sliding it toward her before regaining her military stance. 'I'll be making a full report of course miss.' She then ushered Dee Dee inside, gesturing for her to stand to attention also.
Without a word at first, the smiling warden looked the contraband up and down. 'Tut tut tut, oh dear,' she eventually said, dropping it into her desk drawer and crossing her hands behind her head and rocking back on her chair. 'Somehow I didn't think you'd be that stupid Dawson, but clearly I was wrong. You're no different from all the other wasters in here who think they can flout the law under my nose and get away with it. Well let me tell you this Dawson, nothing gets by me, nothing do you hear,' the warden waved her hand dismissively at the waiting officers. 'Leave us will you,' she said, relishing the hold she now had on Dee Dee.
'But miss!' one officer said, approaching the desk. 'Are you sure, she does have a history of violence, you know that.'
'Yes, thank you for reminding me!' the warden snapped, slamming the palm of her hand down on her beech wood

desk. 'Now wait outside, go on get out!' The officer scurried from the room ignoring Dee Dee's jeers.

'Yeah jog on,' Dee Dee laughed, 'there's a good girl.'

'I'll remind you to keep a civil tongue young lady,' the warden said, tapping her pencil hard on her desk, 'and respect my officers. They can make life pretty damned uncomfortable for you, as could I for that matter.'

'Whateva,' Dee Dee sneered. 'Say what ya gotta say and get on wiv it will ya.'

Dee Dee would prove to be a particularly tough nut to crack, the warden knew this, but bigger fish had stood before her in the past and crumbled.

'Drop the attitude!' the warden told Dee Dee. 'It doesn't wash with me, now let's get straight to the point. I have met with your Mr Hamilton, and he has informed me of your impending release. It seems you mix in quite an illustrious circle indeed, but, and there is a but, I am still the warden of this prison and, as I told your esteemed acquaintance, while you are still under this roof you are mine to do with as I see fit. I also informed him that there will be no early release if either you, or your friends, are found in breach of prison rules. I think you can guess where this conversation is headed Dawson, for possession of a banned substance you are looking at a mandatory ten days in solitary. Now I don't care what you have to say in your defence because believe me I've heard every bullshit excuse there is. My dear there is no defence, you're guilty, full stop, the only question remaining is what you are willing to do to avoid those ten miserable days, and believe me they will be miserable I will see to it personally.'

'What you on abaat?' Dee Dee asked. 'Ar'm guilty like ya said.'

'That you are,' the warden smiled, 'but your fate rests in my hands and mine alone, so I have a little proposition for you. If I were to turn a blind eye to this minor indiscretion, then I'd expect you to show your appreciation in some way. That would only be fair, am I right?'

'Ar don't get it,' Dee Dee said confused. 'Am ar goin to the ole or not?'

'Well that my dear, depends on you doesn't it,' the warden replied. 'You see I know you command a certain respect among many of the slags in here so who better I thought to be my eyes and ears out there, until your release of course. I need to know what's happening where and when, who's doing what to whom and why, and more importantly how this damned contraband is getting into my prison without going through me first. And you Dawson, are going to help me find out and nail those responsible to the wall.'

'You want me to grass,' Dee Dee said, startled at the thought. 'Ar'm tellin ya now that aint gonna appen, so ar'd save ya breff if ar was you.'

'Somehow I knew that would be your reaction,' the warden said, emerging from behind her desk and straightening her jacket. 'But I'm sure you'll reconsider when you hear what else I have to say.'

'Like fuck ar will,' Dee Dee said defiantly. 'Like ar said, save ya breff and take me to the ole.'

'Actually, I have a better idea,' the warden smiled. 'Let's say I send one of your friends down there instead, how would you feel about that?'

'You leave them aat of it!' Dee Dee said, lunging toward her. 'It aint nuffing to do wiv them, ar told ya it was mar spliff, they knew fuck all abaat it and thas the troof.'

'So I have your attention,' the warden said, knowing full well she had pressed precisely the right buttons. 'Now let's see, which one,' she pondered, 'I think that halfwit Trisha, she seems the most vulnerable wouldn't you say?'

'You leave er alone!' Dee Dee growled, causing the warden to reach for her mace.

'Think about what you're doing Dawson,' she said, fearing for her life momentarily, 'if you ever want to see the outside world that is.'

Dee Dee backed away with her fists clenched. 'You aint sendin mar mate to the ole, d'you ear me, ar won't let'cha.'

Suddenly feeling more at ease, the warden brushed off Dee Dee's threats and pocketed the mace. 'How long d'you think she'd last down there?' she asked. 'A day, two perhaps at the most, but not a moment longer. I've broken hardened lifers in less than ten days, so how do you think a delicate, and dare I say, unhinged creature like Trisha would fair?' She looked across at the array of disastrous pottery projects that Trisha had showered her with.

Dee Dee was backed against the wall and she didn't like it one bit, but the warden was right, Trisha was fragile and a spell in the hole would have a devastating effect on her.

'You orrible fuck!' Dee Dee said, feeling altogether powerless. 'She might be shit at pottry, but she don't deserve that and you know it, so leave er the fuck alone, d'you ear me.'

'My dear,' the warden said, perched on the edge of her desk, 'whether I know it or not is completely irrelevant, either you agree to be one of my informants, or that simpleton you call a friend will serve your time in the hole. Which is it to be Dawson, and be quick, this offer expires along with my patience, which I might hasten to add is rapidly diminishing.'

Dee Dee's only chance of sparing her friend the nightmare of the hole was to agree to the warden's terms, but somehow, to give in to the aging tyrant would go against every principle she had come to stand for. But before the words, 'Fuck you,' left her lips she noticed a family portrait on the warden's desk with a familiar face in the background.

'Billy Simmonds!' she said, leaning in for a closer look. 'Fuck me, it is im, ow d'you know that piece of shit?'

The warden snatched the photograph from Dee Dee and replaced it. 'He's my nephew and I'll thank you not to refer to him in that way or I'll double her time in the hole and withdraw my offer, do you hear me.'

Dee Dee then took a closer look at the warden's badge on her breast pocket and soon the pieces in her head began to fall into place. 'So you're Ruthy Simmonds, ar ya?' she said, taking a step back and smiling. 'Well, ar'll be fucked, mar grandad told me all abaat you. You used to work the streets daan Manor Park way, screwin the pissed up punters from the Burnell Arms for a poxy tenner a time. And that little scrote Billy there torched the social club off Green Street and set up that Asian firm for it, they never did catch up wiv im did they. Well well well, ar bet your guvnas don't know you touted your arse up and daan the high Street in the Eighties; blowin anyone wiv a couple bob in their pocket. And that you elped Billy stitch up them Bhangra boys, no ar bet they bleedin don't. You musta lied fru ya teef to get this gig ar bet. Iver that or ya stuck ya scrawny arse in the air and let em ride you at the interview.' Dee Dee felt a surge of adrenaline as the balance of power began to shift in her favour. 'Woss up, not so gobby now ar ya?'

'I, I don't know what you're talking about,' the warden stammered, laying the photograph face down. 'My name may be Simmonds, but you have me confused with somebody else, I assure you.' The redness in her cheeks told a different story.

Ruth had indeed plied her grubby trade on the Manor Park streets during the Seventies and Eighties to feed her marijuana and Martini addiction, offering her body up for as little as a pound on occasions.

'Don't gimme all that,' Dee Dee insisted. 'Your phone number's still on the Burnell bog walls, just above the glory ole; oh eight nine eight, slag wunnit?'

'This is preposterous!' the warden stormed. 'How dare you!'

'It is you and you know it,' Dee Dee replied, jabbing the warden with a finger without a care for the consequences. 'An ar got a dozen blokes wiv a cock rash thatta back me up, so just shut the fuck up will ya coz now ar'm gonna tell you ow fings ar gonna go daan.'

The warden wilted before Dee Dee, knowing that she now held the upper hand. 'Listen here Dawson,' she said, pulling out a chair for Dee Dee. 'Or shall I call you Dee Dee, would you prefer that? There's no need for us to go raking around in the past is there. I'm sure we've all got our fair share of skeletons haven't we? Would you like some tea?'

'No, poke ya tea!' Dee Dee told her, putting her feet up on the warden's polished desk. 'First you're gonna say ya sorry for bad maafin me and mar mates, or ar'm gonna make such a fuckin scene in this place that your guvnas are gonna wanna know woss goin on, an ar'm gonna feel obliged to tell em everyfing.'

'Like I said, let's not be too hasty,' the warden said, taking her seat and offering Dee Dee an open box of chocolates. 'Please, do help yourself.'

Dee Dee snatched the box and emptied the entire contents into her pocket. 'Well!' she said, opening a toffee and popping it into her mouth, discarding the wrapper. 'Ar'm waitin.'

Just as Dee Dee had struggled to relinquish her earlier stance, so the warden choked on her words now. 'I er, I'm, I mean I do apologize if I have offended you in any way Dee Dee,' she clenched her fists beneath the desk. 'I hope you believe me when I say it wasn't my intention.'

'You lyin fuck,' Dee Dee snarled, 'you loved evry bleedin minute of it. Well let me tell you this, I aint never gonna be your bitch, I aint never gonna be anyone's bitch, you got that. And secondly, you're gonna drag ya bony arse daan to mar cell and fank Trisha for ya pottry presents, no matter ow shite they are. OK!'

The warden's blood was now boiling in her veins, but her position at the prison meant everything to her, so if she had to gorge herself on humble pie to keep it, then so be it. 'Yes, yes of course, I'll see to it right away,' she told the gloating Dee Dee. 'And of course, I'll overlook the matter of the marijuana joint and her spell in the hole.'

'Too fuckin right ya will!' Dee Dee said, tossing another toffee wrapper across the desk. 'Ar'm glad me and you now got an understandin, now jog on and go see er while ar use that flash karzi of yours, ar bet you got that quilted shit roll aint'cha, er ya don't mind do ya?'

'No, of course not, go right ahead,' the warden said, trying her damnedest to conceal her rage. 'Please, make yourself at home, there's a bottle of sweet sherry in the cabinet. I'll see to it that you're not disturbed.'

'Fanks,' Dee Dee replied, taking the warden's seat as she left and rifling through her desk drawers, pocketing her gold plated fountain pen and popping her designer sunglasses onto her head. 'Woss this shit?' she then said, reaching into the nearby drinks cabinet and retrieving the vintage sherry and sipping from the bottle. 'Jesus!' she said, spitting the mouthful across the warden's desk, 'thas fuckin dire!'

After a good fifteen minutes in the warden's lavish en suite beautifying herself, and dropping a good pound and a half into her gleaming pan and refusing to flush, Dee Dee finally left her office and made her way back to her cell glaring at several officers on the way, knowing now that with the aid of her recent discovery she was virtually untouchable.

'DEEEEEEEEE!' Maizie screamed, elated to see her friend. 'Oh flippin ell Dee, ar fought we'd never see you again mate, ar really did. What appened, ar fought you was goin daan the ole. Trish look Dee's ear!'

'Oh Deeeee!' Trisha squealed. 'Dee mate ar'm so pleased to see ya, ooh before ar ferget listen ar got summink to tell ya, guess what appened while you was gone, guess go on, ava guess.'

'Just tell me ya twat!' Dee Dee snapped. 'What, what appened, come on tell me then!'

'Well,' Trisha said taking a deep breath, 'd'ya know me bedside table fingy that ar said was werf a few quid and you two never believed me, well...'

'Well what for fuck sake!' Dee Dee said, losing her temper somewhat, 'what abaat it?'

'Ar told ya, ar told ya!' Trisha shrieked, taking a fistful of twenty pound notes from her pocket. 'Ar told ya it was wef dough dint I, the warden just come in and gimme free undred quid for it, she said it was just what she was lookin for. Ar knew it Dee, ar got the gift, antiques of the future thas what mar creations ar. Ar tell ya mate when ar get aat ar'm gonna get me a workshop and start knockin em out olesale, wod'ya reckon?'

'Yeah, whatever ya want,' Dee Dee said, letting Trisha have her moment of triumph.

'Ar couldn't believe it Dee,' Maizie said, interjecting, 'free undred quid for that pile a shit!'

Trisha waved the bundle of notes under Maizie's nose. 'Yeah coz iss art ain it, are wouldn't expect you to understand, you got no breedin, iss like silly bollocks and er unmade bed, only someone creative like me could see what she was tryna say.'

'Ar know what she was tryna say alright, the lazy cow!' Maizie snapped. 'Fuck it ar do it later, that shit ain art is it for gawd sake.'

'You're just jealous,' Trisha said, defending her work resolutely. 'You were crap at anyfing like that at school.'

'And you weren't!' Maizie said, retaliating. 'That poxy dolls ouse you banged togevva in woodwork looked more like a bombed aat squat.'

Dee Dee reclined on her bed with her hands clasped behind her head. 'Will you two turn it in!' she said, eager for a rare moments peace.

'She started it!' Trisha moaned, tucking the money beneath her pillow.

'No ar never!' Maizie said in a childish tone, 'Dee tell errrr!'

'AR SAID TURN IT IN!' Dee Dee barked. 'Jesus ar tell ya what, bein banged up in the same bleedin cell wiv you two's enough to drive someone to suicide, it really is.'

'Eeya,' Maizie said, 'funny you should say that, they found some tart on level two this mawnin strung up by er stockins, they tried to revive er apparently but she snuffed it.'

'Yeah, ar knew er,' Trisha added, stretching out on her bunk. 'She was in mar pottry class.'

'Oh that explains it then,' Dee Dee said, tongue in cheek. 'Did they find a note in er cell sayin ar can't put up wiv that stupid bitch anymore?'

'No!' Trisha replied, turning to face her friend. 'No they never actually, she was a bit of a nut nut anyway if you ask me, said she erd voices in er ed tellin er to kill people.'
'Oh, ar get that all the time,' Dee Dee confessed.
'Do ya,' Trisha asked, 'Really?'
'Oh yeah,' Dee Dee laughed, 'ar can ear Maizie of a night time tellin me to smuvva you in ya sleep.'
Trisha glared at Maizie. 'Thas not nice Maize, ar fought we was mates.'
'We are,' Maizie told her, 'when you aint grindin ya teef and chattin shit in ya sleep.'
'Ar don't talk in me sleep,' Trisha said defensively, 'do ar Dee?'
'You do Trish,' Dee Dee said. 'An iss doin mar nut in an'all. Last night you was goin on abaat ridin a green giraffe in the Grand National, ar mean woss that shit all abaat?'
'Oh yeah,' Trisha laughed, 'I av that dream a lot, wod'ya fink it means?'
'It means ya barkin!' Maizie intervened. 'And that crap abaat you and Britney in a barf of baked beans.'
'Ooooh yeah,' Trisha said, clamping her knees together on feeling a twinge in her crotch. 'That gets me proper orny that does, what ar wouldn't do to that bitch ar tell ya.'
'Sick!' Maizie said, turning up her nose at the thought. 'Ar be bleedin glad when we're aat of ear.'
Trisha took a small notebook from beneath her mattress and began scribbling her thoughts, staring into space occasionally for inspiration.
'What you doin?' Maizie asked. 'Woss that?'
'Writin me memrys,' Trisha replied, shaking her pen to increase the flow of ink.
'You mean ya memoirs,' Dee Dee said, correcting her. 'And what d'you know abaat writin?'
'Ar know enough don'tchu worry,' Trisha said, concealing her notebook. 'Ar reckon ar'd make a good orfa, if J K wosserface can do it, ar don't see why ar can't make a bundle at it.'

'What ya writin abaat anyway?' Dee Dee asked. 'Ar didn't even know you could spell.'

'Course ar can!' Trisha said abruptly. 'Ar got a B in English, and Miss Charmers said I ad a very vivid imagination which is just what ya need to be an orfa, ar'm writin abaat us free Dee, an all the shit thas appened, ar'm gonna call it Gissa Fag, catchy ain it?'

'No bugger'd believe it,' Maizie scoffed.

'Well ar'm writin it anyway,' Trisha said defiantly. 'Ar'm just up to the bit where ar shot ya bruvva in the leg, corr blimey that was funny wunnit eh?'

'Not for Bradley it weren't, ya dopey cow!' Maizie snapped. 'You coulda killed im.'

'You carry on Trish,' Dee Dee said supportively.

'Oh fanks Dee,' Trisha chirped, 'thas proper nice of ya.'

'That weren't a compliment,' Dee Dee admitted. 'Anyfing that keeps you quiet is a bleedin bonus, so as far as ar'm concerned if you wanna be an orfa, you crack on.'

'Yeah, yeah ar will,' Trisha said, dismissing Dee Dee's jibes. 'And when ar'm signin shit loads of me books in Waterstones, you'za be proper prouda me won't ya.'

'You reckon,' Maizie scoffed.

'Yeah ar do,' Trisha said. 'And when issa movie, ar be on that red carpet you wait and see. Who'dya want to play you in the film ay Dee?'

'Ar don't give a shit,' was Dee Dee's reply, as she rolled over to face the wall. 'Now let me sleep will ya.'

'What abaat you Maize?' Trisha asked. 'Renny Zelwegga, Kafrine Zeta wossername, ooh ar know, what abaat Kaffy Burke, ar loved er in Gimme Gimme Gimme, proper cockney an'all.'

Maizie too rolled over leaving Trisha to fantasize about her life as an award winning novelist, rubbing shoulders with the literary elite and seeing her name in print in high street bookstores.

'Ar might ask Tulisa to play mar bit,' Trisha rambled, 'we got the same size tits ar fink.' Trisha put pen to paper, laughing out loud periodically recalling their anarchic antics.
'Trisha, ar'm tryna friggin sleep!' Dee Dee growled.
'Sorry Dee,' Trisha giggled. 'Member when you chopped that dodgy Arab's bleedin arm off. "Cop that Sinbad" you said, ar was shittin meself at the time, but when ya fink back it was funny as fuck wunnit?'
'Ar gotta admit mate,' Maizie said turning back, 'that was the bollocks mate, e was gonna kill the lot of us wern e?'
'And we proper fucked them Tibbs's dint we?' Trisha told her friends.
'Yeah we did,' Dee Dee said, rolling over and staring at the ceiling. 'Ar spoze we av done some proper mental stuff aint we.'
The three friends lay on their bunks, reminiscing on days gone by, long into the early hours, with Trisha jotting the manic memories down as they came to mind.

CHAPTER THREE

Three days went by with no word from Clive Hamilton on their impending release, and the girls were beginning to grow restless.

'When we gettin aat Dee?' Maize said, pushing her plate away at breakfast. 'Ar carn eat much more of this shit, ar'm tellin ya, hairy bacon and runny egg, turns mar bleedin guts it does.'

Trisha plucked the bacon from Maizie's discarded plate. 'Ar'll av it,' she said, transferring it to hers before dipping her buttered slice into Maizie's partly cooked egg white. 'Ar love a bitta snot ar do.'

Dee Dee was about to chastise her friend when she heard an all too familiar voice behind her.

'Well, well, well,' Kathy Bennett snarled from the queue. 'If it ain't that cunt Dawson, and er two slags.'

'Bennett,' Dee Dee said, glancing over her shoulder while Maizie and Trisha froze and lowered their heads.

'Shit Dee,' Maizie whispered. 'They musta let er aat.'

Kathy had quite rightly been released from solitary that very morning and had been warned to keep her nose clean, or face a swift return. But she thought this was a small price to pay for exacting revenge upon Dee Dee for belittling her in front of her fellow prisoners, each of whom had been groomed to respect and obey only her.

'Less go Dee,' Trisha said, rising from her seat.

'Sit the fuck daan!' Dee Dee snapped, grabbing her friend's arm, 'we ain't goin nowhere.'

'Me and you got business,' Kathy growled, glaring at the back of Dee Dee's head whilst checking the officers' proximity. 'Ar'm gonna teach you a fuckin lesson you ain't never gonna forget, d'you are me?'

Dee Dee merely raised a finger above her shoulder, barely acknowledging Kathy's threats which infuriated the bloated bully.

'You fuckin ore!' Kathy said, lunging from the queue tray in hand, but she was quickly tugged back by her minions on seeing an approaching guard.

'Is there a problem here Bennett?' the guard asked, fingering her stick in its holster.

'No there aint!' Kathy barked. 'So piss off!'

'Watch it Bennett,' the guard warned. 'You'll get double time in the hole if you step out of line again, you know that.'

Kathy turned her back on Dee Dee and the officer and thrust her tray across the counter. 'Ar want all that bacon,' she said, eyeing at least four portions on the hotplate. 'And don't be tight wiv the beans neeva.'

The caterer hastily heaped the bacon onto Kathy's plate and topped it with a brimming ladle of baked beans. Kathy then snatched the bread from the prisoner's tray in front of her, staring her down when she spun round. 'WHAT?' she snarled. 'Turn raand and jog the fuck on will ya!' The prisoner scurried from the queue and sat some distance away not daring to look back.

Under the watchful eye of the prison officers Kathy and her cronies took their places at a table across the aisle to Dee Dee.

'Ar'm gonna cut'chu open,' Kathy mouthed, giving Dee Dee the eye and shoveling dripping bacon into her mouth. 'You're dead d'you ear me, dead.'

Dee Dee merely smiled in reply, sipping her tea unfazed.

'Dawson!' an officer said, appearing from behind 'You got a call.'

'Who is it?' Dee Dee asked, setting her mug down.

'No idea,' the officer replied, going about her business, 'get off your backside and go find out.'

'We're comin wiv ya,' Maizie said, hoisting Trisha to her feet, not wanting to be left with Kathy and her crew.

'Yeah,' Trisha added, cleaning her plate with the remainder of her bread. 'Fucked if we're stayin ear.'

Dee Dee led the way to the public phone situated in the corridor. 'Ello,' she said, tucking the receiver under her chin. 'Ello, who's that?'

'Hi Dee it's Clive, Clive Hamilton,' Clive said from his office. 'I trust you three are well.'

'Alright Clive,' Dee Dee replied. 'Yeah, not bad mate, woss appnin?'

'Good news,' Clive told her, 'I have a date for your release and it's sooner than expected, it appears the warden there is keen to see the back of you.'

'Ar bet she bleedin is,' Dee Dee smirked. 'So when we gettin aat then?'

'Ooooooh iss Mr Amilton!' Trisha squealed. 'Maize mate we're gettin the fuck aat of ear.' Trisha and Maizie hugged and hopped on the spot.

'Yes, fank fuck,' Maizie shrieked. 'When Dee, when?'

'Shut it will ya,' Dee Dee said, unable to concentrate. 'So Clive, when mate?'

'This Friday, two o'clock,' Clive replied. 'Isn't that great. I was absolutely thrilled when I got the call this morning. Now I've pulled a few strings for you and have found you three somewhere to stay when you get out, it's not much but all I could do in such short notice. Also I've gotten you girls placements in your chosen charities, and as you know it is a condition of your release that you attend for a minimum of five years.'

'When Dee when?' Maizie said, tugging at Dee Dee's arm. 'Come on mate. When!'

'Friday!' Dee Dee snapped. 'Now shut it will ya!'

'Friday!' Maizie cried, shaking Trisha bodily. 'Trish iss Friday mate, ar can't believe it, two days and we're aat, two fuckin days!'

'Friday!' Trisha squealed. 'Really, really Maize?'

'Yeah,' Maizie said, almost beside herself. 'Yeah Trisha, Friday!'

'Ang on a minute Clive,' Dee Dee said, turning to her friends. 'Will you two fuck off for a minute,' she barked.

Trisha and Maizie skipped back to their cell and sat on Dee Dee's bunk brimming with excitement.
'Five years,' Dee Dee said disgruntled. 'We gotta do that shit for five years.'
'Yes,' Clive said, thumbing his notes. 'Like I said it's an unconditional term of your release. The main thing is you'll be out of there Dee, with a fresh start ahead of you, and you never know you may grow to enjoy your new role.'
'Don't old ya breff,' Dee Dee said, raising her eyebrows.
'Right, I best be off,' Clive said, checking his wrist watch. 'I'll be there to meet you on Friday, and Crystal has insisted on joining me, so until then I'll say goodbye.'
'Yeah seeya geez,' Dee Dee said, replacing the handset and standing in quiet contemplation. 'Friday,' she said to herself with a clenched fist, 'Yes!'
'Dee mate, Friday, can ya believe it!' Maizie said on her friend's return. 'What a result!'
'Yeah nice,' Dee said, still mulling over her proposed employment for the next five years. 'You got yer animal job Trish by the way,' she added.
'Really!' Trisha shrieked. 'Brilliant, ar can't wait ar tell ya.'
'Where we gonna stay Dee,' Maizie asked, 'we can't go back to the estate.'
'Mr Amilton's sorted us a gaff aat,' Dee Dee told her. 'Ar dunno where, but e'z meetin us at the gates on Friday and e'z bringin little Crystal wiv im.'
'Ahhhh,' Trisha sighed. 'Ar bin finkin abaat er I av, ar made er summink in pottry.' She rummaged in the holdall beneath her bunk. 'Dya fink she'll like it?'
'What is it?' Maizie asked, looking the tiny figurine up and down.
'Iss me!' Trisha said, holding it beside her face. 'Can't ya see?'
'No,' Dee Dee laughed, 'looks more like Shrek to me.'
'Oh shut uuuup,' Trisha moaned. 'Ar fink issa good likeness, and so does the pottry lady.'

'If you'd bin it by a flamin truck maybe,' Maizie chuckled, snatching it from her. 'It don't even stand up proply,' she added, setting it down on the toilet cistern only for it to tumble down into the pan.

'Oh Maaaaaaaize!' Trisha cried, leaping to her feet and plunging her hand beneath the water, and retrieving her statuette in two pieces. 'Oh naah look what ya gone and done, ya busted me bleedin ed off. Look Dee, she's buggered it right up aint she?'

Trisha then raised her hand to her nose. 'Oh bloody Nora!' she said, screwing up her face. 'Who pissed and never flushed, ay?'

'Sorry mate, that was me,' Maizie said, raising a hand and a smile. 'We was late for breakfast, member?'

'Oh thas just priceless,' Dee Dee said, rolling back on her bunk in fits of laughter.

Trisha set the broken statue down on Dee Dee's bunk and rushed to the sink, running her hands under the hot tap.

'OY!' Dee Dee yelled. 'Kicking the two pieces onto the floor, where they shattered into a dozen or more fragments. 'Get that shit off me bed will ya.'

'Oh Deeeeeee,' Trisha moaned, 'iss proper fucked naah ain it.'

Maizie also fell about laughing while Trisha looked on stunned. 'I aint got time to make anuvva one,' Trisha told them. 'You can't just knock stuff aat like this willy nilly ya know.'

'Course ya can't,' Dee Dee agreed, biting her lip, 'iss art ain it Trish.'

This time Trisha wasn't so naïve. 'Ar know you're takin the piss Dee,' she said, sweeping up the pieces and dumping them in the bin. 'And you Maizie, the paira ya are always takin the piss outta me, and ar'm sick of it!' With that she stormed from the cell, flinging the dustpan to the floor.

'Ooops,' Maizie said, realizing they may have overstepped the mark somewhat. 'Ar feel proper bad now Dee,' she said,

sitting up on her bunk. 'After all, she did make it for Crystal, dint she.'
'Yeah ar know,' Dee Dee said, feeling for her friend. 'Ar'll go get er, you wait ear.'
Dee Dee first looked around the mess hall but there was no sign of Trisha. 'You seen Trish?' she asked Carol, another lifer, delivering books to her regulars.
'No, no I aint Dee,' Carol told her, whilst taping the torn spine of a well read classic. 'Not since brecky mate.'
'Alright cheers,' Dee Dee said, starting along the corridor, popping her head into the gymnasium and games room along the way. 'TRISH!' she called, but got no reply. Rounding the corner she then saw one of Kathy's close allies ducking into the library and on approach began to hear raised voices.
'Fuck wiv me will ya, you little slag!' Kathy could be heard snarling.
Dee Dee pushed open the door to see Trisha sprawled out on the floor with Bennett sat astride her, repeatedly beating the side of her face with a clenched fist. 'Well arm gonna fuck you up bad.'
'OY GET THE FUCK OFF ER!' Dee Dee screamed, lunging forward. But she was then suddenly grabbed from behind and held with her arms pinned to her side by two of Kathy's crew.
'Oh, nice of you to join us,' Kathy said, wiping the hair from her face. 'When ar'm finished wiv this cunt you're gonna get yours, but for now you can watch me tear your mate to bits.'
Dee Dee squirmed to get free but was held fast by the bisexual brutes. 'LEAVE ER YOU BITCH!' she yelled, seeing Trisha's head tossed from side to side by Bennett's pounding blows. 'FUCKIN LEAVE ER ALONE, AR SWEAR AR'LL KILL YA. AR'LL FUCKIN KILL YA AR WILL!'
Trisha had lost consciousness and a good deal of blood as Kathy, now reveling in the blood bath, slid a screwdriver

from her boot. 'Say goodbye,' she said, staring at Dee Dee through wild eyes.
'NO, NO DON'TCHU FUCKIN DARE!' Dee Dee said, knowing full well that Kathy would stick Trisha and think absolutely nothing of it. With very little time to lose Dee Dee flung her head back violently, catching one of the girls holding her on the bridge of the nose causing her to release her grip and break away clutching her face. With one arm now free she grabbed a handful of the remaining girl's lank yellow hair and pulled her face toward hers. 'Fuckin slag!' she snarled, biting down on her right ear and shaking her head from side to side until the majority of the ear was ripped away, spattering both their faces with blood. The girl let out a blood curdling scream, and dropped to her knees trying to stem the flow with her trembling hands.
Kathy clambered to her feet leaving Trisha battered but breathing. 'GET UUUUUUP!' she screamed at her reeling girls, who lay cowering beneath Dee Dee. 'GET UP AND FUCKIN KILL ER!'
Dee Dee looked down and spat the portion of ear, and a quantity of blood, at its former owner and wiped her mouth smearing the remainder of blood from her lips across her face. To Kathy's complete surprise Dee Dee kicked the girls aside and turned the key in the door locking them inside. 'Me and you Bennett, less fuckin av it!' she said, raising both fists.
'Niiiiice,' Kathy said, relishing the moment and flinging the screwdriver from one hand to the other. 'Come on, cunt. COME ON!'
Dee Dee approached with caution and circled Kathy, looking down at her battered friend.
'Ava good fuckin look!' Kathy said grinning. 'Coz thatta be you soon enough.' Kathy then lunged at Dee Dee wielding her weapon with a maddening expression. 'Grrrrrrr come ear!' she said, striking out again and again missing Dee Dee by a matter of inches on each occasion.

Seizing an opportunity Dee Dee lashed out herself catching Kathy's jaw and splitting her lip. 'Av that, bitch!' Dee Dee said, skipping on her feet. 'Want some more do ya?' she added, goading Kathy. 'Well come get it you fat fuck!'

Incensed, Kathy charged bull-like toward Dee Dee, swinging her weapon and fist wildly and catching Dee Dee off guard knocking her to the floor.

'Yes, fuck ya!' Kathy said, raising the screwdriver above her head and plunging it toward Dee Dee who rolled to the side as the tool was thrust into the oak segmented flooring.

Springing to her feet before her opponent could compose herself, Dee Dee rammed a fist into Kathy's side and the other directly after into her face a total of seven times in rapid succession, causing her to drop the screwdriver and stagger backwards into a tall bookshelf, sending it and its heavy contents crashing to the floor. In an attempt to defend herself from any further onslaught, Kathy grabbed at the scattered novels and began flinging them in Dee Dee's direction. Two of which struck her about the body.

It was then that several prison officers could be heard rattling the door handle and radioing for further backup. 'OPEN THE DOOR!' one of them yelled, bearing down on it with her stick. 'OPEN THE DOOR, NOW!'

Kathy dragged herself to her feet once again, wiping the sweat from her forehead. 'You're dead,' she said, now blowing hard. 'Dead Dawson.'

The girl whom Dee Dee had butted made a grab for her leg in an attempt to assist her boss, but was instantly rewarded with the heel of Dee Dee's shoe to the side of her face. 'STAY DAAN!' Dee Dee yelled, kicking at her ribs also.

Kathy suddenly made a grab for the tool and with an explosion of raw power flung herself at Dee Dee, grabbing her right arm with one hand and jabbing the driver into her thigh with the other. 'Cunt!' she said, wrenching it clear and thrusting it deep once more.

'FUUUUUUCK!' Dee Dee screamed, pulling back on Kathy's hair and raining down blows onto her face. Over and over she pummeled Bennett's head whilst receiving a crushing bear hug. Eventually, with the officers pounding at the door, Kathy could withstand no more and released her grip and staggered backward, tripping and falling amongst the strewn books. But Dee Dee hadn't finished with her. With her leg oozing blood from the two jagged puncture wounds, she hobbled toward Kathy and dropped at her side.

'Fuck you Bennett!' she said, panting herself.

Kathy's energy levels were spent as she floundered trying to raise a fist to continue the fight. 'Dead Dawson,' she mumbled, 'you're dead.'

With the red mist descending fast Dee Dee grabbed a fist full of Kathy's greasy hair and lifted her bloated head from the pile of books and beat down on her face with pure aggression and ferocity.

'Ar told ya to leave mar fuckin mate alone you dirty fat fuck!' Dee Dee said, watching Kathy's eyes glaze over.

Bennett was beaten and bloodied but Dee Dee was unstoppable at this point, flinging Kathy's swollen head down she scoured the pile for the heaviest of books, eventually grabbing a large eighteenth century bible some three inches thick, raised it above her head and unleashed some divine retribution of her own, slamming it down on Bennett's head hard over and over, both of them pretty soon dripping with her blood.

Suddenly the library door burst open under the weight of several shoulders

'DAWSON STOP!' an officer yelled. 'I SAID STOP RIGHT NOW!'

Dee Dee continued her raging onslaught until the bible was snatched from her spattered hands, and she was wrestled from Kathy's side. 'DIE YOU CUNT!' she screamed, still kicking out at Kathy's pulverized body.

The warden followed her officers inside and stood aghast at the bloody scene. 'WHAT THE BLOODY HELL?' she said, with her hands on her hips 'DAWSON I MIGHT HAVE KNOWN.'

Medics rushed to attend to Trisha and Kathy, checking first for a pulse.
'Is she alright?' Dee Dee asked, whist being manacled, her right trouser leg awash with her own blood. 'IS SHE ALRIGHT? OY ANSWER ME!' she yelled, wrestling with the restraining officers. A medic nodded in reply helping lift Trisha onto a stretcher.
'What on earth happened here Dawson?' the warden asked, stopping Dee Dee as she was being led from the room. 'Was this your doing?'
'No, no it weren't,' Dee Dee said, spitting more of Kathy's minders blood from her mouth and glaring at Kathy, wanting more of her. 'That fat fuck battered mar mate, look at er, look at Trisha the poor cow. DIE BENNETT TOU FUCKIN ORRIBLE BITCH, FUCKIN DIIIIIIIIE!'
At this point dozens of inmates had gathered outside as did Maizie in search of her friends. 'DEEEEEEE, DEEEE!' she called out, seeing Dee Dee dragged from the room limping with her hands fastened behind her back. 'DEE MATE, WHAT APPENED?'
'Iss alright Maize, iss alright,' Dee Dee told her, wanting to spare her the gruesome details.
'Oh mar gawd!' Maizie said, breaking through the crowd and rushing to the stretcher. 'TRISH!'
Trisha came to for a second or two, opened one eye and took Maizie's hand.
'Oh no, no no no,' Maizie said holding Trisha's hand to her cheek. 'Trish look at'cha mate, who done it?' Bennett's body was then stretchered out by six panting guards.
'YOU, YOU YA FUCKIN SLAG!' Maizie cursed, lunging at the stretcher with flaying fists, but was immediately subdued by the squad of officers. 'LEMMY GO, LEMMY GO. AR'LL KILL ER!' she yelled, kicking out and catching Bennett's dangling arm.
'Calm down, calm down,' she was told. 'Go with your friends, go on.'

'MAIZE COME ON,' Dee Dee called back over her shoulder. 'WE GOTTA GET TRISH SEEN TO!'
Maizie ran to Dee Dee wedging her head under her right arm to take the weight from her injured leg.
'Fanks,' Dee Dee said, wincing.
'What appened Dee?' Maizie asked, looking down at her friend's bloodied clothes. 'Was it Bennett?'
'Yeah,' Dee Dee said, clutching her wounds. 'She jumped Trisha in the library and give er a proper beatin.'
'And you an'all by the looksa fings,' Maizie said, wiping the blood from Dee Dee's chin.
'That aint mine,' Dee Dee informed Maizie. 'Iss that fat fucks.'
'Bleedin ell Dee,' Maizie gasped. 'Wod'you do to er?'
'Not enough,' Dee Dee said defiantly. 'Ar wonnid to kill er Maize, smash er face to pieces, ar would of an'all if the screws never showed up.'
Kathy was taken to the waiting prison ambulance and whisked off to nearby Saint Pancras hospital as the injuries she had sustained were deemed life threatening, while Dee Dee and Trisha were given adjoining beds in the infirmary.
'What the bloody hell happened in there?' the warden barked, following behind. 'Dawson, did you instigate this because by Christ if you did I'll...'
'No ar bleedin never!' Dee Dee replied, watching her trouser leg being cut from her heel to her hip. 'That bastard Bennett and er bitches jumped Trisha and was gonna do er over wiv a screwdriver.'
One of the warden's officers then produced the said weapon in a clear plastic bag. 'Bennett stole it from class earlier this morning miss,' she told her boss. 'And there's at least twenty girls willing to corroborate Dawson's version of events.'
'I bet there bloody is!' the warden said, glaring over her spectacles at the three girls. 'Bennett may have started this fracas Dawson,' she added, wagging a finger, 'but I do

believe you used excessive force in retaliation. Wouldn't you say?'
'Ar was just gettin started,' Dee Dee said, swallowing the painkillers handed to her, 'she got off lightly if you ask me,'
Snatching the evidence, the warden stormed from the infirmary to file her report, heaping all blame on Bennett and painting Dee Dee whiter than white, a wise move considering the hold she had over her.
'Is she alright?' Dee Dee then asked the prison medics attending to Trisha's facial injuries.
'Yes, she'll be fine in a few days,' one of them told her. 'There doesn't appear to be anything broken.'
'Fank gawd for that,' Maizie said, sitting at Trisha's side. 'Iss mar fault ain it Dee, if I adn't wound er up abaat er art stuff she would be lyin ear all busted up would she.'
Trisha gathered the strength to prod her friend, shaking her head to spare her friend the guilt.
'It is mar fault an ar'm sorry mate,' Maizie said, leaning to kiss Trisha's rapidly swelling cheek. 'Ar shouldn't take the piss aat of ya pottry, yer right ar couldn't do it, I aint got the patience for one, nor the eye for it like you av.'
Trisha could not speak, she merely clawed at Maizie's leg until their hands met, and then reached out for Dee Dee.
'We're still ear aint we,' Dee Dee said, clinging to her tightly. 'Unfuckinstoppable, thas what we are. Unfuckinstoppable!'
Dee Dee then swatted a medics hand away. 'Leave it!' she said looking across at Trisha. 'Sort er out first will ya.'
The prison doctor gestured to a colleague to attend to Trisha while she continued to disinfect and anesthetise Dee Dee's leg, in readiness for stitching. 'You'll be alright mate,' Dee Dee told her friend.
Tears of gratitude streamed from Trisha's blackened eyes as she struggled to speak.
'Shhh, shh shh,' Dee Dee told her. 'Ar know mate, ar know, ya don't av to say a word believe me.'
Maizie took a tissue from her pocket and tenderly dried Trisha's cheeks. 'Iss alright Trish mate,' she said

sympathetically, 'you'll be good as new in a coupla days. Won't she doc, ay?'
'Yes, I don't see why not,' the doctor replied, preparing a mild sedative. 'With plenty of rest that is.' She then applied a cold compress to Trisha's face to relieve the swelling, checked the dilation of her pupils with her torch and gently teased open her blooded mouth. 'I'm amazed you're still in one piece young lady,' she added, swabbing the majority of the blood before pulling the sheets up around Trisha's chest. 'Bennett usually sends them here in a much worse condition.'
'She's tough as old boots our Trish is,' Maizie said, patting Trisha's knee. 'Aint'cha mate?'
Trisha managed a half smile, which judging by the rigidity of her body, pained her to do so.
An attending officer took Maizie by the arm. 'Come on, back to your cell now,' she said, checking the digital clock above the door. 'Ten minutes and it's lockdown,'
'Carn ar stay ear tonight,' Maizie pleaded. 'Please, ar'll kip on the floor if I av to, ar don't mind, ar just wanna make sure me mates are alright.'
'Out of the question!' the officer barked. 'That's strictly against prison policy, now come on, away with ya.'
'Go on Maize,' Dee Dee told her. 'Ar'll keep an eye on Trish, don't worry.'
'Don't worry!' Maizie said, throwing her hands in the air. 'Look at the paira ya. Beat to fuck an ar weren't there to elp ya. Ow d'ya fink that makes me feel ay, course ar'm gonna worry abaat ya'z!'
'Ar know that,' Dee Dee replied. 'But there aint nuffing you can do that these quacks aint doin is there, go on bugger off.'
'You sure you're alright?' Maizie asked, breaking away from the officer. 'Ar don't wanna be on me own tonight wiv you'z two stuck in ear.'

'Maizie!' Dee Dee snapped, in no mood for her friend's foolish behavior. 'Piss off to bed will ya, come and see us in the mawnin, we aint goin nowhere are we.'
'Only if ya sure,' Maizie said, tapping Trisha's toes. 'Ar see ya first fing tomorra,' she said, shaking her head at the battered wreck before her.
Following the officer from the infirmary Maizie made her way back to their cell mulling over scenarios in her head like how different the outcome may have been should she have been at her friends' side.
'Fuckin bitch!' she cursed, still furious with Bennett and wishing her dead, which was closer to reality than she could have imagined.

Kathy had been rushed to theatre at Saint Pancras where a team of neurosurgeons worked tirelessly to relieve the clotting blood around her brain. Three times the Holloway lifer's heart stopped beating, a blessing to all those that had been victimized by the Bradford born bully, many of whom would quite gladly dance on her grave, rejoicing in her passing should she not recover.
The surgeons, knowing nothing of Kathy's history, battled to save her and after several long hours it soon became evident that she would live, but in a vegetative state. Starved of oxygen and badly bruised, her brain would never fully regain its former capacity prior to the onslaught, leaving her needing long-term specialist care, the mental aptitude of a five year old and having to be spoon fed for the remainder of her life.

Five minutes from lockdown, while Maizie sat on the edge of her bunk unable to settle, there was a knock at their door. 'Piss off!' she said, seething at being separated from her friends. The door was slowly pushed open and a group of Kathy's subservient followers entered, looking sheepish to say the least, each of them clutching a tin of sorts

containing half their weekly wage from their respective work detail.
'Woda'you want?' Maizie barked, standing with her knuckles raised expecting a fight.
'To pay,' one of them said, setting down her tin. Kathy had insisted on the weekly taxation of her followers in return for her protection so to speak.
'Pay. Pay what?' Maizie asked, still on her guard.
'Dee Dee,' another said, offering her dues. 'Kathy took...'
'Ar don't give a fuck what that bitch took from ya!' Maizie growled, pushing her hand away. 'Ar don't wonnit and neeva does Dee Dee. Now get the fuck outta mar cell. GO ON, OUT!'
'But we've always paid,' another insisted, fearing they would be left to face the general population without a leader's blanket of protection.
'Ar said get out!' Maizie barked defiantly, ramming the tin back into its owner's hands. 'Go on, fuck off. Mar mates bin bashed to buggery cozza you'z cunts and ar'm in the mood for some payback, so ar'd do one if ar was you'z.' Her convincing tone had the girls backing out the door.
'Come on you lot,' a passing guard said, brandishing her stick, 'lockdown's in two minutes, get a bleedin move on!'
The girls left, scurrying to their respective cells, each of them uneasy and uncertain of their future inside, knowing only too well that retaliation and revenge would be heading their way in the coming days, weeks and months to follow. What goes around would most certainly come around for Bennett's broken battalion of bullies.
In the infirmary Trisha and Dee Dee had been administered pain killers for their collective wounds and were settling down for the night in unfamiliar surroundings, while Maizie paced their cell unable to relax, her head spinning and awash with emotion.
It was close to dawn before Maizie's eyelids grew heavy enough for her to succumb and lie fully clothed on her bunk, leaving a bedside light on to comfort her in her solitude.

'NUUUUURSE!' Dee Dee yelled the following morning, woken by a searing pain. 'NUUUURSE!'
Trisha woke too having slept well, under the circumstances.
'Yes, yes what is it Dawson?' the duty nurse said, rushing from her room donning her glasses. 'What's the matter?'
'Ar got a friggin toof ache!' Dee Dee replied sarcastically. 'Wodya finks a bleedin matter, me poxy legs urtin like fuck, gimme some more of them appy pills will ya. You alright mate?' she then asked Trisha, who raised a thumb and nodded in reply.
'Urry up will ya!' Dee Dee said cringing.
'I'm sorry,' the nurse told her, 'I'm not allowed to issue medication until the doctor arrives, prison policy you see. Would you like a cup of tea?'
'TEA!' Dee Dee yelled. 'What fuckin good is that, come to think of it what fuckin good are you, if ya wanna get me a drink get me a large JD and coke!'
'I'm sorry,' the nurse said sheepishly, 'alcohol is strictly forbidden.'
'I know that you melt!' Dee Dee snapped, in some considerable pain at this point. 'If you aint got no pills you might as well jog on, coz you aint no good to man nor beast are ya, unless your finkin one of us might need our arse wiped, which we don't, do we Trish?'
Trisha then raised a hand and nodded,
'Oh you aint folla'd fru av ya mate?' Dee Dee asked in disgust. 'You dirty bitch!'
'No problem,' the nurse said, taking a pair of blue latex gloves from her pocket. 'I'll see to it right away.'
Trisha couldn't help but smile although her cheek bones were still heavily bruised and tender.
'Corrr flippin ell yeah!' Dee Dee gasped, getting a whiff as Trisha rolled on her side to be bathed. 'You definitely ad the minestrone yesterday dintcha.'

The cocktail of drugs that Trisha had been given the previous night had had a devastating laxative side effect on her, releasing the entire contents of her bowel as she slept.
'Oh my word!' the nurse said, gagging as she lifted the sheet. 'We have been rather volatile haven't we.'
'Fair play to ya mate,' Dee Dee said, pulling her sheet up over the bridge of her nose. 'You couldn't pay me enough to wipe er shitty ring ar tell ya.'
Fifteen minutes, and three rolls of prison issue toilet paper later, Trisha rolled back and wriggled into a pair of disposable paper panties. 'Mawnin mate,' she said, struggling to speak. 'Ow you feelin Dee?'
'Me leg urts like fuck,' Dee Dee replied, rubbing her dressing. 'Ar be alright when the poxy doc gets ear and doses me up. What abaat you mate, ow's ya face feel?'
'Sore Dee,' Trisha admitted, patting her left cheek gently. 'Ow do ar look mate?'
Trisha looked as though she'd been ten rounds in the ring with a heavyweight boxer, but Dee Dee wasn't about to let on. 'Not that bad really Trish mate,' she told her, lying through her teeth. 'Ar've seen you look a lot worse after a night on the jager bombs - wiv ya lippy smudged and ya mascara runnin daan ya neck. Coupla days mate and you'll be brand new.'
'But we get out tomorra Dee,' Trisha moaned. 'Ar can't go out all bashed up can I.'
At that point Maizie came onto the ward carrying two plates with aluminum lids over them. 'Alright, ow ya feelin?' she asked, setting the plates down and examining Trisha's face. 'Oooh that looks sore, is it mate?'
'Mmmmm,' Trisha moaned. 'Yeah it blinkin is, do ar look that bad Maize?'
'No she don't,' Dee Dee snapped. 'Does she Maize?'
'Oh, no,' Maizie said, realizing her mistake. 'You look great Trish, ardly a mark on ya, in fact.'
'Oh shut up Maize,' Trisha said with a smile. 'I aint that stupid.'

'Really?' Dee Dee joked.

'Ar brought ya some brecky,' Maizie said, handing Dee Dee a knife and fork and a plate of scrambled egg and hot buttered toast.

'Corrr ansum. Cheers mate,' Dee Dee said, tucking in straight away.

'Ar fought you might ave trouble swallowin,' Maizie told Trisha, 'so ar got ya summa yesterday's minestrone soup.'

'Don't you flippin dare!' Dee Dee said, spitting egg across her bed. 'She's just finished downloadin the last blinkin lot, can't ya smell it?'

Maizie turned up her nose. 'Come to mention it yeah, as some poor bugger died in ear or summink. Jesus!'

'Ar could'n elp it,' Trisha explained, 'ar never even knew ar done it.'

'Arf the bloody prison new ya done it!' Dee Dee complained. 'An arm in the next poxy bed. NURSE AR WANNA DISCHARGE MESELF!'

The nurse came scurrying back, having incinerated Trisha's contaminated knickers, as well as her entire uniform and donned a replacement. 'I'm sorry Deborah, you cannot leave until you've completed a course of physiotherapy.'

'Fuck that!' Dee Dee scoffed. 'Gimme an andful of pills and a paira crutches and ar'm offski.'

'But Deborah, your leg,' the nurse protested.

'Thas right, it is mar leg,' Dee Dee said, stopping her in her tracks. 'An if ar say ar wanna get the fuck out of ear, you sure as ell aint gonna stop me, you got that.'

The doctor then arrived onto the ward, first checking the sole of his shoe having inhaled the lingering aroma of Trisha's minestrone mishap.

'Nurse open a window will you,' he insisted, retrieving his notes.

'Good morning ladies,' he then said officiously, 'I trust you slept well?'

'No ar never!' Dee Dee snapped. 'Ar'm in a shit loada pain and dippy bollocks there won't gimme any tablits!'

'I'm sorry,' the doctor replied, examining Dee Dee's dressing, 'the nurses aren't permitted to administer medication out of hours. But we should be able to fix you up with a little something now.'

'Little somefing!' Dee Dee exclaimed. 'Ar don't wanna friggin aspirin geeza, gimme somefing thas gonna knock seven kinds of shit outta me, that way ar won't feel a fing, and smell a fing neeva, if she lets anuvva load go.'

None the wiser, the doctor gestured to his nurse to fetch the medicine trolley. 'And you my dear,' he said, turning to Trisha, 'any discomfort?'

'Well, apart from me jaw doc,' she told him, unable to fully open her mouth 'an a bangin ed, ar slept like a baby.'

'Yeah, don't we know it!' Dee Dee scoffed. 'Get er a nappy doc coz she aint ready for trainin pants thas for sure.'

'Oh shut up Dee,' Trisha moaned. 'It was an accident, ar told ya.'

The doctor lifted the lid on Trisha's breakfast. 'You're not eating your soup then?' he asked.

'No she aint!' Dee Dee snapped. 'Unless you wanna clean up the carnage mate!'

'Ahh I see,' the doctor said, realizing from whence the odious aroma had emanated. 'I take it we had a movement during the night?'

'A what?' Trisha asked quizzically.

'A SHIT!' Dee Dee informed her. 'You call it what ya like doc, just give er summink to stiffen it up will ya.'

'Yes, yes of course,' the doctor said, taking a bottle of capsules from the trolley. 'Shall I ask nurse to fetch you a bed pan?' he asked Trisha, whilst popping two on her tongue.

'Any more of that pissin soup,' Dee Dee laughed, 'and ya better get er a flippin gravy boat, an a mop and bucket mate ar tell ya.'

The doctor handed Maizie Trisha's bowl of minestrone. 'Be a dear and fetch your friend a slice or two of dry bread will you,' he asked. 'Better safe than sorry.'

'A'll get er a coupla crackers an'all,' Maizie replied, heading for the door.

'Er doc!' Dee Dee said abruptly. 'You forgotten summink av ya?'

'Excuse me,' the doctor replied, distracted by Trisha's dietetic disaster.

'Me poxy leg!' Dee Dee reminded him sternly.

'Oh yes, yes I am sorry,' he said, handing Trisha a glass of water. 'How is it nurse?'

'Weeping a little this morning doctor,' the nurse said, tossing her soiled swabs into the bin. 'But Deborah is keen to be up and about right away, aren't you?'

'Yeah I aint stayin in ear,' Dee Dee told the doctor. 'Like ar told ya nit nurse ear doc, gimme an andful of orse pills an a paira crutches an ar'm gone.'

'That's preposterous!' the doctor said, examining her wounds for himself. 'You'll need at least another forty eight hours bed rest before you can even attempt to walk on that leg.'

Trisha turned away, knowing Dee Dee's reaction would not be a pleasant one.

'You listen to me you jumped up twat,' Dee Dee growled, the stabbing pain diminishing her patience, 'eeva you dose me up and get me them crutches, or ar'm draggin meself aat of ear on me ands and knees. Woss it gonna be?'

The doctor looked stunned at her outburst. 'But you can't,' he said, foolishly attempting to pull rank.

'Can't!' Dee Dee snapped, tossing back her sheets. 'You fuckin watch me mate!'

'WAIT!' the doctor said with his hands in the air. 'My dear you need complete rest.'

'Don't tell me what ar need, doctor dick!' Dee Dee raged. 'Gimme summink for this bleedin pain right naah, or ar'm gonna proper kick off, and believe me mate you don't wanna be araand when ar do.'

The doctor hastily rummaged in the medicine trolley. 'Nurse. Fetch - Deborah is it?'

'Yes sir,' the nurse replied, keeping her distance.

'Fetch Deborah some water,' the doctor said, retrieving a strip of powerful pain relieving tablets. 'Here, take two of these three times a day,' he told Dee Dee. 'And try to keep the leg elevated as much as you can. Do we have any crutches nurse?' he asked.

'Yes doctor, just the one pair I believe,' the young nurse said, heading for the store room.

'Ar'll av em!' Dee Dee said insistently. 'Right, elp us up will ya Maize,' she then asked her friend.

Maizie stood at her side taking much of Dee Dee's weight. 'You sure abaat this Dee?' she asked, seeing Dee Dee's contorted face as she lowered her injured leg to the floor.

'Yeah, ar be alright,' Dee Dee said, clinging to the mattress for added support. 'You stay where you are Trish,' she said, wagging a telling finger. 'Rest up ear anuvva night to be on the safe side yeah,'

'But Deeee,' Trisha said, looking around at the empty ward. 'Ar'll be all on me own in ear mate, carn ar come wiv you two?'

'Don't worry Trisha,' the nurse said, returning with Dee Dee's crutches. 'I'm on again tonight so I'll keep you company.'

'There ya go,' Dee Dee said, trying the crutches for the first time and a little unsteadily.

'I'll need to change that dressing again tomorrow morning,' the nurse told Dee Dee, dragging a chair out of her path. 'Try to take smaller steps, it'll help with your balance,' she advised her.

The doctor gathered his notes. 'I'll be back to check on you this afternoon young lady,' he told an apprehensive Trisha. 'And nurse, do see to it that she gets a generous portion of ice cream at lunch, it'll help with the swelling.'

'Oooh ansum,' Trisha smiled, 'mint choc chip fanks.'

'I'll ask chef,' the nurse told her, jotting down her dietary request. 'And what would you like for supper, do you have any allergies I need to be aware of?'

'Well....,' Trisha said, pondering. 'Ar bought this snide Ralphy top daan Rommie market and it gimme chronic nipple rash the bleedin fing did, ar paid a blinkin tenner for it an'all.'
'No, no I meant...,' the nurse said, attempting to intervene.
'Oh and,' Trisha rambled on, 'the airs off me nan's Pekinese mutt Pricilla get right up my oota they do, poxy little fing it is, wiv a squidged up face, always shaggin the Enry oova.'
'She's on abaat the grub you doughnut!' Maizie said, steadying Dee Dee.
'Oh yeah, course.' Trisha said, pressing an ice pack to her cheek once again. 'Errrrr,' she added, thinking long and hard. 'Ar don't fink so, ar love me grub ar do, just don't gimme nunna that cous cous shite, proper bungs me up it does.'
'OK,' the nurse laughed, 'I doubt it's on the menu anyway but I will mention it to chef.'
'I aint surprised!' Trisha told her, 'Ar dunno what them tree shaggin ippies see in it anyway.'
'Uggers you melt!' Dee Dee said, correcting Trisha. 'They're tree uggers!'
'Shaggin, uggin,' Trisha said, shaking her head. 'Whateva them scruffy fuckers are doin ain't right if you ask me. Me uncle Morris chained imself bollock naked to a chestnut tree once coz the council was gonna chop the bleedin fing daan.'
'Really?' the naive nurse said, whilst Dee Dee and Maizie slipped away having heard enough already.
'Yeah,' Trisha laughed, 'e won't do that again in an urry ar tell ya, coz arf the kids on the estate pelted iz bare arse wiv conkers, black and bleedin blue e was.'
While Trisha filled the nurse in on her extended family's chaotic life experiences, raising an eyebrow on more than one occasion, Dee Dee and Maizie headed for the mess hall, both of them famished. The hall at that time of morning was full to capacity and ringing with a riotous din. Hobbling toward the snaking queue Dee Dee paused and looked around as table by table suddenly fell deathly quiet, each of

the inmates nudging their friends to warn of Dee Dee's presence. The catering staff also silenced their serving spoons having learned of her recent altercation in the library.

'Jesus Dee!' Maizie whispered, uneasy at the atmospheric shift. 'Woss goin on?'

'Fuck knows!' Dee Dee replied, unsure herself whether trouble was about to come her way yet again. But instead, each of the sixty or so in the queue ahead of them turned and filed past the two of them and took their place behind them leaving Dee Dee at the head. 'Er, bacon and bubble,' Dee Dee said, approaching the counter tentatively.

'Certainly Miss,' the caterer replied, spooning a more than ample portion onto both their plates. 'Take a seat,' she added, handing the trays to her assistant, 'Janice here'll bring them over for you.'

Dee Dee and Maizie looked at one another, perplexed by the preferential treatment. 'Two teas an'all, yeah,' Dee Dee said, turning to face her seated and solemnly silent fellow inmates.

'Where we gonna sit Dee?' Maizie asked, craning her neck.

'Gawd knows,' Dee Dee replied, with her injured leg throbbing somewhat.

Instantly, four prisoners on the table nearest to them leapt from their seats, each of them known associates of Kathy Bennett.

'What the fuck?' Maizie gasped, expecting some form of reprisal, but instead they gathered up their trays, clearing the table swiftly, depositing their unfinished breakfasts at the counter before shuffling away, making very little eye contact with the two friends.

'Dee that was...,' Maizie said, hesitating until they rounded the corner out of sight.

'Yeah ar know,' Dee Dee said, preempting Maizie, 'Bennett's bitches.'

Janice then appeared with their trays, setting them down on the empty table. 'There's plenty more where that came from,' she told them, which in itself was unheard of. 'I'll fetch you some freshly squeezed orange juice in just a moment.'

'Yeah, cheers,' Dee Dee said, scooping a fork full of fried mash into her mouth.

'Good bubble Dee,' Maizie added, wiping her chin.

Gradually, while Dee Dee and Maizie sat in surreal surroundings, the hall returned to normal, although the topic of hushed conversations had obviously shifted. Dee Dee's notoriety had spread throughout the prison like a rampaging bush fire, growing ever more exaggerated with every hastily told version of events.

Whilst still very much in the throes of youth, beyond her delicate exterior many of them imagined lay a simmering dragon which, when riled, would unleash a merciless firestorm. So, for the most part Dee Dee was best avoided.

Janice returned once again carrying two tumblers of chilled orange juice. 'There we are,' she said, setting them down and rummaging in the pocket of her pinny for two chocolate wafer biscuits. 'Have these with your tea,' she told the girls. 'And there's plenty more bacon if you'd like some.'

'Fanks, ar got enough,' Dee Dee told her, growing tired of her fussing, and although usually placid, Maizie herself found her irritating.

'Yeah fanks!' she too said abruptly.

Janice smiled politely and backed away to rejoin her colleagues who were busy dishing out the regulatory rations to the whispering queue.

Trisha in the meantime had been left alone, while the nurse returned to her staff room nearing the end of her shift. Trisha lay gazing out the window at the clear blue sky, switching the rapidly melting pack from one side of her face to the other.

Periodically, passenger laden planes departing from London's Heathrow passed overhead, leaving their wispy white trails behind them; transporting Trisha with them in thought alone to far off places where the sun drenched coral sand warmed the soles of her feet and the margaritas quenched her thirst. This conjured thoughts of her once opulent and altogether extravagant existence, when being draped on the deck of an A-list actor's yacht moored at Monaco was common place, and vomiting in the gutters of Magaloof was just a distant memory.

Dragging her trousers from the back of the chair beside her bed Trisha took her tiny notebook and pencil from her pocket and added to her scribbled and scrawled memoirs, reliving the previous day's nightmarish events - although painting herself in an altogether more flattering light. Her burgeoning passion for the written word, however dyslexic, would soon consume her and compel her to share with the world her inner most thoughts and fantasies, all written in her hometown dialect of course.

'Oh balls!' she suddenly cried, having broken the lead of her pencil. 'Shit, shit!' she added, checking the drawers of her bedside cabinet for a sharpening implement. 'Oh bugger!' she cursed, with a literary gem at the forefront of her mind.

'ELLO!' she called out, 'SCUZE ME!' But there was no reply, the doctor and the day shift were out on the wings visiting expectant mothers and the warden who had been complaining of an irritable bowel, the onset of which oddly coinciding with the arrival of Dee Dee and her friends.

'ELLOOOO!' Trisha cried yet again. 'OY ANYONE THERE?'

Setting down her notebook, she threw back her sheets, eager to resume her penciled prose. Swaying a little with a rush of blood to her swollen head, she slipped her feet into her shoes and stood for a moment to catch her breath before taking a few tentative steps, clinging to the bed at first. 'Shit!' she cursed, lifting her hospital gown to examine her midriff and the bruising Kathy had inflicted when sat astride her. Once clear of the bed, Trisha shuffled awkwardly across the polished floor toward the staffroom. 'ELLOOOOO!' she yelled, in need of some assistance at this

point. 'CAN AR GET SOME BLEEDIN ELP EAR?' But again there was no reply. 'What kind of fuckin ospital is this?'
Throwing open the staff room door with some venom, Trisha first looked for a member of staff to vent her anger on, but found nobody. Broken pencil in hand she dragged open several nearby drawers and rummaged through the paper clips, and surgical swabs, tossing them onto the side in her frustration. Stooping to open the refrigerator Trisha removed a bottle of milk, swigging greedily from the neck before wiping the white mustache from her top lip and holding the chilled bottle to her right eye. 'Result!' she then said, catching sight of a glass display cabinet containing surgical sharps. And prising open the door she removed a stainless steel scalpel and began whittling her pencil. But in time honored tradition the lead repeatedly broke and the pencil became shorter with every scathing slice. 'FUCK IT!' she said, barging open the door that lead to the roof top terrace in search of better light. Almost immediately the wind whipped up her hair and toyed with her surgical gown, blowing open the rear to reveal her pert bare buttocks. But Trisha gained an enormous sense of freedom being outside and away from the ever watchful guards.
Finally, Trisha chiseled a perfect point to her greatly diminished pencil and popped it behind her ear with a contented grin. But on turning to head back inside the same gusting autumnal breeze blew the heavy fire door shut trapping her outside. 'Oh shit!' she cried, hobbling over and tugging at the handle. 'ELLO, ELOOOOOO!' she yelled, pounding on the door with the palm of her hand. 'ELLOOOOOOO!' The door was locked fast with a seven lever security latch and could only be opened from the inside with a key. 'Ohhhh flippin eck,' Trisha said, growing increasingly agitated, 'just mar pissin luck that is.'
The winds whirling around her were fast becoming strong to gale force, as Trisha clung to her loose fitting gown to prevent it being torn from her back. Voices could be heard in the exercise yard some four storeys below her, so Trisha

shuffled to the guard rail and peered over the side with her hair buffeting around her face. 'OYYYYYY!' she cried, waving to attract attention still clutching the scalpel. But her words were extinguished by the winds no sooner had they left her mouth. 'OYYYYYY UP EAR YA DOUGHNUTS!' Still nobody looked skywards. So in her abject frustration, Trisha stooped and wrenched a roof tile free and hurled it down toward the yard, uncaring at this point whether it struck anything, or anybody for that matter.

The hurtling clay tile smashed down onto the concrete floor within feet of a pacing guard, stopping her in her tracks. 'WHAT THE...?' she shrieked, immediately looking up toward the roof and seeing Trisha waving frantically in her prison issue gown, brandishing a glinting blade. 'Oh my god!' she cried, wrenching her radio from her shoulder strap to notify her superiors.

What was to follow could only be described as a catastrophic series of unfortunate events, the outset being that the prison system had a strict protocol in place that had to be adhered to rigidly in the unlikely event of a rooftop protest. Lessons had certainly been learned from the riotous revolts of the eighties and nineties; number one being that nobody but a trained negotiator should approach or attempt to communicate with any aggrieved inmate for fear of exacerbating the situation and force a possible suicide scenario, which would land the prison authorities in very hot water indeed.

The stunned guard was told to sound the general alarm and get all inmates inside, and lock down the yard so that the perpetrators could not be goaded in any way by their fellow prisoners.

'WHERE YA GOIN?' Trisha yelled. 'OY YOU IDIOTS, UP EAR!'

Soon the yard was deserted and the warden informed.

'WHAT? Who the hell is it?' she bawled at her officers.

'We don't know miss,' one of them replied, 'but they're armed, extremely aggressive and in the process of vandalizing the prison roof.'

'JESUS!' the warden shrieked. 'I'll see to this, just you wait and see!' She leapt from her chair but was instantly halted by her second in command.

'You can't!' the number two said, barring her way. 'You know the rules. I've already contacted the police and requested a negotiator. The bad news is that they aren't expected to arrive here for at least another three to four hours.'

'WHAT?' the warden cried, pacing her office and dreading the inevitable media attention, and more importantly that of her superiors.

Susan, the warden's secretary arrived with the section eight document listing quite clearly the limits of their powers in an event of this magnitude, their *do's*, and as stated in bold black type, their *don'ts*.

'Damn those bastard bureaucrats,' the warden snarled, tearing the document from Susan's hands and screwing it into a tight ball.

Meanwhile, Trisha stood livid at her apparent treatment. 'Wankers!' she said, kicking several more tiles loose and watching them slide down the steep roof slope and tumble to the yard below.

Susan raised a hand. 'Shall I contact the governors miss?' she asked the pensive warden.

'NO!' the warden snapped, wanting them left out of the loop for as long as humanly possible, in the hope of an early resolution. 'Let's not bother them just yet. Thank you Susan, that'll be all.'

Susan went about her business in her side office, pausing to update her social network status, informing her friends of the exciting event unfolding at her place of work - unbeknown at the time that the news would spread throughout her contacts and extended family and far beyond in a very short space of time, eventually going viral in up to fifteen countries. The telephones soon began ringing, one after the other, as reporters from around the globe bombarded the warden's office pleading for information on the breaking story having exhausted every avenue open to them on the birth of the new royal baby.

'How in God's name did those jackals find out so bloody fast?' the warden ranted, slamming the phone down yet again. 'And where the hell is that blasted negotiator. SUSAN GET ME A COFFEE DAMN YOU!' Several officers wanted to take matters into their own hands and storm the terrace, but were threatened with severe disciplinary action if they were to go anywhere near the infirmary.

The outside temperature was plummeting as was Trisha's patience. 'OYYYYYY FUCK YA!' she screamed, kicking and beating at the door. 'LET ME IN OR AR'LL KILL THE BLEEDIN LOTTA YA!' Although her threats were merely a figure of speech, desperation was beginning to set in and with it an uncharacteristic rage. Her meds were also wearing off and her wounds were beginning to take their toll on her.

'AR MEAN IT!' she growled. 'LET ME THE FUCK IN OR ARLL RIP THE FUCKIN ROOF OFF, D'YOU EAR ME!' There was absolutely nobody in earshot of the cursing Trisha as police sirens rang out on the approach road.

'Damn it!' the warden snarled, watching as many as four squad cars and six riot vans enter through the main gates. 'That's all I bloody need, I'm up for appraisal in a fortnight!'

The heavy police presence had been sent on the orders of the Home Office to quell any potential mass riot, as inmates began to learn of the rebellious rooftop vigil unfolding above them.

'Woss goin on Dee?' Maizie asked, hearing the raised level of conversations around them.

'Dunno mate,' Dee Dee replied, taking a look around for herself. Suddenly the shutters were pulled down and bolted at the serving counter and the catering staff beat a hasty retreat.

On the roof terrace Trisha stood flapping her arms around her waist in a bid to keep warm, cursing under her breath. The whirring blades of a helicopter from a well-known satellite news channel startled her. 'Flippin eck!' she said, backing against the wall. 'What the fuck!'

Soon there were others circling the prison, capturing the unfolding drama and beaming it live across all four continents.

'GET ME CLOSER!' one eager reporter barked at his pilot. 'Are you getting this?' he then asked his cameraman, to which he received an acknowledging pat on the back. Looking through the lens of his own camera he zoomed in on Trisha's face. 'Blimey she's beaten black and blue!' he said, hastily jotting notes. 'LOWER, LOWER!' he yelled, opening a tiny side window. 'WHY ARE YOU DOING THIS?' he yelled down, putting an ear to the window.

'WHAAAAT?' Trisha replied, with one hand to her ear and clutching the scalpel in the other.

'WHY ARE YOU DOING THIS?' the reporter yelled again, gesturing to his pilot to move in a little closer.

'WHYYYYY?' Trisha replied angrily. 'AR FOUGHT THAT WAS FUCKIN OBVIOUS, AR BIN LOCKED AAAT CAN'T YA BLEEDIN SEE!'

'What did she say?' the reporter asked his crew.

'I think,' the cameraman said, attempting to read Trisha's lips, 'she said she's been knocked out.'

'Jesus Christ!' the reporter gasped, writing feverishly, eager for the scoop. Such a story would undoubtedly secure his position as head news anchor at the station. 'DID YOU SAY YOU'VE BEEN KNOCKED OUT?' he called out, the helicopter blades adding to the turbulent conditions and distorting each and every spoken word.

'YES YOU FUCKIN IDIOT!' Trisha screamed. 'AN AR'M PROPER PISSED OFF ABAAT IT!'

Waving the scalpel in the air Trisha hurled another roof tile down toward the debris littered yard.

'This is priceless!' the cameraman said, capturing the action in high definition.

Tempers were definitely beginning to fray in the warden's office as she observed yet another riot van arriving on the scene. 'Damn it. DAMN IT!' she barked, kicking her beloved Bobby's bowl across the office.

'Miss!' Susan called from her office. 'Miss, the governor's on the phone, shall I patch him through?'

'Ohhh great!' the warden cursed, hovering her hand over her phone, wracking her brain for a plausible excuse. 'Morning Sir David,' she eventually said sheepishly. 'To what do I owe this unexpected pleasure?'

'ARE YOU SERIOUS?' the head of the prison service roared down the phone. 'WHAT THE BLOODY HELL'S GOING ON DOWN THERE?'

'Nothing Sir David,' the warden said, trivializing events. 'Well, when I say nothing, it's just a minor disagreement I assure you. And one that will be dealt with swiftly, you have my word on that. I do intend to keep a tight lid on things.'

'It's too bloody late for that!' Sir David barked. 'Open your eyes woman, we're live on every damn channel!'

Global news networks had become embroiled in a fierce bidding war for the first images of the drama at Holloway, while printing presses at all major newspapers and broadsheets were halted while the new and more newsworthy story was hastily prepared.

'Well?' Sir David asked, in need of an instant explanation. 'I'm waiting!'

'Sir David I, I...' the warden stuttered. 'I can assure you Sir David, I can handle this, you have absolutely nothing to worry about.'

'Are you out of your mind woman!' Sir David yelled, pacing his own office. 'I stuck my neck out giving you that position, and this is how you repay me. I'm up in front of the board in half an hour, what am I supposed to tell them – "Don't worry it's all under control". I'll have your head for this, do you hear me!' With this Sir David slammed down the receiver, leaving the warden visibly shaking.

The media storm was in full flow at this point, reporting of Trisha's apparent protest at the brutality she'd suffered at the prison. Of course, nothing could be further from the truth, but once the baying press and wider media had gotten their teeth into a story of this importance, there was no stopping the journalistic juggernaut. A soon to be iconic image of Trisha with her scalpel raised in her clenched defiant fist, allegedly fighting against the injustice and inhumanity within the prison service, was splashed across every front page.

Trisha herself had by now lost all sense of reason, and feeling in her fingers and toes for that matter. And the prison roof was now minus some fifty or so tiles, whilst the warden was fast approaching a nervous breakdown.

'Do we know who the hell it is up there?' she asked her officers. 'I swear if I had a gun I'd shoot the blasted bitch down myself!'

Amid the speculative conversations around the mess hall tables, word was rapidly spreading that the television in the recreation room was showing live footage of the protestor's plight.

'COME ON!' one inmate cried, rounding up her friends, 'ISS ON THE TELLY!'

The trickle of prisoners leaving the mess hall soon became a stampede as the gossip hungry women fell over one another, such was the hysteria whipped up by Trisha's antics.

'D'you ear that Dee,' Maizie said, rising to her feet. 'Come on, less av a look!'

'Naah, fuck it,' Dee Dee said, without batting an eye, 'ar can't be arsed.'

'Oh come on Dee,' Maizie pleaded, 'iss proper excitin!'

'You go Maize,' Dee Dee told her, 'iss just some soppy tart givin it the biggun. I ope she jumps and breaks er fuckin neck ar really do.'

'Oh don't say that Dee,' Maizie said sympathetically. 'Well ar'm goin anyway,' she added, tucking her wafer biscuit into her pocket. 'A'rll let ya know woss appnin.'

'Don't bovva,' Dee Dee grunted, 'coz I aint bleedin interested.'

Maizie left her friend and followed the stragglers along the corridor toward the recreation room, where garbled cat calls could be heard, all of them aimed at the LCD screen on the wall.

'GO ON GIRL!' one inmate cried, 'POWER TO THE FUCKIN PEOPLE!'

'YEAH GOOD ON YA!' another yelled, each of them wholeheartedly in support of their downtrodden comrade.

Maizie muscled her way between the jostling ladies, only catching a fleeting glimpse of the screen. 'Who is it?' she asked the prisoner beside her.

'Dunno,' was her reply. 'Looks like a proper nutter though, she's got a blade and everyfing.'

'Shit, really?' Maizie said, standing up on her toes. 'Ar can't see a bleedin fing!'

Suddenly the inmate directly in front of Maizie turned, and recognizing her as a member of Dee Dee's firm, swiftly stepped aside. 'Sorry,' she said, tapping on the girl in front of her to do the same.

Maizie inched forward as the crowd parted before her. 'Cheers,' she said, now within a few feet of the television with a clear view of the screen and the studio reporter.

'In a moment we will be going live to her Majesty's Prison Holloway,' the presenter said, shuffling her notes, 'where our man in the field has been watching the drama there unfold and keeping us up to date, so you have the news as it happens, wherever it happens.'

'GET ON WIV IT!' an irate inmate yelled, throwing a ball of paper at the screen. 'SHOW US OLLOWAY AGAIN!'

'But before we cross over,' the presenter continued, 'a quick word with the governor in chief of the prison service, Sir David Clemments. Sir David, can you tell us why this lone prisoner is protesting?'

'Well, well I,' Sir David said via video link, 'I assure you this is an isolated incident and we are doing all we can to bring matters to a swift and peaceful resolution.' In true politician speak Sir David avoided the probing question entirely.

'I'm well aware of that Sir David,' the presenter said, keen to prise out the truth. 'But what can you tell us about the rumors of prison officer brutality at Holloway? The prisoner in question does appear to have been mistreated in some way, as I'm sure our pictures will show.'
Sir David fidgeted nervously in his chair, crumbling under cross examination. 'Well, I couldn't possibly comment,' he said, mopping his brow with his spotted handkerchief. 'Until there has been a full and thorough enquiry, which I intend to head myself, starting at the very top.'
'The warden you mean?' the presenter asked, preparing to go live to the prison. 'I am told it was you personally who appointed Miss Simmonds to the current position. Am I right Sir David?'
'Well I!' Sir David stammered. 'I er, I did yes. But I'll admit in hindsight I may have been a tad hasty in my decision, but like I say, a thorough enquiry will be undertaken and I can assure you that if heads must roll because of this, then roll they will.'
'Thank you,' the presenter said, turning to the camera. 'Sir David Clemments there, governor in chief of the prison service. OK, we can now go live to Holloway where I am told the protestor is growing increasingly agitated. Officials there have grave concerns for her safety following an incident in the late nineties, when two women leapt to their deaths in an apparent suicide pact. Simon, can you tell us what's happening right now?'
'Well Rachel,' Simon said from within the helicopter. 'I can tell you that I have been in contact with the prisoner and she told me, exclusively I might add, in her own words, I quote "I've been knocked out and I'm bleeding pissed off."'
'Knocked out you say?' Rachel asked, wanting to clarify things for the viewers. 'And you say she's armed?'
'Yes knocked out, that's what she said. And that's right Rachel, she is armed with some form of blade. Dozens of police officers have arrived and I am told that a trained negotiator is on the way to attempt to talk her down, but if

that fails there is a possibility they may shoot her from a distance with a tranquilizer dart. But apparently this will only be used as a last resort because as I'm sure you are aware there are certain risks involved; only last year a prisoner in Massachusetts was fatally wounded when the dart punctured a major artery and he bled to death before paramedics could reach him.'

'Shit!' Maizie gasped at the thought, while the helicopter circled to get a closer view of the alleged aggrieved and armed roof top protestor.

'TRISHA!' Maizie suddenly cried, surging forward to within inches of the screen, seeing her friend on the windswept terrace. 'WHAT THE FUCK?'

Trisha, unaware of the gravity of the situation and the media circus' worldwide attention, thrust her blade skyward once again at the circling helicopters.

'LET ME IN OR AR'LL FUCKIN KILL THE LOTTA YA'Z!' she screamed at the top of her voice.

'What's she saying now?' Rachel asked her reporter.

'Well apparently,' Simon said, considering how best to word what little he could make out. 'She said she'll kill us all.'

'My god!' Rachel said, looking across at her producer who gave her the thumbs up, meaning the story was a certain ratings winner. 'Any news on the negotiator?' she then asked Simon, while Maizie stood open mouthed.

'No, not as yet,' Simon replied, tweaking his earpiece. 'I dare say if the situation worsens, and judging by the prisoners mood it will considerably, then the likelihood of a police sniper being used is highly probable.'

'SHIT NO!' Maizie said, with one hand on the screen. 'YOU CAN'T FUCKIN SHOOT ER!'

'D'you know er?' a fellow inmate asked, tapping Maizie's shoulder.

'Yeah, course ar do!' Maizie said, shrugging her hand away. 'She's me bleedin mate!'

'She's a bleedin fruit loop if you ask me,' another prisoner laughed.

'Ar know that!' Maizie snapped. 'But she's still mar bloody mate!'

Maizie shoved several prisoners out of her way making for the door. 'DEEEEEEEE!' she cried, elbowing her way through the crowd. 'DEEEEEEE!' Breaking out into the corridor Maizie sprinted toward the mess hall, knocking over a cleaner's bucket of soapy water in passing.

'DEEEEEEE ISS TRISHAAAAA!' Bursting through the mess hall doors she stood panting. 'DEE ISS BLOODY TRISHA!'

'What?' Dee Dee asked, sitting alone and sipping the last of her tea. 'What you on abaat?'

'ISS TRISHA!' Maizie yelled again. 'ON THE PISSIN ROOF!'

'WHAT?' Dee Dee cried, paying more attention. 'WHAT D'YA MEAN ON THE BLOODY ROOF?'

'SHE'S ON THE TELLY, AVA LOOK!' Maizie said, beckoning. 'FUCK KNOWS WHY, BUT THE DOZY BITCH IS ON THE ROOF WIV A BLADE. AND DEE THEY SAY THEY'RE GONNA SHOOT ER!'

'WHAT THE FUCK!' Dee Dee cried, leaping to her feet. 'WHAT D'YA MEAN SHOOT ER? AND WOSS SHE DOIN WIV A BLADE?'

'AR DUNNO!' Maizie said, holding open the door. 'COME ON!'

The pair of them ran back to the recreation room and forced their way to the front of the jubilant crowd. 'Out me fuckin way!' Dee Dee growled. 'Oy you, aat me way!'

'LOOK!' Maizie cried, pointing out their friend raging on the roof top.

'What the fuck?' Dee Dee said, approaching the screen aghast. 'What is she doin up there?'

'Fuck knows!' Maizie replied. 'You know what she's like Dee.'

'Jesus!' Dee Dee gasped, listening to the reporter's version of events. 'Thas a loada bollocks that is, she aint bin knocked aat by the bleedin screws, but ar'm gonna give er a bleedin fump when ar get me ands on er!'

'Don't be like that Dee, they're gonna shoot er,' Maizie informed her.
'They aint gonna shoot er ya lemon,' Dee Dee said dismissively. 'Why would they wanna do that for fuck sake?'
'Not proply shoot er!' Maizie said, tugging Dee Dee's sleeve. 'Wiv a tranquilizer dart fingy, but iss proper dangerous apparently Dee.'
'We gotta get er daan,' Dee Dee said, looking around the room for a guard.
'JUMP!' a prisoner behind them yelled, still loyal to Kathy Bennett, cupping her hands to her mouth. 'JUMP YOU TWAT!'
'OY!' Dee Dee snarled, turning and grabbing the girl by the throat. 'Thas mar mate up there you slag!' The colour immediately drained from the inmate's face when she realized who she had inadvertently upset.
'If she fuckin jumps,' Dee Dee added, 'ar'll drag your scrawny arse up there meself and fro you off after er, alright!'
'Yeah, yeah sorry ar didn't mean it,' the girl said, holding her hands up in defense. 'Ar'm sorry.'
'DEE COME ON!' Maizie said, dragging her friend away. 'WE GOTTA STOP EM SHOOTIN ER!'
A police marksman had already taken up position in an adjacent clock tower and had Trisha trained in his cross hairs, waiting patiently for the word, his finger hovering over the trigger.
'OY!' Dee Dee yelled at a guard at the door observing proceedings. 'TELL EM ISS ALRIGHT, WE KNOW ER!'
'I beg your pardon Dawson,' the guard replied, with her hands folded behind her back.
'The bird on the roof you idiot!' Dee Dee said, approaching her with Maizie in tow. 'Iss a mate of ours, so tell your lot iss alright we'll get er daan.'
'I don't know what you're talking about Dawson,' the officer said blankly. She and her colleagues were incensed at the scandalous rumors concerning their ill treatment of the

inmates, and the lack of respect shown to them by the metropolitan police officers.

'It's out of our hands now Dawson,' she told Dee Dee. 'So quite honestly, I couldn't give a damn who it is up there, and whether they shoot the girl or not.'

'Do what?' Dee Dee said, perplexed at the officer's lack of cooperation. 'You listen to me you jumped up fuck, you get us up there right naah, d'you ear me?'

'Sorry,' the officer said, looking down at her wrist watch. 'It's time for my break so it'll have to wait.'

'Wait!' Maizie cried, barging past Dee Dee. 'It can't bloody wait, we gotta get er daan you idiot. Call em up on ya walkie talkie fing and tell em we know er.' But the officer merely switched off her radio and left the room.

'What the fuck?' Maizie said, throwing her hands in the air. 'Can you bloody believe that Dee, what a complete...'

'Sod er!' Dee Dee snapped. 'We'll go tell the warden, she'll bleedin listen, ar know she will.' Shoving several inmates aside the two girls burst out into the corridor and headed for the stairs.

Meanwhile Trisha was becoming increasingly enraged by the constant buzzing of the news and police helicopter blades above her head.

'PISS OFF WILL YA!' she cried, wrenching a shoe from her right foot and hurling it in the air toward them. 'WHAT'CHU LOOKIN AT, AY?'

Meanwhile the warden was having a heated discussion on the telephone with the met commissioner. 'Where the hell is this negotiator of yours?' she raged. 'I need this siege brought to an end right now, god damn it!'

'I'm sorry Miss Simmonds,' the commissioner said from his Scotland Yard office. 'It appears our man is delayed and cannot reach you for at least another hour. How are things down there?'

'Oh just bloody wonderful!' the warden said sarcastically. 'I've got half your bloody force here standing around with their heads up their backsides, while a deranged girl is tearing the damn roof off my prison. HOW D'YOU THINK THINGS ARE DOWN HERE? FOR HEAVENS SAKE, JUST SHOOT THE DAMN GIRL WILL YOU!'

Startled by her outburst the commissioner checked the clock on the wall. 'It has been some time, I'll grant you that Warden,' he told her. 'I'll speak to my men on the ground, and if the situation worsens I'll discuss the possibility of deploying a tranquilizer. But as you know that is not without some considerable risk.'

'I don't give a damn!' the warden replied angrily. 'Just get her the hell off my roof!' With this she smashed the receiver down. 'IMBECILE!' she cried, shaking her head in despair.

The met commissioner had come under mounting pressure from Parliament too to bring the situation under control, and whilst fearing for his own job he telephoned his superintendent at their makeshift command centre within the prison gymnasium. 'Jeffries, it's the commissioner here,' he said, feeling the heat from above. 'What's happening down there?

'Morning sir,' the superintendent replied, checking his monitor which had been linked to the prison security cameras. 'Deteriorating rapidly by the looks of things sir. The prisoner, in my opinion, is mentally unstable and could jump at any moment.'

'Good grief!' the Commissioner gasped, foreseeing a future disciplinary hearing for himself and his colleagues at the Yard. 'Do you have a shot?' he asked; while Dee Dee and Maizie raced toward the warden's office.

'Yes sir, we do,' the superintendent said, getting the thumbs up from his second in command. 'Do we take it sir?'

The commissioner stood pondering the possible repercussions of his decision.

'Sir, do we take the shot?' his superintendent asked, a little more forcefully.

'We wanna see the warden!' Dee Dee yelled at the two officers outside her door. 'Get aat the fuckin way!'

'Hang on Dawson,' one of them barked, stopping the girls in their tracks. 'Where d'you think you're going?'
'To see the friggin warden!' Dee Dee snapped. 'Ar just bloody told ya did'n I.'
'Sorry, not today,' the officer replied, barring the way. 'The warden's far too busy. Can't it wait?'
'No it bloody can't!' Maizie insisted. 'We know who's on the bloomin roof, iss our mate Trisha.'
'Like I said,' the officer told them, 'the warden's busy. I'll be sure to pass on message if you like.'
'You don't understand!' Maizie yelled. 'We can get er daan, so get the bloody warden will ya!'
'I'm sorry, we have our orders,' the second officer said, putting her hand on Dee Dee. 'Now please return to your cell at once.'
'Get your fuckin and off me,' Dee Dee barked, 'and I aint goin nowhere till ar see the warden, d'you ear me. WARDEN!' she then cried over the officer's shoulders. 'OY WARDEN!'
'Be quiet Dawson,' one of the officers said, shoving Dee Dee aside. 'I told you to get back to your cell. Now move it!'
Maizie side stepped the officers and beat on the warden's door. 'WARDEN, WARDEN ISS TRISHAAAAAA!'
'What the devil!' the warden barked, throwing open the door. 'What the hell do you two want? I'm busy for Pete's sake.'
'Warden iss Trisha,' Maizie panted, leaning on the door frame.
'What is?' the warden asked, annoyed, to say the least, at the intrusion.
'On the bloody roof!' Dee Dee told her.
'TRISHA!' the warden shrieked, clasping her hands to her head. 'What's that moron doing on my roof for god sake. Does she know the trouble she's caused me.'
'Probly not,' Maizie said, clutching her beating chest, 'if ar know er.'

'You gotta stop the old bill shootin er,' Dee Dee said, grabbing the warden's sleeve. 'Get on the blower and tell em will ya.'

'Shoot her,' the warden scoffed, 'I hope they blow the damn girls head off, I really do. I've got the governor breathing down my neck, and I could lose my job because of that blasted girl.'

'Well, let us get er daan then,' Dee Dee reiterated. 'The quicker she's off ya roof the better, don'tcha fink?'

The warden thought for a moment. 'I'll call the commissioner,' she told the girls, 'get him to stand his men down.' But on dialing, the warden was greeted with a continuous engaged tone. 'Blast, where the devil is he?' she cursed, summoning one of her officers. 'Get down to the gym right away,' she told her, holding open the door. 'Tell the superintendent the police marksman will not be necessary.'

'Yeah, and urry up!' Maizie said. 'Go on, get yer arse daan there, what ya waitin for ya doughnut.'

But up on the roof things were beginning to take a turn for the worse. Slate grey storm clouds had moved in, dropping the first spots of icy rain, a prelude to the deluge to come.

'Oh fuck!' Trisha cried, looking to the sky and considering desperate measures. 'IF YOU'Z AINT GONNA GET ME DAAN!' she yelled at the reporters above, 'AR'M GONNA SHIMMY DAAN THE BLOODY DRAIN PIPE, YOU SEE IF AR DON'T!'

With this she gripped the freezing guard rail and swung her right leg over. 'SHIIIT!' she shrieked, feeling the cold steel against her bare inner thigh, 'ar shoulda wore me blinkin fermals.'

A gasp rang out in the gymnasium on seeing Trisha's attempted suicide, or so they thought.

'Sir look, the girl!' a constable cried.

'Christ!' the superintendent gasped. 'Get me the shooter on the radio. NOW, HURRY MAN!'

Dee Dee shoved the warden aside. 'Fuck it, ar'm goin up there, come on Maize,' she said, heading for the stairs.

'You can't!' the warden yelled after them. 'YOU CAN'T I SAID!'

'YOU TRY AND STOP ME!' Dee Dee called back over her shoulder, vaulting three stairs at a time.

'Yes sir,' the police marksman said, answering his radio. 'Do we have a green light Sir?'

'AFFIRMATIVE!' the superintendent barked clearly. 'Take the shot, I repeat, take the shot now!'

Trisha's trembling hands gripped the rail, watched by tens of millions around the world; many on the edge of their seats having warmed to her and her apparent plight, unified in horror at the treatment she had supposedly received. As far away as the Congo, tribes people gathered round a generator powered TV, peering from behind their tribal shields whilst praying for her in their native tongue.

'Bugger!' she cursed, teetering on the rail and finding it difficult to fling her other leg over as the now near torrential rain beat down on her, causing her flimsy night gown to become completely see through and her hair to cling to the sides of her shivering face.

Taking aim, whilst Dee Dee and Maizie raced to the infirmary, the marksman gently squeezed his finger on the trigger letting fly a tranquilizer dipped dart; but at that precise moment Trisha's hand slipped on the sodden rail and she lurched forward.

'OHHHHHH FUUUUCK!' she cried, falling down onto the scarcely tiled roof as the dart whizzed over her head.

'Damn it!' the marksman said, reloading and taking aim a second time.

Trisha struggled to regain her footing with her gown riding up over her bare bottom, giving the reporters, and the viewers for that matter, a close up of her rear end.

'TRISHAAAAAAA!' Dee Dee and Maizie yelled, bursting into the infirmary and heading for the staffroom. 'TRIIIIIIIISH!'

Firing a second shot, this time the police marksman found his target.

'ARRRRRRRRRGH FUUUCK!' Trisha squealed, as the dart struck her right thigh, 'SHIIIIT WHAT THE FUUUCK?' Reaching for the dart, Trisha released her grip on the rail and immediately slid several feet down the rain spattered tiles. 'WOOAAAAAAW!' she cried, clawing at the roof, 'SHIIIIIIT!'

A unilateral gasp could be heard within households the world over, the majority of those viewers covering their eyes momentarily for fear of witnessing her death live on television.

'TRIIIIISH!' Dee Dee said, reaching the door which was locked fast. 'TRIIIIIIISH!' she cried, peering out the side window. 'Jesus Maizie, she's gonna fall!'

She and Maizie rammed the door with their shoulders, desperate to help their stricken friend.

'IT AINT SHIFTIN DEE!' Maizie said, peering out herself. 'OH FUCK DEE SHE'S IN PROPER TROUBLE MATE!'

'Ar can see that!' Dee Dee yelled. 'There's gotta be a bloody key ear somewhere, elp me look will ya!'

The two of them hurriedly scoured the staffroom, turning out every drawer onto the linoleum floor.

Outside amid the thunderstorm, the powerful tranquilizer was beginning to take effect, but rather than having the desired incapacitating effect on her and enabling her rescue, it was about to assist in her death. Growing rapidly drowsy, her grip on the tiles weakened and as her eyelids grew heavy so she slipped further toward the edge of the roof.

'Got em!' Maizie shrieked, snatching a bunch of keys from a tin above the microwave. 'Shit Dee which one is it?'

'Give em ear!' Dee Dee insisted, trying one after the other of the dozen or so keys, before finally kicking open the door.

'TRIHSAAAAA!' she screamed, peering over the guard rail. 'TRIHSAAAAAA!' But her friend had lost consciousness and lay slumped dangerously close to the gutter line and a drop of well over ninety feet.

'TRIIIISH!' Maizie cried, while the cameras overhead continued to roll. 'TRIIIIIIISH, CAN YOU EAR ME. WOSS APPENED TO ER DEE? DEE WOSS UP WIV ER?'
'Them fucks've shot er, thas woss bloody up wiv er,' Dee Dee snarled, 'ar'll fuckin kill em ar will.'
Aliens could have landed on earth and not a single newspaper or broadcast would have changed their lead story. Trisha was the news, in thirty five languages throughout the civilized world and occasionally beyond.
'Ar'm gonna get er!' Dee Dee said, mounting the rail without a thought for her own safety. 'You stay there Maize, ar said stay there!'
'But Dee,' Maizie protested.
'BUT NUFFING!' Dee Dee yelled over the pounding rain. 'JUST STAY THE FUCK THERE!'
Inching down onto the tiles, which ran with a river of rain, Dee Dee sat and slid slowly on her bottom toward Trisha. 'TRIIISH!' she called, but got no answer. 'TRISH MATE, ISS ME, DEE!'
'Please be careful Dee!' Maizie begged, leaning over the rail as police and prison officers alike raced up the stairs.
'Are you getting this?' Simon asked his cameraman from the helicopter above.
'Yeah man,' he was told, 'course I am. This is pure gold dude, pure gold.'
Dee Dee lost her footing for a split second and slid some six feet in an instant.
'DEEEEEEEE!' Maizie screamed, 'DEEEE PLEASE, PLEASE BE CAREFUL.' Maizie had tears streaming down her face, which were washed away in a flash. 'Please get er Dee, please, please just bring er back.'
Dee Dee stretched out a hand grasping Trisha's gown, but the flimsy cotton material tore from her back when tugged. 'Fuck!' Dee Dee cursed, dropping another foot or so to take her friends hand. 'AR GOT ER!' she called out to Maizie. 'AR GOT ER MAIZE!'

Maizie clutched her beating heart with one hand, whilst reaching out with the other. 'BRING ER UP DEE!' she cried, 'QUICK!'

Dee Dee clawed at the exposed roof battens, dragging her friend's motionless body inch by pains taking inch up toward the rail.

'GRAB ME AND DEE, GRAB ME AND!' Maizie shrieked, leaning way over the rail.

Suddenly a tile Dee Dee had depended on came away in her hand and she and Trisha began to slide to the roof's edge.

'NOOOOOOOOOO, NOOOOOOOOO DEEEEEEEEE!' Maizie screamed, mounting the rail herself and clambering down using the holes as foot holds. 'DEEEEEE!'

Dee Dee had dug her nails into the clay tiles, breaking several of them, to slow their descent.

'MAIZE!' she yelled, reaching out. 'AR CARN OLD ER, ELP FOR FUCK SAKE!'

As the officers burst out onto the terrace, Maizie summoned what little courage she had and let go of the tiles to slide to her friends.

'OHHHHH FUUUUCK!' she cried, crashing into the two of them and hugging Dee Dee and Trisha tightly. 'I aint gonna let ya go,' she said, spitting the rain from her mouth. 'Never d'you ear me. If we go, we go togevva, ar mean it Dee.'

Two officers climbed gingerly over the rail held by their colleagues, another then joined them to form a chain, while the two girls clung to Trisha so tightly they could have quite literally squeezed the life from her. Nothing could have parted them at that moment, absolutely nothing.

'TAKE MY HAND!' an officer told Maizie, as he approached with extreme caution. 'HERE, TAKE MY HAND!'

'NOT WIVOUT ME MATES!' Maizie called back, shaking her head. 'WE'RE COMIN UP TOGEVVA, ALRIGHT!'

The officer beckoned to more of his colleagues who quickly joined the chain, taking Dee Dee and Maizie by the hand and grabbing Trisha's wrists.

'Don'tchu let go of er!' Dee Dee told them, as they were hoisted toward the rail with the punishing rain continuing to fall, hampering their efforts somewhat.

Maizie refused to relinquish her hold on Trisha, entrusting only Dee Dee and herself with her safe return.

'GET HER OVER HERE!' the superintendent said, offering a hand himself knowing they were far from out of the woods.

The world watched and waited, holding their collective breaths as Trisha's body was lifted from the broken tiles up onto the rail, her robe now in tatters. Then, and only then, did a resounding cheer ring out across the countless viewing nations from Perth Western Australia to Latin America. Trisha had touched them all.

The Congo tribesmen rejoiced, beating their spears on their decoratively painted shields, dancing and wailing.

'Thank god!' Simon's cameraman said overhead, having warmed to her himself.

'Fetch some blankets!' the superintendent told his men. 'HURRY!'

Dee Dee and Maizie were also bundled back onto the storm lashed terrace where they stood shivering, clinging to Trisha, with adrenaline surging through their veins and looking down at the yard below that could so easily have claimed their lives.

'Fank fuck,' Dee Dee sighed, wet through.

'Let's get them inside,' the superintendent told his officers, as warm blankets were tossed around the girl's shoulders.

The warden was stood inside with her hands on her hips.

'WHAT THE HELL WAS SHE THINKING?' she yelled. 'THAT STUPID GIRL, I'LL, I'LL...!'

'Leave it!' Dee Dee growled, with Trisha in her arms. 'Just leave it will ya.'

Dee Dee set her friend down on her bed and wiped the dripping hair from her face. 'You did'n av to shoot er, you fuckin idiots!' she said, addressing the surrounding officers. 'Who's fuckin idea was it, ay, ay?'

'I gave the order,' the superintendent said, stepping forward. 'For the prisoner's own safety.'

'Do what?' Dee Dee snarled. 'Firstly mate,' she added, pointing a thrusting finger, 'she aint just a fuckin prisoner, she's our mate; and secondly, you twat, you coulda bleedin killed er!'

'But,' the superintendent said, knowing full well that Dee Dee was right, and had things turned out differently and a fatality, or three, had occurred, then it would have been his carcass dragged across the political coals and trashed by the merciless media who had taken Trisha, or the cash cow as they saw her, to their hearts and wallets.

'But nuffing!' Dee Dee barked, with the bit now firmly between her teeth, while Maizie pulled the curtain around Trisha's bed to remove what little remained of the robe still clinging to her rain battered body.

'Who the fuck put you in charge anyway?' Dee Dee raged, intent on having her say. 'You might fink you're top cop geez, but believe me you couldn't run a fuckin barf ar tell ya, you two bob melt!'

Many of the superintendent's officers around him cupped their hands to their mouths smothering their laughter, finding the verbal onslaught hilarious, and mostly agreeing whole heartedly.

'YOU LOT, GET OUT!' he yelled, shoving one or two of them and following them to the door, keen to distance himself from Dee Dee's scathing tongue and offering no retort.

'Dawson!' the warden snapped, going nose to nose with Dee Dee.

'In all my years as warden of this prison I have never ever felt the compulsion to reinstate the death penalty as much as I do right now. That, that damned fool girl has been a thorn in my arse, let alone my side, ever since she set foot in here. So you listen, and you listen good and hard, I want all three of you out of here the minute your friend Hamilton arrives to collect you. And if you ever, ever, find yourselves on the wrong side of the law and heading back this way, let me tell you that you'll spend the rest of your miserable lives chained to one another in the deepest darkest corner of this prison and left to rot. And that Dawson is a promise, do I make myself clear? I don't care whatever it is you think you have over me, it'll be worth it to destroy you and your pathetic friends.'

Uncertain of her future following the drama, the warden stood white with rage with clenched boney fists and pursed quivering lips.

'You finished?' Dee Dee asked unfazed.

'Grrrrrrr, damn you three!' the warden said, storming from the infirmary, filled with dread at having to explain to her superiors, and knowing her written statements would undoubtedly be demanded in triplicate and that her beloved career teetered on the edge of a political precipice.

The commissioner also sat at his desk with his head in his hands, his telephone ringing nonstop, his force would be brought to bear for their actions which were played out all too publicly.

Dee Dee and Maizie's daring roof top rescue had already received more YouTube hits than the entire top ten videos combined, and internet chat rooms were buzzing with the new controversially trending topic.

Prison governors up and down the land were also having a hard time of things, with copycat crusading criminals finding their way onto the roofs of Parkhurst, Pentonville and Wandsworth alike. Even the Queen herself had expressed her concerns and displeasure at the apparent breakdown of law and order within the institutions.

Prime Minister's question time in The House of Commons saw a heated debate between Labour and the Conservatives; MP's on either side slinging insults back and forth across the floor both attacking the incompetency of the other. All of this testament to the theory that a single snowflake can soon become an avalanche.

Dee Dee and Maizie soon found themselves alone with their friend in the infirmary, both wet through, panting and thoroughly exhausted from their grueling ordeal, while Trisha lay wrapped tightly in her blankets unaware of the impact and sheer scale of her recent actions.

'Jesus Dee, ar fought we lost er,' Maizie said, wringing the water from her hair. 'Ar was proper shittin meself aat there mate, weren't you?'

Dee Dee said nothing for a moment, with water dripping from the end of her nose, struggling to come to terms with their brave but also foolhardy rescue on the roof in treacherous conditions.

'What the bleedin ell was she playin at?' Maizie asked, tucking the blanket up under Trisha's chin, and brushing the remaining strands of hair from her eyes.

'Ar dunno,' Dee Dee said, in a less than sympathetic tone, 'but ar'm gonna find aat.' Grabbing their dozing friend by the shoulders, Dee Dee shook her violently. 'Trisha, what the bleedin ell you bin up to you stupid bitch?' she ranted.

'DEEEEEE!' Maizie cried, wrestling her friend. 'DEEEE LEAVE ER MATE, SHE AINT WELL!'

'AINT WELL!' Dee Dee barked, shrugging Maizie off. 'She aint bin friggin well since the day she fell aat of er muvva's ole!'

'Deeee please!' Maizie cried, wedging herself between the two of them. 'Ask er when she wakes up mate!'

'Ar will!' Dee Dee told her. 'WAKE UP YOU DOZY MARE!' she then yelled, tugging at Trisha over Maizie. 'WAKE UP SO AR CAN SLAP THE SHIT AATA YA!'

'Shit, Dee stop it!' Maizie insisted. 'You'll urt er!'

'URT ER, URT ER!' Dee Dee cursed. 'Urt er, ar'll bleedin kill er!'

'What's going on?' a voice behind them then called out. It was the doctor and his nurse, allowed back into the infirmary for the first time. 'Step away from the bed please!' Pushing the two girls aside he removed his torch from his pocket, pulled open Trisha's eyelids and shone it onto her pupils. 'How long has she been out?' he asked.

'Baat twenny minutes,' Maizie told him. 'Ar fink she it er ed doc.'

'No shit,' Dee Dee scoffed, 'dropped at bleedin berf probly.'

Drying their hair, Dee Dee and Maizie looked on while the doctor and nurse gave Trisha a thorough examination.

'There doesn't appear to be anything broken,' the doctor finally said.

'Not yet there aint!' Dee Dee said, with a clenched determined fist.

'Deeeeeee,' Maizie moaned, keen to hear what the doctor had to say. 'When's she gonna wake up doc?'

'Anytime soon I'd hazard a guess,' the doctor replied, turning to his nurse. 'Fetch the smelling salts will you,' he told her.

'Let me do it!' Dee Dee said, lunging forward before being tackled by Maizie once again.

'Dee, for fuck sake, leave it will ya!' Maizie snapped, losing it somewhat. 'Just leave it!'

Dee Dee was taken aback momentarily by Maizie's ferocity, such was her desire to see her friend's health restored.

'She's bin fru enough!' Maizie added, standing firm between them. 'Leave er!'

'Here doctor,' the nurse said, returning with a tiny brown bottle. Taking it from her, the doctor removed the lid and waved it under Trisha's nose.

'What the hell was she doing out there?' he asked, over his shoulder.

'Thas what we wanna know,' Maizie said, clinging to Trisha's hand. 'She's a proper nut nut believe me doc, but ard'a never fought she'd do anyfing like that, not suicide, not er.'

'Hmmmm!' Dee Dee growled, choosing to say nothing at that point.

'That's it, that's it Trisha,' the doctor said, seeing Trisha's nostrils twitching, followed by a pitiful rasping moan.

'Trish!' Maizie cried, squeezing her hand. 'Trish mate iss me Maizie, can you ear me?'

'Oy soppy nuts!' Dee Dee couldn't help herself saying. 'You awake or what?'

Maizie gave Dee Dee a disapproving look.

'What?' Dee Dee asked, shrugging her shoulders. 'Ar'm only askin.'

The moaning grew louder and there was now movement under the blanket.

'She's wakin up Dee!' Maizie said excitedly. 'She's wakin up mate!'

'Whoop de fuckin doo!' Dee Dee said, distinctively unimpressed, with an ever increasing pool of water at her feet.

'Triiish, Trish mate,' Maizie said softly, 'iss alright, me and Dee are ear.'

'What appened?' Trisha said, barely able to open an eye.

'You tell me!' Dee Dee barked, rubbing herself with her blanket. 'What the fuck was you doin on the roof?'

'The roof?' Trisha replied, still delirious from the dart's effects. 'The roof?'

'Yes the pissin roof!' Dee Dee said, in no mood for games.

'Oh, oh yeah,' Trisha said, recalling fragments of her ordeal. 'Ar broke it did'n I.'

'Ar know ya broke the roof, ya doughnut!' Dee Dee said angrily. 'There's a dirty great ole in it and arf the category A nut jobs on B wing are moppin aat their cells cozza you.'

'No you idiot!' Trisha said, rubbing her eyes and reaching behind her ear. 'Me pencil, ar broke me pencil.'

'Woss that gotta do wiv it?' Maizie asked, with the doctor and his nurse also listening intently.

'Ar was lookin for a sharpener,' Trisha told them, plucking the remainder of the pencil from behind her right ear. 'Ar went aatside to sharpen it, an ar got locked aat, and them fuckers wouldn't let me back in.'

'Locked aat!' Maizie said in disbelief. 'Locked aat!'

'Yeah!' Trisha exclaimed. 'Can ya believe it?'

Dee Dee put a hand to her head as the others looked on stunned, realizing that the incident that had sparked a

global outcry had in fact stemmed from something as paltry as a broken pencil. 'Ar don't bloody believe it,' she said dropping into a chair.
'Ar know,' Trisha agreed, 'thas what ar get for buyin paand shop pencils ar spoze, ya get what ya pay for thas what me nan used to say, ar make er right an'all though Dee, coz them pennywise panty pads aint werf two bob are they, ya gotta wear arf a dozen of the bleedin fings to stop the claret runnin daan ya leg aint'cha?'
The doctor and his stunned nurse looked on as Trisha's mouth slipped into a higher gear. 'In the war though, me nan said they never ad nunna them fancy fangled fings wiv gussets and wings up yer ole,' she rambled yet again, 'they ad to make do wiv a spam fritter or an andfull of parachute lastic, thas proper bulldog spirit that is ar tell ya.'
'Trisha!' Dee Dee said, attempting to silence her friend, but to no avail.
'Ar member our Jimmy gettin stuck on the roof of the Masonic lodge on the Mile End road,' Trisha said, blissfully unaware, 'while them dodgy andshake fuckers was in there beatin eachuvva's bare arse wiv a cricket bat and slashin some poor goat's froat, e was nickin the lead and avin it away wiv the satellite dish, e got two undred hours community service for that e did.'
'Trishaaaaa!' Dee Dee said, with increasing gusto.
'Ya never guess what they made im do,' Trisha waffled. 'Go on Dee, ava guess,' but before Dee Dee could interject Trisha was off again, 'e only ad to scoop the poop aat the Battersea pooch pens wiv a shovel, and summa them big old mutts can really dump a load ar tell ya. We ad a dirty great Doberman when we was kids, d'ya member Dee, Kong iz name was, always shittin in the road e was, bloody great logs like speed ramps they was, me grandad ripped the arse aat of iz Morris Minor on wunna Kong's sun dried Richards.'
'Richards?' the doctor said quizzically.
'Richard the fird,' Dee Dee informed him. 'Turds, mate.'

'Oh, oh I see,' the doctor said, turning his nose up. 'Right, well I suggest you get plenty of rest young lady,' he told Trisha. 'And do try to stay out of trouble.'

'Thas easier said than done doc,' Maizie said at Trisha's side. 'She's a bleedin magnet for it, aint'cha Trisha mate?'

'Ar told ya, it weren't mar fault,' Trisha said in her defence. 'Ar just popped aat to put a point on me pencil and ended up gettin...'

'TRISHAAAAAAA!' Dee Dee eventually screamed, stopping her babbling friend in mid-sentence.

'What?' Trisha asked innocently. 'Woss up Dee?'

Maizie was about to intervene when Dee Dee held up a warning hand. 'So!' Dee Dee said abruptly. 'Lemmy get this bleedin straight, me and Maize ear almost died riskin our necks to save ya, an all because you broke ya fuckin pencil.'

'Ahhhhh thas nice of ya,' Trisha said, rubbing Maizie's hand. 'You did'n av to though, coz ar was gonna shimmy daan the drain pipe.'

'But Trish,' Maizie reminded her, 'you couldn't coz they shot ya.'

'What, who did?' Trisha asked, having no recollection of the darting.

'The old bill,' Maizie told her, 'they fought you was gonna jump or summink.'

'Jump!' Trisha exclaimed. 'You're avin a laugh aint'cha, ard'a broke me bleedin neck.'

'Shame you didn't,' Dee Dee growled. 'You'da saved me and Maizie an ole lotta grief.'

'Ohhhh don't say that.' Maizie moaned. 'You wanted to get er back as much as ar did, dint'cha?'

Dee Dee said nothing, refusing to admit her true feelings.

'Dint'cha Dee?' Maizie said, pressing Dee Dee for an answer. 'Go on admit it, you was worried an'all.'

'Oh alright!' Dee Dee snapped. 'Yeah, yeah ar was, but that don't mean I aint pissed off wiv er. She does it every blinkin time, wunna these days she's gonna get us all killed, you wait and see.'

'Well, if ar do Dee,' Trisha piped up, 'you can say ar told ya so, can't she Maize?'
'No, ar can't!' Dee Dee raged, 'coz ar'll be fuckin dead you idiot!'
'Oh,' Trisha said with a smile, 'yeah, course ya will, silly me.'
'Ar gotta get aat of ear,' Dee Dee said, heading for the door, unable to contain herself a moment longer. 'Wunna these days Trisha,' she warned. 'WUNNA THESE FUCKIN DAYS!'
Maizie sat beside Trisha adjusting her bedding. 'Don't mind er Trish mate.' she told her friend. 'Ar know she loves ya really, we bofe do, you just shit the life aat of us thas all.'
'Ar'm sorry Maize,' Trisha said, overcome with emotion. 'Ar love you'z an'all, ar'm a proper pain in the arse ain I? Praps you shoulda left me aat there, ay?'
'Don't be daft,' Maizie scoffed dismissively. 'You're our mate, there aint nuffing we wouldn't do for ya. Don't worry abaat Dee Dee she'll calm daan, ay and don't forget we're gettin aat tomorra aint we.'
'Shit yeah Maize, we are aint we!' Trisha replied, wriggling with excitement. 'Ar promise Maize,' she told her dear friend sincerely, 'when we get aat ar be the bestest mate you ever ad, onest, ar won't cause you no more trouble you wait and see.'
'Ar know Trish,' Maizie said, knowing full well that Trisha couldn't go a single day without getting into some form of pickle, after all, the chaos theory was written specifically with her in mind.
'Oy!' a guard then yelled at Maizie from the doorway. 'Come on, back to your cell!'
'Alright ang on a minute!' Maizie replied, hugging Trisha closely. 'You get a good night's sleep yeah,' she told her. 'This time tomorra we'll be free, so behave yaself alright.'
'Ar will,' Trisha replied. 'You aint got nuffing to worry abaat Maize, ar promise.'
Maizie left with the fingers on both hands tightly crossed, praying for a smooth and trouble free departure the following day.

'Oh Maize!' Trisha called out from her bed. 'Don't worry mate!' she added, poised with her pencil. 'Iss all goin in the book!'
Maizie rolled her eyes and left Trisha hastily scribbling another chapter of her non fictional memoirs, which was fast becoming a work of such literary fantasy that Tolkien of the Hobbit fame himself would have been hard pressed to match.
Needing no outside inspiration, Trisha filled page after page from her wealth of life experiences, with enough material to draw from the pen a trilogy, and then some.
'You alright Dee?' Maizie asked, rejoining Dee Dee in their cell. 'Ar'v left er writin that book fing of ers.'
'Hmmmm,' Dee Dee growled, sitting in quiet contemplation.
'She aint never gonna change is she Dee?' Maizie added, stretching out on her bunk. 'One minute she's all sweetness and light, and the next she's startin world war free aint she. Ar know she winds you up summink chronic Dee, but you wouldn't see any arm come to er would ya?'
Again Dee Dee remained tight lipped.
'Would ya Dee?' Maizie probed.
'Spoze not,' Dee Dee mumbled, relenting a little.
'Ahhhhh, ar knew it,' Maizie smiled, snuggling into her pillow. 'Ya carn elp but love er can ya.'
'Ar wouldn't go that far,' Dee Dee said, with a wry smile.
'Deeeeee,' Maizie teased, 'go on admit it, you do love er, not in a weird lezza way or nuffing, ar mean as a mate like me, coz ar love you bofe an I ain afraid to say it neeva.'
'Hmmm whateva,' Dee Dee said, turning to face the wall on her bunk. 'Course ya me mates,' she said evading the point.
'Yeah ar know that Dee but,' Maizie pressed the subject further, 'but do ya love us?'
'Oh shut up Maizie!' Dee Dee said, beating her pillow, feeling a tad uneasy. 'You know ar do.'
'Well say it then,' Maizie said tongue in cheek. 'Go on, it won't urt ya.'

'Oh flippin ell Maize, leave off will ya!' Dee Dee moaned, 'woss a matter wiv you, you're as mad as that dozey mare you are!'

Maizie lay in silence for a moment or two. 'Well?' she eventually said, staring at Dee Dee's back.

'OH FOR FUCK SAKE!' Dee Dee yelled, realizing there would be no peace. 'COURSE AR LOVE YA, BOFE OF YA. Ar dunno why, ar must want me nut examinin coz the paira ya drive me up the pissin wall ya do. There, ar said it, you appy naah?'

'Yeeeeah!' Maizie smiled. 'Ar knew ya did, ar just wonnid to ear you say it thas all.'

'Right, well shut up and get some kip will ya,' Dee Dee growled. 'We got a proper big day tomorra, member.'

'Oooh yeaaaaah!' Maizie said excitedly. 'Ar don't reckon ar be able to sleep though Dee, me guts ar goin ten to the dozen, ar can't wait mate ar really can't, can you, Dee? Dee can you?'

Dee Dee had chosen to ignore her friend's continuous banter, losing herself instead in her thoughts.

'Oh sod ya,' Maizie eventually sighed, rolling back to face the ceiling to picture the life that awaited them on the outside.

Trisha in the meantime lay engrossed in her notes, describing in her own inimitable way how the three of them had stolen the Red Sea Ruby from Sheik Abdullah Hussain, and how Dee Dee had hacked off his arm with his own sword in the process. 'Oh bugger!' she soon cursed, turning the last page and looking around her for further writing material, with a head full of enthralling memories to delight her future readers.

Finding herself alone once again Trisha was about to throw her sheets aside and leave her bed when Dee Dee's warning words rang out in her head. 'Shit!' she said, thinking better of it and remembering the promises she had made her friends.

Her notebook now full to capacity, Trisha grew increasingly restless and agitated. 'ELLO!' she called out, as she had done earlier, but this time there was an instant reply.
'Coming!' said Suzette, the nurse from the previous nightshift, hurrying onto the ward and removing her coat. 'God Trisha, I've been so worried,' she added, scurrying to Trisha's bedside. 'I haven't been able to sleep a wink. I've been glued to the television, what on earth happened?'
'Oh that,' Trisha said, shrugging off the day's catastrophic events, still scanning the immediate area for a sheet or two of paper. 'Ar broke me pencil did'n I.'
'You did what?' Suzette asked, checking the medical notes at the end of Trisha's bed. 'Sorry I don't understand.'
'Me lead,' Trisha said, offering up her pencil, now a mere inch and a half in length. 'Ar broke it and went lookin for a sharpner.'
'On the roof!' Suzette said, unable to fathom how the two incidents were related. 'I'm sorry I...' she then paused, clasping a hand to her forehead. 'Oh no, oh no, it's all my fault!' she cried, removing her woolen hat.
'What you on abaat?' Trisha asked. 'You never broke me pencil.'
'No no!' Suzette said, pacing in despair. 'I only popped out for a cigarette, I must've forgotten to lock the door. Oh god, it's all my fault, they'll dismiss me for certain!'
'What?' Trisha asked, watching the nurse toing and froing. 'Stand still will ya!' she snapped. 'Right, naah what you on abaat?'
'The balcony door!' Suzette said, unable to settle. 'I forgot to lock it when I came back inside, that's how you managed to escape.
'Escape!' Trisha scoffed. 'Don't be daft, I only nipped aat for a minute and the poxy wind blew the door shut din it.'
'There'll be a disciplinary hearing, I know it,' Suzette said, wringing her hands. 'Oh god Trisha, I really need this job, my mother has MS and I'm her sole carer. How could I have been so stupid. God I could kick myself!'

'Ang on a minute,' Trisha said, stopping the nurse in her tracks. 'They don't know you left the bleedin door open, nobody's bovva'd to ask me yet actually.'
'You don't understand,' Suzette said at Trisha's side, 'there'll be an enquiry there always is, and that'll be the first question they ask, believe me Trisha I know.'
Trisha thought for a moment. 'Look,' she eventually said, 'ar'll tell em it was locked when ar went in there, an ar faand the key meself. What can they say, ay?'
'Oh Trisha, would you?' Suzette said, clasping her hands together. 'Really?'
'Yeah course, it aint no skin off mar nose is it,' Trisha told her. 'Ar'm gettin aat tomorra anyway, don't worry mate ya job's safe, trust me.'
'Oh would you?' Suzette asked. 'That's fantastic. Oh I'd be eternally grateful, really I would. Can I get you anything: coffee, tea perhaps?'
'Well,' Trisha said, waving her notebook. 'Ar don't spoze ya got any paper av ya, ar'm writin me memries ya see.'
'Paper,' Suzette said, eager to please, 'yes, yes of course, I'll be right back.' She hurried to the staffroom returning moments later with a new three hundred page A5 writing pad. 'Here you are,' she said, handing it to Trisha along with a fist full of biros.
'Oh fanks!' Trisha said, ditching her minuscule pencil and setting down her notebook. 'Ar'm gonna get it published when iss done.'
'Really!' Suzette said in awe. 'I've always wanted to write but I simply wouldn't know where to begin.'
'Yeah, ar nart ya mean,' Trisha said, sounding every bit the seasoned author. 'It ain everyone's cuppa tea thas for sure, iss wunna them fings ar spoze, ya'v iver got it or you aint.'
'Well I must say I'm impressed,' Suzette told Trisha. 'If you don't mind me saying, you really don't look the type, is this your first novel?'
'Me first what?' Trisha asked bemused.
'Your novel,' Suzette said, pointing out Trisha's notebook.

'Oh this, naah,' Trisha said proudly. 'Ar bin writin since ar was a nipper, me muvva always said I ad a way wiv words, ar rit a poem once for me uncle Freddie's funeral and ad em all in tears when a read it aat in the church. D'ya wanna ear it?'
'Oh, I'd love to,' Suzette said, sitting at the foot of Trisha's bed. 'That is if the memory of your dearly departed uncle isn't too painful.'
'Naaaah iss alright,' Trisha replied, composing herself. 'Ang on, ar see if ar can remember it.'
'Take you time, it's ok' Suzette said sympathetically.
Taking a deep breath, with one hand on her heart, Trisha sat up in bed; the ode she had written some fifteen years earlier certainly did have the congregation in tears, but those of hysteria instead of abject grief.
'Ear goes,' she said, making the sign of the cross and looking to the heavens. 'This is for you again Uncle Freddie, ope you can ear me. Oh by the way, if ya can, can you ask me nan up there for the recipe for er rhubarb casserole, ar still aint got the ang of it, iss me dumplins ya see, like bleedin bullets they are.'
'Er, your poem?' Suzette said, halting Trisha's impending ramble.
'Oh,' Trisha said, 'yeah ok, sorry.' She took another deep breath. 'Ahem,' she said, clearing her throat. 'Sorry, this ain easy.'
'No, no I can imagine,' Suzette replied, with one hand on Trisha's leg.
'Right ear goes,' Trisha said resolutely, as though in preparation for a spellbinding speech,

'We all miss you dear Uncle Freddie
You snuffed it before you was ready
Was you finkin of us
When you was squished by the bus
or the affair you bin avin wiv Eddie.'

Suzette could hardly believe her ears.

'Ang on, there's more,' Trisha said solemnly,

'Ar remember the fun in ya Mazda
Goin feevin in Lidl and Asda
It was there to be taken
So you nicked the bacon
An ar filled me pockets wiv pasta.'

Suzette's eyes grew wider and wider with every line.
'Good ain it,' Trisha said proudly.
Suzette was about to reply when Trisha launched into her final verse,

'Uncle Freddie we'll miss you forever
Me, me mum and our Trevor
There's a tear in our eye
As we wave ya goodbye
In ya heels, ya hot pants and levva.'

Suzette sat mortified at Trisha's eulogy.
'Wod'ya reckon?' Trisha asked. 'D'ya fink e woulda liked it?
'Well,' Suzette replied, searching her soul for a fitting answer. 'It certainly is a moving tribute, you must've spent some time composing it no doubt.'
'Naah not really,' Trisha said glibly. 'Ar rit it on the back of a fag packet goin in the church, e was a real queen me uncle Freddie, fuckin great tash an a wardrobe me and you'd die for ar tell ya, proper villain an'all though, an a real nasty bastard when e wonnid to be, e once battered a geeza arf to deff wiv a stiletto for callin im a faggot.'
'So er,' Suzette said, keen to change the subject, 'do you have a title for your memoirs, and you honestly think you'll get them published one day?'
'Oh yeah no probs,' Trisha said, picking up her work and clutching it to her heart. 'Ar'm callin it "Gissa Fag". Catchy ain it?'

'Yes rather,' Suzette agreed. 'I'm sure it'll do extremely well with your obvious talents.' The ever grateful Suzette toyed with Trisha's ego in exchange for her silence over the recent security breech.

'Ar'm waitin for me gran to snuff it,' Trisha said, without a shred of remorse, 'coz ar rit ers already. D'ya wanna ear it?'

'Oh no, no please don't,' Suzette said, having heard enough. 'We don't want to tempt fate now do we.'

'Fate aint got nuffing to do wiv it,' Trisha replied, nibbling on a biro. 'She's on er last legs anyway, she ain ad a lotta luck though the daft old mare.'

'Oh I am sorry to hear that,' Suzette said with true feeling. 'They do say that bad luck has a habit of following some people around but I don't know how true that is.'

'Fuck me ar'd say!' Trisha laughed. 'Ow she aint copped it by naah ar don't know. She was bombed aat of er bungalow durin the war, turfed off the Titanic in a rubber ring and crash landed at Alicante airport on a Saga oliday, she's a bloody jinx ar tell ya, she's ad that mad cows fingy, swine flu, bird flu and any uvva friggin flu ya can fink of, mumps, measles an mange an'all.'

'My word, I see what you mean,' Suzette gasped, dumbstruck by the lengthy list.

'Woss for dinner anyway?' Trisha asked, going off on a completely different tangent. 'Ar'm that ungry ar could eat a scabby cat ar tell ya. We ad a scabby cat once, well e weren't scabby when we got im, little tabby fucker e was, always runnin up the curtains and jumpin on yer ed.'

Suzette's head was spinning with Trisha's meandering tales.

'Anyway,' Trisha waffled, 'me muvva tripped over the bloody fing in the kitchen and dropped a bowl of boilin blackcurrant jelly on iz back.'

'Oh no!' Suzette said, putting a hand to her mouth.

'Yeah, all iz air fell aat an e was covered in boils an blisters for a coupla days before e dropped daan dead.'

'My god it must've been so upsetting for you,' Suzette said horrified.

'Yeah, ar was gutted to tell the troof,' Trisha admitted. 'Ar was lookin forward to that jelly, iss me favrit flavour, me and Dee made a loada Sambuca shots wiv it once and got proper bollocks'd on em.'
'No, no!' Suzette said. 'I meant losing your poor cat in such a horrendous way.'
'Oh im,' Trisha said with little regard. 'Ar never did like the little bleeda, we never buried im, ar bagged im up and swapped im for a set meal for two at Changs Palace on the Romford Road. Ar do like their crispy duck ar do.'
Suzette turned her nose up yet again. 'You are kidding, right?' she asked, never having been a huge believer that the oriental fast food industry would stoop so low as to use domestic animals as a supplement for beef, lamb and even chicken.
'OK, well maybe it aint proper duck,' Trisha admitted. 'But at least they're keepin the pigeon population daan, filfy fuckers shittin all over the bleedin place.'
Suzette at this point had heard enough. 'I'll go see what's for supper,' she said, heading for the door having absolutely no appetite herself.
'Oooh yeah, lovely!' Trisha called after her. 'If iss meatballs again tell em ar like mine deep fried in chip fat, ar let em go cold ya see and then ar lick the lard off em.'
Suzette's stomach turned on hearing this. 'I'll er, I'll see what I can do,' she said, leaving Trisha alone once again. But Trisha was content at least to stay put, with enough writing materials to occupy her for some time.
Although the supper menu did in fact include spicy meatballs Suzette opted for the gammon steak for her one and only patient, the thought of Trisha licking the fat from the congealed savories was more than she could bear.
Dee Dee and Maizie had skipped supper themselves opting for an early night after the day's events, hoping the worst of times were now behind them and awaiting a new dawn which would hopefully herald a fresh start for the three of them, if that were at all possible.

'Gammon!' Trisha said with real distain. 'Oh bleedin ell, is that all they got?'
'I'm sorry, I'm afraid it is,' Suzette said, telling the smallest of white lies. 'Is there a problem?'
'Well yeah,' Trisha moaned. 'They used to ram that shit daan our necks at the Caflic school, wiv a poxy pineapple ring on it an'all, Muvva Superior used to boil the buggers to deff she did and beat the shit out of us if we puked em up.'
'Oh, I am sorry,' Suzette said, feeling the slightest bit guilty. 'I got you desert though, it's black forest gateau with vanilla ice cream.'
'Oh, naah ya talkin!' Trisha said, snatching the bowl with a grin. She then set about mixing the two together with her spoon, scraping the bowl in the process until she'd created a pink blancmange-like mess which she shoveled into her mouth greedily.
'I'll get rid of the gammon then,' Suzette told her, removing the plate and in doing so dropping the fork.
Trisha froze with the fork en route to her mouth looking down at the nurse's shapely bottom with the line of her flimsy thong clearly visible beneath her neatly pressed figure hugging skirt. 'Oy oy!' she said unashamedly, 'take ya time.'
'I'm sorry,' Suzette said straightening her back.
'Don't be sorry darlin,' Trisha smiled, spooning the last of her desert into her mouth and tossing the bowl onto the side. 'Ar was just admirin the view.'
'I don't understand,' Suzette replied, unaware of Trisha's lusty advances.
'Ar don't spoze yer into birds are ya?' Trisha asked, getting straight to the point. 'Coz you gotta fantastic figure if ya don't mind me sayin.'
'Birds?' Suzette said naively. 'I'm sorry I...'
'Girls!' Trisha said, stopping her short and running her eyes up and down Suzette, a brunette of medium build, strong athletic legs, dreamy hazel eyes and a bosom that had Trisha grinding her knees together under her sheets.

'Girls!' Suzette said, clasping one hand to her chest. 'Oh dear god no. No no, no, I'm happily married thank you. Why in heavens name do you ask, are you a...?'
'I ain a lezza if thas what ya finkin,' Trisha informed her. 'Well, not a proper one, ar'm a bisexual ya could say, mind you iss bin so bleedin long since I ad a dick ar reckon ar forgot what one looks like, so er, this geezer of yours,' she said fishing, 'is e sortin you aat proper is e?'
'What do you mean?' Suzette asked, finding the topic of conversation disconcerting. 'We're very happy together, if that's what you mean.'
'No, it aint what ar mean,' Trisha replied, hoping to sway her opinion. 'Ar mean, does e make ya scream and tense up like ya backs gonna snap when e'z daan there bitin on ya bean?'
Suzette looked puzzled to say the least. 'We er, we get by,' she said, blushing somewhat.
'Get by!' Trisha scoffed. 'Ar know what ya mean by gettin by love, e comes in from the boozer shit faced and stinkin, grabs yer arse, squeezes ya tit and bends you over the kitchen table puffin and blowin like a friggin asthmatic, iz limp dick floppin all over the place and iz beer belly bangin on ya back. Am ar right?' Trisha had in fact described Suzettes one sided ritualistic romps to a tee.
'Well, we both work hard and are just so tired half the time,' Suzette told her, seeking an excuse for her lackluster love life. 'It's hard you know.'
'Not ard enough ar bet,' Trisha laughed.
Suzette set the plate down once again and sat at the end of Trisha's bed. 'But us girls have a way of making do, don't we,' she said, hinting toward inanimate battery powered penetration.
'Yeah ar know but,' Trisha sneered, 'I aint faand one yet that gets right raand the rim if ya nart ar mean.'
'Yes, yes I do,' Suzette smiled, finding herself suddenly more at ease. 'But it lasts a damn sight longer than James, I'll say that. When he's been out all day with his rugger friends

he's absolutely useless. I doubt he'd even realize if I slipped out halfway through and made myself a cup of tea.'
'Niiiiice,' Trisha said, picturing the scene and happy that she has the option of switching to the other side. 'You never even fought abaat it?' she asked, stalking.
'About what?' Suzette asked, losing her train of thought for a moment.
'Goin bi,' Trisha told her, doing her upmost to look alluring even with her facial bruising.
'Me!' Suzette gasped. 'Oh, I really couldn't. I mean, I'm not saying there's anything wrong with it, it's just not for me that's all.'
Oh,' Trisha said, with an air of disappointment. 'And ar spoze a limp dick is, is it?'
Suzette looked down at her wedding ring, spinning it nervously on her finger. 'We do have our problems James and I,' she confessed, 'but I do love him and would never do anything to hurt him.' Suzette collected the plate and left Trisha's bedside.
'Fink abaat it!' Trisha called after her. 'Ya might like it!'
The idea had never once crossed Suzette's mind, but she knew she'd be lying to herself to deny she hadn't found the subject mildly titillating; many a modern day neglected housewife had sought comfort, and even passion, in the arms of another of the same sex. Closing the staffroom door behind her, Suzette set down the plate and slumped back against the table gripping the edge between her whitened knuckles and breathing heavily. Trisha had evoked feelings deep within her that, since the heady days of her whirlwind adolescent romance, she'd assumed were lost forever. But if the truth be known, she simply wasn't ready at that particular moment in time to explore unfamiliar, but albeit tempting territory. Although if she were to endure much more of James's alcohol fueled fumbling incompetence then she mightn't be so hesitant should the situation present itself again, and judging by her vocational surroundings with its exceptionally high bisexual and lesbian population, the

once frowned upon forbidden fruit would be offered up with increasing abundance.

Trisha wrote feverishly into the small hours before dozing off pen in hand, her head full of memories, some heart wrenching but the majority chaotic and completely random in description.

CHAPTER FOUR

The following morning, although having slept very little, Trisha had risen, taken a cocktail of pain killers and dragged on her clothes.

Suzette emerged from the staffroom, where she had spent a restless night tossing and turning on the sofa, to find Trisha's bed empty and a note on the pillow with a contact telephone number for her on the outside (namely her mother's), three kisses and an X-rated PS describing in some erotic detail what Trisha would like to do to her given half the chance.

Blushing and weak at the knees Suzette thrust the note into her pocket and, with nobody looking, ran a quivering hand over the sheets that had once covered Trisha's naked body.

The moment that Trisha stepped out onto the wing she was accosted by a patrolling guard. 'Oh, mawnin,' she said, feeling a firm hand on her shoulder.

'Where d'you think you're going?' the officer asked, looking over Trisha's shoulder. 'Who said you could leave the infirmary?'

'Iss alright,' Trisha explained, 'ar'm goin ome today, ar just need to get back to me cell. Ooh ar like what you done wiv your air,' she added, prodding the officers tight plait. 'You look like that bird aata Star Wars, Princess Wosserface.'

'Get off me!' the officer barked, swatting Trisha's hand. 'Follow me, we're opening up now anyway.'

'Okey dokey,' Trisha replied, saluting the uniformed officer and trailing behind. 'Can ar do it, please miss?' she then asked, taking the key from the officer and turning it in the lock, she then burst inside her cell kicking over the bin and shaking the foot of Dee Dee and Maizie's bunk.

'RIGHT YOU SLAGS GET YER ARSES UP, THIS IS A CELL SEARCH!' she yelled, trying not to laugh. 'DAWSON AR KNOW YOU GOT ARF A PAAND OF CRACK UP YA BACK END, AND YOU SOPPY BOLLOCKS!' she added, kicking out at

Maizie's trailing foot, 'AND OVER THE CHARLIE YOU SCUMBAG!'
'What the fuck!' Dee Dee said, lifting her bleary-eyed head from her pillow. 'Piss off screw!'
'Yeah, fuck off!' Maizie snapped, dragging a pillow over her head. 'We aint got no bleedin drugs so do one will ya!'
'TRISHAAAAA!' Dee Dee growled, opening one eye. 'WHAT THE BLEEDIN ELL?'
'Mawnin!' Trisha said chirpily. 'You two gettin up or what?'
'You soppy bitch!' Maizie said, emerging. 'Wadda you fink your playin at?'
'Oh come on,' Trisha moaned. 'Ar'm only avin a laugh, come on shift yer arses will ya, brecky's in ten minutes and we gotta get our shit togevva, come on!'
'Trisha, for fuck sack, ar was avin a lovely dream ar was,' Maizie moaned, tossing her pillow in Trisha's direction. 'Johnny Depp was lickin Lemonade off me left tit in a caravan at Walton on the Naze, proper orny it was.'
'Oh ar love Walton,' Trisha said with fondness. 'We used to go crabbin daan there in the six weeks oliday, mind you the only fing I ever caught was a couple welly boots an a tampax.'
'Trisha!' Dee Dee again snapped. 'Shut the friggin door will ya, and shut ya maaf an'all while yer at it, you know ar carn andle your shit first fing in the mawnin.'
'We stayed in a chalet,' Trisha said, dismissing Dee Dee's aggression, 'wiv an ole in the roof. If it was pissin daan, which it always was, me dad ad to get up evry coupla'v ours to empty the bleedin bucket, wunna the wheels ad sunk in the mud an'all so it was proper wonkey, mind you wadda ya want for a tenner a week, you come daan there wiv us once dint'cha Dee?'
'Yeah, never again,' Dee Dee said, sitting up in her bunk. 'The gaff was crawlin wiv fleas, riddled wiv risin damp, no lectric and the poxy septic tank kept backin up and fillin the pan wiv shit.'

'Well, it ad a five star ratin,' Trisha said, in the dilapidated chalet's defence.
'Compared to what?' Dee Dee stormed. 'A friggin cardboard box!'
'Oh it weren't that bad,' Trisha whined, 'we did av a proper laugh dint we.'
'You mighta done!' Dee Dee said with a hint of bitterness. 'You never ad to kip in a piss stained sleepin bag at forty five fuckin degrees, listnin to the ruddy rain drippin into a tin bloody bucket did ya?'
'Oh!' Trisha said, stunned to say the least. 'You never said.'
Dee Dee paused for a moment to catch her breath. 'No, no ar never,' she said in a calmer tone. 'Coz ar knew ya muvva scrimped and saved up all er coupons to take us on oliday. I aint sayin I aint grateful so don't fink I aint, ar know she ad it ard like mar muvva did, god love er. Ar just wished we ad lectric an a telly at the time thas all, it mighta made it a bit more bearable nart ar mean.'
'We ad Kerplunk,' Trisha reminded her, recalling the candle lit evenings sipping value cocoa from chipped china mugs.
'Kerplunk!' Dee Dee laughed. 'We only ad two marbles an arf the bleedin sticks were missin, what kinda games that, ay?'
Fully dressed and waiting by the door Maizie tapped her toes on the steel door. 'You two comin for breckie or what?' she asked. 'Iss our last one in this shit ole ain it.'
'Yeah alright,' Dee Dee replied, pulling her sweater over her head.
'We played "I Spy",' Trisha said, joining Maizie.
'Oh yeah!' Dee Dee scoffed. 'And ow many times did you say B for bleedin bucket, ay?'
'Well,' Trisha said, thinking back, 'there wern a lot else in there was there.'
The chalet, if it could be described as such, was indeed sparsely furnished with nineteen fifties floral linoleum on the floor, a brown three seater corduroy sofa with questionable staining, and three mismatched ladder back

chairs. Situated in a bramble covered corner of The Happy Sands holiday park, which itself was a good mile and a half hike from the nearest beach via the stinking landfill site, home to hoards of huge mutated rats that now thrived on the very poison set down to annihilate them. All in all, an experience never repeated and best forgotten.

'Mind you,' Dee Dee chuckled, 'ar left em a few choice comments in the visitors book ar tell ya, an a paira me shitty knickers under the grill, ar bet they was proper ripe when the old git come to clean the place.'

The old git Dee Dee was referring to was Arthur Grimley, owner of Happy Sands, and in stark contrast to its name was quite possibly the most miserable man to ever have worked within the hospitality industry. A devout Christian with a distinct hatred of children, and anybody for that matter below pensionable age, Grimley would make the lives of his guests a living hell during their stay with his constant moaning, and mowing at five thirty in the morning and preaching the gospel in an attempt to convert whomever he could corner outside the freezing shower block.

'God yeah ar member what a wanker that old boy was,' Trisha agreed. 'Member when ar pissed on iz radishes on the way back from the beach.'

Arthur's pristine vegetable plot was his one and only pride and joy, winning him countless rosettes at the local village fair. Weeded religiously, the neatly furrowed rows of spring greens and root vegetables were nurtured by his hand and his hand alone.

Trisha had scrambled over the barbed wire perimeter fence, tearing her leggings in the process, and while old man Grimley was reciting the Scriptures to a group of petrified campers she squatted over his ripened radishes and urinated with a satisfied grin on her face; payback as she saw it for the ferocious verbal assault he had inflicted on them that very morning for the most trivial of misdemeanors.

'I only left the fuckin gate open did'n I,' Trisha reminded her friend. Unbeknown to them at the time, a Welsh cob cart horse had strayed from a neighboring farm onto his property and eaten the titanic turnips he was due to show the next day, a sure fire winner he had confidently assumed and one that would gift him a record breaking ninth golden rosette and his name immortalized and engraved on the coveted Walton Growers cup. Consequently, he was humiliated with a third place bronze for his courgettes and was forced to endure the gloating jibes of his bitter rivals.
'D'ya wanna tea Dee?' Maizie asked, handing Dee Dee and Trisha a tray at the counter.
'Yeah ta,' Dee Dee replied, eyeing the mornings offerings.
'Got any marmalade?' Trisha asked the serving girls, whilst plucking two slices of burnt toast from the rack. Trisha was handed three pre packed individual servings of thick cut marmalade. 'Ooooh cheers love,' she said, licking her lips. 'Me nan used to make er own,' she told her two friends.
'Shuttup Trisha!' Dee Dee said dismissively. 'Ar don't wanna ear it.'
'What?' Trisha asked. 'Ar was only gonna say...'
'AR SAID!' Dee Dee reiterated, 'ar don't wanna ear any more of your bollocks, ar'm avin me breakfast, alright!'
Trisha looked round at Maizie for support.
'Yeah, give it a rest Trish mate,' Maizie agreed. 'Less just av our last breckie in peace yeah.'
'Oh,' Trisha said, stunned somewhat. 'Ar just wonnid to tell ya ow she made it thas all.'
'We ain interested,' Dee Dee scoffed, handing over her empty plate. 'Scrambled please,' she said, turning her back on Trisha. 'And two ash braans an'all, yeah.'
Trisha too offered her plate across the counter. 'Beans please,' she said, keen to have her fill.
'You got marmalade aint'cha!' Maizie reminded her.
'Yeah,' Trisha said abruptly. 'Ar know.'
'Beans and marmalade!' Maizie said, almost sick at the thought.

'Yeah,' Trisha said nonchalantly. 'You avin some?'
'No ar bleedin aint!' Maizie snapped, reaching for the cereal. 'You aint right girl, d'you know that?'
'Ar'll av ers,' Trisha said, holding out for a second scoop. 'And stick a sausage on there an'all will ya,' she added.
Dee Dee and Maizie watched horrified at the table as Trisha tore open her marmalade portions one by one and prised out the contents with a plastic knife onto her toast and beans and proceeded to stir in the preserve and lick the tiny cartons clean.
'Luuuuuvly,' Trisha said, wide eyed.
'Jesus!' Dee Dee said in complete disgust. 'You must av cast iron guts, ar swear it Trish.'
'Ar was brought up proper,' Trisha replied, whilst spooning the sweetened beans into her mouth. 'We ad to eat what me muvva give us or we went ungry back in the day. But arf the time she buggered off aat to the bingo and left us to do our own dinner, thas ow ar learned to cook,' she told them, dunking her toast. 'We never ad a lot in most of the time, so I ad to mix and match, if ya nart ar mean.'
'Yeah, ar do,' Dee Dee said, looking down at Trisha's plate. 'Iss filf if you ask me.'
'Yeah Trish, sort it aat will ya,' Maizie added, tucking into her own breakfast.
'Well, woss that shit then?' Trisha asked, eyeing Maizie's bowl.
'Muesli,' Maizie told her, stirring the contents.
'Moosly, what the fuck's moosly ay?' Trisha asked. 'Look like a loada bleedin sawdust and rabbit shit to me.'
'Iss elfy!' Maizie informed her. 'Iss got ardly any calories in it.'
'Iss got bugger all in it,' Trisha laughed. 'Elfy my arse, ar know ya gotta coupla paand to shift off ya back end, but it don't mean ya gotta eat that shite. Get some beans in ya Maize, you'll shit the bleedin weight off ar'm tellin ya.'
'Ooh no, ar don't eat beans,' Maizie told her, sneering at her plate. 'Ar never av.'

'Oh, ar fergot you was proper spoilt weren't ya,' Trisha said, waving her spoon in Maizie's face. 'When me and Dee was sittin raand eatin bread and butter sandwiches, warmin our ands on a friggin candle, you was stuffin ya face wiv roasty beef and sweatin ya tits off wiv ya poncey central eatin weren't ya.'

It's true to say that Maizie's parents were mildly better off financially than that of her two friends, but they were far from comfortable.

'We ad it ard an'all ya know,' she said, wiping milk from her chin. 'Ar never got a telly in me room till ar was ten, and that ad a nob missin.'

'Oh, your breakin mar fuckin art you are Maize,' Trisha said sarcastically. 'D'you ear that Dee, er telly ad a nob missin, least you ad a bleedin telly,' she snapped, with her mouth full. 'We ad to put up wiv me old man's pissin projector playin ome movies on the chimney breast, night after bloody night, an e only ad two of em, our first oliday in Camber Sands when we buried me nan up to er neck and she was shit on by a buncha seagulls, and me first birfday which used to embarrass the fuck outta me coz they dressed me as Minnie bloody Mouse for the first five years of me life. Ar still av nightmares about them ears ar tell ya.'

Dee Dee had been listening intently and had heard enough.

'What the fuck are you two on abaat?' she asked.

'Errrr!' Trisha said, gesturing to Maizie. 'She never ad to share a barf wiv er nan and grandad did she, or get up at the cracka dawn to nick the neighbors milk.'

'Come to fink of it Maize,' Dee Dee agreed, 'you ad it proper easy dint'cha.'

'Oh shuttup Dee!' Maizie protested. 'Just coz we ad ardwood deckin and laminate all over the ouse, don't mean we was minted does it.'

'Laminate floorin, you stuck up bitch!' Trisha scoffed. 'Thas more than we ad ar tell ya.'

'Ardwood deckin!' Dee Dee added, siding with Trisha for once. 'Ardwood bloody deckin, we ad a winda box fulla nettles an a plastic windmill.'
'We ad gnomes,' Trisha said, remembering with fondness. 'Loads of em, me muvva was obsessed wiv the fings, give em names an everyfing.'
'Yeah,' Dee Dee said, recalling the gayly colored garden figures. 'What was it wiv er and them bloody gnomes ay?'
'They elped er wiv er stress,' Trisha told Dee Dee.
'Ar'm not surprised she was stressed!' Maizie laughed. 'Avin you as a flippin daughter.'
'Ar was a bit of a nightmare at the time ar must admit,' Trisha confessed, pushing away her polished plate. 'We was bunkin off school free or four times a week weren't we Dee, sittin over the rec wiv twenny fags an a bottla cider. Them were the days weren't they mate.'
'Yeah, course they was,' Dee Dee agreed, 'listnin to Madonna, sittin on the slide wiv them boys from Barking.'
'Me muvva wus up the school evry week the poor cow,' Trisha said, cupping her mug of tea. 'No wonder she went off er ed an started paintin gnomes, it was iver that she told me, or the booze, and me old man was already on that. Thas why e didn't give a shit what ar did, e was up at arf four evry mawnin on the dust carts and in the pub by lunchtime, bang on the light and bitter pissin iz wages up the wall.'
Maizie tossed her spoon down into her bowl. 'E aint like that naah though is e Trish,' she said, wiping her mouth on her sleeve. 'E don't drink does e?'
'Not a drop,' Trisha told her. 'Not since ar bought em their chalet bungalow in Clacton, an a camper van. The pair of em bugger off all over the place naah, they was in Romania a coupla weeks ago ar got a card off em.'
The girls were then approached by a prison officer. 'You three,' she said abruptly. 'The warden wants you in her office.'
'Tell er she'll av to wait,' Dee Dee said, cutting into her hash brown. 'We're avin breakfast.'

'Now Dawson!' the officer insisted, sliding her stick from its holster. 'Get up!'
Dee Dee grabbed the stick and thrust it away from her face. 'Ar said,' she growled, 'ar'm avin me breakfast so piss off!'
'Come on Dee, it might be important,' Maizie said, not wanting to rock the boat any more than it had been of late. 'Ar've finished anyway, you av an'all aint'cha Trish?'
Trisha drained her mug with a resounding slurp and a burp. 'Yeah ar'm stuffed,' she said, rubbing her stomach. 'Mind you, if you ain eatin that sausage Dee ar'll av it,' she added, reaching across the table.
'Piss off!' Dee Dee snapped, stabbing the back of Trisha's hand with her fork.
'OWWW! Trisha squealed, recoiling.
With the officer breathing down her neck Dee Dee refused to rush her meal, draining her mug to the last. 'Right ar'm ready,' she told the irate officer.
The three girls were led to the warden's office where the furious head paced the room. 'What kept you!' she yelled at her officer. 'I said bring them to me straight away did I not?'
'Yes ma'am but, but,' the officer stammered.
'But, but. Don't give me buts woman!' the warden stormed. 'I gave you a direct order!'
'They were having breakfast ma'am,' the officer pleaded. 'I tried, honestly I did.'
'Oh, just get out!' the warden said, dismissing her subordinate. 'I SAID GET OUT!'
'Later'z!' Dee Dee laughed, watching the guard slope from the office.
Slamming the door behind her, the warden marched behind her desk.
'Mawnin!' Trisha chirped, as though the two of them were firm friends.
'What?' the warden snapped, glaring over her spectacles.
'Ar said mawnin!' Trisha replied, bobbing on the balls of her feet. 'You alright?'

'Am I alright!' the warden snarled, digging her manicured nails into the inlayed leather on her desk. 'Are you out of your mind? Of course I'm not alright, as you put it. There's to be a judicial enquiry into your attempted escape and consequent roof top protest, and I'll be dragged over the coals for this for sure. I'm told they are already lining up a replacement warden, some spotty bitch just out of bloody training pants no doubt!'
'Shit appens,' Dee Dee said, in a cold dry tone.
'Not to me it doesn't!' the warden complained. 'At least it didn't until you three wretches arrived.'
'Oh thas nice!' Trisha said, rolling her eyes. 'We aint blinkin terrorists ya know!'
'I wouldn't be so sure,' the seething warden replied, reaching into her desk drawer for a fist full of papers. 'I've had your friend Hamilton on the phone. He'll be here within the hour and you are to be signed over into his care. God have mercy on him.' Dividing the papers into three equal piles, she first offered Dee Dee a pen. 'At the bottom of each page,' she pointed out abruptly.
Trisha and Maizie stood pensively waiting their turn, whilst their friend completed the formalities and pushed her release papers back across the warden's desk.
'Is that it then?' Dee Dee asked the warden, who said nothing, handing the pen to Maizie who hurriedly scrawled her signature eager to be free.
'Right, now you!' the warden said, offering the pen but refusing to release her grip on the biro at first. 'If I ever see you again I swear,' she growled. 'I'll, I'll...!'
'Yeah, thatta be nice,' Trisha said, preempting the warden. 'We could go for a posh coffee or a panini or summink, ar like them frapuccinos fingys meself wiv loadsa cream on top. I aint keen on them croissants though, bit overrated if you ask me, ar know the Frenchies love em but they would wouldn't they, dirty bleedas.'
'Just sign the damn papers!' the warden snapped, releasing the pen and shoving her toward the documents.

'D'you like mozzarella and meatballs?' Trisha asked, signing the first sheet with separate firm capital letters.

'What?' the warden said, bemused at the relevance of her question. 'What the hell are you talking about girl?'

'In ya panini?' Trisha added. 'Ar prefer the bacon and brie meself. But the meatballs aint bad, they just repeat on ya a bit thas all, we got a megabucks in the high street wiv big comfy levva chairs and they play that poncey opra music while ya slurpin ya latte.'

'No, thas a Costa,' Maizie said, correcting her.

'You sure?' Trisha asked, turning to her friend and abandoning the documents.

'Yes ar'm sure,' Maizie told her sternly, 'our Bradley used to work in there on a Saturday, where d'ya fink me muvva got all them coffee cups from.'

'No, not that one!' Trisha said, nibbling the biro with the warden's patience dwindling. 'The one next to cash money converters, or whatever the bleedin place is called, robbin bastards they are, they only gimme a fiver for me straighteners an a buncha Whitney cds, mind you ar cut the plug off the straighteners and scratched the cds to fuck.'

'JUST SIGN THE DAMN PAPERS!' the warden yelled, clasping a hand to her forehead. 'Sign the bloody things and shut the hell up will you!'

'Alright, alright!' Trisha said, turning back.

'Oh yeah, ar know the one,' Maizie then piped up, 'opposite Londis next to the bus stop.'

'Yeah, thas it!' Trisha said, stopping once again. 'Nice in there ain it, bit pricey though, free an arf quid for a panini iss a fuckin liberty if you ask me.'

'TRISHA!' Dee Dee snapped, losing her rag somewhat. 'If you don't sign them fuckin papers you aint never gettin aat of ear, d'you ear me!'

'Yeah alright,' Trisha moaned, resuming the official formalities yet again. 'Oh bugger,' she then cursed, 'the bleedin pen's run out, ang on ar'll give it the lucky rub.'

'Here,' the warden barked, reaching for another. 'Just get on with it will you!'

Scrawling her name with her tongue clenched between her teeth, Trisha was all but done when she stopped and threw her hands in the air. 'Oh bleedin ell!' she cried. 'Ar'v only gone and spelt me flippin name wrong ain I, got any tipex?'

'For fuck sake, Trisha!' Dee Dee groaned, growing ever impatient. 'What is it wiv you, everyfing's a fuckin drama ain it.'

'What?' Trisha asked innocently. 'Ar carn elp it, me tablits must be wearin off coz me ed's proper bangin an ar can't concentrate.'

'You got summink to sort er aat?' Dee Dee asked the warden, who was eyeing her stainless steel letter opener on her desk, her mind wandering for a moment imagining thrusting the blade into Trisha's neck, curing her headache for good, and doing all of humanity a great service in the process.

'Well?' Dee Dee said, pressing for an answer. 'You got any tablits or what?'

'What?' the warden said, rejoining the real world. 'Oh yes, yes I do but after the trouble your friend has caused me I don't see why I should give them to her.'

'Oh alright, well put it this way,' Dee Dee told her, crossing her arms across her chest, 'the longer silly nuts takes fillin them forms aat, the longer you gotta put up wiv er, nart ar mean.'

'Oh right,' the warden replied, seeing the error immediately and reaching into her cabinet. 'Take two of these,' she said, handing Trisha a strip of five hundred milligram capsules. 'Take the damn lot for all I care.'

'Oh ta!' Trisha said, tearing open the packet. 'Got any milk? Me muvva always gimme warm milk wiv me tablits and sung me the tablit song, you must've erd it.'

'If ya wanna get better take a taaablit,
Mummy knows best and don't forget it,

It'll take away ya pain,
And wash it daan the drain,
Take a tablit for yer ed,
An a tablit for ya tummy,
If ya don't wanna be dead,
Listen to ya mummy.
If ya wanna get better take a taaablit,
Coz mummy knows best and don't forget it.'

Dee Dee, Maizie and the warden stood in stunned silence, never having heard such a ditty.
'What the fuck was that?' Dee Dee asked, looking at Maizie, the pair of them as puzzled as the warden.
'Just take the flippin fings!' Maizie said, shoving Trisha. 'And urry up will ya. The tablit song my arse.'
'Dint ya muvva sing it to you?' Trisha asked her friend.
'No!' Maizie said resolutely. 'No she never, coz she weren't a bleedin fruit loop thas why, just get the bleedin fings daan ya!'
With her patience painfully thin at this point, the warden handed Trisha a bottle of water. 'No, I haven't got warm bloody milk for heaven's sake. Here!'
Trisha washed two capsules down. 'Right, where was I?' she asked.
'Fillin the fuckin forms aat!' Dee Dee told her. 'Just sign em Trish or ar'm gonna give you such a bleedin slap ar'm tellin ya.'
'Ar'm doin it ain I,' Trisha moaned, 'gimme a bleedin chance!' Dotting her final child-like signature Trisha handed the pen back to the warden.
'Keep it,' the warden said, shuffling the papers and slamming them in her cabinet.
'Oh fanks!' Trisha said, showing it to her friends. 'Look, iss got Olloway on it, like a sorta souvineer or summink.'
'Whoop de fuckin doo,' Dee Dee sneered, unimpressed to say the least.

Trisha turned to the warden. 'Ar got me muvva a pen from the paand shop once,' she told her. 'It ad a fit geezer on it an evry time you turned it upside daan e got iz nob aat, she loved it she did.'

'Is that it then?' Dee Dee asked again, ignoring Trisha in the process. 'Can we go?'

'Soon enough,' the warden replied. 'When Mr Hamilton arrives, until then you'll be taken to a holding cell at the main gate.'

There was then at knock at the warden's door and an officer entered.

'Excuse me ma'am,' she said sheepishly. 'The governor's here to see you.'

'Oh god!' the warden said, the colour draining from her face.

'And the board of directors ma'am,' the officer added. 'Shall I show them in?'

'What?' the warden cried. 'All of them?'

'Yes ma'am,' the officer replied. 'They do insist on seeing you right away?'

The warden paced her office once again biting at her nails.

'Mama?' the officer asked. 'What shall I tell them?'

'You three get out!' the warden barked, shoving Dee Dee and her friends toward the door. 'Back to your cell and pack whatever shit you have. Hemmings here'll take you to the gate.'

Trisha offered the warden her hand. 'Fanks a lot,' she said with a grin, 'iss bin a proper laugh onest. Well summa the time anyway.'

The warden looked down at Trisha's hand with utter contempt, suddenly the governor stormed into the office, side stepping the girls.

'How dare you keep me waiting!' he barked, shaking a fist in the warden's face. 'This is an outrage!'

'Ahhh, Governor I'm so sorry, I was just,' the warden bleated.

'I don't care what you were doing woman!' the governor yelled, cutting the warden short. One by one the board of directors filed into the warden's office ashen faced.

'Morning, good morning,' the warden said, attempting to shake their hands and lighten the mood, but she was snubbed each time. 'Would you like some tea?'

'Good luck wiv that,' Dee Dee said, winking at the warden before leaving the office. 'Watch er,' she then told one of the directors, referring to the trembling warden. 'Proper dodgy she is ar tell ya.'

'See ya!' Trisha said, skipping behind her friends. 'Wouldn't wanna be ya!'

'No, me neeva,' Maizie added, eyeing the lynch mob.

The warden sank into her leather chair with a dozen grimacing faces surrounding her desk.

'Was that a no to tea?' she asked with a dry mouth.

'Forget the damn tea,' one of the directors stormed. 'We'd like an explanation and we'd like it right now!'

'Quite right,' one or two of his colleagues echoed, baying for the warden's blood.

Leaving the warden to face the music and plead for her position, Dee Dee and her friends hurried to their cell in high spirits.

'Oh flippin ell!' Trisha cursed, checking herself in the mirror, while Dee Dee and Maizie gathered what little belongings they had. 'Ar can't go aat like this Maize, looka the state a me.' Her bruising had manifested itself fully around her right eye and cheek bones.

'Come ear,' Maizie said reaching for her make up bag. 'Nuffing a bitta blusha and faandation won't sort aat.'

'Oh fanks mate,' Trisha smiled, perching on the end of her bunk whilst Maizie set about concealing her wounds.

'Urry up you two,' Dee Dee said impatiently. 'Mr H'll be ear soon.'

'Yeah ang on,' Maizie replied, holding the mirror in front of Trisha. 'Wodya reckon?' she asked. 'Ya can ardly see a mark mate.'

'Yeah, nice one Maize,' Trisha said, turning her face to either side. 'You shoulda stuck at that beauty course shouldn't ya.'
'Yeah ar spoze,' Maizie said, thinking back to her BTEC tuition. 'Ar never liked the teacher though, right stuck up bitch she was, always gobbin off abaat how she done the make up on four weddins an a fuckin funeral, and copped off wiv Hughey Grant in iz trailer. She was fulla shit if you ask me.'
'Oh, ar like Hughey Grant ar do,' Trisha told her friend. 'Proper toff ain e.'
'If ya say so,' Maizie said unimpressed. 'E aint mar cuppa tea to be onest.'
'Maizie!' Dee Dee barked. 'Shut up and get ya shit togevva will ya!'
A prison guard then entered the cell. 'Come on you three, time to go.' she said, standing rigidly in the doorway.
'Yeah ang on.' Trisha said, darting around the cell. 'Ar can't find me air brush,' she added, checking under her bunk.
'Eeya use mine,' Maizie told her, running it through her own hair one last time. 'Don't be gettin no nits in it though, ya soapy cow.'
'Piss off, I aint got no nits!' Trisha said, snatching the brush. 'Not anymore any way, ar dunked me ed in a bucket of stale piss and killed the lot of em.'
'You what!' Dee Dee gasped. 'You never!'
'Yeah!' Trisha admitted. 'Ar read it in the National Geographical magazine. The aborigines in Australia do it to get the bugs aat their dreadlocks.'
'Sick bitch!' Maizie sneered.
'Just urry up will ya!' Dee Dee said, joining the guard.
'Ang on,' Trisha insisted, dropping her leggings and knickers and squatting on the pan in the corner. 'Av ar got time for a dump?' she asked. 'Iss the beans I ad this mawnin, they're givin me gyp.'
'Oh flippin ell Trish!' Maizie cursed storming out the cell. 'I aint angin abaat while you drop one thas for sure.'

The officer and Dee Dee ducked out of the cell on hearing Trisha's thunderous ablutions.

'Dirty mare!' Dee Dee said, standing with her back to the corridor wall. Several minutes later Trisha emerged wrestling with her waistband. 'There's summink wrong wiv the flusha,' she told the officer. 'Ya might wanna get wunna ya mates to sort that aat in there, coz iss chuckin up summink chronic ar tell ya.' She then tossed her bag over her shoulder and marched past her friends. 'Well come on then,' she said over her shoulder. 'D'you two wanna gat aat of ear or what?'

Dee Dee and Maizie both looked at one another, as they had done countless times before, speechless at their friend's stupidity.

'Lead on geeza bird,' Trisha told the burly officer, who glared back at her.

'In there!' the guard eventually said, opening the door to the holding cell, a halfway house between captivity and freedom.

'This is nice ain it,' Trisha said, reclining on a sumptuous leather sofa and popping her feet on the matching foot stool.

'Wanna cuppa tea?' Maizie asked, availing herself of the refreshments.

'No fanks,' Dee Dee said, gazing out the window which afforded her a view of a nearby park where couples strolled hand in hand, and kissed on wrought iron benches. Travis her former lover crossed her mind for a fleeting moment, before a familiar voice brought her to her senses.

'Good morning ladies,' Clive said, a little out of breath. 'I got here as quickly as I could.'

'Oh ello Mr H,' Maizie said, tossing her tea bag back into the caddy. 'Ar narf glad to see you ar tell ya.'

'Hiyaaa,' Trisha chirped. 'You alright mate?'

'Trisha, my god what happened?' Clive asked. 'You've been all over the news. What on earth possessed you to escape onto the roof, and with your release so close?'

'It weren't me, it was that lot,' Trisha said, referring to the establishment.
'It was you Trisha!' Dee Dee said angrily. 'It's always you ain it!'
'No, no it aint!' Trisha protested. 'Dee it ain always me, what abaat when you got us all barred from the Green Dragon, that weren't mar fault.'
'Yes it bleedin was!' Dee Dee snapped. 'You flippin idiot, you coulda got us all killed!'
The girls had gate crashed the wake of a local heavy in search of a good time and a free buffet. But in her naivety, and in an attempt to cheer up the sombre gathering, Trisha, with a belly full of vol au vents and vodka, hijacked the sound system and cranked out at full volume a medley of her favorite tunes. And considering the occasion, a burial at that, her selection of *Going underground, Down down deeper and down* and *Always look on the bright side* hadn't quite had the desired effect on the congregation. The recently deceased's wife suffered a minor stroke when Trisha dragged her from her seat and marched her round in front of her yelling 'LESS ALL DO THE CONGA, LESS ALL DO THE CONGA, LA LA LA LAAAA!'
Consequently, her close relatives and criminal associates of the family were far from impressed, producing a cache of weapons which had been concealed about their persons and plotting a second, although untimely, burial that same day. And if it wasn't for Dee Dee's quick thinking and flying fists, they may have had their way. Flooring the first to approach them, Dee Dee shoved her two friends out the door and into a waiting taxi with the menacing mob pouring from the saloon bar doors behind them.
'You just don't fink do ya!' Dee Dee scolded.
'Oh ang on Dee,' Maizie said, in Trisha's defense. 'Ya must admit mate it was a bleedin laugh though wern it. When that old dear's baggy drawers fell daan and she stacked it into the prawn ring, ar nearly pissed meself ar tell ya.'

The mortified mourners rushed the grieving widow to hospital, where she underwent surgery to replace her dislocated artificial hip, but the trauma had taken its toll and she never fully recovered, living out the remainder of her days being spoon fed in a nursing home.

'Er ladies,' Clive said, tapping impatiently. 'Shall we go?'

'Oh bugger me, yeah,' Maizie said, grabbing her bag. 'Less get the fuck aat of ear.'

'Shit Dee this is it,' Trisha squealed, springing to her feet clapping her hands excitedly. 'Yes, yes, yes!' she giggled. 'Come on Dee!'

A waiting guard lead the four of them through a series of locked gates to the main entrance.

'Ready?' Clive asked the girls, who had been incarcerated for almost two years.

'Not arf,' Trisha replied, taking both her friends by the hand.

Pulling a huge iron bolt to one side the guard swung open the heavy door within the main gate, and a gust of wind instantly hit the three of them in the face.

'Niiiice,' Dee Dee said, taking in a lung full.

'Let's go,' Clive told them, ushering the girls through the door where, to their complete surprise, a bank of camera wielding paparazzi were waiting behind a police cordon.

'TRISHA, TRISHA OVER HERE!' several of them yelled, her impending release had been leaked to the press at a price by a group of guards, eager to supplement their meager wages, a regular occurrence at Holloway with high profile inmates.

'Ooooh ello!' Trisha said, welcoming the attention.

'Trisha leave it, come on!' Maizie said, tugging at her friend's sleeve.

'Oh ang on a minute,' Trisha replied, pouting and posing as though on a movie premiere red carpet. 'Iss like comin aat the Big Bruvva aas ain it, ar might get in the papers, wod'ya reckon?'

'Trisha, come away please,' Clive asked, keen to keep their release low key, which in Trisha's case was nigh on impossible.

'Oy silly bollocks!' Dee Dee called. 'Get yer arse over ear will ya!'

Alongside the media reporters and photographers were hoards of well wishers, offering poses of flowers and waving homemade banners with a myriad of supportive messages.

'Ahhh fanks,' Trisha said, taking a fluffy dog from a small child and signing her mother's tee shirt. 'Thas nice ain it,' she said, turning to her glaring friends.

Microphones of all description were thrust under her nose whilst supporters clambered for a photograph.

'Trisha, how would you describe your stay at Holloway?' one pushy journalist asked. 'Would you say you were brutalized during your stay?'

'Oh yeah!' Trisha agreed. 'Me mate Dee Dee gimme a Chinese burn one night when ar nicked er toof paste, an it urt like fuck.'

Dee Dee merely beckoned to her troublesome friend. 'Trish ar'm gonna give you such a fuckin slap,' she growled.

'Trisha please,' Clive insisted. 'You're not to talk to the press, it's one of the terms of your release.'

'Yeah, yeah alright,' Trisha replied, signing the front page of a daily newspaper with her headline making photograph on it.

'How does it feel to be free?' a reporter from CNN asked.

'Oh iss great mate,' Trisha replied, whilst posing with a group of Austrian tourists who had just happened by. 'Ar know how Nelly Mandela felt naah,' she added.

'TRISHAAA!' Dee Dee barked, storming over and pushing the Austrians aside. 'Piss off Fritz!' she said, taking her friend by the arm. 'Come on you, before ar lose me rag.'

'Oh, but Deeeee,' Trisha moaned, eyeing a particularly attractive blonde reporter and handing her the fluffy dog. 'Ar reckon ar'm on a promise ear.'

'If you don't get a move on,' Dee Dee said through gritted teeth, 'ar promise ar'll beat the shit aata ya, ow's abaat that.'

'Oh alright,' Trisha said begrudgingly, snatching an autograph book from a horny teen, scrawling a contact telephone number on it and thrusting it into the blonde's hand. 'Call me babe,' she said with a wink. 'Ahh that was nice of em wern it,' she told her two friends, who looked down their noses at her. 'What?' she asked. 'Well it ain often people are pleased to see me is it.' The favorable attention was indeed a welcome surprise, and one that would rarely be repeated.

'No, it bleedin aint!' Maizie said angrily. 'You ever wondered why, ay?'

With the paparazzi still furiously snapping to the last, Clive lead the girls to a waiting polished black four by four. 'Quickly, get in,' he told them, eyeing the approaching crowd who were all rhythmically chanting Trisha's name.

'Seeeeyaaa!' Trisha yelled, waving frantically as Dee Dee and Maizie climbed inside.

'Oh ello,' Dee Dee gasped, on seeing Crystal and her mother sat in the rear. 'Maizie, look who it is.'

'Hiya,' Sarah said, inching over for Dee Dee to slide in beside her. 'Crystal insisted on coming to see you, she hasn't been able to sleep since her father told us you were to be released. It's great to see the three of you again, it really is.' Sarah hugged Dee Dee tightly and took Maizie's hand.

'Ello gorgeous,' Maizie said, planting a kiss on Crystal's cheek. 'Look at you, you look all grow'd up.'

'Mummy done my hair like a real grown up lady,' Crystal told her, toying with her layered fringe. Crystal unfastened her safety belt flinging her arms around Maizie's neck and kissed her face three times before leaping into Dee Dee's arms.

'Crystal, sit down,' her mother said, attempting to prise her free.

'She's alright for a minute,' Dee Dee said, hugging the delighted child tightly. 'Blimey, ar've missed'ya,' she said, rocking Crystal back and forth. 'You all better now are ya?'
'Yes look,' Crystal replied, lifting her cardigan to reveal a neat three inch scar, the result of her bone marrow surgery. 'And guess what?' she added, grinning from ear to ear. 'I don't have to take that yucky medicine anymore.'
'Oh, thas brilliant!' Dee Dee told her, squeezing a little harder. 'Ar'm so pleased ar really am.'
'She's made a remarkable recovery,' Sarah told the girls, as Trisha clambered aboard having treated the photographers to a risqué photo opportunity, her bottom flashed for all to see that is.
'Oh ello!' Trisha cried, on seeing Sarah and her daughter. 'Dee look who it is!'
'Ar know ya doughnut,' Dee Dee said, dragging her friend to her seat. 'Ar bin sittin ear talkin to em waitin for you, what ya bin doin?'
'Trishaaaaaa!' Crystal cried, stretching out her arms.
'Oooh you're a big girl now, aint'cha,' Trisha said, taking her from Dee Dee. 'D'ya wanna sit next to me?'
Crystal nodded with a broad smile. 'Yes, yes, yes please,' she said overjoyed.
'Come on then, put ya seat belt on,' Trisha told her, securing the child.
'It's lovely to see you,' Sarah said, leaning across to adjust her daughter's belt. 'What happened on the roof Trisha?' she asked. 'Clive and I were so worried.'
'Ar broke me pencil,' Trisha began to explain, snuggling up to Crystal.
'I beg your pardon? I'm sorry I don't understand,' Sarah said quizzically. 'What pencil?'
'Never mind,' Dee Dee said, intervening as Clive started the car. 'It was just Trisha bein Trisha, as bleedin usual, thas all ya need to know.'
'Oh, I see,' Sarah smiled. 'Well, you created quite a stir I must say,' she laughed.

'We got ya picture,' Dee Dee told Crystal, producing the child's artwork her father had given them. 'Iss proper brilliant ain it.'
'Oh yeah,' Maizie agreed. 'You're so clever Crystal. Are could never do nuffing like that.'
'Oh, that reminds me,' Trisha said, delving into her bag. 'Ar got summink for you.'
She retrieved the jumbled jigsaw that she had toiled over during her stay at Holloway. 'Are want you to av this,' she told Crystal, 'issa one off.'
'You can say that again,' Dee Dee laughed.
'What is it?' Sarah asked, looking closely. 'Is it a giraffe?'
'No, course it aint,' Trisha said, turning her puzzle on its side. 'Iss a buncha flowers ar fink.'
'Oh, yes of course,' Sarah said, appeasing Trisha. 'I see it now, it's lovely, isn't it darling.'
Crystal laughed on seeing sections of cereal packet gummed in place of mislaid segments.
'Ar've signed it an'all for ya,' Trisha told her. 'In case iss werf summink one day, ya never know do ya.'
'Er, ar think we do,' Dee Dee said with a sarcastic tone. 'What does she want wiv that Trish, you shoulda left it behind like ar told ya.'
'No, no I want it,' Crystal said, hugging her gift. 'Thank you Trisha.'
'You're welcome darlin,' Trisha said, ignoring her friend's scathing remarks.
'I did another one of you Trisha,' Crystal said, pulling a piece of paper from her backpack. 'I did it from the telly.'
'Ahhh look,' Trisha said, proudly displaying her picture. 'Iss me on the roof, nice ain it!'
Crystal's elaborately coloured sketch depicted Trisha's rooftop rant to a tee, with her hurling tiles with the angriest of expressions.
'Iss beautiful,' Trisha said, kissing Crystal. 'Ar'm gonna get a frame for it I am.'

Dee Dee looked over her shoulder at the menacing prison gates as they left, vowing never to return.

'Where we goin?' Maizie asked. 'Ar mean, where we gonna stay, ar spoze ar could ring me mum she'll put us up.'

'There's no need,' Clive told them. 'I've taken the liberty of renting you three a flat, it's not much, but it's somewhere to call home while you get back on your feet.'

'Oh, nice one!' Maizie said appreciatively. 'Dee, we got a flat, result ay.'

'Yeah, nice one,' Dee Dee added, 'fanks a lot geez.'

'Iss gonna be such a laugh,' Trisha chirped. 'All livin togevva.'

'Oh Christ,' Dee Dee moaned, having been cooped up with Trisha for long enough.

'I'm afraid it's only a two bed,' Clive said over his shoulder, 'so two of you will have to share. I'm sure you don't mind, do you?'

'Ar'm avin me own room,' Dee Dee insisted. 'Coz if I av to share wiv er,' she said, prodding Trisha's back. 'Ar swear ar'll end up back inside in a week for murderin the dozy cow.'

'Oh Deeee,' Maizie whined. 'Why do I av to share wiv er.'

'Coz ya do!' Dee Dee said resolutely. 'And thas that.'

'Oh, thas nice ain it,' Trisha said, upset at being shunned by her closest friends. 'After all ar've done for you'z two.'

'Yeah!' Dee Dee snapped. 'Iss cozza what you done that ar don't wanna share wiv ya, you're a flippin liability, scuze mar language.'

Trisha turned to face Dee Dee. 'Oh, well what abaat when you'z two wonnid to share wiv me in Gran Canaria then ay, you wern't that fussy then was ya.'

'And why was that?' Maizie stormed. 'Ar'll tell ya why shall I, coz some effin idiot lost the keys to our apartment thas why, we asked you to look after em for two minutes while we went on a jet ski dint we.'

'Ar did,' Trisha said, defending herself to the hilt. 'Ar put em somewhere safe while ar went to get an ice cream.'

Sarah and Clive, and Crystal for that matter, listened intently to the girls quarreling.

'And why don't you tell us where you put em for safe keepin,' Maizie asked. 'Come on, tell us.'
'Ar buried em,' Trisha said sheepishly, 'in the sand, ar put arf me baguette on top of em so ar could find em again, but the seagulls ate it, so it aint mar fault really is it, it was the seagulls, they ate me tuna melt.'
'You're the melt!' Dee Dee snapped.
Sarah by now was giggling behind her hand at the squabbling friends.
'Ar did try to find em though din I,' Trisha said, appealing to their better natures, which at that point were virtually non-existent. 'Ar paid undred and fifty euros for that metal detectin fing ar did, but ar reckon ar was proper mugged off wiv that, coz ar was aat there till two in the mawnin and all ar got was a san miguel bottle top an a pedlo peddle. Ar tell ya, ar musta dug a faasand oles before ar realized it was me steel toe capped Converses that was settin the poxy fing off, ar can still ear it now, bleeeeep bleeeeeep bleeeeeep, evry coupla bleedin foot.'
'Oh stop, stop please!' Sarah laughed, clutching her aching ribs. 'You three are absolutely hilarious, you really are.'
'Ar weren't laughin at the time,' Maizie told her. 'Free of us in a single bed, wiv er snorin, figitin, fartin and grindin er teef, it was like playin twister wiv a tanked up tramp ar tell ya.'
'Oh, it weren't that bad,' Trisha said with fond memories.
'Weren't that bad!' Maizie laughed. 'I ad Dee's finger in me ear all night and your toe up me...'
'Language,' Dee Dee reminded her friend.
'Oh sorry babe,' Maizie said, stroking Crystal's hair. 'Ar shoulda slept on the floor wiv the cockroaches, ar reckon arda've ad a better kip.'
'Ooooh no,' Trisha said cringing. 'They was big buggers them weren't they.' She was referring to the giant beetle infestation that had plagued their resort on the Canarian isle.

'Ar know,' Dee Dee agreed. 'Ar stubbed me toe on one of em comin aat the barfroom, proper buggered up me nail varnish it did.'

'Great big scary fings they was,' Trisha said, teasing Crystal who hid her face in her hands. 'Hoooooge massive monsters, wiv long legs and googly eyes.'

'Trisha!' Dee Dee barked. 'Your scarin er you doughnut, pack it in will ya.'

'I'm not really scared,' Crystal said, emerging and putting on a brave face. 'We have a mouse that lives in our shed, and I call him Mr Nibbles because he eats all the chocolate I leave for him.'

'Well, ya woulds bin scared of these cockroaches,' Trisha told her. 'A buncha the bleedas carted off our fridge in the middle of the night and we never see it again.'

'Really!' Crystal gasped, buying into Trisha's exaggerated tale.

'Yeah really,' Trisha replied tongue in cheek. 'They musta bin after me bacon and banana sandwiches.'

'Bacon and banana!' Crystal said, screwing up her face in disgust. 'Yeeeeuk!'

Dee Dee turned to Sarah who was equally aghast. 'You fink she's jokin don'tcha,' she said, having witnessed Trisha's culinary concoctions on numerous occasions.

'Well,' Sarah said, finding the scenario a little far-fetched.

'That dozy mare'd eat anyfing,' Dee Dee continued. 'Ar once see er fry an egg and stick it in a peanut butter sandwich, proper turned mar guts it did.'

Clive had to brake suddenly on hearing this, for fear of rear ending the car in front.

'Sorry,' he told his passengers, holding up one hand. 'It was the egg and peanut butter.'

'Yeah, lovely it was,' Trisha said, licking her lips. 'Iss gotta be a snotty egg an'all.'

'Oh shuttup!' Maizie protested. 'You're an animal you are Trisha, ar swear it.'

'Here we are,' Clive eventually said, stopping to reverse between two parked cars outside a three story Georgian terrace with original, but albeit neglected, sash windows.
'Where are we?' Dee Dee asked, having paid little attention during their journey and finding herself in unfamiliar territory.
'Your new home,' Clive said, taking a set of keys from the glove compartment. 'It's on the second floor, 26b.'
'No, ar mean, where are we?' Dee Dee asked again. 'This aint mar manor.'
'Oh I see,' Clive laughed. 'No, sorry this is Islington. I thought a change of scenery and a fresh start would be good for the three of you. It's not a million miles away from your old haunts I assure you.'
'Norf London,' Dee Dee said, somewhat displeased. 'Gooner country.'
'I'm sorry, what?' Clive asked.
'The Arsenal,' Maizie informed him. 'We're West Am fru and fru.'
'Oh I see,' Clive replied, handing Dee Dee the keys. 'I'm sure you'll be far too busy to be thinking about soccer rivalry.'
'Ar dunno abaat that,' Dee Dee moaned. 'Old abbits die ard.'
'Yes quite,' Clive said, not really understanding the inter club passion that ran deep throughout the sport. 'Your employment details are on the hall table along with some monies to get you started. Of course you'll receive an allowance through your chosen charities to cover your weekly expenditure and also buy a few luxuries no doubt. Sarah has very kindly freshened up the place, changed the bed linen and left you a few essentials in the kitchen. I've also left my telephone number should you need to contact me. Oh yes, there are three pay as you go mobiles, I'm afraid they're not the latest gizmos but I'm sure they'll suffice.'
'Fanks Clive,' Trisha said, kissing Crystal. 'And you Sarah mate, fanks a lot yeah.' Trisha stepped from the car and Maizie followed suit.

'Norf London,' Dee Dee mouthed looking out the window hesitantly.
'It won't be forever,' Clive said reassuringly. 'I'm sure you'll make new friends in no time.'
'Not if they're Gooners,' Dee Dee moaned, giving Crystal a tight hug. 'See ya later darlin,' she said, kissing her cheek. 'You come visit us whenever ya want yeah. Cheers Sarah mate, and you Clive, you done well good gettin us aat.'
'Think nothing of it,' Clive replied. 'Promise me you'll stay out of trouble won't you.'
'Yeah, no worries,' Dee Dee said, stepping out onto the pavement and closing the door behind her.
'Seeeeyaaaa!' Trisha squealed, waving.
Crystal and her mother waved back as Clive pulled away, leaving the three girls at the roadside, on the brink of a new beginning and chapter of their lives.
Dee Dee pulled her collar up around her ears. 'Norf London,' she mumbled, as though the place were cursed or plague ridden.
'Oh, it aint that bad Dee,' Trisha said, eyeing the neighbor's neatly trimmed front garden. 'Look, they got a water feature fing an everyfing. Back ome in Chadwell Eaf me neighbors ad a free piece suite an a burnt aat Skoda in their front garden, me muvva tried to keep ers tidy though, but arf the soddin cats on the estate used er bark chippins as a bleedin litter tray, proper chucked up it did if ya disturbed it, ar tell ya.'
While Trisha perused the floral displays of the adjacent property Dee Dee and Maizie headed for the front door.
'Oy ang on, wait for me!' she said, trotting after them, whilst waving at the twitching curtains next door. 'Hiyaaa!' she yelled, attempting to introduce herself, but the elderly occupant ducked back out of sight fearful of the *hood rats,* as she described anybody of youthful appearance.
'Oooh iss excitin ain it,' Trisha said, joining her friends at the heavy panelled powder blue street door.
'Norf bleedin London,' Dee Dee muttered, looking over her shoulder.

'Go on, open it!' Trisha squealed.

'Yeah, come on Dee,' Maizie added, stomping her feet. 'Iss flippin freezin aat ear.'

Turning the key, Dee Dee shoved open the creaking door and stepped into the narrow entrance hall with her friends in tow, their shoes clattering on the recently renovated bare boards. But on closer inspection it was obvious that the remainder of the decor had yet to be overhauled in the same way. Dated and scarcely adhered fresco wallpaper clung to the walls, heavily gouged at waist height from countless bicycle and push chair users.

Maizie flicked the grubby light switch to illuminate the stairs, but a buzzing blue flash had her leaping back.

'Fuck that!' she cried. 'The poxy fing nearly lectricuted me!'

'Niiice,' Dee Dee said apprehensively.

Trisha snatched the keys from Dee Dee's hand, skipping by her and Maizie and starting up the stairs. 'Urry up you two!' she called back.

A door at the foot of the stairs opened an inch or so as they approached, and a small boy no older than three or four peered out with huge doe-eyes, wearing the filthiest of babygros.

'Ello,' Maizie said, stooping, 'woss your name?' A hand then gripped the boy's shoulder and yanked him back inside, raised voices could then be heard in an Eastern European tongue, chastising the child, before the door slammed firmly shut in Maizie's face.

'Oh, thas nice ain it,' Maizie complained.

'Great,' Dee Dee said, looking up the steep flight of stairs with some trepidation, wondering if the house possessed any welcoming qualities so to speak. The raised voices grew louder as the boy's extended family of nine squabbled over control of the TV remote and the last of the Polish sausage.

Dee Dee contemplated beating on the door. 'I aint puttin up wiv too mucha that shit,' she told Maizie.

'Come on Dee!' Trisha called down from the landing, having seen their flat for the first time. 'Iss alright mate, we got a telly an everyfing!'
'Yeah, come on Dee,' Maizie added, tugging at Dee Dee's sleeve. 'We gotta make the best of it mate, aint we?'
'We got booze an'all!' Trisha shrieked, brandishing two bottles of white wine, a gift from the Hamiltons.
'Amen to that,' Dee Dee said, pushing Maizie aside and sprinting up the stairs, grabbing at the heavily painted chocolate brown banister.
'Oy, wait for me bitch!' Maizie yelled, following behind.
Passing a Pears print of a crying boy which hung on the landing wall, Dee Dee and Maizie bundled into their new flat behind Trisha.
'Wod'ya reckon?' Trisha asked, clutching the wine to her chest and kicking the door closed. 'It aint bad is it, least iss warm ay.'
On renting the property Clive had insisted the central heating system was first serviced with winter rapidly approaching, and the broken glass be replaced in the bathroom window.
'Yeah, toasty warm ain it,' Maizie agreed, shedding her coat.
Although the furnishings were dated, Sarah had indeed given the place a woman's touch, steam cleaning the paisley patterned carpets and scrubbing the kitchen and bathroom surfaces.
'Ar need a piss,' Dee Dee told her friends. 'Crack that plonk open will ya,' she told Trisha.
Whilst her friend retrieved three mugs from the narrow galley kitchen cupboard, Dee Dee and Maizie surveyed the bathroom with its pale yellow matching suite and gaudy blue briquette tiling. 'Flippin ell!' Dee Dee gasped, pulling the light. 'Psyca-bleedin-delic or what!'
'Not arf,' Maizie agreed, while her friend squatted on the pan having wiped the seat several times. 'It won't be forever though will it Dee,' Maizie reminded her, over the sound of trickling pee. 'Iss gotta be better than Olloway ain it.'

'Yeah ar spoze,' Dee Dee said, with her chin resting in her hands. 'No, you are right mate,' she then said in a more positive tone. 'TRISH YOU MELT WHERE'S THAT VINO?' she yelled.

'Comin!' Trisha called back, biting at the seal around the neck of a Chardonnay, before pouring three large measures.

'Eeeya,' she said, joining her friends in the bathroom. 'Oh, this is nice,' she added, complementing the décor. 'Me nan ad a suite like this, but er bog ad a chip on it that scratched yer arse to fuck.'

Toasting one another, the three friends hung out in the bathroom as though it were a nightclub loo chatting feverishly. 'We got shit loadsa grub an' all,' Trisha explained. 'Pizzas, cheese, chicken and them gravy granule fings that look like kitty litter.'

Shaking herself dry, Dee Dee wiped and flushed letting the lid drop with a resounding bang.

'Oooh, ya made me jump!' Maizie said, clutching her chest and wiping wine from her chin.

Making their way through to the lounge, Trisha retrieved the remote from the top of the television set and dropped into an armchair beside the sofa, neither of them matching the other. Dee Dee and Maizie sat together draining the remainder of the bottle into their mugs.

'Oy Trish, go get the uvver bottle,' Maizie told her friend, who was busily switching channels.

'Oh flippin ell!' Trisha moaned, checking her own empty mug. 'Fanks a lot!'

'Go on!' Dee Dee insisted. 'We're gonna need a refill in a minute.'

Trisha reluctantly stormed through to the tiny galley kitchen with its basic budget units, worktop and ruffled flooring. Again the stench of disinfectant hung in the air as it had in the bathroom, Sarah had scrubbed and polished to remove all trace of the previous occupants, whose hygiene practices left far too much to be desired - the ring of scum around both sinks and a thatch of human hair being a prime example.

In the meantime Maizie switched channels while Dee Dee's gaze wandered to a nicotine stain on the high vaulted ceiling, vaguely resembling da Vinci's Mona Lisa, a remnant out of Sarah's cleansing reach.

'Wod'ya wanna watch Dee?' Maizie asked. 'Dee!'

'Ay, what?' Dee Dee replied, returning her gaze and righting her tilted mug in the process.

'Wod'ya wanna watch?' Maizie asked again. 'Corrie's on ITV and Ollyoaks is on four.'

'I aint bovvad,' Dee Dee told her, stretching out her legs and relishing their new found freedom before plucking a glossy girly mag from the coffee table, again a gift from the Hamiltons.

Flippin eck!' she then said, eyeing the front page having lost touch of recent celebrity gossip. 'She's gotta be some sorta twat aint she,' she added, referring to the glamorous pouting A-lister adorning the mag, having been snapped by the ever vigilant paparazzi snorting cocaine and indulging in lewd oral acts with a fellow actor on location, whilst professing to be madly in love another.

'Dirty slapper!' Maizie said, looking over Dee Dee's shoulder. 'They're all the same that lot ar tell ya, give em all the money in the world, a flash mota an a tasty geezer and they still want more. Makes ya sick dunnit.'

'Oh Maaaize!' Trisha said, returning with the second bottle. 'Ar wonnid to watch me Dragons whatsit, iss on the uvver side.'

'Ya snooze ya lose,' Maize laughed, reclining.

'Oh Maaaaaize, let me watch it mate,' Trisha begged. 'Ar like that shit ar do, ar got this idea for a new invention.'

'Oh fuck,' Dee Dee mumbled, ducking behind her magazine and wanting none of Trisha's nonsense.

Trisha nestled in between her two friends jostling for elbow room, and topping up theirs and her own mug with wine.

'No listen,' she told them, wriggling her bottom to the back of the sofa.

'Get off will ya!' Maizie barked, narrowly preventing a spillage. 'Sit over there will ya!'

'No, listen will ya!' Trisha said, determined to get her point across. 'Me Chihuahuas made a mint dint they.'

'Yeah ar spoze,' Maizie agreed. 'But ar'm tryna watch the telly Trish, carn it wait. Tell Dee, she wants to ear it, don'tcha Dee?'

'Oh fanks!' Dee Dee said, thumbing her mag. 'Why av I gotta listen to er shite.'

'Oh sod ya then,' Trisha sulked. 'I aint tellin ya, all you two do is take the piss anyway, ar'm fed up wiv it I am. For once ar gotta proper idea and you'z two av to diss me.'

There was a moment or two of silence before Maizie gave in.

'Oh alright,' she said setting down the remote. 'What is it, come on tell us ya dopey idea, coz we aint gonna get no bleedin peace till ya do, are we, ar know you.'

'Gastric pants!' Trisha blurted out . 'For the fatties. They're not as dangerous as the real gastric band fingy coz the lastic's on the aatside, the lumpy buggers'll lap em up ar tell ya. Wod'ya reckon?'

Before her friends could ridicule her outlandish business venture Trisha continued her sales pitch. 'Ar'm gonna make em vibratin an'all, to tone up ya belly and ya back end at the same time. Ar don't want no cheap shit, ar wanna go strictly designer, leopard print and crushed velvet for them lard arse loaded celebs. Ar could let you av a pair at cost Maize if ya like.'

'You cheeky bitch!' Maizie snapped. 'I aint lardy!'

'Gastric pants!' Dee Dee said, looking across from her magazine. 'Are you sure?'

'Oh yeah!' Trisha replied. 'Ar done me ome work an everyfing, ar was surfin the prison web fing in the afternoons, there's a supplier in Kurdistan that can do me forty five mile of grade A industrial strenf lastic for two an arf undred quid. An ar reckon the crafty Koreans can elp me aat wiv the lectrics.'

'Lectrics!' Maizie cried. 'Wod'ya want lectrics in em four?'

Dee Dee and Maizie had inadvertently allowed themselves to be dragged into another of Trisha's farcical ramblings, caught once again, hook line and sinker so to speak.

'For the motas,' Trisha said enthusiastically. 'See the longer the fat fucks spend on the tread mill the more they charge up the wobbly waist band fing, believe me Maizie this is gonna be big, specially in the States coz them buggers ar yooge over there aint they.'

Dee Dee and Maizie both looked at one another thinking the exact same thing, had Trisha stumbled across a highly lucrative cure for the worlds ever increasing obesity problem, with the potential of netting billions from countrys such as the United States with its multinational fast food conglomerates making it head and shoulders, and stomachs for that matter, ahead of the rest of the world? Or on the other hand, had she just wasted the past ten minutes of their lives as they would put it, 'chattin shit!'

'Ar bin workin on a jingle for me telly advert an'all,' Trisha told them, eager to share. 'D'you wanna ear it?'

'No!' Dee Dee snapped, ducking back into her magazine.

'Well, av a listen anyway,' Trisha told them. 'Let me know what ya fink coz iss always important to get feedback, thas what Richie Branson says, an e'z minted ain e.'

Trisha took a deep breath before blurting out the jingle she had composed for her latest business venture; Gastric pants.

'Iiiiiiiiiif ya stuff ya face wiv jelly,
And ya stuff ya face wiv chips,
Does it linger on ya belly,
Does it linger on ya hips.

Do ya waddle when ya walk,
Do ya rumble when ya run,
Put daan ya knife and fork,

Put daan ya bagel and ya bun.

Don't ya worry, don't despair,
Coz whatever ya circumstaaaaaance,
Grab yaself a paira,
Trisha's Gastric paaaaants!'

'Catchy ain it,' she added, chuffed with her efforts.
Dee Dee and Maizie sat quietly mulling over what they had just heard, before exploding in fits of hysterical laughter.
'Oh mar gawd!' Maizie said, almost choking on her words. 'Thas brilliant that is!'
'Fuckin ell Trish!' Dee Dee laughed. 'Ar don't believe it, ar'd buy em just for the jingle mate!'
Trisha's two friends then attempted their own rendition,

'Iiiiiiif ya stuff ya face wiv jelly,'

They sang, swaying their hips,

'And ya stuff ya face wiv chips,
Does it linger on ya belly,
Does it linger on ya hips.'

Moments later the three of them were swaying arm in arm, warbling the tag line at the tops of their voices,

'GRAG YASELF A PAIRA TRISHA'S GASTRIC PAAAAAAAANTS!'

'Quality!' Dee Dee chuckled. A thumping sound on the ceiling below then brought them to their senses, followed by a garbled Romanian rant.
'PISS OFF!' Dee Dee yelled down toward the carpet, stamping a defiant foot in reply. 'YOU KNOW WHAT TO DO IF YA DON'T LIKE IT, DON'TCHA!'
'Well, can we watch it?' Trisha asked Maizie.

'What?' Maizie replied, still humming the melodious and altogether addictive Gastric pant jingle. 'Do ya waddle when ya walk, do ya rumble when ya run,' she sang with a beaming smile. 'Ar love it, you should stick it online, itta go viral in no time, you wait an see.'

'Maizieeeeee,' Trisha moaned, 'me Dragon's whatsit!'

'Oh shit yeah!' Maizie said, making a grab for the remote. 'What side was it on?'

'Ar dunno,' Trisha said, bouncing on her bottom from sheer frustration. 'Urry up will ya!'

'Oh, sorry mate iss finished,' Maizie informed her friend, whilst viewing the closing credits of the penultimate episode in the series, in which an elderly farmer from the Scottish Highlands had been awarded a fifty thousand pound investment for his idea to allow advertising companies to shave their slogans onto the sides of his prized herd of Aberdeen Angus, and dye them in a multitude of colors. His cash cows were set to make the octogenarian a very wealthy man indeed.

'Oh bugger it!' Trisha sulked, crossing her arms.

'Never mind mate,' Dee Dee said, topping up her friend's mug. 'Get that daan ya.'

'Yeah fanks,' Trisha replied, slurping at her wine. 'Corr, thas lovely ain it, proper stuff ar mean, not like that snide shite Maizie's muvva used to knock aat. Prosecco my arse, that stuff used to turn ya teef green din it.'

'Wod'ya want for two quid a bottle,' Maizie protested. 'You got enough of it daan ya neck dint'cha,'

'Well yeah,' Trisha admitted, 'only coz we was potless thas all, gawd knows what was in it, but it proper got us off our faces, ar know that.'

'Not arf,' Dee Dee agreed, 'but it give us the muvva of all angovers an'all.'

The cut price vino Maizie's mother fenced on behalf of her villainous sister Janice, was not processed in the vineyards of Bordeaux or the Chateau region, more a lock-up garage off the Streatham High Road using a concoction of domestic cleaning agents and chip shop vinegar. For Janice it was a side line from her acid and ecstasy business that afforded her a seven bedroom palatial country mansion in rural Essex, but also lead to her demise in a police shoot out in 2005.

Maizie retrieved the brown envelope from the hall table. 'Woss this all abaat?' she asked, tearing open one end and spilling out the contents onto the coffee table.

'Oooh phones!' Trisha said, snatching one of the three handsets. 'Flippin ell,' she then cried, 'they got bloody buttons, ar can't use this for fuck sake.'

'Shut up you melt,' Dee Dee said, thumbing through the documents included.

'Woss it say Dee?' Maizie asked, looking around for a socket to plug in her charger.

'Iss the details of our jobs,' Dee Dee said, turning page after page with a disapproving look on her face. 'We gotta start Monday mawnin apparently, ar can't wait.'

'Oooh ar'm gonna be a vet lady,' Trisha squealed. 'Ar can't wait to get me ands up a dogs arse.'

Maizie spat the wine she had just supped across the floor, spattering Dee Dee's legs in the process.

'MAIZIE, FOR FUCK SAKE!' Dee Dee barked, lashing out at her friend.

'Ar'm sorry Dee, iss that dirty bitch,' Maizie said, wiping her mouth. 'Ar could'n elp it onest.'

'TRISHA!' Dee Dee yelled, turning her attention. 'Looka me ar'm pissin soaked!'

'What?' Trisha said innocently, as she had done a thousand times before. 'Ar don't see what ya problem is Maize, ya gotta be prepared to get stuck in aint'cha.'

'Stuck in!' Maizie said in disgust. 'If thas your idea of a good time, fistin a buncha mangey mongrels you want ya bleedin ed testin. Don't she Dee?'

'Ar don't even wanna fink abaat it,' Dee Dee replied. 'Eeya thas yours.' She handed Trisha her employment details, the whereabouts, local train and bus timetables etc; Sarah and

Clive had been quite thorough in their preparation for the girls' release and reintegration into society.

'Where we gotta go Dee?' Maizie asked, looking over Dee Dee's shoulder.

'Wood Green,' Dee Dee told her. 'Issa right karzi from what ar remember.'

'Ahhh, ar'm lookin forward to it Dee,' Maizie said, snuggling up close to her friend, 'aint you. Summa them people wiv learnin difficulties are proper lovely.'

The two of them looked across at Trisha who was beating the buttons on her mobile phone, which was basic to say the least.

'And some of em aint,' Dee Dee laughed. 'What you doin ya doughnut?' she asked a frustrated Trisha.

'Tryna get Wifi,' Trisha growled. 'Ar can't flippin work this fing, it ain even got Facebook!'

'Just leave it will ya,' Dee Dee snapped. 'It's a phone for phonin thas all, put mar number in it will ya, and Maizie's in case ya get yer ed stuck up a badgers bullet ole or summink.'

Trisha frowned at her friends as Maizie once again burst out laughing. 'You'z two aint got the balls to work wiv animals thas your problem,' she said angrily, wagging a finger. 'I aint scared of em, ar member mar nan's yorkie swalla'd a lumpa lego and couldn't shit it aat, so I ad to finger it aat of iz bum ole, kept draggin iz little arse raand the front room carpet e did the poor little bleeda.'

'Oh shut up Trishaaa,' Maizie said, a little squeamish at times. 'You done that in Faliraki an'all dint'cha, that poor donkey ar reckon you traumatized the bleeda, thas your answer to everyfing ain it, ram yer and up their back passage.'

'Yeah but,' Trisha protested, 'ow was ar spozed to know it only ad a stone in its oof.'

'Coz the fuckin fing was limpin, thas ow!' Dee Dee said, raising her voice.

'Ar fought it mighta swalla'd some lego an'all,' Trisha said, pleading her case.

But Dee Dee was having none of it. 'Well, it certainly shit a brick when you started rummagin araand in its rear thas for sure,' she chuckled.
'Can we please change the subject,' Maizie asked, having heard quite enough of Trisha's veterinary practices. 'Ar'm starvin, woss for dinner?'
'There's a coupla menus ear,' Dee Dee said, producing leaflets from two local takeaways, again supplied by the Hamiltons.
'Oooh, can we av a ruby?' Trisha asked, snatching one of the glossy flyers. 'I ain ad a good ring stinger in ages.'
'Yeah, that ain a bad idea,' Dee Dee agreed. 'That shite they called curry in the nick was bleedin dire wern it.'
'Gawd yeah,' Maizie said, 'it was dull as friggin dishwater, as me muvva used to say.'
'Ar wanna naaga,' Trisha said, scanning the menu from the Bengal Baji restaurant at the end of the street. 'Wiv a pishwari naan to dunk in the sauce, ooh an a mushroom rice.'
Clive had left the girls three hundred pounds to use as they saw fit until their first pay cheques arrived.
'Wod you want Maize?' Trisha asked, handing her friend the menu.
Maizie's eyes lit up as she drooled over the sumptuous spicy selection. 'Ar dunno,' she said at first, 'ar wonnit all.'
'Giss it ear,' Dee Dee said, dialing the restaurant's number. 'Ar'll get a load and we'll divvy it up yeah.'
'Oh yeah, thas a good idea,' Maizie said, content to let her friend decide. 'Get free bottles of Cobra an'all, ar like that Indian lager.'
'Fuck it ar'll get six,' Dee Dee said, before the restaurant owner answered the telephone. 'Alright geez. D'you deliver?' she asked. 'Good, right ar'll av...' Dee Dee rattled off a lengthy list of savories from the Bengal Baji's extensive menu. 'Six bottles of Cobra, oh and summa that mango shit yeah, ow long's it gonna be?'

The owner totted up her bill. 'Half an hour please miss, and that will be twenty seven pounds forty five, if you please.'
'Yeah whateva,' Dee Dee replied. 'Just urry up will ya, d'you want the address?'
'No, I have it from your telephone number,' she was told.
'Sorted then,' Dee Dee said, hanging up the phone. 'Arf hour,' she told her ravenous friends. 'Trish, get the plates will ya, and the weapons.'
Trisha stomped through to the kitchen once again. 'Trish get this, Trish get that,' she moaned. 'WUNNA YOU'Z COULD GET OFF YER ARSES AND DO SUMMINK YA KNOW!' she yelled through to the living room.
'Woss she on abaat?' Maizie asked, turning up the volume on the television.
'Aint got a scooby,' Dee Dee said, flicking through her magazine. 'Just ignore er.'
Trisha rummaged through the kitchen cupboards, aggrieved at being treated as though she were the hired help. 'EEYA!' she said, emerging and clattering the plates down onto the dining table. 'I aint doin nuffin else so don't even fink abaat askin me, alright!' She sat at the table spinning her plate in her hands.
'Trisha,' Dee Dee said a short while later, hearing a car pull up outside. 'Go get the ruby will ya,' she handed Trisha thirty pounds, barely taking her eyes off her read.
'Ohh flippin ell Deeeee,' Trisha complained, screwing the notes up in her hand. 'Ar mean it, I aint doin nuffing after this ar swear it.'
'Yeah whateva,' Maizie laughed. 'Urry up before it gets cold will ya.'
'Yeah and don't forget the change,' Dee Dee insisted. 'We aint made a money.'
Dee Dee and Maizie took their seats at the table awaiting Trisha's return while she trudged downstairs as the doorbell rang for the third time. 'COMIN!' she yelled, but immediately tripped on a pile of shoes outside the

Romanians' door. 'Shit, fuuuck!' she cursed, staggering into the hall radiator with a clang. 'What the bloody ell!'
The door opened beside her and a tall, dark haired, thick set man appeared mumbling obscenities in his native tongue, while repositioning the shoes belonging to the nine fellow countrymen currently sharing his flat.
'Do what?' Trisha replied, as the doorbell rang once again. 'YEAH ANG ON!' she called out. 'You speaky English?' she asked her Eastern European neighbour, who ignored her completely. 'OY!' she added, rubbing her bruised shoulder. 'Ya can't leave them stinkin shoes there geeza, iss bloody dangerous.'
The Romanian glared at her before ducking back inside, the shoes were in fact stinking after he and his friends had completed a twelve hour shift laying concrete on the motorway.
'Nob!' Trisha said, kicking the shoes and boots out of line before opening the street door. 'Sorry mate, ow much is it?'
Handing over the notes and waiting for the change, which the delivery driver reluctantly gave her, Trisha took the three carrier bags from him and slammed the door in his face.
'Ar don't like that geeza daanstairs,' she said, kicking their flat door closed behind her. 'They got all their shit aatside their door, ar fell arse over tit ar did.'
Maizie hurriedly retrieved a bottle opener from the kitchen drawer and prised the caps off three bottles of beer, while Dee Dee and Trisha unpacked. 'Cheers,' she said, taking a mouthful and toasting her friends.
'Up ya bums!' Trisha said, following suit.
Dee Dee served up the meal as she had always done. 'Eeya soppy nuts,' she said, dishing Trisha an extra onion baji. 'Don't say ar never do nuffing for ya.'
'Oooh ta,' Trisha said, shattering the pile of poppadums with a prodding finger.
'Ar got a bhuna,' Dee Dee told Maizie. 'Ar know ya like that.'

'Mmm thanks,' Maizie replied, dipping a baji into her curry sauce.

Toasting one another with more Indian lager the three girls set about devouring their mountainous feast, then mopping their plates clean with a torn naan.

'Fuck me ar'm stuffed,' Dee Dee said rolling back on her chair and massaging her stomach. 'That was the nuts.'

Trisha swigged greedily from her bottle to cool the fire in her mouth before burping loudly. 'Jesus that naaga's flippin ot ar tell ya.'

'Serves ya right,' Maizie told her, having opted for a milder dish. 'You never learn do ya.'

'I aint complainin!' Trisha told her friend, while wiping a bead of sweat from her forehead and supping some more. 'Ar love me chilli sauce me, you know that, me and me cousin Barry done the ot wing challenge at the Romford Rib Shack on iz eighteenf berfday. We done fifty two wings between us in arf hour wiv shots of tabasco in between, we got tee shirts an everyfing.'

Still to this day, the photograph of Trisha and her cousin has pride of place on the Romford diner's wall of flame; and their gluttonous feat has yet to be bettered, with countless courageous contenders falling at the fiery wayside. 'Done me up like a kipper though they did,' Trisha explained.

'Ar don't wanna ear this,' Dee Dee said, leaving the table to peruse their new home. 'Ar'm avin this room,' she told her friends, looking in on what was to be the master bedroom, with a queen size divan dressed in fresh new bedding.

'Oooh, where's mine then?' Maizie asked, leaving Trisha.

'Ours ya mean,' Trisha said, springing from her chair.

'Oh flippin ell, Dee,' Maizie complained, checking out the second and all together smaller room, with two single beds in opposite corners. 'Iss a blinkin box room for gawd sake.'

'Iss alright,' Trisha said, looking over her shoulder. 'Tell ya what mate, we can push the beds togevva like we used to do when we was kids, be proper cozy wunnit.'

'Over mar dead body!' Maizie frowned. 'I ain avin you spoonin me arse again ar tell ya, ar'd rarva sleep wiv a rottin corpse ar would.'
'Oh Maaaaize,' Trisha whined. 'Don't be like that mate, you used to love comin raand mine to play camp in the front room, be just like old times ar reckon.'
'We was five!' Maizie reminded her. 'Anyway, you weren't battin for the uvva side then was ya!'
'Woja mean battin?' Trisha asked naively.
'Lezzin up uvva birds!' Maizie said, testing the mattresses.
'Oh, don't start all that again Maize,' Trisha moaned. 'If you weren't such a bleedin prude ya might try it.'
'No bleedin way!' Maizie said insistently. 'Ar'll stick to dick if ya don't mind.'
'So tell me this then,' Trisha asked, stretching out on what was to be her bed. 'What would you rarva av, a coupla minutes avin yer air yanked aat the back of yer ed by some boozed up bloke who just wants to empty iz sack and don't give two fucks abaat ya feelins, or two hours of sensual caressin leadin to an erf shatterin orgasm? Issa no brainer Maize ain it.'
Maizie thought back for a moment to her formative years and the late night drunken fumblings in the park shelter long after closing, with some spotty youth's mouth clamped to her neck and his loveless hands tearing at her knickers. And Trisha was right, after precisely two minutes of grunting, groaning and gurning, the lad would discard his rubber with its meager contents and reach for another can of stolen cider, leaving her hoisting up her leggings, dissatisfied to say the least, and having to conceal the love bite, or shag badge as they were known for the next few days. 'Ar couldn't Trish,' she told her friend. 'Ar dunno why, ar just couldn't.'
'Suit yaself,' Trisha replied, reminiscing herself but with an altogether more explosively erotic outcome, a school camping trip on which she shared a tent with a new girl recently transferred to their Catholic school, and if it were

possible, more brazen than she. Rebecca Knight was a name that Trisha would never forget, having concealed half a bottle of whiskey in her backpack she shared it with Trisha, using the cap as a makeshift shot glass in the dead of night, but that wasn't the only thing she shared in the Gloucester field using the excuse that she had forgotten her sleeping bag to share Trisha's. Both girls completely intoxicated, and cold for that matter, snuggled up close and drifted off to sleep. But Trisha was woken a short while later by a probing hand, and although startled at first, soon succumbed to Rebecca's charm and the rest is history. 'Ya better off bein bi Maize, seriously,' she told her reluctant friend. 'Ar don't mean wiv me, coz we're mates an all that, but find yaself a quality bitta totty and see what ya bin missin, thas all ar'm sayin, you get the best of bofe worlds then, nart ar mean.'
Maizie lay staring at the stippled artex ceiling mulling over Trisha's theory, maybe she was right, maybe the secret to true erotic bliss lay in the arms of another woman. Maybe she'll see for herself one day, after all, her track record with men had been nothing to write home about - her one true love Enrique had ditched her at the first hurdle after pledging his eternal devotion.
'Eternal my arse!' she said to herself, recalling his betrothal on bended knee.
'Do what?' Trisha asked looking over.
'Nuffing,' Maizie replied, with a hint of bitterness. 'I aint sayin ya right,' she told Trisha. 'An I aint sayin ya wrong. Oh fuck it, ar dunno what ar'm sayin anymore, ar bin fucked araand by so many bleedin blokes maybe ar should go the uvva way.'
'Oy!' Dee Dee then said, leaning into their room. 'You two dykes wanna go for a beer or what, iss only arf nine and we just got aat of nick for fuck sake, we gotta celebrate or summink aint we, there's gotta be a boozer raand ear somewhere.'
'Yeah fuck it!' Trisha agreed, leaping from her bed. 'We're celebratin aint we!'

'Yeah but Dee,' Maizie said hesitantly. 'We aint got a lotta dough av we, we can't blow it all on booze mate.'
'Maizie!' Dee Dee reminded her. 'When was the last time we ad to buy a beer in a boozer, ay?'
'Yeah come on Maize,' Trisha added, checking herself in the wardrobe mirror. 'There's always some mug that'll splash iz cash if ya flash im a bitta flesh, am ar right?'
'Yeah you're right,' Maizie smiled, joining Trisha and tugging her top down to reveal a little more bosom.
'Come on you two,' Dee Dee beckoned, 'ar'm gaggin for a Jack and coke.'
'Yeah and pork scratchins,' Trisha squealed. The three of them trotted down the stairs in high spirits and out onto the North London streets.
'Where to Dee?' Trisha asked, looking both ways. 'I aint got a scooby where we are, av you?'
'This way,' Dee Dee said, marching to the left. 'Ar can smell a boozer from a mile away.' With her two friends in tow, Dee Dee walked the unfamiliar streets with a chill wind blowing at their heels. 'Ava look!' she then said, rounding a corner and finding herself outside the Volunteer public house.
'Fank fuck!' Maizie said, heading inside without hesitation. 'Ar'm flippin freezin.'
Dee Dee followed with a broad smile, as the smell of stale beer and brass polish greeted them.
'OY OY!' a group of lads at the bar called out, the Volunteer was a regulars pub and hardly ever attracted new, let alone attractive, clientele.
'Flippin eck!' the landlord gasped, pulling his ale spattered tee shirt down over his rotund stomach and ditching his scampi fries. 'Yes ladies, what can I get you?'
'George!' a delighted customer called out. 'Ar'll do that.'
'Oh fanks,' Dee Dee smiled, leading her friends. 'Like candy from a fuckin baby,' she whispered sitting beside the lads.

'Yeah fanks,' Trisha said, clambering onto a bar stool being sure to give the drooling punters an ample eyeful. 'Can I av a pint of Guinness please?'

'Guinness!' the landlord said bemused. 'You sure?'

'Yeah,' Trisha nodded. 'An a baga scratchins an'all if thas alright.'

'Yeah course,' the eager drinker said, digging in his back pocket for his wallet. 'And what you two avin?'

'JD and coke geez,' Dee Dee replied. 'Large.'

'Can I av a spicy rum an coke please,' Maizie asked, doing her utmost to look alluring.

'Ave what ya like darlin,' the admirer told them. 'Ar'm Dave by the way,' he added, offering Dee Dee his hand. 'This ear's Jimmy, thas Terry and the little fucker on the end is Bazza.'

'Leave it aat Dave,' Barry protested, stretching up on his toes. 'Some birds like em small, don'tcha,' he added, addressing the girls.

'Whateva you say stumpy,' Dee Dee replied, supping her spirit and adding more coke.

Barry's friends fell about laughing. 'STUMPY!' one of them roared, ruffling his hair. 'For a leprechaun mate, you don't ava lotta luck do ya.'

'Oh leave im alone,' Trisha said, hopping from her stool and putting a consolatory arm around Barry's shoulder, bringing an instant smile to his otherwise solemn face. 'Mine's a Guinness if ya buyin,' she told him, draining her glass and playing the pint sized punter. 'Can I av a Baileys in it an'all, oh and get a raand of shots in while yer at it, might as well get this party started ay.'

'Er, yeah alright,' Barry said, peeling a fifty pound note from his pocket.

'Dee what you avin?' Trisha asked, seeing Barry was flush.

'Oh fanks Bazza,' Dee Dee said, necking her drink and rattling the ice. 'Large JD geez fanks, Maizie wod'you want?'

'Oh Barry you are a darlin,' Maizie said joining Trisha, and planting a kiss on his crimson cheek. 'Spicey rum, a blue wicked an a bag a cheesy biscuits if ya don't mind.'

Having been put well and truly on the spot Barry had no choice but to agree. 'No, no course ar don't,' he smiled, puffing out his broad chest. 'Av what ya want.'
'Forty seven fifty,' George said, plucking the fifty from Barry's hand and handing him back a pittance.
'Right come on!' Dee Dee said, raising a shot glass. 'Up ya bums!'
The four cock-sure guys toasted their new found friends, each of them certain they were on to a good thing.
'Same again George,' Terry said, retrieving his wallet. 'Keep em comin yeah.'
Aside from the four friends and the girls, the pub was relatively deserted, save for an elderly couple in the corner sipping two halves of shandy and sharing a torn open packet of crisps.
'Flippin ell is this it?' Dee Dee asked, sinking another shot in one.
'Yeah mate,' Dave told her, eyeing her up and down. 'Used to be a proper bangin boozer this ar tell ya, din it George, live music and dirty strippers on a Sunday afternoon.'
'Wiv roast tayters on the bar an'all,' Terry piped up.
'Where is everyone then?' Maizie asked, sipping her alcopop through a striped straw.
'Who cares,' Barry said, slipping an arm around Trisha's waist. 'Anuvva shot girls?' His intentions were obvious, to ply the girls with drink to loosen their inhibitions, and their knicker elastic for that matter, but the girls were bar room veterans with cast iron constitutions and wouldn't roll over lightly.
'Oy ya saucy sod!' Trisha laughed, peeling Barry's hand from her bottom. 'Get the sambucas in, ya randy little fucker!'
'You gotta watch im,' Dave warned the girls. 'E'z like a dog on eat rand a bitta skirt.'
'Put some music on George,' Dee Dee asked the leering landlord, and put ya tongue away will ya, ar know ya probly don't get a lotta fanny in ear but ya gonna trip over ya dick if ya not careful.'

'Yeah sort it aat George,' Maizie added. 'Stick a cd on or summink.'

'E'z only got one,' Dave informed them. 'And that jumps like fuck.'

'Yeah less av some music,' Trisha cried, gyrating her hips. 'What ya got?'

'ABBA!' Dave and his friends said in unison. 'Iss always bleedin Abba!'

'Ar like Abba,' George said, retrieving his one and only cd, heavily scratched and coated in ale.

'Whack it on Georgey boy!' Maizie said, necking a large sambuca.

Dave and his friends put their heads in their hands having heard the compilation dozens of times in that week alone while Dee Dee, Maizie and Trisha swayed to the classic hits of the Seventies and singing along.

'DAAAAANCIN QUEEEN, FEEL THE BEAT ON YA TAMBEREEEEN OH YEAAAAAH!' But immediately the cd began to jump. 'D d d d d d d d d dancing queeeen!' But George and the girls didn't seem to mind, each of them lost in a wave of musical nostalgia.

Arm in arm Dee Dee and Maizie jived with their glasses in the air croakily accompanying the Swedish quartet, whilst Trisha did her level best to fend off Barry's ever lecherous advances. 'Fuck me you're like a friggin octopus aint'cha,' she told him, batting a hand from her boob.

'You're right there girl,' Dave laughed. 'E ain ad a bunk up in ages av ya Baz, iz old lady's a proper nasty fucker. Oy Baz when was the last time your Sandra dropped er drawers?'

'Fuck knows,' Barry told them. 'But ar reckon ar might be on a promise this weekend, ar've decorated the front room, the kitchen, put shit loadsa shelves up all over the flippin ouse and bought er a foot spa an'all. If that aint werf a jump ar dunno what is.'

Barry had indeed bent over backwards, accumulating numerous brownie points, in the hope that his fiery wife of

nine years would finally allow him some form of conjugal relief.
'You got more chance of knittin fog aintcha Baz,' Terry joked, knowing Sandra of old. 'Ar reckon her gusset's proper seized up by now, wod'ya reckon?'
'You aint wrong Tel,' Barry agreed. 'But ar bin knockin me bollocks aat on that ouse, so ar reckon ar'm due a sniff at least, unless Trisha ear wants to elp us aat.' With that he slid a hand down onto her bottom once again.
'Get the beers in an ar'll fink abaat it,' Trisha said, winking to her friends who were bopping along to a jittery version of Mama Mia.
'Mamma Mia ow can ar resist ya,' they warbled, followed by, 'Fank you for the music, for giiiiivin it to meeeeee!'
'Ar need a piss Dee,' Maizie eventually said in between numbers.
'Yeah, me an'all,' Dee Dee replied, setting her glass down on the sticky bar 'Where's the ladies geez?' she asked George, who was busy tearing another packet of peanuts from the wall.
'Sorry, the ladies is aat of order,' George told them, stuffing a handful of nuts into his mouth. 'Iss bunged up wiv fanny rags, you'll av to use the gents, first door on the right.'
'I aint got a problem wiv that,' Dee Dee said, leading Maizie by the hand. But on entering the gents the stench of stagnant urine immediately hit them.
'Jesus!' Dee Dee gasped, fanning her nose. 'This rat ole aint seem a bottla bleach in years, wod'ya reckon Maize.'
Maizie covered her mouth while tip toeing through a puddle of pee emanating from a brimming trough, the outlet blocked with copious amounts of gum, wads of swollen toilet tissue and empty cocaine wraps. Ducking into adjacent graffiti littered cubicles the girls peered through a fist sized glory hole at one another, while hovering inches above the pubic hair laced pans.

'That Barry's a pervy fuck ain e Dee,' Maizie told her friend, flinching as her cheeks made contact with the putrid porcelain.
'Not arf,' Dee Dee replied, whilst scratching at a scribbled inscription on the cubicle wall which read *We love Arsenal* with her fingernail, the result now reading *We love Arse.*
'Bugger!' Maizie then cursed. 'Ar got no bum roll in ear Dee.'
'Eeya,' Dee Dee said handing a dozen or so sheets through the hole. The pair wiped and wriggled their knickers and leggings back over their bottoms, both of them refusing to flush for fear of contracting a deadly disease from the cistern handles.
Washing her hands Dee Dee eyed the row of vending machines on the wall offering condoms, cock rings and sexual supplements of various descriptions to aid a gentlemen's flagging libido. 'Got a coupla paand Maizie?' she asked holding out her hand.
'You aint gettin johnnies are ya Dee,' Maizie asked, delving into her pocket.
'No ya doughnut!' Dee Dee laughed. 'Ar want summa these,' taking two coins from Maizie Dee Dee popped them into a machine marked ERECTO PLUS.
'Wod'ya want them for?' Maizie asked, watching two packets of the powerful penile stimulant drop into her hand.
'It aint for me ya daft cow,' Dee Dee said, slipping them into her pocket.
'Well, who's it for then?' Maizie asked, unaware of Dee Dee's intentions as they left to rejoin the others.
'Shhhh,' Dee Dee said, putting a finger to her lips.
'Urry up Dee!' Trisha called, from the bar. 'We got yager bombs!'
'Quality,' Dee Dee replied, covertly cracking all eight capsules of the blue powder into her hand and dropping the lot into a glass of rampant bull energy drink and handing it to Barry with the accompanying glass of Jägermeister. 'Get that daan ya neck,' she told him, whilst toasting the others.

Barry dropped the shot glass into his tumbler and downed the drink in one gulping mouthful, unaware he had just ingested five times the recommended daily dose of stimulant, which in conjunction with the spirit and caffeine laced energy drink would very soon send his heart racing and the blood pumping to his nether region.

'So, are you'z Gooners?' Dee Dee asked the lads.

'Course we are!' Jimmy replied rolling up his sleeve and trouser leg to reveal two large tattoos of his team's famous cannons. 'What are you, Spurs?'

'Your avin a fuckin laugh aint'cha!' Dee Dee scoffed. 'There's only one team in London mate, and thas West Am.'

'West Am!' each of the four friends laughed. 'Leave it aat,' Dave added, 'iss all abaat the Arsenal, look at us, we're top of the league, top of the fuckin league girl, and where are you'z, fird from bottom as usual.'

The boys puffed out their chests and began chanting. 'AR-SE-NAL, AR-SE-NAL, AR-SE-NAL, ARRRRR-SE-NAAAAAL!'

Dee Dee and her friends retaliated, raising their hands in the air and singing at the tops of their voices. 'AR'M FOREVA BLOWIN BUBBLES, PRETTY BUBBLES IN THE AIR, UNITED, UNITED, UNITED!'

'Alright, alright thas enough!' George said, leaning across the bar fearing a riot. 'Settle daan will ya!' Then, in an attempt to quell the impending uprising, started his much coveted CD once again.

It was Terry that first noticed a distinct bulge in Barry's jogging bottoms, who incidentally was still trying his damnedest to worm his way into Trisha's under garments.

'Ava look, Bazza's got a soddin stiffy on!' he cried, spitting the head of his pint across the bar toward George. 'Bazza you dirty little fucker!'

'Jesus Baz!' Dave laughed. 'What ya got in there mate, a bloody bazooka!'

Barry's joggers offered little resistance against his throbbing manhood, which jutted out like a ballet dancers cod piece.

'NO I AINT!' he cried turning away and tugging his bomber jacket down, but to no avail.
'Oooooh Barry!' Trisha squealed. 'You av got yer dander up aint'cha.'
'Shut up, no I aint!' Barry cursed, thrusting his loins against the bar, his cheeks reddening rapidly. 'I aint!'
'Yes you fuckin av!' Terry teased, before chanting, 'BARRY'S GOT AN ARD ON, BARRY'S GOT AN ARD ON LA LA LA LA!'
Jimmy, Dave, the girls, and even George at this point, joined in the barracking. 'BARRY'S GOT AN ARD ON LA LA LA LAAAAA!'
The elderly couple in the corner hurriedly gathered their winter coats, hats and gloves and made for the door, disgusted at the raucous behavior.
'Night Ted!' George called from the bar. 'Night Phyllis!' The couple barely acknowledged the publican's goodbyes, but were almost bowled over as the saloon doors were thrown open and Barry's seething wife stormed in clutching a steaming value ready meal.
'Ar knew you'd be in ear you useless bastard!' she snarled, as the couple ducked behind her. 'Six o'clock ar told you, six o fuckin clock!'
Barry's friends lowered their heads and stared nervously into their pint glasses, well aware of Sandra's venomous capabilities.
'Sandra love!' Barry stuttered, forgetting his prominent erection momentarily and turning to greet her.
Sandra swung the packaged meal over her head and hurled it toward her cowering husband, narrowly missing his face and splattering a glass fronted fridge on the other side of the bar.
'Now calm daan Sandra!' George said, holding his hands in the air. 'Please darlin, calm daan.'
'Piss off George!' Sandra growled, staring her husband in the eye. 'Four an arf minutes ar bin standin in front of that microwave doin your dinner, four an arf fuckin minutes like

a complete cunt, while you're in ear pissin it up wiv these fuckers!'

'Sandra listen ar was just..,' Barry pleaded, whilst George scraped the toad in the hole from his fridge.

Sandra lunged at Barry prodding his chest. 'If you fink ar'm slavin in the friggin kitchen anymore,' she said, standing in her carpet slippers, 'you got anuvva fink comin you little shit.' She glared at Dave and his friends who said nothing.

'And who's this?' she asked, eyeing Trisha up and down,

'No one love, onest!' Barry said, physically shaking at this point. 'Ar'v only just met er. Ar'm just avin a quick arf wiv me mates, ar was on me way ome, wern I Dave?'

Dave again said nothing in his friend's defence, for fear of antagonizing Sandra further.

Sandra then clapped eyes on her husband's bulging jogging bottoms. 'Woss that then you dirty bastard?' she asked. 'Eh tell me!'

'Nuffing!' Barry cried, covering his embarrassment. 'Nuffing love!'

'That aint nuffing!' Sandra said, making a grab for his protruding penis. 'Thas a bloody boner, thas what that is you pafetic little prick!'

'OW, OW OW! Sandra love please!' Barry begged, as his wife sank her manicured nails deep into his manhood. 'OW! Sandra babe, ar never done nuffing. OW babe, onest!'

'You two timin tosser!' Sandra, now incensed, barked. 'Just you wait till ar get you ome, ar'm takin the bloody belt to that bloody boner of yours you see if ar don't, and don't you ever fink you're comin near my ole wiv that fing, coz it aint never gonna appen. D'YOU EAR ME, NEVER!'

Dee Dee and her friends looked on and laughed as Barry was dragged from the bar, his once crimson cheeks white with abject terror.

'What the fuck?' Dee Dee said, shaking her head.

'That was Sandra,' Dave told her, breathing a sigh of relief. But Sandra popped her head back inside waving an aggressive finger. 'And as for you ya dick-ed,' she yelled across to Dave, 'ar've phoned your Julie, she's on er way an'all!'

'Shit!' Dave said, draining his glass and grabbing his coat, as did his two remaining friends. 'Sorry girls, ar gotta go,' he said, making for the side door. 'Mar Julie's worse than that nut job. Seeya later George!'

Jimmy had paid for a round of drinks before bolting, which George had already poured. 'D'you still want these?' he asked the girls, setting down a tray of seven tequila slammers.

'Course we bleedin do!' Maizie said, snatching two, as did Dee Dee and Trisha. 'Appy days!' she said, toasting her friends and the empty bar stools beside them. 'Now, that's how to booze on a budget,' she told her friends.

'Dee we ardly spent a bean,' Maizie reminded her, necking the first of her drinks and wiping her mouth dry.

'Eeya George?' Dee Dee said, slamming her own glass on the bar. 'You wouldn't appen to av any Abba by any chance would ya?'

Maizie put her hand to her chest laughing with a mouthful of her second drink. 'Shut up Dee!' she spluttered, rocking back on her stool. 'Ar nearly choked to bleedin deff than.'

Whilst George stacked the pub chairs onto the tables and collected what little empties there were, Dee Dee and her inebriated friends belted out another round of Abba gold.

'DAAANCIN QUEEEEN, FEEL THE BEAT ON MAR TAMBEREEEEEEEN, OH YEAHHHHH, OOOOOH SEE THAT GIRRRRRL, WATCH THAT SCEEEEENE, DIGGIN THE DANCIN QUEEN!'

'Drink up ladies,' George said, interrupting the choral trio. 'Aint'chu got omes to go to?'

'Ome ya mean,' Maizie told him. 'We live togevva.'

'Yeah, we sleep togevva an'all,' Trisha said, teasing the landlord and snuggling up to Maizie, who for once didn't push her away.

'Really!' George said, becoming instantly aroused at the thought.

'Oh yeah!' Dee Dee laughed. 'Proper scissor sisters we are, at it all the bleedin time wiv strap-ons, dildos, nipple clamps, the lot mate.'

'No really!' George gasped, drooling a little and rubbing his hands on his grubby apron. 'Corrr ar'd love to see that ar would.'

'Ar bet'chu bleedin would,' Trisha said, licking Maizie's face to raise his blood pressure a little higher.

'Ar spoze you're into all that kinky shit an'all aint'cha,' George said with a head full of fantasies.

'Oh gawd yeah!' Dee Dee replied, stringing him along. 'Ar tell ya what ar like to do to Trisha shall I.'

'Yeah, yeah, yeah go on!' George replied eagerly. 'What, what?'

'Ar lock er in the freezer,' Dee Dee chuckled.

'The freezer!' George gasped, his groin now twitching. 'Wod'ya do that for?'

'Well,' Dee Dee explained, 'ar leave er in there for arf an hour till she's proper stiffnin up, then ar get er aat and give it to er good an ard, iss just like doin a deadun, ar love it!'

'Jesus!' George said, alarmed at the near necrophile act. 'Thas some fucked up shit that is ar tell ya, proper orny though.'

'Thas nuffing,' Maizie joked. 'You wanna see what we do wiv the battry drill, bubble wrap and baked beans. Now that is proper naughty.'

'What, what tell me!' George begged, fidgeting. 'Wod'ya do wiv it, come on.'

'Anuvva time Georgy boy,' Dee Dee said, hopping from her stool. 'You got enough wankin material to keep ya goin for a coupla weeks aint'cha.'

'Not arf,' George smirked, logging their farcical fantasies. 'When you comin back?' he asked, in anticipation of further revelations.

'Soon mate,' Trisha told him. 'If ar can walk straight,' she then blew seductively into Maizie's ear maintaining eye contact with the leering landlord, who by now had visions of the three of them indulging in every sordid act conceivable running through his mind and desperately wanting to be alone with his thoughts to relieve the mounting pressure in his pants.

'Laters yeah!' Dee Dee said, leading her friends out the door.

'Yeah, yeah!' George said, hastily locking the doors behind them, turning off the lights and bolting for the stairs, tugging at his zipper en route.

'Now that was a quality night,' Maizie said, swaying in the street, with her arm around Dee Dee's shoulder.

'Oooh yeah!' Trisha agreed, stumbling as the cool air hit her head on.

'Come on you!' Dee Dee said, steadying her. 'You never could old ya booze like us could ya.'

'Oh shut up Dee!' Trisha protested. 'Ar'm alright mate, ar could do that lot again ar tell ya.'

It was late and the North London back streets were relatively deserted.

'D'you member the way back ome Dee?' Maizie asked, watching Trisha collide with a litter bin.

'Yeah, ar fink so,' Dee Dee told her, looking either way at a cross road. 'It all looks the bleedin same in the dark dun it.'

'Ar feel sick,' Trisha moaned, lagging behind having consumed a bizarre cocktail of drinks that evening.

'Don'tchu puke on me!' Dee Dee barked, keeping her queasy friend at arm's length, whilst doing her utmost to remember the way home. 'Ar member that Scooby Doo mota,' she said pointing out a gayly coloured camper van.

'Slow daan will ya,' Trisha moaned, tottering in her heels with the taste of vomit in her mouth.

'Come on urry up will ya!' Maizie said, tugging at Trisha's collar,

'Don't yank me abaat!' Trisha said, clutching her stomach. 'Ar mean it, ar'm gonna chuck in a minute. Eeya do us a favour Maize, stick ya fingers daan me frote, ar can't do it it makes me gag.'

'Thas the idea you dopey cow!' Dee Dee snapped. 'Now come on if ya gonna yak bleedin get on wiv it!'

'Serves ya right,' Maizie told her, having absolutely no sympathy for her retching friend.

Trisha clung to a light pole for support, hunched over with her hair hanging either side of her pale face. 'Shit!' she cursed. 'Me guts are goin raand and raand.'

Dee Dee and Maizie stopped and waited leaning on a low wall. 'Come on chuck it up then!' Dee Dee told Trisha. 'We aint got all bleedin night ya know.'

'Ar'm tryin!' Trisha said, spitting morsels of alcohol stewed naaga onto the pavement.

'Ohhhh nice,' Maizie said, turning away.

'Go on girl!' Dee Dee laughed, unflinching as a torrent of steaming vomit gushed from her friend's mouth spattering her legs and patent shoes in three surging projectile waves, leaving her panting and visibly shaking.

'Thas a waste of good grub,' Dee Dee told her. 'There's arf a baji there if ya still ungry.'

'Ohhhh don't,' Trisha cried, gagging again and again before spitting the remains from her teeth. 'Oh bugger, look at me leggins,' she moaned, flicking a piece of partly digested poppadum from her knee.

'Don'tchu come near me!' Maizie warned her friend, starting off along the street so as not to come in contact with Trisha. 'Ar mean it!'

'Ar know where we are naah,' Dee Dee said, turning into their road. 'Ear we are.'

Maizie began humming a melodious tune which instantly aggravated her. 'Oh fuck it!' she cursed. 'Ar can't get that pissin tune aat me ed.'

'What tune?' Dee Dee asked. 'Dancin Queen?'

'Naah,' Maizie said, breaking into song. 'Do ya waddle when ya walk, do ya rumble when ya run!' Her two friends then joined her in a cat's chorus, 'PUUUUUT DAAAN YA KNIFE AN FORK, PUT DAAAN YA BAGEL AND YA BUN, DON'TCHA WORRY DON'T DESPAIR COZ WHATEVA YA

CIRCUMSTAAAAAAAAAANCE, GRAB YASELF A PAIRA TRISHA'S GAAAAAASTRIC PAAAAAAANTS!'
The curtains on either side of their flat began to twitch, as did several on the opposite side of the street and one by one the neighboring lights were illuminated.
'Come on Dee, ar need anuvva piss,' Maizie said, hopping from one foot to another as Dee Dee struggled to find the keyhole.
'Fuck it!' Dee Dee cursed, picking the key from the floor for the third time, herself feeling the effects of the night's heavy drinking. 'Got it,' she said triumphantly, pushing open the door which crashed against the passage wall denting the dado rail in the process.
Trisha was the last to enter, slamming the door behind her and waking the remaining heavy sleepers.
'Shush will ya,' Dee Dee said, fumbling for the light switch.
'Shit Dee, I aint gonna make it!' Maizie shrieked, bobbing up and down. 'Ar'm drippin in me knickers for gawd sake!'
In her haste Dee Dee tripped on a builder's boot outside the neighboring flat. 'Pissin fings!' she cursed, lashing out. 'Eeya Maize, you wanna waz, fill that fucker.' She handed Maizie the offending boot insistently.
'Ar'm gonna av to,' Maizie said, with crossed legs and a damp patch emerging. Snatching the boot she thrust it beneath her and wrenched at her leggings. 'Fuuuuuck thas good,' she sighed, peeing for almost a minute filling the boot above the ankle, before replacing it beside the other.
'Good girl,' Dee Dee told her, making for the stairs.
The girls bundled one another into their flat as an elderly Romanian looked out into the hall, checking their footwear but seeing nothing untoward.
Dee Dee flopped down onto the sofa with Maizie falling on top of her.
'Get off me wiv ya pissy draws!' Dee Dee cursed, tossing her friend onto the floor. 'Trisha put the kettle on there's a good girl!' she then called through to the kitchen, where Trisha

had stripped to her underwear having loaded her sick stained clothing into the washing machine.
'Yeah, yeah, yeah alright!' Trisha replied, reaching for the mugs. 'You two got anyfing for the wash?'
Maizie appeared moments later wearing the kangaroo onesie her mother had sent her in prison. 'Eeya!' she said, handing Trisha her dampened clothing.
'Don't give it to me!' Trisha said, thrusting it back and wiping her hands on her knickers.
'Ar want two sugars in mine,' Maizie told her, loading the machine and rejoining Dee Dee.
'ONE IN MINE TRISH!' Dee Dee yelled, reclining with a contented smile.
It was past midnight and there had been no guards doing the rounds, invading their privacy and turning out the lights. The girls were free at last, albeit with certain conditions. Trisha clattered around the kitchen in her intoxicated state, slamming the cupboard doors in search of tea bags.
'Woss she doin in there?' Maizie asked, looking over her shoulder from the armchair.
'Gawd knows,' Dee Dee replied without a care. 'While she's aat there fuckin araand she's leavin us alone, thas all ar know.'
'Ar make ya right,' Maizie agreed, cuddling a cushion close to her chest. 'Nice ain it Dee,' she then said, 'bein aat ar mean.'
'Pukka,' Dee Dee said, putting her feet up and rubbing her hands together as Trisha returned with three piping hot mugs.
'Corrr ansum,' Maizie said in anticipation. 'Thanks babe.'
'Trish!' Dee Dee said abruptly, after receiving hers. 'Why the fuck as mar tea got an ed on it?'
'Ar dunno?' Trisha said sitting beside her and sipping hers.
'Jesus Trish!' Maizie cursed, spitting a mouthful back into her mug. 'Woss this shit?'
Dee Dee followed suit with equal venom. 'Fuckin ell Trisha what d'you put in that?'

'What?' Trisha said still supping unflinching. 'Woss up wiv it?'

In her drunken state she had inadvertently added heaped tea spoons of baking soda to the hot beverages instead of the regulation sugar.

'You sure the milk ain off or summink?' Maizie asked, sliding her mug across the coffee table as did Dee Dee.

'And woss that bleedin noise?' Dee Dee asked, looking toward the kitchen hearing a repetitive thud.

'Iss the washin machine,' Trisha told her, dunking a biscuit. 'Ar stuck me stilettos in an'all.'

'Great!' Dee Dee moaned, putting a cushion over her head. 'Thas worse than listenin to your bullshit that is.'

'You not drinkin that?' Trisha asked, reaching for Dee Dee's mug having drained her own. 'Ya know the one fing ar've really missed bein banged up is a proper cuppa rosy.'

'That wern a proper cuppa rosy, you doughnut!' Maizie blasted. 'You carn even get that right can ya, less face it Trish, you're a fuck up waitin to appen aint'cha.'

'Oh leave off Maize,' Trisha said, cradling Dee Dee's mug in her hands. 'You could've got off yer arse and made it, and you Dee. I av to do everyfing.'

Maizie got up and made a dash for the bathroom. 'Ar gotta brush me teef,' she said in parting. 'That shits burnin me tonsils ar swear it!'

'Yeah me an'all,' Dee Dee said, leaving Trisha sat on her own,

'Stuck up bitches,' Trisha scoffed, dragging Maizie's mug toward her.

In the bathroom Maizie and Dee Dee loaded their tooth brushes and scrubbed as best they could, spitting over and over to rid themselves of the foul taste.

'Flippin ell!' Maizie moaned. 'It aint goin away is it Dee.'

'No it bleedin aint,' Dee Dee gargled, filling her mouth from the tap. 'Musta bin the milk.'

'Oy Nigella!' Maizie said sarcastically, swigging the remains from a beer bottle and glaring at Trisha. 'Sling that poxy milk will ya, iss gotta be a mumf aat of bleedin date ar reckon.'
'Milk?' Trisha replied struggling with a magazine crossword. 'What milk, we never ad any.'
'What?' Dee Dee asked, joining them. 'Woja mean never ad any, woja put in the pissin tea then, ay?'
'Squeezy cheese,' Trisha said nonchalantly, before burping into her hand, a side effect of the baking soda.
'SQUEEZY FUCKIN CHEESE!' Maizie cried. 'WHAT THE FUCK?'
'What?' Trisha said, starting her third mug. 'Iss all the same ain it.'
'NO!' Maizie barked. 'No it ain all the bloody same you retard!'
In her naivety Trisha had assumed that any of the vast array of diary derivatives could be added to hot beverages. 'Me nan swears by it,' she told her dumbstruck friends. 'We only ad the creamy cheddar, but ar prefer the garlic an erb meself.'
'Sick bitch!' Maizie snarled, heading back to the bathroom to brush again.
'It all comes aat of a cow's arse dunnit Dee,' Trisha said, tearing her aborted crossword from the magazine and screwing it into a ball.
'It certainly tastes like it,' Dee Dee replied, in no mood to explain the milking process to her bewildered friend.
'What dick does crosswords anyway?' Trisha cursed, tossing the ball across the room having endeavored to cram a nine letter word into a four letter answer; one of the few nine letter words in her limited vocabulary.
'Ar'm gaana bed,' Dee Dee said, kicking off her shoes. 'Ar can't stand that poxy racket.' Trisha's stilettos on a spin cycle reverberated throughout the flat. 'Ar be surprised if ya got any eels left on them shoes when iss finished,' she told Trisha, who was busy scrutinizing two photographs in a spot the difference competition.

'Gotcha ya little fucker!' Trisha said, circling an extra chicken in the right hand picture. 'Thas more like it!' she said, looking extremely pleased with herself having calculated there were some twenty differences when in fact there were only five. 'Sorted. Do what Dee?' she asked. 'Oh yeah, ar'm turnin in an'all mate ar'm cream crackered.'

Maizie returned, having brushed gargled and rinsed three times more. 'Dee, Trish!' she called, peering into the living room, wincing at the clattering sound emanating from the kitchen.

'Alright Maize!' Trisha said, already tucked in bed by the time Maizie entered the bedroom. 'Can ya leave the light on please mate?' Having been bolted in a twelve by eight cell for the past two years the simplest of things were now a greatly appreciated luxury.

Stepping from her onesie Maizie slipped into her own new bed, which in contrast with her prison bunk felt like a warm slipper, the posturepedic mattress a sheer delight.

'Ar got two pillas Maize,' Trisha told her friend, 'I ain ad two pillas in ages.'

'Trisha!' Maizie snapped, turning her face to the wall. 'Ar'm knackered an ar wanna go to sleep, alright!'

'Oh yeah,' Trisha said, pulling her duvet up under her chin, 'sorry.' Fluffing her pillow and turning several times she eventually settled. 'I ad that light shade once,' she said, staring at the ceiling. 'Ar got it from the paand shop, mine was yella though, wiv butterflies on it.'

'Trisha, will you shut the fuck up,' Maizie mumbled, half asleep at this point. 'Ar mean it, if you start ar'm gonna ring ya bleedin neck d'you ear me, d'you ear me!' Maizie looked over her shoulder, but Trisha had dropped suddenly into a deep sleep wheezing and snorting and occasionally breaking wind. 'Bloody marvlus!' she said, pulling her own duvet up over her head and ramming her fingers in her ears.

CHAPTER FIVE

Maizie, having slept very little, woke the following morning to the sound of Trisha's warbling voice singing along to the kitchen radio.
'FOR FUCK SAKE, SHUT UUUUP!' she croaked, slamming her fists down either side of her.
But Trisha was too busy chipping the blackened omelette she had cremated from the saucepan with a bread knife, destroying the Teflon coating in the process and proving the lifetime guarantee worthless.
'Oh sod it!' she said, conceding defeat and binning the pan in favor of the toaster. 'BRAAN OR WHITE MAIZE?' she called out to her friend, dropping two slices of wholemeal in for herself. 'MAIZIE, D'YA WANT BRAAN OR WHITE TOAST?'
She turned to see Maizie glaring at her from the kitchen door.
'Ar don't want nuffing from you,' Maizie said, still wrapped in her duvet. 'You bin chewin on ya bleedin gums all pissin night you av, and turn that shit daan.'
'Ohhh Maize,' Trisha moaned, standing between her friend and the radio. 'You know ar like me Motown, ar was brought up on it wern I.'
'Just turn it daan will ya,' Maizie insisted, heading for the sofa. 'Or the poxy fings goin aat the winda.'
'Woss appnin bitches?' Dee Dee then said, appearing with a laden carrier bag, having risen before her friends and ventured outside. 'Ar bin daan the road for a paper and a four pinta, so we aint gotta av no more of that squeezy shite in our tea.'
'Ar fought you was still kippin Dee,' Maizie said, pulling her feet beneath her duvet. 'What time d'you get up then?'
Before Dee Dee could answer, Trisha turned up the radio on hearing the intro to one of her all-time favorites. 'SH SH SHHHH!' she told her friends before singing along on cue. 'NUFFIN YOU COULD SAY COULD TEAR YOU AWAY FOR MAR GUUUUY, NUFFIN YOU COULD DO COZ AR'M STUCK LIKE

GLUE TO MAR GUUUUUY. Oh shit, talkin of glue Dee,' she then said, taking her stilettos from the washing machine minus their heels, 'you aint got any av ya?'
'No ya doughnut,' Dee Dee laughed. 'Ar told ya what'd appen din I.'
'Yeah but,' Trisha said, 'I aint got nuffin else to wear, ar give me prison pumps back when we left.' Her beloved patent leather shoes had disintegrated during the high temperature cycle, loosening the stitching and removing the sheen completely. 'Five undred Euros they were, in a Paris boutique,' she moaned. 'What mar gonna do, ar can't go aat wiv nuffin on me feet can I?'
'Ang on Trish,' Maizie said, darting back into their bedroom and into the built-in wardrobe, 'ar see these when ar was puttin me gear away.' The previous occupants and their children had left several items of clothing behind that were overlooked by the Hamiltons. 'You got little feet aint'cha,' she said, returning with a pair of child's trainers.
'Oh leave off Maize!' Trisha said on seeing the brightly coloured shoes. 'Thomas the friggin Tank, your avin a laugh aint'cha!' Trisha's feet were petite and would easily slip into the size sevens, but she had grave reservations as each of them were in the design of a steam locomotive with wheels on either side and a smiling face on the toe. 'Ar'm gonna look a proper winda licker in them ain I.'
'Sod ya then,' Maizie said, turning away. 'But me and Dee are goin aat later, so unless you got a better idea it looks like you're stayin at ome dunnit.'
'Ohhhhh,' Trisha whined. 'Can't ya buy me a paira wedges or summink, we got some dough aint we.'
Dee Dee snatched the trainers from Maizie and thrust them into Trisha's hands. 'We aint wastin our dough on no shoes,' she told her. 'So you eeva wear these or stop in, woss it gonna be?'
'Ohh flippin eck,' Trisha replied, looking the trainers over. 'You're windin me up aint'cha?'

'No, no I aint,' Dee Dee said, doing her damnedest not to laugh. 'Ar fink you'll look the nuts in them, wod'you reckon Maizie?' Maizie was fit to burst and had to leave the kitchen.

'Seeeee are told ya,' Trisha protested. 'Oh please Dee, don't make me wear these flippin fings.'

'Iss them or nuffing!' Dee Dee said, having to leave the kitchen herself and ducking out of sight to conceal her hysterics.

Trisha could be heard cursing in the kitchen slipping the trainers on her feet. 'Ar tell ya what!' she then called out. 'They narf comfortable!' Despite their ridiculous outward appearance the juvenile footwear was a perfect fit with padded tongues and cushion soles for maximum support. 'Ohhhh look Dee they light up an'all!' she squealed, prancing up and down in the kitchen. Trisha could hardly contain her excitement as a series of red and yellow neon lights flashed on and off with every step. 'Wicked!' She then attempted a stumbling moon walk but only succeeded in backing into the refrigerator. 'Shall ar make a cuppa?' she called to her friends, steadying the rocking vase.

'NO!' Dee Dee barked, reaching in and dragging her friend from the kitchen. 'Get aata there you doughnut, ar wouldn't trust you to boil a bleedin egg ar wouldn't. Maizie put the kettle on mate!'

'I ope you got proper sugar,' Maizie said, delving into Dee Dee's bag.

'Yeah but Deeee,' Trisha said, wrenching her arm free. 'It aint that easy boilin an egg ya know, arf a minute eeva way and you got a bowl of snot or a ruddy bullet, mind you me grandad ad it sussed, e always done me a pukka egg wiv soldiers an everyfing.'

'Ar don't wanna ear it!' Dee Dee said, raising a hand. 'Ar'm gonna shit shower and shave me legs so leave me alone will ya.' Retrieving her towel and wash bag Dee Dee beat a hasty retreat into the bathroom bolting the door and raising the lid of the pan.

'Iss all abaat timin thas what e used to say,' Trisha said, following Maizie into the kitchen and hopping up onto the side, her friend doing her best to ignore her whilst preparing the tea.

'D'you want sugar?' Maizie asked over her shoulder, but Trisha was oblivious.

'E used to sit me on the side like this,' Trisha rambled, 'and cut iz toenails in the sink.'

'What?' Maizie asked, breaking her concentration. 'What you on abaat?'

'Toenails,' Trisha told her. 'Great big curly buggers they was, like pork scrachins. Anyway by the time e'd lopped off the last one me eggs'd be ready, and done proper nice an'all, mind you summa them gnarly nails never made it daan the plug ole, they pinged all over the pissin place, we used to find em days later in the muesli, macaroni and mung beans.'

'Mung beans!' Maizie said, snared again by another of Trisha's waffling tales. 'What the bleedin ell's a mung bean when iss at ome?'

'Gawd knows,' Trisha replied, shrugging her shoulders, 'me nan was into er lentils and shit thas all ar know, anyway she got wunna the bleedas stuck in er frote an ad to be air lifted to ospital.'

'What, a mung bean?' Maizie asked, ignoring the whistling kettle behind her.

'No ya prat,' Trisha laughed, 'a two inch toenail. She'd made a macaroni cheese and choked on the bloomin fing, it was touch and go ar tell ya. You makin that tea or what?' she then asked, watching the steam rising behind her friend. 'Come on Dolly daydream, ar'm garspin for a brew.'

'What, oh yeah,' Maizie said, having pictured the air ambulance hoisting Trisha's nan into the air with her husband's toenail firmly wedged in her throat.

'That reminds me,' Trisha said, plucking the tin opener from a tub of kitchen utensils. 'Ar gotta do mine.'

'You aint doin that in ear!' Maizie barked, covering her mug and the open bag of sugar fearing a similar fate.

'D'ya reckon Dee'd let me do em in the barfroom?' Trisha asked, hopping down and admiring her flashing feet.
'Yeah course she will,' Maizie replied, knowing full well what her fiend's reaction would be. 'Go on, go and ask er.'
'Deeeee,' Trisha said, tapping the opener on the bathroom door. 'Deeeeeeee.'
'WHAT?' Dee Dee yelled back, lathering herself under the shower head. 'WOJA WANT?'
'Can ar come in and do me nails?' Trisha asked, trying the door handle.
'NO!' was Dee Dee's immediate response. 'AR'M AVIN A SHOWER!'
'Oh but Deeeee,' Trisha whined, 'ar can sit on the bog and do em, ar won't be no bovva onest.'
'AR SAID NO!' Dee Dee growled, tipping her head back and working shampoo into her hair. 'SOD OFF WILL YA, CARN AR GET FIVE FLIPPIN MINUTES TO MESELF!' Dee Dee then chose to ignore Trisha's constant pleas until she eventually gave up and tossed the tin opener onto the sideboard.
'Sod ya then!' Trisha moaned, dropping onto the sofa with her arms folded across her chest. 'Ar can't do nuffing ar can't.'
'Shut up you prat and drink that,' Maizie said, handing Trisha a chipped mug and switching on the television in time to catch the mid-morning news.
'Oooh look iss me!' Trisha cried, sitting bolt upright and spilling a quantity of her tea onto the arm of the sofa. 'Maize ava look!'
Sure enough the day's lead story was Trisha's release from Holloway, with footage of her speaking to reporters outside the gates being beamed around the world.
'You idiot!' Maizie snapped, shoving Trisha's shoulder. 'We was spozed to keep it quiet.'
'Ar carn elp it if ar'm a natral in front of the lens,' Trisha said in her defence.
'Ar'll give you natral!' Maizie warned. 'You coulda buggered it up for all of us.'

'Oh leave off Maize,' Trisha laughed, 'we're aat now so it don't matter who knows does it, fuck em anyway thas what ar say.'
But in his newly acquired corner office at New Scotland yard the girl's nemesis D I Pritcher was rocking back in his chair incensed at the news, having worked so tirelessly to put them behind bars.
'WHAT THE FUCK!' he yelled, lashing out at the photocopier. 'WHO LET THOSE BASTARDS OUT?' He stormed from his office colliding with an inspector with an arm full of files. 'Out of my bloody way!' he cursed, heading for the elevator and leaving his subordinate scrambling for his strewn papers. The D I was furious at his superior's betrayal, as he saw it. Ascending to the top floor to have it out with the top brass, 'Stupid fucks!' he cursed, kicking out at the stainless steel lift paneling. 'Stupid fucking fucks!'
Marching toward the chief constable's office, yanking at the knot of his tie, he rapped on the smoke glass door with his whitened knuckles seeing several blurred figures sat round the meeting table inside.
'I'm afraid Sir David is in a meeting,' a secretary called from behind. 'If you'd like to come back this afternoon I'll pencil you in.'
'No, I wouldn't like to come back this afternoon you dozy bitch!' the D I barked, swiveling on his heels. 'I want some fucking answers and I want em now, you got that!'
'Yes but,' the girl said, taken aback by his ferocity.
'Yes but fuck all!' the D I said, throwing open the chief constable's door. 'Sir, what the bloody hell's going on?' he said, marching in unannounced. 'I put those slags away and some dick ed has gone and let em out!'
'Pritcher, what the devil!' the chief constable yelled, leaping to his feet enraged at the intrusion. 'I told Jennifer I wasn't to be disturbed, now get out!' Several foreign dignitaries were sat around his table and each were equally surprised at the outburst, having travelled to the UK to discuss modern policing techniques.

'I don't know what you're talking about Pritcher!' the chief constable said angrily. 'And quite frankly I don't care. I'm in a meeting so get out of my office!'
'Dawson and her slag mates!' the D I insisted. 'I banged em up for double murder a coupla years ago and I've just seen the fuckers walk free, what's goin on?' The D I was well known for his insubordinance and disregard for authority, but on this occasion he may have overstepped the mark.
'I SAID GET OUT!' the chief Inspector yelled, pushing the D I toward the door. 'I'm sorry, gentlemen,' he said over his shoulder to his bemused guests. 'Bear with me for just a moment please.' Once outside he quickly closed his office door and glared at the D I. 'What the devil d'you think you're doing man? Can't you see I'm in a meeting. You're skating on very thin ice Pritcher, very thin ice indeed.' He then turned to his secretary, 'Jennifer I thought I told you I wasn't to be disturbed, if you can't do your damn job properly I'll find somebody who can. Do I make myself clear!'
'But sir,' Jennifer pleaded, 'I tried to tell the detective inspector but...'
'But nothing!' the chief constable snapped. 'You have a job to do, so just you bloody well do it, do I make myself clear!'
'Yes sir, sorry sir,' Jennifer replied, busying herself with the morning's mail.
'And as for you Pritcher,' the chief inspector said, his face now reddening. 'I suggest you get back to work or you'll be facing another suspension!'
'But sir, the girls,' D I Pritcher said, standing firm. 'That was my collar sir, why was I kept out of the bloody loop?'
'If you must know Pritcher,' the chief inspector explained, 'their release was sanctioned by the highest authority. And one that's way above your pay grade, and mine for that matter, now I suggest you drop this nonsense and return to your desk. I have a meeting to attend.'
'Them pricks in parliament!' the D I cursed. 'They don't know their fuckin arse from their elbow!'

'But they pay your damn salary,' the chief inspector reminded the bitter D I, 'and don't you forget that. Now get out of my sight!' With this he returned to his office closing the door behind him, leaving the D I fuming with clenched fists.

Jennifer thumbed her appointment book. 'I've got a fifteen minute window at three thirty if you'd like to make an appointment,' she told the D I who paced the lobby mumbling obscenities under his breath.

'What?' he said, stooping with his hands on Jennifer's desk.

'Er three thirty,' she replied sheepishly. 'If you'd like to make an appointment.'

'No ar fuckin wouldn't!' the D I growled, swiping her in tray onto the floor. 'SHOVE IT UP YER ARSE!' he yelled, storming back to the elevator.

Dee Dee emerged from the bathroom some fifteen minutes later with a towel wrapped around her head and another around her upper body. 'Gimme a coupla minutes an ar be ready,' she told her friends.

'Dee you missed it!' Trisha said excitedly. 'Ar was on the telly!'

'Ay?' Dee Dee said, rubbing her backside dry. 'What you on abaat?'

'This prat,' Maizie said, shoving Trisha again. 'She's all over the friggin news.'

'Oh great,' Dee Dee sighed, wagging a finger, 'so much for low pissin profile.'

'You're just jealous,' Trisha said, slurping her tea and leaping from the couch. 'Ar'm the photogenic one aat the free of us and you'z know it, you watch ar'll probly be on daytime telly wiv me own game show or summink, as long as it aint Blankety bloody Blank ar can't stick that shit. The closest our lot ever come to bein on the telly was me sister in law Stacey goin on Jeremy Karl, or whateva iz name is, she ad five kids by four different dads, slept wiv er muvva's boyfriend on their weddin night and wanted a blood test coz

she reckoned e was the farva of er unborn triplets, proper fucked up bitch she is ar tell ya.'
'Was e the dad?' Maizie asked, recalling the story vaguely.
'Naah,' Trisha said, taking her empty mug through to the kitchen sink. 'It was me uncle Davey in the end, apparently she copped off wiv im in the back of iz mini cab coz she never ad the fiver fare.'
'E is a dirty sod your uncle Davey,' Maizie agreed. 'E wanted a blowy offa me once to take me to the boozer.'
'Ya didn't give im one did ya?' Dee Dee asked, recollecting a similar incident.
'Naah course not,' Maizie laughed. 'Ar bashed iz bell end wiv me belt buckle and done a runner, when ar told me dad e kicked seven shades of shit aat of im the dirty bleeda.'
'Ar didn't need me dad,' Dee Dee said, having endured Trisha's uncle's slobbering advances in the past. 'Ar dragged im aat the mota meself wiv iz traazers raand iz ankles and broke iz bleedin jaw in free places. I aint never seen im since. What appened to the nonce?'
'The pikeys got im,' Trisha called through. 'E fucked em over for a coupla've undred quid, so they andcuffed im to the wheel of iz cab, filled it wiv forty five gallons of nicked diesel and torched im on the wasteland by the gasworks.'
'Serves im right,' Maizie said, slipping on her shoes. 'Where we goin Dee?'
'Fought we'd go daan Rommie woja reckon?' Dee Dee replied, shaking the towel from her head. 'See a few of the old faces.'
'Oh yeahhh!' Maizie chirped. 'Nice one, a'll get me tracky top on, iss proper freezin aat ar bet.'
'You aint wrong,' Dee Dee told her.
Trisha skipped from the kitchen, her trainers lighting the way. 'Can we get pie and mash Dee?' she asked, wide eyed. 'Please mate, ar've really missed it I av.'
'Corrr yeah, me an'all,' Maizie said, licking her lips. 'Can we Dee, ay?'

'Fuck it yeah,' Dee Dee smiled, having longed for the east end favorite herself for some time. 'Why not, ay?'

Locking their door a short while later the three girls made their way downstairs to where the entire Romanian family were gathered in the hallway ranting over the mysterious water filled boot.

'Iss probly the plumbin,' Dee Dee said, pointing out the cracked ceiling cornice above their heads. 'Shit appens like that in these old gaffs.'

'Eeva that,' Trisha said in passing, 'or some dirty bleeda's pissed in ya boot.'

'Shut it will ya!' Maizie snapped, shoving Trisha out the front door, leaving the Eastern European travelers considering the burst pipe possibility, several of them dipping a finger in the boot and offering it to their lips, the youngest of the family grabbing at the boot in his father's hand and tipping the contents into his mouth gulping greedily and ignoring his mother's protesting cries.

'Don't worry love!' Maizie laughed, whilst gagging a little. 'Ar reckon there's plenty more where that came from.'

The head of the family herded his crowd back inside their flat gathering up the remaining boots and shoes, and in doing so poured the remainder of Maizie's alcohol tainted urine down the leg of his trousers cursing the gods, and the day he and his family set foot in the UK, the father of six ordered his considerably younger wife and tenants to begin packing immediately, planning an early return to his impoverished homeland.

'We gettin a cab Dee?' Trisha asked, zipping her jacket tight up under her chin.

'Naaaah fuck that,' Dee Dee replied, keeping a firm grip on their finances. 'We're gonna get the train.'

'The train!' Maizie said, stopping in her tracks. 'When was the last time the free of us was on a bleedin train?'

'Ar dunno!' Dee Dee said abruptly. 'But ya better get used to it, coz we aint gettin no poxy cabs thas for certain.'

'We used to jump the barrier at Chadwell Eaf,' Trisha reminded her friend, 'dint we Dee.'
'Yeah ar member that,' Dee Dee replied, beckoning to Maizie. 'But we're gonna pay our way this time, so get a bleedin move on will ya.'
'Come on Maize!' Trisha urged, trotting close behind Dee Dee. 'Ar know ya don't like the escalators ya soppy tart.'
'Shut up!' Maizie moaned, starting after them. 'They're proper dangerous them fings ar tell ya, if they aint got no stairs I aint goin ar swear down.'
'Oh leave it aat Maizie,' Dee Dee laughed, quickening her pace against the chill wind, 'you ain a bleedin kid anymore.'
'Ar know that Dee,' Maizie said, catching her friends up. 'Ar dunno what it is, ar just don't like em. Ar member gettin me bobby socks caught in one at Kings Cross on a school trip, Sally Cafcart told me there was a monster livin underneaf draggin little girls in an eatin em, gimmie nightmares for mumfs that did ar tell ya.'
'And you believed that shit,' Dee Dee laughed, rounding the corner with Highbury and Islington station in sight. 'Sort it aat Maize for fuck sake.'
Trisha's flashing footwear turned more than the occasional head as they entered the station, side stepping a man in a panda costume shaking a bucket and claiming to be collecting for a world wildlife charity.
'I aint givin fuck all to the pandas!' Trisha told him, in no uncertain terms. 'Nasty buggers they are, ar was tryna get a phota of one layin on iz back scratchin iz nuts, but it copped the ump an rubbed its shitty arse up the glass, ar mean that aint nice is it, ar don't feel sorry for em one bit me ar tell ya, ar'd rarva give mar dough to the penguins, ya don't ear them moanin abaat not avin enough bamboo and shit do ya.' The collector stood open mouthed, bemused at Trisha's response.
'OY, COME ON YOU!' Dee Dee called from the ticket window. 'Free to Romford mate,' she told the cashier, slipping a note under the glass.

'I ope you got stairs!' Maizie said over Dee Dee's shoulder.
'Shut it will ya,' Dee Dee snapped, retrieving the tickets and handing them to her friends. Having descended the stairs, which pleased Maizie no end, the three girls stood on the drafty platform, stamping their feet to increase their circulation and reading the many movie posters that lined the tiled walls.
'Told ya we shoulda got a cab,' Maizie said, looking along the line and blowing into her hands. 'Dee, ar said ar told ya we shoulda...' she said again, but Dee Dee and Trisha had wandered along the platform in search of a vacant bench.
'Oh thas flippin nice ain it,' Maizie moaned, she was about to start after them when to her surprise a young busker with a weathered guitar started up behind her playing a deeply hypnotic melody. With her friends in sight Maizie found herself rooted to the spot, in awe at the ease in which he coaxed a tune from his instrument. His outward appearance hadn't captivated her quite so much, faded threadbare denims, leather sandals and a psychedelic tie dye tee shirt clung to his scrawny body, but that mattered very little because the moment he opened his bearded mouth and began to sing Maizie's heart melted, the soulful lament which he had penned himself told the tale of a lonely traveler in search of a soulmate. Passengers filled by the busker barely acknowledging his efforts and refusing to drop the smallest of denominations into his open guitar case.
'TWO MINUTES MAIZE!' Dee Dee yelled, checking the overhead screens. 'WHAT YA DOIN?'
Ignoring her friend Maizie approached the singer and stood with her hands in her pockets and a broad smile on her face, swaying ever so slightly. 'That was lovely that was,' she said when the song had ended. 'Ar mean it, proper lovely.'
'Thank you,' the young musician replied, toying with several beaded dreadlocks in his otherwise curly blonde hair. 'Thank you so much, I er, I have a cd if you'd like to buy one, they're only five pounds.'

'Ar've only got a quid,' Maizie said, turning her pockets out. 'But ar do love your music.'
'Take it,' the young man said, taking a disc from his backpack and handing it to Maizie. 'I'd rather give it to somebody that appreciates it, than sell it to someone that doesn't.'
'You sure!' Maizie gasped, holding the album to her chest. 'Ahhh fanks, thas really nice of ya, take this anyway,' she added, dropping her pound into his case. 'Me name's Maizie,' she said, offering a hand. 'Me and me mates just moved in raand ear.'
'Frankie,' the lad replied. 'But my friends call me Bird.' Rolling up his sleeve he showed Maizie a magnificent hawk in flight clasping a serpent in its talons tattooed on his forearm. 'I have this thing for birds you see,' he added.
'Thas good to know,' Maizie laughed. 'Coz ar got this fing for blokes an'all.' She then stood for a moment in an awkward silence while Frankie tuned his g string, wanting so desperately to strike up an intelligent conversation of sorts. 'Me mates call me Maize,' she blurted out, to regain his attention. 'Well they call me a lotta fings, but ar can't repeat arf of em, nart ar mean.'
Frankie had the bluest of eyes and wispy sideburns that wrapped around his face and met under his chin, not Maizie's type at all, but unbeknown to her she hadn't let go of his hand shaking it gently, jangling his tribal beaded bracelets and taking a step closer.
'MAIZE ISS COMIN!' Dee Dee then yelled, bringing her friend to her senses. 'LEAVE THE IPPY ALONE AND GET YER ARSE OVER EAR!'
'Shut up Dee!' Maizie said angrily. 'Sorry abaat er,' she told Frankie, who reluctantly pulled his hand free. 'Oh sorry!' Maizie said, blushing somewhat.
'That's quite alright,' Frankie replied, readying his guitar as the train pulled into the station.
'MAIZE!' Trisha yelled, approaching the opening doors. 'COME ON YA GONNA MISS IT!'

'Sorry ar gotta go,' Maizie said, taking Frankie's hand once again. 'Iss bin really nice talkin to ya, are you ear all the time?'

'You too,' Frankie smiled. 'And most days I'm down here, yes. Let me know what you think of the album if you would.'

'MAIZIE FOR FUCK SAKE!' Dee Dee cried, holding the doors open. 'COME ON WILL YA!'

'Ar will, course,' Maizie told Frankie over her shoulder, as she left. 'See you again yeah.'

'I'd like that!' Frankie said, strumming the intro to another of his melancholy tracks.

'Where ya bin?' Dee Dee asked Maizie, as she hopped aboard the train and the doors closed behind her.

'Talkin to that buska,' Maizie told her, slipping her disk into her pocket. 'E was really nice e was, and what a lovely voice, makes ya go all tingly it does.'

'Ar don't give a toss if ya pissed ya knickers over im,' Dee Dee said angrily. 'Me and Trish've bin oldin these poxy doors open for ya and this lot've bin moanin like fuck.' Maizie ignored the packed carriage and the disgruntled passengers looking her way as the train pulled away, she pushed her way to the window and waved at Frankie in passing.

'Looks like wunna them tree shaggers if you ask me,' Trisha laughed, looking over her shoulder. 'Scruffy bleeda.'

'You leave im alone!' Maizie warned. 'E'z really sweet e is, iz friends call im Bird apparently, nice that ain it.'

Dee Dee and Trisha burst out laughing.

'Bird!' Dee Dee said, putting an arm around Trisha. 'What the fuck's that all abaat?'

'Shut up!' Maizie yelled, shoving her friend. 'Ar fink iss nice!'

Navigating their way around the tube network the girls boarded their final train to Romford which again offered very little in the way of seating.

'Me legs ar bleedin killin me,' Maizie moaned, stepping out of her heels for a moment. A group of young Asian youths were at the end of the carriage were being particularly rowdy, jostling one another and goading their seated friend to check out the shapely girl standing in front of him who, as Dee Dee noticed, was wearing a *baby on board* badge on her lapel. The lad, no older than fifteen, sporting a bandana and baggy vest top eyed the girl's legs rubbing his crotch and gesticulating to his friends. Weighted down with shopping bags and rubbing her aching back the girl looked about the carriage but not a soul would relinquish their seat.

'Oy, cheese dick!' Dee Dee said, attracting the lad's attention. 'Why don't you get off yer arse and let the girl sit daan, ay. Can't ya see she's up the duff.'

The youth glared at Dee Dee, showing her a finger. 'Fuck you, bitch!' he said, which amused his friends greatly and had the surrounding passengers looking away fearing confrontation.

'Yeah fuck you!' one or two of his crew said from a safe distance. 'Tell er Sanjay blud.'

'You laary scrote,' Dee Dee said menacingly. 'You aint werf two bob ya chavvy little shit, look at'cha.'

This also had Sanjay's friends howling. 'She dissed you baaaaad blud!' one of them laughed, clicking his fingers together.

'Yeah, fuck that bitch up Sanj man!' another yelled.

'Yeah, yeah fuck this shit!' Sanjay said, leaping to his feet flexing what little muscle he had and sauntering toward Dee Dee, leaving one of his cackling crew to jump into the vacant seat ahead of the pregnant girl.

'If ar was you geez,' Trisha warned the advancing youth, 'ar'd back the fuck off while ya still got ya bollocks intact.'

'Go on Sanj man!' his friends said, egging him on. 'Dems only girls blud!'

Sanjay shoved one hand beneath the waistband of his jeans which hung precariously at his hips, pushing the boundaries of common decency to the very limit, sneering and brandishing a raised finger again. 'See you'z bitches,' he said, jostling his genitals. 'You'z can suck mar dick!' He then turned to acknowledge the riotous applause of his friends.

'Sanj man you'z told dem hoes blud,' one jeered, but not daring to assist in any way; neither did any of the surrounding passengers come to the girls' aid, many of them of foreign origin where chivalry was perhaps not the cultural norm.

Dee Dee towered over the scrawny youth who had foolishly assumed that women were the weaker sex and were to be treated with contempt, just as his father had treated his long suffering mother in time honored tradition.

'Gobby little prick ain e Dee,' Maizie said, looking the lad up and down.

'Don't take dat from dem Sanj!' a gang member told his friend. 'Fuck em up blud, fuck dem up bad, num sayin!' Another held his mobile phone aloft recording events to add to previous footage in which elderly passengers were tormented, and some beaten without an apparent motive.

'Yeah proper gobby,' Trisha added. 'Like ar said little man,' she told him, 'best you bugger off back to Ben Ten and the Tweenies over there before you really piss mar mate off.'

This infuriated Sanjay, and his friends for that matter. 'Who you'z callin little man?' Sanjay said, puffing out his pigeon chest and shoving Trisha. The train pulled into Seven Kings station and many of the passengers around them scurried out onto the platform and into the carriage behind, out of harm's way.

'Ar've ad enough of this shit,' Dee Dee said, lunging at the Asian assailant and grabbing him by his crotch, twisting and squeezing with ferocious intensity. 'You ad ya chance ya fuckin shitbag!' she snarled, watching the colour literally drain from his face.

'OW, OW, OW SHIT BLUD!' Sanjay squealed, as Dee Dee hoisted him up onto his toes and dragged him toward her.

'You need to learn some fuckin manners,' she told him, while the pregnant girl looked on in admiration.

'Ar warned ya,' Trisha laughed.

'Get off me bitch. OW SHIT STOP WILL YA!' Sanjay cried, looking to his friends for support, but they were doubled over laughing at their stricken friend.

'Shit Sanj man dat looks well painful blud,' a gang member said wincing and clenching his knees together.

Sanjay reached into his pocket and produced a knife. 'Ar'll cut you'z bitches!' he said, squirming in Dee Dee's hand. Many around them gasped on seeing the blade in his hand but Dee Dee was unfazed, snatching it from him in an instant she tossed it out onto the platform.

'You gettin this?' Dee Dee said, addressing the hysterical youths, several of them now filming her retaliation in high definition.

Sanjay lashed out at Dee Dee, striking her on the side of the head with his clenched fist. 'Ar said let me go bitch!' he cursed, his feet now off the ground. Maizie and Trisha looked on with a knowing smile well aware of the outcome and feeling no need to assist their friend.

'Is that all you got you cocky little cunt!' Dee Dee growled, raising the lad higher before slamming him to the floor of the carriage. In an instant she then bent down grabbing the baggy bell bottoms of his low riding jeans and whipped them from his legs with ease, leaving him squirming in his boxers. His so called friends surged forward to capture their homie for posterity.

'Gimmie Dem, gimmie dem!' Sanjay cried, reaching out with one hand over his crotch.

'Fetch, ya little fucker,' Dee Dee laughed, flinging them from the train and watching the humiliated youth scramble after; Trisha kicking his backside in passing with a flashing foot.

'You'z want some an'all!' Dee Dee snarled, now in the mood for a fight and willing to tackle them all.

'Fuck dat!' one lad cried, leaping from the train where his friend was wrestling with his jeans much to the amusement of fellow passengers. His crew collectively followed suit before the doors closed behind them, forced to abandon their journey way ahead of their destination.

'BITCH!' Sanjay raged at a smiling Dee, as the train pulled slowly away. 'YOU'Z DEAD, AR SWEAR DOWN, DEAD!'
'Thank you,' the pregnant girl said, taking the now vacant seat and stroking her stomach, 'that's very kind of you.'
'Thas alright love,' Dee Dee replied, 'you just gotta speak their language thas all.'

Alighting at Romford the girls strolled along the precinct, taking in the sights, sounds and smells of their former stomping ground, their heads filled with the fondest of childhood memories.
'Member gettin chased out of Woollies wiv our ands full of pick and mix,' Maizie laughed, recalling just one of their many narrow escapes.
'Yeah course,' Dee Dee told her. 'If ar never pelted the prat wiv me peppermint creams e woulda caught us an'all.'
'Iss still there Dee!' Trisha said, pointing out the shoe store where the three of them had worked upon leaving school. Although it was now run by Mrs Sanjeef, since divorcing her philandering husband and taking him for every penny, following a string of affairs.
'Two pies, one mash and liquor,' Dee Dee said, queuing in the famous Robins of Romford.
'Ar want stewed eels an'all,' Trisha piped up. 'If we can afford em Dee, you know ar love em.'
'Yeah ar spoze,' Dee Dee said, collecting the spoons and forks, taking her plate and sitting at one of the familiar marble topped tables.
'Corrr ar'm proper lookin forward to this,' Trisha said, joining her friends. 'Pass the vinegar Dee mate.'
Dee Dee and Maizie polished their plates clean and sat supping their orange squash, watching their friend sucking on her stewed eels, slurping the juice and generally making a pig of herself.
'Looka that Maize!' Trisha mumbled with her mouthful. 'That girl's got a Nitro tee shirt, and a matchin phone case an'all.' Her two friends looked over their shoulder to see a

fan of Maizie's brother listening to his latest album on her mobile, with liquor on her chin which her mother duly wiped whilst raising her eyebrows.

Bradley's, aka D J Nitro, musical career had gone from strength to strength in recent years; dueting with the greats and selling out stadium after stadium.

'Ar'm dying to see im,' Maizie said, having given her brother strict instructions not to visit during her incarceration. 'Gawd knows where e is right now, probly sunnin iz arse on that bloody great boat fing of iz ar bet.'

'Give im a bell!' Trisha told her friend. 'You know iz number don'tcha.'

'Yeah, yeah course ar do,' Maizie replied, pushing her plate aside. 'He's probly busy though, ar ring im later.'

'Shut up Maize,' Dee Dee said, piling the plates. 'You know you wanna talk to im so just ring the doughnut.'

Maizie took out her mobile. 'He's probly changed iz number,' she said tapping at her screen. 'Iss ringin, iss ringin!' she then said excitedly.

'Whoop de fuckin doo!' Dee Dee said with less enthusiasm.

Bradley's PA answered his phone. 'Ello!' Maizie said, bobbing on her seat. 'Who's that?'

'This is Jill Moran,' the PA replied. 'To whom am I speaking?'

'Iss Maizie!' Maizie said, giving her friends the thumbs up. 'Ar you wunna've me bruvva's tarts?'

'I beg your pardon!' Miss Moran replied, taken aback. 'Who are you and how did you get this number?'

'Iss Maizie ya melt!' Maizie insisted. 'Bradley's bleedin sister, go get me bruvva will ya.'

'I'm sorry,' Miss Moran replied from her desk. 'Mr Nitro gave strict instructions he wasn't to be disturbed, if you'd like to leave a message I'll see he gets it at his earliest convenience.'

'Earliest fuckin convenience!' Maizie cried. 'Ar'm iz pissin sister you dozy tart, now go tell im right now, coz ar promise ya e won't be appy if e finds aat you mugged me off.'

'You're his sister you say,' Miss Moran said, not having heard her mentioned but wanting to keep her highly lucrative position all the same. 'Well I suppose I could just check if he'll take the call.'
'Yeah, you go check why dont'cha,' Maizie told her, gesturing to her friends what a complete moron the PA was.
'Hold the line please,' Jill told her, scurrying from behind her desk and marching through Bradley's palatial residence to the pool house. 'Mr Nitro,' she said, tapping on the ornate gold leaf doors, 'Mr Nitrooo.' She could hear laughter and splashing in the pool from inside and tapped a little harder. 'There's a call for you Mr Nitro,' she said, raising her voice and turning the door handle. But, she then immediately gasped at the sight on the other side; Bradley was in the midst of playing pool volleyball with upwards of twenty topless cheerleaders from the Miami Dolphins, whom he had invited over after singing at the opening of the Superbowl in New Orleans a month earlier.
'JIIIIIIIL!' Bradley called from the shallow end. 'GET'CHA KIT OFF GIRL AND GET IN HERE!'
'Oh no, I really couldn't Mr Nitro,' Jill said sheepishly, tip toeing around the pool amongst the empty champagne bottles and discarded bikini tops. 'I'm sorry to disturb you sir, but there's a call for you,' she added.
'Not now Jills,' Bradley said dismissively, whilst batting the ball to a buxom redhead. 'Take a message yeah.'
'But sir it's...,' Jill said, leaping back as a wave engulfed her feet filling her polished stilettos. Bradley dived beneath the water and through the legs of several of his guests, surfacing moments later with a thong between his teeth.
'Yeah, das what ar'm talkin bout!' he said, tossing it toward his PA who side-stepped the flying underwear. 'Jill babe, whoever it is, get rid of em yeah,' he told her wiping water from his face. 'I'z bin tourin for over a year and now iss time to partaaaay, num sayin girl. So if you'z aint gonna get nekid leave me be yeah.'

'But it's your sister sir,' Jill said, avoiding another encroaching wave from the cavorting girls. 'Maizie is it?'

'MAIZIE!' Bradley cried. 'ON THE PHONE! WHY DIDN'T YOU'Z TELL ME BLUD?'

'I was trying to sir,' Jill said. 'You did say you weren't to be disturbed under any circumstances.'

'Yeah but iss me sis,' Bradley said, fending off an intoxicated hotty and climbing from the pool, swigging from a guilt glass and donning his crimson silk robe.

'Sis,' he said, taking the phone from his PA. 'Maize is dat you?'

'BRAD!' Maizie said, having waited patiently at the other end. 'Yeah Brad iss me bruv, you'll never guess where me Dee and Trish are, ar swear down you won't...'

'Banged-up aint'cha!' Bradley said, as another of his girls draped herself around him.

'We was,' Maizie replied, 'but the Amiltons got us aat, we're avin pie n mash in Rommie bruv!'

'Shut the fuck up no!' Bradley gasped. 'You'z is free!'

'Yeah, proper good ain it,' Maizie said with a brimming smile. 'Where ar ya Brad, somewhere proper nice like the Maldives ar bet.'

'Naaah sis,' Bradley said, whilst having his right ear licked. 'Ar'm in Essex babe, you know I'z always wanted me own castle yeah, well I'z bought one up norf yeah an ad it shipped daan saaf and put back togevva. Iss proper good sis, you gotta come see it.'

Bradley had indeed purchased a seventeenth century castle from an estate in Lanarkshire and paid a small fortune to have it dismantled and shipped to a fifteen acre plot of land in rural Essex, and then painstakingly rebuilt with several modern additions; the Olympic size swimming pool, ice rink and cinematic theatre to name but a few.

'I'z tell ya what,' he said, fending off a wandering hand. 'What you'z doin now?'

'Nuffing,' Maizie said, shrugging her shoulders. 'Just checkin aat the old manor.'

'Well come see me,' Bradley told his sister. 'I'z gonna send a car for ya'z, stay put yeah.'
'Yeah, deffo!' Maizie said, almost beside herself. 'Ar can't wait bruv, ar really can't.'
'Ar'll get Jills on it sis,' Bradley told his sister. 'Be good to see you'z too, tell Dee I'z still got the ragin orn for er yeah.'
'Tell er yaself bruv,' Maizie replied knowing only too well what her friend's reaction would be, having fended off Bradley's advances on more than one occasion. 'Listen bruv,' she added, 'd'you wanna make wunna your fan's day?'
'Yeah course,' Bradley replied, having one of the best rapports with his fan base in the business.
'Scooz me!' Maizie said, attracting the young girl's attention on the opposite table.
'Me,' the girl said, removing one of her headphones.
'Yeah,' Maizie smiled. 'You like Nitro do ya?'
'Like im, ar love im!' the girl said, holding her phone to her heart. 'Ar fink e'z gorgeous, ar got all iz stuff.'
'Yes, I can vouch for that,' her mother said, having shelled out hundreds of pounds on her daughter's obsession.
'D'you wanna talk to im?' Maizie asked.
'What?' the girl said with a stunned look on her face. 'Woja mean talk to im?'
'E'z mar bruvva,' Maizie smiled, 'ar got im on the phone.'
'No way!' the girl gasped. 'You aint, no ar don't believe it, no way, you aint!'
'She as,' Trisha told the girl. 'And Brad, ar mean Nitro is er bruvva.'
'Shut uuuup,' the girl cried, with her hand to her mouth. 'Shut uuuuup ar don't believe it!'
Maizie handed the frantic girl her phone. 'Go on,' she said, 'iss Nitro, say ello.'
'Shut uuup, it aint!' the girl, now trembling, said. 'Ello.'
'Yo baby girl!' Bradley said, strolling around his pool with the phone to his ear. 'Iss D J Nitro comin at'cha faaaast and furious, nart ar mean!'

'Oh mar god, oh mar god, oh mar god,' the girl said over and over, hopping up and down. 'Iss Nitro, Mum iss Nitro, oh mar god iss D J Nitro!'

'S'appnin girl?' Bradley asked, wedging the phone behind his ear and popping the cork on another bottle of vintage bubbly and kicking the ball back to his bouncing babes.

'Oh mar god!' the girl said yet again. 'E asked me woss appnin, Mum. D J Nitro asked me woss appnin. Me! Can you believe it, oh looka me ar'm shakin!'

'Well talk to im then,' her mother said, attempting to calm her ecstatic daughter.

'Oh mar god ello,' the girl said, kissing the phone. 'Ar got all your stuff D J, all of it, the duvet, the jim jams, the lunch box the lot, ar just love you so much, ar fink you're triffic ar really do!'

'Fanks baby girl, das real nice of ya,' Bradley told his adoring fan. 'Tell ya'z what, ow'z about ar send you'z back stage passes for me Glastonbury gig later dis year and a signed pillow case, I'z slept on myself yeah.'

'Oh mar god, oh mar god!' the girl shrieked. 'Yes please, oh yes please Nitro, oh mar god ar don't believe it, me arts beatin like iss gonna burst.'

'Woss ya name baby girl?' Bradley asked filling several of his guest's glasses and returning their blown kisses.

'Is Jessica!' the girl said excitedly. 'Jess for short, thas what all mar mates call me. Oh flippin ell ar can't believe ar'm actually talkin to ya.'

'Jess baby girl,' Bradley said, preparing for an impromptu rap. 'Check dis out, dis one's for you;

'Jess, Jess ar gotta confess,
Mar heart's in a spin an mar head's in a mess,
Jess Jess mar number one girl,
Number one girl coz ya rock mar world.

Rock me fast and rock me slowly,
You're mar number one girl, you're mar one an only,
Jess Jess ar gotta confess,

Mar heart's in a spin an mar head's in a mess.'

'Oh mar god, oh mar god!' Jessica cried, shaking uncontrollably with tears streaming down her face. 'E sung to me, Mum e sung to me, oh mar god!'
'Seez ya later baby girl,' Bradley told the weeping girl. 'Dem Passes are on their way yeah, wait wiv me sis and me chauffeur guy'll sort you out.'
'Thank you, thank you, thank you,' Jessica said, quivering as she handed Maizie her phone back. 'E sung a song abaat me,' she said in sheer disbelief. 'Ar gotta tell me mates,' Jessica dropped into her seat and began tapping furiously into her phone. 'Ello, Paige is that you,' she said when her best friend answered, 'you will die when ar tell ya what just appened to me, ar swear daan your gonna die.'
'Thank you,' her mother told Maizie, never having seen her daughter so overjoyed. 'I would've been the same if I'd spoken to the Bay City Rollers.'
'The who?' Trisha asked, knowing absolutely nothing of the seventies pop heartthrobs.
'Shang Alang!' Jessica's mother said, hoping the mention of one of the band's greatest hits would jog their memory.
'Naaah ya lost me love,' Dee Dee told her. 'Right Maize woss appnin?' she asked.
'We're goin to Brad's,' Maizie told her friends. 'E'z only gone and got imself a flippin castle of all fings, in Essex an'all. Well, it weren't at first but it is now.'
'What you on abaat?' Dee Dee asked. 'Is now, woja mean is now?'
'Oh ar dunno,' Maizie said, scooping a finger full of liquor from the side of Trisha's plate. 'We're goin there anyway, e'z sendin a driver bloke to pick us up, be good to see im wunnit.'
'Yeah!' Trisha said, swatting Maizie's hand from her plate. 'Ar've only ever bin to one castle, wiv the school, member Dee we got slung aat for snoggin them forf year boys in

Annie Boleyn's bed. Just fink Dee, that fing adn't seen no action since that fat fucker Enry rolled araand in it.'
'Shit don't remind me,' recalling the rampant romp with the senior boys on the sixteenth century antiquated bed. 'That mattress proper fucked mar back up, ar tell ya.'
Jessica hadn't come up for air whilst filling her friend in on her earth shattering conversation with their pin up. 'Ar couldn't believe it, ar couldn't believe it Paige onestlyyyy,' she rambled, still in a state of shock.
After another round of orange squash the door opened and Bradley's butler come driver entered. 'Miss Maizie?' he said, looking around the restaurant.
'Yeah thas me!' Maizie said, rising to her feet. 'Come on you two,' she told her friends.
'And er,' the butler added, 'is there a Miss Jessica here also?'
'Jess, Jess,' her mother said, nudging her daughter to silence her. 'This geeza wants ya.'
'Ay what?' Jessica said. 'Ang on Paige, ar call ya back,' she told her friend. 'What?' she asked again. 'Woss up?'
'Miss Jessica I presume,' Bradley's butler said, approaching her table and removing his chauffeur's hat. 'Master Nitro requested I give you this.' He handed Jessica a neatly folded silk pillow case with the words *To Jess wiv love* written on one corner. 'And this envelope.'
'For me!' Jessica squealed, cradling the pillow case and taking her back stage passes for her and a friend from the envelope. 'Oh mar god, oh mar god. Fanks, oh mar god ar gotta phone Paige!' Her mother raised her eyebrows again as her daughter dialed her friend, almost peeing herself with sheer excitement.
The girls left the ecstatic teen and her mother. 'Fanks love,' Dee Dee told the ladies behind the counter. 'Bleedin ansum that.'
Bradley's butler led the three of them back through the precinct to where his master's gleaming Bentley was parked. 'Allow me,' he said, holding open the rear door.

'Oooh fanks,' Trisha said, hopping inside and stretching out on the luxurious cream leather seat.

'Shove over,' Dee Dee told her, climbing in behind her. 'You work for Bradders then do ya?' she asked the butler, as he closed the door behind them and climbed in front.

'If you mean am I in the employ of Master Nitro young lady,' he replied as only a former Eaton scholar could, 'then yes I have been hired to run his estate and personal affairs whenever he chooses to visit his UK residence.'

'Blimey,' Maizie said, impressed to say the least. 'Me bruvva's got imself a posh nob to sort iz shit aat, ar fink thas what e means.'

'Do help yourselves to refreshments,' their driver told them, flicking a switch to release the lid of the drinks cabinet beside them.

'Fanks, woss ya name geez?' Dee Dee asked, taking three champagne flutes and a bottle of Moet from the chilled cabinet.

'Call me Spencer ma'am,' the driver replied. 'I'll be at your service during your stay.'

'Cheers Spence me old son,' Maizie said, wrestling with the champagne cork.

'A'll do it!' Trisha said, making a grab for the bottle. 'Let me, ar know ow to do em ar do.'

'No you flippin don't,' Dee Dee said, intervening. 'Ya nearly took Maizie's flippin eye aat last time ya fucked araand with wunna these ya doughnut.' Dee Dee teased the gold foil from the neck of the bottle and twisted the retaining wire ever so slightly, but Trisha's violent yanking of the bottle had shaken the contents and increased the pressure tenfold behind the cork which, without warning, burst from the bottle with a resounding pop striking Trisha point blank in the side of the head.

'OW OW ARRRRRGGGHHH YA FUCKIN SHOT ME!' she cried, clutching her head while Spencer veered across the road having ducked his own head.

'What on earth?' Spencer asked, correcting his steering and checking the rear view mirror. 'Are you alright back there?'

'NO, THE FUCKERS SHOT ME AN IT FUCKIN URTS!' Trisha squealed, rocking back and forth while her two friends fell about laughing.

'Serves ya right ya dozy mare,' Maizie giggled, 'you shook the fucker up dintcha!'

'OW ME BLEEDIN ED!' Trisha continued to moan, with a pained expression. 'Ar fink ar got a brain emridge!'

'Ya need a fuckin brain for wunna them,' Dee Dee laughed. 'Stop bloody moanin, it aint that bad.'

'Aint that bad!' Trisha cried, still rocking. 'Ar fink ya've fractured me ed bone or summink.'

Spencer reached into his glove compartment. 'I have a first aid kit if that's of any use,' he said, handing it over his shoulder. 'Is ma'am ok?'

'No ma'am aint fuckin ok!' Trisha snapped. 'Woss all this ma'am bollocks anyway, me name's Trisha ya stuck up twat!'

'OY!' Dee Dee snapped, poking her friend. 'E'z only tryna elp so don't av a pop at im, you shook the shit up. Sorry abaat that Spence.'

'That's quite alright ma'am,' Spencer replied, having heard more than his fair share of colourful language from his master of late. 'If mistress Trisha requires, I have a fine cut of fillet steak back at the estate which would help ease any swelling.'

'Fillet steak!' Maizie gasped. 'Ar wouldn't waste a two bob value burger on that dopey cow, that aint nuffing to what she's put us fru ar tell ya.'

Dee Dee tried to comfort her injured friend but with the broadest of smiles. 'Sorry mate, it just went off in me and, less ava look.'

Trisha's earlier bruises from her prison beating were now fading, but a new and equally painful contusion was now manifesting itself on her upper temple with the word Moet clearly stamped in the centre. 'Quality,' Dee Dee laughed.

'Ar got a ringin in me ear,' Trisha told her friends, shaking her head from side to side.
'Thas me phone you idiot,' Maizie told her, taking out her mobile.
'Where you at sis?' Bradley asked, reclining poolside on a lounger and having his pale scrawny body massaged by eight oil smothered hands.
'On our way bruv!' Maizie told him. 'Ya geezer come got us.'
'Spencer,' Bradley said, stroking a bikini clad bottom. 'Yeah e'z a top bloke das for sure, listen ar got some friends comin over laterz yeah for a jam, a smoke an a wicked party, num sayin sis. We'z gonna celebrate you'z gettin aat big time.'
'Fanks bruv thas proper nice of ya,' Maizie told her brother. 'We can't stay though, we gotta go work tomorra.'
'Work!' Bradley laughed. 'Shut the fuck up sis, you don't need to be doin no work shit blud.'
'Yeah we do bruv,' Maizie replied. 'Look a'rll explain when ar see ya yeah.'
Bradley set down his phone and rallied his girls. 'Yo me bitches,' he told them, 'owz abaat we go try my new Jacuzzi yeah, you'z gotta lose dem panty hoes though, num sayin.'
The willing cheerleaders wriggled out of their bikini bottoms and ran naked toward Bradley's eighteen foot heart-shaped jacuzzi, the young rapper watching their pert peach like rears as he wrenched his own boxers to the floor and scampered after them like a horny dog, leaping in amongst them then ducking below the foaming surface to tickle a fancy or two.
'YEAHHHHH!' he cried, surfacing with a mound of lather on his head. 'Dis is what ar'm talkin bout blud.'
Stacey, a stunning leggy brunette, took off an earring and purposely dropped it into the water in front of young Bradley. 'Oops,' she said, with a lustful smile and a glint in her eye. Maintaining eye contact with him she slowly submerged with absolutely no intention of searching for her missing hoop, groping for his manhood instead and wrapping her rosy lips around him.

'SHIT YEAH!' Bradley cried, squirming as one by one her girlfriends followed suit, pleasuring him to the brink of eruption. 'Oh yeah, oh yeah, das it, das it me bitches, ooh ooooh ahhhhhhhhhh.' Bradley slumped back, his knees trembling as his bathing beauties surfaced, each of them aroused and wanting more. 'Gimmie a minute yeah,' he told them, fending off their numerous advances. But his limp and lifeless member was resurrected in record time on seeing the nymphs frolicking with one another and engaging in a raunchy bisexual synchronized routine.
'Das it, ar'm back!' he cried, leaping amongst them with his bony arms outstretched.

With Trisha nursing her throbbing head the sleek limousine cruised out into the Essex countryside through villages and fields of corn stubble. 'Master Nitro's residence,' Spencer told the girls, pointing out Bradley's stately home with newly pointed ramparts and a flag fluttering overhead; one that he had specially commissioned featuring a Staffordshire bull terrier with knotted iPod headphones around its neck, in a ring of lager cans - a striking coat of arms to say the least.
'You're avin a laugh aint'cha!' Dee Dee gasped on seeing the towering castle standing stark against the skyline, dwarfing anything within a twenty mile radius.
'I assure you not ma'am,' Spencer replied, leaving the road and sweeping through a set of enormous golden gates.
'Flippin eck!' Maizie said, with her nose pushed to the glass watching teams of digger drivers tearing up the surrounding manicured lawns and ancient woodland in preparation for Bradley's colossal karting track; an ambitious project which once completed would rival the likes of Dubai, Le Mans and Silverstone. Thirty five high powered pimped up hatchbacks like that of his own beloved super nova were rolling off the production line in readiness, each equipped with the customary two hundred and forty decibel bass box, neon

under mounted strip light and colour changing LED hub caps.
The castle's former limestone statues of past kings, queens, dukes and duchesses had been tossed into a builder's skip, replaced with exquisitely chiseled replicas of Tupac, Biggy, Puffy and the like.
'E'z lost the blinkin plot ain e,' Dee Dee said, shaking her head at a grizzly bear, aptly named Pooh, pacing inside a fortified enclosure.
'E'z always ad a fing for bears,' Maizie pointed out. 'E ad this scruffy little two bob teddy when e was a baby and carried the bleedin fing everywhere he went. E was devastated when me muvva give it to the charity shop wiv me old man's tank tops, cried imself to sleep evry night till e was fifteen e did, then e discovered internet porn and that was the enda that.'
Spencer, a distant relative of the royal Spencers, circled his master's fountain; cut from the finest Italian marble it featured three nude and pouting females, the icy water cascading down their erect breasts, built of course to Bradley's own depraved specification.
'Flippin eck iss massive ain it!' Maizie said, stepping from the car. 'Cheers geez,' she told Spencer, who held open the door tipping the peak of his cap.
'My pleasure ma'am,' he replied courteously.
'Oh mar gawd,' Dee Dee said, emerging to the awesome spectacle. 'Massive aint the bleedin word mate, iss fuckin yooge, thas what it is.'
'So is the poxy lump on my ed!' Trisha moaned, joining them on the gravel drive. 'Ar bin proper JFK'd ain I.'
'Oh shutuuuup,' Dee Dee said, climbing the stone steps at the entrance.
Suddenly the huge redwood doors were thrown open and Bradley appeared wearing nothing but a towel around his narrow waist, his hair and entire body dripping and showing signs of sexual ill treatment at the hands of his lusty American guests.

'YO ME BITCHES!' he cried, arms outstretched. 'WOSS APPNIN?'
'Ar tell ya woss appnin!' Trisha raged. 'That bloody...'
'Tha bloody what?' Dee Dee snapped. 'It was your own stupid fault as usual, now stop ya bleedin whinin!'
'Yeah shutup Trish for fuck sake,' Maizie said, adding her weight. 'Ar dunno what ya moanin abaat.'
Trisha did her level best to put her point across but her two defiant friends were having none of it. 'Oh sod ya!' she eventually said, storming past Bradley. 'Got any tablits?' she asked.
'Good to see ya bruv,' Maizie said, flinging her arms around her brother's neck.
'You too sis,' Bradley replied, dripping onto his sister's shoulder. 'Deeeeee babygirrrrrrrrl!' he then cried, beckoning to Dee Dee and in doing so letting the towel slip from his hips. 'You'z bin banged up wiv dem bitches so long blud you'z must be gaggin for a bitta man meat, an I'z got dat shit right ear for ya sista, num sayin!'
Dee Dee gave his manhood a contemptful glance in passing. 'Man meat,' she sneered, 'ar'd rarva go veggie mate.'
Spencer, a closet bisexual eyed his master up and down as he ran a chamois cloth firmly over the limousines bonnet, rubbing his groin on the gleaming grill.
Bradley hastily covered himself and stepped from the puddle he had created. 'Yo me Jills!' he called, as his PA crossed the grand entrance hall to greet the girls. 'Sort dese ladies aat yeah, give em whateva day want, me got a coupla tings me need sortin, nart ar mean?'
By 'tings' Bradley meant there were one or two cheerleaders that he hadn't yet had the pleasure of, and time was of the essence as their coach was due anytime to whisk them off to the airport and home in time for the NFL playoffs.
'Right you are sir,' Jill replied, offering her hand. 'Hi, which one of you is Maizie?' she asked.

'Thas me,' Maizie said with a firm shake. 'We spoke on the phone dint we, ar fought you was wunna've iz Doris's.'
'Excuse me?' Jill replied abruptly. 'I don't know what you mean.'
'Iz fuck buddy,' Dee Dee interjected.
'Oh heavens no!' Jill said resolutely. 'Of course not, he er, he has a number of lady friends you could say, that he has intimate relations with.'
'You mean e'z shaggin em,' Trisha added, grasping fragments of her convoluted explanation.
'Quite,' Jill said, her cheeks flushed. 'I'm his personal assistant. I take care of Mr Nitro's business interests.'
'Oh riiiiight,' Maizie said, looking around. 'Where's Chantelle?'
Chantelle was Bradley's first glamour model girlfriend to throw herself at him on the eve of signing his multimillion pound recording contract.
'Chantelle left several months ago, the night after their wedding in the Caribbean in fact, taking a huge slice of his personal fortune, the villa in Tuscany and custody of their twelve Chihuahuas. Shortly after she sold her story to the tabloids for a six figure sum and I understand she's currently in the Big Brother house flirting with an aging Hollywood A lister.'
'Money grabbin whore!' Maizie said angrily. 'If I ever see er ar'll kick er fuckin teef in ar swear.'
'Ar bet e was well gutted wern e,' Trisha said, with an ice cube she had taken from the limousine to her head. 'Ar know e loved er.'
'Devastated would be a more accurate analogy,' Jill explained. 'Since she left Mr Nitro has partied harder than ever, barely sleeping a wink, living on a diet of ginger beer and cola bottles. And on the odd occasion when he does make use of his extensive recording studio, he'll be in there for days working tirelessly on, if I may say, some of his most imaginative work to date. His recent album *Hear Me Now*

has just gone double platinum in the US. Can I get you ladies a drink?'

'Got any yager?' Trisha asked.

'You ain avin no yager!' Dee Dee insisted. 'You get proper messy on that shit an a right pain in the arse an'all.'

Jill intervened. 'I was thinking more along the lines of a latte perhaps,' she told them, leading the way to the kitchen.

'Oh, woss that?' Trisha asked.

'Froffy coffee to you,' Maizie told her friend, following her brother's PA into his comprehensively equipped and spacious kitchen. 'Flippin eck!' she gasped, 'iss like that Master Chef shite ain it.'

'Not arf,' Dee Dee agreed, running her hand along the polished stainless steel work surfaces. Trisha on the other hand made straight for the enormous refrigerator, yanking open the double doors and snatching a pack of frozen prawns from the freezer section and clasping them to her pounding head, much to the annoyance of the kitchen's head chef Marcelle who was busy preparing canapés for Bradley's illustrious visitors who were due to arrive that afternoon.

'WHAT?' Trisha asked, returning his glare. 'Me ed's bangin like a shit ouse door in the wind mate, so don't even fink abaat givin me grief, alright!'

The fuming head chef belched a string of vile obscenities under his breath whilst ferociously chopping onions.

'Woss up wiv im?' Maizie asked.

'Oh don't mind Marcelle,' Jill told the girls, 'he's extremely highly strung, but passionate about his food. The man's a genius in the kitchen without a doubt, from one of the finest Parisian restaurants, I'll have you know, with no less than six Michelin stars to his name.'

'Genius my arse,' Trisha scoffed. 'You aint tasted mar liver and lemon curd cookies av ya, they're the bollocks mate, ar sent the recipe into wunna them cookry programs but never erd back from em, no doubt them airy bikers av got their feevin ands on it, ar wouldn't put it past the beardy buggers

ar tell ya.' Trisha rummaged inside the refrigerator once again. 'If ya got all the gear ar'll knock ya some up,' she said, with her backside in the air.
'Oh no, no that's quite alright!' Jill said, dreading the thought. 'I'm er, I'm a vegan you know.'
'You're a what?' Trisha asked, retrieving six eggs and a block of butter.
'A vegan,' Jill said again, 'I don't eat the flesh of animals.'
'Oh neeva do I,' Trisha said, hunting for a rolling pin. 'Or the arse oles an eyeballs neeva, so ar spoze ar must be wunna them an'all, ar do love a bitta liver though don't you.'
'No, no you don't understand,' Jill said, keen to explain her chosen doctrine.
'Save ya breff love,' Dee Dee told her, with a hand on the PA's shoulder. 'She wouldn't know a vegan from a ventriloquist the dopey cow. And believe me, you really don't wanna know what she eats, arf the shit'd choke a blinkin billy goat ar swear. Leave it Trish we ain intrested.'
'Oh but Deeeee,' Trisha whinged, 'ar faand all the gear, got a pukka lumpa liver ear an'all.'
'Liver and lemon curd,' Jill said, bringing up a small quantity of stomach acid into her mouth. 'Are you sure?'
'Oh yeah!' Trisha smiled. 'Ar chop up the liver like chocolate chips and mix it with the lemon curd, whack in a nob of butter, an andful of flour, oh and some gravy granules to ficken up the mix. Bake the buggers for arf hour and Bob's yer uncle, liver and lemon curd cookies a la Trish. Thas gotta be werf wunna them michelin fings ain it.'
'I very much doubt it,' Jill said, heading for the coffee machine, content to leave Trisha to her own devices - flouring the work surface and cracking several eggs into a bowl under the ever watchful eye of Marcelle. 'Is she always like that?' she asked Dee Dee.
'Like what?' Dee Dee replied.
'Like that,' Jill said, looking over her shoulder at a frustrated Trisha attempting to roll a sticky ball of liver infused cookie

dough flat, cursing the mix which clung to the roller and her hands for that matter.

'Retarded ya mean,' Maizie laughed. 'Yeah, yeah she is ar'm afraid.'

'Look love,' Dee Dee added, 'ar know what ya tryna say, she's mad as a boxa friggin frogs she is and you'd be bang on, yeah she's a mate of ours but ar'm tellin ya arf the bleedin time ar'd like to stick the dumb fuck in a sack and draan er.'

Jill was taken aback by Dee Dee's apparent loathing for her close friend. 'Well I'm sure she must have some redeeming qualities, for you three to remain such good friends.'

Dee Dee turned to Maizie, 'can you fink of any?' she asked.

'Nope!' Maizie said without hesitation. 'She's like a boil on the cracka my arse she is.' Maizie's colourful analogy amused the PA, as she lead the two girls on a VIP tour of Bradley's lavish home, leaving Trisha clumsily cooking up an unpalatable storm in the kitchen.

Climbing the winding stone staircase Dee Dee and Maizie marveled at the stately grandeur of the castle which had been transported from the highlands and painstakingly rebuilt at a cost of thirty six million pounds.

'The master bedroom,' Jill told them, throwing open the doors to Bradley's lavish sleeping quarters, with his vast oval bed revolving in the centre of the room surrounded by a white deep shag pile rug.

'Blimey!' Maizie said, stepping inside and setting off motion detectors which activated a thousand tiny star like spot lights in the vaulted ceiling above them.

'Iss like Willy Wonka's!' Dee Dee laughed at one of several vending machines attached to the walls, offering a vast array of confectionary, drinks and flavored sexual protection. The room was indeed every alpha male's dream with foosball, air hockey and video arcade games of all description.

'Is there anyfing me bruvva aint got?' Maizie asked, toying with the remote to his ninety six inch 3D screen.

'One or two things,' Jill explained. 'But I'm working on those. Mr Nitro is a must have kinda guy and why shouldn't he be, he has amassed a personal fortune that puts most global artists of the day to shame, to put it bluntly, he's earning it way faster than he could ever spend it.'

'Bloody Nora!' Maizie gasped. 'Ar knew e was popular but Jesus e'z a bleedin megastar ain e.'

'You could say that yes,' Jill said proudly. 'He has a great team behind him, myself included.'

'Woss wiv the poxy bear?' Dee Dee asked, gazing at the hulking beast from the window. 'Saands like e'z gone a bit whacko Jacko if you ask me.'

Jill joined her. 'Just one of his many eccentricities,' she said, raising an eyebrow. 'Only yesterday he asked if I could arrange to have the Moscow state circus visit, along with several members of the Korean women's Olympic gymnastic squad, in gym slips of course.'

'E'z off iz bleedin trolley,' Dee Dee sneered. 'Thas just ridiculous that is.'

'Nevertheless,' Jill said, straightening one of the many framed platinum discs on the wall, 'they arrive in the morning. Mr Nitro had me charter three private 747s to collect them from Zagreb and Chungnam. The circus will leave on Monday but the gymnasts, he hopes, will stay a little longer.'

'Ar bet e bleedin does,' Maizie said, knowing her brother only too well.

While Jill showed Dee Dee and Maizie around the opulent first and second floors, Trisha was growing increasingly frustrated with her stubborn and sticky cookie dough, which adhered itself to just about everything within arm's reach.

'Excuse me,' one of Marcelle's assistants said, in a bid to end the farcical spectacle. 'If you don't mind me saying, you may find it a little easier if you flour your roller.'

'What?' Trisha snapped, having obliterated the electric blender. 'Yeah ar do mind ya sayin actually, ar bin bakin these cookies since you was a tadpole in yer old man's nut

sack, so do me a favour and jog the fuck on.' The assistant turned tail and left Trisha flicking the putty like mix from her fingers and, of course, reaching for the flour.
Marcelle by this time had seen enough and after a volley of Parisian abuse he too left, hurling his pinny into the kitchen sink in a fit of rage.
'Yeah whatevaaaa!' Trisha said defiantly. 'Speak English ya froggy fuck!' With the help of the flour, Trisha soon got a handle on her cookie dough, smiling and puffing out her chest whilst cutting random freehand shapes and placing them on a baking tray; becoming ever more flamboyant in her technique, going so far as to frost her creations with icing sugar before popping them into one of the kitchen's three fan assisted ovens. Leaving her work station looking like a culinary crime scene, Trisha scrubbed the residue from her hands and under her fingernails and hacked a tangled portion from her hair using the closest thing to hand, a pizza cutter. 'Sorted!' she finally sighed, leaving to join her friends. 'DEEEEEEE, MAAAAAAAIZE!' she called out in the entrance hall. 'WHERE ARE YA?'
'UP EAR!' Maizie replied, leaning over the banister on the third floor. 'YOU WANNA SEE SUMMA THE SHIT ME BRUVVA'S GOT IMSELF!'
'ANG ON, AR'M COMIN UP!' Trisha replied, taking the stairs two at a time at an awkward jaunt, pausing at the first floor to catch her breath.
'Oh shit,' Dee Dee sighed, having relished their brief separation.
'Shit ar'm shagged,' Trisha puffed, bent over wheezing. 'Ar gotta get more bleedin exercise.' Eventually trudging the final flight clinging to the banister she met Jill and her friends outside Bradley's favorite room of all.
'This is where Mr Nitro likes to unwind, so to speak,' Jill told the girls who followed her into Bradley's *womb room*, as he called it.
'Bloody Nora!' Maizie gasped, yet again taken aback by its unconventional appearance. The entire thirty by thirty room

had been painted a stark matt black, complete with black carpet and accompanying furniture; in fact the room and its contents were completely devoid of any other colour but black. It had been commissioned for Bradley by the controversial Belgian designer Phillipe Cantrelle who believed the room symbolized a return to the mother's womb, a calm and tranquil environment free from the rigors and corruption of the outside world. The ceiling and a large portion of the roof above had been removed and a single toughened sheet of glass set in its place. This was no ordinary glass though, it was purchased from the NASA space program and was constructed to give the viewer fifteen times magnification, turning Bradley's bolt hole into a state of the art observatory come night fall, with Orion's Belt, the rings of Saturn and the entire Milky Way clearly visible with the naked eye. Self-tinting in direct sunlight too, the glass cost the young rapper a staggering three quarters of a million pounds, a small fortune to most but merely pocket change to Bradley. In the centre of the room sat his custom built chill-out chair, fashioned in black Kevlar this was no ordinary piece of furniture, weighing in at a colossal ton and a half the recliner comprised of no less than eight surround sound speakers hooked up to a gloss black Dolby stereo system loaded with the sounds of migrating humpback whales and the mating call of a newly discovered Patagonian toad - considered by those in the know to be as hypnotic as the Sirens of Greek mythology, who lured passing sailors and their vessels to shipwreck with their haunting cries.

'Woss this for?' Trisha asked, hopping into the chair and laying back gripping the arm rests. 'Is this where e gets iz barnet cut?' She began tinkering with the control console mounted beside her. 'Shit, ava look!' she said, as a drawer slid open containing some fifty or so pre rolled marijuana joints, as fat as her thumb and twice the length. 'Fuck me, ar knew e liked a dooby,' she said, fingering the stash, 'but these fings are fuckin torpedoes. Look at em.'

'Purely recreational you understand,' Jill said, closing the drawer. 'Shall we press on?'

Bradley was now out front seeing his departing guests to their coach, each of them dressed in matching figure complementing pale blue lycra, dragging their hand luggage and clutching a tiny crimson ribboned box containing a bejeweled Cartier bracelet, a farewell gift from their horny host. Receiving a tongue probing kiss from each and every one of them, under the watchful and envious eyes of the beavering digger drivers, Bradley then watched their firm and rotund rears climb the steps and take their seats. The ever grateful girls were waving and blowing sensual kisses to the rapper, standing in his baggy Y fronts, and planning a hasty return as bunnies in his very own playboy mansion.

Leaving Bradley's eccentric man cave Jill escorted the girls back down the winding castle staircase.

'Ar feel like a Princess,' Trisha said, attempting to walk sedately with her nose in the air.

'Well you look like a freak,' Maizie laughed.

'Oh shutup!' Trisha said frowning. 'Ar might get meself wunna these gaffs when me gastric pants kick off.'

'Don't old ya breff,' Dee Dee smirked, 'you'll be lucky if you get a tenner an a two man tent.' Maizie burst out laughing at this.

'Ar tell ya what!' Trisha snapped. 'You'z two aint got no bleedin faif in me av ya, ar bin told ar got a good ed for business I av.'

'My arse you av,' Dee Dee said with a dismissive tone.

Trisha raised a rigid finger and was about to retaliate when Bradley appeared at the bottom of the stairs dressed from head to toe in white top hat and tails, carrying an ivory cane and sporting a pair of polished white snakeskin boots.

'Fuck me!' Dee Dee laughed. 'Iss the Pillsbury Doughboy!'

'Woss appnin niggas?' Bradley chirped, tipping his velour hat. 'Wod'ya fink of me crib, iss proper righteous blud ain it?'

'Yeah iss well nice bruv,' Maizie said, descending to join him. 'Ar can't believe you got all this from ya rappin.'
'What can ar'z say,' Bradley said proudly. 'De bitches dig me, de hoes dig me, even the President of the United States digs mar shit. Fanks Jills babe,' he then told his PA, 'go chase up dem gym girls will ya, and tell em to shave der pits yeah coz I'z know what dem Rusky tarts is like.'
'Right you are sir,' Jill said, heading for her office with Bradley leering after her.
'Wunna dese days yeah blud, I'z gonna ram raid dat milf I'z tellin ya,' Bradley began humping his cane with little regard for his guests. 'Mmmm, mmm, mmm, mm, oh yeah bitch, you gonna get yourself some papa's gooooood lovin.'
'Oy, cheese dick!' Dee Dee said, shoving Bradley. 'We aint come ear to watch you jizzin on ya stick.'
'Oh, yeah,' Bradley said, snapping out of his sadistic daydream. 'Listen, ar got someone you'z ar gonna wanna meet yeah, diss way.' Bradley lead the girls through the castle's ancient corridors, now gayly coloured with images of his favorite childhood Marvel heroes pinned to the walls. Bradley had truly transformed every square inch of the once mighty fortress - where it is believed that Robert the Bruce, King of Scots himself, resided during his reign plotting the now legendary war of independence against the English.
Stepping out into the rear garden Bradley proudly displayed his enormous Olympic size swimming pool, complete with high board.
'Flippin eck!' Maizie gasped, gazing up at the battlements high above them. 'This is some gaff bruv ain it?'
'Yeah, but ya know what sis,' Bradley said, taking a minute to survey his property. 'I aint dat keen on it ya know, so I'z gettin Ronnie and Pete from the old manor to come pebble dash de place for me next week, dat shit's proper class ain it, wod'ya reckon?'
'Proper council,' Dee Dee smirked.

'What about that plastic claddin gear?' Trisha said, offering her opinion. 'Me nan's got it on er aatside shit ouse, it looks the bollocks ar tell ya.'
'Shut up you melt!' Dee Dee said, disregarding Trisha's idea with utter contempt and strolling poolside.
'Diss way, diss way!' Bradley said, heading for the pool house, itself larger than the average three bedroom semi. From several meters away Bradley and the girls could hear the sound of music being played at a deafening number of decibels from within the pool house.
'What the fuck?' Dee Dee laughed, catching one or two of the sexually suggestive lyrics. 'Bradley ya nob, is that you?'
'Yeah course blud!' Bradley said, swinging his cane and grabbing at his crotch in preparation for a live performance. 'Iss called treesome innit, check this shit blud.'

'Yo bitch hows about a date,
Hows about a treesome wid you and your mate,
Ar want you bofe, ar wanna be between ya,
Ar've had this bone ever since ar seen ya,
You, me and ya mate makes tree,
One on mar face and one on mar knee.
Hows about a treesome ar'm ready an waitin,
Tonight dere'll be no hesitatin,
Num sayin blud!'

'Yo bitch ar wanna be ya mista,
Hows about a treesome wid you and your sista,
A bottle a Jack an a game a twista,
Twista twista ar wanna be your mista,
Hows about a treesome wid you and your sista,
Come on bitch I'z ready an waitin,
If you'z iz angels den ar'm your Satan,
Tonight dere'll be no, hesitatin.'

'Come on bitch ar hear you'z holla,
You'z want mar dick and ya want mar dollar,

Treesome, treesome I'z gaggin for a treesome,
Don't ask why coz ar got no reason,
So come on bitch hows about a date,
Hows about a treesome wiv you and your mate,
Come on bitch ar wanna be your mista,
Hows about a treesome wid you and your sista,
Come on bitch don't keep me waitin,
Tonight dere'll be no hesitatin,
Num sayin blud!'

'Ar watch it all alone dat treesome porn,
Ar've had diss bone ever since ar was born,
Ar'm gaggin for a treesome so much ar can taste it,
Ar got diss bone iss a shame to waste it,
So come on bitch hows about a date,
Hows about a treesome wid you and your mate.
Come on bitch ar wanna be your mista,
Hows about a treesome wid you and your sista,
Treesome treesome I'z gaggin for a treesome,
Num sayin blud
Num sayin!!!'

'Like ar said,' Dee Dee reiterated. 'What the fuck?'
'Ar like it!' Trisha squealed. 'Minds me of a freesome I ad wiv a coupla lezzbos in Miami, proper naughty they was an'all, ar fought ar knew all that dyke shit but them girls ad me trussed up like a chicken in a bin liner wiv a tangerine up me bum ole and me noo noo wired up to a twelve volt battry.'
'Shut uuuuup,' Maizie said in disbelief. 'You kinky bastard.'
'Don't knock it till ya tried it,' Trisha said, defending her debauched encounter.
'Tried it!' Dee Dee exclaimed wide eyed. 'Oh yeah course we av, only a coupla days ago Maizie rammed the rough end of a pineapple up me poopa and connected me knockers to the national fuckin grid!'
'Urrrrgh Deeee,' Maizie winced, 'thas disgustin!'

Snapping out of their conversation Bradley rapped on the pool house door with the head of his cane. 'YO ME BREDRIN!' he called out. 'WOSS APPNIN HOMIE?'
It was then that an all too familiar voice yelled out in reply. 'JOG THE FUCK ON WILL YA BRADDERS MATE, AR'M GETTIN ME NUTS IN!'
'Fuck me thas Terry,' Trisha said, turning the handle and shoving the pool house door open in time to see their good friend West Ham Terry in a shocking pink mankini with Bradley's head housekeeper Gloria. Gloria, a thirty two stone West Indian, was bent over before him, her gargantuan breasts swaying at her knees.
'Shit, shit Trish!' Terry cried, whipping himself out and darting behind the sofa to conceal his lower half. 'What the fuck. What you doin ear?' he asked, panting breathlessly, his body heavily marked from Gloria's grappling hands. 'Ar mean, ar knew you was aat, but ar weren't expectin ya thas all.'
Gloria hastily crammed her blubbersome breasts back inside her bra on seeing her lord and master at the door. 'I'z sorry Mister Bradley,' she cried, gathering up her uniform and tugging her rope-like thong up over her mountainous rear, that too showing the battle scars inflicted by the palm of Terry's right hand. 'I'z sorry, surely I iz Mister Bradley sir,' she said. Barging past the girls and almost knocking them from their feet, the Haitian house maid waddled as fast as her bloated legs could carry her back to her quarters.
'Tel blud, woss appnin?' Bradley asked, aghast to say the least at Terry's choice of conquest, having offered him the pick of his vivacious visiting cheerleaders. But Terry's tastes for the more curvaceous female forms had lead him on many occasions into the gelatinous arms of the morbidly obese - one or two of them house bound and bed ridden and needing the assistance of a hydraulic winch to raise their hulking frame onto their bent and buckled bed pans. But he loved them, every inch and yard of them, diving into

their cavernous creases with wanton desire and a lustful glint in his roving eye.
'Iss not what ya fink geez,' Terry said, pulling on his shirt and yanking the boxers from his ankles.
'Oh give over Tel,' Dee Dee laughed, 'you was angin aat the back end of er ya pervy fuck.'
'Deeee mate iss good to see ya,' Terry said in an attempt to mask his obvious embarrassment. 'Ar fought you'z was in for at least anuvva five.'
'The Amiltons got us aat,' Maizie told him, peering behind the couch at his lily white legs, 'cozza what we done for Crystal and them. Anyway what you doin ear?
'Ar'm still on the run ain I,' Terry explained. 'Pritcher was beatin every door daan back ome, so Brad offered to put me up, din'tcha mate?'
'Yeah, course Tel,' Bradley said, spinning his cane in his fingers. 'You'z me bredrin ain'tcha, mar crib is your crib, num sayin blud!'
Dee Dee raised her eyebrows at Bradley's constant street speak. 'Give me fuckin strenf,' she sighed. 'Got any booze Tel?' she asked, dropping onto his sofa, as did Maizie and Trisha.
Terry gave Trisha's Thomas trainers a sideways glance, but under the circumstances chose to say nothing. 'Does the Pope wear a dopey at,' he said, heading for his kitchenette. 'Ar got Tenants, Stella or easy rider. Wod'ya fancy?'
'Ar'll av a cider Tel,' Trisha said. 'What you avin Brad?'
'Nuttin for me yeah, fanks,' Bradley replied, hovering at the door. 'I'z got some VIPs comin over, we gonna jam and lay down a track for some good cause bullshit, num sayin?'
'Yes you melt!' Dee Dee said, snatching a can of cider from Terry. 'We num what ya bloody sayin. Whatever the fuck that means.'
'Ar'll av a Stella please Tel mate,' Maizie piped up. 'Cider gives me the shits summink chronic.'
'Me bruvva in law makes iz own cider,' Trisha told her friends, taking a tinny from Terry. 'E puts a shit loada bashed

up Cox's orange pippins in the barf, two tona sugar an a dead cat.'

Dee Dee and Maizie by now would have usually switched off, but Trisha's outlandish tale had them hooked from the onset.

'A dead fuckin cat!' Dee Dee said, opening her can which sprayed across the rug at their feet.

'Yeah, a ginger one,' Trisha continued. 'E left it in the barf for a mumf an arf till it was proper rank, well it wern as if im an Michaela used the poxy fing the soapy paira bleedas. Ritchie even ad a ring raand iz neck and gawd knows what under iz finger nails on iz weddin day the dirty sod. Anyway where was I?'

'Er, the dead ginger cat in the bloody barf!' Maizie reminded her.

'Oh yeah,' Trisha laughed. 'Course, when the gear ad a rancid ed on it e strained it fru a string vest, filled up shit loadsa fruit shoot bottles and flogged em to the kids on the estate for a pop. A coupla swigs and the little scrotes was off their tits ar tell ya.'

'Trish!' Maizie said, wiping the neck of her can with her sleeve before tugging the ring. 'What the bleedin ella you on ay?'

While Maizie and Trisha squabbled amongst themselves, Dee Dee filled Terry in on their Holloway antics.

'Kaffy Bennett!' Terry said, opening a second can having drained the first in two gulping mouthfuls. 'Yeah ar've earda that bitch, used to run a little firm outta Befnal Green. Small time shit though, runnin a bitta weed across the channel, coupla bettin office blags ear and there and leanin on the Bangladeshi's for protection. Proper nasty Doris from what ar've eard. You'za got some bollocks takin er daan ar give ya that.'

'Well,' Trisha said, leaning into the conversation. 'Ar weren't takin none of er shit ar tell ya, ar don't give a toss who she is.'

'Shut up you melt,' Maizie laughed. 'She beat the fuck outta ya.'
'Yeah but...,' Trisha sulked.
'Yeah but, nuffin!' Dee Dee added, taking Maizie's side as she often did. 'If you adn't got er poxy back up in the first place, ar wouldn't av ad to save your dopey arse would I?'
'Oh!' Trisha said, sitting upright. 'So iss mar fault is it?'
'Yes!' her friends replied adamantly. 'Iss always your bleedin fault!'
Terry could contain his curiosity no longer at this point. 'Trish mate ar gotta ask, woss wiv the Thomas the tanks?'
'Ay? Oh these?' Trisha replied, swinging her feet. 'Good aint they?'
'Your avin a bubble aint'cha!' Terry chuckled. 'What are you,' he asked Dee Dee and Maizie, 'er full time carers or summink?'
'Tell me abaat it,' Dee Dee scoffed, 'iss a full time fuckin job ar tell ya, look at er, she's as daft as a boxa bleedin Christmas tree lights.'
Whilst Trisha headed for the refrigerator for a second can, unfazed by her friends scathing remarks, Maizie peered from the window. 'Who's that lot?' she asked, seeing two silver limousines and three coaches pull into Bradley's drive.
'Ar dunno mate,' Terry said, joining her and shoving his venetian blind to the side. 'Bradders did say summink abaat recording a new track fing wiv a coupla mates. Could be anyone doll, a coupla days ago we ad Suzie Boyle ear poncin a Nitro sample for er new album.'
'Can we go see Dee!' Trisha asked, dashing to the window. 'Oh come on Dee ar like Suzie Boyle.'
'You are a pissin boil!' Dee Dee growled. 'On the cracka my bleedin arse.'
'Oh shutuuup,' Trisha smiled, craning her neck as the cars and coaches disappeared out of sight. 'Can we, can we go see, pleeeeeeease Dee?'
'Oh for fuck sake alright!' Dee Dee said, knowing there would be absolutely no peace until Trisha had her way. 'But

ar'm tellin ya if it is Suzie flippin Boyle ar'm comin straight back alright!'

With Terry in tow the girls left his bolt hole and made their way back inside Bradley's regal residence, where teams of technicians were scurrying about the place wheeling large black tour boxes toward the great hall and laying mile upon mile of sound and lighting cables.

'Scuze me!' Trisha said, stopping a young musician wheeling a giant harp. 'Is it Suzie Boyle? I ope it is coz she minds me of me auntie Pat, big old lump she was wiv fat rosy cheeks an a bowel disorder.'

'I'm sorry, I beg your pardon?' the young lady replied, buckling under the weight of her instrument. 'Suzie who?'

Before Trisha could elaborate the red faced harpist was ushered along by her conductor. 'Hurry girl,' he snapped, taking one end of her harp. 'Quickly. Quickly now.'

'Can we watch geez?' Maizie asked, trailing behind. 'Brad's me bruvva.'

'Yes yes,' the conductor puffed. 'But I cannot stress enough the need for absolute silence, this is a live recording after all.'

'Don't worry we'll keep shtum geez,' Dee Dee said, holding the door open for Trisha. 'Won't we!' she said, looking her friend in the eye.

'Oh yeah,' Trisha agreed. 'Even if I av to old me breff, ar done it under water for free minutes daan the lido once for a dare, ar coulda done longer ar reckon but the piss was stingin me eyes.'

Dee Dee and her three friends shuffled inside and took a seat at the back, watching the entire Royal Philharmonic Orchestra take up their positions and fine tune their gleaming instruments.

'Bloody Nora!' Trisha whispered. 'Bit posh ain it.'

Bradley appeared shortly after, having changed from his white top hat and tails to one of shimmering gold. 'Is Suzie Boyle ear?' Trisha asked expectantly.

'Trisha!' Dee Dee snapped. 'Will you shut the fuck up abaat Suzie soddin Boyle, you're doin mar bloody swede in!'
'Nah blud,' Bradley laughed. 'Suzie B was ear de uvva day, ar spit the bitch a rhyme for a quarter of a mill an a fifty fifty split on da sales yeah. Nah today we'z doin a track for dat Amnesty charity fing, me and me new homie's mar main man Elton and me booty bitch Mariah.'
'Shut the fuck up!' Dee Dee gasped. 'You mean you're singin wiv Mariah and Elton, ear today?'
'Yeah course blud,' Bradley smiled. 'Well I'z rappin innit, dem two's doin de singin shit.' Bradley had been coerced into collaborating with the two recording megastars to highlight Amnesty International's heroic efforts to free the countless so called prisoners of conscience held captive around the world by tyrannical governments, many charged with high treason when in fact their only crime was to have spoken out and opposed the often brutal torturous regimes.
'We'z got an orchestra an everyfing sis, how cool iz dat?'
Dee Dee and her friends looked over Bradley's shoulder in the hopes of catching an early glimpse of the visiting A-listers. 'Where are they then?' she asked impatiently.
'Who?' Bradley replied, mulling over his forth coming rap.
'Marge n Omer Simpson ya melt!' Dee Dee said sarcastically, rolling her eyes. 'Who'dya bleedin fink?'
'Oh Elton n Mariah,' Bradley laughed, 'dems in da green room wiv a bottla Hennessy warmin up and shit.'
Three further coaches had recently arrived carrying one hundred and fifty gospel singers, part of the world renowned Sister Petunia tabernacle choir hailing from Memphis Tennessee. Dressed in long black matching robes, their hair shimmering with coconut oil, they each clutched a tall white candle as they filed into the hall and took up their place opposite the seated orchestra.
'Flippin eck!' Trisha gasped. 'This is some serious shit ain it.'
The visual director then approached Bradley. 'We're ready for you now Mr Nitro,' he said, whilst receiving directorial instruction through his ear piece. 'FIVE MINUTES LADIES

AND GENTLEMEN, FIVE MINUTES!' he yelled, silencing the gathering. 'CUE SMOKE. LIGHTS!'

The orchestra conductor tapped his baton three times on his music stand to ready his musicians and stood poised.

Bradley stood in the centre of his stage head bowed, cane in hand, with wisps of white smoke billowing around his torso.

The sound engineer raised his right hand. 'We go in five... four...,' he said, then silently gesturing the final three numbers, which was the cue for the cameras to begin rolling and the orchestra's percussion section to burst into life with a thunderous drum roll.

'YO CHECK DISS!' Bradley yelled, snatching the microphone with a confident sneer. 'LISTEN UP YEAH, I'Z ABOUT TO LAY SOME SERIOUS SHIT ON YA'Z!'

The girls were on the edge of their seats, never having witnessed such a spectacle with the illustrious Philharmonic to their right and the hordes of gospel choristers to their left.

Bradley gave his scrotum his trademark jostle before opening the track entitled *Your Voice,* which he himself had penned in permanent marker on the bonnet of his beloved Bugatti; the one of a kind super car was then gifted to the amnesty organization to be auctioned, and the proceeds used in their fight against global injustice. The wind and string orchestral sections then accompanied the drums and suddenly all eyes were on the young snarling rapper enshrouded in smoke, and then it began...

'I aint gonna spit about racial tension,
Ar'll tell you da shit da uvvas won't mention,
Issa crime against humanity,
Dat borders on insanity.
Iss rough enough for one so tough,
To comprehend da gravity,
Issa a certain kinda nonsense,
To be caged for your conscience,

Someday we'll be together

Set dem free, set dem free, set dem freeeee.'

'Day say what you believe ins,
Worse dan robbery an feevin,
To speak your mind is so unkind,
But who are day deceivin.
Iss your opinion dat day fear,
So day make you disappear.
Set dem free, set dem free, set dem freeeee.'

'Sittin on da floor of a nine by four,
Twenny four, twenny four, twenny four.
Chained like a dog and for what, for what
Beaten and flogged and forgot, forgot!
Taken in da night it aint right deres no reason.
We're gonna fight, fight for your freedom.
We're gonna fight coz dere aint no reason,
We're gonna fight, fight for your freedom.'

Clenching his cane and punching the air triumphantly Bradley took a step back, it was then and only then that Elton and Mariah appeared hand in hand, also dressed in white. Clasping their mic's they began belting out the rousing chorus as only they knew how, with the gospel choir humming and repeating every line in synchronized harmony....

'We are your voiiiiice, we rise and we will staaaaand,
We are your voiiiiice, together hand in haaaaand,
And we're tearing down the wirrrrre,
We're putting out the firrrrre,
We are here behind you,
To break the chains that bind you,
And set you free, set you free, set you freeeee.
We are your voiiiiice,
Together hand in haaaaand,

Someday we'll be together

We are your voiiiiice,
We'll rise and we will staaaaand.
WE ARE YOUR VOIIIIICE,
WE ARE YOUR VOIIIICE,
WE ARE YOUR VOIIIIIIIIICE!'

Bradley then stood shoulder to shoulder with the two musical giants, beat boxing as they repeated the chorus not once, but three times, rattling the leaded windows in their frames with all one hundred and fifty choral singers looking to the heavens and belting out those immortal words;

'WE ARE YOUR VOIIIIIIIIICE,
WE ARE YOUR VOIIIIIIIIICE,
WE ARE YOUR VOIIIIIIIIIIIIIIICE!'

Bradley hurled his top hat into the air. 'DASS WHAT AR'M TALKIN BOUT. GIVE IT UP FOR MAR MAIN MAN ELTON AND MAR LADY BITCH MARIAAAAAAAAAAH. COME ON SHOW DEM SOME LOVE, NUM SAYIN?'

Bradley turned to Elton hugging him tightly as the great hall erupted in tumultuous applause. 'Das some powerful shit bruv,' he said, giving Mariah the thumbs up. 'Nice one princess,' he told her. Bradley and his co stars then took a unified bow before the cameras ceased rolling.

'Wonderful darlings!' the floor manager squealed, slapping at his clipboard 'That was simply divine!'

'Yeah man, that was the bollocks blud!' Bradley yelled, turning every head in the great hall.

Trisha and her two friends also stood in awe, honored at having been privy to the making of a musical masterpiece. 'Fuckin awesome!' Dee Dee was forced to admit.

Maizie stood clapping frantically with the broadest of smiles, raising her fingers to her mouth to let out a periodic piercing whistle. 'BLOODY ELL BRUV!' she cried proudly. 'THAT WAS BRILLIANT!'

As the trio on stage hugged and returned the orchestra and choir's applause, Terry raced to Mariah's aid, helping her down the steps stage left. 'Alright Maz ar gotcha,' he said

with an arm around her waist whilst eyeing her bountiful curves.
'Why thank you,' she replied courteously. 'Thank you so much.'
'Thas alright babe, no worries,' Terry smiled, pouring his own inimitable charm.
'Sorry I didn't catch your name,' Mariah said, offering her hand. 'I'm Mariah.'
'No shit!' Terry laughed. 'Ar know who the fuck you are girl, me ex misses loved all your shit she did. Mind you she loved a lotta fings an a big black cock was one of em, the dirty two timin cunt, pardon me French.'
Mariah was taken aback by Terry's bitter hatred toward his long term girlfriend Cindy, whom he'd met and fallen big time for at the Dagenham and Redbridge centre for sexually transmitted diseases during his annual venereal scrape. 'West Am Tel,' he said, shaking her hand with a builder's grip. 'Ar'm surprised you ain erd'a me.'
'West Am Tel?' Mariah said, shaking her head. 'No, no I can't say that I have. Are you a friend of Nitro's?'
'Who?' Terry asked, hoisting up his waistband.
'DJ Nitro,' Mariah reiterated, pointing toward her co star.
'Oh Bradders, yeah course,' Terry smiled. 'E's an old china plate a mine. Fuck me yeah, we go way back, e used to sell a bitta puff for me on the estate, now look at him the little shit's minted.'
Mariah attempted to break away, realizing the two of them were professionally and intellectually worlds apart. 'I'm sorry I really do have to be getting along,' she told him, eager to distance herself.
'Listen, old up!' Terry said, making a grab for her wrist. 'Ar bin finkin, ar got me own rap ya know, owsabaat you and me doin a little duvet duet togevva?'
'Oh really, you're an artist too?' Mariah said changing her tone, and keen to boost her flagging UK sales. 'Are you big in Great Britain?'

'Big! Ar'm fuckin massive love,' Terry boasted. 'I aint too sad in the traazer department neeva.'

'So you'd like to collaborate?' Mariah asked, leaning a little closer.

'Woss that?' Terry replied. 'Saands proper naughty to me, ar'll give anyfing a go, but less get one fing straight, I ain avin nuffin up the Gary Glitter alright!'

'I meant the two of us working together,' Mariah said, although if it meant pipping her bitter rivals to the coveted number one slot then she wouldn't be adverse to a little flirtatious liaison, in the name of business of course.

'Yeah, thas what ar meant an'all,' Terry said, lying through his recently whitened teeth. 'Ar tell ya what, ar got a vintage bottla Blue Nun back at mar gaff, wod'ya say me and you go back and er, collaborate or summink.'

Terry's silver tongue had coerced countless conquests to his bed chamber, many of them hesitant or even unwilling at first, but a glass and a half of cheap plonk would more often than not soothe the savage beast, and with a little help also from his coveted Barry White cd - or the knicker dropper as he liked to call it - this age old combo had stood Terry in good stead over the years, notching up a staggering six hundred and fifty women on disc one alone.

'Laters girls yeah,' he said, passing Dee Dee and friends with a snake like arm around Mariah's midriff and that look in his roving eye.

Dee Dee and Maizie stood aghast at his laddish audacity, whilst Trisha curtsied at the pop diva who paused looking down at her garish footwear. 'Oh you poor thing,' she said. Assuming Trisha was mentally deficient in some way and wanting to make a charitable gesture, she raised Trisha's chin with an exquisitely manicured finger and looked her in the eye. 'A pretty little thing like you should wear couture my darling,' she said, beckoning to her assistant. 'Tamara, my shoes please. Size five am I right?' she said, hazarding a guess.

'Yeah miss, yeah I am,' Trisha smiled. 'We all got little feet in our famly, iss me great grandad's fault, e ad a low sperm count apparently, iss a miracle me great nan ad any kids at all from what ar've erd, e tried everyfing goin e did, ipnosis, acupuncture, leaches the lot. But if god only give ya two tadpoles in a ball bag fulla blanks ya fightin a losin battle aint'cha.'

Mariah's breathless assistant appeared carrying a designer travel case. 'Thank you Tamara honey,' the sultry singer said, flicking the catch and opening the case to reveal several pairs of stunning stilettos. 'Take your pick my dear,' she told Trisha, displaying her shoes, none of which were purchased for less than five thousand dollars.

'Corrrr, fanks!' Trisha shrieked, kicking off her flashing pumps and plucking a pair covered completely in tiny pink Swarovski diamonds. 'These are a bitta me,' she smiled.

'Fuck me,' Dee Dee smirked, 'ar fought the Thomas the tanks were laary.' Indeed the dazzling designer one-offs would undoubtedly bring far more attention than her former fashion faux pas.

'Oh shut up, ar love em,' Trisha said, slipping her feet in. 'Ow much are they?'

'No, no they are a gift,' Mariah said, handing back the case and dismissing Tamara. 'You have a very good eye, those are my favorite too.'

'Yeah whatever,' Terry said, eager to get the diva alone. 'Come on girl we gotta do summa that collaboratin shit.'

'What,' Maizie asked, 'woss e on abaat?'

'Mr Am Tel and I,' Mariah replied, 'are going to combine our musical minds and thrash out a track for my forthcoming album.'

'West Am Tel ya spanner!' Terry laughed. 'And yeah, we're gonna proper frash one aat, nart ar mean.'

'Ar bet'chu are ya filfy fucker,' Dee Dee said, well aware of Terry's clandestine intentions.

'You're so lucky,' Mariah told the girls, 'being surrounded by such creativity and talent. I mean, Mr Am Tel, sorry I mean

Mr West Am Tel, has been telling me all about his meteoric rise to fame and his plans for a nationwide tour.'

'Ave ya now?' Dee Dee asked Terry, who replied with a sly wink.

'Well, well yeah course,' he said semi confidently, 'ar fought ar'd start at the Flyin Orse, then maybe the Phantom and Firkin and finish at the Dirty Bishop.'

Mariah of course assumed these crass back street venues were world renowned stadia with colossal crowd capacities where the likes of Bon Jovi, U2 and Oasis may have strutted their stuff.

'Blimey!' Maizie said sarcastically. 'Let me know when ya playin the Firkin won'tcha, me uncle Eddie's got an ot dog stand on the corner ar'll tell im to get an extra arf dozen buns in.'

'Yeah,' Dee Dee laughed, 'it'll be like the Chuckle Bruvva's playin Wembley Arena with two tramps and a pissed off ticket tout in the audience.'

'Oy!' Terry snapped. 'Don't get lemon Dee, ar'm workin on a new rap thas gonna make me bundles you watch. Iss called "what ar wouldn't give for a dirty Doris."'

'What's a dirty Doris?' Mariah asked, struggling with Terry's terminology.

'Get yaself back to mar gaff girl,' Terry told her, slapping her bottom playfully, 'an ar'll show ya.' The majority of his former victims, so to speak, may not have been dirty Doris's when they first met, but after the aforementioned wine, whispered sexual innuendos and his hypnotic lava lamp, every one of them without exception turned to the dark side willingly, performing carnal acts that would have once repulsed them.

'I have to admit,' Mariah confessed, 'I haven't as yet heard any of your material but I am intrigued to say the least.'

Trisha tugged at Terry's arm, 'Do ya rap Tel, go on mate,' she urged. 'Oh miss,' she added, turning to Mariah, 'you gotta ear the West Am Tel rap, iss the nuts.'

'Yeah Tel,' Dee Dee said, 'do the Al Pacino bit, that shit cracks me up ar swear.'
'D'you wanna ear it babe,' Terry asked Mariah, who nodded excitedly in reply.
'Right, coppa loada this,' Terry said, striding confidently toward the stage. 'RIGHT YOU LOT!' he yelled, standing in front of the mic addressing all and sundry. 'SHUT YER NORF AND SAAF'S!' The orchestra, who had begun to disassemble their instruments stopped in their tracks, as did the gospel choir. 'Oy, you lot!' he asked the musicians, 'd'you know the feme tune to funderbirds?' The bemused musicians looked at one another, then one by one nodded. 'Right well sit yer arses daan!' Terry barked, 'get'cha trumpets and banjo's aat and play that shit, and you lot,' he added, addressing the confused choristers, 'just do what ar do yeah!'
'YEAH BLUD!' Bradley cried, clicking his fingers. 'LAY DAT SHIT DAAN TEL BRUV!'
Mariah stood with the girls twitching with anticipation, whilst Terry lit a cigarette and took a long drag. 'RIGHT, EAR GOES!' he said, blowing a stream of smoke as he spoke. 'PIN YA LUG OLES BACK AND CHECK THIS SHIT AAT.' Gesturing to the orchestra to begin Terry grabbed the mic with a snarl and a swagger,

'Back in the day ar was wunna the faces,
A diamond geezer oldin all the aces,
Laced up boots, corduroys and braces,
Laced up boots, corduroys and braces,
Ar'm a diamond geezer an ar'm wunna the faces.'

The swaying choristers hung on his every word. 'He's a diamond geezer and he's one of the faces,' they sang, before Terry belted out his second verse.

'Ar'm ya sexy beast ar'm yer Al Pacino,
Ar got more class than a glassa vino,
Ar got more class than Al Pacino,

Ar'm a sexy beast wiv a glassa vino.'

'See me dance ar'm Michael Flattly,
An ever ready bunny wiv a brand new battry,
When ar leave the floor the ole fings smokin,
Ask for more you must be jokin,
Ar'm kinda reem but I aint well jell,
A one man team AR'M WEST AM TEL!'

'Ar got arf a dozen Doris's wrapped araand me,
Every wunna them Doris's glad they faand me,
Ar love me slags and sluts but me mum's a darlin.
Ar love a baga nuts an a pinta Carlin,
Ar love a baga nuts and me mum's a darlin,
Ar love me slags and sluts an a pinta Carlin.
You can find me at the boozer proppin up the bar,
Or tuggin at me pecker in me girlfriend's car,
Tuggin at me pecker or proppin up the bar,
Sittin in the boozer or me girlfriend's car.'

Mariah, Dee Dee and the others were also swaying in time with Terry's boisterous ballad and accompanying the gospel choir.

'Laced up boots, corduroys and braces.
Ar'm a diamond geezer an ar'm wunna the faces,
Laced up boots, corduroys and braces,
A diamond geezer oldin all the aces.
Ya sexy beats ar'm yer Al Pacino,
Ar got more class than a glassa vino,
Ya sexy beast wiv a glassa vino,
Ya sexy beast wiv a glassa vino.
See me dance ar'm Michael Flattly,
An ever ready bunny wiv a brand new battry.
Ar'm kinda reem but I aint well jell,
A one man team AR'M WEST AM TEL!
A one man team AR'M WEST AM TEL!'

'Ar got all mar Doris's wrapped araand me,
All mar Doris's are glad they faand me,
Ar love em big an ar love em lumpy,
If you're Snow White ar must be Grumpy,
If you're Snow White ar must be Grumpy,
Gimme em big and gimme em lumpy.'

'Laced up boots, corduroys and braces,
Laced up boots, corduroys and braces,
Ar'm a diamond geezer an ar'm wunna the faces.
Ar'm kinda reem but I aint well jell,
A one man team AR'M WEST AM TEL!
Ar'm kinda reem but I aint well jell
A one man team AR'M WEST AM TEL!
AR'M KINDA REEM BUT I AINT WELL JELL!
A ONE MAN TEAM AR'M WEST AM TEL!
WEST AM TEL, WEST AM TEL, WEST AM TEL!'

Soon every red blooded male in the great hall began to feel a surge of testosterone and a certain empathy with the cockney character clenching their fists and singing along under their breaths, a primeval flush of admiration manifesting itself for the first time for many of them. Eventually technicians, musicians and evangelical choristers alike could no longer contain their inner caveman and with girded loins and raised voices they joined Terry in his rousing chant, uncharacteristic as it was for many of them.
'WEST AM TEL, WEST AM TEL, WEST AM TEL, WEST AM TEL!'
Terry turned the microphone on his band of brothers, united as though side by side on the terraces, he had reminded each and every one of them that it was no longer politically incorrect to be a man in a man's world - it was their god given right. Several members of the choir tore off their robes and beat their bare chests, there was a new Messiah in town and the Messiah's name was Terry, and as

though foretold in ancient scriptures he would lead them to the promised land, a land of beer, footy, fags and totty.
'YOU KNOW THAT SHIT!' Terry cried, soaking up the adoration heaped upon him. 'Ar was born for this shit,' he told himself.
Elton, and Bradley's driver-come-chauffeur Spencer, stood in the wings casting a wanton eye over Terry's manly form - each mulling over the prospect of bedding the rapping rogue and scratching the eyes out of the other in a screaming bitch fight.
Mariah by now was well and truly convinced that Terry was the opportunity she'd been waiting for, the chance to reassert herself in Europe and the wider world, and being the cold calculating business woman that she was she was prepared to do just about anything to seal the deal. But little did she know that Terry would take full advantage of her willingness to please, bulldozing any sexual barriers and reservations she may have had to have his depraved and debauched way, ram raiding her relative innocence into submission leaving her ravaged and ransacked, disheveled and discarded like a threadbare rag doll. Had she had the slightest inkling of Terry's demonstrative carnal demands, then perhaps she would have ditched the lucrative lure of the limelight and opt wisely to fade graciously into obscurity.
Three violinists and a trombone player surged forward urging Terry to sign their instruments, thrusting a permanent marker in his hand.
'Do yaself a favour geez,' he told one of them, while scrawling his name and two crossed hammers on his Stradivarius, 'get shotta this banjo and get yaself a proper guitar, you'll bang a shit load more birds ar'm tellin ya.'
'You really think so?' the violinist asked, having been starved of female attention for longer that he'd care to mention.
'Course me old son!' Terry said reassuringly. 'Ar used to dabble meself and ar tell ya what mate, I ad to fight the fanny off wiv a fuckin stick ar did.'

'Fight them off you say,' the violinist said, all ears at this point and wondering if his chosen profession had indeed been the catalyst for his sexual drought.

'Fuck me, ar'd say!' Terry continued. 'Ar bought a two bob acoustic from that cash converter gaff, fucked abaat wiv it till I ad "Summer of Sixty Nine" sussed, then ar was quids in. Ar'm tellin ya ar was nuts deep in Doris's in no time, believe me.'

'Nut's deep!' the violinist gasped, on the verge of a premature eruption. 'Thank you, thank you so much,' he said, scurrying from the great hall, discarding his Stradivarius in the process.

Stepping triumphantly from the stage to tumultuous applause, Terry eyed a young bassoonist in a plunging halter neck dress. 'Eyar girl,' he said, leaning across her music stand and daubing his mobile number on her right breast. 'Gissa bell sometime yeah, ar gotta blindin bugle you can blow on, nart ar mean?'

'Well I never!' the startled musician cried, horrified at Terry's preposterous proposition.

'Maybe you aint,' Terry said with a lecherous smile, 'but don't knock it till ya tried it ay girl. Ar bet you can proper bang aat a tune wiv them lovely lips.' Jostling his bulging crotch and knocking her sheet music to the floor Terry infuriated the young musician.

'Damn you, you horrid man!' she snapped, rummaging at her feet.

'Dyke!' Terry said on leaving, assuming her to be of that persuasion - after all, he thought, what other reason could there possibly be for her to repel his advances so robustly.

'Right, get'cha coat girl,' Terry told Mariah, tugging at her arm, 'iss time to get daan to business.'

Mariah hesitated on seeing platter after platter of the finest cuisine being ferried into the hall by a team of caterers. 'Do you mind if we grab a bite to eat first honey?' she asked. 'The last meal I had was two days ago in Seattle, and I'm famished.'

'Leave it aat girl,' Terry said, eager to consummate their partnership. 'Tell ya what, ar can do better than that shite, ar gotta baga twiglets an a coupla ding dinners back at mar gaff an if ya play ya cards right you can av arfa me pukka pie an'all.'

Never having sampled such simple pleasures Mariah relented, snatching her chinchilla throw from her assistant. 'Call the BBC will you please Tamara darling,' she said, taking Terry's arm, having oringinally planned to appear that evening on their top rated ten o'clock chat show alongside One Direction, the inventor of the year's best selling mobile app featuring a tiny flapping bird, and a former playboy bunny girl turned author whose kiss and tell memoirs of life in the Beverley Hills mansion had taken the literary world by storm. 'Tell them I'll be late.'

'But, but miss,' Tamara replied, deeply concerned for her tight UK schedule, 'may I remind you this is the BBC, they won't wait.'

'Damn you girl!' Mariah snapped, in true diva fashion. 'Everyone waits for Mariah!'

'Yeah,' Terry said in addition, 'tell the jumped up pricks to jog the fuck on, like ar said, we got business aint we babe?' Running his probing hand the length of Mariah's muscular hips it was all that Terry could do to contain the savage throbbing beast pounding at the straining zip of his stay press chinos.

'You're damn right we have,' Mariah agreed, incensed at her assistant's impertinence. 'You tell them to keep those snot nose kids and that bunny girl bitch talking till I get there, or you'll be flipping patties at MacDonald's for a buck fifty an hour. Am I making myself crystal clear Tamara?'

'Yes ma'am,' Tamara said, wilting somewhat, 'I'll get right on it.'

Mariah had guested coast to coast on every US talk show from Letterman to Larry King, each time unfazed by the predominately male host's notorious celebrity status, assuming whole heartedly that she out-ranked and outclassed them by a mile. But as many a celebrity before her had lived to regret, Mariah had become complacent, believing that the pristine pedestal on which she was placed by millions the world over would stand forever, and in doing so ignoring the bitter truth. Her global sales were dwindling in the wake of a growing tide of increasingly youthful competition, the majority of which dredged from an infinite pool of wannabes hungry for a slice of the lucrative pie and a glimpse into the world of their idols.

The latest being a seven year old Columbian, Chicco, who had beaten over a thousand of his country folk to be crowned winner of Venezuela's got talent. Chicco, once a street urchin begging for table scraps and dancing for tourists on a sodden sheet of cardboard to support his mother and five siblings had it all; the moves, the voice and an uncanny resemblance to a young Elvis Presley. His raw natural talent was limitless, Chicco was Jackson, Bieber, Timberlake and Williams rolled into one. Plucked from obscurity and a tin hut with no sanitation and fast tracked to the dizzy heights of mega stardom within a matter of weeks, Chicco Gonzalez soon had his very own Californian beach front condo complete with private mooring for his colossal ocean going catamaran, a gift from Sony, as well as a seven album deal reported to be worth around seventy five million dollars.

In the light of all this Mariah was becoming increasingly paranoid as the up and coming juveniles nipped at her heels, eating away day by day at her share of the public purse.

Throwing all her eggs into one basket and pinning her hopes on a rank outsider, Mariah nestled into Terry's broad shoulder. 'Come on,' she said with an alluring smile. 'Let's go make music.'

'Sweeet,' Terry grinned, reading heaps more into her proposition than she dared have implied.

'Laters yeah Tel,' Dee Dee said, raising a hand. 'Ar know where you are now, so we'll stop by for anuvva bevvy sometime.'
'Yeah nice one,' Terry said in parting. 'Gissa bell though mate, case ar got anuvva Doris raand an ar'm sunk to the nuts.' His reference to being balls deep, as it were, went way over Mariah's head.
'Too bleedin right ar will!' Dee Dee replied, the image of Bradley's hunched over housekeeper still very much a fresh in her mind.
'Oh flippin eck!' Trisha moaned, seeing Elton whisked away by his entourage. 'Ar wonnid iz autograph for me uncle Dennis, e'z still in intensive care apparently, but ar know e'z a proper fan.'
'Woss that nob gone and done now?' Maizie asked, knowing Trisha's hapless uncle had a long and rather painful history of epic fails. His most recent being a near terminal spinal injury, caused when the microlight aircraft he was piloting high over the Andes was struck by a flock of some seven hundred vampire bats returning to their roost after a night of gorging on sheep's blood. The winged rodents clogged the tiny craft's rotor, stalling the 50cc engine immediately and sending it spiraling toward the rocky slopes below. The horrific scene was recorded for posterity on his headcam, as were his gargling cries and groveling prayers to the almighty. After the violent bone crunching impact, Denis lay unconscious in a pool of his own blood for twenty four hours, his body contorted and barely recognizable. His saving grace was a lowly pine tree, which partially broke his fall, but punctured his pelvis in the process. Eventually coming too in excruciating pain, he was forced to drag his battered body three and a half miles over treacherous terrain to the nearest village.
'Oh gawd knows,' Trisha said, shrugging her shoulders. 'The twat's bin tryna get in that bloody booka records for donkey's years. All ar know is e launched imself off the white cliffsa flippin Dover a fortnight ago, wiv a blinkin

mobility scooter strapped to iz arse an a week later they brought im back in a full body cast, mind you e'z ad worse.'

'Worse!' Dee Dee laughed. 'E fell aat the fuckin sky for fuck sake, woss worse than that, ay?'

'Frostbite,' Trisha explained. 'The bell end wonnid to be the first bloke to trek to the Norf pole stark in iz birfday suit, yeah stark bleedin naked, well you ain't gotta be a friggin genius to work aat the obvious dangers av ya, wivin a coupla days e'd bin ravaged by a ruddy polar bear, pecked to pieces by a packa pissed off penguins, lost free toes on iz right foot an iz black and blue ball bag shriveled and disappeared up iz arse ole.'

'What a twat,' Maizie laughed. 'E'll kill imself wunna these bleedin days if e keeps that shit up, arm tellin ya.'

'Yeah ar know,' Trisha agreed. 'E'z bin told to jack it in but e'z a stubborn fucker, ar member e done forty nine bungee jumps in one day once tryna top the record, made iz own lastic an everyfing, well we aint got no bridges in Chadwell Eaf so the pillock jumped off the top floor of our tower block the nutter. E was one away from a new record when iz two bob bungee broke and shoved im ed first fru the roof of a Dagenham dairy's milk float, you shoulda seen it, it was like a semi skimmed Tsunami it was, e broke six ribs, iz collar bone, bofe arms, oh and firty five fat free yoghurts. Me muvva ad the ravin ump coz she always has one wiv er muesli, whatever the fuck that is, ar'd rarva eat a bowla bleedin gravel wouldn't you, ay?'

Dee Dee and Maizie had switched off long before the culmination of Trisha's rambling tale and were chatting amongst themselves, mostly about the dreamy clarinet player in the third row whom each of them longed to tie to his chair, and ride bareback until the early hours of the following morning and when he was screaming for mercy ride him some more until they were duly satisfied.

'Deeee,' Trisha said, nudging her friend, 'wod'ya reckon on muesli?'

'What?' Dee Dee said angrily, having lost her debauched train of thought. 'What the fuck you on abaat you idiot?'

'Muesli!' Trisha reiterated. 'Weren't ya listnin?'

'Wod'you fink,' Maizie said without averting her gaze.

'Muesli?' Dee Dee said quizzically. 'Ar fought you was chattin shit abaat yer uncle Dangerous Denis?'

'Yeah, ar was,' Trisha frowned. 'Oh ar don't know why ar bleedin bovva sometimes, ar really don't.'

'That makes free of us,' Maizie smirked, snapping out of her dizzy daydream.

'Yo me bitches!' Bradley said chirpily, having bid Elton a fond farewell. 'You'z gonna stick araand for de after party yeah? I'z got a bangin buffet on de go, wiv all dat poncey shit and stuff, mar bredrin Dizzy's gonna dj till six in de mawnin blud, an I'z got enough booze in de house to get us all smashed for a mumf, ya num sayin?'

'Naah, not for me geez,' Dee Dee said uncharacteristically. 'We gotta be up for work in the mawnin.'

'What?' Maizie said, stunned to say the least. 'Dee iss a party mate, sort it aat.'

'Yeah Dee,' Trisha said, adding what little weight she had to the argument. 'We bin banged up for gawd knows how long mate, less get shit faced yeah?'

'Ar said no!' Dee Dee replied firmly. 'Listen ar was appy to stay where ar was and do me bird, but you'z two wonnid to take the government's shitty deal dint'cha, bofe of ya. So thas what we're gonna do, go do our crummy bloody jobs till iss all done and dusted, then we can party like fuck if ya want. OK!'

'Yeaaaah alright,' Trisha said reluctantly, 'ar spoze.'

'Sorry bruv,' Maizie told her bouncing brother, 'we gotta shoot mate.'

'Well look,' Bradley said, taking a cheque book from the back pocket of his Armani jeans. 'You'z must be brassick yeah, lemmy give ya some spends, a coupla mill or summink.' Signing the cheque, Bradley then paused before tearing it from the book. 'Oh take what ya want yeah, ar got shit loadsa dosh and bundles comin in every day innit.'

'No fanks,' Dee Dee said, which astounded her friends further. She tore the blank cheque in three and handed the pieces back to Bradley. 'Ar know ya mean well an all that,' she told him, 'but I aint never took an and aat in me life, ar've earnt it or robbed it, but I aint never ponced it.'

'Deeeeee,' Trisha moaned, hanging on her arm. 'We've ardly got a pot to piss in between us and you're turnin daan milyons.'

'Yeah Dee, av you lost the flippin plot or summink,' Maizie added, siding with Trisha for the first time in ages. 'We could do a lot wiv that dough, we could move aata that shit ole of a flat for a start, get summink nice on the river, wunna them yuppie gaffs.'

'Ar could buy me lastic,' Trisha piped up, 'for me gastric pants, get me business started. Oh Dee, pleaaaaaaaase.'

'Shut up you tart,' Dee Dee laughed, 'you aint never gonna get them fat fucks to lose weight wiv ya vibratin lastic knickers.'

'Why not?' Trisha asked defensively. 'Maizie you'd wear em won'tcha, ar swear mate you'd lose that baggy back enda yours in a coupla days ar promise, or ya money back.'

'What baggy bleedin back end!' 'Maizie growled, groping her rear. 'What av ar told you abaat takin the piss aata my arse, ay?'

'Well look at it!' Trisha said, ridiculing her irate friend. 'Iss as big as a bloody banjo, ain it Dee.'

'Ooh you orrible bitch!' Maizie snapped, grabbing Trisha's right arm and forcing it behind her back. 'Ar mean it ar'll break ya friggin arm if you keep that shit up ar will!'

'Deeee, Deeeee!' Trisha squealed. 'Get er offa me will ya, Deeee, ow, owwww, Maaaaaize that urrrrts!'

'Will you two pack it in,' Dee Dee yelled, tearing the two apart, 'or ar'll batter the bleedin paira ya. We aint takin the dough and thas that, d'you ear me?'

'Yeah but...,' Trisha said, red faced.

'Yeah but nuffin!' Dee Dee insisted. 'We got a few bob so we'll manage.'
'Alright Dee babe,' Bradley said, pocketing the cheque book. 'But you'z know where I am yeah.'
'Yeah course,' Dee Dee replied, silencing Trisha with a hand to her mouth. 'Shut it, ar don't wanna ear it,' she told her, 'and you Maizie, stop ya bitchin and get yer arse into gear, we're offski.'
Bradley summoned Spencer. 'Yo Spence blud,' he called. 'Give me bitches a ride to der crib yeah, and make sure der's shit loads in de mini bar bruv.'
'Certainly sir,' Spencer said. 'I have an excellent Chilean merlot on ice as we speak.'
'Fuck that,' Maizie replied, 'get some wickeds an a bottla yager.'
'Deeeee,' Trisha said, looking dejected. 'Ya dint mean what ya said abaat me lastic pants did ya, ay Dee? Ar fought it was a blindin idea, specially wiv me jingle an'all.'
'Look!' Dee Dee stormed. 'You know what ar fink abaat the lazy lardy fucks don'tcha!'
Dee Dee had voiced her opinion on numerous occasions as to the root cause of the obesity epidemic that was rapidly sweeping the globe, unloading a volley of unsympathetic abuse on all those that dare suggest that water retention, or an inactive metabolism, was to blame for their excess blubber. Double XL was fast becoming the norm in everyday society, with junk food and inactivity at the very heart of the problem.
'Yeah ar do,' Trisha said, resolute in the belief of her product. 'Ar member you slaggin off our Janice at me nephew's christnin, mind you she ad narf whacked the weight on adn't she.'
'Whacked it on!' Dee Dee exclaimed. 'Ar'd say, the greedy bitch'd et arf the bleedin buffet before the little fucker'd even got iz ed wet, and then the dozy mare ad the front to tell me she was big boned or summink. Big boned! Ar wern avin any of that bollocks ar let er av it right there in the

church hall in front of everyone, ar said "see you ya salad dodgin ungry fuckin ippo, ar'll tell you what your flamin problem is shall I? You're a lazy greedy fat fuck that needs to get off er arse and jog furver than the poxy fridge and back!"'

Janice, along with the hundred or so well wishers attending young Presley's christening, was stunned into mortified silence for a moment or two before she eventually broke down and vomited the contents of her enormous stomach right there on the floor; some thirty buffet pork pies, twenty or so mini scotch eggs, several fistfuls of cheesy nibbles from puffs to straws to triangles, an entire stack of dinosaur shaped reformed ham, three prawn rings, nine swiss rolls half chocolate half vanilla and a strawberry trifle.

Now some may criticize Dee Dee for her complete lack of tact considering Janice's delicate mental state, but the boot camp style barracking she unleashed had a profound effect on the overweight thirty something. And after numerous hypnotherapy sessions, the fitting of a wire mesh muzzle and a stringent celery soup and string bean diet, within eighteen months she had managed to shed a colossal thirteen stone from her frame taking her down to a size fourteen, and in doing so earning herself a six figure sum and a makeover in a top women's magazine. Before the amazing transformation most men were repulsed to say the least by her outward appearance, only ever making sexual advances in an inebriated and incoherent state, or as part of the new shag-it-nominate-it craze which followed the internet driven alcohol related fad. This recent pathetic past-time saw moronic males filming themselves performing lewd sexual acts in public places with the obese or physically deformed, earning them the highest respect, kudos and status among their like-minded peers.

Janice now turned men's heads and induced spontaneous erections like never before, and of course she reveled in it, throwing out her live-in slob of a lover and dating a string of virile athletic beefcakes half her age. Her confidence soared and all thanks to Dee Dee's brutal criticism hitting home where all else had failed.

'We should go into business togevva Dee,' Trisha said, having a brief epiphany. 'You bollock em an ar'll flog em me lastic pants, wod'ya reckon ay, slag em and bag em we could call it.'

Dee Dee couldn't help but laugh at Trisha's preposterous proposal. 'Fuck me that just might work,' she said, draping an arm around Trisha's shoulder. 'Thas just what the lardy bleedas need, an ar reckon they'd pay top dollar for it an'all.'

The girls said their goodbyes to Bradley and followed Spencer to the door.

'Ow's it go Trish?' Maizie asked, with a rhythmic saunter. '*If ya stuff ya face wiv jelly, if ya stuff ya face wiv chips…*'

Her two friends joined her in Trisha's jaunty jingle;

'Does it linger on ya belly, does it linger on yer ip's,
Do ya waddle when ya walk, do ya rumble when ya run,
Put daan ya knife an fork, put daan ya bagel an ya bun,
Dont'cha worry, don't despair,
Coz whatevva ya circumstaaaaaaance,
Grab yaself a paira Trisha's gastric paaaaaaaants.'

Spencer glanced over his shoulder whilst descending the stone entrance steps. 'I have an aunt who is, shall we say over exuberant at the dining table, and hence has ballooned far beyond the realms of the clinically obese,' he explained, hoping Trisha and Dee Dee's unorthodox approach to weight loss would save her, since the medical fraternity had all but given up on her and put a figure of a matter of weeks on her life expectancy - after three consecutive heart attacks following her exhaustive efforts to remove the lid from a jar of blackberry preserve, which she would often lather over bread and beef dripping to appease her relentless hunger pangs. 'Do you think you and your gastric garments could help her, she has a sizable estate so I assure you money would be no object.'

'See Dee!' Trisha squealed, nudging her friend. 'There's faasands of em just like er, wiv potsa dough gaggin for a paira mar pants an a kick up the arse, ar'm tellin ya mate we're gonna be proper minted you wait and see. Ar was workin on a prototype fingy in the nick, ar stuck a nappy an a nine volt battry on the chaplain's cat, but the bleedin fing ad a spaz attack, pissed on the battry an taser'd iz tiny todger. Poor bleeda, I ad to flush im daan the toilet like a big ginger turd ar did, but don't worry ar fink ar've ironed aat all the problems an ar reckon ar've got it sussed.'

'Ar bleedin ope so!' Dee Dee snapped. 'Or the vicar's mangey moggy won't be the only lectrified pussy, nart ar mean.'

'Don't worry Dee,' Trisha reassured her, 'ar'm gonna stick a rubber fanny flap in the gusset an arf a yard of earf cable raand the back end, them fings'll be so safe mate they'll be able to wivstand a direct it from a bolta bleedin lightnin wivaat singin a single curly pube.'

'You better be right,' Dee Dee said, having grave reservations once again. 'Uvverwise they'll be queuin up left right and centre wiv their no win no fee bollocks to sue the shit aat of us.'

'Dee mate,' Trisha reiterated, climbing into Bradley's limousine behind her friends, 'every new business as its ic ups don't they, ay?'

'Ic ups!' Dee Dee laughed. 'Ic up's? If them poxy fings go wonky we'll be banged up on anuvva friggin manslaughter charge.'

'Yeah Trisha,' Maizie added, 'I aint goin back inside mate, not for you, not for no one d'you ear me.'

'Ohhhh shuttup you two,' Trisha moaned, 'we'll test em good and proper first won't we.'

'Test em!' Dee Dee scoffed, reclining as Spencer pulled away, 'who the fuck's gonna be stupid enough to test your lectrifyin lastic knickers, thas what ar wanna know?'

Trisha glanced across at Maizie who was busy fastening her seat belt.

'Ohhhhhh no!' Maizie said, wagging a finger. 'Ohhh no, you aint testin them fings aat on me, ar don't give a flyin fuck if they got a rubber piss flap or not. I aint doin it, alright. Ar seen the look on the chaplain's cats face when you switched the buggers on, poor little fucker was jiggin araand gang nam style foamin at the maaf before e kicked the bucket. An ar never forget the stench, Jesus that was rotten wern it?'

'Maizie!' Dee Dee snapped. 'Someone's gotta take one for the team, an it aint me.'

'Yeah Maize,' Trisha said, edging away. 'You're the only one carryin a coupla've extra paand aint'cha.'

'You bitch, no I aint!' Maizie barked defensively. 'If you say that one more time ar swear ar'll...'

'Shuuuutup,' Dee Dee said, intervening whilst helping herself to the mini bar. 'We'll be quids in if these fings work.'

'IF!' Maizie shrieked. 'Wod'ya mean, if! What if they don't ay, ar'm the poor bleeda wiv the cremated crotch for gawd sake, not you'z two.'

'Oh don't be daft,' Trisha laughed, 'aint'chu ever licked a battry before?'

'No!' Maizie barked defiantly. 'Not wiv me flippin fanny I aint, get some uvva mug to wear em coz I ain intrested.'

Dee Dee and Trisha suddenly closed ranks in a rare show of solidarity.

'What'chu two lookin at?' Maizie asked, allowing her paranoia to get the better of her. 'Ar said I aint wearin em and thas that!'

'Yeah I erd ya,' Dee Dee replied, nudging Trisha. 'I erd ya good and proper, ar won't mention it no more ar promise. Just like ar won't mention the time ar saved your arse from a beatin aatside the Chadwell chippie neeva, or the time ar sat up all bleedin night wiv you rubbin ya back wiv you yackin daan the pan after you necked a pinta cockles swimmin in tequila ya dopey cow. Or the undreds of times ar've lied fru me teef to ya muvva sayin you was stoppin at mine when you was coppin off wiv creepy Kristos in the back of iz kebab van ya dirty bitch.'

'Oh shut up e was lovely,' Maizie protested, having heard enough. 'Ar used to get a chicken shish, a shag an a shandy every Friday in a lay by on the one two seven.'

'Yeah ar bet,' Trisha teased. 'Did e do ya doggy for a doner an'all?'

'Get kinky for a kofti did ya?' Dee Dee added, ribbing her friend to near breaking point.

'ALRIGHT, ALRIGHT!' Maizie eventually yelled, throwing her hands in the air. 'Alright, ar'll wear the poxy fings, but ar'm tellin ya Trish, ar'll av the ravin ump if you lectrify mar landin strip ar swear it. D'you ear me!'

'Yeah yeah,' Trisha replied, with a blasé air. 'Ar promise ya mate, ar reckon ar've almost perfected me prototype, on paper anyway.' Trisha delved into her clutch bag and produced a crudely drawn crayon interpretation of her intended invention. 'Ar gotta mail this over to a Mumbai sweat shop so they can knock me up some samples, ar got a great deal an'all coz they pay their five undred free year olds two bob a mumf to work them machines twenny four seven till they drop, the little bleedas.' Trisha had indeed sourced her suppliers and manufacturers thoroughly whilst sitting a level three creative computing course at Holloway, one which she duly failed to graduate in after inadvertently downloading a ferocious virus to the prison system which wiped no less than thirty three motherboards clean of all course work, incurring the immediate wrath of her fellow classmates.

'Two bob a mumf!' Maizie gasped. 'Thas disgustin that is.'

'Ar know,' Trisha agreed. 'The greedy little fuckers ar takin the piss if you ask me, ar'd give em a bowla porridge an a dry slap ar would, the snot nosed shits'll wanna blinkin tea break next won't they, give em an inch and they'll take a bleedin liberty thas what ar say.'

The unscrupulous clothing manufacturer Trisha had approached was not adverse to courting controversy, flouting countless health and safety regulations whilst completely disregarding its predominantly juvenile employees' human rights in the process. Gupta Garments, with its lower than low price market strategy, attracted some of the world's leading brands from sporting goods to haute couture catwalk designer wear, worn by the rich and famous alike, all of them blissfully unaware of the appalling conditions under which they were made.

'Ar should boycott the bleedin fings,' Maizie said, having ethical reservations, the plight of the minor Mumbai machinists pricking at her conscience. 'Just like ar done wiv them fox fur fongs Black Mickey was knockin aat daan the market, it aint right ar'm tellin ya.'

'You aint wrong mate,' Dee Dee agreed. 'Them mangey flea bitten fings gimme a ruddy rash like you wouldn't believe, ar looked a proper wrongen scratchin me muff on the Met line every mawnin ar did.'

'You got off lightly Dee,' Trisha informed her. 'Our Sandra copped a dosa ringworm, rabies and rheumatoid arfritis off er badger skin basque, the poor cow. She lost all er air, er top teef and two toes on er left foot.'

'Thas what ar'm talkin abaat,' Maizie said, leaping gallantly onto her high horse. 'Iss karma if you ask me, for murderin them poor little bleedas in the first place.'

'Yeah yeah alright muvva flippin Theresa,' Dee Dee scoffed, as Spencer cruised by the Angel underground station. 'Chuck a left ear geez!' she told him, 'then first right fanks!'

'All ar'm sayin,' Maizie continued, determined to get her point across, 'iss that we aint cavemen anymore, we don't av to unt wild animals for a fur coat, we got man made shit now aint we?'

'Women!' Trisha piped up.

'What?' Maizie asked, turning sharply. 'What you on abaat?'

'Cave women,' Trisha said pedantically, 'you said cavemen dint'cha.'

'Oh shut'cha face,' Maizie sneered, 'you know what ar mean.'

'Left ear geez!' Dee Dee told their driver. 'Just behind the silver Skoda, yeah thas it.'

Spencer reversed alongside the kerb with a sigh of unmitigated relief, his head now spinning having endured the girl's chaotic conversation for what seemed like an eternity.

'Fanks Spence,' Trisha said, stepping from the passenger seat and slamming the door with some vigor which incensed the chauffeur somewhat.

'Yeah cheers mate,' Maizie added. Spencer leapt from his seat taking hold of the rear door as Maizie alighted to prevent further mistreatment of his master's beloved automobile.

'Nice one mate,' Dee Dee said, taking a crumpled five pound note from her purse and tucking it into his lapel pocket. 'Get'cha self a light and lager or summink.'

'Madam, there really is no need I assure you,' Spencer said, reaching to return the cash.

'No you av it!' Dee Dee insisted. 'I aint no piss taker I always pay me way.'

Spencer was in no mood to argue, and judging by the determined look on Dee Dee's face to do so would've been of little us.

'Very well Madam,' he said, closing the rear door carefully and wiping a smear from the rear windshield with a neatly pressed handkerchief, 'then I'll bid each of you good day.'

'Yeah laters,' Maizie replied, heading along their garden path.

'Wouldn't wanna be ya!' Trisha chirped, skipping behind. 'Seeya!'

Spencer waved half-heartedly with a judgmental look at his surroundings before hopping back into the limousine. 'I say!' he called, winding down his window as Dee Dee turned away. 'Master Tel, I mean West Ham Tel or whatever the devil his name is.'

'Yeah,' Dee Dee said, stopping at the aging wooden gate, 'what abaat im?'
'Does he em?' Spencer probed. 'I mean I can see he's obviously a ladies man but um, I mean has he ever been known to er, shall we say stray from the path of the accepted norm, so to speak?'
'You what?' Dee Dee asked again, confused at his convoluted questioning. 'What the fuck's that spozed to mean?'
'Deeeeee come on!' Maizie called, holding the street door open against the powerful overhead spring. 'What'cha doin?'
'I suppose what I'm trying to say,' Spencer continued, a little flushed around the cheeks, 'is, ar Master Tel's carnal preferences limited purely to the female form?'
'You mean does e swing bofe ways?' Dee Dee replied, finally getting the gist. 'Does e take it up the Gary Glitter, is e a ravin ruddy cock jockey, an arse bandit, a rear gunner, a...'
Spencer raised a hand having heard quite enough of Dee Dee's homophobic connotations. 'Young lady I'll have you know,' he said defensively, 'it is no longer PC, shall we say, to refer to a person's gender in that repulsive manner.'
'Oh I aint got nuffing against em,' Dee Dee replied, toying with the rusting gate latch, 'I ain even omaphobic. We got a coupla wooftas in the famly an ar get on great wiv em, proper she-males though the paira've em, bawlin their bleedin eyes aat at a chick flick an a broken friggin nail, and proper shite at DIY nart ar mean. Mind you, if ya need a facial or a bikini wax the boys ar blindin, anyway ar gotta go geez Corrie's on in arf hour and talkin of batty boys, Ken's just been caught bendin young Chesney over a Boddington's barrel at the backa the Rovers slippin im a lenf, ar reckon iss payback though coz Deirdre give it to Gail good and proper in Rita's Jacuzzi.'
Spencer's head was soon spinning again not being a fan of the long running family favorite himself. 'I er... I really should be going,' he said, starting the car.

'Give Tel mar love won'tcha,' Dee Dee said in parting, 'just don't give im AIDS or nunna that shit, nart ar mean.'
Spencer smiled in anticipation of soon making a lecherous move on the self-styled diamond geezer.
'Come on Deeee, flippin ell!' Maizie moaned. 'Ar've ad to nick a gnome aata next doors to wedge the friggin door open.' Maizie removed the ridiculous stone statuette and tossed it back across the adjacent fence with complete disregard for the resulting flattened fuchsia's and the now traumatized tabby dozing therein.
Trisha, who had bolted up to their flat, peered down from the landing. 'Deeee, we're aata fanny rags!' she yelled. 'Ar've ad to tuck a tea bag in me drawers.'
'Oh great,' Maizie sighed, 'ar reckon ar'm due meself.'
'Iss alright Maize,' Trisha said, greeting her friend at the top of the stairs, 'we got a boxa two undred bags and they're erbal an'all, so they're proper good for ya.'
'Not if they're stuffed up ya flu they aint!' Dee Dee informed them.
But Trisha dismissed her scathing criticism. 'Ar prefer the pyramids meself though,' she said, following Dee Dee and Maizie inside. 'They don't chaff so much and the strings proper meaty, there aint nuffing worse than the bugger snappin off in yer and, and ya gotta rummage raand daan there wiv a soddin soup spoon to winkle the bleeda aat. Right, who fancies a brew?'
Although her two friends were particularly parched and craving a cuppa Trisha's over descriptive analogy had turned their stomachs. 'Well ar'm avin one,' she said, getting no reply and sauntering through to the kitchen.
Dee Dee sat in the armchair with her hands clasped to either side of her head.
'You alright Dee?' Maizie asked, leaning across from the sofa. 'Wossup mate?'
'Ar got a bangin ed ache,' Dee Dee replied, with a furrowed brow.

'Ar know ow ya feel,' Maizie said, looking in the direction of the kitchen. 'She's proper doin mar swede in an'all.'

'No,' Dee Dee added, with her eyes clenched shut, 'me ed is proper bangin like fuck.'

'Shit really,' Maizie said, somewhat concerned now. 'TRIIIIISH!' she yelled, causing Dee Dee to wince. 'WE GOT ANY TABLITS? OY SOPPY NUTS!'

'What?' Trisha replied, emerging with a dripping dish cloth in one hand and a plunger in the other.

'What ya doin?' Maizie asked, forgetting Dee Dee momentarily.

'Plungin me porridge,' Trisha said, reenacting her recent endeavors with said plunger. 'Ar lobbed arf a bowl daan the plug ole this mawnin, an iss proper bunged up the U bend, makes ya wonder what that shit does to ya guts dun it. Me aunt Libby spent free weeks in ospital after a lump of it set rock ard in er lower intestine, whatever the fuck that is, anyway the poor cow couldn't crap for love nor money no matter ow much cod liver oil and stewed prunes they chucked daan er froat.'

Maizie attempted to intervene at this point noticing the anguish on Dee Dee's face, but her efforts yet again proved pointless.

'In the end,' Trisha waffled, 'they got a coupla plumbers to bend er over and ram a coupla've drain rods up er back passage. Mind you Aunt Libby was proper backed up by then if ya nart ar mean, so the poor bleeda on the end of em got smuvvered from ed to toe in prunes, poop and porridge, ar tell ya e wern an appy bunny. Woss up Dee?' she then asked, seeing her friend rocking in her chair. 'You got ed ache or summink?'

'YES!' Dee Dee barked. 'You soppy twat, Maizie asked ya for some bleedin tablits!'

'Oh,' Trisha replied, 'we aint got none.'

Dee Dee with her throbbing head pounded the arm of her chair. 'Why dint'cha just TELL ME THAT IN THE FIRST PLACE

YOU DOZY MARE!' she raged, 'insteada chattin bleedin shit abaat ya flippin aunt Libby an er BUNGED UP BUM OLE!'
Trisha stood stunned for moment or two. 'Ar tell ya what,' she eventually said, recalling an old wives tale.
'Ar'd rarva you never!' Dee Dee snapped, but Trisha ducked back into the kitchen unhindered and began throwing open the cupboards, causing Dee Dee further discomfort.
'Iss summink me nan used to use,' Trisha mumbled, 'whenever me grandad got one of iz eds.'
Dee Dee reclined closing her eyes to alleviate the pain, while Maizie thumbed the TV pages.
'Eeya,' Trisha chirped, emerging carrying a sugar coated slice of bread and butter. Before Dee Dee knew what was happening Trisha pasted it square onto her forehead. 'Twenny minutes of that and you'll be as right as ninepence.'
'WHAT THE FUCK!' Dee Dee shrieked, leaping from her seat and peeling the offending slice away leaving the sticky residue. 'Woss this you soppy bitch?'
she raged, turning to check herself in the mirror that hung above the mantle.
'Iss alternative medicine,' Trisha said in her defence, 'iss all the rage apparently. I erd Tommy Cruise and Michelle Phifer ar proper into it, mind you ar bet they got some poncy Gucci bread or summink.'
'Ar'll give you Gucci bread!' Dee Dee snarled, hurling the slice toward Trisha who ducked swiftly out of harm's way.
'Dee, give it a chance mate,' she squealed, 'don't knock it till ya tried it an'all that.'
'Yeah Dee, give it a go,' Maizie laughed, which only fuelled the flames of Dee Dee's wrath.
'Give it a go!' Dee Dee cursed. 'If you fink for one minute ar'm sittin ear lookin like a complete dick coz soppy bollocks there reckons iss friggin alternative medicine, you got anuvva fink comin ar tell ya.' Dee Dee then stormed through to the bathroom to scrub the buttery mess from her face. 'IS THIS BLEEDIN SUGAR?' she called out angrily.

'Yeah,' Trisha said, popping her head through the door. 'Iss meant to exfoliate ya skin, good ain it, eeya d'ya know what Dee ar fink ya lookin better for it already mate.'

Dee Dee's flushed complexion could have easily been mistaken for a youthful glow, if it were not for the look of bitter hatred in her eye. 'TRISHA!' she screamed in reply, kicking the door closed in her face. 'FUCK OFF!'

'Leave er alone will ya,' Maizie said, beckoning to Trisha, who as usual could not see the error of her ways.

'Ar know itta take time to catch on over ear,' Trisha said, flopping down beside Maizie, 'but you watch, the NHS'll be dishin aat buttered baps for boils, back ache and bubonic bloody plague before ya know it.'

'Will you shut up!' Maizie insisted, switching channels. 'You're givin me a flippin ed ache an'all. And before ya say it,' she said firmly, 'no ar don't want arf a sarnie stuck to me bonce fanks.'

Trisha sat in silence swinging her legs and wishing she hadn't offered to help however outlandish her methods. The two of them sat through several soaps, which Trisha continuously commented on. 'So Kevin's shaggin the geezer's daughter in the dry cleaners,' she'd blurt out after a brief period of silence, 'but what they don't know is that Gary from the garage is givin iz old lady a full service and toppin up er fluids.'

Maizie did her level best to ignore her irritating friend until, during an episode of Strictly, she happened to mention that the popular children's television presenter was in her words 'ridin the arse off his beautiful Bulgarian dance partner.'

'Iss bleedin obvious,' she said, watching the pair Rumba into the semi finals, and further agitating her friend in the process. 'E'z got a ragin boner, look, and she can't keep er ands off im, I always knew e was a wrongen ar did, ar mean ow can ya spend arf ya life wiv ya right and stuck up a fluffy ducks arse in the name of entertainment, ay?' She was referring to the children's teatime TV show 'Daisy duck and Dufus' featuring a purple domestic duck and her best friend

Dufus the donkey; a huge hit with the under-fives netting millions through merchandising and its West End stage adaptation.
'Thas it!' Maizie screeched, tossing the remote control into Trisha's lap and springing from the couch, 'ar'm gaana bed!'
'What, ay?' Trisha said bemused. 'Ar fought you wonnid to watch Artbeat, iss on in arf an hour.'
'Ar did!' Maizie snarled in parting. 'What ar don't want though is you bendin my bleedin ear, tellin me who's bangin who, and who's trussed up like a ruddy chicken in a levva gimp mask givin it to their neighbour's friggin dog!'
'Oh,' Trisha replied, stunned to say the least. 'OK.'
Maizie disappeared into the bedroom slamming the door behind her, leaving Trisha alone to her own devices. Dee Dee herself had slipped unnoticed into her own room giving her wittering friend a wide berth.
'MAIZIE!' Trisha called out several moments later. 'MAIZE, MAAAAIZE!'
'WHAT?' Maizie snapped, wrenching open the bedroom door with vigor. 'Ar mean it Trish I ain in the mood, we gotta be up for work in the mawnin, member.'
'Yeah, ar know that,' Trisha replied. 'Ar've set me alarm an hour early so ar can av a dump and do me air, tell ya the troof Maize ar'm too excited to sleep ar've always wonnid to work wiv animals, you know that.'
Before Trisha could get into her stride with another meaningless meandering tale Maizie raised a hand. 'TRISHA!' she said firmly. 'Wod'ya want?'
'Oh yeah,' Trisha smiled, backtracking. 'It was the doddery old chief inspector bloke.'
Maizie looked puzzled. 'What you on abaat?' she asked, her patience wearing extremely thin at this point.
'In Artbeat!' Trisha said, raising her eyebrows. 'E's the one trussed up like a ruddy chicken in a levva gimp mask, in case you was wondrin.'
Maizie stood for a moment, her nails penetrating the painted door frame. 'The only fing ar was wondrin,' she

growled, 'was when you was gonna shut the fuck up and do us all a friggin favour!' With that Maizie slammed the door shut a second time.

With very little regard for her friends' fraying tempers Trisha popped her feet up onto the coffee table and settled down into the remainder of the soaps that had been denied them during their imprisonment. 'Flippin eck!' she would shriek from time to time. 'Ar never see that comin ar must admit!'

Eventually her eyelids grew heavy and the remote slipped from her dangling hand to the floor with a thud. 'Urrrgh, what?' she slurred, scratching at her head.

Hauling herself from the sofa, she turned off the television and trudged through to the bedroom, switching on the light.

'Trishaaaaa!' Maizie moaned, dragging her duvet up over her head and kicking out at her irritating friend, having slipped into a peaceful slumber. 'Turn it off will ya!'

'Ang on,' Trisha replied, dragging her top over her head and reaching behind for her bra catch, before slipping it from either shoulder. 'Ear Maize,' she said, tapping at Maizie's feet. 'Ya know that bird wiv the nose, Tara summink or uvva, you know, the one that used to do the wevva on the telly, then she done that dancin on ice cobblers, got er baps aat in the celebrity jungle and shagged that rugby bloke. Oh what was iz name, big Welsh twat wiv cauliflower ears and a toof missin.'

Maizie by now had both index fingers rammed firmly into either ear, but this only muffled Trisha waffling.

'She done that photo fing for OK magazine completely starkers,' Trisha continued, turning the sleeves of her Peter Andre pj's out the right way. 'Well sorta starkers,' she added, 'she ad free dollops of vanilla ice cream coverin er noo noo and er nips, she looked a proper lemon ar tell ya, all she needed was an andful of undreds and faasands and a flake stuck up er arse and she'da bin a ninety nice, the dozy mare. Oh woss er name?'

Maizie could take no more, springing from her bed she shoved Trisha to her own and thumped the light switch. 'Go to fuckin sleep!' she barked, ensnaring herself in the straps of Trisha's discarded bra whilst returning to her bed. 'Shit, fuck!' she cursed, staggering blindly in the dark before colliding head on with the bedside cabinet.

'Oh friggin ell, turn it in will ya Maize,' Trisha said, having snuggled beneath her sheets. 'Ar'm tryna get to sleep for gawd sake.'

'DO WHAT?' Maizie yelled, lashing out and clawing at her tethered feet. 'TRISHA AR'LL FLIPPIN KILL YOU!'

'Don'tchu stretch mar straps,' Trisha said, peering down at Maizie's feet, her eyes having grown accustomed to the dark.

'Stretch em!' Maizie screeched, shredding the flimsy garment with ferocious venom. 'Stretch em!' Maizie wound the lacy elastic around either hand forming a crude garrotte. 'Stretch em, ar'll stretch em raand your fuckin neck and frottle the fuckin life aata ya.' Leaping onto her friend's bed Maizie wrestled to tear the sheets from Trisha's cowering head.

'Get off, get offa me!' Trisha cried, thumping on the wall that adjoined their room with Dee Dee's. 'DEEEEEEEE!' she yelped, fending off Maizie with her feet. 'DEEE, SHE'S TRYNA KILL ME, DEEEEEEE ELLLLLLLP!'

Moments later, during the ensuing melee, their bedroom door flew open clattering and distorting the chipboard wardrobe.

'DEE FANK GAWD!' Trisha begged, breaking cover momentarily.

Seizing the opportunity Maizie strung the taught elastic around her slender throat, not once but twice for good measure.

'AR'VE AD ENOUGH AR TELL YA!' Maizie screamed, foaming ever so slightly at the mouth. 'ENOUGH!'

'Deeeeee,' Trisha gargled, stretching out a pleading hand. 'Deee mate, ar can't breev.'

Dee Dee paused, her head still thumping, contemplating Trisha's mortality; on one hand to deny Maizie her divine retribution would mean that Trisha would live to plague them another day, the thought of which sent a cold shiver the length of her spine; but on the flip side, no matter how attractive, Trisha's demise would be somewhat messy and unless the body could be reliably disposed of, then the murderous crime would attract the long arm of the law and land her and Maizie straight back in the slammer for the remainder of their days.

'Maiiiiize, get off er,' she said, choking on her words. 'OY, MAIZE!' she then yelled, getting no response. 'Believe me if ar fought we could get away wiv it ar'd cave er ed in meself, but we can't so leave er alone.'

'But Deeee,' Maizie snarled, maintaining her grip on the ever tightening straps and watching Trisha's face turn a flushing crimson. 'Ar don't give a toss if ar get banged up, ar really don't, itta be werf it. Ar know ar've said it a faasand times before but ar really av ad enough.' Maizie glared at the wheezing Trisha. 'Ar bleedin love ya, but ar can't live wiv ya, me nerves ar shot to bits so die ya soddin bitch!'

Dee Dee, seeing Trisha moments from an agonizing death at the hands of her life long friend, stepped in to intervene and avert a heinous crime in the process. 'MAIZIE!' she yelled, wrenching at her wrists. 'Ar said let er the fuck go will ya!' Dee Dee dragged the raging Maizie clear of Trisha's bed, and tore the straining straps from her whitened knuckles. 'Ar'm sicka this shit,' she added, 'me ed's bangin like a shit ouse door in a fuckin funderstorm and you'z two ain elpin one bloody bit!'

'Ohhhh, looka me bestest bra,' Trisha whined, clambering from her bed, clutching her throat with one hand and retrieving the flimsy remains.

'You're lucky Dee Dee come in ar tell ya,' Maizie growled, still very much restrained at this point.

'She's off er ed Dee,' Trisha complained. 'Ar never done nuffing, onest mate.'

'Trisha!' Dee Dee said, shoving Maizie back onto her bed. 'Ar don't believe a friggin word you're sayin, ar know what'cha like, gobbin off like a ravin bloody loon till one of us snaps and goes for ya froat.'

'Oh thas a bit strong ain it Dee,' Trisha said, attempting to piece together her tattered bra.

Maizie slithered beneath her duvet, mumbling threatening obscenities under her breath.

'You,' Dee Dee told Trisha, 'get yer arse into mar room, ar'm stoppin in ear wiv Maizie, uvverwise you aint gonna make it fru the night.'

'Oh she's alright,' Trisha said, suddenly making light of her friend's recent grievous actions. 'Aint'cha mate?' Maizie disappeared beneath her covers.

'You dunno when to stop do ya?' Dee Dee said, snatching Trisha's tattered bra from her and hurling it across the bedroom. 'Go on, piss off in the uvver room while ya still breevin.'

Trisha reluctantly stomped from the room while Dee Dee, still nursing her head, climbed into her bed and turned off the bedside light. Trisha on the other hand could be heard shuffling the knotted pine wardrobe and chest of drawers from one end of Dee Dee's room to the other and nudging the bed with her knees to the opposite wall.

'Now what?' Dee Dee cursed. 'TRISHAAA, WHAT THE FUCKA YOU DOIN?' she called, thumping at the wall. 'ISS THE MIDDLE OF THE PISSIN NIGHT!'

'SORTIN AAT ME FENG SHUI!' Trisha replied, tossing the pillows to the opposite end of the bed. 'ISS ARSE UPWARDS IN EAR, ALL ME POSITIVE ENERGY'S GOIN AAT THE WINDA!'

'YOU'LL BE GOIN AAT THE FRIGGIN WINDA IF YOU DON'T TURN IT IN!' Dee Dee screamed in reply.

To add to Dee Dee's woes the father downstairs began prodding at the ceiling firmly with the handle of their shaggy mop, barking in his foreign tongue. 'DO ONE YOU DICK!' she yelled, hanging her head from the bed. The prodding ceased forthwith, but the neighbour's door was then heard being flung open and heavy footsteps treading hastily up the stairs toward them.

'Shit Dee, e'z comin,' Maizie said, edging against the wall.

'Like ar give a fuck,' Dee Dee replied, flinging her sheets aside and lunging toward the bedroom door.

'Deeeee don't,' Maizie warned, 'they're nutters that lot.' But Dee Dee's wrath would not be curtailed, and as the roused Romanian raised a fist to beat on their door, baying for British blood, Dee Dee tore the door open toward her.

'WHAT?' she yelled, wild eyed with a porcelain pig clenched in her right fist, snatched from the gate leg hall table in passing.

The Romanian's fiery fury was immediately doused by her rigid confrontational stance, tipping him suddenly onto the back foot.

'WHAT?' she asked again, standing her ground and defending her door, just as her ancestors had done steadfastly before repelling marauding foreign invaders.

Raising the glazed porker to the Romanian's eye line and backing him to the banister, Dee Dee positively foamed at the mouth. 'You fink you can come up ear givvin it the fuckin biggun,' she said, shaking the pig. 'Puttin the frighteners on us, well let me tell you summink, ar don't back daan ta no one, least of all the likes of you, not one fuckin inch d'you ear me.'

The Romanian would-be aggressor, realizing he could possibly be verbally outgunned, and physically for that matter, inched toward the top step.

While Maizie cowered beneath her quilted floral duvet, Trisha ventured out into the hall. 'Oh ello!' she said, waving to their departing neighbour. 'If yer after sugar we just run aat, but ar got a coupla sweetners ar can let you av.'

'Trisha!' Dee Dee said, spinning on the spot to confront her friend and allowing the Romanian to beat a hasty retreat. Her steely glare was enough to send Trisha scurrying to her bed, looking back Dee Dee caught sight of the retreating coward disappearing into his ground floor flat, pushing his curious wife inside in the process. 'Wanker,' she mumbled, slamming the pig down and the door closed simultaneously.

'Has he gone?' Maizie asked, sitting upright on Dee Dee's return. 'Ar was just comin to give you an and.'
'Yeah course you was,' Dee Dee said, managing a smile under the circumstances. 'Next time you can go then, yeah?'
'Well,' Maizie replied hesitantly, 'well er'm.'
'Go to sleep Maize,' Dee Dee told her, turning out the light yet again.
Seconds later there was the faintest of tapping on the bedroom wall. 'Deeeeee, Maaaaaaize,' Trisha called softly from her darkened room, to which Maizie and Dee Dee both barked, 'WHAT?'
'Niiight,' Trisha said, laying her head down. 'Love yaaaaaaaa.'
Hoping this meant an end to Trisha's foolishness the two of them rolled their eyes and replied, 'Nuniiiiight!'
'Love yaaaaaa,' Trisha said once again, pushing her luck to the very extreme and receiving nothing in reply.
With very little left in the way of a night's sleep, the three friends eventually settled, each of them pondering the outcome of the following day with the onset of their first day's employment in quite some time.

Meanwhile, back at the pool house of Bradley's country estate, Terry too was turning in for the night having bid a fond farewell to the lovely Mariah, after some three and a half hours of gratuitous and at times acrobatic sex. Her wanton wailing, howling, and insistent pleading for deeper and harder penetration, had resonated far beyond the detached poolside premises -dispersing flocks of roosting crows, pipistrelle bats and an ever watchful tawny owl - in the orgasmic process. His shag pad, as he affectionately called it, now reeked of sweat and spattered bodily fluids and closely resembled a ransacked and war torn ghetto. 'Quality bird,' he said to himself, stretched out on his ruffled bed with his stomach in the air, one hand behind his head and the other clutching a glowing cigarette.

After having filled Mariah's head with empty promises, blatant lies and bucket loads of bullshit to bed her, Terry blew several contorted rings into the air whilst flicking the deposited ash from his chest hairs and grinning like the proverbial Cheshire cat. Eventually ditching the smoldering butt, Terry tapped at his Blackberry, updating his online status; naming no names but bigging up
his recent performance to almost Olympian standards, with a smattering of overly graphic innuendos, and ending his bragging text with a resounding 'Hashtag sexy fuckin beast or what.' He finally discarded his phone, retrieved a trapped testicle from between his legs and turned onto his side, letting out an extended reverberating trump in doing so.

An hour or so later, unbeknown to the slumbering Terry, Spencer had tip-toed from his quarters within the castle wearing nothing but his crimson satin house coat and carpet slippers, intent on furthering relations with their curvaceous cockney guest. Throwing caution to the wind and unable to curtail his burgeoning feelings, the man-hungry man-servant, with his chest beating rapidly with heightened anticipation, slipped quietly out of the drawing room french doors and made his way cat like through the walled garden toward the pool house, which by now was cloaked in darkness.

Looking furtively over his shoulder Spencer took the master key he had stolen from the housekeeper from his breast pocket and stooped to fumble for the lock, letting himself in as covertly as he could. Once inside and after easing the door closed he merely followed the nauseous nasal rumblings emanating from Terry's room. Moments later, cracking his shin on the upturned dining table that Mariah had earlier straddled, Spencer covered his mouth to muffle his cursing objections. Terry's bedroom door was ajar, and slithering through Spencer could just make out the waistband of his lurid market bought Gavin Klein boxer shorts, as he rarely slept beneath the sheets.

Such was Spencer's lust for Terry that even the lengthy succession of tiny bottom burps did not dissuade him, nor did the grinding of teeth. Now within inches of Terry's back, Spencer tipped his robe from either shoulder letting it fall to the floor, his manhood soon pulsating in his right hand. He was momentarily startled when Terry muttered in his sleep, 'Pinta Carlin an a baga nuts please Trace,' a reference to his Sunday afternoons propping up the bar at the Chequers where he'd leer at their regular weekend wench. 'Any chance of a tit wank an'all?' he asked, still very much asleep. Beside himself and trembling, Spencer put a knee up onto the polyester mattress and gripping the headboard pulled himself up behind Terry and sank gently beside him, content at first to lay within a hairs breadth of him, but soon his hand crept onto Terry's side and ever so gently brushed his skin with a gossamer touch.

Terry, who'd earlier plied Mariah with not one but three bottles of cut price vino and had supped more than his fair share of Bradley's vintage vodka which he had liberated from his host's Elizabethan cabinet that afternoon, did not stir.

Growing in confidence and taking Terry's inactivity as an open invitation to proceed, Spencer slid his quivering hand over and around Terry's waist and nuzzled his face into his ear.

'Mmmmm,' Terry groaned, stirring somewhat. 'Alright Maz,' he croaked, 'you come back for anuvva ammerin av ya.'

Spencer sighed, rubbing Terry's belly in a circular motion and blowing gently onto his cheek.

'Corrrr you dirty bitch,' Terry said, becoming aroused instantly. 'Get olda that,' he said, gripping Spencer's hand and forcing it down inside his boxers and around his stiffening shaft.

Spencer could hardly believe his luck and began massaging with increasing vigor.

'Niiiiiiice,' Terry moaned, readying himself for another marathon mauling. 'Go on girl, give it some,' he added, with his back to the butler. Spencer, whilst administering the firmest of hand relief he could muster, nestled in a little closer spooning into Terry's back, and in doing so thrusting his own throbbing erection at the crease of his bottom pushing his flimsy fashion fakes deeper within.

Terry stiffened his back suddenly, opening his eyes and staring at the blank wall in front of him, but then relaxed a tad, assuming Mariah had brought along a plastic playmate to spice up the party. 'If you're gonna use that fing ya betta grease the bleeda,' he said, wriggling his boxers to his knees in readiness.

'Oh I will,' Spencer said, running his tongue the length of Terry's left cheek.

'DO WHAT?' Terry gasped, detecting a masculine tone and running a hand along Spencer's forearm, brushing back the tell-tale hairs.

'WHAT THE FUCK?' he cried, wrenching Spencer's hand from his genitalia and flinging it aside.

'WHAT THE FUCKIN FUCK?' Swinging his stubby legs out in front of him, Terry rapidly dragged himself from his side of the bed.

'WHAT THE FUCKIN FUCKIN FUCK?'

Pounding at the light switch Terry shrieked and fell back against the wall. 'Arrrrrrrgh, fuck me Spence, what the fuck, what you doin ear you dirty bastard?'

'Sharing your bed,' Spencer replied calmly. 'Do you mind?'

'MIND!' Terry yelled, clasping his hands to his head. 'MIND! COURSE AR FUCKIN MIND. JESUS FUCK, WOSS GOIN ON, GET THE FUCK AATA MAR BED YOU FILFY FUCKER!'

Spencer remained reclined on Terry's bed. 'Oh come now Terry darling,' he replied, clearly displaying his crotch. 'You don't really want me to go do you?' His eyes tracked down to Terry's prominent phallus.

'Fuuuuuuuuck!' Terry cried, looking down in disgust. 'Fuck, what the fuck?' His boxers were still at half mast. 'What you done you dirty nonce?'

'Nothing you didn't want me to do darling,' Spencer smiled.

'Do what?' Terry cried yet again. 'Ar never, ar mean ar fought you was… Urrrrrgh you dirty bastard, get the fuck aata mar bed. I aint no shit stabber for fuck sake!' Slapping his penis which projected like a rod of iron, Terry clawed at his boxers, pulling them high above his bulging waistline. 'You touched mar dick you fuckin faggot,' he yelped, inching away a little. 'If you don't fuck right off, ar'm gonna kick the fuckin shit aata ya you batty bastard!'

'Oh I don't think you're going to do that Terry darling,' Spencer said, remaining calm considering Terry's threatening stance.

'Ar fuckin will!' Terry growled, raising a fist. 'And stop callin me darlin, I aint ya fuckin darlin. I aint no cock jockey neeva, so do one ya nancy fuck before ar proper lose me rag.'

Spencer, still unfazed, slipped from Terry's bed and stooped for his house coat giving Terry an eyeful of his bottom in the process.

'Fuck, shit!' Terry cried, screwing up his face and turning away. 'Ar mean it you fucker, ar'm gonna knock you into next fuckin week for this.'

'I doubt that very much,' Spencer informed him. 'You wouldn't want me to let slip how aroused you became at the hands of another man now would you?'

'DO WHAT?' Terry screeched. 'YOU BETTER FUCKIN NOT AR'M TELLIN YA. Anyway, ar fought you was a Doris ar swear ar did!'

'I believe you darling,' Spencer said, tying the cord around his waist. 'But I'm wondering if your friends and associates would be quite so convinced, after all, mud sticks you know.'

'You fuckin what!' Terry snarled, for the umpteenth time. 'You better not say nuffin or ar'll kick your bleedin ed in. D'you ear me!'

'Has anyone ever told you,' Spencer laughed, 'you're damned attractive when you're angry. Rather like Joe Pesci in Goodfellas.'

'You're avin a fuckin bubble aint'cha!' Terry barked, incensed at being likened to the Hollywood A lister. 'I outta cut your nuts off ya little prick!'
'See what I mean!' Spencer said, reminding Terry of Pesci's iconic line. 'Go on, say it again,' he pleaded, 'ya little prick, ya little prick!'
'Ar'll give you little prick!' Terry raged.
'Oh it's not that little, believe me,' Spencer said, raising his hand to his nose which disgusted Terry further.
'Just get the fuck aata've ear!' he said, hurling a pillow across at Spencer, who caught it and buried his face into it.
'What'chu doin?' Terry asked, sickened to the stomach at this point.
'I love the scent of a man,' Spencer informed him. 'And you my darling are one hell of a man. Mmmmmm, I will leave Terry darling, but not without a memento.'
'A what?' Terry asked, none the wiser. 'What'chu on abaat?'
'A trophy,' Spencer replied cheekily, gesturing toward Terry's boxer shorts. 'A keepsake to remember our time together. To buy my silence, so to speak.'
'ME PANTS!' Terry shrieked, gripping his beloved undergarment. 'You're avin a fuckin laugh aint'cha, you can fuck right off ya pervy poof!'
'Well then, have it your way,' Spencer said, heading for the door, 'but I must warn you I am an insatiable gossip.'
'WOAW, WOAW!' Terry yelled, raising his hands. 'Old up, old up ar got me rep to fink of ain I, you can't go raand spreadin that sorta shit, ar'll be bullied off the bleedin terraces ar will.'
'So er,' Spencer smiled at the bedroom door, 'do I get my memento then darling?'
Terry was backed against the wall, literally. 'Oh leave off geez,' he whined, 'just bugger off and keep ya norf and saaf shut will ya.'
'Look babes,' Spencer insisted, 'it's the knickers or nothing. So what's it going to be?'

'I aint ya babes,' Terry cursed, 'or ya bleedin darlin. This shit aint right ar'm tellin ya.'

Spencer stood with one hand on his hip and the other outstretched expectantly.

'Oh shit, come on mate,' Terry pleaded, 'gissa break will ya.'

Spencer remained steadfast, beckoning with his fingertips.

'Friggin ell!' Terry sulked, relenting and wriggling his boxers to his ankles with his right hand whilst covering his nether region with the left. 'Eyar!' he said, flinging them across the bed toward Spencer, who snatched them from the air.

'Mmmmmm thank you hun,' he said, cupping them to his face and inhaling Terry's mucky scent. 'I shall treasure them I promise.'

Terry snatched the remaining pillow to cover his modesty. 'You got what ya want, now piss off!' he told the elated Spencer. 'And you keep schtum abaat the and job fing, or ar swear ar'll av ya.'

Spencer draped the boxers over his shoulder. 'You can have me anytime you like darling,' he said provocatively, before disappearing out the door.

'FUCK!' Terry said aghast, with a hand to his forehead unable to come to terms with what had just taken place.

Dashing through to the bathroom Terry leapt into the shower cubicle, shuddering at first at the icy water, then turning the temperature as hot as he dare, Terry wrenched the sponge from the riser rail dousing it with copious amounts of fragrant shower gel and proceeded to scrub his crotch vigorously. 'Dirty bastard,' he sobbed, until his manhood appeared enflamed.

Terry remained beneath the power shower for quite some time, hoping to cleanse himself of any trace of homosexuality that may have tainted him. He then emerged in a heady daze, flinging his West Ham towel around his waist and walking zombie like through to the kitchen where he poured himself a generous measure of vodka and sat at the table staring into space, letting fly the occasional obscenity, disgusted with himself for allowing Spencer the liberty of groping him so intimately. Downing his glass in seconds, causing him to shudder, Terry poured another and then another, but was unable to drown the graphic images circulating his mind. 'Oh mar gawd,' he said, rolling the glass in his hand and contemplating the fallout and irreparable damage to his reputation should the details of the sordid affair ever reach the streets of his home town.

Distraught, disheveled and traumatized beyond consolation, Terry pounded at the linen table cloth looking toward the heavens for some semblance of forgiveness; an absolute first for the devout atheist who had only ever visited the house of god on two occasions. The most recent would have been his cousin Martina's wedding day, on which he arrived P'd as the proverbial newt howling a line or two of the Real Thing's 1976 hit *You to me are everything,* with his shirt tails exposed and his checkered tie askew. Prior to that would have been to steal the lead flashing from the 17th century slate roof and three pounds from the collection box set aside to repair that very roof.

Eventually, by the time Terry had swigged the dregs from the vodka bottle, he had worked himself up into such a guilt ridden state that he could stand it no longer. 'Fuck this!' he said, tossing the bottle aside. He staggered to his chest of drawers and emptied his entire collection of Sergio Tacchini track suits onto the bed. Cramming his bottom and stomach into one classic with unflattering horizontal stripes, Terry pulled the zipper up tight under his chin and stepped into his beloved Adidas. The remainder was hastily stuffed into a drawstring duffle bag along with seven pouches of tobacco, his jumbo bottle of *Pagan Man* aftershave, which had stood him in good stead with the less refined ladies over the years, and fifteen hundred pounds in cash, which Bradley had kindly given him on his arrival for essentials and such like.

Staggering and bouncing off the pool house walls Terry peered cautiously outside, petrified that Spencer may be lurking in the shadows wielding the erection that had probed him so intimately, but desperate on the other hand to flee the sordid scene, choosing instead to take his chances on the streets of London and run the risk of having his collar felt by the ever diligent D I Pritcher.

Trudging the length of the gravel drive switching his laden bag from shoulder to shoulder, Terry finally flagged down a passing motorist at the gate, using two fifty pound notes and promising another in exchange for a ride to his native East London. The spotty youth snatched the cash and told Terry to buckle up before wheel spinning away, mounting a grass verge and taking the first corner at break neck speed.

'Go on my son!' Terry urged. 'Give it some!'

CHAPTER SIX

A dawn chorus in rural England would usually consist of plump cooing pigeons, feisty sparrows and the occasional magpie calling to its mate, but on the North London street where Dee Dee and her friends now resided the adjacent neighbours, postmen and refuse collectors within earshot where treated to a more anarchic vocal volley.

'TRISHAAAAA, YOU GOT MAR LIPPY?' Maizie called, rummaging through her handbag. 'TRISHAAAA!'

'WHAAAAT?' Trisha replied from the bathroom.

'YOU GOT MAR LIPPY?' Maizie said, looking out into the hall.

'YEAH!' Trisha replied, smacking her lips together in front of the mirror. 'BUT THERE AINT NONE LEFT!'

Maizie charged into the bathroom and snatched the dispenser from Trisha's hand. 'Oh fanks a lot,' she raged, 'thas the only one ar got, ar can't go aat wivaat any.'

'Well neeva can I,' Trisha said, preening herself. 'Ya know what they say Maize, ya snooze ya lose.'

'Ar'll give you snooze ya feevin bitch!' Maizie yelled, shoving Trisha back against the bath.

'Ang on, ang on a minute,' Trisha pleaded, fearing an early morning slap. 'D'you want some lippy?'

'Course ar do ya prat!' Maizie barked.

'Well gissa kiss then,' Trisha said, lunging at her friend pouting. 'You can av summa this.'

'Piss off ya lezza bitch,' Maizie cried, covering her mouth and backing away.

'WILL YOU TWO URRY UP IN THERE!' Dee Dee called from the living room, where she crawled around on her hands and knees in search of her missing shoe.

'ISS ERRRR!' Maizie replied, fending Trisha off, 'SHE'S TRYNA SEX ME UP!'

'We done it before,' Trisha reminded Maizie. 'When we was skint, member?'

'Yeah ar do,' Maizie said, with her back to the wall. 'But thas before you was munchin muff left right and flippin centre, ya dirty cow.'

'Ow many more times av ar gotta tell ya,' Trisha protested, 'I ain a proper lezza, ar'm a bisexualist an ar don't wanna shag ya. D'you want some lippy or not?'

'Yeah course ar bloody do,' Maizie said, dodging Trisha's lips. 'But I aint swappin spit wiv you to get it.'

Dee Dee pushed her way into the bathroom and sat to pee. 'What the bleedin ell you two doin?' she asked, buttoning her blouse.

'She's nicked all me lippy Dee,' Maizie explained. 'Now she's tryna give it back.'

'Looks like yer swappin spit to me,' Dee Dee said, hoisting up her leggings and leaving Maizie alone with Trisha once again.

'No, no we aint, onest!' Maizie cried, wriggling free. 'We aint Dee!' she added, joining Dee Dee in the kitchen. 'We weren't swappin nuffing mate.'

Trisha retrieved her coat from a hook in the hall. 'Right ar'm off,' she told her friends. 'Ar gotta be there at arf eight an ar don't wanna be late, ar done you'z two some sarnies, they're in the fridge. We never ad no Tupperware so I ad to make do. See ya later.'

Trisha left for her induction into the RSPCA full of beans and bursting with enthusiasm.

'We better make a move in a mo Dee,' Maizie said, opening the fridge. 'What the fuck?' she then gasped, seeing two recycled bean tins with a ham sandwich rolled and crammed into either on the top shelf. 'Ava look Dee.'

'What a retard,' Dee Dee scoffed. 'She knows ar don't eat mayo an'all.'

'That aint mayo,' Maizie informed her on closer inspection. 'Thas banana yoghurt that is.'

'Do what?' Dee Dee recoiled. 'That girl's a friggin savage ar tell ya.'

Maizie stomped firmly on the refuse bin's pedal and dropped the makeshift lunch boxes inside. Supping the remainder of their tea, Maizie and Dee Dee donned their jackets, Maizie champing at the bit but Dee Dee dragging her heels.
'Come on Dee,' Maizie urged, 'iss only for a year and ya never know, ya might like it.'
'Don't old ya breff,' Dee Dee moaned, following her friend begrudgingly out of the flat.
The door at the bottom of the stairs opened as the two girls descended. 'Mawnin!' Maizie said, on seeing the mother emerge. But before she could reply courteously her husband dragged her back inside, fearing another confrontation. 'Weird,' Maizie said, as the door slammed in their faces.
'Ar wouldn't lose no sleep over it,' Dee Dee said, side stepping her friend and opening the street door.

Trisha had already boarded the number 43 bus, dropping into a seat beside a thickset middle aged gentleman.
'Mawnin!' she said, rubbing her hands together in anticipation of the day ahead. But the gentleman turned his face to the window with a stern expression. 'Oy!' Trisha said, with a little more conviction. 'Ar said mawnin.'
'Feck off!' the man snapped, in a broad Donegal brogue.
'Oh you're a paddy,' Trisha said, unfazed by his negativity. 'Me aunty Sal married a paddy, from Limmrick ar fink.'
'Limmerick!' the gentleman growled, annoyed at her mispronunciation.
'What?' Trisha asked. 'Oh yeah, thas what ar said, anyway Dougal iz name was, funny little bugger. Used to work on the roads layin the drains, up to iz neck in turds and tarmac e used to say, well andy at a barby, coz e proper reeked e used to keep the blue bottles off the burgers, nart ar mean. Where you from then, ay?' Again the gentleman chose to ignore her, but he hadn't reckoned on her tenacity.

'Dublin. You look like Dublinish to me,' she said, hazarding a guess and having very little geographical knowledge of the emerald isle.

'Am I bollocks!' her fellow passenger barked, his ancestors hailing from the North, sworn enemies of anyone south of the border. 'Belfast born and bred and damn proud of it, sure I wouldn't give ya shite for the south girly.'

'Ar know what ya mean,' Trisha said, recounting London's own feudal past. 'Me dad never went saaf of the river, bandit country e called it, e said them fuckers'd turn over their own muvvas for a coupla bob. Ar brought this fella ome once from Millwall, well me old man went ballistic bein an Ammers fan an'all that, e chased the poor bleeda aat the ouse wiv iz Black and Decker and frettened to cut iz gonad's off if e ever see im our sida the water again.'

Trisha's tale brought a wry smile to the Irish gentleman's otherwise sullen face. 'If you ask me girly,' he said leaning closer, 'the fecker got off loytly, we'da nailed the bastard to the floor, shot his knee caps to shite and set the bleed aloyt, sure we would.' Such was the bitter hatred vented between Catholic and Protestant in days gone by, which nowadays quietly simmered on the back boiler.

'Ar'm Trish,' Trisha said, offering her hand. The Irishman looked her up and down, hesitant at first to make her acquaintance. 'Don't worry, ar don't wanna shag ya,' Trisha informed him. 'Me dad brought me up proper e did, always look someone in the eye and shake their and e said.'

Admiring her old school values the gentleman relented, wrapping his hand around hers. 'Seamus,' he said. 'Where ya headin girly?'

'Ar'm gaana work,' Trisha told him. 'For the animal society mob, iss me first day an ar'm proper excited.'

'Sure, I can tell,' Seamus laughed . 'Ya haven't sat the feck still since ya got on the bus sure ya haven't.'

'Yeah ar know, ar'm wettin me crusties finkin abaat it,' Trisha squealed, bobbing up and down. 'Ar get a uniform an everyfing, ar probly won't get me taser straight away though coz arm a newbie.'

'A taser!' Seamus said, raising his eyebrows. 'What the feck?'

'Oh yeah,' Trisha said, convinced her new employers would equip her with tactical riot weaponry. 'Ya can't be too careful, summa them barmy bitches wiv an ouse fulla stinkin cats don't give em up wivaat a fight, but I aint takin no shit from em ar tell ya, a coupla smoke grenades, a face fulla pepper spray an a punch up the froat'll sort em aat.'

'Blimey O'reilly!' Seamus gasped, having assumed the organisation adopted a slightly less hands-on approach in their dealings with the general public. 'Don'tcha tink a taser's takin tings a tad too far?'

'Naaaah course not,' Trisha replied, defending her self-appointed right to bear arms. 'Anyone who urts them poor animals deserves a faasand volts up the gusset ar'm tellin ya.'

'Sure it's not the wretched animals I'm worried about, sure it isn't,' Seamus said, with a shred of sympathy for the unwitting owners who would very soon have the angel of death beating on their door, in the shape of this hormonal Essex beauty, and her venomous vengeance brought down upon them. Had they had prior warning they would surely change their spiteful ways, end the neglect, abuse and exploitation of the creatures entrusted to their care and beg for their immediate forgiveness.

'This is mar stop,' Trisha then said, looking over the shoulder of the passenger in front. 'See ya later geez.'

'Goodbye to ya missy,' Seamus said, tipping his cap. 'And the besta luck to ya, although I doubt you'll be needing it, sure ya won't.'

'Ahhhh fanks,' Trisha said, pressing the bell three times, antagonizing the driver no end. 'An the besta British to you an'all mate.'

Alighting and leaving Seamus to continue his journey, contemplating what on earth had just occurred and having, like so many before him, been touched by her inimitable presence. Trisha then dropped several coins into a homeless man's Styrofoam cup, unaware that the Sisters of Mercy had just visited the down and out, bringing hot soup and a comforting word as they did every morning. Grateful, but a tad peeved, the vagrant fished around in his mulligatawny with his grubby fingers to retrieve the cash, which to his disgust amounted to a paltry fourteen pence. The faithful mongrel at his side licked the copper coins clean and nuzzled in beside him against the prevailing wind.

Feeling good about herself after her charitable act, Trisha waltzed along the busy street toward the society's headquarters.

'Oooh oooooh!' she called, shoving the revolving doors and addressing the receptionist. 'Alright mate!'

'Can I help you?' the receptionist asked, looking over her spectacles from behind her desk.

'Ar'm ear for the job,' Trisha replied, in awe of her surroundings. 'When do ar get me uniform?'

'I take it you have a name,' the receptionist asked sarcastically, whilst checking the day's appointments.

'Course I av ya doughnut,' Trisha joked, peering across. 'Thas me there look. Trisha.'

'Yes, yes I see,' the receptionist agreed, reviewing her notes. 'It appears you're here on a placement, fresh out of prison I see. Tut tut.' She gave Trisha a disapproving glance. 'We've had your type here before.'

'Wod'ya mean mar type?' Trisha asked angrily. 'So ar bin banged up, big deal, ar paid me dues now ar wanna elp your mob aat, woss wrong wiv that, ay?'

'Well I for one do not approve,' the fifty something told Trisha, with her arms crossed in defiance. 'This is a respectable charity with Her Majesty's royal approval, and the likes of you and your kind would only tarnish our good name.'

'Now you listen ear you stuck up...,' Trisha was about to unleash a tirade of abuse upon the overly officious receptionist, when the adjacent elevator door opened and a young lady in her early thirties appeared wearing a figure hugging pin stripped suit.

'Ahhh, you must be Patricia,' she said, in a more welcoming tone. 'I'm Susan. Susan Sharpe, head of human resources here at headquarters.'

Trisha climbed down from the receptionist's desk and took Susan's hand. 'Iss Trisha actually,' she said, looking Susan up and down admiringly. 'Ar'm ear abaat the job.'

'Yes of course,' Susan smiled. 'I've been expecting you. Come on up and we'll take a few details from you. I suppose you could do with a cup of tea, I know I could.'

'Yeah fanks,' Trisha said, flicking the sour faced receptionist a firm middle finger. 'Spin on this, bitch!' she said, while Susan's back was turned. 'Woss er problem?' she then asked, once the elevator doors had closed.

'Oh you mean Martha,' Susan smiled, selecting the third floor. 'I must apologise if she gave you a hard time. She's been with us for quite some time, twenty five years I believe, and can be a little cranky at times, but she's part of the furniture around here now.'

'Cranky!' Trisha exclaimed. 'Is that what ya call it. She's lucky ar didn't punch er up the froat for lookin daan er beak at me.'

'She does have a way of rubbing people up the wrong way I'll grant you that,' Susan agreed, finding Trisha's attitude mildly refreshing. 'Tea or coffee?' she asked, passing through the main office.

'Ar'll av a cuppa rosy cheers,' Trisha said, having forgone her morning brew. 'Got any biscuits?'

'I'll er, I'll see what I can do,' Susan said, tapping a colleague on the shoulder. 'Kerry could you be a darling and rustle us up two teas please,' she asked, 'and if we have any biscuits that'll be marvelous.'

'Jammie dodgers if ya got em,' Trisha piped up, tapping the opposite shoulder. 'And leave me bag in ar like it strong enough to make ya teef rattle.'

'Yes miss,' Kerry said, leaving her monitor.
'When do ar get me uniform?' Trisha asked, following Susan into her office and nosing at the framed photographs adorning the walls which documented the society's illustrious history.
'We'll get you kitted out soon enough,' Susan replied, taking a file from her cabinet and sitting at the desk. 'We just have the formalities to take care of first. Please, take a seat.'
Trisha remained standing, scanning the photographs and the society's personnel therein for signs of weaponry, but of course there were none. 'Hmmm,' she said pensively. 'Wod'ya do when someone gets proper stroppy and won't roll over.'
'You mean the owners?' Susan said, looking up.
'Yeah, the scumbags,' Trisha said, remaining steadfast at the wall. 'D'you lot do some ninja shit on em or summink?'
'Oh heavens no!' Susan laughed. 'We have the backing of the police force who are readily at available should a situation get out of hand, so to speak, which on occasion they do, as I'm sure you'll understand.'
'Ar don't need the old bill to sort mar shit aat,' Trisha told the HR manager. 'Just gimme a taser an a paira Doc Martins an ar'll get a result every time, ar promise ya.'
'A taser!' Susan chuckled. 'I admire your enthusiasm Patricia, I mean Trisha, but we aren't authorised to use such a degree of force. Although, and this is purely off the record you understand, there are some owners whose actions have turned my stomach, and are whole heartedly deserving of such recourse, or maybe even worse if you get my drift. But like I say, those are my personal views and not those of the society.'
'Yeaaaah ar get ya,' Trisha smiled, taking Susan's remarks as a green light to unleash her own brand of retribution on anyone who would dare harm a hair, or feather for that matter, of any living creature. She would champion the cause with a manicured fist of iron; smiting those responsible, freeing the oppressed, the mistreated and the

exploited who had no voice of their own, and embarking on a fearless valiant crusade in the name of justice. 'Forget Noah and his ridiculous ark,' she thought to herself, animals would flock to her in their droves and nestle into her bosom.
'Trisha, Trisha,' Susan said, pen in hand.
'Oh sorry, what?' Trisha said, snapping out of her exuberant daydream. 'Woss that?'
'It's our waver,' Susan explained. 'Absolving the society of any blame should you be bitten, scratched or even mauled whilst carrying out your duties. It's merely a formality, but I'm sorry our insurance company insists on it. You do understand?'
'Oh yeah, course,' Trisha agreed, reaching to scrawl her signature. 'Ar know what them robbin fucker's are like. Me uncle Ronnie got that bird flu bollocks when e was scrapin the pigeon shit offa Nelson's whatsit, the poor bleeda was laid up in ospital for mumfs on a ventilator fingy before e snuffed it.'
'Oh dear, I am sorry to hear that,' Susan said, clutching her chest. 'How awful!'
'Yeah not arf,' Trisha said, handing back the pen. 'Me aunty Rita was expectin bundles in compo coz e paid into some shite scheme for years, she went aat and bought a new mota, a conservatory an a Nintendo Wii whatsit for the kids on the strenf of it, and booked a two week stay at Disneyland Paris, all bloody inclusive an'all. Well you should've seen the look on er face when they sent er a cheque for six undred quid wiv some bullshit excuse that e weren't wearin an ard at or summink, she was proper gutted ar tell ya.'
'Yes, yes I dare say she was,' Susan said, losing her train of thought entirely. 'Right er, where were we?'
'Ar've signed all ya fings,' Trisha told her, slapping her thighs expectantly. 'So what appens naah, do ar get kitted aat wiv me uniform and gadgets or what? Ar want wunna them telescopic truncheons the old bill use for whackin the backa

the bastards legs, an a walkie talkie, yeah ar want wunna them.'
Susan was about to quash Trisha's outlandish expectations of the society's limits but, like so many before who had attempted to intervene, her words fell on the deafest of ears.
'Can ar be whiskey tango?' Trisha asked, requesting her own personal call sign. 'Me and me mates used to get off our tits neckin that aata plastic cups at the yoof centre, that and some Campari shit that Maizie nicked aat the Co-op. Get the bloody Baileys ar told er, but oh no, not er, soppy nuts arf inches a bottla sherry and that dishwater. Ar said to er even me nan wouldn't give ya the steam off er piss for it, we draaned it wiv diet coke and drunk it though coz we ad fuck all else.'
'Thank you Kerry,' Susan said, taking the refreshments from her assistant.
'I'm sorry miss, we have no biscuits,' Kerry told Trisha politely.
'Thas alright mate,' Trisha smiled, taking a crumpled candy bar from her pocket and dunking it. 'Ar'll finish off me wham bar.'
Kerry looked on in abject amazement and then across at her boss, who shrugged her shoulders in silent reply.
Trisha slurped and gargled until her sweet was no more, and then proceeded to pick at her teeth. 'Ar love em, but they bugger up me fillins,' she told Susan, as Kerry left them to inform her colleagues of Trisha's apparent vulgarity.
'Well Trisha,' Susan said, a short while later once the formalities were complete. 'I'd like to take this opportunity to welcome you to our organisation and thank you personally in advance.'
'Thas alright,' Trisha replied, knotting her sweet wrapper and tossing it onto Susan's desk. 'It was iver you'z lot or the omeless, and to be onest wiv ya, arfa them lot earn more than you, me and Richard bloody Branson, poncin a coupla

bob off anyone mug enough to give it to em. Fuck em, thas what ar say.'

Susan sat stunned at Trisha's brutal honesty and colorful command of the English language. 'There by the grace of God Trisha,' she said, hinting that a twist of fate was all that stood between them and a bitter existence on the mean and unforgiving streets.

'Do what?' Trisha asked - the metaphor wasted on her completely.

'I mean the shoe could quite easily have been on the other foot,' Susan explained, she was then forced to elaborate seeing Trisha's blank expression. 'We really should count our blessings and think ourselves lucky it's not us out there sleeping rough in all weathers. Don't you agree?'

'Naaah,' Trisha said confidently. 'Me auntie Janice says as long as she's got an ole in er arse there'll always be somewhere for me to get me nut daan at er place, mind you, iss a back bustin zed bed wiv a saggy mattress an a wonkey leg, but I ain't complainin. Ar use to knock er up at all hours of the night when ar'd done me cab fare on double Smirnoff's and couldn't be arsed to walk ome.'

It was Susan's turn with the blank expression now, lost in Trisha's tedious tale. 'Yes, quite,' she said, coming too. 'Right, let's see about that uniform shall we?' she added, rising from her desk. 'Then there'll be a short video presentation explaining the society's objectives and what not. You'll begin your duties tomorrow morning. I've put you out on patrol with one of our more senior members to show you the ropes, so to speak.'

'Yeah nice one,' Trisha replied. She followed Susan from her office, her hand hovering inches from her swaying buttocks, wanting so much to squeeze and caress them through her tight tailored skirt.

Dee Dee and Maizie meanwhile had made their way to the tube station for their brief journey to the Westmoreland centre for the mentally impaired. Built in the late eighties,

the centre housed twenty three full time residents of all ages, with a further fifteen beds available for respite stop overs.
'Ar can't wait, can you Dee?' Maizie said, looking along the platform for any sign of the young busker she'd recently made a connection with.
'You gettin on this friggin train or what?' Dee Dee said, wrenching her friend's coat sleeve.
'Ar was sayin ar can't wait can you?' Maizie said again.
Dee Dee merely answered the question with a look that said it all.
'Oh come on Dee, you'll enjoy it ar promise ya,' Maizie chirped, in an attempt to raise her friend's spirits.
'You reckon,' Dee Dee grunted, having had very little sleep that night; with this she nestled against the glass divider at the end of the row of seats and closed her eyes.
Moments later Maizie was nudging Dee Dee's arm. 'Dee, we gotta get off ear,' she told her dozing friend. 'Blimey mate, you was aat for the caant there, ar tell ya.'
'Mmmmm yeah,' Dee Dee mumbled, rubbing her eyes and dragging herself from her seat.
Exiting at Finsbury Park station along with a tide of bustling commuters, the two girls perused the directions they had been given before crossing the street, taking their lives into their own hands in doing so as a speeding motorcycle courier swerved and narrowly missed them.
'GET OUT THE ROOOOOAD!' he yelled in passing.
'YOU GET AAT THE FUCKIN ROAD YA PRICK,' Dee Dee barked, picking up a cola can and hurling it after him. 'Wanker!' she growled, in no mood for such an altercation.
'What a dick ay Dee?' Maizie agreed, ducking between the parked cars. By the time the two of them arrived at the centre Dee Dee was positively fuming, having fended off a ravenous spaniel and the advances of an inebriated Rastafarian supping special brew and slurring sexual innuendos.

'Mawnin!' Maizie said, entering the foyer with Dee Dee lagging behind.

'Hello there!' a well groomed young gentleman in a baby pink shirt and flannel trousers said, emerging to greet them. 'You must be our new girls. Deborah right?' he added, offering Maizie a hand.

'Naah thas Dee,' Maizie informed him, 'ar'm Maizie.'

'Oh I do apologize,' the man said, tapping at his identification on his breast pocket. 'Well as you can see my name's Richard. I'm the assistant manager here at Westmoreland and we're so glad to have you two on board. We're not quite full to capacity at the moment, but that's not to say we aren't rushed off our feet. As you can imagine our residents require round the clock care and supervision, and with our governmental funding being slashed to the bone year in year out that sometimes just isn't possible I'm afraid.'

'Saands abaat right,' Maizie sighed, 'they got plenny of dough to bomb the shit aatta some poor bleedas arf way raand the world, but ask em for a coupla bob for the needy in this country and you'll get fuck all.'

Maizie's rant struck a chord with the assistant manager who'd been pleading with his local MP, and the wider government, for increased funding for their ill equipped and under staffed centre, but had been rebuffed on each application.

'Well, I wouldn't have put it quite like that,' he smiled, 'but yes, I believe you have it in a nutshell my dear.'

'It aint right is it Dee?' Maizie told her friend, who had been tinkering with her mobile phone the whole time.

'What?' Dee Dee said, looking up. 'What aint?'

'The government!' Maizie insisted. 'They won't give em enough dough to look after these poor buggers proper.'

'Wod'you expect!' Dee Dee sneered. 'Them arsewipes are too soddin busy linin their own pockets, ridin araand in two flippin jag's and screwin the rest of us over.'

It was clear to Richard that there was absolutely no love lost between Dee Dee and the powers that be. 'Yes, quite,' he said, having to agree no matter how brash Dee Dee's reply. 'Right, well, I'll show you around so you can get a feel of the place, and run through your duties.'
'Yeah fanks,' Maizie said enthusiastically. 'Come on Dee,' she urged her trudging friend.

That evening Dee Dee and Maizie arrived home first, having had an extensive tour of the centre and been introduced to many of the residents. Maizie had been on a high the whole way home, bending Dee Dee's ear. 'Oh they were lovely though weren't they Dee, ay?' she said, flinging her coat over the back of the sofa. 'Don'tcha fink?'
'Oh give it a rest Maize will ya,' Dee Dee moaned. 'You're doin mar nut in you are.'
'Sorry mate but,' Maizie continued, unable to contain herself, 'them little Downes kiddies were gorgeous weren't they, are just wonnid to scoop em all up and bring em ome ar did.'
'You're off your ed you are,' Dee Dee scoffed, kicking off her shoes. 'Mar friggin feet ar killin me,' she added, massaging her toes, 'we ain ardly sat daan all bleedin day av we.'
'Ar can't wait till tomorra,' Maizie squealed, 'we get to feed em an everyfing.'
'Whoop de bleedin doo,' Dee Dee sneered, rolling her eyes. 'Ar'm bleedin ecstatic abaat it an'all.'
Maizie folded her arms across her chest and glared at her friend. 'Dee, them poor gits never asked to be born like that did they, no they never, so the least we can do is elp em aat ain it. What if you give berf to a beautiful kiddy and they told you it was disabled ay, if it was me ar'd love em no matter what, ar would.'
'Well!' Dee Dee snapped. 'Seein as I ain't plannin on avin kids that aint likely to appen is it. Ar know you and Trish want a shit load of ankle biters but it aint for me, ar wanna

live mar life wivaat some screamin, shittin rug rat angin araand me.'
'Speakin of Trisha,' Maizie said, looking about the place, 'where is she?'
'Ar don't care,' Dee Dee replied, 'she ain ear so thas a blessin in mar book.'
'Oh Deeee,' Maizie whined, 'ar know she's a proper, proper pain in the arse but it narf quiet wivaat er ain it. Ar mean, it just aint the same is it?'
'Aint the bleedin same!' Dee Dee cursed. 'You wonnid to rip er friggin ed off last night, member?'
'Well, well yeah ar did I admit it,' Maizie agreed, recalling their violent interlude. 'But iss bin like that since we was kids ain it, but ar still love er, don'tchu?'
Dee Dee paused for a moment, then was about to concur when there was a rattling of a key in the door and that all too familiar voice.
'Hiyaaaaaaaaaaa,' Trisha called, slamming the door behind her, toppling three pictures which hung in the hall from their mounts, and waltzing through to the living room. 'Tadaaaaaaaaaah!' she sang, spinning to display her new society uniform. 'Coppa loada this, do ar look the bollocks or what, ay?'
'D'you want me to answer that?' Dee Dee smirked, looking her friend up and down. 'Who you come as, postman pissin Pat?'
'Oh shutuuup Dee,' Trisha said, posing proudly in her pressed navy jacket with her peaked cap tilted to one side. 'Ar got shiny buttons, steel toe bovva boots an a pukka belt for all me gadgets.'
'Gadgets!' Maizie said, looking closely. 'What bleedin gadgets?'
'Well I aint got em yet,' Trisha explained, 'coz ar'm on probation ain I, but when ar do ar'm gonna proper kick some arse ar tell ya.'
'Oh ar get it,' Dee Dee laughed, 'ar bet'chu asked em for a flippin taser din'tcha, ay?'

'Well yeah,' Trisha replied. 'But like ar said ar'm on probation so ar gotta wait a coupla mumfs for me bits and bobs, ar get a walkie talkie though tommora when ar go aat on patrol.'
'Patrol!' Maizie chuckled. 'You aint doin a tour of Afghani-fuckin-stan ya know.'
'Ya gotta be prepared for anyfing,' Trisha informed her mocking friends. 'Ar'm finkin of takin up that ultimate cage fightin shit, in case any of them badger baitin or dog fightin geezers get aat their prams.' Trisha stood preening and plucking tiny particles of fluff from her jacket sleeves. 'They showed us a video today, ar missed most of it coz ar was textin and stuff, but what ar did see was so sad, there was this skinny orse called Ted they rescued off the pikeys, firty five scabby cats livin in a one bed flat, a yooge massive swan fing wiv a fishin net wrapped raand its neck, a namster wiv a gammy leg, oh and this poor pitbull named Freddie whose cock of an owner burnt sixty free times wiv a fag butt and beat wiv a baseball bat till e was unconscious, e'z alive but terrified of blokes naah.'
'Bastard!' Dee Dee growled. 'If ar got me ands on im ar'd bend the slag over and butt fuck im wiv iz own bleedin bat ar would.'
'Yeah me an'all,' Maizie added, 'wiv no lube neeva, make the fucker wish e'd never bin born.'
'Then there was these gorgeous little fluffy ducklings,' Trisha said, sitting beside Maizie and removing her cap. 'In the middle lane of the M25 at Potters Bar, the little perishers caused a fifteen mile tail back coz a nice man from Eddie Stobarts wouldn't squish em wiv iz forty footer.'
'Ahhh thas nice of im,' Maizie sighed, 'and you lot got em off safe and saand did ya?'
'Yep, we did!' Trisha said proudly. 'Every one of em, and took em back to their muvva.' She then sprang from the sofa. 'Ar meant to show ya this Dee,' she said, lifting the hem of her jacket and thrusting her bottom in Dee Dee's

face. 'Look at me traasers, they go right up the cracka me arse and show off me fong, nice aint they?'

'Put the kettle on now yer ome,' Dee said dismissively, shoving Trisha aside.

Trisha's heart sank having ran the quarter mile or so from the bus stop to share the day's experiences with her best friends. 'Yeah alright,' she sulked. 'How was your day anyway?' she asked, heading for the kitchen.

'Yeah it was dead good!' Maizie called after her. 'We aint got a uniform like yours but we met some lovely people, dint we Dee?'

'Hmmmmm,' Dee Dee grunted, paying very little attention once again.

'Oh Trish, there was this one little boy,' Maizie explained, 'Domonic iz name is, e'z got that Downes fingy, oh e'z lovely Trish e really iz. Ar played connect four wiv im and e beat me the little bleeda. E'z muvva brings im daan there every day so she can av a break, but some of em live there all the time, don't they Dee?' Maizie again got no response from Dee Dee who merely turned the volume up a little louder. 'Once we've ad our trainin,' Maizie continued unabated, 'they reckon we can take em aat an everyfing. Ar'm really lookin forward to that.'

It was clear that Dee Dee had made her mind up to spend the remainder of her time doing as little as possible for the charity, and with absolutely no emotional attachment whatsoever.

'Oh I almost forgot,' Trisha said, retrieving her bag from the hall. 'Ar got us summink nice for tea, to celebrate if ya nart ar mean. Iss ya favrit Dee, chicken kievs wiv boil in the bag ballsmatic rice, they was on a bogof at appysavers so ar got a shit load of em.'

Dee Dee spun round at the mention of the culinary treat. 'Ooh yeah nice one Trish,' she said with renewed vigour. 'Ar got some cans of cider in the fridge we can crack them open an'all.'

'Yeah,' Maizie said, hurriedly setting the tiny teak table with its flaking varnish and cigarette burns, while Trisha emptied the contents of her shopping bag into the microwave. 'Iss like bein back on the estate ain it?' Maizie added, flicking a dead blue bottle across the room. The chipped mismatched crockery, dated decor and lurid linoleum was a far cry from their former glamorous surroundings, but somehow being together as they had been throughout the best and worst of times was enough. After all, they had come from next to nothing so it was hardly a culture shock, more a reality check for the three friends.

Dee Dee filled three mugs with value cider. 'Cheers,' she said, taking a sip. 'God thas dire that is,' she gagged, looking down into the fizzy brew.

'It aint Moet ar give ya that,' Maizie agreed, 'but ar've ad worse. Member that shit your dad used to make in iz garage? What did e call it, donkey punch wern it?'

'Hmmmmm,' Dee Dee growled at the mention of her father, who had abandoned her and her mother many years previous to start a new life with a close family friend. 'Eeya, av some more,' she said, filling Maizie's mug and changing the subject. 'Trisha where's that bleedin dinner?'

'COMIN!' Trisha called, dishing up their supper. 'There you are, get that daan ya necks,' she added, setting the plates down in front of her flat mates. 'Eat it while iss ot ok, oh an ar got some squirty cream an'all.'

'What for?' Maizie asked. 'Woss for afters?'

'Nuffing,' Trisha said, looking puzzled, 'iss for the kievs.' She then proceeded to spray a swirling foam peak onto her processed chicken portion.

'Jesus Trish!' Dee Dee said in absolute disgust, 'you really aint right d'you know that!'

'Triiiiiiish,' Maizie said, toying with her rice. 'Why is there melted plastic in me grub?'

'Dunno,' Trisha replied, tucking in without a care.

'Er,' Maizie added quizzically, 'you did boil the rice dint'cha.'

'No,' Trisha said, with her mouth full, 'ar ding'd it.'

'Trisha you dumb fuck!' Dee Dee snapped. 'Iss boil in the bag rice, for fuck sake!'

'And?' Trisha replied, in between further mouthfuls and scooping cream from her chin. 'It was only a minute an arf in the nuke, if you don't want that ar'll av it.'

'Fill ya boots,' Dee Dee said, pushing her plate away and shaking her head. 'Fancy a sarnie?' she asked Maizie.

'Yeah go on,' Maizie said, discarding her own dinner also.

'There's gratitude for ya!' Trisha moaned. 'Ar won't bovva next time.'

'Don't!' Dee Dee and Maizie both told her in no uncertain terms.

While Dee Dee prepared an alternative to Trisha's catastrophic creation, Maizie drained her mug of value cider. 'We got any more booze Dee?' she asked, 'ar'm proper gettin me drinkin ed on.'

'Yeah me an'all,' Trisha said, swigging hers to the end.

'Naah thas the last of it,' Dee Dee told them. 'Ar got a pony in me pocket if ya wanna nip daan Kareem's. Can ya get us ten fags while ya there?'

'Baat time you jacked them in ain it Dee,' Maizie preached. 'Me and Trish give that shit up ages ago.'

'Ar don't give a monkey's what you two done,' Dee Dee said, waving a bread knife in their direction. 'If ar wanna fag ar'm gonna av a fag, alright!'

'All we was sayin Dee,' Trisha said, siding with Maizie, 'is that they aint no good for ya mate, why don'tcha get wunna them lectric fags, ar seen em at Rommie market.'

'Coz ar don't wanna look like a complete cock,' Dee Dee told them sternly. 'If you'z aint gonna get em for me ar get em meself.'

'Alright ar get em,' Maizie said, swiping the twenty pound note from her hand.

'Me cousin Shelly,' Trisha said, whilst licking her plate.

'Oh fuck ear we go,' Maizie said, rolling her eyes.

'No, no listen!' Trisha added, waving her fork in the air. 'She went an got erself ipnotised she did, wiv doctor Kasmagaani or whateva iz name is, e'z got a place above the ninety nine p shop on the Barking Road.'

Dee Dee and Maizie both looked at one another with that *do we really want to hear this* look.

'Anyway,' Trisha continued unhindered, 'she ad six sessions wiv im a coupla years ago and she aint ad a fag since, mind you ar reckon e musta felt er up or summink while e was doin iz voodoo shit, coz er two year old Michaela's definitely got a bitta Bengali in er ar don't care what ya say.'

'Oh shut up you idiot,' Dee Dee said dismissively, 'thas all bollocks that is.' She handed Maizie a cheese and pickle sandwich and headed for the sofa, but before she was seated Trisha rose from the table and thrust her fork into her friend's forearm. 'What abaat akipuncha?' she said, jabbing again and again.

'ARRRGH WHAT THE FUCK?' Dee Dee yelled, leaping aside, her sandwich slipping from her plate in the process. 'You soppy bitch what ya doin?'

'Akipuncha!' Trisha replied, stooping to retrieve the sandwich. 'Ar see this documentry on it, iss all abaat ya nerve endins apparently.'

'Nerve endins!' Dee Dee raged. 'Ar'll give you fuckin nerve endins!'

'What, what?' Trisha said, dusting off the sandwich. 'Ar was only tryna elp, it looks a piece a piss, ar reckon ar could sort you aat in a couple've hours.'

Dee Dee raised a fist. 'Ar'll sort you aat in a coupla minutes!' she yelled, lunging at Trisha baring her teeth.

'Deeeee leave er!' Maizie said, stepping between them. 'She aint werf it mate, you know that, sit yaself daan ar'll get ya fags.'

'Wunna these days Trisha,' Dee Dee said, nursing her punctured arm. 'Wunna these bleedin days ar swear.'

'Er Deeee,' Trisha said, pushing her luck beyond all acceptable levels. 'If you don't want this sandwich can I av it?'

'No you bleedin can't!' Dee Dee snarled, leaping from the sofa and snatching the snack and hurling it into the bin. 'Your muvva shoulda draaned you at berf ar swear it.'

Trisha stood in stunned silence for a moment before being dragged toward the door by Maizie. 'Come on you,' Maizie told her, grabbing their coats en route. 'You're comin wiv me daan the mini mart before she gives you a right ander, or summink worse.'

'Oh alright,' Trisha agreed, still reeling from Dee Dee's verbal assault. 'Only if ar can get a scratch card. Me cousin Darren won seventy grand for gettin free pigs in a row on one of em on New Year's day, the lucky bleeda. Im an iz mate ad two weeks on the piss in Torremolinos on the strenf of it.'

'Maizie!' Dee Dee barked from the sofa, unable to concentrate on her dvd. 'Get er the fuck aat of ear will ya, ar wanna watch this!'

'Oh thas a good film that Dee,' Trisha piped up.

'Shutup!' Dee Dee snapped, sensing an impending spoiler. 'Ar don't wanna know,'

'Come on will ya!' Maizie urged from the hall, but Trisha could hardly contain herself.

'Don't say it!' Dee Dee warned Trisha. 'Just piss off aat.'

'Ar won't tell ya the endin Dee,' Trisha said, fit to burst. 'But Sandra Bollock there, she cops off wiv er best mate's geeza who turns aat to be a proper nut job and tries to draan er in the barf, but she stabs im in the eye wiv er toofbrush.'

'Oh fanks a fuckin lot,' Dee Dee said, folding her arms. 'You've ruined it you retard!'

'No, no I aint,' Trisha said, in her defence. 'Coz e aint dead, e comes back later wiv a pirate patch fingy and kidnaps er dog, but she unts im daan and shoots im in the nuts wiv a crossbow. Issa quality film mate you'll love it.'

Maizie took Trisha by the arm and dragged her to the door. 'Get aat will ya!' she said, sensing an explosive situation. 'Leave er alone coz she'll bleedin batter ya.'

Dee Dee sat seething once again as her friends made their way down the dimly lit communal stairs to the street door. It was late evening and the North London back streets were relatively deserted, save for a few drunken revellers leaving the Ship and Shovel.
'OY OY GORGEOUS!' one of them yelled across the street, grabbing at his crotch. 'WANT SUMMA THIS DO YA?'
Maizie looked the bloated scruff up and down. 'AR TELL YA WHAT MATE!' she yelled back, 'EVEN THOUGH AR'M TEMPTED, I AINT GOT THE TIME AND YOU AINT GOT THE STAMINA. SO TAKE THAT PENCIL DICK OF YOURS AND JOG THE FUCK ON!'
The drunk's friends fell about laughing at Maizie's retort, pushing and shoving their friend. 'Pencil dick, thas fuckin priceless,' one of them said, ruffling his hair. 'She's proper mugged you off mate.'
'Dykes!' he replied, breaking free and kicking out at a parked car.

Ambulance and patrol car sirens occasionally pierced the eerie city silence, but being now commonplace, they hardly caused a stir among the complacent residents.
'Wanna wine gum?' Trisha asked, taking a crumpled packet from her pocket and popping two into her mouth. 'Ar've only got green ones left and there a bit ard, but iss better that nuffing ain it.'
'Ar dunno abaat that,' Maizie sneered, eyeing the jaded jellies. 'Where d'ya get them from anyway?'
'Ar faand em at the flat,' Trisha said, taking another. 'Daan the side of the fridge, if ya suck the fluff off of em they aint that bad, go on get involved.'
'No fanks!' Maizie said, turning away. 'You dunno ow long they bin there do ya.'
'Oh shuuuut uuup,' Trisha laughed. 'You're too fussy Maize thas your trouble, ar member me nan used to av the same casserole on the go for mumfs, every coupla days she'd

chuck in anuvva mutton bone and an and fulla sprouts, friggin ansum it was ar'm tellin ya.'

Following Maizie into Kareem's mini mart to the sound of his two tone door alarm, Trisha was instantly drawn to the Punjabi grocery isle where the sights and smells tantalized her senses. 'Woss this, woss that?' she asked, darting from one side to another, thrusting packets of spices under her nose and scrutinizing the illegible table of contents of the Eastern produce. 'What are these?' she asked the assistant, offering up what at first appeared to be shriveled tomatoes.

'Scotch bonnet chillies madam,' the Pakistani owner told her. 'Very very hot. Very hot indeed.'

'Ooooh nice, ar can do wunna me chilli con carnes,' Trisha said, popping half a dozen into a brown paper bag. 'We can av it wiv a jacket tayta tommora night,' she told Maizie in the opposite isle. 'Ar do some chips wiv it an'all if ya like, or would ya rarva av mash, wod'ya reckon?'

'Mash!' Maizie said confused momentarily. 'Wiva jacket potato?'

'OK mash it is then,' Trisha said, putting three large baking potatoes into a bag along with a packet of smash.

'Mash and potato,' Maizie said again, expecting the penny to drop in Trisha's tiny mind.

'Yes alright, ar got it!' Trisha said, pointing out the packet in her basket. 'Ar'll get a treacle tart for afters an'all shall I?'

'Yeah whateva,' Maizie said, adding a litre of vodka to her basket. 'We avin mash wiv that an'all are we?'

'Don't be daft Maize!' Trisha laughed. 'Ar get anuvva tin of squirty cream for that, ooh an owbaat pineapple?'

'Class,' Maizie said, paying very little attention.

While Maizie checked their limited funds, Trisha skipped around the isles swinging her basket. 'Oy go easy!' Maizie called. 'We aint got shit loadsa dough ya know!'

'Yeah ar know,' Trisha replied, thumbing the magazines. 'Alright geez?' she then said to a midget standing beside her with his nose in a copy of *steam locomotive enthusiast*. 'Oh, ar know what you come in ear for mate,' she told him, 'you

don't av to be embarrassed.' With that Trisha snatched the magazine from his hands and tossed it back onto the rack.
'What, but I...,' the man, measuring no more than three feet, said aghast.
'Yeah ar know what ya want,' Trisha said, dropping her basket, stooping and grabbing him around the waist and hoisting him up into her arms as though he were a child. 'There ya go geez,' she added, pointing out the pornographic glossies on the top shelf. 'Wod'ya want: *Boobs n Butts*, *Bent over Babes*, *The Doggers Digest*, of if yer into some proper shifty shit they got *Pissin for Pleasure*. Oooh look, ya get a free shower cap wiv that one, thas andy ain it.'
'Put me down!' the miniature man cried, wriggling and kicking his tiny legs. 'Put me down!'
'Oh ar get it,' Trisha said, eager to please. 'You're into that degradin lark aintcha? Alright a'rll give it a go ya stumpy little fuck, ow's that, does that do it for ya, look at'cha, ya knee high to a friggin garden gnome ya pervy little ponce.'
'Trisha!' Maizie cried, rounding the isle after hearing the commotion. 'Put im daan!'
'I am for fuck sake!' Trisha replied, taking the dwarf's thrashing as a sign of ecstasy. 'The little fucker's lovin it an'all, look at im go.'
'No, let him go will ya!' Maizie insisted. 'E don't wanna be picked up.'
'No I damn well don't,' the man cried, wriggling free and dropping to the floor. 'I... I've never been so insulted in all my life.'
'Oh fanks,' Trisha smiled, 'glad ar could elp.'
'Come ear will ya!' Maizie snapped, dragging her friend clear.
'Ar tel ya what Maize,' Trisha said, looking back at the midget brushing himself down. 'It never ceases to amaze me ow some people get their jollies, still, it takes all sorts ar spoze. Ooh speakin of Allsorts, can ar get a bag for Dee, ar know they're er favrit.'

'Yeah go on,' Maizie said, handing over the last of their cash. 'Ar've paid for this lot, ar'll wait aatside.'
Trisha approached the counter. 'Alright geez,' she said, sliding three pounds toward the till. 'Can I av a scratch card an'all, the one wiv the pigs please.'
Mr Kareem tore off a card from the roll, scanned the sweets and handed Trisha the change. 'Oh please,' he said, retrieving the brown paper bag. 'You forgot your chillies.'
'Oh fanks,' Trisha replied, stuffing the chillies and Allsorts into her coat pocket. 'Ar'm doin a chilli con carne tomorra.'
'Oh very good,' Mr Kareem smiled. 'Please be very very careful with the scotch bonnets miss, they are oh so hot, and do not be rubbing your eyes when you are preparing them, this is very dangerous indeed.'
'Oh yeah ar know,' Trisha said, taking a twenty pence coin and rubbing her lottery card on the counter. 'We rubbed the seeds off wunna them on the karzi roll at me cousin Kenny's comin aat party. I always knew e was a woofta, ya can tell can't ya?' The mini mart owner looked on bemused while Trisha waffled with a queue forming behind her. 'E always ad a way abaat im, d'ya nart ar mean, laary shirts and tight arse shorts. Mincin araand like e was toutin for business, never drunk pints, always a whiskey mac wiv a slice a lemon an a cocktail cherry, ar mean if that don't say bend me over and fist me roughly ar don't know what does.'
Maizie, having waited patiently outside pushed open the door, 'TRISHAAAA, URRY UP WILL YA!' she yelled.
'Yeah ang on,' Trisha replied, paying very little heed to the tutting customers behind her. 'I only need one more pig for a tenner, ooohhh balls issa rabbit, thas your fault that is Maize, gissa paand mate ar'll av anuvva go.'
'No, you've ad all the blinkin money!' Maizie barked, entering the shop once again to drag her friend from the counter. 'Come on, ar wanna go ome,' she said angrily. 'Stop pissin araand will ya!'
'Oh but Maaaaaize,' Trisha moaned, eyeing the reel of scratch cards.

'NO!' Maizie snapped. 'COME ON!'

On leaving, the pair passed the midget flicking through the locomotive magazine again. 'Alright little legs!' Trisha said, ruffling his hair which enraged him further. 'Look!' she then said, snatching the steam enthusiast glossy from him yet again. 'Put that shit daan, ar told ya ya don't av to be embarrassed.' She then took down a copy of *Squirting Wives* and held it in the air. 'SCUZE ME!' she yelled, attracting Mr Kareem's attention. 'BILBO BAGGINS EAR WANTS THIS WANK MAG, OW MUCH IS IT?' Trisha then grabbed the shell shocked shorty by the arm and dragged him through the queue toward the counter. 'Iss *Squirtin Wives*,' she said, waving the mag. 'Can ya scan it for us?'

'Let me go, let me go!' the crimson cringing man shrieked.

'Excuse me,' an elderly lady brandishing a bottle of bleach said behind them. 'I believe I was next.'

'Oy leave it aat love,' Trisha said, appealing to her better nature. 'This poor little fucker's gaggin for a tug, ava flippin art won'tcha.'

'TRISHA!' Maizie yelled from the door. 'Ar'm goin, you comin or what?'

'Yeah, yeah ang on!' Trisha said, waving.

'Oh I am sorry,' the elderly woman said, taking a packet of tissues from her pocket. 'Here,' she said, thrusting them into the midget's hand. 'You'll be needing these you dear little man,' she then placed a twenty pound note onto the counter. 'Put the fellow's magazine on my bill please,' she told Mr Kareem.

'Ahhh thas nice ain it,' Trisha said, looking down at the so-called train enthusiast, who by now was wishing he were a million miles from the mini mart, but instead of flinging the tissues in her face he quickly pocketed them, snatched the water sports magazine and ran as fast as his tiny legs could carry him from the store, side stepping Maizie in the process.

'Ahhhhhh,' Trisha sighed. 'Give ya a right warm fuzzy feelin elpin someone aat dunnit?'

'Yes, yes it does my dear,' the pensioner replied, leaning across the counter. 'Mr Kareem,' she said, lowering her voice. 'Do you have my husband's TV magazine.'

'Yes Mrs Pardew,' the owner replied, reaching under the counter and slipping a copy of the gender bending monthly, *Swap Till You Drop*, into a plain paper bag. 'Please tell Mr Pardew,' he too whispered, 'I now have those nylons he was asking for.'

'Oh yes he'll be thrilled I'm sure,' Mrs Pardew said, dropping the magazine into her tartan trolley.

'Jesus Trish,' Maizie said, swapping the heavy carrier bags from one hand to the other, 'what the fuck was that all abaat?'

'Just elpin the little geeza aat,' Trisha said, leaving the mini mart. 'Ar mean, it can't be easy for em can it ay, d'ya member me uncle Dickie's boy Danny, e was a short arse little shit wern e, always sniffin raand yer arse and proper creepy wiv it an'all.'

Maizie raised her eyebrows and headed for home with the babbling Trisha in tow.

'Well me and Chantelle,' Trisha waffled, 'you member Chantelle don'tcha Maize, sat behind us in maffs, lived above the bookies on the high street.'

By now Maizie had switched off completely, counting the cracks in the weathered precinct pavement.

'Anyway,' Trisha continued aimlessly, 'we caught dirty Danny lickin the ladies lav seats at the lido, so we bog washed the little bastard and rammed the rough end of a karzi brush up iz rear end, ar fink e got the message.'

'What, ay?' Maizie asked, catching the tail end. 'Oh yeah ar reckon e did, who you on abaat anyway?

'Danny Pearce!' Trisha scoffed. 'Weren't ya listnin?'

'Oh yeah, course,' Maizie replied, lying through her teeth. 'Danny Pearce.'

Making their way through the near derelict arcade, a stone's throw from home, Maizie suddenly felt a rough hand on her shoulder.

'Get in ear you slag!' a voice said, tugging her into a doorway, where a switchblade was thrust against her throat. 'And you bitch!' Trisha was told. 'If you don't wanna see your mate opened up like a canna fuckin beans.'
'What, what ya doin?' Trisha asked, aghast, whilst Maizie stood rigid in abject horror against the fly posted roller shutter.
'Get the fuck in ear!' the hooded male insisted. 'Or ar'll cut er ar swear ar will!'
'Please, please don't,' Maizie gasped, letting the carrier bags slip from her fingers. 'We aint got nuffing onest!'
Trisha joined them with some trepidation. 'Let er go mate. Please geez,' she said, attempting to prise the two of them apart.
'Shut up, cunt!' the man said, slamming Trisha against the aluminum shutter. 'Now ar want everyfing you bitches got, phones, dough, bling the lot. So urry the fuck up abaat it.' His heavy hood concealed much of his face, leaving only his stubbled chin and cracked lips on show, while his breath reeked of cheap scotch and cigarettes.
'We done all our dough at the mini mart mate,' Trisha told him, putting a hand in between the blade to ease her friend's discomfort.
'Get your fuckin ands off!' the assailant growled menacingly. 'Don't gimme that bollocks, ar know you got summink.'
'Please,' Maizie croaked, now shaking uncontrollably. 'Ar got a shitty pay as ya go phone, you can av that if ya want.'
'An ar got a baga licorice allsorts,' Trisha added, hoping to win him over.
'You takin the fuckin piss!' the mugger raged, pressing hard enough on the blade to break Maizie's skin.
'No, no please!' Maizie squealed. 'We really aint got nuffing, onest mister!'
The semi inebriated attacker eyed Maizie's distinctive earrings. 'What abaat them then you lyin bitch,' he said, swaying a little. 'Gimme em or ar'll cut'cha bofe, come on, and em over!'

'Oh please,' Maizie cried, shaking her head. 'Not these, they was me nan's they aint werf nuffing onest, she left em to me when she snuffed it.'

'Ar said,' the man snarled insistently, 'gimme the fuckin fings or ya dead. I aint fuckin araand!'

Trisha attempted to intervene. 'Ohhh, they was er nanny Marge's they was,' she said, knowing the cheap costume imitations true value lay in their sentimentality. 'There must be summink else we can do for ya.' She dragged a teasing finger across the crotch of his faded fatigues. 'What abaat a wank?'

Maizie immediately glared at her friend, mortified at her suggestion. 'Trisha, no!' she barked, while their hooded attacker stood relishing the power and control he had over the pair of them.

'Yeah go on then,' he said. 'You toss me off while missy ear gives me the bling.' With that he unzipped his fly with one hand and rummaged inside dragging his manhood free.

'TRISHA DON'T!' Maizie snapped. 'Don'tchu dare!'

'Shut it you slag!' the attacker said, nose to nose with Maizie. 'When ar'm ready, you're gonna take it in that pretty maaf of yours and swolla the fuckin lot, d'you era me!'

But while he was otherwise distracted Trisha reached into her pocket and plucked a fiery scotch bonnet from the paper bag and pulverized it in her hand. 'Go on, get old of it,' the attacker told her, stiffening steadily.

'Alright, if thas what ya want,' Trisha replied, thrusting the fleshy paste complete with searing seeds onto the head of his penis, massaging it in vigorously.

'Ooooh yeeeeah,' he first said, sensing a mild tingling sensation. 'Fuck me thas good, mmmmmmm go on girl work it arder.' But his ecstasy was soon stifled by the bonnet's burning on such a sensitive area. 'Shit! Shit, what the fuck!' he said, looking down. 'What the fuck?'

'Woss a matter?' Trisha laughed, massaging with a firmer grip. 'Don'tcha like it?'

The heat soon quadrupled in intensity. 'Shit what you done to me?' he groaned, letting the blade slip from his hand and cupping his throbbing phallus in both hands.
'Ay, what?' Maizie said, none the wiser.
'I aint lost me touch av I Maize,' Trisha said, wiping her hands across the back of their hunched over assailant. 'Does that float ya boat ay geez?' she asked.
Seizing the opportunity, Maizie wasted no time in bringing her knee up sharply into the whining man's contorted face. 'Av that you fuckin ponce!' she snarled, pushing him out into the street where he tumbled into the gutter and inadvertently transferred a quantity of the scorching chili from his hands to his blooded face.
'ARRRRRRRGH, FUUUUUUCK!' he screamed, writhing in agony across a recently deposited pile of dog poo. 'ELP ME, PLEASE ELLLLLP!' he cried.
Maizie stooped and picked up the blade, and for a split second considered plunging it to the hilt into the reeling robber's neck, still shaking from her harrowing ordeal.
'It aint werf it Maize,' Trisha said, taking the knife from her and tossing it into a nearby refuse bin, before approaching the befallen bundle of stinking rags. 'You fucked wiv the wrong coupla slags dintcha,' she said, planting a defiant stiletto heel on the back of his right hand and baring down with increasing malice.
'Ar'm sorry, ar'm sorry,' he cried, with the chili's furnace like effects peaking at excruciating levels.
'Come on Trish,' Maizie said, retrieving her bags. 'Less get the fuck aat've ear.'
'Yeah alright,' Trisha said, shifting all nine stone of herself onto her right foot and shattering the hand that had threatened her friend.
'OH GOD FUUUUUUUCK!' the floored thief cried out, whilst pinned to the pavement 'OW! AR'M SORRY. SORRY1 PLEASE STOP, PLEEEEEEASE!'
Trisha then looked down at her other foot. 'Oh now look,' she moaned. 'Ar got shit on me bleedin shoe,' in one last act

of defiant degradation before leaving, Trisha dragged the side of her stiletto across the man's stubbled chin as though he were a door mat. Battered, bruised and badly burned he lay coiled in the litter strewn gutter twitching, slipping in and out of consciousness; the soft touch he had assumed would roll over and eagerly surrender their possessions had turned and served him a bitter helping of rough justice, causing him to question their sanity and his own career choice.

'Laters bell end!' Trisha scoffed, taking Maizie by the arm and starting for home.

'Fanks mate,' Maizie said, nestling into Trisha's shoulder. 'Ar fought we was proper fucked for a minute there, ar still got me nan's earrings though fanks to you. You're the nuts Trish you really are mate.'

A broad smile crept across Trisha's face as she savored the rare accolade. 'D'ya reckon, really?' she asked, fishing for further compliments.

'Yeah course,' Maizie added, 'ar fink e'da slit me froat if you adn't chilified im. You got some guts girl ar'll give ya that.'

'Well, we're mates aint we,' Trisha said, taking the key from Maizie and opening the door to their flat.

'Jesus, where you two bin?' Dee Dee asked, rising from the couch and shaking her empty tin. 'I ope you got some booze.'

'Yeah course.' Maizie put the bags down on the table. 'Ohhh Dee,' she added removing her coat.

'You never guess what appened mate, it was bleedin awful ar tell ya, ar nearly shit a brick mate.'

'Let me tell er!' Trisha squealed, discarding her jacket. 'Go on Maizie let me!'

'Tell me what?' Dee Dee asked, joining them at the table. 'What appened?'

'Well,' Trisha said, pre-empting Maizie, 'ar wonnid free pigs yeah, but I only got two an a flippin rabbit din I.'

'What?' Dee Dee asked, bemused. 'What the fuck you on abaat?'

'Me scratch card!' Trisha said, taking the liquorice from her pocket. 'Oh ar got ya these by the way, ar know ya love em, sorry I et all the coconut ones.'
'Tell er what appened for gawd sake!' Maizie insisted. 'Never mind ya poxy scratch card.'
'Oh yeah, course,' Trisha laughed. 'Sorry Dee, yeah there was this little geezer jizzin over the train mags coz e couldn't reach the ard core shit, so ar give im a bunk up an e kicked off, the ungrateful little tosser. Ya carn elp some people can ya?'
'No you twat!' Maizie raged. 'The geezer in the arcade. Oh ar'll tell er!'
'Oh, oh yeah that!' Trisha said excitedly. 'Well, there was this orrible oody bloke in the arcade yeah, an e grabbed Maizie and stuck a knife up er froat.'
'A knife!' Dee Dee said, checking the tiny slit on Maizie's neck. 'You alright mate?'
'Yeah ar'm alright,' Maizie said, shrugging off her injury. 'Fanks to er.'
'Trisha?' Dee Dee said with an air of disbelief.
'Yeah me,' Trisha said proudly. 'Ar see the fucker off good and proper ar did.'
'Bleedin ell, well done you,' Dee Dee said, praising her friend for her heroics. 'Wod'ya do, punch im up the guts or summink?
'Naah,' Trisha said, producing the bag of chillies. 'Ar burnt iz bell end wiv me bonnets.'
'What?' Dee Dee said, peering into the paper bag. 'Ow the ell, er actually ar don't fink ar wanna know.'
Maizie gave Trisha an impromptu hug. 'Fanks again Trish mate,' she said, cracking open the vodka and hurriedly rinsing their three mugs under the water heater.
Dee Dee and Maizie sat toasting Trisha with generous measures of neat vodka, until one by one they each passed out slumped at the table.

The following morning Dee Dee and Maizie were awoken by the sound of a rattling spoon on a chipped china cup.

'Mawnin!' Trisha chirped, setting two more down in front of her friends. 'Nice cuppa rosy for ya.'

Raising their thumping heads, the two wiped the dribble from their chins and cupped their tea in their hands, struggling to focus with their sleep clogged eyes.

'What time is it?' Maizie asked, blowing into her tea.

'Arf six,' Trisha said, busying herself. 'Ar know iss early but ar'm too excited to sleep. Iss me first proper day on the job, ar can't believe it Dee, ar'm gonna be a vet lady or summink like that.'

'ARF SIX!' Dee Dee yelled, dragging herself to her feet and heading for the sofa. 'We aint gotta be up for anuvva hour an arf you dozy mare!'

Maizie joined her, still cradling her cuppa. 'Ar forgot what iss like, drinkin on a school night. Jesus me ed's bangin.'

Trisha threw open the curtains. 'Ar do ya'z some brecky thatta sort you aat,' she told them, heading for the kitchen. 'We aint got a lot in, but ar'm sure ar can rustle up summink.'

'Don't bovva!' Dee Dee snapped, covering her face with a cushion. 'And shut them fuckin curtains!'

Ignoring Dee Dee, Trisha rattled around the kitchen fishing what little they had from the cupboards and clanging the pots and pans in the process. 'TRISHAAAAAAAAA!' Maizie yelled, snuggling into Dee Dee's shoulder 'D'YOU AV TO?'

'Yeah!' Trisha called back. 'Me muvva always said iss the most important meal of the day!'

'Ar'll kill er,' Dee Dee moaned.

'Me an'all,' Maizie added, turning her nose up at her tea. 'And she aint put no sugar in me tea.'

'Ar know coz iss bad for ya!' Trisha called out again. 'What av we told ya abaat ya fat arse, thas ow ya got it in the first place!'

'I AINT GOT A FAT ARSE!' Maizie protested. 'YOU KEEP THAT SHIT UP AN AR'LL FUMP YOU ONE!'

'You av Maize,' Dee Dee agreed. 'Who has four sugars in their tea anyway?'
'Ar do,' Maizie said in her defence. 'Ar just got a sweet toof thas all.'
'An a fat arse!' Trisha said, whilst igniting the gas ring.
Some thirty minutes later, after Maizie and Dee Dee had drifted back off to sleep, Trisha slammed two plates down on the coffee table in front of them. 'Eeyar!' she said, licking tomato sauce from her fingers. 'Get that daan ya, ar gotta go in a minute, ar'm gettin picked up.'
'Well piss off then,' Maizie groaned, forgetting so soon how her friend had literally saved her life the previous evening.
'Ar done ya some sarnies an'all,' Trisha told them, 'for ya lunch. We aint got no Tupperware shit but don't worry ar sorted it.' A horn then sounded three times in the street outside. 'Ooh thas for me!' Trisha shrieked. 'Ow do ar look?'
'Like a twat,' Dee Dee sneered, looking over the back of the sofa at Trisha in her uniform.
'Right, ar'm off,' Trisha said unfazed. 'Get up you two, you only got arf hour.'
'Whateva,' Dee Dee said, wincing as Trisha slammed the door behind her. 'What the fuck?' she then said, opening one eye at a time and dragging her plate toward her. 'Jesus!'
Trisha's lavishly prepared breakfast consisted of alphabet spaghetti, toast cut into bizarre animal shapes, a sprinkling of corn flakes and for good measure a random marshmallow floating in the mix.
'Ava look Maize,' Dee Dee said, nudging her friend. 'That girl definitely aint right ar'm tellin ya.' Trisha's empty plate in the washing bowl was a clear indication that she had devoured her share.
'Fuuuuck me,' Maizie gasped. 'The nob's only rit bollocks in me sketty letters.'
'Ar dunno abaat you,' Dee Dee said, heading for the pedal bin and scraping her plate, 'but I aint that ungry.'
'Me neeva,' Maizie said, ditching her breakfast too.

Meanwhile Trisha had skipped downstairs and out into the street. 'Oooh oooooooh!' she yelled, waving to the driver of a white minivan with the royal society's logo emblazoned on the side. 'Hiyaaaaaa!' she said, opening the door and hopping into the passenger seat. 'You alright?' Before the driver, a middle aged portly man with a greying beard, could respond, she clicked her seatbelt into place and continued her conversation. 'Mar name's Trish, or Trisha, whateva takes ya fancy, ar can't tell ya ow excited I am, really, ar love animals, all of em, elephants, pandas, even them stinky skunk fings. Mind you ar wouldn't want one araand me ouse, iss bad enough wiv mar cheesy boots, corr they proper chuck up ar tell ya.' The driver sat stunned into complete silence. 'Adrian, thas a nice name,' Trisha babbled, checking the badge on his breast pocket. 'I ad an uncle Adrian ar did, but e'z Adelle naah, since they turned iz balls inside aat.'

Adrian offered his hand. 'Hello,' he said, cramming a word in. 'You're the new girl I take it?'

'Yeah thas right,' Trisha replied. 'Well sorta new, ar've ad a bit of experience in the game over the years I av, me nephew got a newt stuck up iz nose when e was five an ar coaxed it daan wiv a lettuce leaf, ar got a way wiv em ya see, ar spoze you av an'all aint'cha.'

'Yes, yes I suppose I have,' Adrian said, backing out of the parking place and starting along the street. 'I have your two way radio in the back, I'll give it to you when we next stop.'

'What?' Trisha said, thrilled at the prospect. 'Ar got a radio. Fuck that ar'm avin it naah,' with that she slipped from her seatbelt, turned and leant over the back of her seat with her backside in the air.

'Trisha, Trish!' Adrian said, with his view limited. 'I said you can have it when we stop!'

But Trisha was having none of it, she wanted her walkie talkie real bad and was not about to be denied. Dragging a bag into the front she rummaged inside retrieving her very

own two way radio. 'Corrrrr, pukka!' she smiled, tossing the bag over her shoulder.
'What are you doing?' Adrian asked, watching from the corner of his eye as she began tweaking the dials. 'Trisha you mustn't.'
'Iss alright,' Trisha assured him. 'Ar can do it. Ello ello, anybody there? It aint friggin workin,' she moaned. 'Woss up wiv it?'
'You have to switch it on my dear,' Adrian informed her. 'But we shouldn't use it willy nilly.'
'Ello ello this is whiskey tango!' Trisha said, paying no heed. 'Anyone there, copy copy!'
An authoritative voice then came over Adrian's radio. 'Two four, two four, come in two four, what is your position? I repeat, two four, what is your position?'
Trisha looked on in awe as Adrian lifted his mic and pressed the button on the side. 'Two four receiving,' he replied. 'Yes Sheila we are currently approaching the junction of the Caledonian Road and Copenhagen Street, over.'
'Two four,' the royal society's controller replied, 'could you proceed to number 13. I repeat number 13 Glenby terrace. That's number 13 Glenby Terrace. We've received a report of a goose, I repeat a goose, in distress. Over.'
'Two four receiving,' Adrian replied. 'Thirteen Glenby Terrace, got it. I know where that is, over.'
'Thank you two four, report when you are clear,' the controller said, signing off.
'Will do Sheila,' Adrian smiled, replacing his handset.
'Is it a shout?' Trisha said, almost beside herself at this point.
'Yes,' Adrian said, turning in the road. 'And it's a goose of all things. A baptism of fire for you my dear.' Trisha didn't quite understand what Adrian meant by this, but was too enthralled to ask.
Geese and their renowned violent nature had long been the bane of the society's staff lives, causing countless minor injuries and on the rare occasion the odd fatality.

Trisha tweaked her snug fitting uniform. 'Don't spoze ar get a shoota?' she asked, checking her utility belt for a holster attachment.
'I beg your pardon?' Adrian said, navigating through the heavy morning traffic.
'A shoota!' Trisha said again. 'D'you lot carry em, do ya, for pit bulls and shit?'
'Oh heavens no,' Adrian laughed. 'We have a catch pole for dangerous dogs which is more than adequate.'
'Oh.' Trisha said, disappointed to say the least, 'ar see.' She sat thinking for a moment or two. 'What abaat a taser? Now that'd come in andy ay, ar see this programme in the nick abaat a grizzly bear that ad this bloke pinned to the graand and was gonna rip iz froat aat. Well the geezer whips aat iz taser and zaps the bastard in the ball bag, saved iz bleedin life it did. Ar reckon we should ava word wiv the guvnors, wod'ya reckon? Ar mean we're aat ear riskin our lives wiv nuffing to defend ourselves.'
Adrian sat mortified at the thought of being armed whilst carrying out his day to day duties. 'My dear Trisha,' he said, stopping at the lights. 'Firstly we seldom come across the likes of a grizzly bear in our line of work, especially on the streets of London. But if, and this is a huge if I might add, we were to encounter such a beast, then the constabulary's armed response team is more than adequately equipped to dispatch the creature in any event.'
'Oh,' Trisha sulked. 'Don't spoze they got any jobs goin av they?'
Adrian looked across at Trisha, unable to ascertain if she were joking or in fact deadly serious. 'Here we are,' he then said, turning off the main road. 'Glenby Terrace. The last time I was here Mrs Barnard at number 72 had reported a mange ridden fox living beneath her garden shed, plaguing hers and the neighboring cats. Now there's a dangerous fellow when cornered I'll tell you. If it wasn't for my gauntlets and Kevlar vest I'd have sustained a scratch or two

for sure. And then there's the threat of rabies to contend with.'
'Ar know what arda done,' Trisha said, counting down the door numbers to her left. 'Arda smoked the bastard aat wiv a burnin Michelin tyre, and clobbered im raand the ed wiv a nammer.'
'Christ no!' Adrian protested. 'That's hardly ethical my dear.'
'Effical!' Trisha exclaimed. 'Ar don't give a toss if it's effical or not. If some flea bitten fucker's comin at me wiv its claws aat to scratch me mascara off, ar'm lettin im av it good and proper.'
Adrian looked at Trisha in abject disbelief. 'You er...,' he said hesitating. 'You did watch the training video at headquarters I presume?'
'What?' Trisha replied. 'Oh, oh yeeeeah corse, well sort of, ar got a text from me aunty Rita, er Jade's avin triplets at Newham General.'
'Oh my word!' Adrian gasped. 'The poor girl.'
'Oh naaaaah she's alright,' Trisha explained, 'she's got five kids already so the little bleedas aint gonna touch the sides, if ya nart ar mean.'
'No,' Adrian said bemused. 'Sorry I don't.'
'Ar mean,' Trisha smiled, 'she's got an ole like a friggin builder's bucket.'
'Ahh here we are, number 13,' Adrian said, red faced and changing the subject rapidly. 'Be a dear Trisha and hop out and see me into that space will you.'
'Yeah, course,' Trisha said, stepping from the van and standing at the roadside while Adrian reversed. 'Keep comin, keep comin,' she called, beckoning. 'Come on yer alright!' There was a moment or two of silence before the rear of the society's van collided firmly with the parked vehicle behind, creasing the front bumper and shattering the number plate.
'What the...?' Adrian cried, leaping from the van. 'Trisha!' he shrieked.
'What?' Trisha replied, looking up from her phone.

'What do you mean, what!' Adrian said, examining the rear of his vehicle and the scattered fragments strewn beneath. 'I don't believe it!'

'Me neeva!' Trisha said, holding her phone aloft. 'That was Aunty Rita. Jade's ad the littluns but there was four of the buggers up er flu insteada free. Woss the chances of that, ay?' Trisha then peered around the back of the van where Adrian stood, stroking a large dent in the rear quarter. 'Ooooh!' she gasped, 'what ya done?'

'What have I done?' Adrian exclaimed. 'What have I done? You were supposed to be seeing me back!'

'Yeah ar know but,' Trisha replied, 'ar got the text, then I ad to put it on Facebook, then ar sent a whats app fingy to me mum tellin er abaat me new job an'all that. Oh look don't worry abaat it, me cousin Billy's a panel beater and e'z the bollocks ar tell ya. E sorted aat me nan's mobility scoota after she wrapped it raand a pelican crossin.'

Adrian stood open mouthed at Trisha's long winded reasoning. 'What about the third party?' he asked, eyeing the battered car behind. 'I'll have to leave our insurance details.'

'Fuck em!' Trisha told him dismissively.

'Oh no, I couldn't possibly,' Adrian said, jotting the society's particulars down, tearing the page from his notebook and tucking it under the windscreen wiper of the other car.

Opening the rear door which now creaked due to a damaged hinge, Adrian reached inside and handed Trisha a hessian sack with a small hole in one corner. 'Woss this for?' she asked, holding the grubby sack between her thumb and forefinger.

'It's for aggressive wildfowl,' Adrian explained. 'To contain their flapping wings and flaying claws. Simple but effective.'

'Oh right,' Trisha said, unimpressed to say the least. 'Ar don't get a nammer then, no?'

'No my dear,' Adrian laughed. 'You don't get a hammer, or a taser, or an AK47 for that matter. It's a goose for heaven's sake.'

Ringing the doorbell of number 13 Adrian and Trisha stood admiring the owner's exquisite collection of china thimbles lined along the window sill, when the door suddenly opened and a hunched over elderly lady with thinning hair and an aran sweater stepped out to greet them. 'Oh hello!' she said cheerfully. 'Ar you hear about the gas, my pilot light's gone out you see, and I want to cook a suet pudding for my supper.'

'No madam,' Adrian smiled. 'We're from the RSPCA. We had a call about a goose.'

'My gas, yes do come in,' the resident said, leading the way. 'I'll show you where the meter is. Would you like a cup of tea?'

'No thank you madam,' Adrian insisted. 'It's the goose we're here for, not the gas.'

'Oh the goose, yes of course,' the elderly lady replied, clearly hard of hearing, and possibly in the early stages of dementia. 'Please call me Margaret,' she told them. 'Right the meter's under the stairs behind my late husband's vintage pornography. Did you both say yes to tea?'

'Ar'll av a cuppa fanks,' Trisha said, looking round at the pre decimal décor.

'Margaret love,' Adrian said, placing both hands tenderly on her shoulders. 'We're not from the gas company. We had a call saying you have a problem with a stranded goose. Goose not gas.'

'Yes, yes I know,' Margaret said irritably 'The poor devil's outside in the garden. I fed him some cheese and tried to shoo him away, but I think his wing might be broken.'

'Don't worry Margaret,' Adrian told her reassuringly. 'We'll see to the poor fella.'

'Oh thank you young man,' Margaret said, rubbing her hands together. 'I'll prepare the suet pudding while you two get to work. There's a light under there,' she added, pointing beneath the stairs. 'Do let me know when I can light the gas won't you.'

Trisha and Adrian looked at one another, deducing that the aging Margaret may lack a little something upstairs.

'Goose!' Trisha snapped, showing very little tact. 'We're ear for the friggin goose, not'cha ruddy gas!'

'Yes I know that deary,' Margaret replied, heading for the kitchen. 'I told you he's in the garden, do go on through.'

Throwing her hands in the air Trisha followed Adrian through to the rear garden.

'There he is,' Adrian said, pointing out a large Canadian goose sitting quietly beneath a magnolia tree.

'Would you like some tea?' Margaret asked again, joining them outside.

'Yeah, ar said ar'll av a cup!' Trisha said, losing her patience. 'An ar'm still waitin.'

'Off you go,' Adrian told Trisha, gesturing toward the goose. 'Just pop him in the sack.'

'What, me?' Trisha said hesitantly.

'Yes, yes it's quite alright,' Adrian reassured her. 'Unless you don't think you're up to it that is.'

'Me. Course ar'm up to it,' Trisha said, taking a cautionary step forward before mumbling under her breath. 'Fuck a friggin duck.'

'Would you like some tea deary?' Margaret asked yet again from Adrian's side.

'Yeah ar said ar'll av a ruddy cup!' Trisha barked, without taking her eyes off the roosting goose.

'Not for me Margaret love,' Adrian smiled, watching her scurry inside. 'Sweet old thing,' he added.

'Sweet!' Trisha laughed. 'Er lift don't go to the top floor if you ask me.'

With the sack outstretched Trisha crept slowly across the manicured lawn. 'Right goosey,' she said, addressing the stricken bird. 'You're gettin in this bag wevva ya like it or not, d'you ear me.' The goose turned and stared as she approached, letting out a single quack. 'Yeah thas right,' Trisha said, edging closer. 'You, in the bag, got it.'

Suddenly the goose rose to its webbed feet causing Trisha to stop dead in her tracks. 'Woaw!' she gasped, seeing the huge bird in its entirety. 'You're a big bugger aint'cha.'

'Go on, go on,' Adrian urged her from the relative safety of the patio. 'Get him in the sack, head first mind.'

'Ed first, right,' Trisha said to herself, taking smaller steps now as the petrified goose backed away. 'Oy, where you goin?' she asked.

Margaret then appeared, minus the tea of course having forgotten the moment the set foot inside. 'I say, young man,' she said, tugging Adrian's sleeve. 'I'm afraid I still can't light my gas, would you take another look at it for me, only I want to cook a suet pudding for my supper you see.'

'Margaret love,' Adrian said sympathetically. 'We're not from the gas company, you rang us about the goose, remember?'

Margaret looked puzzled. 'But I'm not having goose dear,' she said innocently. 'I'm having suet pudding and mash potato.'

'THIS RUDDY GOOSE!' Trisha yelled, closing in on her quarry.

'Oh my word!' Margaret cried, clutching her chest. 'How on earth did that thing get in here?' Adrian merely shook his head and turned away.

Opening the neck of the sack Trisha finally lunged at the goose. 'Get in here!' she cursed, making contact with the bird's back which sent it waddling away. 'Come ear!' Trisha growled, following behind hunched over. The startled goose was now quacking repeatedly circling the garden with Trisha in pursuit.

'You will be careful won't you deary!' Margaret said, wringing her hands.

Adrian found the whole thing mildly amusing, having tangled with the Canadian visitors on numerous occasions. 'That's it, that's it!' he urged. 'You've got him cornered.' But once again the goose evaded capture.

'Come on you friggin fing!' Trisha puffed, darting left then right. But the fleeing bird, with wings outstretched and chest puffed, nimbly outran her.

'I say!' Margaret called. 'I say, young lady!'

'WHAT?' Trisha roared, red faced,

'Would you like some tea?' Margaret asked, having absolutely no recollection of having earlier offered.

'Ar you takin the fuckin piss?' Trisha said, with her hands on her hips.

'Trisha!' Adrian warned. 'We have a duty of care to the general public, as well as the animals, I'll have you know.'

'Yeah, sorry geez,' Trisha relented. 'Ar know she carn elp it, but ar don't need er bollocks when ar'm up to me neck in shit an fevvas.' The goose had fouled the lawn and shed a fistful of breast feathers whilst fleeing from Trisha and the ominous sack in her hand. 'Oooh, ang on!' she said, seeing the breathless goose pinned between the fence and the bird table. 'Got'cha naah ya mangey muvva.'

'That's it Trisha girl!' Adrian called. 'Careful now, careful!'

'Get in this fuckin bag!' Trisha cried, leaping with the sack aloft but the goose wriggled free and hopped aside, as Trisha crashed head long into the bird table showering herself with its contents of wild bird seed, fat balls and a bowl of icy water. 'Shiiiiit!' she cursed, thumping the ground.

'Ooooh,' Adrian said, wincing at her catastrophic collision. 'I er, I think he's tiring,' he added, offering moral support.

'Ar bleedin ope so,' Trisha wheezed, brushing seed from her hair. 'Coz ar'm proper fucked ar tell ya.

Margaret raised a hand. 'You will mind my petunias won't you deary,' she told Trisha, who merely glared at her in reply, remembering Adrian's warning.

'Oh and I almost forgot,' Margaret added. 'Where are my manners, I haven't offered you both a cup of tea.'

Trisha signaled to the chuckling Adrian. 'You tell er geez before ar lose me rag,' she said, turning back to the job in hand.

While Adrian explained with all the diplomacy he could muster that in fact she had already offered a beverage, Trisha rolled up her sleeves and gritted her teeth. 'Right duck!' she said positively seething. 'You're proper muggin me off naah, so ar suggest you get your arse in this ear sack, or fings ar gonna turn proper nasty, nart ar mean.'
The cornered Canadian goose flapped its huge wings and waddled along the fence line, flattening Margaret's seedling petunias in its path, before darting through the open shed door and ducking behind the hand tools and garden canes.
'Got'cha naah ya little fucker!' Trisha smiled, following the goose inside and closing the door behind her.
The larch lap shed was dimly lit by a single perspex window to one side, and was heavily cluttered with all things horticultural. 'Shit!' Trisha cursed, stumbling over Margaret's muddy boots. 'Where are ya ya bleeda?' she said, flinging a garden fork aside startling the bird which hissed and quacked in the corner. 'Ar see ya,' she said, clambering over the electric lawn mower. 'There's only gonna be one winner goosey,' she said, striking her knee on Margaret's potting bench. 'Shit, fuck it!' she cried, examining the tear in her new trousers. 'You're really startin to piss me off naah ya little bugger,' she told the cowering goose. But leaning a little closer she inadvertently thrust her entire face into a dust covered spiders web, complete with stranded midges and the odd cocooned wasp. 'Yaaaaaaargh, fuuuck, eurrrrrrrrgh!' she cried, clawing at her face and hair in a blind panic.
'Is she alright in there?' Margaret asked, wiping her silver hair from her eyes.
'Yeah, she'll be fine,' Adrian said, with his fingers crossed behind his back.
Straining her eyes in search of further arachnid webbery, Trisha's patience had all but worn through and with the panting goose within arm's reach she readied her sack and inched closer, assured of bringing the wild goose chase as it were to a conclusion. 'Come on ar won't urt'cha,' she said,

but the flightless bird reared up and hissed menacingly toward her. 'You keep that shit up!' she said, backing away, 'an ar'll ring ya fuckin neck!' Trisha's aggressive tone sent the goose into a flap, clawing and scratching at the shed wall. 'Get in ear!' Trisha said, making a grab for an outstretched wing. 'Got'cha!' she cried, pulling the bird toward her through the canes and garden netting. But she realised she may have met her match seeing the frantic goose at close quarters. 'Bleedin Nora!' she gasped, snatching her face away from its snapping beak. 'Calm daan, caaaalm daaaan!' she yelled, attempting to pull the sack over its bobbing head, but the goose was having none of it, hissing and defecating in unison. 'Urrrrgh ya dirty bleeda!' Trisha yelled, wiping poo from her jacket sleeve. But while she was pre-occupied the squawking goose broke free, leaving Trisha with a fist full of feathers. 'Ooooh ya bleeda!' she snarled, but instead of fleeing to a darkened corner, the angered goose turned on her pecking wildly at her legs. 'SHIT, GET OFF, GET OFFA ME YOU MANGEY BIRD!' she yelped. It was now Trisha that was backed into a cobweb covered corner. 'Urrrrgh bugger!' she cried, floundering among the leaning rakes, forks and pruners.
'What the?' Adrian said, growing a tad concerned.
Now on her back amid the spiders and spades, Trisha kicked out to defend herself against the rampaging gooses attack, with its hissing snapping beak within inches of her face. 'Piss off ya peckin ponce!' she cried, fending off its snaking neck. Struggling to find her feet Trisha grabbed at a sack of grass seed, toppling the contents over her head also. 'Bollocks!' she gasped, spitting out a mouthful of grain, unable to see through the cloud of rising dust. 'Arrrrrgh ya fucker!' she squealed, receiving half a dozen or so nips to the side of the face from the beast's beak. Fearing the goose would pluck out her eyes Trisha grappled either side of her on the shed floor, eventually grasping the shaft of Margaret's trusty trowel. 'AR SAID GET OFFA ME!' she screamed, lashing out blindly, the final swing making contact with the goose's skull

with a resounding thud. The Canadian goose dropped onto Trisha's beating chest, fluttering its wings once more, it quacked its last quack and lay lifeless. 'Euuuuurghhh!' Trisha cried, shoving the deceased bird aside and scrambling to her feet, knocking a pile of plastic plant pots from the bench. 'Shit!' she panted, looking out the window at Margaret waiting expectantly outside with Adrian at her side with a furrowed brow. 'AR GOT IM!' she yelled, rummaging for the sack. 'E'Z ALRIGHT!' Ramming the bird head first as instructed and pulling its beak through the hole, Trisha tucked its sagging body under her arm supporting its limp head with her index finger. 'There's a good goosey,' she said, emerging from the shed victorious.

'Oh well done deary!' Margaret said, clapping frantically. 'Well done, I say would you like a cup of tea?'

'Only if you're gonna make the friggin fing,' Trisha replied, jerking the goose from side to side as though it were struggling to break free. 'Woaw, woaw there goosy, woaw!' she said, wrestling with the sack. 'E'z a feisty little fucker ar'll give im that.'

Margaret reached out to pet the goose's head. 'He's a beauty isn't he,' she smiled.

'Watch it Mags!' Trisha warned. 'E'll av ya bleedin arm off e will.'

'Oh really!' Margaret said, snatching her hand away. 'I must say you're incredibly brave young lady. I bet you'd love a cup of tea.'

Adrian couldn't take his eyes off the goose, his suspicions aroused by the look of sheer terror etched on its face. 'Yes, yes be careful Margaret love,' he told her, sparing her feelings. 'They'll give you a nasty nip and think nothing of it.'

Trisha had worked up quite a thirst during her arduous battle with the stranded bird. 'Ow'z abaat that tea then Mags, ay?' she asked, bobbing the goose's beak up and down. 'An a saucer of milk for me mate ear.'

'Tea?' Margaret replied quizzically. 'Oh I am sorry deary I haven't got any. I never touch the stuff you see.'

'What?' Trisha said angrily. 'You bin chattin shit abaat a cuppa ever since we got ear ya dozy mare.'

Adrian then thought it best to intervene, having tangled with the elderly and infirm on dozens of occasions. 'Right er,' he said, taking Trisha's arm. 'I think it best we get this poor fellow to the veterinarian ASAP, get him checked over and such.'

'Ay?' Trisha said. 'Oh, oh yeah, get the quack to av a look at im, d'ya get it?' she said, realising the pun. 'Get the quack to av a look at im.'

'Oh very good,' Margaret smiled. 'The quack. Yes, very good.'

'Right we best be on our way Margaret love,' Adrian said, making his way back through the house.

'You won't forget about my gas will you,' Margaret said, scurrying behind. 'Only I'd like to cook a suet pudding for my supper.'

'You need to call the gas company Margaret. Gas,' Adrian said, doing his damnedest to remain calm. 'We're here for the goose.'

'Oh, yes right,' Margaret said, hanging her head. 'I was going to make a crumble for desert you see.'

'Scuze me!' Trisha said, barging past goose in hand. 'Ar gotta get this little bleeda in the van before it as me friggin eye aat.'

Margaret backed against the wall giving the goose a wide berth. 'Yes, yes deary you do that. I do hope he makes a full recovery, it'll be simply splendid if he does.'

'Itta be a fuckin miracle thas what itta be,' Trisha laughed in parting.

Once outside Adrian opened the rear door. 'He's dead isn't he?' he said under his breath, whilst waving goodbye to Margaret.

'As a fuckin door nail,' Trisha replied, tossing the Canadian's corpse inside with little regard. 'E tried to peck me oota so ar caved iz ed in good and proper.'

'You er, you did watch the training video?' Adrian asked again.
'Yeah course!' Trisha said, tongue in cheek, whilst fastening her safety belt.
Margaret darted back inside, returning moments later carrying a porcelain pudding bowl. 'I say, I say!' she called, as Adrian pulled away. 'What about my suet pudding?'
'Poke it up yer arse!' Trisha yelled back, winding up her window.
'Trisha!' Adrian snapped, whilst trying desperately not to laugh.
'Wellllll!' Trisha sighed. 'She was proper doin mar swede in.'
'Yes, I know what you mean,' Adrian was forced to admit, raising a smile. 'Fancy a cuppa?'
'You takin the piss?' Trisha barked.
'No, no I mean at the café,' Adrian explained. 'There's a smashing little Greek place I use whenever I'm in this neck of the woods. They do a fry up to die for.'
'Well ar've ad a gut buster already this mawnin,' Trisha told him. 'But ar reckon ar could andle anuvva.'
Parking outside Aphrodite's on the Seven Sisters road, Adrian led the way inside the elaborately decorated cafeteria, with its Corinthian columns and Mediterranean murals. 'Morning Stelios!' he called to the olive skinned owner.
'Ahhhhh, Mr Adrian, good to see you again!' Stelios smiled, wiping his hands on his apron and rounding the counter to greet them. 'How are things with you?'
'Good, yes thanks, very good,' Adrian said, receiving the firmest of handshakes. 'Oh this is Trisha, she's our new trainee.'
'Alright geez,' Trisha nodded, whilst eyeing the menu board.
'Ahhhh beautiful lady,' Stelios crooned, taking her hand and smothering it with kisses. 'A goddess to equal Aphrodite herself.'
'Flippin eck,' Trisha said, snatching her hand away. 'E'z a smoov talkin fucker ain e.'

'Please, take a seat,' Stelios said, straightening a table and pulling a chair out for Trisha. 'Madam,' he added, sliding it beneath her bottom.

'Two teas please Stelios,' Adrian said, handing Trisha a menu.

'I already know what ar'm avin,' Trisha said, knife and fork in hand. 'Ar'll av the juggernaut please geez,' she told Stelios.

'Ar you sure?' Adrian asked leaning across, knowing full well what the monstrous special included.

'The juggernaut!' Stelios too said wide eyed. 'Young lady the juggernaut is not for the faint hearted.'

'Who you callin faint arted!' Trisha snapped, glaring at the owner. 'You gonna gimme the bloody breckie or not?'

'Yes, yes indeed,' Stelios relented. 'One juggernaut for the lady, OK. I like her Mr Adrian,' he added, 'she's a spirited one.'

'Yes, isn't she just,' Adrian replied half-heartedly. 'I'll have my usual please Stelios,' he said, handing back the menus.

'Two eggs, beans and brown toast, correct?' Stelios said, hazarding a guess.

'You got it,' Adrian smiled.

'What ice cream ya got?' Trisha asked, perusing the desert menu.

'Ice cream?' Stelios said a little confused. 'We have chocolate and vanilla, but I doubt you'll have room for desert young lady.'

'Who's talkin abaat desert,' Trisha replied, 'stick a dollop of vanilla on toppa me ash braans will ya.'

Stelios stood open mouthed. 'On top of the hash browns?'

'Yeah,' Trisha said without batting an eye.

'On top of the hash browns,' Stelios said once again.

'Yes!' Trisha insisted. 'On toppa me bleedin ash braans, now jog the fuck on and get me me juggernaut will ya, or we're buggerin off to the Caribbean gaff daan the road!'

'Very well, very well if you insist,' the confused owner said, returning to his kitchen mumbling in Greek under his breath.

The juggernaut as it was aptly named, consisted of four cumberland sausages, six rashers of smoked back bacon, three fried eggs, fried tomatoes, black pudding, mushrooms, baked beans, bubble and squeak, two buttered toast, three hash browns and a fried slice. It was a gargantuan culinary colossus of a meal, that had got the better of all but a few fool-hardy enough to tackle it.

'Oh damn it!' Adrian said, suddenly rummaging through his coat pockets. 'I've forgotten my wallet, how embarrassing. I don't suppose I could ask you to stump up the cash for breakfast Trisha, and I'll return the favour tomorrow?'

'You're avin a laugh aint'cha,' Trisha replied, emptying three postage stamps and a bus ticket from her purse. 'I aint got a bean mate.'

'Oh dear,' Adrian moaned. 'I wonder if I could persuade Stelios to let us have it on tick until tomorrow.'

'Naaah fuck that,' Trisha said, springing from the table. 'You leave this to me.' With that she left the cafeteria, leaving Adrian bewildered.

'What the?' he said, when she returned moments later with the dead goose draped over her shoulder.

'Oy Stelios me old son!' she called, heading through to the kitchen to proposition the grease spattered Greek. 'Sorted,' she said, rejoining Adrian several minutes later.

'What on earth have you done?' Adrian asked, leaning across to confront her.

'Sorted aat our breckies for the next coupla weeks,' Trisha smiled, looking ever so pleased with herself. 'Ar give im the goose for iz goulash, the fucker's over the friggin moon wiv it ar tell ya. Ar told im ar'd bring im all me deaduns and fill iz freezer up if e looks after us.'

'All your deaduns,' Adrian remarked. 'Trisha may I remind you our mantra is to preserve animal life wherever possible, it was pointed out quite categorically in the training video, did you watch any of the damn thing?'

'Well like ar said, sort of,' Trisha said, toying with the salt shaker. 'Ar did nip aat for a dump, so ar mighta missed that bit if ar'm onest.'
'That bit!' Adrian exclaimed. 'My dear the entire presentation explains our goals and objectives.'
'Our what?' Trisha asked. 'OY GEEZ, WHERE'S ME CUPPA. AR'M SPITTIN PISSIN FEVVA'S EAR!'
Stelios's daughter Karina came scurrying from the kitchen catching Trisha's eye immediately, her waist length auburn hair tied in a neat French plait and stocking tops barely visible. 'I'm sorry,' she said, setting two mugs down. 'I, I scolded myself with the hot water boiler.'
'Ooooh less av a look sweatart,' Trisha said, taking her slender hand in hers. 'That looks proper nasty,' she said, examining the rising blister and looking into Karina's smouldering eyes. 'Put that under the cold tap darlin, as quick as ya like, go on urry up,' letting her hand slip away Trisha leaned to watch Karina's buttocks jostle beneath her tight pleated skirt as she hurried to the sink. 'Corrr what ar wouldn't do to that,' she said, making no attempt to conceal her bisexual feeling.
'I beg your pardon?' Adrian said, halting with his mug of tea at his lips.
'That smokin piece of arse,' Trisha pointed out. 'Ar'd proper ruin er ar tell ya.'
'You mean Karina?' Adrian asked in disbelief.
'Is that er name?' Trisha said, without averting her gaze and resting her chin on the palm of her hand.
'Yes, yes she's Stelios's daughter,' Adrian explained. 'One of twins I might add.'
'Twins!' Trisha gasped, sitting bolt upright, an instant sordid fantasy flashing through her degenerative mind. 'Fuuuuuuck me, what a win double thatta be.'
Adrian thought it best at that point to come right out and ask the question playing on his mind. 'Trisha are you a lesbian by any chance?'

'Me!' Trisha laughed. 'Gawd no geez, ar do like a bitta cock an'all from time to time, mind you I ain ad a descent lenf in ages.'
Adrian spluttered his tea across the table at Trisha's descriptive reply. 'Sorry, I'm sorry,' he said, hastily mopping the table cloth with his napkin.
'What ar wanna know,' Trisha added, causing Adrian's eyebrows to rise even further. 'Is if ar give im a goose for me breckie, what av ar gotta give im for iz girls, a fuckin rhinoceros!'
'Well I'm glad to say my dear,' Adrian said, mopping his brow, 'we don't come across too many of those on our rounds.'
'Shame,' Trisha mumbled, figuring it to be a fair exchange. 'If we do though ar'm avin it, Stavros or whatever e'z bleedin name is can spit roast it while ar spit roast iz daughters.'
Again Adrian spat his tea across the table. 'My God girl!' he coughed, mopping the spillage once more. 'You really are insatiable aren't you.'
Trisha was miles away at this point. 'Oh mar gawd!' she then said, as Stelios's second daughter Christina emerged from the kitchen with their breakfasts in either hand, her blouse unbuttoned enough to reveal a partial glimpse of her lacy baby pink bra. 'Ello gorgeous,' Trisha said, as she bent to lower the plates offering Adrian the juggernaut. 'Sorry thas mine,' Trisha said, swapping plates to Christina's amazement. 'Woss your name love?'
'Christina,' the waitress replied. 'Can I get you anything else?'
'Yeah,' Trisha said leering. 'A strap-on an a tube a lube.'
'Sorry, what? Christina asked, checking the menu naively while Adrian sat staring red faced at the wall.
'What ar'm offerin ain on the menu babe,' Trisha told her, pouring a spoonful of beans over her ice cream. 'But if it was, itta come wiv a side order of melted chocolate an a pair of edible undies.'

Christina hadn't the foggiest idea what Trisha was implying.
'No, no we're fine thanks Christina,' Adrian said, dismissing the girl.
'Enjoy your breakfasts,' she said, tucking her note pad inside her bra and giving Trisha a sideways glance, as the trainee animal welfare warden spooned the bean smothered ice cream into her mouth.
'Fuckin aaaansum,' Trisha gurgled, scooping the drips from her chin.
Adrian looked on, tucking into his paltry breakfast, while Trisha worked her way methodically from left to right through her mammoth meal, pausing occasionally to burp and jostle the contents of her stomach. 'If you ain eatin that ar'll av it,' she told Adrian as he sat in awe.

Dee Dee and Maizie's morning hadn't been quite so chaotic on the other hand. After the obligatory staff briefing at 8.45, the two were separated; Maizie sent to assist with resident recreation and Dee Dee to deliver refreshments to those confined to their rooms.
'Carn ar just watch telly wiv em?' Dee Dee asked the staff nurse, hoping for an easy ride.
'Absolutely not!' she was told in no uncertain terms by Agnes, a retired volunteer. 'Roll up your sleeves young lady and get stuck in.'
Wheeling a tea trolley and dragging her feet, Dee Dee studied the notes outside each resident's room, as per instructions, to ascertain whether tea, coffee or juice could be given.
The majority of the patients housed at the centre were assigned anti spill, two handled infant training mugs, a little degrading Dee Dee thought, but a health and safety requirement nevertheless.
'Mawnin,' she said, pushing open the first door, not knowing quite what to expect. 'Alice ain it?' she asked, checking the door plate.

'Teaaaaaaaaaaaaaaa, teaaaaaaaaaaaaa, teaaaaaaaaaaaa!' Alice shrieked, sitting up in bed and clapping jubilantly. Alice, one of the centre's more senior residents, had been with them from the very beginning. Suffering from severe brain damage as a result of childhood seizures, the seventy one year old rarely left the comfort of her room.
'Yeah ar got ya tea love,' Dee Dee said, filling Alice's monogrammed mug.
'Teaaaaaaaaaaaaaaa, teaaaaaaaaaaaaa!' Alice cried, snatching at the mug.
'Careful!' Dee Dee warned, watching her sipping greedily. 'D'ya wanna biscuit?' she added, opening a packet of digestives.
'Teaaaaaaaaaaaa!' Alice said again, grabbing four biscuits and tucking them under her pillow. Whilst Alice supped greedily, Dee Dee looked around at the contents of her scarcely furnished room, albeit clean and extremely warm. The one thing that struck Dee Dee as odd was the distinct lack of photographs, knowing full well that her own grandparent's house was festooned with family portraits, holiday snaps and crudely drawn crayon gifts from loving grandchildren. Alice was alone in every sense of the word.
'D'ya want ya telly on?' Dee Dee asked, taking Alice's remote from her side table. Alice nodded whilst toying with her hair and staring blankly at a tiny tear in the wallpaper.
'Wod'ya want?' Dee Dee said, channel hopping. 'Crap in yer attic, a shit ole in the sun, what?'
Alice said nothing until Dee Dee switched to her favorite garden makeover programme. 'Yes, yes, yes, yes, yes, yes, yes, yes!' she shrieked, bobbing up and down and in doing so obliterating the digestives she had just stashed.
'Oh you like a bitta Charlie Dimock do ya,' Dee Dee said, setting her remote down. 'Ar like er meself, mind you she's got a massive paira lils aint she, ar'm surprised they aint draggin in the dirt when she's diggin er dandelions or whatever the fuck it is she does.'

Alice hardly acknowledged Dee Dee's presence, staring wide eyed at the TV as the horticultural hottie grappled with an overgrown rhododendron. 'Ar leave ya to it then,' Dee Dee said, tugging at the corner of her duvet and tucking her sheet; a glimmer of compassion however unintentional. 'Seeya later,' she said, but getting no reply.

Maizie in the meantime was sat amongst a group of Down's children, having the time of her life painting their faces, the boys being tigers and the girls butterflies. 'Ava look,' she said, showing each of them a mirror, causing a ripple of infectious laughter. Dominic, whom she had met the day before, put a finger into the pallet of paint and daubed Maizie's nose, again delighting him and his friends no end. 'Oy ya cheeky bleeda,' Maizie laughed, rubbing the red smudge. One by one the rest of the class delved into the paints and surrounded Maizie with hands outstretched. 'No, no, no!' Maizie said, wriggling back on her behind. 'No no!' But the pack of giggling children set about her, smothering her face with their spattered hands, coating her with an array of colours. 'Oy, no!' she cried, as she was eventually pinned to the floor by the boisterous group. 'You little bleedas, no!' she chuckled, beneath the pile of bodies.
Richard then popped his head into the room to check on her, and immediately burst out laughing. 'Children, children!' he said, pulling one or two from the pack. 'It's Maizie's first day, we don't want to scare her away just yet do we.'
'Ar'm alright,' Maizie said, surfacing with her technicolor coating. 'Ar couldn't get em off me though thas all.'
Richard stood back, astounded at her appearance. 'My God, they have gotten the better of you haven't they.'
'Yeah, ar love it though,' Maizie replied, taking a quick selfie on her phone and posting it online.
Dee Dee during her rounds came across a door that appeared to be locked, peering through the tiny viewing window she could just make out the figure of a young girl

sat at a desk facing the wall. 'Ello!' she said, knocking. 'Ar got some tea if ya wonnit!' The girl did not stir.
'Ellooo!' Dee Dee called again. 'Ar got juice an all!' Again the girl sat motionless. 'What the fuck?' Dee Dee said to herself, looking around for help, but the corridor was deserted. It was then that she noticed a number of keys hanging on a string on the underside of the trolley. 'Gotcha!' she said, trying each in the lock until the door eventually swung open.
'Ello, want some juice love?' she asked, venturing inside. 'Ar got black currant an orange. You alright?' she asked, edging closer and getting no reply.
The girl sat rigid as though frozen, staring straight ahead. In her hands were a pair of plastic scissors and a magazine, and strewn across her desk were an assortment of images cut from glossies, each of them featuring an A list female celebrity and oddly enough with one thing in common, long blonde hair.
'You must be Bonnie,' Dee Dee said, checking the name on the key fob and the notes hanging at the end of her bed. 'Thas a lovely name that is, like Bonnie and Clyde, whoever the fuck they are, scuze me French.'
Bonnie's heart was racing at the sudden intrusion and her eyes flitted rapidly from left to right with very little head movement.
'Woss it gonna be?' Dee Dee asked, in an attempt to get a response. 'Orange or black current, ar got wafer biscuits and wagon wheels an'all if ya fancy it.' Still nothing. 'Ar do ya an orange,' Dee Dee decided, filling a mug. 'An ar leave ya one of each,' she added, popping two treats onto Bonnie's desk. 'What'cha doin anyway?' she asked, looking over Bonnie's shoulder at the scattered clippings of Ga Ga, Zellwega, Paltrow and Diaz, onto each she had scrawled a solitary word in lilac felt pen, *Mum*.
'That aint'cha muvva,' Dee Dee said, plucking a photograph of Marilyn Monroe. Had Dee Dee been fully informed of Bonnie's situation then maybe she never would have entered her room, let alone tampered with her belongings.

The girl, no older than fifteen, suddenly flew into a violent rage.
'ARRRRRRRRRRRRRGH, ARRRRRRRRGH, NOOOOOOOOOO!' she screamed, snatching back the clipping and swiping the mug of orange onto the floor, causing Dee Dee to jump back. 'ARRRRRRRGH, ARRRRRRRRGH, ARRRRRRRRRGH!' Bonnie repeatedly cried. 'ARRRRRRRRRRGH!'
'WOAW!' Dee Dee said, raising her hands. 'Woaw caaaalm daaan, caaalm the fuck daan will ya!'
But Bonnie's rage intensified, pounding on her desk with both hands, shaking her head from side to side. 'NOOOOOOOOO, NOOOOOOOOO, NOOOOOOO!' she screeched.
'What the fuck?' Dee Dee said, backing a little further away, while the enraged girl set about systematically ransacking her room, tearing the mattress and sheets from her bed and wrenching the curtains from the window.
'Woss your problem?' Dee Dee asked, naively.
Suddenly, two members of staff came sprinting into the room. 'Bonnie love, calm down,' one of them said. 'There's a good girl, come on Bonnie, put that down.'
'What are you doing in here?' the other barked at Dee Dee. 'You shouldn't be in here, get out. I said get out!'
'Ar was givin er a drink,' Dee Dee replied. 'Thas all.'
'Bonnie no, Bonnie please!' the men said, in an attempt to soothe her. 'Come on Bonnie, give me that,' she was told as she wielded a bedside lamp above her head. 'I SAID GET OUT!' one of them yelled at Dee Dee.
'Alright keep ya fuckin air on!' Dee Dee replied, incensed at their tone toward her.
Dragging the drinks trolley from the room she then encountered Richard in the corridor. 'Deborah what's going on?' he asked, peering over her shoulder. 'Were you in Bonnie's room?'
'Yeah,' Dee Dee replied, finding it hard to see what all the fuss was about. 'Ar was givin er a drink, woss wrong wiv that?'

'My dear,' Richard said, taking Dee Dee to one side. 'Bonnie is a very unstable young lady and only those that she truly trusts are permitted to enter her room.'
'Woss up wiv er then?' Dee Dee asked, her curiosity getting the better of her. 'She frightened the bleedin life aata me ar tell ya.'
'Bonnie came to us when she was just three years old,' Richard explained. 'The police found her clinging to the body of her dead mother in a squalid Highgate flat.'
'Jesus,' Dee Dee gasped at the thought. 'Poor little fucker.'
'Yes indeed,' Richard continued. 'The mother, a prostitute and heroin addict, had been dead for just over a week when they broke in and found them. Neighbours reported the smell you see. Bonnie only survived by drinking water from the lavatory and scavenging what little food she could find in the lower cupboards, raw vegetables and such. The child seemed almost feral when she arrived here, hissing and spitting at staff and barely uttering a legible word. They told us she was brushing and tying ribbons in her mother's hair when they found her.'
'Was it blonde?' Dee Dee asked.
'I'm sorry, what?' Richard replied, losing his train of thought.
'Er muvva's air,' Dee Dee added, 'was it blonde?'
'I, I really couldn't tell you,' Richard said, pouring himself a tea from the trolley. 'Why do you ask?'
'Oh, no reason,' Dee Dee said, recalling the magazine clippings. 'Why d'you keep er banged up anyway, she aint doin bird is she.'
'Oh heavens no,' Richard laughed, dunking a biscuit. 'Bonnie insists on her door being locked at all times. Oh bother!' he then cursed, losing half his digestive in his mug.
'Ar fink ar need a cuppa meself,' Dee Dee said, dropping a tea bag into the remaining mug. 'Me nerves are shot to shit ar'm tellin ya.'
Bonnie was eventually calmed by the staff members and settled back at her desk once again, but occasionally after

the door was secured she would glance over her shoulder for any sign of the mystery girl.

'Where's the rest of her family then?' Dee Dee asked, blowing into her mug. 'Er muvva must've ad bruvvas and sisters or someone.'

'Not that we know of,' Richard replied. 'As far as we know the poor girl has nobody.'

'Thas bullshit!' Dee Dee remarked. 'Everyone's got someone.'

'I agree,' Richard said, fishing in his mug. 'But social services used all the resources at their disposal and drew a blank, it's a crying shame it really is. She tolerates certain staff members, but that's as far as it goes. I'm afraid Bonnie has been institutionalized and will remain that way for the rest of her life.'

Dee Dee was allowed, as she'd first requested, to sit in the day room with the more mobile residents and watch the television, albeit fleeting images as Muriel, a hyperactive patient, constantly switched channels and muted the sound whilst skipping in circles, which infuriated Dee Dee but she bit her lip sparing a thought from time to time for Bonnie.

'Oh Dee ar've ad the best time ever!' Maizie said, walking on air on the way to the station that evening, with traces of water colour still visible around her ears. 'The little bleedas painted me ed, and then smuvvered me wiv sticky stars, ar looked a proper state ar tell ya. Dominic's a little darlin mate, e really is, strong as a bloody ox an'all, you wouldn't wan a right ander off im. You alright Dee, Dee?' she asked, noticing her friend's sullen expression. 'Woss up mate?'

'Nuffin,' Dee Dee said, descending the station stairs. She didn't utter another word until they arrived home. Maizie on the other hand was full of the day's events, recounting in the minutest of detail every exhilarating moment spent with the centre's children.

'Oh give it a rest Maize for fuck sake,' Dee Dee moaned, kicking off her shoes and trying the bathroom door. 'Trish you in there?' she asked, with her ear to the door.

'YEAH AR'M AVIN A SHOWA!' Trisha yelled back, whilst stood in the bath lathering her body.
'Great,' Dee Dee sighed, wanting to soak the day away.
'Ar'll make us a cuppa,' Maizie said, hanging up her coat. 'Oh an anuvva fing Dominic done,' she added, driving Dee Dee to distraction, 'e drew me a lovely picture of an airplane, iss proper good it is, ar got it on me locker.'
'Marvlus,' Dee Dee mumbled, disinterested to say the least and reclining on the sofa. 'We got anuvva five friggin years of this shit.'
The two of them were relaxing when Trisha emerged from a steamed filled bathroom wrapped in a towel. 'Alright!' she said, with an energetic tone. 'I ad to av a wash, ar was covered in orse shit. Our last shout was a flippin nightmare, ar tell ya, two pissin ponies got aata their ruddy field and run amuck in Enfield taan centre. Ar chased em into T K Max, Bootsie's and Claire's friggin accessories, but ar couldn't get old of em. We ad em cornered at one point in the Carphone whatsit, but they kicked the shit aata the pay mumfley smart phone fingeys and jumped fru the winda, ar did manage to get olda wunna the buggers by the tail in the Forntons chocolate gaff but the bastard shit all over me and kicked me up the guts, ava look.' Trisha lowered her towel to reveal a horseshoe shaped bruise around her belly button. 'Proper urt it did, ar tell ya.'
'Flippin ell, ar bet!' Maizie said, taking a closer look. 'And that's only the first bleedin day.'
'Oh yeah,' Trisha agreed. 'And don't even get me started on the ruddy goose, but ar do love it though, ar wouldn't change it for nuffing. Ow was your day Dee, wod'ya get up to?'
'Made the pissin tea,' Dee Dee said unenthusiastically.
'What, all day?' Trisha said, sitting down opposite.
'Yes!' Dee Dee snapped. 'Oh an ar watched some telly an'all.' Dee Dee neglected to mention her encounter with Alice and Bonnie, but the two residents, with their contrasting set of circumstances were constantly at the

forefront of her mind. 'Woss for tea?' she asked Trisha. 'An ar don't want nunna your shite wiv undreds and faasands on it, d'you ear me, ar just want proper grub.'

'Yeah course,' Trisha said, heading for her room. 'Let me get me onesie on an ar'm gonna do me chili con carne just like ar promised, wiv jacket tayters.'

'Mmmm yeah,' Maizie said, rubbing her grumbling stomach. 'Ar could andle that right naah. Eeya what appened to the ponies then?'

'Oh them,' Trisha said, peering from her room. 'A bunch of airy bikers raanded em up in Morrison's car park and we shushed em into a norse box.'

'Ahhhh that was nice of em wunnit Dee,' Maizie smiled.

The Potters Bar chapter of the infamous Hell's Angels had indeed ridden gallantly to the rescue on their gleaming Harleys, encircling the frantic ponies and herding them toward the open horse box to the cheers and rousing applause of the mid afternoon shoppers.

'Ar fought they was all nut jobs that lot,' Maizie remarked. 'Bitin the eds offa chickens and stuff.'

'Naah nuffing like that,' Trisha said, zipping her onesie. 'They was proper lovely they was, one of em let me steer iz chopper bike fing wiv im on the back, but wunna them trolley dolly dopes pulled aat in front of us an ar stacked it into the arse end of a Fiat flippin Panda, e didn't mind though coz ar let im coppa feela me tits on the way raand.'

Whilst Trisha prepared the evening meal under Maizie's watchful eye, several police vehicles sped by outside with two tone sirens piercing the night. 'Woss goin on?' Maizie asked, peering from the window in time to see them disappear out of sight at the end of the street.

'Gawd knows,' Dee Dee said, thumbing the pages of the previous day's paper. 'Take ya pic Maize, a muggin, stabbin, shootin, anyfing goes in this shit ole of a city naah.'

'Yeah you're right Dee,' Maizie agreed, dropping the curtain. 'Fings are gettin proper aat of and aint they.'

Within a matter of a few months the capital's crime rate had spiked to an all-time high, coinciding some would say with the recent influx of Eastern European gypsies hell bent on looting London; a soft touch as they saw it full of rich pickings and a government only too willing to invite them in to do so.
'I erd me auntie Rose got turned over by a coupla beggars up Saint Paul's way,' Trisha said, saucepan in hand. 'When she only give em fifty pence they stuck a blade to er granddaughter's froat and took every penny she ad, even the little girl's christenin bracelet, the orrible bastards. They was on CCTV doin it an'all but the old bill wern interested, ar know what arda done if ar got old of em,' she said, gritting her teeth. 'Arda skinned em alive wiv a fuckin cheese grater, smuvvered em in salt and laughed me flippin ed off while they died a very slow and painful deff.'
'Blimey,' Maizie gasped. 'Fuck bringin back angin, you got mar vote wiv ya cheese grater, ar love it.'
The spate of appalling callous crimes had shocked even the hardest of home grown criminals, with the young, old and even disabled targeted, contravening the strict unwritten code that British blaggers lived by.
'Yeah good shout Trisha,' Dee Dee nodded. 'And skin the fuckers that let em in in the first friggin place an'all.'
'Right, dinner's nearly ready!' Trisha called from the cooker.
Dee Dee rose from her seat. 'Not for me Trisha,' she said, heading for her room.
'What?' Trisha replied, leaning from the kitchen. 'Ar fought you like chili con carne Dee. I aint put nuffing moody in it, av ar Maize?'
'Naah nuffing,' Maizie said, shaking her head and sitting at the table. 'Ar bin watchin er Dee.'
'I aint feelin all that,' Dee Dee replied. 'Ar'm gonna get me nut daan.'
'You alright mate?' Maizie asked. 'You gotta eat summink.'

'Yeah Dee,' Trisha reiterated, 'ar put a coupla scotch bonnets in it so iss a proper ring stinger, just the way you like it.'

'Yeah fanks Trisha,' Dee Dee smiled. 'Ar just ain all that ungry mate, ar see yers bofe in the mawnin yeah.'

'Alright mate,' Maizie said sympathetically. 'Night!'

'Ar leave ya some in the nuke Dee,' Trisha called. Moments later she set two plates down on the table. 'Eeya Maize,' she said, darting back for the cutlery. 'Dee aint right is she,' she remarked, sitting with her friend. 'She's never turned daan a chili con carne before.'

'Ar know mate,' Maizie said, carving her jacket potato. 'It aint like er to go to bed this early neeva. Corrr fuck me Trisha this is hot.'

'She's probly got wunna them bug fings,' Trisha said, tucking in without a care. 'Woss up wiv ya, ya wuss I only put two bonnets in it.'

'Yeah ar know,' Maizie said, mopping her brow. 'An ar reckon ar got bofa the bastards.' Maizie took three more mouthfuls before admitting defeat. 'Sod that!' she said, pushing her plate away. 'Thas otter than a friggin vindaloo that is.'

'Ar'll av it if you don't wonnit,' Trisha said, scraping the remainder onto her own plate. 'Me muvva always said ar got cast iron guts, ever since she caught me chewin the budgie's cuttlefish and swiggin the white wine vinegar.'

Maizie had hurried into the kitchen, taking the last of the milk from the refrigerator and guzzling it at the sink in an attempt to cool her burning mouth. 'Flippin ell Trish!' she moaned, fanning her dripping tongue. 'Me maaf's on flippin fire!'

'Ohhhhh shutuuuup,' Trisha laughed, clearing her plate and licking the cutlery clean. 'That was bleedin aaansum that was.' Taking her plate through to the kitchen she was almost bowled off her feet meeting Maizie dashing in the opposite direction.

'Aaat me way!' Maizie cried, with a sense of urgency. 'Ar need a turn aat and ar need one bad!'
'Ang on Maize!' Trisha called after her, but Maizie had slammed the bathroom door behind her and leapt onto the pan, wriggling out of her leggings and uttering a sigh of relief as her bowels emptied with very little resistance, while Trisha waited outside expectantly. 'Trishaaaaaaaa!' Maizie yelled, right on cue. 'Where's the friggin bog roll?'
'There aint none left,' Trisha called, whilst clearing the table. 'Ar used the last coupla sheets gettin me mascara off!'
'DO WHAT?' Maizie raged, now stranded on the lavatory. 'WELL GET ME SUMMINK TO WIPE ME BLOODY ARSE ON YA DOZY MARE!'
'Like what?' Trisha asked. 'We aint got nuffing!'
'OH FLIPPIN ELL!' Maizie cursed. 'Well do summink ya doughnut, ar can't friggin move off the flamin karzi, and urry up for gawd sake!'
'Oh, yeah right,' Trisha said, looking about the place. 'Shit, shit,' she said, throwing open the kitchen cupboards, but hardly taking much notice of their contents.
'TRISHAAAAA, WHAT YA DOIN?' Maizie asked, unable to leave the pan.
'A'RM LOOKIN, AR'M LOOKIN!' Trisha replied, exhausting all possibilities. 'Tell ya what, ar'll ask the neighbours!' she added, heading for the door.
'Ay, what?' Maizie said, hearing the door close behind her friend. 'Where ya goin, they won't give ya sod all that lot, Trisha. TRISHAAAAAA!'
Trisha had hot footed it downstairs to the Romanian's door, forgetting their previous feud, pressing her finger on the buzzer repeatedly. 'Ello, ellooooo!' she called. 'Ellooooo, anybody there?'
Moments later the door opened an inch or so and a young woman appeared. 'What do you want?' she asked, swatting the inquisitive children at her feet.

'Bum roll,' Trisha replied, gesturing to her bottom. 'Me mate's got the trots and we run aata shit paper, you aint got arfa roll we can borra av ya?'

'I am sorry I do not understand,' the woman told Trisha. 'What is this?'

'Karzi roll!' Trisha said with some urgency. 'You lot do use it don'tcha?'

'You mean the paper for the lavatory?' the Romanian asked. 'Yes I have it, but my husband is not home right now, I am sorry.'

'Ang on, wait!' Trisha said, jamming her foot in the door. 'Look woss ya name?'

The Romanian girl paused. 'Tatyana,' she said sheepishly. 'But I cannot help you.'

'Tatyana, thas a nice name,' Trisha told her. 'Can ar call ya Tatty?'

'If you wish,' Tatyana replied, cursing the children behind the door.

'Look,' Trisha said, appealing to the girl's better nature. 'Ar know Dee ad a proper dig at yer old fella, but thas just er way, nart ar mean.'

'I am sorry I do not understand,' Tatyana said, once again struggling with Trisha's dialect.

'Can ar come in?' Trisha asked, attempting to strike up a rapport with her neighbour. 'Just for a minute?'

Although hesitant, Tatyana eventually relented and opened the door. 'Please,' she said, inviting Trisha inside. 'I will get what you need.'

'Ohhh ello!' Trisha smiled, ruffling the hair of the two young boys at her feet. 'You'z two are gorgeous aint'cha.'

The giggling tots ran to their grandparents who were sat in front of the TV in the living room, having encountered very few strangers. 'Hiyaaaaaa!' Trisha said, waving to the octogenarians who barely acknowledged her presence.

'Please, this way,' Tatyana said, ushering Trisha through to their tiny kitchen before rummaging in the cupboard for a roll of toilet paper.

'This is nice,' Trisha said, looking around and lying through her teeth, a tad shocked at their humble existence.
'It is shit,' Tatyana replied bitterly. 'We had beautiful house in Bucharest, but my husband, he bring us here.'
The two girls were of a similar age but it would be true to say that Tatyana had lived a lifetime, already enduring hardship and famine as a child in her homeland. 'Would you like some tea?' she asked, reaching for the kettle.
'Naah sod that, you got anyfing stronger?' Trisha asked expectantly.
'Only my husband's vodka,' Tatyana said, producing a bottle from the bread bin. 'But I am forbidden.'
'Forbidden my arse,' Trisha laughed, snatching the bottle and two plastic beakers from the draining board. 'Arfa nip won't urt'cha.'
'No please you mustn't!' Tatyana begged, having lived in fear of her husband, who was some twelve years her senior. 'I told you I cannot touch his drink.'
'Oh shuuutuuuup,' Trisha said, pouring two generous measures and pressing one into Tatyana's hand. 'Get that daan ya girl, itta do ya the worlda good.'
Hesitant but intrigued at the same time, Tatyana sipped at the vodka wincing at the strength. 'Neck it!' Trisha insisted, tipping the beaker and forcing her to down the measure in one.
'It is horrible,' Tatyana spluttered.
'Good though ain it,' Trisha smiled, sinking hers with ease. 'Fancy anuvva?' This time throwing caution to the wind Tatyana nodded offering her beaker. 'Oh, ar'm Trish by the way,' Trisha said, filling both beakers to the brim. Then toasting Tatyana she looked her up and down, her unflattering clothes and lank hair aged her beyond her years. 'D'you know what?' she said, offering some constructive criticism. 'You'd be an arf tidy bird if you done summink wiv yer air and spent a coupla bob on a new outfit or two.'

Tatyana toyed with her hair. 'Oh no, my husband does not allow it,' she said, her words tinged with regret. 'I would dearly like to look like the ladies on the television, but I must respect his wishes.'

'Thas bollocks that is,' Trisha said angrily. 'I aint never been told by no geezer, ar tell ya what, you got an air brush an a bitta make up?'

'Yes, yes I have these things,' Tatyana said, the alcohol flowing through her system for the very first time. 'This is good,' she added, sipping constantly.

'Go on, get ya shit togevva,' Trisha told her, 'ar'll show you a coupla tricksa the trade. What time's the old man back?'

'Not until tomorrow,' Tatyana explained. 'He visits his brother twice a week and gambles with the cards, sometimes he loses all our money and comes home drunk and angry.'

'Just get yer gear love,' Trisha insisted. 'What e don't know won't urt im will it.'

Tatyana ran to her room, returning moments later with her brush and cosmetics bag that had seldom been used.

'Right sit yer arse daan,' Trisha told her, freeing Tatyana's hair from the grubby ribbon. 'Ar tell ya what,' she said, running her fingers from end to end, 'there's a lotta them birds on the telly thatta die to av air like this, iss gorgeous.'

'Thank you,' Tatyana replied, unaccustomed as she was to compliments.

Forgetting completely that her friend was stranded on the toilet upstairs, Trisha set to work styling her neighbour's hair, taking a pair of scissors from the side and trimming the split ends away and layering the fringe that had partially obscured her vision.

'That looks better already,' Trisha said, brushing out the knots and sweeping it to one side, 'ava look.'

Tatyana took a mirror from the wall and clasped a hand to her mouth. 'It is beautiful,' she said, welling up inside.

'No, you're beautiful,' Trisha told her. 'And don'tchu let any bugger tell ya different.' Delving into Tatyana's meagre make up bag Trisha clasped Tatyana's chin in one hand. 'Right, pucker up,' she said, applying a pale red lipstick and a little blusher to the cheeks. 'Bleedin stunning,' she commented, standing back. 'You need to get dolled up more often girl, ar'm tellin ya.'

Tatyana stood in awe of her reflection, she had been transformed in a matter of minutes from dowdy housewife to dishy debutant.

'Right less av anuvva voddy shall we,' Trisha said, grabbing the bottle. This time with a belly full of Dutch courage Tatyana offered no resistance, instead thrusting her beaker toward Trisha thirsty for more. 'There's a good girl,' Trisha smiled. 'Less av some tunes shall we,' she added, turning on a dated transistor radio on the window sill. 'Woss this shit?' she said, turning her nose up at the preset melodies.

'It is Romanian channel,' Tatyana informed her, checking herself in the mirror once again.

'It is shite!' Trisha sneered, turning the dial. 'Less av a bitta Magic,' she added. 'Proper old school this is. OH YES!' she shrieked, before singing along to one of her all-time favorites. 'Girls just wanna av fuuuuun, they justa wanna, thay justa wannaaaaaaa, girls just wanna av fuuuuuuun. Come on Tatty!' she said, dragging Tatyana to her feet. 'Ang on a minute,' she said, looking her dress up and down. 'Where's them friggin scissors?' Before Tatyana knew what was happening Trisha had set about hacking two and a half feet from the hem of her dress.

'What are you doing?' Tatyana asked in a heady daze, whilst bobbing in time with the music.

'They justa wannaaaaaaa, they justa wannaaaaaaaaa,' Trisha warbled, tossing the fabric over her shoulder and swinging Tatyana around the kitchen.

'They justa wannaaaaaaa,' Tatyana sang, with the broadest of smiles.

'Thas it!' Trisha laughed. 'Girls just wanna av fuuuuuuuun!'

Tatyana was becoming increasingly intoxicated, eventually snatching the bottle from Trisha and swigging from the neck as they sang and danced, much to the children's amusement at the kitchen door. The Grandparents on the other hand sat solemn faced, disappointed at Tatyana's behavior, but too grateful for the roof over their heads to object.

'Fuck me girl, you got some moves,' Trisha remarked, as her new friend grew increasingly confident twerking against the kitchen table and attempting a slut drop or two.

Upstairs Maizie was beside herself with rage. 'Ar'll kill er, ar'll fuckin kill er!' she snarled, her backside now numb on the pan. 'Trisha, Trishaaaa!' she growled, not wanting to wake Dee Dee. 'Trisha, you back yet ya doughnut?'

Oblivious, Trisha marched around the folding table with Tatyana following suit. 'Ar would walk five undred miles!' she sang. 'An ar would walk five undred more, da da da da, da da da da, la la la la la la la la la la laaaaaaaaa!'

Tatyana stumbled after Trisha, the room now a blur. 'Byeeeee byeeeee miss American pieeeeeee,' she slurred, literally having the time of her entire life, the children rejoiced never having seen their mother so happy. Trisha grabbed their tiny hands and the four of them danced around in circles.

'Oh this is wunna mar faves!' Trisha shrieked. 'Never gonna give you uuuuuup, never gonna let'chu daaaaaaan, never gonna tell a lieeeeee and urt youuuuuu, never gonna give, never gonna give, never gonna give.'

Turning up the volume the two girls belted out Rick Astley's meteoric eighties classic, Tatyana following Trisha's lead enthusiastically. 'Never gonna make you cryyyyyy, never gonna say goodbyeeeee, never gonna tell a liiiiiiie and urrrrrt youooooo!'

The children soon tired and joined their grandparents on the sofa, while Trisha and Tatyana polished off the remainder of her husband's vodka and boogied like never before to everybody from Marvin Gaye to Diana Ross and the Supremes. Eventually Tatyana's elderly relatives barked at the kitchen door, reminding her of the lateness of the hour and the deafening music, but instead of relenting Tatyana

slammed the kitchen door in their faces and shook her hair provocatively whilst writhing against the freezer.
'Ar better be goin Tat mate,' Trisha explained. 'Ar'm up early in the mawnin and them coffin dodgers wanna get some kip.'
Tatyana flung her arms around Trisha's neck giving her a friendly peck of gratitude on the cheek. 'Woss that for?' Trisha asked, looking into her hazel eyes, but then instinctively returned the favour not once but twice before locking lips with the Romanian beauty who, although startled, reciprocated pulling Trisha toward her feeling a closeness that had been denied her for so many years. 'Flippin eck!' Trisha said, coming up for air, her head spinning. 'Thas well nice,' she moved in for another lingering kiss, the pair of them under the influence of the powerful Polish vodka and wrenching at one another's clothes. Suddenly one of Tatyana's children called out to her, 'Mamaaaaaaaaa, mamaaaaaaaaaaa!' Tatyana pulled away reluctantly, her hair ravaged by Trisha's frantic hands, breathless but not breaking eye contact.
'Mamaaaaaaaaa!' the child cried again.
'You better see to im,' Trisha told her. 'Ar gotta go anyway, like ar said ar'm up early in the mawnin. Listen ar've ad a proper good night, can we do it again sometime?'
'Yes, yes I'd like that,' Tatyana said, throwing herself at Trisha yet again.
'Easy, easy!' Trisha laughed, returning her smothering kisses. 'See to ya kiddies babe, ar'll come see ya anuvva time.'
Groaning, Tatyana broke away, light headed and hungry for more. 'You will come back,' she said eagerly. 'Promise me you will, promise me, say it, say you will!'
'Alright, ar said ar would babe,' Trisha smiled, heading for the door. 'Just get plenty of voddy in.'
'Yes, yes I will,' Tatyana said, trailing behind. 'And thank you, for my hair I mean.'

'No probs,' Trisha replied, pecking Tatyana's lips and starting up the stairs a little worse for wear. 'Never gonna give you uuuuuuup,' she sang, swaying into the wall. 'Never gonna let'chu daaaaaaan, never gonna tell a liiiiiiiie and urt'chaaaaa.'

Slamming their door behind her, she waltzed through to the bathroom. 'Never gonna give you uuuuuuuup. Oh ello Maize,' she said nonchalantly. 'You alright?'

'ALRIGHT!' Maizie yelled, her backside positively throbbing. 'ALRIGHT!' She was about to launch into a bitter tirade when Trisha interrupted,

'Ohhhh Maize, what a night ar've ad ar tell ya, ar went daanstairs and met this proper gorgeous bird. Tatyanus or summink, anyway we done all of er old fella's voddy and boogie'd to some pukka eighties Magic. Ar done er air coz she looked proper council but ar tell ya summink Maize, she done arf scrub up well mate. Anyway one fing led to anuvva and we ended up snoggin. Oh it was wicked mate you shoulda bin there.'

'BIN THERE!' Maizie screeched. 'Ow the fuck could I av bin there when ar've bin stuck ear on this crapper waitin for the bog roll ya friggin idiot!'

'Oh,' Trisha said, with absolutely no recollection. 'You shoulda said Maize, ar'da got ya some.'

'You mean you never got sod all!' Maizie raged, clenching her rolled down leggings in her whitened knuckles.

'Well ar did get summink,' Trisha admitted. 'An andful of Tatty's arse and a damp patch in me DKNYs.'

Maizie, whose legs by now were numb with temporary paralysis, reached out to grab her friend. 'Come ear you soppy bitch so ar can beat the shit aata ya,' she said, clawing at Trisha's leg.

'What, what av ar done?' Trisha yelped, backing away. 'It aint mar fault.'

'There was arf a roll left!' Maizie cursed. 'You tell me who uses arf a bloody roll to wipe their arse. You tell me!'

'Ar didn't use it all on me arse,' Trisha explained. 'Ar made an origami chicken wiv the rest, you shoulda seen it Maize, it was the nuts ar'm tellin ya.'
'YOU DONE WHAT?' 'Maizie said beside herself.
'A chicken,' Trisha replied, fluffing her hair in the mirror. 'Ar wonnid to do a kangaroo, but I aint never seen one so ar wouldn't know where to start, nart ar mean. You wanna try that origami Maize iss proper feraputic.'
'Ow the bleedin ell am ar gonna do that then?' Maizie growled. 'WIV NO PISSIN BOG ROLL!'
'Alright, alright,' Trisha said, attempting to calm her furious friend. 'Ang on, ar see what ar can do.' Leaving Maizie marooned once again, she scoured the living room returning shortly after with a well-thumbed glossy mag rolled in her hand. 'Eeyar!' she said, slipping it onto Maizie's lap. 'It aint much cop for ya clingons but iss all we got, just mind the seduko on page eight, ar done it wiv a permanent marker an it aint dried yet.'
Maizie examined the far from absorbent alternative. 'You're avin a fuckin laugh aint'cha,' she scoffed, tearing off a strip and checking the cover story. 'Ohhh great,' she grimaced, 'ar got Posh, Becks and Miley friggin Cyrus goin up me bum ole.'
'Ooh errrr,' Trisha laughed. 'Ar'll leave ya to it shall I?'
'Yeah, you do that!' Maizie said glaring. 'Fuuuuuuck!' she then yelped, reaching behind.
'What, woss up naaah?' Trisha replied from outside the bathroom.
'WOSS UP?' Maizie yelled wincing. 'Iver Beckham just bit my arse or ar got a pissin paper cut, thas woss up!'
'Niiiiice,' Trisha said, beating a hasty retreat.
With gritted teeth Maizie spent the next five minutes shredding the magazine and dabbing at her reddened rear, plotting the demise of her faltering flatmate.

The following morning Dee Dee was the first to rise, having slept solidly for some nine hours. 'Mawnin Dee!' Trisha said, joining her in the kitchen. 'If ya makin a cuppa ar'll av one.'

Maizie trudged in behind her, yawning and scratching her head. 'Mawwwnin,' she said, stroking Dee Dee's back. 'Ow ya feelin?'

'Oh ar'm glad you asked,' Trisha said butting in. 'Ar've ad a poxy night ar tell ya.'

'Not you!' Maizie snapped, still miffed at her toilet vigil. 'Ar'm talkin to Dee!'

'Yeah, not bad fanks,' Dee Dee replied, topping up the cheap plastic kettle with water. 'Ar feel better for that kip.'

'Well ar'm glad you got some,' Trisha moaned. 'I aint slept a bleedin wink I aint, ar dunno what was in that dodgy polak vodka that Tatty bird gimme, but iss proper done me up like a kipper as me old nan used to say.'

'Tatty bird?' Dee Dee said, resting against the sink while the kettle gurgled. 'What you on abaat?'

'Ar'll tell ya shall I,' Maizie moaned. 'Silly bollocks ear leaves me stuck on the karzi wiv no bum roll and buggers off daanstairs to that Romanian lot. Apparently she got steamin drunk wiv em and lezzed up the geezer's misses.'

'Do what?' Dee Dee asked.

'Yeah, it was pukka!' Trisha smiled. 'She was orny as fuck an'all.'

'Oh that aint the worst of it,' Maizie continued, folding her arms across her chest. 'When the dozy mare did eventually come back she forgot the pissin bog roll, ar'm surprised you never erd me Dee, ar was proper goin mental at er.'

'Ar give you a magazine din I,' Trisha piped up. 'There aint no elpin some people is there Dee.'

'Next time don't bovva!' Maizie snarled, dumping two sugars into her mug. 'That shit ripped me to bleedin bits it did.'

'What you an abaat no bog roll?' Dee Dee asked, reaching into the cupboard above the microwave. 'There's arf a dozen rolls in ear.'

'Do what?' Maizie said glaring wild eyed looking for Trisha who had slipped away unnoticed to the safety of her bedroom. 'Trishaaaaaaaa!' Maizie yelled after her.
Dressing hastily and slipping from the flat to avoid Maizie's simmering wrath, Trisha hot footed it down the stairs almost colliding with Tatyana who was also leaving for one of several cleaning jobs she held down. 'Oh, mawnin babe,' Trisha said, expecting maybe a repeat of the previous evening's passionate clinch. But instead Tatyana dropped her head red faced and ducked quickly back inside her door. 'Tatty!' Trisha called, bemused. 'Tat, you alright?'
Tatyana stood with her back to the door, racked with guilt but at the same time her heart skipping a beat having, against her better judgment, cherished their intimate liaison.
The street door then opened and Tatyana's hungover husband stomped in giving Trisha the meanest of looks as he rattled his keys. Trisha stood for a while listening at their door as the overbearing brute barked at his petite wife and the children, demanding breakfast and mocking her newly cropped hair. 'Wanker,' Trisha said, wanting so much to kick in the door and beat him to a bloody pulp with his empty vodka bottle, which he duly noticed had been drained, causing him to fly into a violent rage hurling cups, saucers and Tatyana's beloved china cat to the kitchen floor.
Checking her phone Trisha stood at the end of the garden path, looking left then right along the street and occasionally over her shoulder toward Tatyana's flat. Soon Adrian's van came into sight. 'Hiyaaaaaa!' she said, stepping into the road between two parked cars and waving. 'Mawnin.'
'Good morning Trisha,' Adrian said, watching her climb in beside him. 'I have to tell you Trisha, I've had the top brass on the phone this morning and it wasn't pleasant.'
'Oh, right,' Trisha said, buckling up. 'Why, what you gone and done?'

'ME!' Adrian remarked. 'It seems you caused quite a stir on your first day with the society. The switchboards handled a record number of calls from the general public - the majority of them complaints I might add.'

'Complaints!' Trisha smirked. 'Oh you don't wanna worry abaat nunna that shit Ade, some people aint got nuffing better to do mate.'

'You do remember what happened yesterday don't you?' Adrian asked, pulling away. 'We do have procedures in place for capturing escaped horses, and I'm afraid screaming *come ear you four legged fuckers* and waving a badminton racket isn't one of them.'

'Oh yeah ar member that,' Trisha laughed. 'Ar got that in *Sports for You* when ar chased the buggers up the escalator, that and a paira Nikey's for me cousin Shelly's two year old Riley. Ohhh you wanna see im, e'z a proper ansum little sod e iz.'

'Well, the manager of *Sports for You* is one of many demanding compensation for the damage caused by the stampeding ponies, apparently his store is now in need of a complete re-fit.'

'Ar spoze ar'm up the road then am I?' Trisha said, hanging her head. 'Ar was only tryna elp.'

'Fired!' Adrian said jokily. 'Oh heavens no, it appears that during the debacle you saved the chief commissioner's wife from being trampled by pushing her into a cabinet of frozen fish in the supermarket, oddly enough he's considering a commendation.'

'For me!' Trisha gasped. 'Bloody Nora!'

'Indeed,' Adrian added. 'You, my dear, are one very lucky young lady.'

'Well, me muvva always said,' Trisha replied, 'if ar fell in shit ar'd come up smellin of roses. When ar was eight an arf ar burnt daan me pre-school wiv me grandad's lighter, cost em arf a mill to rebuild it apparently, but when they dug the new faandations they faand a stasha roman shit werf millions. Ar never got a bean though which proper pissed

me muvva off at the time coz we was potless, all ar got was me picture in the paper and an M&S vaacher which me old dear used on a paira big knickers.'
Adrian's head was swimming at this point, at the mention of arson, archeology and Trisha's mother's under garments - all blurted in a single breath. 'My word!' he gasped, turning onto the high street. 'Anyway I've been ordered to keep you on a tight leash from now on,' he told Trisha.
'Oh yeah,' Trisha smiled. 'You into that shit are ya, listen mate ar don't mind a bitta levva an all that, and maybe a bitta playful slappin, but if the shit gets aat of and ar'll av ya nicked ya pervy fuck.'
'Oh no, no, what I meant was!' Adrian said, back tracking.
'Ar know what ya meant alright,' Trisha interjected, 'you're as bad as me uncle Jerry you are, that dirty bleeda used to make iz old lady drag im raand the ouse in a muzzle an a studded staffy collar. The poor cow ad to worm im twice a week, and watch im drag iz shitty arse across the friggin carpet.'
'Trisha!' Adrian insisted. 'Management merely want me to keep an eye on you, that's all, nothing more.'
'Oh,' Trisha said, deflated somewhat. 'Well why dint'cha say?'
Adrian was about to explain when the radio operator interrupted them. 'Two four, two four, come in two four!'
Trisha snatched the receiver before Adrian had a chance to reply. 'Alright mate!' she chirped. 'This is Whisky Tango and Papa Bear receivin ya, over!' She then put her hand over the mouthpiece. 'Ar fought ar'd call ya Papa Bear,' she told Adrian, 'ya don't mind do ya?' Before Adrian could object Trisha addressed the controller once again. 'Sorry mate, wossup?'
'Two four?' the controller said, having received an unfamiliar reply.
'Yeees!' Trisha snapped. 'Ar told ya, we're receivin!'
'Oh, er right you are,' the controller replied hesitantly. 'Well er, I need you to proceed to the Tower of London. I repeat

the Tower of London. Apparently one of their ravens has gotten itself stuck inside a sixteenth century cannon of all things and is making quite a racket.'
'Yeah OK mate,' Trisha replied. 'We'll sort the bleeda aat, laterz!' Hanging up, Trisha turned to Adrian, who was staring in disbelief. 'What?' she asked innocently. 'Well come on, what ya waitin for?'
'Whiskey Tango?' Adrian grimaced. 'Papa Bear? Trisha may I remind you our call sign is *two four* for heaven's sake.'
'Two four, two four,' Trisha laughed. 'What kinda shit is that, don'tchu worry me old mukka ar'll learn em.'
Adrian gave his passenger a sideways glance before turning onto the dual carriageway.

Dee Dee and Maizie had left shortly after their friend, with Maizie, as usual, eager to get back to the centre. Meeting Tatyana at the foot of the stairs Dee Dee couldn't help but notice the reddened hand print on the side of her face and the ripped breast pocket of her cleaner's apron; the result of a struggle to resist her husband's demanding sexual advances.
'You alright?' Dee Dee asked, as Tatyana wiped a tear from her cheek.
'Yes, yes I'm fine,' the Romanian said, scurrying to the street door.
'Suit yaself,' Dee Dee said nonchalantly.
'Woss up wiv er Dee?' Maizie asked.
'Thas bleedin obvious ain it,' Dee Dee sneered, listening to the husband's drunken verbal abuse directed at his boisterous children. 'She wouldn't give up the goods so the prick give er a slap.'
'Bastard!' Maizie snarled.
'Tell me abaat it,' Dee Dee said, quietly seething and having no time for perpetrators of domestic violence in any way shape or form, for all her father's faults he had never once raised his hand in anger toward her mother, or his voice for that matter.

Taking the short walk to the station the girls were greeted by a police cordon at the main entrance with a placard appealing for witnesses. 'Woss all this?' Maizie asked, following commuters through the side door.
'Another stabbing,' a station official told them, directing passengers to an alternative platform. 'Lovely young fella an'all.'
Maizie then noticed a blood spattered beaded tribal bracelet lying beneath a wooden bench. 'What young fella?' she asked, recognizing it instantly. 'Tell me, who was it?'
'Couldn't tell you his name,' the official replied, shrugging his shoulders. 'Used to busk down here regular, great voice and fantastic on that guitar of his.'
'Bird!' Maizie gasped, recalling the young busker's nickname. 'Is he alright, is Frankie alright? What ospital did they take im to?'
'More like the morgue I'm afraid love,' the official told her in a hushed toned. 'They tried for forty minutes to resuscitate him, but he'd just lost far too much blood, such a shame, it really is.'
'Who was it Maize?' Dee Dee asked, handing her friend her return ticket.
'Bird, ar mean Frankie,' Maizie said, stunned and staring into space. 'Ar met im ear before.'
The station official put a hand on Maizie's shoulder. 'They'll get the so-and-so's that did it, we got em on CCTV,' he then stooped to retrieve the bracelet.
'Can I av that?' Maizie asked, holding out her hand. 'Please?'
'Well,' the underground official said, observing her obvious distress. 'I shouldn't really, but it seems you knew the lad, so go on then.'
'Fanks,' Maizie said, trembling as he slipped the bracelet over her outstretched fingers. 'Oh Dee look,' she said examining the traces of Frankie's blood, the stuff of life that had flowed through his talented veins. 'Look.'
'You liked im then?' Dee Dee asked.

'Yeah, yeah ar did,' Maizie replied, clenching the bracelet in her tightening fist. 'I only met im once, but there was summink abaat im, summink in iz eyes. Ar'm gutted mate, proper gutted.'

'Thas why the old bill were flyin abaat last night,' Dee Dee remarked. 'Ar told ya London's proper fucked up naah. Come on mate.' Dee Dee led her shell-shocked friend to the edge of the platform, then left her to her thoughts during the tube journey.

Walking the busy streets to the Westmoreland centre Dee Dee paused outside a Turkish newsagents. 'Ang on a minute,' she said, leaving Maizie slumped against a light pole and popping inside. Dee Dee emerged a short while later with three magazines rolled up in her left hand, a packet of sweets stuffed in her jacket pocket and a chocolate bar in her right. 'Eeyar mate,' she said, handing Maizie the Mars. 'Ar know ya like these,' this small token from one friend to another was in no way meant to ease her distress, it was merely a gesture that in Maizie's eyes spoke volumes. Dee Dee was there for her as she always had been, a rock to lean on and a pillar of strength.

'Fanks mate,' she said, taking the treat. 'You're right it is me favrit.'

Dee Dee slipped an arm through Maizie's and walked closely with her. 'Sorry abaat ya geezer,' she said, side stepping the broken paving.

'Yeeeah,' Maizie sighed with a dry mouth. 'Yeah, so am I.'

'You gonna be alright?' Dee Dee asked her fiend outside the centre doors. 'Ar'll tell em ya sick if you wanna go ome.'

'Naah,' Maizie said, biting at the chocolate wrapper. 'I aint gonna let the littluns daan, anyway iss probly just what ar need.'

'Good on ya,' Dee Dee said, leading her inside.

Trisha and Adrian had navigated their way through bustling city centre traffic to the gates of the Tower of London. 'Ar come ear wiv the school,' Trisha told her mentor, looking

across at the ominous battlements. 'Ar got a bollocking for stickin a jam samwich to a beefeaters backside, d'ya fink they'll recognize me?'
'I don't know, how old were you?' Adrian asked, leaning to press the buzzer.
'Six,' Trisha confessed, pulling her collar up to partly conceal her face.
'Six!' Adrian laughed. 'My dear, I don't think you have anything to worry about. RSPCA!' he then said into the intercom.
The heavy gates were opened by a tower official and they were ushered inside. 'You're here for the raven I presume?' a Beefeater said, leaning into the driver's window, 'follow me.' Escorting them, he strode with an air of distinction through the cobbled inner roads to Traitor's Gate. 'You'll have to walk from here I'm afraid,' he told them, ascending a stone staircase to the upper terrace which overlooked the swirling river Thames. 'I have no idea how he got in there,' he added, waiting at the top. 'They very rarely leave the Tower green, what with their wings being clipped an'all.'
It soon became apparent which direction the stricken bird was by the gurgling squawks and the ever increasing crowd of inquisitive tourists peering inside one of several heavy bronze cannons. Adrian had with him a large cat basket in which to transport the raven back to the green once released, and a pair of thick leather gauntlets with which to handle the creature.
'Right shift yer arses!' Trisha said, shoving a family of Swedes aside. 'Come on, let the dog see the rabbit.'
'Rabbit?' one of them said, regaining his footing and craning his neck once again.
'Shut'cha noise and gimme some bloody space will ya,' Trisha said forcefully. 'Or ar'll av ya nicked for obstruction, d'you ear me?' Cupping the mouth of the cannon Trisha stooped and peered inside and was immediately greeted by a screeching sound and a ruffle of feathers. 'Ar can't see a friggin fing,' she said, retrieving her phone and turning on

the back light. 'Oh there you are,' she added, illuminating the bird who had somehow turned in the half ton cannon to face her, but had become lodged in the process.

'Here, take these,' Adrian said, offering the elbow length gauntlets.

'Oh don't be daft!' Trisha laughed, draped over the cannon. 'Ar've ad bigger budgies than this bugger.'

'My dear,' a concerned beefeater added, standing alongside her. 'May I remind you these creatures are carnivorous by nature.'

'They're what?' Trisha asked, turning to confront him. 'Ar fought they was crows.'

'Carnivorous,' the beefeater reiterated. 'Flesh eaters, so to speak, so if I were you I'd wear the gloves. And it is in fact a raven.'

'Well you aint me are ya!' Trisha replied, angered at having her apparent authority undermined in front of the jostling tourists. 'In fact what the bleedin ell are ya?' she eyed him up and down in his traditional crimson garb complete with neck ruffle and black velvet hat.

'Trisha!' Adrian barked. 'Calm yourself please, and remember where you are.'

'Yeaaaah alright,' Trisha sneered, rolling up one sleeve. 'Just get ready wiv the bloody basket will ya.'

'He's right, you should really wear the gauntlets,' Adrian said, opening the cat box. 'They are carnivores after all.'

'They're what?' Trisha said, turning from the cannon.

'Carrion,' Adrian explained. 'It's a term to describe...'

'It's a bloody crow!' Trisha said, tired of the repeated interruptions.

'Raven,' the Beefeater said, raising a finger to correct her once again.

'Oh shut it you!' Trisha snapped. 'And you!' she added, snatching the basket from Adrian. 'Gimme that fing!' Puffing her chest and playing to the gathered crowd, she bent and thrust a hand into the cannon, ramming her arm in to the shoulder and grabbing with her outstretched fingers. 'Come ear ya bugger,' she puffed, with the bird inches out of reach. 'Oooh ya bleeda,' she repeatedly cursed.

'Would you like me to try?' Adrian asked, tapping Trisha's shoulder.

'Naah ar got it,' Trisha insisted, rounding the cannon to thump her clenched fist at the rear in an attempt to startle and possibly dislodge the raven.

'Please, you'll frighten him,' the Beefeater begged, tugging at Trisha's sleeve.

'Ar know what ar'm bloody doin!' Trisha barked, tapping at her lapel badge. 'Ar work for this bleedin lot dun I.' Trisha's haphazard approach did in fact stir the bird causing it to shuffle an inch or so however awkwardly. 'Right less av ya,' she said purposefully, groping inside once again with a concerned Adrian looking on. This time Trisha was able to swipe the raven's face with her probing fingers, causing it to squawk louder and lash out with its enormous beak clamping down on her index finger with a vice like grip. 'ARRRRRRGH YA FUCKER!' Trisha yelped. 'FUUUUUCK, FUUUUUUCK ISS GOT ME. THE BASTARD'S GOT ME!' The gathered visitors backed away several steps, startled at her distress call. 'SHIT, SHIT, GET IT OFFA ME!'

'I did warn you,' the smiling Beefeater told her.

'Shut up you cock!' Trisha barked, shaking the bird's beak from side to side. 'And get this cuntin crow off mar fuckin fingaaaaa!'

'I told you it's a raven,' the Beefeater said, offering very little in the way of assistance.

'ARRRRRGH!' Trisha cried, as the razor sharp beak pierced her skin. 'ADRIAN FOR FUCK SAKE DO SUMMINK WILL YA!'

'Oh yes, yes of course,' Adrian said, pounding the cannon to distract the raven's attention, while camcorders, iPads and smart phones were trained on them.

Suddenly the frantic raven released its grip to take another nip and Trisha pulled her hand free sharply. 'Shit, shit, shit!' she cursed, shaking and cupping her bloodied finger. 'Oooooh you bastard!'

'You'll need a tetanus jab for that young lady,' the Beefeater said, shaking his head knowingly.

'And you'll need a punch up the froat!' Trisha barked in reply.

'Trisha please!' Adrian said in an authoritative tone.

'Well!' Trisha said rocking. 'E ain elpin is e.'

'Here, let me take a look,' Adrian said, examining her hand. 'That'll need a stitch I'm sure of it,' he told her. 'I'll deal with the raven, you sit this one out. If you'd like to wait in the van there's a first aid kid behind my seat with a lint dressing inside.'

'Do what?' Trisha said, refusing to admit defeat. 'Gimme that glove fing,' she added, snatching a gauntlet. 'Ar'll sort this slag aat meself.'

'But Trisha, your hand!' Adrian winced, watching her pull the gauntlet up to her elbow.

'Fuck it!' Trisha said, still in some considerable pain. 'I aint lettin this fucker beat me ar'm tellin ya, and before you say a blinkin word,' she told the beefeater, 'ar don't give a shit if iss a raven, a crow or a friggin cockatoo, the bleeda's comin aat and thas that.'

The belittled beefeater had met his match with Trisha and opted for crowd control instead. 'Please keep back ladies and gentlemen!' he said, with arms outstretched. 'Keep well back please, sir, I won't tell you again!'

Taking a deep breath Trisha once again beat down on the cannon's barrel half a dozen or so times. 'Get ready wiv that flippin basket,' she told Adrian, before delving inside with a determined grimace.

'Go on my sweet,' an elderly bystander said, holding an antiquated camera aloft. 'Get the black bastard!' she continued, much to the horror of the Jamaican standing beside her.

'What de hell did you saaay womaaan,' the Rastafarian said, spinning to confront her. 'Dat be some raaaacist shit right dere.'

'OY CHEWBACCA!' a cockney cabbie called from behind, his view now obscured by the Jamaican's traditional dreads and floppy hat. 'GET'CHA BLOODY BEANIE AAT THE WAY!'
'You hush ya mote!' the Rasta raged, his colourful woollen hat stuffed with matted hair.
'OR WHAT?' the cabbie sneered over a party of Parisians. 'What'chu gonna do ya scruffy fucker?'
Trisha clawed at the raven's feet unfazed this time by its thrusting beak, whilst the unrest within the crowd boiled over. A German father lashed out when the Jamaican inadvertently stepped on his son's foot whilst surging through the sea of bodies toward the goading cabbie.
'PLEASE!' the beefeater said, waving his hands in the air. 'Please settle down, otherwise I'll have to ask you all to leave.' Soon a full scale brawl broke out when a twenty eight stone Ghanaian woman waded in with bloated fists flying to defend the Rastafarian against the obvious racial attack.
'Got'cha you mangey fuck!' Trisha blurted, grasping the raven by the neck while Adrian edged away from the turmoil unfolding at his side.
'Hurry up Trisha please,' he said, dodging a hail of projectiles, including soda cans, ice creams and a selection of ceramic souvenirs ranging from red route master busses to the trademark telephone boxes.
Trisha tugged red faced, inching the squawking bird toward the mouth of the cannon. 'Ar got'cha,' she puffed, dragging the distressed creature clear.
The beefeater beat a hasty retreat, fearing for his life after sustaining a cut to his right eye from a flying handbag. With the raven now free, in a flurry of feathers it began flapping its colossal wings in an attempt to escape Trisha's grasp. 'Get the bloody basket!' she screeched, holding the thrashing bird at arm's length. 'Ade get the fuckin basket will ya!'
Adrian cowered at her feet as though in a missile strewn war zone, offering the open basket up to her, as the

metropolitan police arrived in force to break up the cross continental chaos.
'Get in there ya bleeda!' Trisha groaned, ramming the raven's backside into the plastic basket which angered it no end, having just been freed from one confine. 'Shut the fuckin door!' she barked, pulling her hand free and breathing a sigh of relief, before looking over her shoulder. 'What the fuck?' she gasped, seeing the brawling tourists resisting arrest aggressively, the melee having escalated to near riot proportions much to her surprise. 'Woss up wiv that lot?' she asked, ducking a launched lolly.
'God only knows,' Adrian cried, wiping ice cream from his sleeve. 'Let's get the hell out of here shall we?'
Hot footing it down the stone steps to their vehicle, the two narrowly escaped a falling bench hurled from the battlements. 'Friggin ell!' Trisha cried, watching it obliterate an unoccupied sentry box. 'They're off their fuckin eds that lot ar tell ya!'
Adrian leapt behind the wheel, and fumbling with the keys wondered if in fact the chaos theory was written specifically with Trisha in mind.
'OY GEEZER!' Trisha yelled, leaning from the window as they left the scene and approached the traumatized beefeater. 'EAR'S YA CROW BIRD FING!' she tossed the basket into his arms in passing. 'If ya get any more trouble wiv the fuckers gissa bell yeah!' Flopping back into her seat, she fastened her seat belt. 'Sorted' she said, smacking her hands together as Adrian shook his head and pulled aside to allow a riot van to pass them.
'I definitely need a cuppa,' Adrian said, his heart still pounding and his society uniform spattered with overpriced Mr Whippy ice cream.
'Oooh yeah,' Trisha smiled, 'an ar could murder anuvva wunna them juggernaut's an'all, but this time ar wanna nuvva fried slice an a couple more ash braans.'
Adrian looked across wide eyed, having seen the colossal breakfast at close hand. 'Another fried slice?' he said,

finding it hard to imagine how anybody could put away that many calories in one sitting and still ask for more.

Maizie had steadied her nerves with two cups of fortifying tea and a hug from Dee Dee. 'Ar know e was nuffing to me Dee,' she said, taking a calming breath. 'But some people come into ya lives for a reason don't they,' she immediately realized the gravity of her statement. 'Oh ar'm sorry Dee mate, ar didn't mean to...,' she added, stroking Dee Dee's shoulder. 'Ar shouldn't say fings like that cozza what appened to Travis an'all that, sorry mate.'
'Don't worry abaat it,' Dee Dee replied, concerned only with her friend's feelings at that point it time. 'But ar do know what ya mean though mate.'
'Come on,' Maizie smiled, pulling herself together and sparing Dee Dee any further heartache, 'less go to work.'
'Yeah, too right,' Dee Dee said, donning her apron and heading for the kitchen. 'Ar'll catch you at break yeah.'
'Alright mate!' Maize said, putting on a brave face for the centre's children already seated in the play room. 'Elloooo mate!' she laughed, when Dominic ran to hug her legs and tugged her by the hand toward the rest of the group who had made a make shift camp in the middle of the room from chairs and blankets.
'It's our castle,' Dominic shrieked. 'Come in, come in!'
Maizie followed Dominic inside on all fours, ruffling the hair of his two friends within.

Dee Dee loaded her trolley with an urn of tea, a pot of coffee and a supply of soft drinks and tasty treats for the residents. 'Ello darlin,' she said, rattling the trolley into Alice's room.
'Teaaaaaaaaa, teaaaaaaaaa!' Alice clapped, bouncing as she had done during the previous weeks, months and years.
'Ar got ya summink special,' Dee Dee said, pulling the packet of sweets from her pinny pocket. Alice snatched the bag and pressed it to her face in an attempt to read the label. 'Eeya,'

Dee Dee said, taking it back and tearing off a corner, Alice popped out her tongue allowing Dee Dee to feed her. 'Thas it,'

Dee Dee smiled, watching Alice's expression change. 'Cherry flava, d'ya like it?' Alice took back the packet and hastily unwrapped several more, popping them one by one into her mouth until her cheeks were bulging. 'Easy mate,' Dee Dee chuckled, observing her taste overload.

Alice grabbed at Dee Dee's hand, pulling it close to her chest with the widest of smiles on her dribbling face. 'Love, love,' she gurgled.

'Yeah ar know,' Dee Dee said, welling up somewhat and straightening Alice's hair. 'Ar love ya too mate.'

Alice tucked the remainder of the packet under her pillow and held a hand out for juice.

'Orange or blackcurrant?' Dee Dee asked.

'Ringe, ringe, riiiiiiinge!' Alice shrieked, sucking the sticky dribble back into her mouth.

'There ya go,' Dee Dee said, handing her the cup before cracking open her window to allow the autumn breeze to penetrate her stifling room. Alice closed her eyes and faced the window, still sucking the boiled sweets and loving the caress of the wind on her cheeks.

'Hmmmmm, hmmmmm, goooood,' Alice said, swaying from side to side, 'hmmmmmm.'

'Catch'ya later,' Dee Dee said on leaving, but Alice did not respond. Dee Dee's heart sank pausing at the door to observe the sorry sight, Alice was happy in her own sweet way, but had been denied so many of life's pleasures that the majority of the planet's inhabitants had taken for granted.

The tea urn was all but empty when Dee Dee approached Bonnie's room. The introvert was once again sat at her desk fingering a pile of clippings. Dee Dee retrieved the magazines she had purchased from beneath the trolley and one by one slid them under Bonnie's door, pushing the trolley away before the girl had time to turn.

Bonnie spun and froze for a moment at the unfamiliar scene, then slowly approached the door looking out of the glass in time to see Dee Dee leaving. Dee Dee had chosen well, the content of the magazines was above and beyond Bonnie's expectations. Hurrying to her desk she savaged the glossies with her scissors turning occasionally to glance at the door. The girl she had exploded at the previous day had redeemed herself tenfold and pricked something deep inside the orphan. Although the centre's staff had provided Bonnie with the occasional periodical for her scrapbook, Dee Dee was different, she had no agenda, no vested interest and had returned after initially being shunned so robustly.

Maizie read to the children over and over as each of them thrust their favorite fantastical tale into her hand. 'Yeah, yeah ang on,' she laughed, 'lemmy finish this one first.' Dominic lay in her arms looking up at her mouth as she read his beloved picture book out loud.

Richard looked in from time to time, commenting to his passing staff at Maizie's natural aptitude for the otherwise demanding position. Maizie waved from within the huddle before having her head turned back toward the page by Melissa, a bubbly three year old. 'Again, again!' she said, bobbing. 'Again, again, again, again!'

'I'll leave you to it,' Richard smiled, closing the door.

CHAPTER SEVEN

Having settled, however chaotically, into their new roles the three friends were true to their word and attended ritually without fail. Trisha putting her own inimitable stamp on the royal society, Maizie gradually coming to terms with the fact that she needed the children in her life as much as they needed her, whether it be a calling or a vocation, it completed her and for the first time she knew contentment. Dee Dee's burgeoning affection for Alice had blossomed, with the hardened Essex girl choosing to spend more and more of her time with her. But although Alice seemed in her own sweet way pleased to see her, Dee Dee began to wonder if her feelings were being reciprocated, or whether the mentally deficient resident could indeed differentiate between her and the regular members of staff.

Dee Dee continued to slip carefully selected material beneath Bonnie's door over a period of weeks, each time slipping away unnoticed or so she thought. Until one afternoon during her rounds she stooped to pluck a copy of OK from her trolley and almost spat the gum from her mouth when confronted by Bonnie's smiling face at the glass. 'Jesus, ya scared the shit aata me!' she said, clutching her chest. Bonnie laughed, waving a fistful of clippings. 'Ar got some more,' Dee Dee said, composing herself but still shocked at Bonnie's apparent change of manner toward her. 'Shall ar put em under the door?' Bonnie shook her head and beckoned to Dee Dee. 'Ar can't mate,' Dee Dee said, looking left and right along the corridor. Bonnie nodded vigorously pointing down toward the lock.

'Ar got a proper bollockin last time,' Dee Dee told her sympathetically, but Bonnie persisted, hopping on the spot with a pleading expression. 'Alright, alright,' Dee Dee relented, taking the key from the trolley and after checking the corridor once more, cautiously opened the door. 'You alright mate,' she said softly, as Bonnie invited her in. 'Look ar'm sorry abaat touchin ya stuff last time,' she told her, but

Bonnie said nothing, she merely took Dee Dee's hand and lead her to her desk. 'Oh thas lovely,' Dee Dee smiled, checking Bonnie's collage of some fifty or so celebrity clippings. 'Thas er aata the Sugar Babes ain it,' she said, tapping at one of them. 'She just ad a tit job, a tummy tuck and anuvva kid by er usband's bruvva, ar'm sure they do that shit just to get in the papers, woja reckon?' Again Bonnie said nothing, she tugged Dee Dee toward the chest of drawers beside her bed. 'Woaw ang on!' Dee Dee laughed, sitting beside Bonnie as she then rummaged through the top drawer flinging her underwear aside. 'What ya lookin for?' Dee Dee asked, Bonnie pulled a crumpled photograph from the rear of the drawer and lovingly straightened the dog eared corners. 'Who's that?' Dee Dee asked, looking over Bonnie's shoulder. Without uttering a word Bonnie kissed the photograph and placed it into Dee Dee's hand. On closer inspection Dee Dee could make out a woman, possibly in her twenties, complete with babe in arms. 'Is that you?' she asked, tapping the toddler. Bonnie merely smiled. 'It is ain it?' Dee Dee said, checking the rear of the polaroid for an inscription, but there was none. 'And that must be ya mum,' she added, turning the photograph back.

'Mum,' Bonnie said, which startled Dee Dee, but before she could react an orderly marched into the room. 'What the hell are you doing in here?' he barked, rounding the bed toward them. 'You were told!'

But this time Bonnie leapt to her feet and stood between him and Dee Dee. 'NO, NO!' she yelled, beating his chest and shoving him back a step or two. 'NO, NO!'

'Ar better go,' Dee Dee said, rising to her feet. Bonnie shook her head and pushed Dee Dee back down onto her bed, shielding her and shoving the orderly once more. 'GO!' she snapped.

'Are you sure Bonnie?' he asked, backing to the door. Bonnie nodded, seeing him out of the room and slamming the door behind him. 'Mum,' she said, once more rejoining Dee Dee and tapping the photo.

'Ohhhh she speaks,' Dee Dee smiled.

'Mum,' Bonnie said again, stroking the image.

'Yeah she looks lovely,' Dee Dee agreed. 'And look at'chu wiv er, wiv ya chubby little legs.' Bonnie ran her fingers through Dee Dee's golden hair. 'Ya mum's is like mine,' Dee Dee said tugging at her locks. 'Woss er name?'

'Mum,' Bonnie replied, taking back the photograph and smothering it with kisses.

'Ahhhh fanks for showin me,' Dee Dee told her. 'And ya picture fing, iss proper good that is.'

Bonnie tugged at Dee Dee's embroidered identification. 'Deb, debr, debrrrr' she mouthed.

'Just call me Dee Dee,' Dee Dee laughed. 'Only me mum calls me Debra, oh and me dad, but we won't talk abaat im.'

'Dee,' Bonnie said smiled.

'Yeah thas it!' Dee Dee said, taking her hand. 'Dee Dee, everyone calls me Dee Dee. Well, all me mates anyway. You got any mates in ear?'

Bonnie looked at Dee Dee with a furrowed brow having never formed a meaningful friendship within the institution.

'Mates,' Dee Dee reiterated. 'There must be someone in ear you like, wunna the staff?'

Bonnie prodded Dee Dee with her finger and then her own chest. 'Yeah, yeah ar be ya mate if ya want,' Dee Dee told her. 'Right what abaat ya juice, ar got ya some mini eggs an'all.' The pair sat sharing the candy coated eggs and sipping blackcurrant, with Dee Dee attempting to coax more than a monosyllabic conversation out of the shy and retiring girl.

'Dee you comin?' Maizie eventually said, popping her head into Bonnie's room. 'Iss arf four mate. Oh ello,' she added, waving to Bonnie.

'Is it!' Dee Dee gasped. 'Blimey where's the bloody time gone today. Oh Maize this is Bonnie. Bonnie this is me mate, Maizie.'

'Alright!' Maizie said, raising a hand once again. 'Come on Dee ar wanna get ome to watch the Chase, ar'm proper ooked on that shit naah.'
'Yeah ang on,' Dee Dee said, rubbing Bonnie's back. Bonnie leapt toward her wrapping her arms around her waist and pressing her cheek to her chest. 'Woaw, woaw ya stranglin me!' Dee Dee wheezed jokily. 'Ar'll be back tomorra, don't worry, ar promise.'
Bonnie reluctantly let her one and only friend go. 'Dee Dee,' she then said with her hand raised. 'Dee Dee.'
'Yeah ar know,' Dee Dee smiled. 'Ar see you in the mawnin, yeah.'
The two friends sat on the tube savouring the events of the day as they had done on many occasions. 'Ow ya feelin?' Dee Dee asked, slipping an arm through Maizie's.
'Ar'm alright mate,' Maizie said, snuggling into her friend's shoulder. 'Ar've ad a proper good day wiv the kids I av.'
'Yeah,' Dee Dee said, counting the stops. 'Yeah, ar've ad a pukka day an'all.'
Shoving open the door of their flat Dee Dee dropped the keys onto the hall table and removed her coat. 'TRIIIISH!' she called out, in need of a cuppa. 'TRISHAAAAA!'
'Don't look like she's in yet,' Maizie said, discarding her own coat and heading for the television. 'Ar got five minutes before the Chase,' she told her friend, turning on the set. 'Woss all this?' she asked stepping back.
'What?' Dee Dee said, joining her. The lead news story of the day was the apparent sinking of one of the two passenger ferries that crossed the River Thames repeatedly from North to South Woolwich. Helicopter and shore mounted cameras were beaming images of the drama as the stricken ferry lay listing to one side, partly submerged against the South terminal. A flotilla of boats plucked frightened passengers from the icy water ferrying them to safety, while salvage tugs and cranes raced to the scene. 'Shit!' Dee Dee gasped, having used the ferries countless times as a child. 'What the fuck?'

'Woja reckon Dee, terrorists?' Maizie asked, dropping onto the couch and leaning toward the television.

'Dunno,' Dee Dee said, sitting beside her. 'Why the fuck would they wanna blow up the Woolwich ferry for gawd sake, woss the point in that?'

Dozens of dripping passengers lined the quayside wrapped in foil blankets and sipping hot beverages, while eager reporters vied for their attention.

'Here we are at the South terminal with survivors of the disaster,' Kate Simmons of Sky news said, facing her cameraman. 'Officials are trying to piece together the events that lead up to the apparent sinking of one of these historic ferries. It is not yet known whether there have been any fatalities as there is no passenger manifest. The ferry company have to rely on CCTV footage for an accurate headcount, the forty or so vehicles that were on deck at the time have all been lost to the murky depths of the river.'

'Flippin ell!' said Maizie aghast. 'Ar don't believe it.'

'Excuse me miss,' The Sky reporter said, addressing a young lady. 'Could you tell us please in your own words what exactly happened?'

The girl turned, spilling her tea over her hand. 'Shit, fuck shit!' she cried.

'Oh mar gawd!' Dee Dee cried. 'Oh mar fuckin gawd. Trisha!'

'What the?' Maizie said, dropping to her knees in front of the set. 'Dee iss Trisha!'

'Ar can see that!' Dee Dee said, pushing Maizie aside. 'Get aat the bleedin way will ya!'

'Woss she doin there?' Maizie asked.

'Well,' Trisha said, shaking her scolded hand. 'Where d'ya want me to start?'

'From the beginning I guess,' Kate said, thrusting the microphone a little closer.

'You sure?' Trisha asked, pulling the foil up under her chin.

'Yes, yes,' Kate replied, eager for the scoop. 'It's as good a place to start than any other.'

'Well if ya sure,' Trisha said, readying herself. She then took a deep breath. 'Right well,' she said, wiping her sodden hair from her face. 'Ear goes, me and me mates got the sack from the Rommie shoe shop coz Dee Dee was late and we give that bitch Julie a loada lip. Then we nicked twenny graand aat the safe and faand the video of Mr Sanjeef doin Julie doggy style in the back room.' Kate looked at her cameraman struggling to see the relevance of Trisha's rant, but as usual she was unstoppable. 'Well, then we robbed a dirty great ruby fing offa Sheik Abby and Dee Dee lobbed iz friggin arm off. Black Mickey got nabbed and bashed up by the Tibbs's, so I ad to lez up their sister to elp get im back. Ar shot Bradley in the leg in the mota but ar done im a favour really. Anyway, then Mr Nakajima and iz ninja mates come over ear to buy the ruby fing wiv the elp of Nikos the nonce. Well the Tibbs's were gettin proper aat their prams so we ad to top the lot of em, but Jimmy the slag stabbed me up and ar snuffed it in ospital, then ar got better and we buggered off to Marbella wiv D I Pritcher up our arses. Well, we ad it sweet for a while, I ad me Chihuahua business bringin in bundles of dough, Maizie was shaggin Schumacca's mate and Dee Dee's muvva buggered off crab fishin wiv er new fella.'

'Excuse me,' Kate said, attempting to intervene.

'Shut up ar'm talkin!' Trisha snapped, taking another breath. 'Anyway that ponce Fitzroy showed up at Dee's ouse wiv some sob story abaat the Amiltons and their baby girl Crystal. Who, by the way, is a proper cute little fing. Anyway we was mugged into goin arfway raand the world to rescue em from a buncha Somali pirates for gawd sake, but Fitzroy bein the slag that e was shot Dee's fella Travis and left us to rot in that shit ole. Arf the country was after us but we made it back ome and Crystal got er operation. Well, Dee Dee was proper pissed off wiv Fitzroy as ya can imagine, so we tracked im daan, er and Maizie shot the shit aat of im and ar taser'd im in the balls. Trouble is, Pritcher nabbed us and banged us up in Olloway where we ad a bit if grief wiv a fat slag called Bennett, ar made friends wiv the warden and made er some pottry prezzies, while Dee Dee was beatin the fuck aata some kiddie murderin bitch in the exercise yard. Anyway then Mr Amilton come to see us and said e done a deal to get us aat but we ad a big barney wiv Bennett and I ended up on the pissin roof, don't ask iss a long story...'

Kate's eyes grew wider and wider at the extraordinary tale.

'Anyway,' Trisha continued, 'we got a flat and jobs an everyfing. Bradley's like this super pukka pop star wiv a massive ouse and shit loadsa birds wrapped raand im, ar'm wiv the animal company an ar've already rescued a goose an a crow fing and Dee Dee and Maizie work in some ome for wonky people or summink. Can I av anuvva cuppa?' she asked a passing policeman.

'But what about the ferry?' Kate asked, exasperated at this point.

'Well ang on,' Trisha blurted, 'ar'm comin to that bit.' Trisha took another polystyrene cup of tea. 'Cheers geez', she told him. 'Anyway me and Ade, thas a fought,' she said, looking around for her partner. 'ADE, ADE, YO ADRRIAAAN!' she yelled.

'TRISHAAA!' Adrian replied, from within the crowd. 'TRISHAAA!'

'OVER EAR!' Trisha said, waving. 'ADE, OVER EAR MATE!'

'Trisha, thank God,' Adrian said, breaking through the gathering. 'Are you alright?'

'Yeah ar'm dandy,' Trisha chirped, 'ow you doin?'

'Well I have to admit I've been better,' Adrian confessed, nursing a swollen wrist. 'What on earth happened?'

'Well,' Trisha said, gesturing to the frustrated reporter. 'Ar was just tellin this bird all abaat it.'

'You haven't told me a thing,' Kate said, raising her eyebrows. 'That's the problem.'

'Yeah alright, alright!' Trisha tutted.

'I'm afraid we lost the van,' Adrian informed her.

'What, and the mangey ginger tom?' Trisha asked.

'I'm afraid so,' Adrian said solemnly. 'We rescued the poor fellow in the morning, and drowned him in the afternoon.'
'Ahhhhh,' Trisha said, 'never mind ay.'
'Er, the ferry?' Kate said, growing ever impatient and the cameraman's batteries dwindling.
'Oh yeah,' Trisha smiled. 'Where was I? Oh yeah, me and Ade was on our way over the saaf side to sort aat some arse wipe wiv a skinny Schitzu. Ade wonnid to take the tunnel but ar spat me dummy aat and talked im into takin the ferry, ar like boats ya see, ar fink ar get it from me grandad, e was a rear gunner on a mine sweeper durin the war. Anyway, me and Ade was avin a breeva on deck when I ad to go for a piss, anyway I erd some old Doris freakin aat coz er bastard Bichon Frise bitch got aat of er flippin Fiat five undred and fucked off daan below. Leave it to me Misses, ar said, ar know what ar'm doin, anyway ar chased the little shit daan five levels to the engine room then raand and raand till ar was proper fucked. Anyway ar fought to meself there's no way ar'm gonna catch the bleeda, so ar nicked a dirty great spanner aata some geezer's tool box and launched it at the bugger, course ar never av bin any good at chuckin so ar missed im and smashed the shit aata some big spinny fing.'
Trisha's ill-timed lob couldn't have been better placed for maximum destruction. The wrench became jammed in one of the ferry's massive turbines, knocking it off its axis with a deafening grinding crunch, the attached piston now unsecured punched a five foot hole in the ferries hull and she immediately began to take on water at an alarming rate.
'Well the next fing ar knew,' Trisha added, 'ar was leggin it upstairs wiv a faasand gallons of shitty water up me arse.'
'So I take it you'll be accepting full responsibility for the disaster,' Kate said, sensing a raise for the scoop.
'Me!' Trisha sneered. 'Like fuck will I, if that dodgy Doris adn't let that poxy dog of ers aat, nunna this would've appened, would it.'
'Well I suppose not,' Kate replied, unconvinced.

'Anyway ar gotta go,' Trisha said, leaving the speechless reporter open mouthed. 'The Chase is on soon, and me and Maizie love that shit. Seeya!'

'Cut, cut!' Kate told her cameraman despairingly, whilst looking round for another eye witness, figuring she had inadvertently approached the one and only raving lunatic to have been on board.

The hulking ferry was now on its side lodged in the muddy river bed, a slick of floating debris drifting away from the scene.

'Ar don't bloody believe it!' Dee Dee said, with a gaping mouth.

Miraculously everyone on board was eventually accounted for, but the clean-up and salvage bill would surely run into tens of millions.

'What am I going to tell the society?' Adrian said, distraught at the quayside looking down at the chaotic scene, as coast guard, river police and salvage crews buzzed around the creaking craft in tiny boats assessing the damage and deploying divers to attach lines to the dozens of vehicles littering the river bed.

'I say, I say young lady!' the owner of the Bichon Frise called, making her way through the crowd with her cashmere sweater hanging down at her knees - having taken on a gallon or two of foul Thames water. 'Did you find my Foo Foo?'

'Ay?' Trisha said, none the wiser.

'My darling Foo Foo,' the lady added, wringing her hands. 'You went below to retrieve him.'

'Oh that little bleeda,' Trisha said, cottoning on. 'Listen, don't talk to me abaat ya fuckin Foo Foo love, if ar'da caved iz ed in wiv that poxy spanner we wouldn't be in this bloody mess.'

'But, but where is he?' the distraught owner bleated. 'I can't live without my Foo Foo.'

'Well love,' Trisha smirked, 'you better launch yaself in the river naah, coz the last time ar saw ya Foo Foo the little

bugger was treadin water wiv an anchor chain wrapped raand iz neck.'
'Oh nooooo!' the lady cried, with a hand over her mouth, her knees buckling beneath her. 'Oh my poor Foo Foo!' She was helped to a waiting ambulance by a paramedic with an oxygen masked clamped to her face. 'Foo Foooooo, Foo Foooooooooooo!' she wailed, struggling to break free and end it all in a watery grave with her lifelong companion. 'Foo Fooooooooooo!'
'Dozy mare,' Trisha scoffed, grabbing a passing policeman by the arm. 'Oy geez,' she said, 'any chance of a lift ome? Me and me mate are on the force an'all ya know,' she tapped at the society's crest on her lapel. 'Us lotta got to stick togevva aint we,'
The policeman gave her a sideways glance then laughed at her audacity. 'Yeah ok miss, I'll see what I can do,' he said, taking his radio from his belt.
'Ar'm gutted abaat the van an'all ya know,' Trisha told Adrian, as they waited for their ride. 'I ad arf a baga bon bons in the glove box and a flaska leak and potata soup.'
Adrian merely stared blankly out across the river, his sodden beard clinging to his face. 'In all my years,' he mumbled, almost grief stricken. 'In all my years with the service…' his partnership with Trisha had taken its toll both physically and mentally.
'Never mind mate,' Trisha said, resting her head on his shoulder. 'Least we got eachuvva, ay.'
Adrian at this point didn't know whether to laugh, cry, or toss himself over the side and join Foo Foo in Davey Jones' locker.
'Terrorists my arse,' Dee Dee said, sitting back against the sofa. 'If Trisha would've bin on board the flippin Titanic ar'da never said it was a bloody iceberg that sunk it, ar'da swore blind that soppy tart ad summink to do wiv it.'
Maizie sat in stunned silence, as did the hundreds of thousands of viewers around the globe, then threw her arms in the air when told that due to extended news

coverage of the disaster the regular episode of the Chase would not be aired. 'Ar'll fuckin kill er!' she said. 'Ar bin lookin forward to that all blinkin day I av.'

Blue lights were then seen flashing through their living room curtains from the street outside. 'Woss that?' Maizie asked, remaining seated.

'Probly anuvva stabbing,' Dee Dee said dismissively.

'Oh don't say that,' Maizie moaned, toying with Frankie's bracelet on her wrist. Moments later the door opened and Trisha waltzed in, complete with foil blanket. 'Hiyaaaaa!' she called. 'Eeya ya never guessed what appened to me today.'

'We know!' Dee Dee and Maizie said simultaneously, pointing at the television set.

'Oh yeah that,' Trisha said dismissively. 'No ar was gonna tell you'z abaat me trip to the Tower of London, proper good it was, ar met the beefeater blokes an everyfing, oh an ar got a crow fing aat of a cannon an'all.'

'Trisha!' Dee Dee snapped, gesturing to the news footage. 'You sunk a fuckin ferry!'

'Yeah well, sort of,' Trisha replied, sitting beside them. 'But ar did get a pukka blanket fing, ar'm gonna use it to do me jacket taytas in. Av ar missed the Chase?'

'You, ya dozy bitch!' Maizie raged. 'Because of you the Chase as bin cancelled!'

'Ohhhh flippin ell,' Trisha moaned, reclining, 'ar bin lookin forward to that all blinkin day an'all.'

'What is it wiv you'z two?' Dee Dee barked. 'She sunk the fuckin Woolwich ferry for fuck sake.'

'Alright, alright Dee,' Trisha said, shrugging her shoulders. 'Iss alright they got a spare one.'

'We see you on the telly,' Maizie told her friend. 'You looked like you just done a marafon or summink in ya bacofoil wrapper.'

'Tell me abaat it,' Trisha sighed, 'ar was proper puffed aat chasin that Foo Foo fucker all over the bleedin place ar tell ya.'

'You alright Dee?' Maizie asked, noticing her friend rocking ever so slightly.
'Yeah,' Dee Dee said, putting on a brave face. 'Just feel like ar wanna chuck up thas all, but I ain ad nuffin to eat all day, ar fink ar'm gonna turn in, ya don't mind do ya?'
'Naah, course not,' Maizie said concerned. 'You sure you're alright though mate, ar don't mind goin daan the road and gettin ya summink if ya want.'
'Naaaah, cheers mate, ar'll be alright onest,' Dee Dee said, clambering to her feet.
'Tell ya what Dee,' Trisha added, 'ar can fix ya wunna me erbal teas if ya want.'
'Listen!' Dee Dee warned, stopping Trisha in her tracks. 'If you fix me any of your shit ar swear ar'll...,' Dee Dee then clutched her chest.
'Trisha!' Maizie snapped. 'Leave er the fuck alone will ya. Dee, let me go get ya summink mate, paracetomols, anyfing.'
'Ar was only tryna elp,' Trisha said, placing a hand on Dee Dee's knee. 'Onest mate, ar weren't bein funny of nuffing, ar love ya, you know that.'
'Yeah ar know,' Dee Dee sighed, rubbing Trisha's hand lovingly. 'Sorry, ar didn't mean to av a pop at'cha. I aint feelin meself thas all, ar be alright after a nights kip, you watch.'
'You sure you don't want no tablits,' Trisha asked, shedding the foil blanket. 'Or an ot water bottle or summink?'
'Naah,' Dee Dee said, heading for her room.
'Shall ar call the doctor?' Trisha asked Maizie.
'You're avin a laugh aint'cha!' Maizie scoffed. 'She don't trust them fuckers as far as she can fro em, not since they told er auntie Rose she only ad shingles and the poor cow died a mumf later wiv a tumor the size of a friggin pomegranate in er ed. Naah, there aint no love lost between Dee Dee and the quacks thas for sure.'

'Oh alright,' Trisha said, somewhat deflated and wanting so desperately to help. 'Ar got a scented candle, d'ya reckon that'd elp?'

Maizie merely looked Trisha in the eye. 'Ar'll leave it shall I,' Trisha said, with a gurgling stomach. 'Oooh woss for dinner, me guts are graalin summink chronic.'

'There's a sausage toad in the freezer,' Maizie told her friend, 'an a bagga wedges. But ar'll av to do em in the oven coz the nukes on the blink.'

Trisha sat separating her matted hair, forgetting that she had microwaved her leak and potato soup that very morning in a stainless steel saucepan. 'Thas weird,' she merely said. 'Eeya, ar got pulled aat the water by this proper orny diver bloke today Maize. I ad to grab im by the balls to yank meself in the boat, ar tell ya what e was ung like a bloody bell rope mate.'

Maizie peered back into the living room from the kitchen. 'Ar fought you was proper lez naah,' she said, questioning Trisha's sexuality.

'Well I am, sort of,' Trisha replied, retrieving a towel from the bathroom. 'Ar mean strap-ons are alright an'all that, but ya can't beat a proper lenf can ya, praps ar need wunna the mafradite bloke bird fings, woja reckon? Maize, woja reckon, shall ar shag a she-male fing or what? Maizie? MAIZE!' Trisha sauntered through to the kitchen to find her friend standing at the sink holding the saucepan Trisha had left to soak.

'What the fuck appened to this?' she said, turning and looking through a gaping hole in the base, caused by an eight hundred watt electrical surge which had blown the fuse and at the same time opened three automatic garage doors at the rear of their building, allowing the local youths to plunder their contents.

'Dunno,' Trisha said, shrugging, 'all ar did was boil a bitta soup.'

The two friends sat opposite one another, dining and sipping cheap cola. 'Eeya Maizie?' Trisha said, after much

deliberation. 'D'ya reckon they used to use proper frogs in this gear?'
'Dunno,' Maizie replied, eyeing her sausage. 'Ar know they used to eat some proper fucked up shit in the olden days. Miss Pealer told us the Romans et orses cocks.'
'Really!' Trisha said, open mouthed. 'Well ar tell ya what, ar'd rarva gag on an orses dick than a filfy frog any bloody day.'
'They aint frogs,' Maizie laughed. 'They're toads ya doughnut.'
'Eeeeurgh what?' Trisha said, tossing her fork down and cringing. 'Ar'm gonna av a bath Maize,' she told her friend, leaving the table. 'Ya never know woss in that bleedin river do ya, ar reckon I ad more chance of angin onto a lil-let than a lilo.'
Maizie put her knife and fork down too, unable to continue after Trisha's repulsive analogy, as her friend disappeared into the bathroom kicking the door closed behind her. 'Wunna these friggin days,' she mumbled, clearing the table.

Despite her earlier reservations at being released by the very government she despised, Dee Dee soon became an integral part of the Westmoreland team, taking on a more supervisory role and thus appointing herself sole carer of Alice and Bonnie. She would sit with them for hours at a time, building the kind if relationship that had been so sadly absent in their lives.
Trisha though was a different kettle of fish indeed, having received her third and final written warning from the society and driven Adrian to a forty a day smoking habit. She had written a new chapter in the annals of animal welfare, adopting a jackboot approach to even the minutest of misdemeanors; kicking in doors after reports of neglect and wrenching kittens from the arms of sobbing children, without a shred of compassion for the traumatized toddlers.

Things were going swimmingly with the girls and was set to continue until one August morning, the seventeenth, a nondescript date with very little historical significance, eight AM to be exact...

'Get off!' Maizie moaned, kicking out at Trisha at the opposite end of the sofa. 'Ar was on ear first.'

'Shut up Maize,' Trisha replied, stabbing at the buttons on the remote control. 'Ar wanna watch Country File, iss abaat otters today, ar love them they're proper funny little bleedas swimmin on their backs an everyfing.'

'Fuck the otters!' Maizie snapped, tugging her duvet from Trisha's legs. 'Sit over there will ya!'

The pair of them continued to tussle with the cover and control of the TV remote while Dee Dee showered. 'Gimme that will ya!' Maizie said, snatching at Trisha's hand. 'I aint watchin no bollocks abaat friggin otters. Jeremy Kyle's on in a coupla minutes!'

'Oh sod off Maize,' Trisha laughed, 'you aint gonna learn fuck all watchin that shit. Well unless you wanna av arf a dozen kids by ya stepdad who just appens to be a cider swiggin wife batterin coke ed.'

Maizie made another desperate lunge for the remote but was fended off by a well-timed swipe from Trisha's cushion. 'RIGHT!' she said, pulling her own cushion from behind her head. 'You started summink naah!' Maizie repeatedly beat Trisha about the head with the velour cushion.

'PISS OFF, PISS OFF!' Trisha cried, lashing out in defence. Very soon a full scale pillow fight ensued, with the two girls tumbling from the sofa yelling obscenities at one another and swinging with increased vigour. 'Av that ya bitch!' Trisha laughed, landing a defiant blow to the side of Maizie's face.

'Ooooh you bastard!' Maizie winced, dodging another and landing a doozy of her own. 'Got'cha ya dumb fuck!' she smirked.

The two girls stood toe to toe trading blows in front of the television and hadn't noticed Dee Dee step quietly from the

bathroom naked, dripping and staring blankly toward the kitchen door, her right hand clutching her chest.
'Dee?' Maizie eventually said, catching sight of her friend whilst ducking Trisha's onslaught. 'Dee woss up?'
Trisha was none the wiser and continued the affray.
'Dee?' Maizie asked again, lowering her cushion and her defenses.
'Yes!' Trisha grimaced, taking full advantage of Maizie's distraction and pounding her head and upper torso with a barrage of blows.
'Trisha piss off will ya!' Maizie said dismissively. 'Dee, tell me mate, woss up?'
'Ar got a lump,' Dee Dee said softly without averting her gaze, her hair clinging to the side of her ashen face and traces of shower gel slipping down her thighs.
'What?' Maizie asked, raising one hand to fend of Trisha's flaying cushion. 'Dee woju say?'
'Ar got a lump,' Dee Dee said croakily, as a pool formed on the laminate at her feet.
Maizie immediately stiffened and her eyes bulged. 'NO!' she barked. 'No don'tchu say that Dee, don'tchu fuckin say that!' Shoving Trisha aside and letting the cushion fall from her fingers she vaulted the coffee table and ran to her dazed friend. 'Dee don'tchu say that, ar'm tellin ya, don't, please don't,' she pleaded, clasping her hands together in prayer.
Dee Dee said nothing, she trembled with a glazed deadpan expression.
'What?' Trisha asked, out of breath somewhat. 'Woss up Maizie, woss up Dee?'
Maizie ever so gently removed Dee Dee's hand and replaced it with her own. 'Oh God no!' she cried, cupping a hand to her mouth. 'No Dee, no.'
'What, what is it?' Trisha insisted.
'She's got a lump,' Maizie said, in a helpless tone. 'Trish mate, elp us will ya.'
The penny suddenly dropped with Trisha too and she flung her cushion aside upsetting the mantle clock. 'Shit Dee!' she

said, attempting the same gymnastic feat across the coffee table but stubbing her toe in the process and toppling awkwardly onto her knees. 'OW SHIT!' she cursed, scrambling to her feet and rushing to her friends. 'Dee woss up mate?' she said, rubbing her friend's goose pimpled back lovingly.

'She's got a bloody lump,' Maizie informed her.

'Do what?' Trisha gasped. 'Shut up, don't fuck araand Maize that shit aint funny.'

'I aint fuckin araand!' Maizie said forcefully.

'Fuck no, no Dee,' Trisha said, feeling an immediate knotting in her stomach. 'No, not you mate,' she raised a hand. 'Can I av a feel? Don't worry Dee I aint gonna lez you up or nuffing.'

Maizie rubbed Dee Dee's trembling arm and caressed her face. 'Trish get er onesie,' she told Trisha, who cupped the side of Dee Dee's breast. 'Trish get er fuckin onesie,' Maizie insisted. 'The poor cow's fuckin freezin!'

'Oh, yeah, yeah sorry Dee,' Trisha said, dropping her hand and scurrying to Dee Dee and Maizie's room, returning almost instantly with Dee Dee's leopard print woolen onesie.

'Come on Dee mate,' Maizie said, dabbing Dee Dee gently with a towel before offering the onesie to her legs. 'Elp me Trish will ya!' she told her friend, who carefully lifted one leg and then the other. 'There ya go mate,' Maizie said, sliding the zip up and over Dee Dee's quivering breasts. 'Come and sit daan.' Guiding her stone faced friend to the sofa she retrieved both cushions and propped them at Dee Dee's back. 'Ar'll make you a cup of tea Dee,' she told her, looking up at Trisha who turned this way and that in a daze.

'What do we do Maize?' Trisha asked, her head spinning with thoughts that no close friend should ever have to endure.

'We need an ospital!' Maizie said, bringing Trisha around. 'Find aat where the nearest one is. DO IT NAAH!'

'Yeah right, yeah course.' Trisha said, clasping a hand to her forehead for a moment before racing to her room. 'AR'LL GOOGLE IT!' she called back from her bedside, phone in hand.
'URRY UP!' Maizie yelled in reply.
Dee Dee sat motionless, her vulnerability that she had fought so hard to suppress had bubbled to the surface as a wave of tensile emotion.
'Eeyar Dee,' Maizie said, taking her hand and placing it onto the handle of her mug. 'Blow it mate coz iss ot,' she warned. 'TRISHAAAAA!'
'YEAH ALRIIIIGHT!' Trisha replied, tapping frantically at her phone. 'AR GOT NO PISSIN SIGNAL!'
'WELL DO SUMMINK!' Maizie barked, sitting beside Dee Dee and wrapping an arm around her. 'Don't worry mate itta be alright,' she said reassuringly.
'Oh fuck it!' Trisha sneered, tossing her phone onto her bed. 'Ang on!' she told her friends, flinging open their flat door and dashing downstairs leaping three at a time. 'TATTYYYYYYY!' she screamed, pounding at the Romanians' door with a clenched fist. 'TAAAAAAAT, TAAAAAAT ISS ME TRISH!' She listened for a moment and heard nothing from within. 'OYYYYYY TAAAAAT, ELLLLLLLLP!' Still nothing, so Trisha dashed to the street door wrestling with the catch. 'SCUZE ME, OY!' she yelled, sprinting down the garden path. 'OY MATE, SCUZE ME!'
A passing postie skidded to a halt on his bicycle, resting his sack on his crossbar. 'You OK Miss?' he called from across the street.
'NAAH, WHERE'S THE OSPITAL?' Trisha asked, burying her nails in the wooden gate rail and forgetting that her pajama top was unbuttoned to the waist. 'WHERE'S THE NEAREST OSPITAL MATE, COME ON TELL ME, WHERE IS IT?'
'I beg your pardon,' the postie said, cupping a hand to his ear.
'THE OSPITAL YA DEFF GIT!' Trisha replied, growing ever impatient.

'TRIIIIISH URRY UP WILL YA!' Maizie called from the lounge. 'AND SHUT THE BLOODY DOOR ISS FLIPPIN FREEZIN IN EAR!'
'ALRIGHT!' Trisha called back, hearing Maizie's faint moaning. 'YOU GONNA TELL ME OR WHAT?' she barked, at the postman. 'AR NEED A FUCKIN OSPITAL AND AR NEED IT NAAAAH!'
'Oh the hospital yes,' the postman smiled, walking his bicycle closer and getting an eyeful of Trisha's chest in doing so. 'You want Saint Pancras, just up from the station,' he told her leering. 'You can't miss it.'
'Yeah just like you can't miss mar tits ya pervy fuck,' Trisha scoffed. 'Cheers mate, now on ya bloody bike.'
The postman, with his cheeks now flushed, flung a leg over his bicycle and bumped down the granite kerb narrowly missing a passing van.
Trisha wrapped her chest and ran back inside. 'AR GOT IT!' she called, dragging herself up the stairs clawing at the banister. 'MAIZIE AR GOT IT!'
'Where is it?' Maizie asked, sitting close to Dee Dee.
'Just up the road apparently,' Trisha puffed, bursting back into the flat. 'Saint Panctus or summink, it aint far from ear, av ar got time for a bowla moosli?'
'No you friggin aint!' Maizie barked. 'Urry up and get dressed will ya!'
'Let er av er museli,' Dee Dee said, speaking for the first time in a while and sipping her tea.
'No Dee,' Maizie urged. 'We aint got time, we gotta get you looked at.'
'Ar'm alright,' Dee Dee said, attempting to calm her close companions. 'Chill aat will ya.'
'Chill aat!' Maizie exclaimed. 'Chill aat. Dee, you got a ruddy lump mate, you know what that might mean as well as ar do, we gotta get you checked aat and we gotta do it naah.'
'Iss probly nuffing,' Dee Dee said, making light of it once again, while sensing the heightened tension. 'Me auntie Renee freaked aat over a friggin cyst.'

'Yeah ar know that,' Maizie said, having none of Dee Dee's cavalier attitude. 'And yer auntie Jackie's pushin up bloody daisies coz of it, now for once Dee ar'm tellin you what to do. D'you ear me, ar said d'you ear me? You're goin to the ospital wevver you like it or not ok. Ok!'

'Yeah, yeah whatever,' Dee Dee relented.

'Iss best Dee ain it,' Trisha said, rubbing her friend's back. 'Get it checked aat ay?'

'Yeah ok, ar said ar'm gonna go din I!' Dee Dee snapped, slamming her mug down. 'I aint goin in me bloody onesie though, ar look a right twat. Oh, an ar gotta do me air an'all.'

'You can get dressed,' Maizie said sternly. 'But yer air's ok. We aint got time for that, now come on shift yer arse.'

Dee Dee smiled at Maizie. 'Bleedin ell,' she smirked, 'where'd you get a paira bollocks from all of a sudden?'

'From you!' Maizie said abruptly, helping Dee Dee to her feet. 'So if you don't wanna right ander ar suggest you do as your flippin well told, and don't gimme any shit.'

'Yes miss,' Dee Dee joked.

'Trisha go wiv er,' Maizie told her friend. 'Elp er get dressed, and no pissin araand, d'you ear me, ar said d'you ear me?'

'Yes!' Trisha snapped, following Dee Dee the pair of them looking over their shoulder at their newly dominant friend with a determined glint in her eye. 'Ar preferred er when she was a pussy,' Trisha told Dee Dee, holding open the bedroom door.

'Oh ar dunno,' Dee Dee smiled, 'iss abaat time she grew some nuts, ar was beginnin to worry abaat er.'

'Yeah, well we're worried abaat'chu Dee,' Trisha replied, throwing open her friend's wardrobe and selecting a miss matched outfit.

'If you fink ar'm goin aat like Ronald friggin Macdonald,' Dee Dee jeered, 'you're avin a fuckin laugh mate.' Dee Dee snatched the gaudy ensemble and tossed it into the bottom of the wardrobe before selecting her own outfit.

Trisha helped her friend out of her onesie and into her leggings 'Is it still there?' she asked, eyeing Dee Dee's breasts. 'Which one is it?'

'This one,' Dee Dee said, allowing Trisha a fleeting feel.

'Fuuuuck,' Trisha said softly. 'Shit Dee, iss big ain it, ow comes you aint felt it before?'

'Ar dunno,' Dee Dee shrugged. 'Ar know we're spozed to check em regular but I aint felt me tits up in ages.'

'You shoulda said mate,' Trisha smirked, making light of things, 'ar'da done it for ya.'

'Ar bet you would an'all you filfy fucker,' Dee Dee laughed.

Maizie then marched into the room having hastily dressed.

'Trisha ar told you no fuckin abaat,' she barked. 'Come on Dee, we gotta go.'

'Ar never done nuffing!' Trisha bleated, pulling the sweater over Dee Dee's head.

'No, you never do,' Maizie said, glaring at her. 'Do ya?'

'I ain a bloody cripple,' Dee Dee said, shrugging Trisha off her arm. 'Leave me alone will ya, ar can do it.'

Trisha herself opted for a burnt orange catsuit, pixie boots and a scrunchie in her hair. 'Ready!' she said joining her friends at the door.

'What the fuck d'you look like?' Maizie asked, looking her up and down.

'A pissin power ranger,' Dee Dee laughed.

'What?' Trisha said, failing to see the funny side. 'Ar got it daan Brick Lane offa wunna them moody stalls, ar fink iss alright, ar look like that tomb raider bird, but she's got bigger ips than me aint she.'

'Shut up Trisha!' Maizie said, leading Dee Dee downstairs as though she were a pensioner. 'I aint got time for nunna your shite ar told ya that.'

'Maizie onest mate,' Dee Dee smiled. 'Ar fink ar can manage a couple bleedin steps.'

'Sorry Dee,' Maizie said, racing to open the street door. 'Ar just want you to be alright thas all.'

'Ar know you do and fanks,' Dee Dee replied, caressing Maizie's hand. 'But seriously mate, ar'm alright.'
'Ar'll believe that when the ospital tells me,' Maizie said, ushering her friend along the garden path.
'Well you know what ar finka them fuckers don'tcha,' Dee Dee said, almost wrenching the gate from its hinges.
'Well we gotta get someone to av a look at'cha,' Maizie said, holding the gate for Trisha. 'Coz we don't know fuck all abaat it.'
'Neeva do they ar reckon,' Dee Dee scoffed.
'Ang on,' Trisha said, turning back. 'Ar forgot me lip gloss, you know ar never go anywhere wivaat it.'
'Trishaaaa!' Maizie snapped. 'Don'tchu bleedin dare!'
Once at the main intersection Maizie ran into the road. 'TAXIIIIII!' she yelled, waving her arms frantically. 'OYYYYYY!'
A black cab traveling in the opposite direction slowed and turned in the road.
'Maizie we aint got no dough!' Trisha reminded her. 'Ar left me purse on the side in the kitchen.'
'Yeah, we can walk it,' Dee Dee said, heading to her left.
'Shut up Dee,' Maizie insisted, raising a silencing hand. 'Leave it to me.'
Again Dee Dee was taken aback by her friend's forthright approach.
'Eeya Maize!' Trisha called at Dee Dee's side. 'You aint gonna offer im a wank ar ya?'
'No ar bleedin aint!' Maizie yelled, spinning on her heels as the taxi pulled alongside.
'Where to love?' the cabbie said, lowering his window.
'Saint Pancras,' Maizie said, leaning inside. 'Listen mate, iss a proper emergency yeah, but we aint got no dough, all ar got is these earrings,' she slipped her beloved gran's earrings from her lobes and offered them to the apprehensive driver. 'They aint werf bundles,' she added, 'but they're werf a lot more than a ride in ya cab, woja reckon?'
'Oooh ar dunno,' the cabbie said hesitantly. 'Aint'cha got a credit card or something?'

'Naah, we aint,' Maizie replied, with a sense of urgency. 'Please mate, you can get a few bob for them easy ar reckon, ar gotta get me mate to the ospital proper quick. Please, please mate.'

The cabbie looked over her shoulder at her two friends at the roadside.

'AR DON'T MIND TOSSIN IM OFF!' Trisha yelled on tip toes.

'Trisha!' Dee Dee barked. 'You aint tossin no one off, not for me anyway, ar'd rarva walk.'

The cabbie finally relented. 'Yeah alright, go on then,' he said, taking the costume jewellery from Maizie and tossing it into his cash tray.

'Come on Dee!' Maizie said, holding open the rear door. 'And you Trisha, shift yer arse.'

'Yeah alright!' Trisha said, slightly disgruntled. 'Who the fuck died and made you the bloody captain, ay?'

'Shut up and get in,' Maizie growled, in no mood for Trisha's antics.

'Saint Pancras ospital yeah?' the driver said, switching off his light and pulling into the traffic.

'Yeah mate,' Maizie replied, leaning forward. 'And don't ang abaat, like ar said iss proper urgent.'

'You're not ready to drop ar ya?' the cabbie asked, looking in his rear view mirror and assuming they were heading for the maternity ward. 'Ar don't want ya water's breakin in mar cab.'

'She ain up the duff mate,' Trisha laughed, eyeing Maizie's rear. 'She's just a lardy bitch.'

'You shut your maaf!' Maizie said, spinning to confront Trisha who nestled in beside Dee Dee to avoid a slap or two. 'Naah mate, nuffing like that,' she told the cabbie. 'Just urry up will ya.'

As Maizie took her seat beside her friends Dee Dee noticed her earrings were missing, and on closer inspection noticed them lying in the cabbie's cash tray. 'Maizie what you done?' she asked, tugging her friend. 'You aint give im them for this ride av ya?'

'Yeah,' Maizie said, as though they meant nothing to her. 'But iss alright Dee they was only a bit of old shit anyway.'

Dee Dee knew different, having grown up around Maizie's Grandmother. 'No, no, no ya don't,' she said, lunging forward. 'Not for me Maize, ar won't let'cha.'

'Dee leave it!' Maizie insisted, pulling Dee Dee back into her seat and pointing a rigid finger at her face. 'Ar told ya they're shit, and even if they was proper bling ar'da done the same. Naah don't fight me on this mate coz ar swear ar won't back daan, not one bit d'you ear me.'

Dee Dee took a moment to process what her friend had sacrificed for her. 'Alright mate, and fanks yeah,' she said softly.

'You shoulda let me toss im off,' Trisha blurted. 'Ar'da got waitin time an'all ar'm tellin ya.'

'Shut up Trish,' Maizie and Dee Dee said simultaneously.

Trisha crossed her arms over her breasts and sat staring out of the window. 'Ar was only tryna elp,' she mumbled. 'Maizie aint the only one that loves ya ya know.'

Dee Dee ran a hand through Trisha's hair. 'Ar know mate,' she said, with a wry smile. 'And believe me, you offerin to toss im off was the nicest fing anyone's ever done for me, ar swear you're a proper mate, you bofe ar, ar dunno what ar'd do wivaat'cha. Ar love the two of ya ar mean that.'

Maizie choked back a tear and looked away. 'Ow much longer mate?' she asked the driver.

'Coupla minutes tops,' the cabbie replied, honking his horn at the slowing traffic whilst Trisha clung to Dee Dee's hand.

'Triiish,' Dee Dee said reassuringly. 'Ar'm alright mate, don't worry.'

The taxi was soon forced to stop in the heavily congested road. 'Go raand em!' Maizie said, tapping at his shoulder. 'Come on go raand the bleedas!'

'I can't,' the cabbie said, pointing out a collision in the road ahead with two drivers standing outside their vehicles trading insults.

'OY!' Maizie yelled from the open window. 'GET AAT THE BLOODY WAY!' One of the aggrieved drivers raised two fingers in her direction and continued his rant. 'YOU WHAT?' Maizie growled, throwing open the door. Dee Dee instinctively sprung from her seat to help. 'Dee sit daan!' Maizie said, pushing her friend back into her seat. 'Ar'll sort this aat.'

'Maizie shut up,' Dee Dee laughed. 'Ar can sort those coupla wankers aat no problem.'

'No!' Maizie barked steely eyed. 'Sit the fuck daan, ar won't tell you again d'you ear me!'

'Ar fink she means it Dee,' Trisha said, seeing her friend in a completely different light.

'Alright,' Dee Dee relented. 'But if you get any bovva from em, gimme a shout yeah.'

'Yeah no worries,' Maizie replied, marching toward the stricken vehicles.

'Is she alright?' the cabbie asked, looking over his shoulder and opting to remain seated.

'Ar fink so,' Dee Dee said, craning her neck to keep a watchful eye on her friend.

'OY!' Maizie barked at the warring drivers. 'YOU GONNA SHIFT THESE FUCKIN MOTA'S OR WHAT?' The sound of frustrated honking drivers behind her filled the morning air.

'Look, do yaself a favour love,' one of the drivers said in a condescending tone, 'get back in ya cab and shut the fuck up.' He had foolishly assumed that because of Maizie's slight stature and youthful complexion that she would be no match for either of them, but Maizie was focused on one thing and one thing only, getting her friend to the hospital and nobody however large and aggressive was going to prevent that from happening.

'Now you listen to me you lanky jumped up streaka piss,' she said, rounding a delivery van to confront him. 'Don't fink coz ar'm a bird ar won't beat the fuck aata you in front of all this lot and mug you right off, coz ar fuckin will.' The second driver backed away and dropped into the seat of his convertible. 'Thas it, now back the fuck up!' she yelled, waving her arms. 'And you!' she snapped, turning to the other driver as the police arrived on the scene, 'you do the same coz ar swear ar can be one proper orrible ormonal cunt when ar wanna be.' The driver stood speechless for a moment or two, his cheeks flushing as the gathered onlookers cheered her audacity. With the bobbies approaching and the pedestrians jeering, the remaining driver reluctantly returned to his dented vehicle and reversed it into a side street. 'Thas all you ad to do you twat!' Maizie yelled, flicking him a middle finger.

'What's the problem here?' one of the policemen asked.

'Ask them coupla dicks,' Maizie told them, stepping aside to allow the delivery van to pass.

'Good on ya girl!' the van driver said, leaning from his window in passing and giving her the thumbs up.

Dee Dee couldn't help but feel a flush of pride as Maizie climbed back in beside her. 'Bleedin ell Maize,' she said, patting her friend's knee, 'you don't take no shit no more do ya.'

'Ar learned from the best din I,' Maizie said, winking. 'Right come on geez, get a fuckin move on!' she said, pounding the back of the cabbie's seat.

Having seen Maizie's wrath at first hand, the cabbie stepped on the accelerator flinging the girls back in their seats. 'Like ar said, a coupla minutes tops,' he told them.

Maizie sat rubbing Dee Dee's knee whilst looking ahead the while time. 'Thissa do mate!' she said, seeing the hospital entrance ahead of yet another red light. 'Come on Dee,' she told her friend, hopping out in the middle of the road and stopping an approaching bus whilst Dee Dee followed. 'Trish get a fuckin move on will ya!' she urged.

'Ar'm comin for gawd sake,' Trisha moaned.

'Fanks mate,' Maizie told the cabbie, slamming his door closed and taking Dee Dee's hand and leading her to the hospital steps. 'Scuze me, scuze me!' she yelled, pushing

through a group smoking at the entrance. 'Come on, aat the bloody way will ya.'
'Look at em,' Trisha scoffed, watching the pathetic gathering huddled round a bin marked butts and gum. 'Iss the bloody cancer club.'
Maizie spun and glared at Trisha, enraged at her insensitivity and the mention of the C word around their friend. 'Trisha for fuck sake!' she snarled through gritted teeth.
'Oh,' Trisha said, hurrying behind. 'Yeah sorry.'
'Scuze me!' Maizie said, again this time dragging Dee Dee to the front of a snaking queue at the reception desk. 'Scuze me miss, can you av a look at mar mate?'
'I'm sorry?' the nursing attendant said, looking up over her glasses.
'Me mate,' Maizie said again, with increased urgency. 'Can you av a look at er, like naah!'
'You'll have to take a number and a seat,' the nurse told her. 'Just like everybody else here.'
'Do what?' Maizie said, unflinching. 'What bloody number, me mate needs lookin at, so get someone aat ear please.'
'Please take a number and a seat,' the nurse reiterated. 'Next!'
'No ang on!' Maizie said resolutely. 'You aint listnin. Me mate's got a lump on er tit that needs lookin at.'
'Have you been referred by your GP?' the nurse asked, holding out her hand for a doctor's note.
'GP?' Maizie said, growing increasingly agitated. 'We aint got a pissin GP!'
'We bin banged up!' Trisha piped up over Maizie's shoulder. 'We ad a doctor in Olloway, but all she ever done was finger our bums.'
'Trisha shut the fuck up!' Maizie snapped, digging an elbow into her friend's ribs.
'No I aint got a GP,' Dee Dee told the nurse. 'Ar just want me bloody lump looked at, thas all.'
'Yes, yes I understand,' the nurse replied with a modicum of sympathy. 'But you'll have to go through triage like the rest

of these good people I'm afraid, and as you can see we are rather busy.'
'Busy!' Maizie said, looking at the multicultural gathering filling the waiting room to capacity. 'Ar tell ya what, the only fing you aint got in ear by the looksa fings is a Mongolian bloody goat erda and a Tibetan monk. Look at em.'
'I'm sorry miss,' the nurse said sternly, 'but we will not tolerate racism of any kind in this hospital.'
'Racism!' Maizie growled. 'Listen love, me grandad was shot to fuck durin the Normandy bloody landins, God rest iz soul. Are you tellin me e give up iz life so this lotta free loadin fucks can bleed this country dry. And before you say ar'm racist I aint got a problem wiv anyone that pays their way; Indians, Muslims, Chinese, whoever, if ya want somefing aat, ya gotta put somefing in.'
Although the nurse knew for herself that the majority of the hospital's day to day patients had made their way to the UK with the promise of free housing, benefits and health care and were a massive drain on the already overstretched and understaffed National Health Service, she was not at liberty to cast an opinion, or indeed express her true feelings for fear of reprisal. 'If you just take a number,' she told the girls, 'you'll be seen as soon as it is humanly possible.'
'Ar got one!' Trisha said, tearing a strip from a nearby dispenser. 'One eighty!'
'Undred and eighty!' Maizie exclaimed. 'What number they on naah?'
'Seventy six,' Trisha said, checking the stub of the Moroccan in front of her.
'Seventy six!' Maizie cursed. 'You're avin a fuckin laugh aint'cha. Oh come on mate,' she pleaded with the nurse. 'Iss me mate.'
'I'm sorry,' she was told in reply. 'You'll have to go through the correct procedure. Now if you'll please take a seat,' she added, taking the Moroccan's ticket from him.

'Come on Maize,' Dee Dee told her friend, heading toward the rear of the waiting room. 'We aint gonna get nowhere wiv this bleedin lot.'

The three friends sat at the end of a row of plastic seats, looking around at the coughing, wheezing and scratching patients. 'I ate these friggin places,' Dee Dee said shortly after. 'Less come back tomorra.'

'No!' Maizie said insistently. 'You're gonna get that fing sorted aat today, d'you hear me?'

'Yeah Dee,' Trisha added, 'iss for the best mate, ar never used to like ospitals neeva but they sorted me aat good and proper when ar got stabbed up dint they.'

'Oh yeah ar know that,' Dee Dee agreed, having seen at first hand the dedication of the surgical team that had brought Trisha back to life. 'We fought we lost ya mate, we really did.'

'Oh don't be daft,' Trisha scoffed. 'I aint goin anywhere me.'

'Oh great,' Maizie sighed, rolling her eyes. The girls then looked at one another and burst out laughing, nudging each other with their shoulders.

'Ar know ya don't mean it,' Trisha said innocently, she then looked across at the Asian lad in his early teens sat beside his clearly irate mother, his left arm heavily bandaged. 'What you gone and done then?' she asked, her curiosity getting the better of her.

The boy said nothing. 'He has been playing that bloody cricket,' his Bengali mother said angrily. 'What good is he now to his father and the market stall, ay, ay?' she asked, slapping the boy about the head. The lad ducked from her flaying hand, nursing his elbow.

'Coulda bin worse ar spoze,' Trisha joked. 'Me uncle Morris got bowled a proper ball breaker e did, shoved one of iz nuts right up inside im it did, poor bugger walks wiv a stick naah, and saands like e'z bin suckin on an elium balloon.'

After a wait of some forty five minutes, and very little movement in the queue, Maizie sprung to her feet. 'Fuck it!' she snapped. 'Ar'll sort this aat.'

'Maizie leave it!' Dee Dee said, grabbing at her wrist.
'No Dee!' Maizie said, breaking away. 'Ar won't leave it, arfa this lot in front of us are only ear for a soddin sick note or summink, and you're sittin there wiv gawd knows what inside ya. I ain avin it. I aint bleedin avin it!' With her friends aghast, Maizie marched along the polished hospital corridor to where a group of four or more doctors were stood examining a patient's x-ray against a light screen. 'OY!' she said, spinning one round by his shoulder. 'Woss your game?'
'I beg your pardon?' the young doctor said, startled to say the least at the intrusion.
'Ar said woss your bleedin game?' Maizie said again. 'There's arf a dozen of you'z ear pullin ya dicks, while the likes of us are losin the friggin will to live aat there!'
'I'm sorry, you'll have to speak to reception,' the doctor said, turning away and continuing his conversation.
'Oy, ar'm talkin to you!' Maizie barked. 'Me mate needs lookin at, and she needs lookin at naah!'
'Young lady,' a slightly older doctor with a roving eye said, slipping an arm around her shoulder. 'You cannot jump the queue, it just simply isn't done I'm afraid.'
Maizie looked at his slithering hand and had his intentions figured in an instant. 'Look,' she said, pulling him to one side. 'Me mate's got this lump on er tit, not a bloody splinter in er friggin finger or a bloody boil on er arse, so iss serious, you should know that.'
'Yes, yes indeed,' the doctor said, winking to his colleagues. 'Yes it is.'
'So,' Maizie said forcefully. 'What av ar gotta do to get er looked at?'
The doctor, in his mid-forties, looked down her gaping blouse. 'Well now, let's see,' he said, with a lecherous smile. 'I think I might be able to pull a few strings, come with me.'
'Ar spoze you want me to pull summink an'll don'tcha,' Maizie said, looking down toward his crotch.

'We'll see,' the doctor said, leading Maizie toward a side room. 'I may have to give you a full examination first,' he said, leering.

'Yeah whatever,' Maizie replied, repulsed by his advances but anguished at her friend's condition.

'This way,' the doctor said, pushing open the door and patting Maizie's bottom to usher her inside. 'Right let's see what you are prepared to do,' he added, sliding his zipper down indicating that oral or manual relief would go a long way to securing medical favours for her friend. But Maizie was no fool, she quickly leapt back out into the corridor and stood with her hands on her hips.

'NO AR WON'T SUCK YA COCK YA DIRTY BASTARD!' she shrieked, turning several heads in doing so.

'What, what?' the doctor cried, yanking at his zip and throwing his hands in the air to silence her. 'What, what are you doing?'

'AR SAID!' Maizie cried, raising her voice a little louder, attracting more attention than the doctor would have wished for. 'I AINT SUCKIN YA...'

'Quiet!' the doctor said, pushing a hand over Maizie's mouth. 'What's the matter with you, I thought we had an understanding.'

'An understandin,' Maizie said, wrenching his hand from her mouth. 'You're avin a fuckin laugh aint'cha, if you fink ar'm gonna go daan on you or give you a wank, ya want ya bleedin ed tested. Naah ar'll tell ya woss gonna appen shall I, you're gonna get a tit doctor to see mar mate right naah, uvverwise ar'm gonna scream this fuckin place daan and tell everyone what a dirty bastard you are.'

'No wait!' the disheveled doctor said, looking this way and that. 'There's no need for that,' he smiled, attempting to slide another arm around her.

'Get the fuck offa me!' Maizie said, shrugging him off. 'Ar mean it, ar'll proper kick off ar will.'

'Ok, ok,' the doctor said, desperate to calm her. 'What did you say was ailing your friend?'

'Ar told ya!' Maizie said, exasperated at this point. 'She's got a dirty great lump on er tit, an ar wonnit looked at right naah. So you gonna elp us or what?'
With his colleagues and a group of nurses looking his way the doctor had no choice. 'OK leave it to me,' he said, with his erection flagging rapidly. 'You need an oncologist.'
'A what?' Maizie asked. 'Woss that?'
'Not what,' the doctor replied, 'who. An oncologist, you see oncology is a branch of medicine that deals with tumors, cancers if you like'
'Ar never said she ad cancer!' Maizie barked, hating to even think the worst. 'Opefully iss a cyst or summink.'
'Well, either way,' the doctor said, eager to distance himself from Maizie, 'an oncologist will be able to put your mind at rest, and I know just the fellow. If you'll please return to the waiting room I'll pop along and see if he is free to see your friend.'
'You better not be pissin abaat!' Maizie warned him. 'Or ar swear ar'll come straight back and kick up such a fuckin stink.'
'No, no I promise!' the doctor said, heading off. 'He'll be right out to see you, you have my word.'
'Sorted.' Maizie said, returning to her seat.
'What is?' Trisha asked.
'Dee's gonna be seen by some specialist geezer,' Maizie told her, sitting beside Dee Dee and taking her hand and kissing her fingers. 'We'll get'chu sorted mate, don't worry.'
'Fanks Maize,' Dee Dee said, still in a state of shock. 'Ar taught you good and proper did'n I.'
'Yeah, yeah ya did,' Maizie smiled. 'And ya know what Dee, it feels bloody marvlus mate.'
'Right!' Trisha said, puffing out her chest. 'Next time leave it to me yeah, ar'll show you two ow to kick arse.'
'Gawd elp us,' Dee Dee laughed.
Several minutes later, just as Maizie was about to lose her cool once again, a tall thin doctor appeared with his

stethoscope draped around his neck. 'Oncology?' he said, looking the girls up and down.

'You what?' Trisha said, eyeing the youthful doctor and leaping to her feet. 'Leave this to me Maize,' she said, turning to her friend. 'Ar'll sort this aat. Listen ear sonny,' she said, prodding the doctor's chest, 'get yer arse back in there and get us a bloody tit doctor or me and you ar gonna fall aat big time, d'you ear me!'

'But, but I'm an oncologist,' the doctor said, backing away.

'Ar don't give a fuck mate!' Trisha said, keen to prove her worth to her friends. 'You could be a fanny ticklin gyno geezer for all ar care, we want a tit doctor and we want one naaaah.'

'But, but,' the doctor stammered again. 'I am a tit doctor, as you call it, oncology as I've already explained is the treatment of tumors, for example those that can often occur in the breast'.

After a moment or two of contemplation Trisha looked down at her feet. 'Oh,' she said, turning slowly to her friends who were both glaring at her.

'You twat!' Maizie snarled, grimacing. 'What is it wiv you, ay?'

'Leave er Maize,' Dee Dee said, rising to her feet. 'Iss me mate, ar need checkin aat please.'

'Right er,' the doctor said, giving Trisha a wide berth, 'come with me.' He made his way back along the corridor with the girls in tow, Maizie clinging to Dee Dee's hand and Trisha skulking behind as they turned left then right several times.

'Bleedin ell, where we goin?' Trisha said, struggling to keep up.

'Shut it will ya!' Maizie barked over her shoulder.

'Ok, here we are,' the doctor said, ushering Maizie and Trisha to a row of seats in the corridor. 'I'm afraid you two will have to wait out here,' he told them.

'Do what?' Maizie said, returning to Dee Dee's side. 'We're goin wiv er mate.'

'Yeah,' Dee Dee agreed, wanting them by her side. 'They're me mates, can't they come in wiv me. Please?'
'I'm sorry,' the doctor said adamantly. 'That's out of the question I'm afraid. If you wish to be seen then I suggest you obey hospital rules, I've already called in a few favours to get you here.'
'He's right ar spoze,' Maizie told her friends. 'Iss more important for you to get checked aat Dee, ain it.'
'Er, yeah,' Dee Dee said apprehensively, she then made a grab for Maizie and Trisha's hands and squeezed them tightly.
'Iss alright Dee,' Maizie said, leaning to kiss her cheek. 'We're gonna be right aat ear, we aint goin nowhere ar promise ya.'
'Er, ar might nip off for a piss,' Trisha said, cross legged. 'I ad a cranberry smoovie this mawnin, an iss bangin away at me bladder summink chronic.'
'Trisha, for fuck sake!' Maizie growled at her friend's insensitivity once again.
'Oh yeah, sorry,' Trisha said, rubbing Dee Dee's back. 'Ar'll old it in, you get yaself in there mate, we'll be ear waitin don'tchu worry.'
'Fanks,' Dee Dee said, as the doctor lead her into the oncology room, letting the door swing closed behind him.
'Love ya!' Maizie called after her friend.
'Yeah me an'all!' Trisha echoed.
'You flippin idiot!' Maizie immediately said, turning to Trisha. 'Dee's proper shittin erself and all you can fink abaat is avin a bloody piss, you call yaself a mate!'
Trisha dropped onto one of the moulded chairs beside Maizie. 'I am er mate,' she said, facing her friend. 'Maize, I am er mate. Just like ar'm your mate.'
'Huh,' Maizie said dismissively. 'You wanna start actin like one, instead of a prize prat all the bleedin time.'
'Oh don't say that Maize,' Trisha whined. 'Please Maize, ar love er just as much as you do, you can't say ar don't, ar love you an'all, ar mean looka the shit we bin fru togevva, ay?'

'Hmmmmm,' Maizie said, staring at the door across the corridor. 'Ar know all that Trish. Iss just sometimes mate, ar could proper stab you to deff and not lose a winka sleep over it, ar really could.'

Trisha sat stunned at Maizie's brutally honest confession. 'Oh,' she merely said in reply, staring at the door also.

Inside Dee Dee was stood beside a large laminated chart featuring several breasts in section, a fleeting glimpse of malignant tumors was enough to turn her head away. The doctor conferred quietly with his nurse at the opposite end of the room, looking across at Dee Dee periodically before summoning her. 'So,' he said, clasping his hands together, 'I believe this is not a GP's referral.' He stood poised, taking a pen from his breast pocket and a clipboard from his desk with a pink form attached.

'Naah,' Dee Dee said, with a dry mouth. 'We aint got a doctor yet coz we bin banged up, like me mate said.'

'I see,' the doctor replied, ticking one or two boxes. 'And have you ever had a breast examination before?'

'Naah never,' Dee Dee said apprehensively. 'Ar know ar shoulda bin checkin em meself, but to tell ya the troof ar just forgot.'

'Ahhhh right,' the doctor said knowingly. 'I'm afraid you're not alone there my dear, despite increased publicity.'

'Ar know,' Dee Dee replied. 'Ar seen all the celebs in the papers coppin a feel.'

'Yes that's right,' the doctor smiled, 'it's a wonderful campaign, but a lot more needs to be done to raise awareness. Right, if I could just get you to fill in section two to five b, then we'll get you looked at. OK?'

Taking the pen and clipboard it was all that Dee Dee could do to stop her hand from shaking. 'Shit sorry,' she said, the cracks well and truly beginning to show. 'Ar ticked the wrong bloody box.'

'That's quite alright,' the doctor told her. 'Just cross it out and initial the mistake, it's fine really.'

'Can ar get a glass of water?' Dee Dee asked, clearing her throat.

'Yes, yes of course,' the nurse replied, retrieving a paper cup from the fountain. 'Here.'

'Fanks,' Dee Dee said, draining it in one mouthful and tossing the screwed cup into the bin beside her. 'Flippin ell, iss ot in ear ain it,' she added, with her heart now racing.

'Take your time,' the doctor reassured her, 'there's no rush.'

'Woss this mean?' Dee Dee asked, tapping at the bottom of the form.

'Oh, that's our legal waiver,' she was told by the doctor. 'Standard hospital procedure I'm afraid.'

'Where've I erd that before?' Dee Dee said, with a cynical smile.

'Would you like another drink?' the nurse asked, observing Dee Dee's perspiring forehead. 'These places have a habit of drying you out don't they. I swear I spend more time at the fountain than my desk.'

The nurse's joking manner fell on deaf ears as Dee Dee scrawled her name. 'No fanks,' she replied, handing back the clipboard.

Outside Trisha's nerves were beginning to manifest themselves, her right knee bobbing uncontrollably. 'Trisha pack it in will ya!' Maizie snapped, slapping Trisha's leg. 'You're doin mar pissin ed in.'

'Sorry ar carn elp it,' Trisha said, bracing herself. 'Woja finks appnin in there?'

'Ow the bleedin ell do ar know!' Maizie said, in no mood for her friend's questioning, but then relenting somewhat. 'Oh look ar'm sorry Trish,' she said, taking her friend's hand. 'Ar know you're as worried as I am. We just gotta be strong for er thas all.' The two girls clung to one another in the stark sterile corridor, their eyes boring into the beechwood door in front of them.

'Iss a cyst, iss a cyst, iss a cyst,' Trisha said, rocking.

'You're bleedin right it is,' Maizie said defiantly, their palms sweating together.

'Ok,' the oncologist said, handing the clipboard to his nurse. 'Deborah if you'd just like to slip your top off, that'll be great.'

Dee Dee took a deep breath before pulling her sweater over her head, shaking her hair loose in doing so. 'And me bra an'all?' she asked.

'Yes please,' the doctor replied, taking a pair of latex gloves from his drawer and stretching them over his fingers. 'Ok, which side is it?' he asked, after Dee Dee had popped the catch on her bra.

'This one,' Dee Dee told him, stiff lipped.

'Ok, if you could just raise your arms for me,' the doctor asked, pulling at his gloves. 'Thaaat's great.'

Dee Dee stood looking away as the doctor, and his nurse for that matter, prodded her breast and arm pit. 'I seeee,' he said, massaging the lump. 'Any itching or discomfort around the nipple?' he asked.

'Naah, not that ar've noticed,' Dee Dee said, without turning back. 'Ar just noticed it this mawnin in the showa.'

'Any trauma to the breast recently?' the doctor then asked, scribbling on the reverse of his form.

'Trauma?' Dee Dee said bemused.

'Yes,' the doctor continued, 'injury or infection, weeping of the milk duct maybe?'

'Milk!' Dee Dee exclaimed. 'I aint got no nippers so why the bleedin ell should I ave milk comin aat me tits?'

'I have to ask,' the doctor told her, 'it's procedure you see. What about an injury maybe?'

'Well, ar've ad a few rucks in me time,' Dee Dee replied, referring to her numerous physical encounters, the majority of which she had emerged the victor. 'But ar give a lot better than ar got ar'm tellin ya,' she added.

'Rucks?' the doctor asked, looking at his nurse for guidance, but she was none the wiser either.

'Yeah rucks,' Dee Dee said again. 'Barneys, punch ups, flippin fights for gawd sake!'

'Oh, oh I see,' the doctor said finally. 'So you're a pugilist.'

'A what?' Dee Dee asked defensively, turning to face him.
'A boxer,' the doctor said, raising his fists. 'I hear it's becoming more and more popular with the ladies. What about you Julia?' he asked his nurse jokily. 'Don't you fancy giving it a go?'
'Absolutely not!' Julia replied resolutely. 'You couldn't pay me enough to step into the ring and get my head beaten in.'
'Naah, not that shit,' Dee Dee told them, 'proper ruckin, bare knuckles and boots an'all.'
The doctor and his nurse looked at one another processing Dee Dee's confession. 'Riiiight,' the doctor said, not knowing quite how to proceed. 'Well er, it does seem that you have quite a substantial growth, which gives me cause for concern.'
'What?' Dee Dee said, stiffening. 'Woja mean concern?'
'Well,' the doctor continued, sitting back on the edge of his desk. 'Most of our patients, and you do as well I don't doubt, are hoping that their growth is some form of cyst.'
'Well yeah,' Dee Dee said, covering her breasts with one arm feeling somewhat uncomfortable. 'Thas what we fought.'
'Well, I'm afraid not in your case,' the doctor replied with a wrinkled brow.
Dee Dee took a single step back. 'What?' she said, visibly stunned. 'You sure?'
'Well, I'd still like you to have a mammogram while you're here,' the doctor told her. 'Julia here is our resident radiologist, and will take good care of you. Would that be alright with you, Deborah? Deborah?'
'Oh yeah, what?' Dee Dee said, rooted to the spot. 'What, what you on abaat?
'A mammogram,' the doctor said again, switching on a large upright machine in the corner of the room. 'Julia, could you give Deborah a screening for me?'
'What is it?' Dee Dee asked. 'What do ar need wunna them for?

'Well, a physical examination is ok,' the doctor told her, 'but a mammogram gives us a better idea of what's happening inside the breast. It's an x-ray so to speak, I suspect your growth is attached to your lymph nodes.'

'Limf what?' Dee Dee asked, looking down at her breast.

'Lymph nodes,' the doctor reiterated. 'Here, let me show you.' He led Dee Dee to the chart. 'Here they are, and as you can see they extend from under your arm down to the breast itself, their purpose as part of the lymphatic system is to filter lymph rather like a net, they also assist the immune system protecting the body against harmful micro-organisms and other such nasty particles.'

'I aint got a clue what you're on abaat,' Dee Dee confessed. 'But if you reckon ar need wunna these memory gram fings then crack on.'

'Mammogram,' the doctor said, correcting Dee Dee. 'Julia, if you could please.'

'Yes of course,' Julia said, handing Dee Dee a surgical gown. 'You might be more comfortable in this,' she told her, watching as Dee Dee slipped the gown over her head. 'That's it Deborah,' Julia said, raising Dee Dee's arm. 'If you could just stand against the plate for me, that's right, now you will feel some discomfort I'm sorry to say because I may need to manipulate the breast so please do tell me if it becomes too painful.'

'Yeah alright,' Dee Dee said, going through the motions with a blank expression. 'And iss Dee.'

'Sorry?' Julia said, looking up.

'Dee. Everyone calls me Dee,' Dee Dee told her. 'So ar'd rarva you did an'all.'

'OK Dee,' Julia smiled, stepping back behind a protective screen as did the doctor. 'Could you just raise your arm a little higher for me and just turn a little more to your right. Thaat's it. OK if I could get you to take a deep breath and hold it until I say.'

Some twenty to thirty minutes later, after both of Dee Dee's breasts had received a thorough screening, Julia switched

off the machine. 'Thank you Dee that's great,' she said, returning to her computer.
'Would you mind popping back in tomorrow?' the doctor said, looking up. 'I'd like to arrange for you to have a biopsy.'
'Woss wunna them?' Dee Dee asked, slipping out of the surgical gown and back into her sweater.
'A biopsy,' the doctor said, standing at her side. 'It's a procedure in which we take a small sample of tissue and cells from the affected area so that we can study them under a microscope and build up a detailed picture of the tumor, and its rate of growth, so to speak.'
'Oh,' Dee Dee said, baffled again by his medical description. 'Alright, if ya fink ar need one.'
'Yes. Yes I'm afraid you do,' the doctor replied. 'You did the right thing coming in to see us by the way, although you really should register with a GP for medication purposes.'
'Medication!' Dee Dee said abruptly. 'I aint takin no tablits if thas what ya mean, ar can't stand tablits.'
'Riiiight I see,' the doctor said, tapping at his keyboard. 'There are a few alternatives I could suggest.'
'I ope so,' Dee Dee said defiantly. 'So what appens naah?'
'Well, like I said,' the doctor said, looking up from his PC. 'I'd like to see you back here tomorrow.' His printer whirred into life. 'Take this to reception and they'll make an appointment for you, and don't worry, you'll come straight to oncology tomorrow and bypass triage.'
'Fank fuck for that,' Dee Dee said, tugging her hair from the neck of her sweater.
'I know it's easy for me to say,' Julia said, placing a hand on Dee Dee's back. 'But try not to worry, hopefully we've caught it at an early stage.'
'It!' Dee Dee said, looking her in the eye. 'Woss it?'
The doctor approached the two women. 'I'm afraid Deborah, sorry Dee, early indications point to a growth attached to your breast and possibly the lymph nodes, as I said earlier. The growth in question I'd say is approaching

five centimeters in diameter, which is a cause for concern but not yet metastatic. By this I mean that it may not yet have spread to your other organs, the lungs, liver, brain and such like. Now I know how you must be feeling right now, it's a lot to take onboard but believe me Dee when I say that it may not be as bad as it all sounds, therefor I'd like to perform a biopsy so we can get a much clearer picture, I hate to use the word tumor at this stage but if it is I can reassure you that most tumors are in fact operable'

'Operable!' Dee Dee exclaimed. 'D'you mean an operation. I ain avin no bleedin operation, just stab me up wiv drugs or summink, or laser the bastard or whatever it is you lot do in ear, but ar don't wanna be cut open.'

'I fully understand your concerns,' the doctor said, adopting a professional stance, 'but sometimes it's the only course of action available to us to rid a patient of this particular type of growth.'

'What type of grofe?' Dee Dee asked.

'Well, let's wait and see shall we,' the doctor replied, sensing her heightened anxiety and sparing her feelings. 'Julia's right, try not to worry, you're in good hands. We have an excellent track record here at Saint Pancras. Here,' he added, handing Dee Dee her appointment form. 'See reception on your way out and please grab a leaflet detailing our counseling connections should you feel you need to talk to a professional. They are really very good and can put your mind at rest on a whole host of matters. Anyway it's something to consider, we'll see you again tomorrow.'

'Fanks,' Dee Dee said, staring at the jumble of words on the page.

'Do you have someone with you?' Julia asked. 'Or is there anyone we could call for you?'

'Naah, me mates are ear,' Dee Dee told her. 'They go everywhere wiv me.'

'Yes you seem very close,' the doctor added. 'I thought one of them was going to give me a thick ear earlier.'

'Oh, thas Trish,' Dee Dee informed him, 'she's off er ed, but proper armless.'
'Well, she had me worried,' the doctor joked. 'They obviously think the world of you, you're very lucky to have them I'd say.'
'Yeah I am,' Dee Dee said, mustering a smile. 'Apart from me muvva they're all ar got in the world them two, ar love em. Yeah even Trish ar wouldn't change er for nuffing.'
'Well, they must be worried sick about you out there,' the doctor said, ushering Dee Dee to the door.
Dee Dee raised a hand, stopping the doctor in his tracks, opting to face her friends alone. 'Shit,' she said under her breath apprehensively. The doctor and nurse returned to the desk to process Dee Dee's scans and prepare for the next patient due to arrive shortly after.
'Are you alright?' Julia asked, seeing Dee Dee hovering at the door.
'Yeah, yeah fanks,' Dee Dee said, without turning, she drew a deep breath and clawed at the door knob turning up the corners of her mouth to form some semblance of a smile.
'Alright!' she said, pulling open the door.
'DEEE!' Maizie said, springing to her feet. 'Dee what is it, are you alright mate?'
'Yeah come on Dee!' Trisha added, leaping up also. 'What did they say, ay?'
'Iss alright,' Dee Dee said, lying through her teeth, unable to break the devastating news and shatter the lives of those she loved the most. 'Iss a cyst.'
'REALLY!' Maizie shrieked, hopping uncontrollably. 'Really, really, really, oh Deeeeeee!' she threw her arms around Dee Dee's neck, hugging her tighter than ever. 'Trish iss a cyst!'
'Oh mar God ar'm so glad Dee,' Trisha squealed. 'Ar bin proper brickin it aat ear, we bofe av aint we Maize?'
'Fuck me not arf!' Maizie smiled. 'Me arts bin in me maaf ever since you went in there. Oh shit ar'm so appy mate ar really am. Trish ain it brilliant!'
'Yeah proper brilliant!' Trisha agreed.

Dee Dee maintained her rigid smile although aching inside. 'Come on,' she told her ecstatic friends. 'Ar gotta make an appointment for tomorra.'

'Why?' Maizie said, her expression changing instantly. 'What for?'

'Oh just anuvva test or summink,' Dee Dee said nonchalantly. 'Nuffing really.'

'You sure?' Maizie asked, probing. 'You aint shittin me are ya Dee, you sure iss a bloody cyst?'

'Yesssss,' Dee Dee laughed, 'naah come on.' With her friends close at her side Dee Dee made her way back through the maze of corridors, but the more she tried to quell the surge of emotion within, the stiffer and more rigid she became.

'You alright Dee?' Trisha asked, clinging to her trembling hand. 'Woss a matter?'

Her face now flushed and a tide of turmoil welling inside Dee Dee struggled to maintain her composure.

'Dee,' Maizie said, as her friend began to falter, snatching at the dado rail to steady herself. 'DEE WOSS UP, TELL ME!'

Dee Dee suddenly bent over double, her face crimson and the veins in her neck protruding.

'Dee mate woss up?' Trisha asked, rubbing her friend's back and looking helplessly across at Maizie. 'Maize woss up wiv er?' she asked. Suddenly a jet of vomit poured from Dee Dee's mouth splattering the linoleum at her feet.

'DEEEEEE, DEEEE!' Maizie cried, glancing back along the corridor with a look of sudden realization etched on her face. 'Cyst my arse. Stay wiv er Trish!' she barked, starting back toward the oncology room.

'MAIZE WHAT IS IT?' Trisha called after her. 'MAIZIE?'

'STAY WIV ER!' Maizie yelled back over her shoulder. 'DON'TCHU FUCKIN LEAVE ER!'

'MAIZE!' Trisha called again, panic stricken. 'What is it Dee, woss up mate?'

Dee Dee slumped to her knees and then down onto her bottom, spitting the remainder of the vomit from her mouth. 'Deee!' Trisha said, dropping at her side. 'What is it?'

Maizie rounded the corner and burst through the doors of the oncology room. 'WHAT WAS IT?' she yelled at the startled doctor and nurse. 'Woss me mate got. Tell me!'

'Excuse me?' the doctor said, taken aback. 'I beg your pardon.'

'Me bloody mate!' Maizie insisted, lunging at him. 'She told us iss a cyst!'

'You mean Deborah,' the doctor said, taking a cautionary step back. 'I'm afraid it's a little more serious than a cyst.'

'WHAT?' Maizie cried, clasping a hand to her head. 'Woja mean more serious?'

'We're just going over her slides now,' Julia told her. 'Dee obviously told you it was a cyst to spare your feelings.'

'Ar bloody knew it!' Maizie growled. 'What is it then?'

'Well,' the doctor said, straightening his coat. 'The results of the mammogram indicate the presence of a cancerous growth possibly attached to Dee's lymph nodes.'

'CANCER!' Maizie gasped. 'Oh fuck no, don't say that please, please mate.' She gripped the edge of the doctor's desk with whitening knuckles. 'Don't...'

'I've asked her to come back in tomorrow for a biopsy.' The doctor told Maizie, switching off his monitor to spare her the heartache of Dee Dee's mammogram results. 'We're confident at this moment in time that it is treatable, but she really should've come in sooner.'

'Shit!' Maizie said, processing the information and looking round at the door. 'Dee.'

'Will you be ok?' Julia asked, but Maizie was already leaving as fast as she had entered.

'DEEEEEEE!' Maizie screamed, sprinting back to her friends. 'DEEEEEE!'

'What is it?' Trisha asked, with a comforting arm around Dee Dee. 'Maizie what is it?'

'Dee, why dint you say?' Maizie asked, ignoring Trisha constant questioning. 'Dee mate why dint you say?'
'Whaaaaat?' Trisha asked yet again. 'Maizie, tell me!'
'It ain a cyst!' Maizie barked, side stepping Dee Dee's vomit and dropping in front of her. 'Iss c, c...,' somehow the word would not leave her mouth.
'What, what Maize?' Trisha begged. 'What?'
'Cancer,' Dee Dee said, emerging from her hands. 'Iss cancer Trish.'
Trisha wriggled back against the wall. 'Fuck no!' she cried, clawing at her hair. 'Fuck no, no, no, no!'
'Dee mate,' Maizie said, sitting beside her without a care for the putrid bile at her side. 'The doc said iss treatable.'
Trisha too buried her face, rocking again with tears streaming down her face but not a sound from her lips. 'Oh shit, oh shit, oh shit Dee,' she eventually blurted. 'No mate.'
'Shut it will ya!' Maizie snapped. 'She don't need it d'you ear me!'
'Ar'm sorry,' Trisha sobbed, inching closer to touch Dee Dee's hair ever so tenderly. 'Dee ar'm sorry mate, ar dint mean to upset ya.'
'Iss alright,' Dee Dee said, taking an extended breath. 'Yeah, e told me itta probly be alright an'all, ar dunno what come over me, sorry you two.'
'Dee mate,' Maizie said, wiping her friend's chin free of vomit. 'You aint got nuffing to be sorry for onest. You're gonna be alright, ar'm gonna make sure of it.'
'Yeah me an'all,' Trisha said, drying her eyes. 'You're gonna get fru this ar promise ya.'
'Fanks,' Dee Dee said, reaching for the dado.
'Ang on, ang on!' Maizie said, clambering to her feet and helping Dee Dee to hers.
'Shit look,' Dee Dee said, stepping over her vomit. 'Ar've puked all over the bloody place, what a melt.'
'Oh shut up Dee,' Maizie said reassuringly. 'They got shit loadsa cleaners in these gaffs, ar wouldn't worry abaat that.'

'Ohhhh iss all up me bleedin legs' Trisha moaned. 'Ar've only just bought these an'all.'
'Shut it you idiot!' Maizie barked, shoving Trisha. 'Iss only a bitta bloody puke for fuck sake.'
'Oh yeah ar know that,' Trisha said, shaking her leg. 'Ar weren't moanin abaat it Dee, iss alright mate ar've ad worse comin aata Faces on a Saturday night. Member when ar shit meself after all them margaritas that time, the cabbie wern an appy bunny was e.'
Trisha's reminiscence brought a smile to Dee Dee's face. 'Yeah you din arf pen an ink din'tcha,' she laughed.
Maizie took the crumpled form from Dee Dee's shaking hand. 'Scuze me!' she said at the desk. 'Me mate needs an appointment for tomorra, iss for the oncology lot.'
'Oncology,' the receptionist said, correcting Maizie.
'Yeah whateva,' Maizie scoffed. 'We gotta come back tomorra so we want one as early as ya got yeah.'
'Right let me see,' the receptionist replied, logging in. 'We have a nine thirty will that be ok?'
'Arf nine!' Maizie said with a sense of urgency. 'Aint'chu got nuffing earlier than that, iss proper important ya know.'
'I'm sorry no,' the receptionist replied, tapping at her keyboard entering Dee Dee into the system. 'Oncology doesn't open until nine you see.'
'Lazy fuckers,' Trisha said, muscling in alongside Maizie. 'No wonder the national elf's proper fucked if them lot won't get aata bed in the mawnin, ay Maize?'
'Shut up you idiot,' Maizie said dismissively. 'Keep an eye on Dee will ya.'
'Oh yeah, right,' Trisha said, turning to Dee Dee who was staring blankly once again. 'Wanna cuppa tea mate,' she asked, seeing signs for the hospital canteen. 'Ar know ar could murder one, after ar've ad a piss though ar'm proper bustin. SCUZE ME WHERE'S THE BOGS?' she yelled over Maizie's shoulder.
'There's a fuckin sign there!' Maizie snarled, glaring at Trisha and pointing behind her.

'Oh, yeah, course,' Trisha smiled. 'Ar can't see for lookin me can I, d'you want one Maize?'

'No,' Maizie said angrily, 'ar don't need a bloody piss now sod off will ya!'

'No, ar mean a cuppa tea,' Trisha said, bobbing cross legged.

'Oh,' Maizie said, rummaging in her pocket. 'Er yeah, ar'll av one fanks, eeyar ar got some change ear.'

'Did ya want one Dee?' Trisha asked. 'A cuppa tea ar mean, not a piss, mind you ar dunno ya might wanna piss an'all ar know ar do, ar fink iss me nerves I always get like this in ospital.' Trisha began to ramble. 'When me cousin Kenny went in to av is appendix aat ar squatted behind iz curtain and filled up two of iz bedpans, iss a good job they never tested it coz ar reckon it was ninety nine percent Sambuca.'

'Trisha!' Maizie said from the desk. 'Piss off and get the teas will ya.'

'Go on ya dozy cow,' Dee Dee smiled, ruffling Trisha's hair.

'OK,' the receptionist said, handing Maizie Dee Dee's appointment card. 'So that's nine thirty tomorrow morning, just go straight to oncology when you arrive.'

'What,' Maizie said sarcastically, 'wivaat takin wunna your poxy numbers and sittin ear like a complete cock for arf me bleedin life.'

'I'm sorry about that,' the receptionist said, without a hint of compassion in her voice. 'Rules are rules.'

'Whateva!' Maizie said, joining Dee Dee. The pair stood at the hospital entrance waiting for Trisha to return. 'Where the fuck is she?' Maizie asked after some ten minutes. 'If she's pissin abaat ar'll kill er.'

Dee Dee said very little, the oncologist had dealt her a hammer blow and drawn a dark cloud over her, one that would be difficult to shake as tens of thousands of women had discovered before her.

'Hiyaaaa!' Trisha eventually called out, appearing with three paper cups.

'Where the bleedin ell av you bin?' Maizie asked, taking a cup from her.

'Ohhhhh don't,' Trisha laughed, raising her eyebrows. 'Like ar said I ad to av a piss first, anyway the bog was backed up and kickin up summink chronic, there was no squeezy soap and the and dryer was on the blink. I only ad enough for two teas.'
Maizie looked at the three cups. 'Don't tell me you wanked em off for the fird cup,' she said, examining her cup for traces of bodily fluids.
'Naaaah, don't be daft!' Trisha said, turning up her nose. 'E weren't mar type, bald ed an a beer belly. Naah ar nicked a fork went back in the bogs and jemmied the fanny rag machine open, ar got over firty five quid av a look!'
She produced a bulging fistful of fifty pence pieces from her pocket. 'We got enough for a cab ome if we wonnit.'
'You soppy bitch!' Maizie barked. 'What if you'da got caught ay, you'da bin banged up in Olloway again and for what, a few measly quid, and then what good would you've bin to Dee Dee ay. You just don't fink sometimes do ya. DO YA!'
'Ar'm sorry,' Trisha said, apologizing for the umpteenth day that day and dropping the coins back into her pocket. 'Ar just wonnid to elp thas all, sorry Dee.'
'Thas alright,' Dee Dee said, sipping her tea. 'Ar fink iss funny as fuck meself.'
'Oh fanks!' Trisha said with renewed vigour. 'Ar got us a loada tampons as well.' She gestured down to her opposite pocket with several strings hanging from it. 'Once a blagger always a blagger ay,' she said proudly.
'Well iss ardly the Brinks Mat bloody bullion robbry is it,' Maizie scoffed.
'Nice one Trish,' Dee Dee said, giving Trisha a break for once. 'Iss the fought that caants mate, ain it.'
'Yeah, yeah thas what ar fought,' Trisha chirped, looking ever so pleased with herself.
Outside the three girls binned their empty tea cups. 'Shall ar get us a cab?' Trisha said stepping into the road.

'Naah leave it Trish,' Dee Dee replied, beckoning her back, slipping her hands into her pockets and facing the prevailing wind. 'Less walk shall we.'
'Walk!' Trisha exclaimed. 'What, like walk walk?'
'Yeah walk,' Dee Dee reiterated, 'it won't urt'cha.'
'Yeah come on Trish,' Maizie said, linking arms with Dee Dee, 'itta do us good to get some fresh air.'
'You reckon,' Trisha moaned, joining her friends, the change rattling in her pocket as the three made their way along Saint Pancras Way.
Shortly after they were approached by a young girl in her teens with matted hair and a hoop through her nose. 'You aint got a coupla bob for a cuppa and a bite to eat av ya?' she asked, extending a grubby hand. 'Ar'm desperate.'
'Piss off!' Maizie said, snubbing the girl.
'Ang on,' Dee Dee told her friends, who barely broke their stride whilst eyeing the girl's shabby sleeping bag in the kebab shop doorway. 'You don't want dough for grub do ya,' she told the girl. 'I aint stupid mate, you wanna get fucked up on shite cider or summink don'tcha.'
The girl looked Dee Dee in the eye, stunned at her candor. 'Er, yeah,' she said sheepishly. 'Yeah ar do as it appens.'
'Come on Deeee,' Maizie groaned, 'leave er will ya.'
'Trish giss the dough,' Dee Dee said, holding out her hand but maintaining eye contact with the girl.
'What?' Trisha said aghast.
'The dough ya nicked!' Dee Dee said abruptly. 'Come on, and it over.'
'You're jokin aint'cha Dee,' Trisha laughed, clasping a hand over her pocket.
'Do ar look like ar'm bloody jokin!' Dee Dee snapped, glaring at her friend. 'Ar said give us the dough, all of it.'
'Oh flippin ell!' Trisha whined, scooping each and every coin from her pocket and dropping them into Dee Dee's hands.
'Eeyar,' Dee Dee said, 'go get yaself proper shit faced on this lot, and the besta luck to ya.'

'Faaanks,' the girl said wide-eyed. 'Fanks a lot mate, er you aint got a spare fag an'all av ya.'

'Now you ar takin the piss,' Dee Dee smiled, starting on her way.

'Deeee,' Trisha said, skipping after her, 'woja go and do that for mate, ar nicked that for us.'

'Exactly,' Dee Dee scoffed. 'Ya nicked it, so it don't matter if we av it or that poor cow does, does it. Ar don't give a shit what she does wiv it neeva.'

'Yeah thas karma that is,' Maizie jeered, 'serves ya right ya feevin git.'

'Karma!' Trisha gasped, stopping abruptly. 'That shit's proper bad ain it. OY!' She called back to the young homeless girl who was sat in the doorway counting the handful of coins with a smile on her filthy face. Trisha ran back to her and promptly emptied the twenty or so tampons into her lap. 'Eeyar,' she said, fearing a further helping of karma. 'Stuff them up ya flu an'all,' she told the startled girl. 'But ya never got em from me, nart ar mean.'

'Ay?' the girl asked, fingering the absorbent mouse like pads.

'Seeya!' Trisha said, skipping back to her friends looking very pleased with herself. 'Thas me karma sorted,' she told Maizie. But no sooner had the words left her mouth she turned and walked head long into a pelican crossing light pole. 'Shit, fuck, fuck!' she cried.

'What was you sayin?' Maizie laughed.

'Shut up!' Trisha moaned, nursing her forehead. 'Flippin ell that urts.'

'You alright mate?' Dee Dee asked, doing her damnedest not to laugh herself.

'She's alright,' Maizie chuckled, 'she aint got nuffing in there to damage as she.'

Opening the street door Maizie ushered Dee Dee inside before letting the door swing back toward Trisha. 'OYYYY!' Trisha said, trailing behind.

'Come on mate,' Maizie told Dee Dee, putting an arm around her on the stairs. 'You can put'cha feet up when we get in, ar make ya summink to eat, you must be starvin ungry.'

'I aint actually,' Dee Dee told her friend at the top of the stairs.

Trisha had just put a foot on the bottom step when the Romanians' door opened beside her.

'Trisha,' Tatyana said emerging, having waited the whole day to catch her and express her true feelings for her.

'Ar can't stop Tat,' Trisha said, raising a dismissive hand, 'me mate's got cancer.'

'TRISHA!' Maizie yelled from the landing, appalled at her friend's insensitivity once again. 'WHAT THE FUCK?'

'What?' Trisha asked, ascending. 'Oh, yeah sorry, sorry Dee,' she added with a guilty smile. 'Sorry mate ar weren't finkin.'

'Jesus, you never blinkin do do ya!' Maizie said, in complete disbelief, opening their door. 'Ar really don't believe er sometimes.'

'Sheee's alright,' Dee Dee smiled. 'Ar wouldn't expect anyfing else from er would you.'

'Ar spoze not,' Maizie agreed, glaring over her shoulder. 'But as soon as you fink she can't possibly get any dumber the soppy cow fucks up on a bleedin monumental scale don't she.'

'Yeah not arf,' Dee Dee laughed, holding the door for their hapless friend. 'Come on you,' she said, tugging Trisha inside. 'Put the kettle on will ya.'

'Bloody Nora!' Trisha moaned. 'Some fings never bleedin change do they.'

'Shuuuut uuuup,' Maizie said, fluffing the sofa cushions for Dee Dee. 'Just do as ya told will ya.'

'Make the tea Trisha,' Trisha whined, stomping through to the kitchen. 'Do this Trish, do that Trish. STICK A BLOODY BROOM UP ME ARSE AR'LL SWEEP THE FRIGGIN FLOOR!'

'YEAH OK!' Maizie called back. 'BUT MAKE THE BLOODY TEA FIRST WON'T YA!'

Trisha mumbled under her breath the whole time the kettle was boiling.
'You sure you don't want nuffing to eat Dee?' Maizie asked. 'Ar can make you a bacon samwich if ya like, ar know ya love a bitta streaky.'
'Naah, seriously Maize,' Dee Dee replied, putting her feet up on the coffee table and dropping her head onto one of the cushions. 'Me stomach's goin ten to the dozen at the moment so ar probly couldn't keep it daan, fanks anyway, ar'll just av me tea.'
'TRISHAAAAA!' Maizie shrieked, causing Dee Dee to wince. 'WHERE'S THE BLOODY TEA?'
'ISS COMIN!' Trisha replied, retrieving the milk from the refrigerator. 'AR'VE ONLY GOT ONE PAIRA BLEEDIN ANDS YA KNOW!'
'YEAH!' Maizie said in reply. 'AND ONE FLIPPIN BRAIN CELL AN'ALL, NOW URRY UP. COME ON DEE'S GARSPIN!'
'Yeah, yeah alright,' Trisha said, handing Maizie Dee Dee's mug. 'Eeyar give er that, and tell er ar got a packet of ginger nuts if she's ungry.'
'She aint,' Maizie said abruptly. 'Neeva am I come to fink of it.'
'I am!' Trisha said, opening the freezer. 'Ya don't mind if ar make meself a coupla kievs do ya?'
'Do what ya like,' Maizie said, leaving her to her own devices and rejoining Dee Dee on the sofa. 'Eeyar mate, watch it iss ot,' she told her friend, handing her the tea.
'Fanks Maize,' Dee Dee said, cupping the mug. 'Listen, you don't av to fuss over me all the time ya know.'
'Shut up Dee,' Maizie said, sitting beside her, 'you'd do the same for me ya know ya would.'
'Yeah probly,' Dee Dee smiled, tucking her feet under her backside and nestling into her friend.
'Love ya Dee,' Maizie said, kissing Dee Dee's shoulder tenderly.

Dee Dee merely smiled in reply, her head spinning with a thousand thoughts, the majority of them centered around her own mortality.

Trisha in the meantime had completely forgotten the devastating events of the day and pranced around the kitchen with a tune she'd heard belting from a teenager's hatchback that very afternoon.

'Ar wanna lick tutti fruity from a big ass booty,' she sang, shaking her bottom and delving into the refrigerator.

'Suck a jelly roll from a big belly ho,
Big belly ho, big belly hoooooo!'

'Listen to that soppy cow Maize,' Dee Dee smiled.

'TRISHAAA TURN IT IN WILL YA!' Maizie yelled.

'Leave er Maize,' Dee Dee said, welcoming the distraction, 'she's alright.'

Trisha emerged some twenty or so minutes later having cremated her kievs in the fan assisted oven. 'Ar can't get that friggin Tutti Fruity song aat mar bleedin ed,' she said, slamming her charred chicken on the table.

'Ar know,' Dee Dee laughed, 'we erd.'

'You ain eatin that are ya?' Maizie asked observing Trisha biting down hard on the blackened morsels, her teeth clogged with carbon deposits.

'Yeah!' Trisha said with her mouth full. 'I aint waistin em, ar was watchin a bitta totty two doors daan angin er washin aat and forgot I ad em in the oven, mind you it was werf it though coz she ad tits like a paira copper's elmets, proper ard they were.'

Maizie and Dee Dee sat quietly whilst Trisha cleared her plate. 'Aaaaansum' she said, wiping her charcoal coated lips. 'Listen ar got a coupla jubblies in the freezer if you'z two wonem, ar'v ad mine, it was drippin daan me chin while ar was pervin over the red ed and er rotary washin line, you shoulda seen er peggin aat er pretty little pussy pouches, got me ringin wet it did.' Getting absolutely no response from her friends Trisha tapped her knife on the edge of her

plate several times. 'Oy!' she said, perturbed at being ignored. 'Woss up wiv you'z two?'
Maizie span to give her friend the fiercest of frowns. 'REALLY!' she said, after a short pause. 'Really!'
'What?' Trisha replied, but a glance across at Dee Dee staring blankly at the lifeless television set brought the harsh reality rushing back to her. 'Oh gawd ar forgot,' she said, clasping a hand to her forehead.
'FORGOT!' Maizie screeched, springing from her seat. 'OW THE FUCK CAN YOU FUCKIN FORGET. YOU STUPID FUCKIN FUCK!'
'MAIZE!' Dee Dee said, pulling her friend back down onto the couch. 'Please mate.'
'Sorry Dee but...,' Maizie said seething.
'Shhhhhhhhhh,' Dee Dee said, with a pained expression. 'It don't matter Maize, onest mate, it don't matter. She's as barmy as a boxa bloody frogs but she's our mate aint she.'
Maizie sat unconvinced.
'Oh fanks Dee,' Trisha said, hopping over and wedging herself in between her two friends.
'Get off!' Maizie moaned, snatching her foot from under Trisha who lay across Dee Dee's lap with her head on her thighs.
'You are gonna be alright aint'cha Dee?' Trisha asked, toying with a thread hanging from Dee Dee's sweater. 'Ar mean ar dunno what ar'd do if ya, well ya know.'
'I aint goin nowhere ya dozy mare,' Dee Dee smiled. 'Ar promise.'
Maizie turned her face away to conceal her tears.
'Good,' Trisha said resolutely. 'You better not.'
Dee Dee lovingly toyed with Trisha's hair as her mother had done when Trisha was a child with exactly the same outcome, Trisha's eyes grew heavy and a contented smile crept across her yawning face.
'Come on mate,' Dee Dee told her, nudging her softly. 'Get yaself off to bed, you're knackered aint'cha.'

The emotional bombshell and the fallout filled aftermath had taken its toll on all of them. 'Ar'm fucked an'all,' Maizie admitted, swinging her legs to the floor. 'Oy soppy nuts!' she added, jostling Trisha. 'Oy, come on, bed.'
'Mmmmmm, ay, what?' Trisha asked, stirring. 'Oh yeah,' she said, stretching. 'Sorry Dee ar musta fell asleep mate.'
'Thas alright babe,' Dee Dee said straightening, having endured a mild cramping. She and Maizie left Trisha looking on fondly and trudging wearily to her own room.
'Night Trish,' Dee Dee said, without turning.
'Yeah night Dee,' Trisha replied, feeling somewhat estranged from her friends.

In the dead of night Dee Dee woke abruptly in the midst of a harrowing dream in which she was looking up at her friends and family from the bottom of a sodden rat infested grave. She lay in her bed, her heart pounding, when from the other side of the wall she could just make out a faint whimper. 'Maize?' she called softly to her friend, but got no reply. Dee Dee put an ear to the blown vinyl wallpaper and moments later threw back the sheets from her bed. 'Shit,' she said, on hearing her friend sobbing uncontrollably in her bed next door. 'Ay, ay, ayyyyyy,' she said, hurrying into Trisha's room and siting beside her. 'Woss up mate?'
'Oh, oh, oh Deeee, ar, ar, ar, ar'm really sc... scared,' Trisha cried, struggling to catch her breath and throwing her arms around Dee Dee's neck. 'Ar, ar'm really really scared Deeeeee.'
'Ay, ay shhhhhhhh. Come on woss up?' Dee Dee asked in an attempt to comfort her distraught friend. 'Come on shhh, shhhhhh, iss alright, what ya gotta be scared abaat?'
'Ar don't wanna lose ya?' Trisha bawled, with her chin on Dee Dee's shoulder and her arms tightening around Dee Dee's neck. 'Me auntie Shelly ad a lump,' she added, rambling aimlessly, 'they, they, they cut er tit off and we dunna sponsored walk to, to send er to Centre parcs but, but she died on er birfday, on er bloody birfday Dee for fuck

sake. Ar fucked up coz, coz me mobile went off in the church and it was some bastard tryna sell me p, p, ppi, ar told em to get fucked and the vicar fru a paddy and chucked me aat.'

'Sh, shh, shhhhhh,' Dee Dee said, rocking her friend and wondering where her conversation was heading. 'Ar told you I aint goin nowhere din I ay. Don't get yaself into a state abaat it mate.'

'Ar carn elp it Dee,' Trisha sobbed.

'Ar tell ya what,' Dee Dee said, cupping Trisha's face. 'D'you wanna come and get in wiv me for tonight, ay?'

'Can I?' Trisha said, wiping her dripping cheek. 'Can I Dee?'

'Yeah course ya can, come on,' Dee Dee told her, tossing her duvet aside.

'Fanks Dee,' Trisha said, following hand in hand in the half light and still sniffing from time to time.

'In ya get,' Dee Dee whispered, so as not to wake Maizie. 'And don't try nunna ya lezza stuff or a'll beat the shit aata ya.'

'Ar won't Dee,' Trisha said, climbing eagerly onto her friend's bed and nestling against the wall. 'Ar promise ar wont.'

The pair clung to one another, Dee Dee gleaning as much comfort from her friend's company as Trisha did from hers.

'Mawnin Dee,' Maizie said softly the following morning. 'Ar made you a nice cuppa tea.'

'You done me one an'all av ya?' Trisha asked, popping her head above Dee Dee's covers.

'What the!' Maizie said aghast. 'Eeya, what'chu doin in there? Dee you aint gone all lez av ya?'

'No ar fuckin aint!' Dee Dee slurred, opening one eye. 'She couldn't sleep so ar got er in ear wiv me.'

'You're mad,' Maizie scoffed. 'Ar'da told er to get stuffed ar would.'

'Yeah well, Dee never did,' Trisha said, cuddling her friend. 'Now jog on and get me tea you muppet.'

'Sod off and make it yaself!' Maizie snapped, leaving the room.

'MAAAAIZE!' Dee Dee called after her. 'DON'T BE LIKE THAT, MAKE ER A TEA WILL YA. PLEASE!'

Maizie reluctantly wrenched another mug from the kitchen cupboard and slammed it down on the counter. 'Make me tea ya muppet,' she mumbled, 'ar'll give er muppet.'

Dee Dee took her tea into the bathroom, running a shower while she pee'd, leaving Trisha sat up in bed expectantly. 'MAIZE WHERE'S ME TEAAAAAA?' she called at the door. 'MAIZE!'

'ON THE BLOODY TABLE!' Maizie replied from the sofa.

'Oh flippin ell!' Trisha said, scratching at her crotch emerging from their room. 'Ar wonnid it in bed.'

'Yeah,' Maizie said sarcastically, 'well ar wonnid to win undred grand on a scratchcard and run away wiv Jason Stayfum, but instead ar'm stuck ear wiv you.'

'Oh,' Trisha said, sitting at the table sipping her tea. 'Ohhhhhh Maaaaize,' she then moaned, 'ya left the bloody tea bag in.'

'Oh did I?' Maizie smiled. 'Sorry maaaate.'

Maizie finished her tea and tapped on the bathroom door. 'Dee mate iss quarter past eight,' she told her friend. 'We gotta be up the ospital for arf nine member.'

The bathroom door opened and Dee Dee came out with a waft of steam and a towel turban. 'Yeah ar know,' she told Maizie, sounding surprisingly upbeat considering her circumstances. 'We got loadsa time.'

'You alright Dee?' Maizie asked, astonished at her turn of mood.

'Yeah,' Dee smiled, rubbing her hair dry. 'Look we can't keep sittin araand feelin sorry for ourselfs,' she told her two friends. 'Yesterday was yesterday and today's today, OK. Whatever they fro at us we face it ed on like we always av, d'you ear me? Trish, ar said d'you ear me?'

'Er, yeah,' Trisha said unconvinced.

'No more cryin,' Dee Dee warned. 'Ar won't av it, ar done some finkin while ar was in the bog and we gotta stay positive uvverwise we're gonna fall apart and that aint no

good for no one is it. IS IT?'
'No,' Maizie and Trisha agreed.
'So!' Dee Dee chirped. 'Get yaselves dressed and less go do this biopsy shit and say bollocks to cancer, we ain avin it.'
'Yeah!' Maizie cried. 'Bollocks to it, ay?'
'YEAAAAAAH!' Trisha shrieked, springing to her feet and upsetting her cup of tea on the table. 'Oh shit fuck!' she said, grabbing at the toppled cup.
Dee Dee and Maizie both looked to the heavens and disappeared into their room, leaving Trisha scooping the spilt tea back into her cup and then into her mouth. 'Yeah fuck it!' she said, joining her friends. 'Er wait,' she added quizzically. 'What was we fuckin again?'
'Cancer you cock!' Maizie snapped, pushing Trisha out of their room. 'Now piss off and get dressed will ya.'
'Oh shit yeah sorry!' Trisha called from outside.
'Ar see this programme once,' Maizie told Dee Dee, as the two of them reached into their wardrobe. 'Where the mafia disposed of a body by feedin it to a loada pigs.'
'Maizie!' Dee Dee said, stopping her friend in mid sentence. 'We aint doin er in, she's our mate for gawd sake.'
'We can get anuvva mate anywhere can't we,' Maizie said, scheming Trisha's demise yet again.
'Not like er we couldn't,' Dee Dee smirked. 'There aint anuvva Trisha anywhere in the world.'
'Ar make ya right ar spoze,' Maizie sighed, put out somewhat by Dee Dee's refusal to be a willing accomplice.
'You two ready?' Trisha asked, shoving open their door.
'Well you obviously aint,' Maizie laughed, ridiculing Trisha's fashion faux pas. 'Really Trish,' she said, with a hand to her chin. 'Jeggin's, crocks and socks!'
'What?' Trisha replied, looking down at her aubergine footwear and tangerine trousers. 'Ar quite like it. Iss a statement ain it.'
'Iss a pile a shit,' Maizie sneered.
'Ar love it,' Dee Dee said uncharacteristically. 'You wear what ya want mate, iss your life.'

'Yeaaaaah,' Trisha said, turning her nose up at Maizie. 'Iss mar life.'
'Not if ar got anyfing to do wiv it,' Maizie said, under her breath.
Leaving the flat the three of them descended the stairs and once again Trisha was accosted by Tatyana in the hallway.
'Trisha please I must talk with you,' the frustrated Romanian begged.
'Not now Tat!' Trisha said, raising a dismissive hand and repelling her advances once again. 'Maybe anuvva time yeah.'
Tatyana ran back into her flat in floods of tears, slamming the door behind her.
'Woss that all abaat?' Dee Dee asked.
'Ar'm playin ard to get,' Trisha confessed, 'anuvva coupla days and ar'll av er eatin aat me ands, and me knickers an'all opefully.'
'Oooh you dirty bitch,' Maizie scoffed, leading Dee Dee to the street door. 'Come on mate,' she said, helping Dee Dee down the single step.
'Maize I ain an invalid!' Dee Dee frowned. 'Jesus, stop fussing over me will ya.'
'Bleedin ell!' Trisha exclaimed, looking out across the street. 'Look who it is. OY OY TEL!'
Dee Dee and Maizie looked up startled to see West Ham Terry standing on the opposite side of the road with a piece of paper in his hand looking across at the terraced houses on their side. 'OY OY SAVALOYYYYY!' he called back, waving. 'Fank fuck!' he added, bowling between the parked cars. 'You gimme the right road, but you never gimme the number Dee!'
'Ello Tel,' Maizie said, meeting him at the gate and leaning to plant a kiss on his cheek. 'What'chu doin ear?'
'Alright Tel!' Trisha chirped, doing the same. 'Woss appnin?'
'Ar need a favour,' Terry told the girls, 'ar need somewhere to get me nut daan for a coupla days.'
'Yeah course,' Dee Dee said without hesitation. 'But ar

fought you ad it cushty at Bradley's.'
'Yeah ar did but...,' Terry was about to tell the girls of his harrowing sexual experience with Spencer when he though better of it. 'I er, ar wonnid to come back to London din I, back to me roots and shit.'
'What appened then?' Maizie asked.
'Well,' Terry said, leaning on the creaking gate. 'An old school mate a mine put me up at iz gaff, but the wanker just slung me aat.'
'Oh Tel why?' Dee Dee asked, feeling for her friend.
'Issa long story Dee,' Terry replied, 'but basically e come ome and caught me angin aat the back end of iz old lady.'
'You was shaggin iz misses!' Maizie gasped. 'Oh Tel for fuck sake mate.'
'Ar know, ar know,' Terry said, holding his hands in the air, 'but it was on a bloody plate Maize. She's always liked me ever since ar felt er up in double maffs, she was a proper dirty little bitch back then an ar tell ya what, she still is naah believe me. She's into all that tantric shit, ar'd never erd of it but fuckin ell we done it for six hour one day, ar got fru arf a dozen viagra and a boxa johnnies, but what a bleedin ride ar tel ya.'
'Ar'm not surprised ya bleedin mate fru you aat,' Dee Dee told him. 'Talk abaat shittin on yer own doorstep, did e proper kick off?'
'Naaaaah,' Terry smiled. 'The geezer's a pussy, e just left me a note and a tenner for me train fair.'
'Ahhhhhh,' Trisha sighed, 'thas nice of im ain it.'
'Yeah course you can stay Tel,' Dee Dee told him. 'You can kip on the settee till you get yaself sorted.'
'Oh nice one,' Terry smiled. 'Ear, where you'z off too naah?'
'Oh we're goin to the ospital,' Trisha blurted. 'Coz Dee's got cancer!'
'TRISHA!' Dee Dee barked, ramming an elbow into her friend's ribs.
'SHUT THE BOX!' Terry gasped. 'No, Dee shut up, you aint av ya babe.'

'Ar don't know for definite,' Dee Dee told him, giving Trisha a cold hard look while Maizie shook her bodily.

'Woss a matter wiv you?' Maizie growled.

'Dee, tell me you're pullin mar dick,' Terry said, taking Dee Dee's hand.

'No Tel I aint pullin ya dick,' Dee Dee laughed. 'And ar wouldn't even if ya paid me. No ar just gotta av anuvva test so we av to wait and see, you can go up and make yaself at ome if ye want. Elp yaself to tea and stuff.'

'Fuck that,' Terry scoffed, 'ar'm comin wiv ya.'

'You sure?' Dee Dee asked. 'You don't av to ya know.'

'You try and stop me,' Terry replied, opening the gate and leading Dee Dee through. 'You alright, careful,' he said.

'Not you an'all,' Dee Dee told him, growing tired of the fussing already.

'Iss your fault!' Maizie told Trisha, shoving her out the gate. 'You and your big maaf.'

'What?' Trisha asked, shrugging Maizie off. 'What av ar done?'

Terry walked with the girls, struggling to come to terms with the earth shattering news. 'Ar really ope you're alright Dee mate,' he told her.

'Ar gotta job Tel!' Trisha cried, skipping alongside him. 'Ar work wiv the animal geezers naah.'

'Oh,' Terry said, disinterested to say the least.

'Ar've rescued a goose, a crow bird fing and a shit loada cats so far,' Trisha continued.

'Don't forget Trish,' Dee Dee said turning. 'You sunk the fuckin Woolwich ferry an'all dint'cha.'

'Shut uuuuup!' Terry gasped. 'Don't tell me that was you Trish, that was all over the poxy telly an everyfing, ow the fuck?'

'Well she was on it Tel,' Maizie said, looking down her nose at Trisha, 'so it was bound to bleedin appen wern it.'

'Flippin ell Trish!' Terry said, wide eyed. 'You're bleedin barkin aint'cha girl.'

'You only just worked that aat Tel,' Maizie smirked. 'We av

to live wiv the doughnut.'
Part way along the Caledonia Road Terry glanced over his shoulder, then suddenly dived into the betting office doorway, and ducked down behind a pile of crumpled boxes.
'Tel, what'cha doin?' Dee Dee asked, but then an all too familiar voice rang out.
'OY YOU SLAGS!' D I Pritcher called from his car.
'Pritcher,' Dee Dee sneered, turning to see the D I slowing at the kerb side. 'COME EAR!' he called, beckoning with a condescending finger. 'AR SAID COME EAR!'
'What the fuck do you want?' Dee Dee asked, approaching the car.
'You can't touch us Pritcher,' Maizie remarked. 'We're legit naah.'
'LEGIT!' the D I smiled. 'Don't make me laugh, you slags couldn't go legit if ya tried, ar dunno why the fuck they let'chu aat, ar'da left you free in there to rot if I ad mar way.'
'Well we are aat,' Maizie scoffed. 'And there's fuck all you can do abaat it, so do one!'
'Watch it you stupid little bitch!' the D I barked. 'Ar could fit you up with whatever the fuck ar like, and not lose a bloody winka sleep over it so ar'd tread very carefully if ar was you.'
'You can't touch us Pritcher,' Dee Dee said defiantly. 'And you know it.'
'What you'z slags doin up ear anyway?' the D I asked. 'Finkin of turnin over that bookies are ya?'
'Naah we're goin to the ospital!' Trisha piped up, and before Maizie could stop her blurted yet again. 'Coz Dee's got cancer!'
'Ow many more fuckin times!' Dee Dee said, spinning to confront her. 'Shut the fuck up will ya!'
'Cancer my arse,' the D I smiled. 'You slags can bullshit whoever you like but that shit won't wash with me, let me tell you that. Ar'll be watchin you, mark my words, and the minute you'z free step aat of line ar'll bang ya'z up for

good.'

Maizie dragged Trisha away to give her a stern talking to, but as usual it fell on deaf, and for the most part dumb, ears.

'Laterz Pritcher,' Dee Dee said, turning her back on the flustered D I and showing him a finger.

'Watch it Dawson!' the Detective Inspector growled. 'And if you ear from that West Am fuck of a mate of yours, you tell im ar gotta cell fulla poofs wiv iz name on it and ar'll make sure they ride iz arse mawnin noon and night. Ar'll av im if it's the last bleedin fing ar do.' The D I pulled away into traffic and into the path of a number 393 bus which honked its horn. 'PISS OFF!' he yelled, sticking two fingers in the air and speeding away.

'ISS ALRIGHT TEL!' Dee Dee called to Terry. 'E'Z GONE!'

'Fuck me that was close,' Terry said, emerging and peeling a banana skin from the leg of his trousers. 'That fucker's bin tryna feel mar collar ever since he banged you free up, e'z got a proper ard on for me, ar dunno why.'

'Iss coz you're a mate of ours,' Maizie told him, having given up trying to drum an ounce of sense into Trisha. 'E won't rest till e'z nabbed ya, that bastard's like a dog wiv a bleedin bone e is.'

'Tell ya what Tel,' Dee Dee said, slipping an arm around Terry's rotund waist. 'You can stop at ours for a coupla days then ar got a contact that can get you aat the country in a container. Black Mickey's still aat in Spain, ar'm sure e'll put you up.'

'Nice one,' Terry replied, checking the coast in either direction. 'But less see what appens wiv ya test first ay.'

Once at the Saint Pancras the four friends made their way through the hospital to the oncology department, Terry leering at one or two of the more heavily set nurses in passing. 'Corrr, iss times like this when ar wished I ad a boil on the enda me nob,' he joked, the thought of penile treatment at the hands of one of those lovelies turning him

on no end.
'Take a seat please,' a young nurse told them, as they hovered outside the oncology suite. 'The doctor will see you in just a moment. I'll just take that,' she added, taking the form from Dee Dee's hand.
Moments later the doctor arrived. 'Dee isn't it?' he said, slipping his hands into his hospital coat pockets. 'I remembered you see. OK, I see your entourage is growing.'
'Woja mean?' Trisha asked alarmed.
'Her friends,' the doctor replied. 'I trust you're all being very supportive?'
'Oh yeah,' Maizie said, putting an arm over Dee Dee's shoulder. 'She's our mate, so course we're gonna look after er.'
Terry then took the doctor by the arm and tugged him to one side. 'Listen geez,' he said, out of earshot of the girls, and taking a roll of bank notes from his inside pocket. 'There's a monkey in it for ya if ya sort er aat alright.'
'A monkey,' the doctor said, unfamiliar with east London slang.
'Yeah, arf a baga san,' Terry reiterated. 'Do the business wiv me mate and the dough's yours, alright.'
'A bag of sand, a monkey!' the doctor said, totally confused at this point. 'What the devil are you talking about man?'
'A baga sand, grand!' Terry told him, growing impatient. 'Arfa baga sand is a monkey, five undred quid for fuck sake. Jesus, you blokes ar spozed to be ejacated aint'cha.'
'I'm sorry,' the doctor told Terry, 'but I cannot accept any monies from patients or relatives, it simply doesn't work that way. Your friend will receive the very best of care the Saint Pancras has to offer, regardless of her financial situation. Now if you'll excuse me, I have a biopsy to perform on her and there isn't a moment to lose.'
'Oh yeah course,' Terry said, slipping the money back into his pocket. 'You crack on doc,' with this Terry planted a firm hand on the doctor's back almost knocking the wind from his sails.

'What was that all abaat Tel?' Dee Dee asked.
'Just gettin a number for that fat old Doris in maternity,' Terry said, sparing Dee Dee the truth.
'Ar see you pervin at er,' Dee Dee said, shoving Terry playfully.
'Dee, shall we?' the doctor said, holding the door open.
Dee Dee looked at her two girl friends, her expression said it all.
'Oh Deeee mate, everyfing's gonna be alright,' Maizie said, showing two hands with fingers crossed. 'We're rootin for ya, evry stepa the way, you know that don'tcha?'
Trisha flung her arms around Dee Dee's neck kissing her repeatedly on the cheek. 'Love ya, love ya, love ya,' she said, refusing to release her friend.
'Ar know,' Dee Dee laughed. 'Ar know ya nut nut, now lemmy go will ya.'
'Oh sorry Dee, course, yeah the tit doctor's waitin, aintcha mate?'
'Er, yes,' the doctor said, blushing. 'But I'm an oncologist actually.'
'Whateva,' Trisha said, kissing Dee Dee over and over to the door. 'Love ya, love ya!' she said, watching her friend dissapear inside. 'LOVE YA DEEEE!' she called after her.
'Come on Trish,' Maizie said, tugging her friend from the door. 'Come and sit daan wiv us, she'll be alright.'
Terry sat with his arms outstretched across the backs of the chairs and his legs splayed, checking out the numerous nurses scurrying along the hospital corridor, while Maizie and Trisha sat hand in hand staring at that very same door as they had done the previous day.
'Riiight Dee,' the doctor said, ushering Dee Dee to a bed. 'I'd like to start by giving you an ultrasound.'
'A what?' Dee Dee asked apprehensively.
'An ultrasound,' the doctor replied. 'We use high frequency sound waves to produce an image of the breast tissue, the same as we do for expectant mothers to produce an image of their unborn babies.'

'Oh yeah right, like a scan ya mean?' Dee Dee said, breathing a sigh of relief.
'Yes that's right,' the doctor told her. 'Now I know you've had a mammogram but the ultrasound provides us with different information about the breast you see, it's quite painless and will only take a few moments.'
'Yes, you won't feel a thing,' his nurse added. 'If I could just get you to undress to the waist and pop this gown on that would be great. Then if you could lie down with your right arm raised above your head please.'
Dee Dee did as she was asked and while the doctor busied himself at his computer, the nurse retrieved her apparatus. 'OK, this piece of equipment is called a transducer,' she told Dee Dee. 'Basically it's a hand held scanning probe. I'm going to move it over your breast and the area under your arm known as the axilla, just here,' she said, pointing. 'Now to gain a clearer image I'll need to apply some gel to the area, so this may be a little cold to begin with, is that ok?'
'Yeah thas alright,' Dee Dee said, wanting the whole thing to be over with.
The doctor looked closely at his monitor and the images produced by the ultrasound while the nurse scanned the affected area. 'Thank you Julia,' he eventually said, when satisfied. Julia and the doctor then conferred in a hushed whisper at the monitor, leaving Dee Dee fretting on the bed.
'Is everyfing alright?' Dee Dee asked, feeling decidedly uneasy, but she received no reply. 'Scuze me? she called again. 'Ar said is everyfing alright?'
'Oh I'm sorry Dee,' the doctor said, looking up. 'We won't keep you a moment.'
Dee Dee looked round the room catching sight of the breast chart once again, which sent a chill running down her tense spine.
'Riiight ok,' the doctor eventually said, rising from his seat. 'Dee, ordinarily I would proceed with an FNA at this juncture.'
'A what?' Dee Dee asked. 'Woss wunna them when iss at

ome?'

'Oh I'm sorry,' the doctor smiled. 'A fine needle aspiration, it's a type of biopsy where we use a fine needled syringe to take sample cells from the breast for analysis. But, judging by the size of your growth, I'd like to perform a core biopsy. Basically I'm going to take a slightly larger sample of tissue this time because we can locate it quite easily with the help of the mammogram.'

'Ohhhhh OK,' Dee Dee said, much of his convoluted explanation going way over her head.

'OK if I could ask you to lie back again,' the doctor asked, assisting Dee Dee. 'I won't keep you a moment.'

Dee Dee stared at a stain on the ceiling for what seemed like an eternity before the doctor returned. 'OK I'm going to give you a local anesthetic,' he said, producing a syringe, 'to numb the area. Is that ok?'

'Yeah crack on,' Dee Dee said, looking away while the side of her breast was injected.

'Thaaat's great,' the doctor said, removing the needle. 'Now I have to ask,' he continued, 'are you taking any asprin at the moment, or any other anticoagulants, blood thinning tablets basically.'

'Naaaah,' Dee Dee replied. 'Ar told you ar don't do tablits.'

'OK let me explain the procedure I'm about to perform,' the doctor told Dee Dee pulling his chair closer. 'So there's no doubt in your mind so to speak. OK, a core biopsy uses a larger needle hence the need for a local anesthetic. We remove tissue as I said from the area of concern. We take tissue rather than cells for more detailed information. OK, because we can't see signs or lesions on the surface of the breast I'm going to have to give you an ultrasound once again so that I can be guided to the growth using the screen. Are you with me so far, or am I moving too fast?'

'Naaah, you're alright,' Dee Dee replied. 'Ar fink.'

'Great, well,' the doctor said, summoning his nurse, 'Julia here will assist with the mammogram.'

'Hi Deee,' Julia said softly. 'You had one of these yesterday

didn't you, so you're familiar with the machine.'
Dee Dee merely smiled, her stomach churning inside. The mammogram plates were then positioned either side of her right breast and pressed quite firmly into place. 'Sorry,' Julia said, observing Dee Dee's discomfort.
The doctor dragged his computer closer and switched on the monitor. 'Right,' he said, checking the image and familiarizing himself with the position of Dee Dee's growth. 'OK I need to make a small incision in the side of your breast Dee so I suggest you look away for a moment. You shouldn't feel anything because I've given you sufficient anesthetic. Is that alright?'
Dee Dee nodded and turned to face the wall. While her friend's waited anxiously outside Dee Dee remained rigid whilst the doctor, with the aid of his nurse and the monitor, guided his instruments towards the growth and retrieved three small samples of her tissue, popping them into a small jar in Julia's hand. 'OK, can you get those off to the lab please Julia,' the doctor asked.
Julia hurried from the room. 'Is she alright?' Maizie asked, as the nurse emerged. 'Woss appnin?'
'Yes she's fine,' Julia replied, slipping the jar into her pocket. 'She won't be too much longer now.'
Back in the room the doctor was applying a dressing to Dee Dee's incision. 'You'll need to keep that on for a day or so,' he told her, 'your breast may be a little numb for a while until the anesthetic wears off, and then a little sore for a while and you will experience some bruising, but this is quite normal I assure you.'
'Yeah ar can andle that,' Dee Dee said, closing her gown and sitting up. 'What appens naah?'
'Well,' the doctor said, sliding back toward his desk on his chair. 'I take it you haven't had a chance to register with a GP yet.'
'Naaah,' Dee Dee said, swinging her legs down from the bed. 'Not yet.'
'OK,' the doctor replied, tapping at his keyboard. 'Well

ordinarily your results would be sent to your GP, but in certain circumstances they would be sent in the post.'

'Ow will ar know what ar'm lookin at?' Dee Dee asked. 'Arfa this mumbo jumbo don't mean nuffing to me.'

'Right, well let me explain,' the doctor said, retrieving a guide from his desk. 'Your core biopsy results will be in a B1 to B5 ratio. B meaning biopsy of course, now a B1 would indicate normal breast tissue, but I'm afraid to say we can already rule that out. B2 would be benign, i.e. not cancer, again I have my reservations. B3 would indicate that the tissue is abnormal but most probably benign.'

'Not cancer,' Dee Dee said, getting the gist.

'Yes exactly,' the doctor replied. 'Now, this is the serious stuff, B4 would indicate to us that the tissue is suspicious and possibly malignant, that means cancer I'm afraid. And B5 is a positive result for a malignant growth.'

'Cancer,' Dee Dee said, preempting the doctor. 'B5's cancer ain it, and B4's probly cancer.'

'Yes , yes you're quite right,' the doctor said, moving back closer to Dee Dee. 'Look I fully understand the position you are in right now. I've seen enough women, and men for that matter, in my time. But like I said to you before, you are in good hands here, we'll be with you every step of the way throughout your treatment, I promise you.'

'What if are get a five?' Dee Dee asked, trembling again. 'Five's bad ain it.'

'Well, let's cross that bridge if and when we come to it,' the doctor replied diplomatically. 'It may be good news after all.'

'Look!' Dee Dee snapped. 'You don't av to shit me, if you got summink to say to me you say it to me face right naah, all this bollocks abaat waitin for ya bloody results, ar know birds thatta bleedin died while they were waitin for em.'

'Well I assure you,' the doctor said, taken aback by her forthright attitude, 'you are not about to die in the near future. We have plenty of options at our disposal to treat you. Now I've put a note on your file so that your results will be sent to the address you provided for us yesterday, but what I would stress to you is that it is important that you are not alone when you open the letter. It is always in my opinion imperative that close friends or family are nearby for support.'

'OK fanks,' Dee Dee said, realizing it would be futile to probe any further. Turning her back on the doctor she slipped from the hospital gown and dressed. 'Is that it?' she asked. 'Can ar go?'

'Yes, thank you Dee,' the doctor said, escorting her to the door.

'Av ar gotta come back?' Dee Dee asked, before leaving the examination room.

'There will be instructions with your results,' the doctor told her. 'Please try not to worry, I know it's easy for me to say.'

'DEEEEEEE!' Trisha shrieked, when her friend appeared. 'Deee mate!' Trisha leapt from her seat, flinging her arms around Dee Dee yet again.

'Ow, watch me tit!' Dee Dee snapped.

'Oh sorry Dee,' Trisha said, pulling away. 'Ar didn't mean to urt'cha mate.'

'Get off of er!' Maizie growled, dragging Trisha clear. 'Dee, you alright mate? Ow was it, what did they do, what did they say, what appens naah?'

'Ang on, ang on!' Dee Dee said, collecting her thoughts. 'Gimme a minute will ya.'

Terry tugged the doctor to one side again. 'Listen doc,' he said, in a hushed tone, once again.

'I've told you,' the doctor said, holding up a hand. 'I cannot take any monies in exchange for medical help. I it simply isn't done, now if you'll please excuse me.'

'No, no, no!' Terry said, tugging the doctor's sleeve. 'It aint that, ar was wonderin if you got time to look at me nuts while ar'm ear.'

'I beg your pardon?' the doctor said quizzically.

'Me nuts, me craan jewels,' Terry explained, 'me gonads. Me balls for fuck sake!'

'Oh I see,' the doctor said, after the penny had dropped. 'You mean your testicles, have you made an appointment?'

'No course I aint you pleb,' Terry told him. 'Ar just wonem checked aat incase ar got anyfing that might interfere wiv me love life nart ar mean.'

'Do you have a GP?' the doctor asked. 'Are you registered with a doctor I mean?'

'Yeah ar know what ya bleedin mean!' Terry said angrily. 'I aint no melt ya know. Yeah ar got a doctor, some Chinese geezer, but I aint seen im in years.'

'Well I suggest if you have cause for concern,' the doctor explained, 'that you visit your GP first and he will examine you before referring you to a hospital.'

'Oh, right,' Terry said deflated. 'You er, you couldn't give em a quick jostle while ar'm ear could ya.'

'I'm sorry,' the doctor said, backing away, 'I have another patient in a couple of minutes. Good luck Dee.'

'Yeah fanks,' Dee Dee said, fending off her fussing friends.

Rounding the corner of their street with Terry in tow, Trisha heard the familiar sound of the Ross's ice cream van. 'Oooooh can we get an ice cream Dee, ohh please Dee, ar wanna ninety nine wiv sprinkles. Dee, can we, can we?'

'Oh flippin ell,' Dee Dee moaned. 'Well, you aint gonna bloody shut up until ya get one are ya.'

'But ar really want one,' Trisha cried, bobbing on the spot.

'Go on then,' Dee Dee said, in no mood to argue. 'TEL, D'YOU WAN AN ICE CREAM MATE?' she called back.

'NAAH LEAVE OFF!' Terry replied, with two carrier bags at his side, one from the Indian takeaway and the other from the cut price off license. 'AR DON'T EAT THAT SHIT, AR'M ON AN ELF KICK.'

'Yeah, looks like it,' Dee Dee smirked.

'Wod you want Maize?' Trisha asked, checking that the van was still there.

'Ohhhh get us a Fab,' Maizie replied. 'If they aint got wunna them ar'll av a feast.'

'Ow abaat'chu Dee?' Trisha asked, checking the van again.

'Urry up e'z gonna go!'
'Ar don't want nuffing,' Dee Dee said, handing Trisha a ten pound note. 'Just get what'cha want.'
'Ohh fanks!' Trisha said, her eyes lighting up. 'ANG ON, ANG ON!' she called to the driver. 'WAAAAAAAAIT, AR'M COMIIIIIIN!'
'Look at that dopey cow,' Dee Dee laughed, watching their friend sprinting with the note in the air. 'She aint changed a bloody bit since the day ar met er.'
Trisha rejoined her friends at their gate with her hands full.
'What'cha got there?' Dee Dee asked, counting six ice creams and Maizie's Fab lolly. 'Ar said ar never wanted one.'
'Ar dint get'cha one,' Trisha replied, licking the cream which was running down the side of her hand. 'These a for me, well you did say get what'ch like, you aint got no change by the way. I owe im a paand, ar said ar see im next time.'
Trisha proceeded to lick each ice cream in turn to prevent them running, but this proved futile and as the entered the street door the ice cream was already nearing her elbow. 'Urry up Maize!' she said, getting herself into quite a state and following close behind her friends on the stairs. 'Open the bloody door!'
'Serves ya right ya greedy bitch,' Maizie laughed, taking her time fumbling for the keys.
'Oh Maizie, don't take the piss,' Trisha cried, licking furiously. 'Ury up will ya!'
When Maizie did eventually turn the correct key, Trisha barged past her friends smearing them with whipped ice cream and dashed through to the kitchen, where she rammed the melted cones into the freezer and proceeded to lick her coated arms clean.
'Oh flippin ell Trish!' Maizie moaned, checking the arm of her jacket. 'Look what'cha bleedin done, iss all up your arse an'all Dee.'
'Oh so what,' Dee Dee said unfazed. 'It don't matter.'
'Yeah see,' Trisha scoffed in Maizie's direction, 'it don't matter.'

'Ar'll give you don't matter,' Maizie barked, retrieving a wad of toilet tissue and dabbing her jacket. 'Ar just bleedin bought this.'

Terry came in moments later out of breath. 'Fuuuck me, them stairs are a bleedin nightmare,' he puffed, setting his bags down on the table.

'You wanna get some exercise Tel,' Dee Dee laughed, 'look at'cha, ow old are ya?'

'Firty eight,' Terry wheezed, taking his cigarette packet from his pocket.

'You aint smokin that in ear Tel!' Maizie barked. 'Not in fronta Dee, and Dee you aint avin no more eeva, d'you ear me!'

'To be onest,' Dee Dee replied, 'ar don't really fancy one.'

'Ohh Maize ar gotta av an oily rag,' Terry said, still very much out of breath. 'Iss good for me breevin.'

'Well ang yer ed aat the winda,' Maizie told him abruptly. 'Coz you aint doin it in ear and thas that.'

'Yeah alright,' Terry said, sliding the bay window sash up and lighting up. 'Corrr thas better,' he said, coughing and spluttering.

'You did say firty eight dint'cha Tel,' Maizie mocked. 'More like ninety eight mate!'

'Oh shut up Maize!' Terry said, standing and cracking his head on the window above. 'Shit bollocks!' he cursed, then clung to his aching back. 'Cor blimey ar shouldn'ta got up so bleedin quick.'

'You were sayin Tel,' Maizie smirked. 'Wanna cuppa tea Dee?' she asked her friend, joining Trisha in the kitchen. 'Looka the bleedin state of you!' she laughed, seeing Trisha wrestling with the kitchen roll.

'What?' Trisha said, getting herself into a sticky state.

Dee Dee opted for an early night once again, while Terry gorged himself on his takeaway and her girlfriends sat at the table wringing their hands. 'What we gonna do Maize?' Trisha asked in a hushed tone. 'Dee proper aint well is she.'

'Ar know that ya doughnut,' Maizie whispered. 'We just

gotta look after er aint we, you gotta stop fuckin up all the bleedin time coz she don't flippin need it.'
Maizie may as well have been asking the sun not to rise in the morning and the tide not to turn, Trisha was Trisha and that was that.
'Ar do me bestest,' Trisha promised. 'Ar promise Maize.'
Maizie had grave reservations herself as to Trisha's ability to change her spots overnight. 'Ar believe that when ar see it,' she scoffed. 'We just gotta make sure she aint left on er own too long any time, thas all.'
'Oh right,' Trisha said, rising from the table. 'Shall ar go get in wiv er naah then.'
'No!' Maizie barked. 'Give er a break will ya, a'rm gunna go to bed naah anyway so ar'll see to er, you bugger off in yer own room. And Dee Dee said no cryin so just you remember that, OK?'
'It ain easy Maize,' Trisha told her friend. 'Me art feels like iss gonna explode sometimes, ar carn elp it.'
'Well you better elp it!' Maizie said, pointing a finger. 'Coz if you upset er ar'll swing for ya ar swear it.'
'OK,' Trisha said sheepishly, 'night Maize.' She trudged through to her own room with her head down.
'Trish,' Maizie called after her feeling somewhat guilty. 'Night mate.'
'Oh yeah!' Trisha said, turning with a smile. 'Night Maize mate, see you in the mawnin yeah.'
'Yeah whateva,' Maizie smirked. 'Seeya. Night Tel,' she said, waving to their bloated friend on the sofa, as he cracked open another can of super strength lager.
'Yeah night Maize girl,' Terry replied. 'Listen babe if you need a bitta man love in the night you know where I am yeah.'
'Not likely Tel,' Maizie smiled. 'But fanks for the offer mate.'
'What abaat'chu Trish?' Terry said, pushing his luck to the extreme. 'Ar know ya battin for the uvver side but ar reckon ar could straighten you aat, no probs.'
'Tel,' Trisha said, pausing at her door. 'Ar'd rarva shit in a

bag and punch it mate.'

Terry sat aghast with absolutely no comeback to Trisha's crass remark, apart from, 'Oh, alright.'

The following morning the girls rose for work as usual.

'Dee what you doin up mate?' Maizie asked. 'You aint gotta go to work, you aint well mate, stay in bed and relax.'

'Fuck that,' Dee Dee said, dressing.

'Ar gotta go in, what abaat Bonnie and Alice, whose gonna look after them? Iss bad enough I aint bin there all bleedin weekend.'

'Leave it Dee,' Maizie replied, urging her friend to forgo her compassionate duties. 'Someone else can sort em aat, they aint your problem mate.'

'They!' Dee Dee snapped. 'Them poor fuckers depend on me, they love me an ar love them, they aint got nuffing else. Besides ar love lookin after em, ar never fought ar would when we started there, but ar really do. D'you know Alice goes to the day room naah all by erself, and Bonnie, God love er, she's learned to write. Some of er poems are bloody brilliant they are, ar'm gonna elp er get em published. No, ar'm goin in and you aint gonna stop me.'

'Alright Dee,' Maizie relented. 'If you're sure mate.'

'Oh fuckin ell look,' Dee Dee said, opening the bedroom door and seeing Terry sprawled on the sofa in his underpants, with one leg on the floor and one hand cupping his privates. 'Looka the state of that!'

'Jesus!' Maizie exclaimed. 'Thas enough to put you off cock for life that is.'

'Thas why ar went lez,' Trisha said, overhearing her friends and emerging from her room in full uniform. 'Dee mate, why you goin to work, you aint well babe.'

'Don'tchu start!' Dee Dee snapped, buttoning her coat.

'Well lemmy do ya some breakfast before ya go Dee,' Maizie told her friend. 'You need summink inside ya mate.'

Dee Dee peered over the back of the sofa at the snoring Terry, with the majority of the chicken biryani he had

bought on the way home plastered around his mouth. 'No fanks,' she said, losing any appetite she may have had instantly. 'I ain ungry.'
'Yeah but Dee mate!' Trisha said, approaching her friend. 'You gotta keep ya strenf up.'
'Trisha!' Dee Dee snapped. 'Sod off to work will ya.'
There was the honking of a horn outside and Trisha dashed to the window. 'Yeah thas Adrian, ar gotta go anyway,' she planted a kiss on Dee Dee's cheek. 'Will you be alright?' she asked lovingly.
'Yeeeees!' Dee Dee said, shoving her off. 'Go on, bugger off will ya.'
'She's just worried abaat'cha,' Maizie said, watching Trisha leave and oddly enough taking her side. 'We bofe ar.'
'Yeah ar know that,' Dee Dee agreed. 'But seriously Maize, ar'm alright onest. Come on, less go ar gotta elp Bonnie wiv er poems.'

Trisha climbed in beside Adrian with less gusto than usual.
'Morning Trisha,' Adrian said, upbeat. 'I trust you had a good weekend.'
'Yeah,' Trisha replied, with her head bowed. 'Yeah, well sort of.'
'Oh dear,' Adrian said, sensing a problem. 'Why, what's wrong?'
'Me mate's got cancer,' Trisha said, unable to control herself. 'Ar'm not spozed to say nuffing but ar carn elp it, iss doin me ed in.'
'Oh no,' Adrian gasped, taking Trisha's hand. 'How awful, I'm truly sorry to hear that Trisha. Look, if you want to stay at home I'll cover for you, it's not a problem I assure you, if you want to be with your friend I mean.'
'Naaah,' Trisha replied. 'Fanks Ade mate, but Dee's goin into work erself, ar dunno why ar tried to stop er, but she's a stubborn bitch at times when she wants to be. So ard rarva be aat the ouse meself, keepin busy, nart ar mean.'
'Yes, yes I fully understand,' Adrian said sympathetically.

'Well, if you feel you need to talk I'm here,' he added.
No matter how much trouble Trisha had caused him ever since they had met, Adrian had warmed to her. He would wake with a smile each morning, apprehensive but also intrigued as to what the day may bring. His partner of some twenty years, Simone, had also noticed a change in him, a change for the better.
'If you're sure,' Adrian asked, starting the engine of their new gleaming van.
'Yeah come on,' Trisha said, sitting up in her seat. 'Less av it!'
'Thaaat's the spirit,' Adrian smiled.

Dee Dee and Maizie left Terry breaking wind and snoring loudly on the sofa, with a note saying *help yourself to whatever you want* at his side.
'D'you sleep alright?' Maizie asked, as they descended the stairs.
'Sleep?' Dee Dee scoffed. 'Woss that?'
'Ohhh Deeee,' Maizie said, concerned.

After a call to a high rise block in Peckham to attend to reports of a cockatiel loose in the lift lobby, which Adrian retrieved by tossing his jacket over the frantic bird, the two animal wardens were later making their way along the dual carriageway at Stratford E15 towards the Bow flyover. When suddenly the traffic ahead of them slowed to a near standstill and a plume of smoke could be seen rising into the air from an adjacent abandoned furniture manufacturers.
'Oh woss appnin naah?' Trisha asked, leaning from her window.
The police were on the scene, awaiting the arrival of the fire brigade and diverting traffic onto the opposite carriageway, which on a Monday created utter chaos. Having moved only a matter of feet in almost ten minutes Trisha threw open the door. 'Ar'm gunna walk up there Ade,' she said. 'Ar see ya when ya get there.'

'Trisha is that wise?' Adrian asked.
'Yeeeeah course,' Trisha said, slamming her door and striding towards the scene where a crowd of inquisitive local residents were gathered. 'Woss appnin?' she asked, muscling between them to the police cordon.
'Kids!' one disgruntled elderly man said. 'Ar've bin ringin the police abbat em for weeks I av. They've bin campin in there of a night smokin their whacky backy and all sorts.'
'Ohhh riiight,' Trisha said unfazed.
'Noisy bastards,' another resident complained. 'Playin their ravin shit at all times of the night.'
Trisha stood watching the towering flames flicking from the factory windows, looking over her shoulder periodically at the queue of traffic and Adrian in the distance.
'It's the dogs ar feel sorry for,' a chain smoking lady then said, causing Trisha to prick up her ears.
'Dogs!' Trisha said, turning sharply. 'What dogs?'
'Ar dunno what they are,' the lady replied, dropping a butt and stamping on it before tugging another cigarette from her packet. 'But ar seen em from me winda goin in and aat every night. I aint seen em come aat this mawnin mind.'
'Oh yeah ar seen them,' another resident remarked. 'Shitzu's ar think they are.'
'DO WHAT?' Trisha cried, leaping over the cordon. 'OY, OY MATE!' she yelled at the two police officers standing guard outside the blazing building. 'You seen a coupla dogs come aata there?'
'Dogs!' one of them replied. 'No love, not this way.'
'RSPCA!' Trisha informed them, flashing her identification. 'We gotta go in an av a look.'
'I'm sorry Miss that's out of the question,' the second officer said, barring the way. 'It's not safe. Look the fire's out of control. I can't let you go in there it's more than my job's worth. The fire brigade are on their way if the dogs are alive they'll find them.'
Trisha looked at the heavily congested road ahead. 'They aint never gettin fru that lot,' she complained. 'The poor

little bleedas'll burn to deff before they get ear.'
'I'm sorry miss,' the officer said, ushering Trisha back toward the cordon. 'Judging by the size of this fire I doubt there's anything alive in there. I know it's a shame, I'm an animal lover myself, but it's just not worth the risk.'
'Iss always werf the bloody risk!' Trisha barked, getting nowhere. 'Just lemmy av a quick look, please!'
'No sorry,' the officer said, a little more forcefully this time. 'Now if you'll please get back behind the tape I'd appreciate it.'
Trisha looked up at the raging inferno as she sloped reluctantly back toward the crowd, but then she heard a faint whimper from somewhere inside. 'D'YOU EAR THAT?' she asked, turning back. 'I ERD SUMMINK IN THERE!'
'No,' the officers both said, shaking their heads.
'YEAH!' Trisha said, darting back to them. 'Ar did, ar fink it was the dogs, we gotta go get em!' She tried to break past them but was immediately restrained.
'Look Miss!' one of them said angrily. 'I've told you no one's going in there, not until the brigade have put out the fire and made the building safe. Now get back behind the line, I won't tell you again.'
'But, but,' Trisha pleaded, 'just let me av a look, I erd em ar tell ya!'
'I said no!' the officer barked. 'This is the last time I'm going to tell you.'
'Alright, alright!' Trisha said, shrugging them off and looking up at the smoke filled sky. Suddenly the sound of a fire engine siren could be heard some way away attempting to creep through the heavy traffic. The officers turned to catch a glimpse of the approaching appliance turning their backs on Trisha who, seizing the moment, ran toward the open factory door.
'OY!' one of the police officers yelled, catching sight of her out of the corner of his eye. 'GET BACK HERE!' But Trisha covered her mouth unflinching and darted into the blackened building. 'HEY MISS, MISS COME BACK!' the

officer cried, starting after her but stopping at the door. 'MISS!'
He was joined by his colleague. 'GET BACK HERE NOW THAT'S AN ORDER!' he too barked. Reluctant to enter, and following police protocol, the two officers backed away, radioing the fire department telling them to hurry and that there were now persons inside the building. But the engine was making little headway, despite the screaming sirens and calls from the fire crew to get out of the way.
'Shit,' Trisha said, looking around frantically inside the smoke filled warehouse, the heat hitting her instantly. 'EAR BOY!' she yelled, cowering. 'EAR DOGGY, COME EAR!' She then heard the whimper again coming from somewhere up on the first floor. Whistling with streaming eyes she leapt the stairs two at a time, dodging from side to side to avoid the burning floor boards. 'WHERE ARE YA?' she called, coughing and attempting another whistle, but the searing heat had dried any moisture from her mouth. 'OH FUCK!' she then cried, leaping clear of a blazing timber which fell from the vaulted ceiling. It was at this point Trisha realized she may have bitten off a little more than she could chew and had been overly foolhardy entering the building, and considered turning back, but a faint barking spurred her on. 'Come on Trish,' she said, pulling herself together, and her lapel over her face. 'You can do this shit.'
The fire had well and truly taken hold and all hope of saving the building were now lost. 'EAR DOGGY!' Trisha called, dropping her lapel occasionally and leaping the burning boards. Again she heard the whimper and darted into a side room, dropping to her knees to avoid the choking smoke. With limited vision and stinging eyes Trisha rummaged on the litter covered floor, tossing beer bottles and fast food containers aside. 'Where are ya?' she called, coughing repeatedly and tearing the knee of her trouser leg. Yet another whimper led her in the direction of a smouldering work bench. 'There you are,' she said, catching sight of a ball of smoking fur quivering against the back wall. 'Ear boy!' she

called, reaching out. On closer inspection, whilst sheltering beneath the bench herself while burning debris rained down from the ceiling, Trisha saw that it was in fact two Bijon Frise brothers. 'Come on you two,' she said, making a grab for them, but one of them growled and huddled with its kin. 'Wossa matter boy?' Trisha asked, edging closer and wiping the tears from her blackened cheeks. 'Iss alright mate, shhhh, shhhh.' The vocal dog retreated further and refused to leave the others side. 'Come on you two, less get'chu aat of ear,' she said, but then noticed that one lay motionless with charred fur, having succumbed to the billowing smoke. 'Ohhhhh no,' she sighed, placing a hand on its side and getting no pulse. Its brother immediately nipped at Trisha's hand. 'Iss alright,' Trisha said, reaching to stroke its head, despite it baring its teeth at her. 'Ay, ay iss alright mate.' The snarling Bijon nestled closer to its deceased brother, nudging him with its nose in a futile attempt to rouse him. 'Ar'm sorry mate,' Trisha said, stroking the corpse. 'E'z gone, we gotta go, come on.' With a defiant bark the Bijon lay across its older brother's lifeless body licking at his face. This tugged at Trisha's heart strings, but the sound of crashing timbers all around brought a renewed sense of urgency.

The crowd outside surged forward having seen Trisha enter the building and not return. 'YOU GOTTA GET ER AAT!' one resident yelled at the confused officers. 'WHAT YOU WAITIN FOR?' One by one her neighbours too voiced their opinions, and called up at the flame filled windows. 'COME AAT, LADY COME AAT!' they cried. The two officers fumbled with their radios having only been with the force a matter of months. 'YOU CAN'T LEAVE ER IN THERE!' they were barracked.
Trisha realizing the situation was becoming desperate, and the chance of her perishing with the dogs increasing with every wasted minute, made a grab for the living brother sustaining one or two bites in the process. 'CAALM DAAAN!' she cried, wrestling with the wriggling hound. 'Shh shh calm daaaan, ar know ya wanna stay but ar can't let'cha.'

Ramming the bereaved Bijon down inside her coat, and patting his brother tenderly, Trisha turned and wriggled from beneath the bench. 'Fuuuuck!' she gasped, seeing her exit was now a wall of ferocious flames, the heat from which forcing her back. 'Shit, shit!' she cried, fanning her face and shoving the Bijon's bobbing head down over and over. She was soon backed against a partition office wall with burning embers raining down all around her. 'Bugger!' she cursed. 'ELLLLLLLLP!'

The fire brigade was now fast approaching and was waved onto the forecourt by the two officers. 'There's a girl in there!' one of them cried, as the fire crew leapt from their appliance. 'Hurry, there's a girl in there, we tried to stop her but she got past us.'

'RIGHT, GET THE HOSES READY!' the superintendent yelled. 'AND SUIT UP DOUBLE QUICK!'

While the fire crew hurriedly donned their breathing apparatus, Trisha cowered against the wall batting glowing embers from her hair. 'Shit fuuuuuck!' she cried, clinging to the barking Bijon beneath her coat. 'YEAH AR KNOW!' she said, pushing back against the dividing wall which gave a little. Spinning Trisha pushed at the flimsy plasterboard divider then began kicking out frantically, cracking the boards without a great deal of effort. 'YA, YA!' she screamed, lashing out with flames rapidly approaching behind her. Soon she had created a hole big enough for her to stoop and crawl through. On the other side she found herself in the abandoned factory's offices which, although not ablaze at that point, were still thick with smoke which seeped between the gaping boards.

Choking now, Trisha distanced herself from the encroaching flames stumbling over discarded filing cabinets and swivel chairs.

'READY!' the superintendent told his crew, leading them through the main entrance as their hoses were livened with water. The ground floor was now completely ablaze and gave the huddled fire crew a mammoth task to bring it under some semblance of control, but the rest of the building was all but lost.

The residents clung to one another now, rooted to the spot, united in hope and horror as Adrian arrived on the scene.

'Triiiish!' he called. 'TRISHAAAA!' He scanned the crowd for signs of his partner. 'Excuse me,' he asked a bystander, 'have you seen a girl in a uniform like mine?'

'Yeah, she's in there mate,' the man told Adrian, pointing up at the blazing building. 'She run in there a while ago and aint come back aat.'

'WHAT?' Adrian cried, clasping a hand to his head. 'Are you serious?'

'Yes mate,' a woman beside him added, 'she went in there for the dogs.'

'Dogs!' Adrian asked, beside himself with dread. 'What dogs?'

'Two dogs sleep in there of a night,' another voice called out. 'She just run in there to get em, the nut case.'

'Oh my God!' Adrian gasped, staggering back. 'What, no, not in there. TRISHAAAAAAA, TRISHAAAAAAAAA!'

Trisha could hear nothing but the sound of breaking glass and crackling flames. 'Elllllllllp!' she called out in a blind panic.

'UPSTAIRS SIR!' one of the fire crew members yelled, aiming his hose at the burning staircase, but before they could ascend the entire fight of stairs collapsed showering the crew with burning fragments.

'BACK, GET BACK!' the superintendent barked, shoving his men toward the door seeing no alternative with the roof beams ablaze above them. 'OUT, EVERYBODY OUT. NOW!'

'BUT SIR!' a crew member said, hesitating, 'THE GIRL'S UP THERE!'

'I KNOW!' the chief replied, pushing him back too. 'WE'LL HAVE TO USE THE LADDER, NOW GET THE HELL BACK WILL YOU!' Reluctantly the fire crew retreated back outside.

'WHERE IS SHE?' Adrian yelled, clambering over the cordon and rushing to confront the firemen. 'Where's Trisha for

christ sake?'
'I'm sorry sir, it's not safe for you to be here,' the superintendent said, intervening. 'Now please get back behind the line.'
'Where's Trisha?' Adrian asked again. 'Where is she?'
'We're going to use the ladders to try to reach her,' the chief told Adrian. 'It's our only hope now I'm afraid, the entire ground floor is impassible. Now please be patient.'
'PATIENT!' a member of the public nearby called. 'SHE AINT GOT TIME FOR THAT. GET ER AAT FOR GODS SAKE!'
Suddenly a huge section of the factory's roof caved in with a resounding crash, the residents gasped clutching their chests and crossing their hearts, some turning away fearing the worst.
'MAN THE LADDERS!' the superintendent barked, looking up at the blazing windows and shaking his head in despair. His crew raised the three triple ladders against the smoking building wall and raced to the top, hoses in hand, pouring gallon after gallon of water onto the ever increasing flames.
'Oh dear God no,' one elderly resident said helplessly. 'God no. That poor child.'
Huddled together willing the flames to recede, the residents - many in tears and Adrian too for that matter - were joined by motorists who had abandoned their vehicles. 'There's a girl in there!' they were told. 'She just ran in after the dogs!'
'That's my Trisha,' Adrian said, his hands clasped in prayer.
'Call for an ambulance,' the superintendent told the police officers, fearing a fatality. 'Hurry man!'
Trisha having sustained several burns to her hands and face, clung to her jacket with one hand and shoved furniture aside with the other. The remaining roof timbers above her groaned under mounting pressure and began to subside. 'Shit, shit, shit!' she said, looking up and cowering with an arm across her face. One by one the timbers tore free and fell toward her 'Arrrrrrrgh fuck!' she screamed, as a hefty burning beam crashed through the floor beside her leaving a gaping hole, exposing the hellish ground floor below. 'Shit,

sorry mate,' she said to the quivering Bijon in her jacket. 'Ar tried.'

Backing into a corner helplessly choking, while the fire crew fought desperately to gain access to the first floor, Trisha felt something sharp dig into her back. Reaching behind with almost zero visibility she immediately scolded her hand on a scorching metal bar. 'Arrrrgh bugger!' she cursed shaking her hand, but on closer inspection she saw that it was the panic bar on a fire exit door. 'Fank fuck,' she gasped, backing toward the flames which now leapt through the battered floor and kicking out, but the door having been painted shut numerous times and rarely used, was stuck fast. 'SHIT!' she cursed, kicking over and over screaming obscenities. 'OPEN YA BASTARD, FUCKIN OPEN!'

Looking over her shoulder, and getting a blast of heat on her face which reduced her eyelashes to shriveled stumps, her breath was sucked from her smoke filled lungs. 'COME ON FOR FUCK SAAAAAAAAAKE!' she cried, kicking with every fibre remaining.

With an aggressive grunt, and the soul of her boot now melting from the near glowing bar, Trisha gave it her all until finally the door flung open and the light from outside flooded in.

'LOOK!' a resident gasped, pointing up at the top of the fire escape on the side of the building, seeing Trisha emerge in a swirling cloud of thick black billowing smoke. 'IT'S HER. IT'S THE GIRL!' A resounding gasp rang out throughout the crowd as she staggered onto the wrought iron landing.

'YES, YES, FUCKIN YEEEEEEES!' a group of builders cheered, having leapt from their van to join the onlookers. 'COME ON GIRL. COME ON BABY!'

Trisha stood sucking in lungfuls of air and spitting the soot from her mouth for a moment, looking down inside her jacket at the frightened dog within, before shakily descending the stairs.

A single resident began a slow clap with a tear strewn face, which soon multiplied a hundred fold to a thunderous

applause. 'YEEEEEEEEES, OH MY GOD YEEEEEEEEES!' they called. 'IT'S THE GIRL, IT'S THE GIRL!'
Adrian himself broke down and sobbed uncontrollably into his shaking hands. 'Thank you, thank you,' he said, looking to the heavens. Cameras and cell phones clicked furiously, capturing her selfless act of heroism first hand. Three firemen raced to the foot of the stairs to greet her. 'Thank God!' one of them sighed. 'What the hell were you doing in there?' Trisha coughed and merely unbuttoned her jacket and removed the charred Bijon, to a resounding cheer which grew in intensity until the fire crew and police officers applauded her too.
'Let me take him,' a fireman said, attempting to prise the dog from her hands.
'NO!' Trisha snapped with a dry throat. 'E stays wiv me!'
'OK love, OK,' the fireman said, seeing the ferocity in her streaming eyes.
'E stays wiv me,' Trisha reiterated, kissing the Bijons face several times. 'Don'tcha mate.'
'Amazin,' one lady wept. 'Absolutely amazin.'
Ambulance crew members ran to clasp an oxygen mask over Trisha's mouth, examining her obvious burns. 'Let's get you to the hospital,' one of them told her, summoning the trolley. Trisha was laid out and led toward the waiting ambulance, refusing at each request to relinquish the tiny dog whose brother had so sadly perished. 'E goes wiv me ar said!' she snapped, batting their hands away.
'OK, OK love,' one of them said, placing a child's mask over the dogs snout. The two of them were loaded into the ambulance with the ecstatic crowd refusing to let up on their appreciative applause. Adrian burst from the crowd and ran to the ambulance as the doors were being closed. 'WAIT!' he cried. 'WAIT PLEASE. Just give me a moment will you,' climbing in beside the trolley he looked down on the sorry blackened sight. 'My God!' he gasped. 'Look at you.'
'Alright Ade,' Trisha mumbled, beneath the mask whilst clinging to the Bijon, which now nestled in her chest. 'Ar got

one of em mate, but the uvver ones a gonna ar'm afraid.'
'God Trisha, you had us all so worried,' Adrain said, taking her bandaged hand. 'You had me so worried, what on earth possessed you?'
Trisha simply raised the dog. 'Im,' she said wheezing. 'Thas what we do ain it.'
'Yes Trish,' Adrian said, his heart filled with pride. 'Yes it is, but some more than others.'
'Excuse me sir,' an ambulance man said, hovering at the door. 'We really have to go.'
'I'll see you at the hospital,' Adrian said, patting Trisha's leg on leaving. 'And well done, well done you.'
With sirens blaring and a police escort, Trisha was driven to the nearest hospital and rushed to the burns unit still clutching the dog she had so gallantly, and some would say foolishly, saved.
The fire crews eventually brought the inferno under control with the factory all but ruined. The overjoyed crowd dispersed, chatting amongst themselves of Trisha's bravery, with the soon to be iconic images shared around the globe.

Dee Dee and Maizie were sat in the staff kitchen sipping lattes with their feet up, oblivious to Trisha's trials and tribulations.
'You aint said nuffing av ya Maize?' Dee Dee said, dunking a digestive.
'Naah course not,' Maizie replied, blowing her steaming mug. 'You told me not to din'tcha.'
'Ar don't want Bonnie or Alice frettin,' Dee Dee told her friend. 'So iss best if we keep schtum abaat it, alright.'
'Yeah whateva ya want mate,' Maizie said, checking the clock above the door. 'Ar gotta get back Dee,' she added, 'me and the kids are makin kites this afternoon.'
'Nice one,' Dee Dee said, rising to place her mug in the sink. 'Ar'm gonna try and get Bonnie aat in the garden.'
'Yeah good luck wiv that,' Maizie smirked, having heard of Bonnie's agoraphobia.

Later that afternoon, whilst Maizie and the children constructed crude kites and decorated them, Dee Dee summoned Bonnie to the window in her room. 'Bonnie mate, ear,' she said, pulling the net curtain aside. 'Ar bet'cha you could write some lovely poems abaat that lot aat there ay. Look there's a robin over there and all them beautiful flaaas.'

Bonnie looked apprehensively around the edge of the window. 'Not for Bonnie,' she said, shaking her head. 'Not for Bonnie.'

'But look at them beautiful roses,' Dee Dee said, coaxing her further. 'Wouldn't you like to smell em, ar bet they smell gawjus.'

'No, not for Bonnie,' Bonnie said repeatedly. 'No.'

'Well what abaat for me?' Dee Dee asked. 'Would ya do it for me?

'For Dee?' Bonnie asked.

'Yeah,' Dee Dee smiled, 'for Dee Dee. Would you come aatside for me?'

Bonnie looked both at Dee Dee and the garden several times before nodding. 'For Dee,' she said, biting at the corner of her finger.

'OK, less get ya coat on then,' Dee Dee said, taking Bonnie's duffle coat from her wardrobe, which had seldom been worn, save for the occasional hospital visit. 'There we go,' Dee Dee smiled, buttoning the toggles up under Bonnie's chin. 'I ad wunna these when ar was a littlun ar did, proper warm aint they. Right ya ready?'

Bonnie looked out of the window once again, filled with trepidation.

'Itta be alright,' Dee Dee reassured her. 'Ar'll be wiv ya.'

Bonnie followed Dee Dee out into the corridor and immediately stopped. 'Come on mate,' Dee Dee urged. 'You'll love it ar promise, for Dee Dee yeah.'

'For Dee?' Bonnie asked again.

'Yeah thas right,' Dee Dee replied, taking her hand and leading the reluctant resident step by tentative step. 'For

Dee Dee.'

Soon the two of them were at the rear french doors. 'Ready?' Dee Dee asked, with one hand on the latch.

'For Dee,' Bonnie said, taking a deeper breath. Dee Dee turned the brass latch and swung the pair of doors outward, but Bonnie immediately took a step back, startled by the brisk breeze that ruffled her hair. 'Iss alright,' Dee Dee said, placing a hand on Bonnie's back. 'Come on, ar got'cha.' Leading Bonnie over the threshold and out into the centre's garden, Dee Dee delighted in seeing the myriad of changing expressions on her face; like when she felt the course grass beneath her sandaled feet for the first time in over a decade, then on seeing a pair of magpie's squabbling over a rotten apple core. 'You like birds?' Dee Dee asked.

'Bird,' Bonnie smiled, tilting her head to one side. 'Bird!'

'Magpies,' Dee Dee told her. 'They're magpies they are.'

'Mag pie.' Bonnie said, holding out her hand and approaching the birds which hopped away. 'Mag pie.'

'Yeah thas right,' Dee Dee smiled. 'Magpies, and thas a blackbird, ar fink.'

Bonnie ran her hand through a clump of flowering lavender, disturbing the bees foraging for pollen within. Dee Dee sat on one of the centre's teak benches and watched the reclusive resident on her voyage of discovery.

Grabbing at a beautiful floribunda rose Bonnie cried out and ran to Dee Dee, having grasped its fearsome thorns. 'Deeeeee Deeeeeee!' she screeched, shaking her hand.

'Iss alright, iss alright,' Dee Dee said, removing the three thorns using her teeth and spitting them out. 'There ya go Bonnie mate, watch aat for the roses they got forns on em.'

Bonnie ran back to the red and yellow roses and hung her nose over the fragrant blooms. 'Niiiice,' she said, taking in the heady scent. 'Niiiiiiice Dee.'

Richard, the centre's manager, caught sight of the two of them from the staff room window and called Maizie. 'Look!' he said in awe. 'How on earth did she manage that?'

'What?' Maizie asked, looking over his shoulder.

'Bonnie!' Richard replied. 'She hasn't been outside in God knows how long, the staff had tried to coax her, but she's been adamant.'
'Thas Dee for ya,' Maizie said, watching her friend fondly, and seeing the joy on her face. 'She's bloody marvlus she is.'
'Yes, Bonnie has really taken to her,' Richard explained. 'It's really quite uncanny, Alice too for that matter. Your friend has a unique gift Maizie.'
Maizie hung her head, her lip quivering.
'What's wrong?' Richard asked. 'Maizie what's wrong?'
'Ar can't say,' Maizie said, keeping true to her word. 'All ar know is ar love er, an ar don't ever wanna lose er,' several tears trickled down her crimson cheeks.
'Maizie what is it, please,' Richard persisted. 'Maybe I can help.'
'No you can't,' Maizie sobbed, clutching the window sill and resting her forehead on the frame in despair. 'There aint nuffing you can do Richard, nuffing.'
Richard put a consolatory arm around Maizie's shoulder. 'Hey, hey,' he said, attempting to sooth her. 'Hey, come on it can't be that bad, can it?'
Maizie suddenly confronted Richard. 'Ow bloody bad d'you reckon cancer is then, ay, ay?'
'Oh my God I'm so sorry,' Richard said, holding up both hands. 'Maizie honestly I didn't... I mean, I don't know what to say.'
Maizie despite having promised Dee Dee whole heartedly that she would not cry, broke down at the window turning away as her friend looked across in her direction. 'Me and Trisha can't lose er,' she said, falling into Richard's chest and gripping his pullover. 'We can't Rich we can't.'
'Look, she's a strong woman,' Richard said, in an attempt to ease her suffering, 'and a real fighter no doubt, Maizie. Maizie?' he said, lifting her chin to look her in the eye. 'I'm sure everything will be alright, and for the record we don't want to lose her either.'
'Fanks,' Maizie sobbed, unable to catch a breath. 'Fanks

Rich,' she looked up into his huge hazel eyes, and in a brief moment of grief and insecurity stood on her tip toes and kissed him; not just a friendly peck, a lingering kiss lasting several seconds. 'Oh shit ar'm sorry,' she said, pulling away. 'Rich mate ar'm really sorry, ar dunno why ar done that.'

'It's alright,' Richard smiled. 'Really, it's OK. I just wasn't expecting it that's all, I mean I like you and everything but...'

This was enough for Maizie, she clasped her hands either side of his face and lunged in for a full on smooch, catching him off balance. This time Richard responded, slipping his hands around her slender waist and pulling her toward him tightly, probing her mouth with his tongue, their breathing became erratic as the two locked lips over and over. 'Hold me tight,' Maizie pleaded, grabbing at his hair. 'Ar need ya,' she told him. 'God ar need someone, ar can't talk to Trisha she's mad as fuck.'

'I'm here,' Richard said, backing her from the window, still locked in a lustful embrace.

Before the pair disappeared out of sight Dee Dee caught a glimpse of the two of them locking lips yet again, she smiled and clenched a fist delighted for her friend, overjoyed in fact, aware of the heartache she must be going through and the anguish yet to come. 'Get in there girl,' she said under her breath, before turning back to Bonnie. 'What'cha got there mate?' she asked, approaching Bonnie who was marveling at the simple complexity of a maple leaf, holding it up to the light to view it's vein like structure. 'Lovely ain it,' Dee Dee said, taking a moment to look into Bonnie's eyes. Although she had been alive she had never lived, until now.

Bonnie flung her arms around Dee Dee. 'Love, love,' she said, kissing her cheek. 'Bonnie love.'

'Ahhhh, fanks,' Dee Dee said, taking the leaf as it was offered to her. 'Fanks a lot, ar love you too.'

'LOVE, LOVE, LOOOOOOVE!' Bonnie yelled, racing around the lawn skipping and jumping, tearing a bunch of marigolds from their stalks and after smelling them, tossing them high

into the air and watching them rain down toward her.
'THAS IT!' Dee Dee yelled. 'THAS IT BONNIE MATE, YOU GO BLOODY MENTAL, GO ON!' Dee Dee urged her to vent all her pent up frustration and scream at the heavens, exorcizing her demons once and for all.
'MUUUUUUUUUUUUUUUUUUUM!' Bonnie screamed red faced at the clouds above. 'WHYYYYYYYYYYYYY MUUUUUUUUUUM. WHYYYYYYYYYYYYY!' She then fell to her knees, and for a moment Dee Dee thought that she may have pushed her too far, but after pounding the turf three or four times with a clenched fist Bonnie relaxed and stood with her arms outstretched toward Dee Dee. 'Love?' she said, beckoning.
'Yeah, course ar will,' Dee Dee said, running to her and sweeping her from her feet. 'Ar'll always love ya.'
Inside Maizie and Richard were locked in a writhing embrace against the staffroom door, their hands exploring one anothers curves feverishly. 'I can't,' Richard said, breaking away momentarily. 'Not here.'
'Yeah OK,' Maizie agreed, then lunged again for another steamy kiss, her hand snaking down his torso to his bulging groin. 'Sorry, sorry,' she said, restraining herself although every ounce of her longed to drop to her knees and tear open his fly taking him in hand, and mouth for that matter.
'Shall we do this properly?' Richard asked. 'Dinner and drinks first and all that?'
'Naah fuck all that,' Maizie smiled cheekily, 'tell me where ya live an ar'll come raand jump ya bones.'
'Oh wow!' Richard said, his eyes lighting up. 'Er OK that would be quite pleasant I suppose.'
'Pleasant,' Maizie said, biting at his lip. 'Itta be fuckin erf shatterin.' A member of staff then attempted to gain access to the staffroom, forcing the two to hastily break their clinch and straighten their clothing.
'Yes OK Maizie,' Richard said officiously. 'If you could read with the children for the next hour it will settle them down quite nicely.'

'Yeah whateva,' Maizie smirked, giving his bottom a tweak out of sight of the orderly in passing. Richard cleared his throat and went about his business, shielding his bulging crotch which Maizie had so skillfully aroused.

For the remainder of the afternoon Dee Dee and Bonnie sat on the bench, Bonnie making the daisy chains that Dee Dee had shown her, while Dee Dee herself sat content and at peace.

'For Dee,' Bonnie said, placing a ring of flowers in Dee Dee's hair.

'Ahhhh fanks,' Dee Dee replied, checking her reflection in her phone. 'Ar love it.'

When the breeze that had soothed them, developed a chill, Dee Dee took Bonnie's hand. 'Come on mate,' she said, rising to leave. 'Less get'chu back inside.'

Hesitant Bonnie looked around the garden.

'Don't worry,' Dee Dee assured her. 'We can come back tomorra.'

Maizie stood waiting at the door, positively bursting at the seams. 'Dee, Dee ar got summink to tell ya!' she said, with the widest of grins.

'You're shaggin Richard,' Dee Dee said, wiping the smile from her friend's face.

'What, ay?' Maizie said, stunned. 'Ow d'you know that?'

'Ahhhhh,' Dee Dee smirked, 'there aint nuffing gets past me. Anyway ar'm appy for ya.'

'Oh fanks Dee,' Maizie said, hugging her friend. 'Ar mean I aint shaggin im yet, but ar'm definitely gonna. You alright Bonnie love, did you enjoy it in the garden?'

Bonnie nodded, handing Maizie a daisy bracelet. 'For me?' Maizie said, slipping it onto her wrist. 'Ohhh fanks Bonnie, thas gawjus that is.' She then turned back to her friend. 'Oh Dee, ya don't mind do ya, abaat Richard ar mean.'

'Naah course not,' Dee Dee told her. 'Like ar said ar'm proper appy for ya, ar mean it.'

After taking the tube home the two friends leapt back

startled across their threshold when confronted by a yapping Bijon.
'What the fuck?' Dee Dee gasped, then was startled even further when Trisha came scurrying after him, her hands and face heavily bandaged.
'What the fuck?' she and Maizie both cried.
'D'ya like im?' Trisha asked, scooping the dog up into her arms. 'E'z proper lovely, ar could eat im all up ar could,' she added, showering the pooch with kisses.
'What the fuck is that?' Dee Dee asked abruptly. 'And what the fuck appened to you?'
'Yeah Trisha!' Maizie added. 'What you gone and done naah?'
'Oh, ar got burned a bit,' Trisha said, shrugging off her injuries. 'But least ar got Rodney ay.'
'Rodney!' Dee Dee smirked.
'Yeah Rodders,' Trisha said, cuddling her new friend. 'Ar called im that coz e'z got the same dopey look abaat im as Del Boy's bruvva ain e, woja reckon?'
'Well, yeah ar can see what ya mean,' Maizie said, on closer inspection.
'Can ar keep im Dee, can I, can I, pleeeeeeeease?' Trisha begged. 'E aint got no one else coz Del Boy's dead.'
'What'chu on abaat?' Dee Dee asked, pushing past Trisha.
'There was two of em,' Trisha replied, following behind cradling Rodney. 'But the uvva one got burned to deff.'
'Ahhhhhh,' Maizie said, patting Rodney. 'Thas a shame ain it.'
'Can I, can I?' Trisha once again pleaded. 'Pleeeeeeeeease Dee, can I keep im?'
'Yessssss!' Dee Dee said.
'Ar wouldn't give a monkeys if ya brought a bloody elephant ome. Where's Tel anyway?'
'Oh, e'z gone to get some fags and lager,' Trisha explained. 'E should be back in a minute.'
'Put the kettle on Trish,' Maizie asked. 'Make Dee a cuppa, ar don't want one though coz ar'm goin aat soon.'

'What, where ya goin?' Trisha asked, watching her friend disappear into the bathroom.

'Shaggin,' Dee Dee told her.

'Shaggin!' Trisha exclaimed. 'Shaggin who?'

'Never you mind!' Maizie said, popping her head out from the bathroom having stripped to the waist. 'Now make Dee that bloody tea will ya!'

Rodney attempted to join Maizie in the bathroom. 'Oy piss off aat of it,' she said, scooting him out with her foot. 'Trisha if e shits on mar bed ar'm rubbin your nose in it, d'you ear me!'

Raised voices could then be heard downstairs as the Romanian husband was preparing to leave for another night of heavy drinking and gambling at his brother's house, taking with him every penny the family possessed.

'But we need to buy food!' Tatyana pleaded. 'And the children, look they both need new shoes.'

'Shut up bitch!' her husband barked, zipping his jacket. 'I will win the money for their shoes, you will see.'

'Win, huh!' Tatyana scoffed. 'You always say this, but you never win, you drink and come home with nothing. You are useless.'

'I SAID SHUT UP!' her husband yelled, lashing out and striking Tatyana across the side of her face with the back of his hand, knocking her to the floor.

'Mummy, Mummy!' her two children cried, rushing to her. But as always the grandparents remained seated in the lounge, just grateful for the roof above their heads.

'Wunna these fuckin days,' Trisha growled, listening to the commotion. 'Ar'm gonna taser the fuck aat of that wanker.'

'Ar wouldn't blame ya,' Dee Dee agreed, reclining on the couch.

Terry returned moments later, opening the street door using the key the girls had given him and was immediately confronted with Tatyana and her husband in the hallway. 'Pleaaaase!' she begged, clutching her swelling cheek. 'Please do not take all our money!' Her husband raised his

fist.
'OY!' Terry barked. 'Woss goin on ear?'
'None of your business English pig,' the Romanian said, looking over his shoulder with contempt. He then took hold of his wife by the throat and thrust her against the hallway wall. 'I said silence,' he snarled.
'Woju call me?' Terry said, dropping his two carrier bags at his side.
'Pig!' The Romanian reiterated, then began slapping his wife about the face with his free hand, whilst the children clung to her legs begging him to stop.
'Please, not in front of the children!' Tatyana cried, hoping to spare them the trauma.
'Oy you piece a shit!' Terry said, grabbing the Romanian's shoulder. 'You lay one more finger on er, an ar'll beat the shit aata ya.'
In an act of abject defiance the Romanian raised his hand higher and slapped Tatyana harder, jolting her head to the side before spitting in her face. 'I do what I want to my bitch,' he said, shaking her bodily.
'You reckon?' Terry barked, yanking the Romanian back against the opposite wall and ramming a clenched fist into his startled face. 'You like to it girls do ya, you werfless fuck!' Terry added. Before the Romanian could retaliate Terry poured on the punches. 'Av that you fuckin prick!' he said, reeling back and butting the husband's nose.
Dee Dee, Trisha and Maizie in her bath robe, ran to the top of the stairs. 'TEL!' Dee Dee called down. 'What'cha doin?'
'STAY THERE!' Terry yelled back, smashing another fist into the bloody Romanian's ribs. 'YOU FREE STAY THERE!'
It was obvious to the girls, seeing Tatyana slumped against the wall, why Terry was dishing out so menacingly his own form of divine retribution. 'Call me a pig will ya!' he snarled, planting the soul of his desert boot squarely on the side of the Romanian's face after he fell to the floor. 'You're the fuckin pig you wife batterin cunt!'
'GO ON TEL!' Trisha cried, punching the air. 'Kick iz fuckin ed

in!'

Terry looked round to see Tatyana's children looking on and ceased his onslaught, wrenching their father to his feet and marching him to the street door. 'Now you get the fuck aat!' he told him with gritted teeth. 'And if I ever catch you beatin your misses again ar'll cut'chu open you slag. D'you ear me!'

With this Terry shoved the battered Romanian out the door and watched him stumble to the ground. 'Go on, fuck off!' he barked, slamming the door.

'You alright love?' he then asked, helping Tatyana to her feet. 'You aint gotta put up wiv that bollocks ya know, ar know people that can urt im proper if ya nart ar mean.'

Tatyana of course didn't know what Terry meant, but was eternally grateful for his timely intervention. 'Thank you, thank you,' she said, kissing his cheek before herding her children back inside.

'YOU ALRIGHT TAT?' Trisha called down. Tatyana nodded and smiled up at her then disappeared.

'Nice one Tel,' Dee Dee said, greeting Terry at the top of the stairs.

'Yeah fanks mate,' Trisha added, planting another kiss on his cheek.

'Quality,' Maizie said, heading back to the bathroom following the trail of drips she had left.

Trisha made Dee Dee and Terry a cup of tea and waited on the two of them hand and foot.

'Ow do ar look?' Maizie asked, emerging from her bedroom having spent almost an hour preening herself for her dinner date at Richard's house.

'Fuckin orny,' Terry piped up. 'Ar definitely would if I ad the chance.'

'Cheers Tel ya dirty bleeda,' Maizie smiled.

'You look lovely mate,' Dee Dee said, approaching her friend. 'E'z a proper lucky bloke and you tell im ar said it an'all.'

'Ahhhh fanks mate,' Maizie said, hugging her friend. 'You sure you're gonna be alright, ar don't av to go if ya don't

want me to.'
'You're goin and thas that,' Dee Dee said adamantly. 'Ar knew you liked im coz ya never take yer eyes off im.'
'Ohh e iz lovely Dee,' Maizie smiled. 'Ar know e'z a bit older an'all that, but ar don't give a shit, iss only a number ain it?'
'Yeah course!' Dee Dee agreed. 'As long as yer appy thas what really matters.'
'OY MAIZE!' Trisha then called from the kitchen. 'YOU GOT YA FUCK ME KNICKERS ON?'
'Course!' Maizie replied, lifting the hem of her leatherette skirt to reveal her skimpy red french knickers. 'Me old faiffulls,' she smirked.
'Niiiiice,' Terry said, leering from the sofa.
'Oh shut up Tel,' Maizie laughed, checking herself one last time in the mirror. 'Right, ar'm off,' she said, donning her shoulder bag. 'Ar probly see you in work tomorra Dee.' Rodney frolicked at her feet. 'Yeah alriiiiight,' she said, stooping to ruffle his fur. 'Ar see you tomorra an'all.'

Maizie took a taxi to Richard's Belsize Park basement flat where she was greeted with champagne, flowers and a table set with gleaming cutlery, neatly folded crimson napkins and the mouthwatering smell of a joint of lamb roasting in the oven. 'Ahhhh this is lovely Rich,' she said, pecking his cheek. 'Ow long's dinner gonna be?'
'Oh I'd say about half an hour,' Richard replied, looking immaculately manicured.
'Quality,' Maizie said, then proceeded to strip. 'Well come on!' she said, unclipping her bra. 'Get'cha kit off!'
'Oh,' Richard said, astonished to say the least. 'Oh yes, right.'
The two discarded the majority of their clothes right there in the dining room and sank to the floor in a frantic embrace.
'Oh fuck yeah!' Maizie gasped breathlessly, when Richard ran his probing tongue the length of her midriff. 'Fuck yeaaaaaah!'
'Oh I do like these,' Richard remarked, tugging at her

knickers with his teeth.
'They're me fuck me knickers,' Maizie informed him, arching her back. 'So you better get on wiv it geez.'
The two of them, not having had an intimate relationship in an age, made up for lost time over and over again until the oven timer signaled a break in the steamy proceedings.
'Fuuuuuckin ell,' Maizie sighed, slumped on Richard's chest. 'That was bleedin marvlus babe.'
'Yes, yes it was,' Richard panted, wiping the sweat from his brow.
The pair dined hurriedly, still semi naked, and without taking their eyes from one another.
'Would you like dessert?' Richard asked, sipping his champagne.
'Woju reckon?' Maizie said, with a devilish grin. Richard grabbed the bottle and Maizie's hand and led her through to the bedroom, closing the door behind them. 'Ooooh you naughty bleeda!' Maizie squealed shortly after from within.

Dee Dee dozed contentedly on the sofa while Terry watched the footy highlights and Trisha played with her new companion on the floor at their feet, unaware of her impending celebrity status. All was well within the group of friends at that precise moment, except for the spectre of cancer which loomed in the wings.

Several days later Trisha was summoned to her charity's head quarters for another dressing down, or so she thought.
'Ahhh do come in Trisha,' one of the board of governors said, holding open the office door.
'Look if this is abaat the flippin snake,' Trisha said, holding up her hands. 'Ar swear ar didn't mean to lectricute it.'
'No, no it's nothing like that,' the governor said, pulling out a chair. 'Please, do sit down.'
'Fanks,' Trisha said, sitting in the company of an ominous looking group of officials.
'It's about the fire and your rescue of the dog,' she was told

by another. 'I don't know if you are aware of the impact you have made.' Trisha was then shown a copy of Time magazine with the image of her emerging from the burning building clutching the charred Bijon.

'You are famous Trisha,' another piped up. 'We have been inundated with calls here at head office - from the media and from countless well wishers wanting to donate to our cause. It's really quite staggering the amount of revenue that has been generated in such a short space of time. Well done you.'

'Oh fanks,' Trisha said, thumbing the magazine. 'Oh look, they got that new Chanel lippy,' she added, disregarding her accolade entirely. 'Thatta go nice wiv me slingbacks.'

'Trisha!' her boss said, taking back the magazine. 'We are here to thank you.'

'Oh thas alriiiight,' Trisha smiled. 'It weren't nuffing really.'

'Well it may be nothing to you,' the vice president of the charity told her, 'but it means a great deal to thousands of people around the world, so it seems.'

'Ohhh thas nice ain it,' Trisha said, pouring herself a glass of water.

'If it's OK with yourself Trisha,' the vice president said, 'we'd like to use you as the new face of the charity.'

'What, like Estee lawda ya mean?' Trisha asked.

'Er, yes, sort of,' the vice president replied. 'And we'd also like you to be an ambassador too, traveling the world raising awareness so to speak.'

'What, give up me day job?' Trisha asked. 'Wiv Ade?'

'Well yes that would be the case,' Trisha was told. 'It's a fantastic opportunity don't you think?'

'No fanks,' Trisha said, pushing her chair back and standing. 'Listen you can put me boat race on all yer adverts, but I aint givin up me job, ar love it alright.' With this Trisha marched from the office leaving the hierarchy gobsmacked.

'Well I never!' the vice president said, slumped in his seat.

Once again Trisha had inadvertently created a media storm and an internet buzz, with videos of her trending on Twitter

daily and going viral worldwide.
'Fancy a full english Ade mate?' she said, climbing into Adrian's waiting van.
'What was that all about?' Adrain asked, starting the engine.
'What?' Trisha said, buckling her belt.
'What do you mean what?' Adrain laughed. 'Your meeting of course!'
'Oh that,' Trisha said, shrugging her shoulders. 'Nuffing really, ar got me picture on some magazine for pullin Rodder's aat the fire.'
'Really!' Adrian gasped. 'Which magazine, I'll have to buy a copy.'
'Oh er,' Trisha said, thinking hard as Adrian pulled into traffic. 'Ar never erd of it meself, iss called Time, ar fink.'
'TIME!' Adrian shrieked. 'Time magazine!' He slammed on the brakes, enraging the lorry driver behind him. 'You are on the cover of Time magazine?'
'Yeah, why woss wrong wiv that?' Trisha asked, putting two fingers out the window to the honking drivers.
'My God, nothing's wrong!' Adrian said, in a mild state of shock. 'Time magazine, Trisha, over the years has featured the majority of the world's most iconic images: Albert Einstein, Abraham Lincoln, JFK for goodness sake, Regan, Obama, the moon landings, Nine eleven!'
'Yeah, yeah alright,' Trisha said, raising a hand to silence her partner. 'But ar still woulda rarva bin on the fronta Bella or Just Seventeen wiv Robbie or Katie Price.'
'WHAT?' Adrain asked in abject horror. 'BELLA! Trisha this is Time magazine we're talking about, you'll go down in history for this!'
'Yeah whateva,' Trisha said dismissively. 'Come on urry up, ar want me brecky.'
'Unbelievable,' Adrain mouthed, heading off to the cafe.

The following morning Trisha rose before her two friends as usual and prepared for work, leaving Rodney asleep on her pillow. 'Ar'll see you two later yeah,' she said when Dee Dee and Maizie walked bleary eyed from their room. 'I aint fed Rodder's yet, so can ya give im iz breakfast when e gets up Maize and take im aat for a shit. Ar've left a coupla pooh bags by the door, oh e might be a bit loose coz ar give im summa me biryani last night. Seeya!'

Before Dee Dee and Maizie could object, Trisha waltzed out the door and down the stairs. Stooping to retrieve the mail from the mat, she whistled whilst thumbing the envelopes but then stopped as a chill ran the length of her spine when she read a nondescript brown envelope addressed to Dee Dee with the words Saint Pancras Oncology dept on the reverse.

'Shit,' she said trembling, and turning back to the stairs, instead of her usaul jaunting vault of two stairs at a time, she trudged ever so slowly without taking her eyes from the envelope.

'Trish?' Maizie said, seeing her re-enter the flat. 'What'chu doin back ear, ar fought you was goin to work.' But she too froze on seeing the brown envelope and the mortified look on Trisha's face.

'Oh shit,' she said.

'What? Dee Dee asked, emerging from the kitchen with Terry. 'What is it?'

'Woss up babe?' Terry asked.

'Iss the ospital,' Trisha said, her lip quivering. 'Dee, iss the ospital mate.' For a moment the flat fell silent, each of them statue like.

'OK,' Dee Dee eventually said. 'Ar spoze we better open it then.'

'Fuck, fuck, fuck,' Maizie said, wringing her hands. 'Fuck Dee ar dunno mate, ar dunno if we should.'

'Maizie,' Dee Dee said, in an attempt to calm her friend. 'Maizie look at me, iss alright, onest mate. We're togevva aint we.' Dee Dee took the envelope from Trisha and sat on the sofa, quickly joined by her girlfriends, one on either side of her scootching up close.

Terry dragged the armchair in front of her. 'You OK Dee?' he

asked, stroking her knee.
'Ar dunno,' Dee Dee replied, clutching the envelope tightly and letting out an extended breath. 'Right, ear goes.'
'WAIT!' Trisha said, kissing Dee Dee's cheek. 'Ar love ya mate,' she said, welling up.
'Yeah me an'all,' Maizie said, kissing the opposite cheek.
'We all do,' Terry added, leaning to kiss her forehead.
'Fanks,' Dee Dee said, taking comfort from their presence. Slipping her thumbnail under the flap Dee Dee cautiously tore open the envelope with her friends watching intently. Looking each of them in the eye she then pulled out the folded letter between her thumb and forefinger.
'Shit, shit, shit,' Maizie mumbled.
'Please, please, please God,' Trisha begged, looking toward the ceiling.
Terry himself was in no way a religious man but he too quietly pleaded with the almighty for good news.
As if in slow motion Dee Dee unfolded the letter. Terry clung to her knee in a futile attempt to transfer his positive energy to her. To Dee Dee the entire page was a blur, a jumble of medical jargon which meant nothing to her, but one short line in bold type stood out, hitting her square in the face. 'Fuck,' she merely said, the hairs on the backs of her arms raising.
'What Dee?' Maizie asked softly. 'What is it?'
Trisha covered her ears with her hands and clenched her eyes tightly shut.
'What is it babe?' Terry asked also.
'Iss B5,' Dee Dee told them croakily. 'Iss B5, iss cancer.'
'Oh fuck no!' Terry said, rocking back in the armchair. 'No Dee, no.'
'No mate,' Maizie said, clinging ever so tightly to Dee Dee's arm. 'Are you sure, praps you read it wrong.'
'No I aint,' Dee Dee told her. 'Look iss there in black fuckin letters.'
Maizie looked down at the shaking letter in Dee Dee's hands, and threw her arms around her neck. 'Oh God no

mate, not you!' she said, fighting back the tears. 'Not you, not you, not you.'
'What?' Trisha said, opening an eye. 'What is it Maize, is it good news, is she gonna be alright?'
Maizie shook her head whilst hugging Dee Dee. 'No mate,' she said, wiping the tears which now ran down her cheeks. 'Iss cancer.'
Trisha immediately clasped a hand over her mouth and let out a muffled squeal, shaking her own head repeatedly from side to side before leaping from the sofa and sprinting to the bathroom to drop to her knees and vomit into the toilet pan.
'See to er please Maize,' Dee Dee asked. 'You know she aint no good wiv anyfing like this.'
'She's alright Dee,' Maizie said, refusing to let her friend go.
'For me Maize, please,' Dee Dee said, listening to the intermittent wailing and vomiting coming from the bathroom. 'Go on, see to er for me.'
'Alright Dee,' Maizie said, stroking Dee Dee's hair tenderly. 'Ar be back in a minute alright. Tel keep an eye on er mate.'
'Yeah course,' Terry said, leaning forward once again and taking Dee Dee's hand. 'Iss gonna be alright mate,' he assured her. 'They'll get that shit aata ya and you'll be brand new, you wait and see.'
Dee Dee said nothing; those tiny symbols B5 burning into the pupils of her eyes.
'You alright mate?' Maizie said, dropping beside Trisha and rubbing her back lovingly.
Trisha sobbed uncontrollably whilst spitting into the pan. 'Ar, ar, ar don't want er,er to die Maize,' she wept, rising with vomit on her chin. 'Ar don't, ar don't, ar don't.'
'Shh, shhhhh,' Maizie said, tearing some tissue from a roll beside them and mopping her friend's chin. 'Me neeva mate, me neeva.'
Trisha lunged at Maizie and the pair hugged, rocking on the bathroom floor, whilst Terry struggled himself to come to terms with the news. 'What er, what else does it say?' Terry

asked, choking back a tear.

'Ar dunno,' Dee Dee said, handing him the letter. 'Ar can't read nuffing else. You read it please Tel.'

Terry, although playing the part of the lovable rogue to a tee, had had a first rate education excelling in maths, english and at least two of the sciences. 'Right,' he said, clearing his throat, 'less av a look.' Studying the letter and breaking down the doctor's speak into layman's English, he deduced that Dee Dee was requested to begin her treatment as soon as possible. 'They er, they want you to go back in Dee,' he told her. 'To talk abaat ya treatment, soon as ya can mate.'

'Oh, right,' Dee Dee said, without thinking.

Maizie then led Trisha from the bathroom. 'Ar'm sorry Dee,' Trisha said, dropping to hug her friend and resting her head against her stomach. 'Ar'm sorry, ar'm sorry.'

'Shhhh iss alright ya doughnut,' Dee Dee said, stroking Trisha's hair. 'Ar'm gonna av me treatment an iss gonna be ok.'

Terry handed Maizie the letter. 'She's gotta go back to the ospital to talk abaat er treatment,' he told her. 'Soon as poss.'

'Right, well thas today then!' Maizie said, taking charge yet again. 'Dee get yaself washed and dressed and we're goin.'

'Not yet mate,' Dee Dee replied, taking her hand. 'Let me just sit ear for a minute, me legs are like jelly mate.'

Maizie looked down her nose and frowned wanting the very best of medical care for her friend right that very moment, but then relented. 'Alright mate,' she said, sitting back down beside her. 'Just for a minute ay yeah.'

The four friends sat in complete silence for four or so minutes before the sound of Adrian's honking horn brought them to their senses. 'Oh shit!' Trisha said, snatching the letter from Maizie's hand and heading for the window. Sliding up the sash she merely waved the letter and shook her head.

'Oh no,' Adrian said, sitting behind the wheel understanding the gesture, having been Trisha's shoulder to cry on on

many occasions. 'OK,' he mouthed, putting a hand to his ear. 'Call me if you need anything.' Trisha nodded and returned to the couch.
'You can go if ya want,' Dee Dee told her.
'You're avin a laugh aint'cha,' Trisha scoffed, scooping up Rodney who had trotted from her room. 'Ar'm goin wiv you and nuffing's gonna stop me, alright!'
'Yeah, we're all goin,' Terry said.
Unified and steadfast the friends clung to one another, while Dee Dee readied herself mentally for what was about to become the fight of her life. 'Right, fuck it!' she eventually said, springing to her feet. 'Less do it!'
'Yeaaaaah!' Maizie agreed. 'Thas it Dee, less fuckin av it ay!'

At the hospital Terry, Maizie and Trisha took up their places outside the oncology room, whilst Dee Dee underwent a further examination before having the various treatments available explained to her, but the list was limited due to the extent and size of her tumor. 'Ar told you ar don't want tablits,' Dee Dee said adamantly.
'OK, OK,' the doctor said, checking his monitor. 'We can start you on a course of chemotherapy, but at this stage I am afraid to say we cannot rule out a mastectomy.'
'A what?' Dee Dee asked. 'Ar've erd of it but what the fuck is it?'
The doctor hesitated for a moment, unsure of the best way to approach the subject.
'Dee,' his nurse said, taking her hands. 'In some cases, to save a patient whose tumor is considered life threatening, it is necessary to remove the offending breast entirely.'
'Me tit!' Dee Dee said, clutching her right breast. 'You aint choppin mar fuckin tit off ar'm tellin ya that naah!'
'Dee,' the doctor said, in a less formal tone. 'For many it's the only course of action left to them. But I assure you, as I've explained to you before, medical science has advanced tenfold in recent years, and the reconstruction team here do a remarkable job, using state of the art equipment and

the latest materials.'

'You mean a plastic tit!' Dee Dee frowned. 'There aint no way ar'm ever avin a bloody plastic tit d'you ear me, ar'd rarva top meself ar would.'

'You mustn't say that Dee,' the nurse urged. 'You have your whole life ahead of you.'

'Do I!' Dee Dee snapped. 'Ow d'you know ay, you aint got a fuckin lump eatin away at yer insides av ya? No, no you aint!'

Despite Dee Dee's aggressive stance the nurse remained calm. 'Look, I fully understand your reservations,' she told Dee Dee. 'And as the doctor explained we have a fantastic network of councillors to help you through the tough times. We are all here to help you, even your friends sitting outside.'

'I aint never needed anyones elp in me life,' Dee Dee admitted, 'ar stood up for meself, and me mates. I ad to.'

'Well, let us all stick up for you now,' the nurse said, hoping to win Dee Dee's trust. 'It is in no way an admission of failure Dee I assure you. It's accepting that we are human, made of flesh and bone just like everybody else, we bleed like everybody else and in certain circumstances get sick like everybody else. But if we lower our defences and allow others to take the reins, so to speak, we greatly increase our chances of survival. It's a proven fact, now I'm not saying don't fight this thing, but you have to let others help you, it's imperative.'

'Yes quite right Julia,' the doctor agreed. 'Dee, we are not saying for definite that you will need a mastectomy, we are just making you aware of the possibilities so you are forewarned, as they say. Now have you registered with a general practitioner?'

'A what?' Dee Dee asked.

'A GP,' the doctor said. 'Somebody local to you.'

'Oh, oh yeah,' Dee Dee replied, 'ar couldn't tell you iz name though, ar carn even say it, iss got two K's four B's an a zed in it.'

'Riiiight,' the doctor smiled. 'Well, we'll need their details so that we can liase with one another on matters of medication and such.'
'Yeah ar got it in me bag,' Dee Dee told him.
'OK great,' the doctor said, returning to his screen. 'Well, like I said, I'd like to start you on a course of chemotherapy and possibly radiation before anything else. I'll explain a little about the chemotherapy to start with, oh and don't worry Dee, it's not in tablet form.'
'Fank fuck for that,' Dee Dee sighed.
'Right well,' the doctor continued. 'You'll be on this particular course from anywhere between three and six months, but you'll be able to go about your usual daily duties, work etc. Now, as with most forms of chemotherapy, I'm afraid you may experience some form of side effects most commonly gastrointestinal, stomach cramps that sort of thing. You also may want to prepare in advance for some form of hair loss, which I understand is particularly hard for women to deal with. You must steer clear of anybody with cold or flu symptoms, because your red and white blood cells will be affected too making you more prone to infection. If you like you can attend one of our chemotherapy classes to gain a greater understanding of how these drugs work and their effects. OK, I've chosen Abroxone for you because it has performed well in all of its clinical trials.'
'Trials!' Dee Dee piped up. 'Ar don't wanna be no friggin lab rat!'
'No, no,' the doctor assured her. 'It's beyond the research stage I'll have you know. OK, before you begin your treatment a blood sample will be taken just to make sure it is OK for you to have this particular drug, but I'm sure you'll be fine. Your chemotherapy will be prepared by our pharmacist and you'll first be given an anti sickness drug, and quite possibly a steroid injection, then a thin tube or cannula will be inserted into a vein in your arm or hand - or sometimes your chest - and the drug is then administered in

drip form, usually over the space of half an hour or so. Now I must warn you that it's possible you may experience some side effects whilst receiving chemotherapy; dizziness, swelling of the face and lips, a pain in the tummy, shortness of breath. If any of these occur you must inform the nurse immediately. You will receive your chemotherapy as a course, or several cycles as we call it, each cycle lasting approximately three weeks. You'll be given more anti sickness drugs to take home with you, and they must be taken exactly as the pharmacist tells you, I cannot stress this enough Dee, it's very important you adhere to the instruction. Do you understand?'

'Yeah, er no,' Dee Dee said, numb from all the jargon.

'Well, the nurse will explain everything in greater detail when you begin your treatment, which I have scheduled for this afternoon.'

'Oh, right!' Dee Dee said. 'What if it don't work, ar mean it saands like ar'm gonna go fru a shit loada pain, and we ain even sure if iss gonna bleedin work are we?'

'Well, let's cross that bridge at a later stage shall we,' the doctor told her. 'Right now it's imperative you begin your treatment.' The doctor had spared Dee Dee many of the drugs side effects, such as: diarrhea, constipation, loss of appetite, bruising and possible bleeding, a sore mouth, tiredness, muscular and joint pain, hot flushes, headaches and numb and tingly hands, an ominous list for any patient to take in in one sitting.

'Ar wanna know!' Dee Dee abruptly. 'What appens if this shit don't work?'

'Well,' the doctor said, looking at his nurse. 'In my honest opinion, if you fail to respond to the chemotherapy and radiation, and if all else fails you, will be looking at a mastectomy I'm afraid.'

'Thas the tit off fing, ain it?' Dee Dee said, scrunching the hem of her top with her whitened fingers.

'Yes, yes if you prefer to put it that way,' the doctor replied.

Dee Dee thought long and hard for a moment or two,

realizing that suicide would hurt all those that she loved so dearly. 'Ar spoze if that's what it takes,' she said, putting on a brave face. 'Course I ain appy abaat it but fuck it, if ya gotta do it, do it.'
'Well that's incredibly brave of you,' the doctor told her, 'and extremely rare. Most women go to pieces at the mere mention of the procedure.'
'Yeah well, I aint most women,' Dee Dee replied, puffing her chest.
'Yes, quite,' the doctor agreed, handing Dee Dee a leaflet. 'Here are some of the do's and don'ts for you to consider whilst undergoing chemotherapy, for instance a woman of your age, if you don't mind me saying, would be considered to be sexually active.'
'Yeah, when ar can be arsed,' Dee Dee scoffed. 'But ar've ad me moments.'
'Well Dee,' the doctor informed her, 'it is advisable to use contraception to protect your partner in case any of the chemotherapy is present in the vaginal fluid. And if you have young children it is also not advisable to breast feed during your course and for a good few months after, to minimize the risk of transmitting the chemotherapy to your infants.'
'Well I aint got no nippers,' Dee Dee told the doctor. 'So ar got nuffing to worry abaat there, and I ain ad a jump since…,' she paused, reflecting on the night aboard the helicopter with her late lover, Travis. 'Well I ain ad one lately,' she opted to say.
'I must say Dee,' the doctor smiled., 'I do find your candor most refreshing.'
'Me what?' Dee Dee asked. 'Woss that when iss at ome?'
'Your frank and open expression,' the doctor replied. 'It's really quite admirable. Don't you agree Julia?'
Julia sat spellbound by Dee Dee's forthright manner, wishing she too could speak her mind more often and shed her sheepish chains. 'Oh yes!' she said, nodding. 'Quite admirable doctor.'
Terry, Maizie and Trisha sat in quiet contemplation outside.

Terry was absent mindedly gouging his name into the arm of the plastic chair with the corner of his cigarette lighter. 'Ar could murder a fag,' her said, tapping his foot repeatedly.
'You're avin a bleedin laugh aint'cha!' Maizie said, pointing up at the oncology sign. 'Ar tell ya what Tel, why don'tchu ask the cancer geezer in there, arm sure e'z got a tailor made tucked behind iz flippin earole.'
'Oh, yeah right, sorry mate,' Terry said sheepishly. 'Ar was finkin of jackin it in meself anyway.'
'Yeah, well do it for Dee Dee,' Maizie insisted. 'Coz she aint never avin anuvva fag neeva, ar flushed all ers daan the karzi this mawnin.'
'Ear she iiiiiiiis,' Trisha smiled, greeting Dee Dee at the door. 'Alright mate woss appnin, what did they say, what did they give ya, when ya gonna get better?'
'Trisha!' Maizie said, tugging her irritating friend aside. 'Leave off will ya. Ow'd it go Dee mate?'
'Yeah alright,' Dee Dee said, clutching the leaflet. 'Ar gotta av chemo for me lump, and they wanna start me on it today.'
'Oh shit Dee,' Trisha said, clasping a hand to her face. 'Chemo, what is it anyway?'
'Ar dunno meself,' Dee Dee admitted, taking a seat to steady her nerves. 'Ar probly gotta av some radio ferapy an'all, so they reckon.'
'Iss probly radio four,' Trisha interjected. 'Or that Smoov radio, that proper chills you aat, wiv all that old time shit ar mean.'
'Shut up you melt!' Maizie snapped. 'They aint gonna give er a digital fuckin radio!'
'Oh,' Trisha said, taken aback. 'Thas a shame, we coulda listened to it in the barfroom when we was slashin and waxin, ar prefer the eighties meself, ar love a bitta Spandou Bally, corrr them bruvvas was gorgeous weren't they, are coulda fucked em to a stand still ar could.'
TRISHA!' Maizie barked, slapping her friend. 'Will you shut the fuck up!'

'What?' Trisha asked. 'Iss better than that garage shit you used to listen to.'
'It was dance!' Maizie said, correcting Trisha yet again. 'And it aint shit!'
'Dance my arse,' Trisha scoffed, 'that aint dance, pointin ya finger in the air wiv a glowstick up yer arse. Naaaah thas proper shite that is, them eighties lot now they ad it sussed, break dancin, dirty dancin, and boppin araaand like a bleedin Egyptian.' Trisha then attempted the Bangles 1986 classic sand dance.
'You look like a proper mong,' Maizie mocked.
Dee Dee raised a smile at her feuding friends. 'Ya bofe wrong,' she told them. 'Mowtaaan mate, now that was music, it ad soul and rivum.'
'Ar like a bitta Ska meself,' Terry chipped in.
'Naaah,' Dee Dee scoffed. 'Me muvva brought me up on Mowtaaan, ar member er playin er tape fingy's: The Supremes, Gladys Knight, The Jackson Five, Marvlus Marvin Gaye ar love em all. Ar've always said at mar funeral ar want 'Someday we'll be togevva' by Diana Ross and er two mates, thas lovely that is.'
'Oh shut up Dee!' Maizie said, springing to her feet. 'I aint talkin abaat that shit, not ear, not naah!'
'Oh leave off Maize,' Dee Dee smiled. 'Ar was only sayin thas all.'
'No Dee, no ar mean it,' Maizie said. 'Ar don't wanna ear it, there aint gonna be no funeral, not naah not never!' With this she stormed off along the corridor, ignoring Dee Dee's repeated calls.
'MAIZIEEEEEE, MAIZE WAIT UP!'
'She'll be alright Dee,' Trisha told her friend. 'Ar know what she means though mate.'
'Look all ar was sayin,' Dee Dee replied, 'is thas what ar want. OK.'
'Yeah OK Dee,' Terry said, rising to his feet too. 'Less change the subject ay.'
Terry and the two girls eventually found Maizie seated in

the corner of the cafeteria, dragging a spoon around the rim of her cup staring blankly into the swirling brew. 'A'm sorry mate,' Dee Dee said, sitting opposite. 'But iss really important you'z lot know what mar wishes are, especially you Maizie.' She looked around at Trisha who was folding a napkin into a bizarre mutated origami goat. 'If ar left it all to soppy nuts there ar'd be carried into the church to the feme tune to the bloody Lego movie.'

'Oooh ar like that!' Trisha said, attempting to stand her creation on the table but the lack of a fourth leg made it impossible.

Dee Dee snatched the goat shaped thing and blew her nose into it before tossing it aside.

'Fancy a brew Dee?' Terry asked, approaching the counter with Trisha in tow.

'Yeah go on Tel, fanks,' Dee Dee said, over her shoulder. 'We got arf an hour before me treatment fing.'

Trisha scanned the display cabinet and the snacks therein. 'Can I av summa them spicy meat balls?' she asked, stabbing the glass with her finger.

'I'm sorry, what,' the lady behind the counter asked, looking down into the cabinet.

'Them there!' Trisha said, jabbing at the glass once more. 'The spicy meatball fings, ar'll av em wiv chips an'all.'

'They're falafels,' the woman replied, returning to her till.

'Fa what?' Trisha asked.

'Falafels,' the woman reiterated. 'This is a vegan cafeteria, no meat, no dairy.'

'No meat!' Trisha cried. 'Well what the bleedin ells in em?'

'Chick peas,' the woman replied, 'coriander and spices.'

'Oh for fuck sake,' Trisha said in disgust. 'That aint grub is it, chick peas, what the fuck's a chick pea, ar might as well eat grass and an andfulla dirt for gawd sake.'

'Three teas love,' Terry said, handing over a five pound note.

Trisha studied the menu unable to make head-nor-tail of the vegan offerings.

'Woss a tofu quiche when iss at ome?' she asked. 'And a bloody lentil dahl, ar mean woss that all abaat ay?'
Handing Terry the teas the lady at the counter soon grew tired of Trisha's foolishness, 'Melinda!' she called over her shoulder. 'Can you see to these customers, I'm going on my break!'
'Yeah OK Jeany,' her young assistant said, appearing from the kitchen and immediately catching Trisha's eye. 'Yes can I help you?' she asked, drying her hands.
'D'ya know what,' Trisha said, standing up on tip toes to eye her voluptuous figure whilst Terry headed for the table carrying the teas, 'ar reckon you probly could. So er, are you wunna these veggie nut jobs then are ya?'
'You mean a vegan, yes, yes I am,' Melinda smiled. 'You should try it, we have some really tasty snacks and salads and a mouthwatering butternut squash soup, which I simply adore.'
'Oh, right,' Trisha said, looking at the display counter once again and Melinda's legs on the other side of the glass. She then caught sight of a tiny button badge on Melinda's lapel which drew her attention, it was the rainbow symbol for gay pride. 'Are you a dyke an'all then?' she asked, thinking she may have struck gold.
'A what, sorry?' Melinda asked, leaning a little closer, close enough for Trisha to be able to smell her heady perfume.
'A lezza,' Trisha said, pointing out her badge. 'Ya know, a rug muncha.'
'Oh I see,' Melinda laughed. 'Yes I am a lesbian and proud of it too. Now what can I get you?'
'Errrrrrr,' Trisha said, 'ya phone number for a start.'
'I'm sorry,' Melinda smiled, 'I couldn't possibly date a non-vegan. Just knowing that she'd eaten the flesh of an animal would make my skin crawl.'
'Well I am wunna you'z lot!' Trisha said, lying through her teeth once again to curry favour with the luscious Melinda. 'I ain ad a bitta meat in ages if ya nart ar mean.'

'Oh really!' Melinda said, changing her tone. 'That's fantastic to hear. It's only by making a unified stand that we can irradiate the cruelty and suffering in world farming, and free the countless thousands of innocent creatures kept in appalling conditions purely to feed the bigoted masses.'

'Ar was only sayin that to me mates this mawnin,' Trisha said, dishing out white lie after white lie, 'while ar was signin up with that Greenpeas lot to go sink a Jap whale boat. So er, what abaat me and you discussin this over a bottla cider or summink?'

'Well I don't know,' Melinda said, mildly intrigued at Trisha's stance. 'Ar you sure you're a vegan?'

'Yeaaaaaah course,' Trisha told her. 'Ar tell ya what, gimme arf a dozen of them fluffels, a mung bean pasty, two spinach muffins an a bottla cabbage water.'

'Oh yes, right!' Melinda replied, hurriedly preparing Trisha's order. 'May I just say you have impeccable taste, the spinach muffins and cabbage water do wonders for your lower bowel.'

'Ya mean it gives ya the trots?' Trisha said, realizing she may actually have to eat the contents of the tray set before her.

Melinda slipped a biscuit on the side of the tray. 'Please try one of our curly kale cookies. I made them myself.'

'Oh yeah?' Trisha said, examining the biscuit closely. 'Iss got green bits in it.'

'That's the kale,' Melinda said enthusiastically. 'It's packed full of iron and scrummy vitamins.'

'Scrummy?' Trisha said, eyeing the revolting treat. 'Yeah OK ar'll er, ar'll give it a whiz.'

'Great,' Melinda said, scrawling her number on a napkin. 'This is my home number but don't call me until after the weekend because I'm away with some activist friends of mine raiding a mink farm in Somerset.'

'Fanks,' Trisha said, eager to impress. 'Yeah ar'm away an'all, me and summa them tree huggin nut jobs ar raidin DFS. It makes me wanna spit finkin of all them poor pines

trees bein turned into coffee tables and bloody corner units.'
Melinda gave Trisha a sideways glance. 'Yeeeees,' she said with less enthusiasm. 'Well I suppose it's good to make a stand for what you believe in isn't it.'
'Oh yeaaah,' Trisha said, taking her tray. 'Listen, if yer ever raidin John Lewis lemmy know yeah, coz they got this lovely diamontey lamp thatta go proper nice wiv mar bedroom curtains, ar give ya a coupla quid to nick it for us.'
'No, no you don't understand,' Melinda tried to explain.
'Don't worry gorgeous,' Trisha said, silencing the waitress, 'ar done a bitta blaggin meself, there aint no shame in it. Listen babe ar gotta get back to me mate coz she's got cancer.'
'Oh, oh dear I am sorry,' Melinda replied. 'Well I wish her all the very best.'
'Ahh fanks hun,' Trisha smiled, leaving the counter. 'Ar'll give you a bell yeah,' she added over her shoulder. 'Oh and if you can get us arf a dozen of them minky fings ar wanna make a fury bog seat cover, iss givin me bleedin piles sittin there vajazzlin me fanny.'
Melinda stood open mouthed as Trisha left to join her friends.
'What the fuck's that?' Dee Dee asked, sipping her tea.
'Fluffles,' Trisha said. 'They got chick peas in em or summink. Eeyar Maize ar got you a muffin, to cheer you up and shit.'
'Oh, fanks Trish,' Maizie said, taking the cake and breaking it in half. 'You now ar love a muffin don'tcha.' But on taking a bite her expression soon changed to one of absolute disgust. 'What the...?' she said, letting the contents of her mouth tumble onto her plate. 'Trisha what the fuck?' she added, swigging her tea to rinse her mouth.
'Oh iss spinach,' Trisha said nonchalantly. 'Us vegans eat em all the time.'
'Vegans!' Dee Dee exclaimed. 'Since when av you been a bleedin vegan?'

'Shhhhhh keep ya noise daaan will ya,' Trisha whispered, looking round at Melinda who was restocking the cabinet. 'Since that lovely bitta cracklin over there gimme er number. Ar tell ya what, ar'm gonna ride the fuck aat of er I am. Maizie can ar borra the battries aata your radio fing coz me vibrator's on a go-slow an ar wanna stick it up er...'

'Yeah, yeah alright!' Dee Dee said, halting her friend in mid-sentence. 'We don't need the bloody details.'

'Get yer own battries!' Maizie said defensively. 'You've already ad em aat the smoke alarm, gawd knows what'll appen if we av a bloody fire, we'll all be proper fucked.'

'These aint that bad,' Terry said, sampling a falafel. 'I aint goin veggie though, not even for a shag. Ar love me bacon baps, wiv a runny egg in em an'all.'

'Ooh yeah,' Maizie smile. 'Naah ya talkin Tel, wiv loadsa daddies sauce.'

'Me an'all,' Trisha said, dunking her curly kale cookie into Maizie's tea, 'but don't tell me bitta totty over there will ya.'

'Oy sod off!' Maizie said, dragging her cup away. 'What is that shit anyway?'

'Iss a cookie ya doughnut,' Trisha said, waving it under Maizie's nose.

'Yeah are know that you idiot!' Maizie said, backing away. 'But why the bloody ell is it green?'

'Coz iss got curly kale in it,' Trisha informed her friend, 'whatever the fuck that is.'

'Ooooh you dirty bitch,' Maizie said, turning her nose up and rejecting her tea. 'You've fucked up me brew naah.'

'Ar'll av it,' Trisha said, dunking her cookie once again and a falafel for that matter.

'You make me wanna puke sometimes Trish,' Maizie said, holding her stomach. 'D'you know that?'

'Ohhhh shutuuuup,' Trisha laughed. 'You aint never lived you aint.'

Terry looked at his fake Breitling wrist-watch. 'What time you avin ya chemo Dee?' he asked, downing the last of his tea and taking the last of the falafels.

'Ooooh shit yeah!' Dee Dee said, checking the cafeteria clock. 'Ar gotta be daan there in a coupla minutes.'
'Listen Dee,' Terry said, taking her hand. 'D'you mind if ar shoot off mate, ar gotta see this mate a mine daan Stepney way. E'z got me a ticket for the FA cup semi's, we got Wigan away which gets proper naughty after the game. Ar love givin it to them norvern monkeys, anyway we owe em a good idin coz last time the slags came to Upton Park they smashed up the Bowleyn pub and turned one of our coaches over.'
'Yeah no worries Tel,' Dee Dee smiled. 'You get off mate, ar'm only avin me meds, you back tonight are ya?'
'Ar give you a bell babe,' Terry told her. 'Coz ar might go an av a couple beers wiv the old man, I aint seen im in mumfs.'
'Alright mate,' Dee Dee said, hugging Terry. 'Fanks for comin yeah.'
'Laterz Tel,' Trisha said, supping her cabbage water before spitting the contents of her mouth across the table at Maizie.
'OY WHAT THE FUCK?' Maizie cried, swiping the drips from her face. 'What ya doin ya soppy bitch?'
'Oh mar gawd thas dire!' Trisha said, spitting the remainder onto the floor and eyeing the bottle. 'Fuck me them veggie nut jobs are bleedin savages if they drink this shite, iss like pissin pond water.'
'Looka the bleedin stata me!' Maizie cursed, rising from her seat and sponging her hoodie with a handful of napkins. 'And it bleedin stinks like fuck an'all.'
Trisha attempted to help, leaning to dab her friend with her origami goat. 'Ya missed a bit,' she said, but only making matters worse as usual.
'Get offa me!' Maizie barked.
Terry leant and cupped Dee Dee's head, kissing her forehead tenderly. 'Ar see ya soon babe yeah,' he told her. 'Bell me if ya need anyfing alright.'
'Fanks Tel mate,' Dee Dee said, patting his hand while Maizie stood fending off Trisha.

'Come ear!' Trisha said, lunging at her friend. 'You got a bit on yer earole.'

'Trisha, stay the fuck away from me!' Maizie raged, snatching the origami goat from her and dabbing her eyes.

'Laterz you two yeah,' Terry said in parting; but the two squabbling girls hadn't heard a thing.

Accompanied by her two best friends Dee Dee strolled apprehensively to her appointment with the chemotherapy nurse. 'I aint sure abaat avin these poxy drugs,' she said, looking to the suspended ceiling. 'Ar've erd some nasty shit abaat em I av, women go bald an all sorts, ar can't lose me air Maize, not me air.'

'You'll be alright Dee,' Maizie assured her friend. 'You won't av to take em for long then you'll be all better mate.'

'Woja reckon Trisha?' Dee Dee said, turning to Trisha who was busy reading a leaflet she had found on becoming an organ donor.

'Ay what?' she asked, looking up.

'The drugs you idiot,' Dee Dee said again, 'woja reckon?'

'Oh ar wouldn't touch em wiv a barge pole,' Trisha replied, not having been privy to the whole conversation, 'it aint werf it. Me cousin Lewis done arf a dozen grams of charlie and a shit loada ketamin at Kelly Patterson's eighteenf, you remember Kelly, big tits an a wonky eye, anyway they faand Lewey the next mawnin in the summer ouse flat aat in a puddle of iz own pooh and puke. The ambulance geezers wouldn't touch im till we ozed im daan wiv the jet washer.'

Trisha then noticed her two friends staring wide eyed at her.

'What?' she asked, discarding the leaflet. 'Well you asked din'tcha.'

'Not them flippin drugs!' Dee Dee snapped. 'Oh never mind.'

Maizie shoved Trisha while Dee Dee knocked on the nurse's door.

'Hi, do come in,' the nurse smiled, opening the door a moment later.

'Can me mates come in an'all?' Dee Dee asked.

'Yes, yes of course,' the nurse replied.

Trisha and Maizie sat to the side watching intently while Dee Dee was first handed a form for her to sign, giving her consent to receive the treatment.
'That's great,' the nurse said, taking the form and handing Dee Dee a small cup containing two capsules.
'Woss that?' Dee Dee asked, looking down her nose. 'Ar don't do tablits, ar told the doctor bloke ar don't do tablits.'
'Those are your anti-sickness capsules,' the nurse informed her. 'It's important you take them during your course of chemotherapy to help with the nausea. It's ok, they're really easy to swallow, not like those chalky tablets. Here,' she said, handing Dee Dee a glass of water.
'Just daan em Dee,' Trisha said from the sidelines, but then received a cold hard stare from both of her friends.
'Just pop them in your mouth one at a time with a little water,' the nurse told Dee Dee. 'Tip your head back and swallow.'
Dee Dee tipped the two red capsules into her hand, took a deep breath and did as she was asked with her eyes clenched tightly shut.
'Excellent!' the nurse smiled, taking the cup. 'OK while those are taking effect if I could just ask you to pop on the scales, I need to measure your weight and height so we can administer an accurate dose.'
'Ar could do wiv wunna them pills meself,' Trisha said, clutching her stomach and squirming while Dee Dee's measurements were taken. 'The fluffle fings ar proper goin to work on mar guts, where's the karzi love?' she asked the nurse.
'You mean the lavatory?' the nurse asked, looking up from her desk where she busily prepared Dee Dee's medication.
'Yeah!' Trisha replied, bent double now. 'Urry up ar'm touchin cloff.'
'Two doors down on the right,' the nurse told Trisha, flicking at her syringe.
Trisha bolted from the room letting the door slam behind her, raising a smile on the faces of her friends.

'Serves er bleedin right,' Maizie said, ecstatic at Trisha's discomfort.

'Ok,' the nurse said, taking Dee Dee's hand. 'I'm about to put a cannula into the back of your hand which can be a little painful, so I'm first going to spray the area with an anesthetic if that's alright with you Dee.'

'Yeah crack on,' Dee Dee told her, eager for the treatment to be over with.

'You alright Dee?' Maizie asked, resting her chin in her hands.

'Yeah babe,' Dee Dee replied, as the line was inserted into a vein. 'Yeah ar can't feel a fing mate.'

'Right, I'm going to start your drip,' the nurse told Dee Dee, checking the bag above her head and monitoring the flow rate. 'Now just make yourself comfortable Deborah, this could take up to forty minutes.'

'Call me Dee,' Dee Dee told her.

'Oh ok, right,' the nurse replied, placing a dressing on the back of her hand to keep the line in place for the duration. 'Now the anti-sickness capsules should help with the nausea like I said, but do let me know if you feel any discomfort whatsoever in your arm or anywhere else for that matter.'

'Yeah alright,' Dee Dee said, watching the bag and the steady drips beneath it.

While the nurse busied herself at her desk, Maizie joined Dee Dee on the edge of the bed taking the other hand. 'Iss gonna be alright mate,' she said, choking up inside. 'You wait and see.'

'Yeah ar know,' Dee Dee replied, squeezing Maizie's hand. 'Ar just wanna get back to work Maize. Alice'll be frettin wivaat me, an ar promised to cut Bonnie's air for er.'

'Don't worry,' Maizie reassured her friend, 'ar spoke to Richard earlier, e'z gonna look in on em imself and let em know you'll be back tomorra.'

'Ahhh fanks mate,' Dee Dee said, taking comfort. 'I appreciate that. Bonnie won't let anyone else touch er air ya see, and me and Alice av a good old sing along wiv them rock n' roll cds ar got er for er birfday. She loves *Great Ballsa Fire* she does, you wanna see er boppin in er bed iss proper funny mate.'

'You love them girls don'tcha Dee,' Maizie said, clinging to Dee Dee during her treatment.

'Yeah, yeah ar do,' Dee Dee admitted, with the bag almost empty. 'It aint like a job no more, ar can't wait to get in in the mawnins and see em, ar tell ya what if ar could live wiv em ar would.'

'Ar'm praada ya Dee,' Maizie told her friend. 'You've bin like a proper muvva to em ain'tcha.'

'Oh ar dunno abaat that,' Dee Dee said modestly. 'Ar just wonem to be appy thas all.'

'They are mate,' Maizie smiled. 'And thas all cozza you, believe me mate ar seen em come alive when they're wiv you, you got the touch Dee. Even Richie says you're a natral.'

'You really like im don'tcha,' Dee Dee said, looking Maizie in the eye.

'Yeah ar reaaaaaaally like im,' Maizie agreed whole heartedly. 'Ar never fought ar'd ever be appy again after Enrique dumped me, but Richie's made me feel wanted again, e treats me like a queen e does.'

'E bleedin better,' Dee Dee warned her friend, 'or e'll av me to deal wiv, you tell im that.'

'Yeah ar did actually,' Maizie laughed. 'E said e wouldn't wanna get on the wrong sida ya, specially after ar told im you knocked aat that bouncer aatside Faces.'

'Oh that twat,' Dee Dee said, reminiscing. 'E fought e could coppa feel of my arse in the queue and get away wiv it dint e, well I aint no bitta meat, ar told im that an'all before ar laid im aat wiv a right ander.'

'Ar know, that was quality,' Maizie said, recalling the altercation. 'E ad to jack iz job in after that coz e got the piss taken aat of im night after bleedin night. Where'd you learn to punch like that anyway Dee,' she asked.

'Me old man taught me,' Dee Dee told her. 'Iss abaat the only good fing e ever done was teach me to fight, oh and take me to the park once a week. E used to say if the boys ever come near ya punch em up the frote and kick em in the nuts. We used to spar in the back garden wiv iz old boxin gloves, ar member e split mar lip once but ar didn't cry ar just done im good and proper wiv a combination to the guts and an uppercut and decked im on the patio. E wouldn't fight me after that, me muvva was proper praada me she was, ar member she got us KFC to celebrate.'
'Shit Dee!' Maizie said, suddenly startled. 'You gotta tell ya mum.'
'Tell er what?' Dee Dee asked.
'Woja mean tell er what?' Maizie said, as the nurse removed the line from Dee Dee's hand and applied another dressing. 'Abaat'cha bleedin lump of course!'
'No!' Dee Dee snapped. 'No ar don't wanna worry er. Not naah she's so appy wiv Ramos an everyfing.'
'But Dee,' Maizie said insistently, 'you gotta look at it from er pointa view mate, if you ad a kid an it was sick you'd wanna know wouldn't ya. You would wouldn't ya Dee, ay?'
'Yeah,' Dee Dee agreed. 'Yeah course but...'
'There aint no buts Dee,' Maizie said resolutely. 'You gotta tell er, if you don't ar will, ar mean it.'
'Alright, alright!' Dee Dee said with her hands in the air. 'You might av to tell er anyway coz ar don't fink ar can.'
'OK mate, ar will don't worry,' Maizie said, attempting to calm her anxious friend. 'Don't you worry abaat nuffing, you just concentrate on gettin better and leave everyfing to me and Trish.'
'Where is that doughnut anyway?' Dee Dee asked.
At that precise moment Trisha entered the room looking decidedly pale. 'Fuuuuuck me,' she puffed, 'the fluffles dun arf go fru ya ar tell ya, ar just battered the bog to buggery.'
The nurse turned up her nose at Trisha's descriptive explanation.

'Ar'm still gonna give er one though,' Trisha said, waving Melinda's telephone number.
'Shut up will ya!' Maizie said, in no mood for Trisha's antics. 'Ar was just sayin to Dee we gotta tell er muvva.'
'Oh gawd yeah!' Trisha agreed. 'Yeah Dee, you gotta tell ya mum mate, ar don't mind doin it if ya want.'
'No you bleedin won't!' Maizie barked, wagging a finger. 'Ar know what you're like, oh ello Misses D, yeah everyfing's alright, oh by the way ya daughter's got cancer,' she said, mimicking her friend to a tee. 'No you aint ringin no one.'
'Oh leave off Maize,' Trisha moaned, 'I aint that bleedin bad.'
'Yes you are,' Dee Dee agreed. 'But ar know yer art's in the right place so fanks for offerin.'
'Well ar wanna do summink,' Trisha said, sitting beside them. 'Ar'm ya mate an'all ain I.'
'Yeah ar know that,' Dee Dee smiled. 'Course ya me mate ya doughnut, you're ear thas all that matters to me.'
'Right ar'm gonna give ya mum a bell,' Maizie said, heading for the door. 'Trish, keep an eye on er will ya.'
'Yeah course,' Trisha said, with one arm around Dee Dee. 'I aint leavin er.'
'Ohhhh great,' Dee Dee laughed.
Maizie made her way to the front entrance and sat perched on a low brick garden wall, phone in hand, going over in her mind the best way to break the news to Pearl. 'Fuck it!' she said eventually, pressing call.
'Ello, elllo is that you Misses D?' she said a short while later, after the international dialing tone. 'Ello, ello iss Maizie, Misses D iss Maizie!'
Pearl and Ramos were painting the hull of their fishing boat in a dry dock when the call came through. 'Ohhhh ello Maizie love!' Pearl said, setting her brush down. 'Ramos love iss Maizie!'
Ramos smiled whilst scraping barnacles.
'Ohhh iss lovely to ear from ya Maize!' Pearl continued, raising her voice above the calling sea birds. 'Ow are ya?

Ow's mar Dee is she alright? And what abaat Trish is she keepin aata trouble? Ow ya gettin on wiv ya jobs? Oh ar narf glad they let you girls aat, ar was frettin every night ar was knowin you'z was banged up.'

'Yeah, yeah we're gettin on alright,' Maizie said hesitantly. 'Trisha's er usual dopey self.'

'What abaat Dee?' Pearl asked again. 'Ow's mar baby girl doin?'

'Well, well thas what ar'm ringin ya for,' Maizie said, her mouth drying somewhat.

'What?' Pearl asked abruptly. 'Woss wrong? Maizie woss wrong babe, woss up wiv mar Dee?'

Ramos set his scraper down and rounded the boat. 'What is it my love?' he asked, placing a hand on his lover's back. 'What's wrong?'

'Ar dunno babe,' Pearl replied, caressing his cheek. 'Maizie tell me love, what is it, is it Dee, is she alright?'

'Well, no Misses D,' Maizie said, biting at her finger nail. 'No she aint.'

'Oh mar gawd what is it?' Pear asked, clinging to Ramos. 'Maizie tell me, tell me woss up wiv mar baby girl?'

'She's er,' Maizie said, the words jamming in her throat. 'She's gotta lump Misses D, on er breast.'

Pearl instantly dropped the tin of marine paint from her right hand and cupped her mouth.

'What is it my love?' Ramos asked, deeply concerned. 'What's wrong, is it Dee?'

Pearl nodded with rapidly swelling eyes unable to speak momentarily. 'Oh God!' she eventually gasped, having held her breath. 'Oh God no, oh God Rammy, iss mar Dee she's got, she's got... Oh fuck ar can't say it babe, where is she Maize, where's mar baby?'

'In ospital at the minute,' Maizie told her, sensing Pearl's anguish, 'avin some chemo, ar just fought you oughta know.'

'Oh mar gawd,' Pearl cried, clutching her heart and staggering into Ramos' arms. 'Oh Jesus no, no not mar baby,

not mar baby, not mar Dee Dee. Please God no, no no pleaaaaaaaase God noooooooooo!'
Ramos took the phone from her trembling hand. 'Hello, hello Maizie this is Ramos,' he said, whilst supporting Pearl.
'Ello Ramos mate,' Maizie said, shaking herself. 'Is she alright?'
Before Ramos could answer Pearl wrenched at his overalls. 'Get me over there babe, get me over there right naah!' she begged. 'Rammy love please take me to er, pleaaaase ar gotta be wiv er!'
'OK, OK my love,' Ramos said, holding her tight. 'We will go right away. I will call my brother he will take us to the airport.'
'Call im, call im naah!' Pearl insisted. 'Call im Rammy love, ar gotta go back ome!'
'Yes, yes right away,' Ramos promised. 'Maizie,' he said, pressing the phone to his ear, 'Pearl and I will be over on the next available flight. Please tell Dee.'
Pearl snatched the phone from Ramos' hand. 'Stay wiv er Maizie babe!' she said, hyperventilating. 'Stay wiv er please!'
'She's alright Misses D,' Maizie said reassuringly. 'She's avin a course a meds an a bitta radioferapy apparently, and she wants to stick wiv er job no matter what, she loves it Misses D.'
'Oh mar poor baby,' Pearl sobbed, unable to come to terms with the horrendous news. 'Oh mar poor Dee. We're comin Maize you tell er that, even if I av to ijack the fuckin plane we're comin today!'
'Alright Misses D ar'll tell er,' Maizie said, choking back a tear. 'And don't worry me and Trish are wiv er.'
'Oh fanks babe,' Pearl cried. 'Fank you, you'za good mates to mar girl.'
'Right ar see ya when ya get ear,' Maizie told Pearl, who clung trembling to her lover on the quayside. 'Give us a bell when ya land an ar'll give you our address. We're in norf London naah, yeah ar know gooner country.'

'Yeah, yeah course ar will,' Pearl said, tugging Ramos. 'See ya soon love, bye, bye.'

'Yeah seeya Misses D,' Maizie said, lowering her phone and exhaling.

Pearl ran to their jeep. 'Come on Rammy love!' she called over her shoulder. 'Urry up will ya, call ya bruvva, call im naah will ya, tell im to meet us at our gaff!'

Racing to their waterfront apartment Pearl tore an armful of clothes from her wardrobe and rammed them into her suitcase. 'Is e comin?' she asked Ramos, who too packed hurriedly. 'Rammy is e comin?'

'Yes, yes my love,' Ramos said, retrieving his wash bag from the bathroom. 'Stefan is on his way, he tells me there is a flight at noon and will book us two seats.'

'Oh fanks babe,' Pearl said, flinging her arms around his neck and sobbing on his shoulder. 'Babe ar'm so scared, iss mar little girl, woss she doin wiv a fuckin lump, she don't deserve that shit, she don't, she don't.'

'Shhh, shhhh, shhhh,' Ramos said, caressing the back of her head. 'She will be ok, Dee is a fighter you know that.'

'Yeah ar do,' Pearl wept, wiping her tear strewn cheeks. 'She's ard as fuck she is, but this is different babe, this is, this is...,' she still couldn't bring herself to say the word, the word that had struck fear and dread into the hearts of countless parents before her.

Stefan, Ramos' younger brother, arrived at their Marbella home in his estate car. 'I came as quickly as I could,' he said as Pearl and Ramos rushed from the door and leapt into the back.

'Quick as ya can please Stefan,' Pearl said, tapping his shoulder and clinging to Ramos's hand.

'What did she say?' Dee Dee asked, meeting Maizie on the hospital steps having completed her first dose of chemotherapy. 'Is she alright?'

'Sort of,' Maizie told her. 'She's upset as ya can imagine, she's on er way over.'

'Ohhhhh Maize,' Dee Dee moaned. 'Ar love er an'all that but ar don't want er fussin over me all the bleedin time, ar don't fink ar could andle it mate.'
'She's ya muvva Dee,' Maizie reminded her friend. 'She's baand to fuss.'
'Yeah ar know that mate but,' Dee Dee said, descending the steps, 'but ar don't need it right naah thas all.'
'Oh Dee itta be nice to see er,' Trisha added, trotting behind. 'Is Ramos comin over an'all?'
'Yeah ar fink so,' Maizie said, taking Dee Dee's arm. 'Come on mate ar got'cha,' she said, fussing. 'Ow d'ya feel?'
'Like shit,' Dee Dee said, clutching her stomach. 'Them anti sickness fingeys aint werf a wank ar tell ya, ar keep feelin like ar'm gonna chuck up any minute.'
'Praps they aint kicked in yet Dee,' Maizie said. 'Did she give you any more of em?'
'Yeah shit loads,' Dee Dee said, producing several packets of capsules from her pocket. 'But they're shite ar tell ya.'
'Ar get us a cab,' Trisha said, waving at a passing taxi. 'OY GEEZA!' she yelled, 'OVER EAR YA NOB JOCKEY!'

'D'ya wanna cuppa mate?' Maizie asked, once they arrived back at their flat.
'Oooh yeah fanks,' Trisha said flinging her coat.
'Not you!' 'Maizie snapped. 'Ar was talkin to Dee.'
'No fanks mate,' Dee Dee said, heading for her room. 'Ar'm gonna lie daan for a minute ar feel like deff.' The chemotherapy drugs were coursing through her veins wreaking havoc with her intestinal system. 'Ya better get me a bucket,' she said over her shoulder, 'just in case.'
'Yeah, yeah alright Dee,' Maizie said, retrieving the washing bowl from the sink and tossing out Trisha's thong that had been left to soak with her thumb and forefinger. 'Eyar mate,' she said, pulling back Dee Dee's bed sheet while she undressed. 'D'you wanna glass a water or summink?'

'Naaah,' Dee Dee said, sitting on the edge of the bed looking disheveled to say the least. 'Ar just wanna get me nut daan, just for a little while mate.'
'Is she alright Maize?' Trisha asked when Maize joined her at the table.
'Course she not alright!' Maizie snapped. 'What kinda dopey question's that? She's ad a shit load of orrible drugs pumped inside er so ow d'ya fink she feels.'
'Well ar dunno,' Trisha said, shrugging her shoulders. 'But ar wouldn't wanna be in er shoes ar tell ya that, ar know we done some pretty naughty shit back in the day but she don't need to be punished no more does she.'
'It aint punishment,' Maizie told her friend. 'Iss life thas what it is, you always know someone's gonna get the cancer fing you just don't want it to be you or ya famly, or ya mates neeva.'
'She is gonna be alright aint she Maize?' Trisha asked. 'She is aint she?'
'Ar dunno Trisha ar really don't,' Maizie replied, looking over her shoulder at their bedroom door.

Pearl and Ramos landed at London Gatwick later that evening and after telephoning Maizie took a taxi directly to North London. 'Ow is she?' Pearl asked when Trisha opened the street door.
'Ello Misses D, ello Rammy mate come in,' Trisha replied. 'She's alright at the minute, they got er on some chemo shit though that proper upsets er guts but we're keepin an eye on er, she just woke up actually.'
'Upstairs is it?' Pearl asked, leaving Trisha and her lover trailing behind. 'DEEEE!' she called out, 'DEE BABE ISS YA MUVVA!'
'Is that you Mum?' Dee Dee said, meeting her mother on the landing and falling into her arms. 'Shit Mum ar narf mist'cha,' she admitted, feeling that unmistakable parental bond instantly.

'Ar've mist'chu an'all,' Pearl said, stroking her daughter's hair. 'Woss appened to ya babe, tell me, tell ya Mum.'
'Ar just got a lump Mum thas all,' Dee said, kissing her mother's cheek.
'Thas all!' Pearl exclaimed. 'Woja mean thas all, iss a pissin lump not a bloody verruca Dee love!'
'Ello Rammy mate,' Dee Dee said, breaking from her mother to greet Ramos. 'Fanks for comin.'
'I go where your mother goes,' Ramos replied, taking Pearl's hand. 'Always.'
'Right!' Pearl insisted. 'Come on get the kettle on ar wanna know everyfing the ospital told ya, an ar mean everyfing.'
'Trisha!' Maizie said expectantly.
'Yeaaaaaah ar know,' Trisha said, trudging through to the kitchen. 'Make the teas.'
Pearl sat holding her daughter's hand, mortified, while Dee Dee explained what she had been told by the medical staff including her chemotherapy regime.
'Ohhhh e'z lovely,' Pearl then said, distracted somewhat when Rodney scampered from Trisha's room and leapt onto her lap.
'Thas Trisha's dog,' Maizie told her, sitting at the table with Ramos. 'She rescued im from a fire and called im Rodney.'
'Rodders!' Trisha said, appearing with five mugs.
'Where ya stoppin Mum?' Dee Dee asked, looking round her tiny flat. 'We aint got no room ear for ya.'
'Oh no we're sorted love,' her mother told her. 'We see an otel on the main road and booked in there, and we're stoppin for as long as it takes for you to get better.'
'Muvva you don't av to,' Dee Dee said, looking her mother in the eye. 'What abaat ya fishin and shit?'
'There are no crab at this time of year,' Ramos informed her. 'We have the boat out of the water, my brother Stefan will see to her maintenance.'
'See,' Pearl said adamantly, 'we aint got nuffing to rush ome for so we're stayin. Right Maizie tells me you're still workin love is that right, and is it wise in your condition?'

'Yes it bloody well is!' Dee Dee said, squeezing her mother's hand. 'Ar love what ar do naah Mum so don't ask me to jack it in coz ar won't.'

'Ya wastin ya breff Misses D,' Maizie told Pearl, handing her the biscuits. 'You couldn't drag er aata that place once she's wiv them girls.'

'Girls, what girls?' Pearl asked. 'What is it you're doin anyway?'

Dee Dee began to explain her relationship with Alice and Bonnie and the reasons she would never desert them.

'Ahhhh thas lovely of ya babe,' Pearl eventually said, cupping her daughter's face. 'Mar little baby girl all grown up, you're like a little Muvva Treeza you are.'

'You stoppin for dinner Misses D?' Trisha asked, taking Rodney from her. 'Ar could do wunna me spag bolls.'

'Er, no fanks Trish love,' Pearl replied, having sampled Trisha's cooking several times in the past, incidents she had lived to regret. 'Ar'd rarva boil me arse in chip fat if iss all the same to you.'

Everyone burst out laughing, everyone that is is except Trisha. 'Oh,' she said despondently. 'Oh, ok.'

'Sorry love,' Pearl told her. 'Me and Rammy are eatin aat later, tell ya what, why don'tchu girls come wiv us. There's a Dixie Chicken next to the otel, woja reckon Dee?'

'Fanks Mum but,' Dee Dee said, clutching her stomach. 'Ar don't fink ar could keep nuffing daan at the moment.'

'Ohhh darlin,' Pearl said, pulling her daughter close. 'Sorry love ar weren't finkin, praps we will stay for spag boll, ay Rammy babe?' Ramos merely smiled in reply.

'Oh leave off muvva,' Dee Dee scoffed. 'If ar can't keep a flippin Dixie Chicken daan me neck ar got no bloody chance wiv er soddin spag boll av I?'

'You don't know what ya missin,' Trisha said, allowing Rodney to lick her face much to Ramos' disgust.

'Oh yes we do!' Maizie sneered. 'The last time you done a spag bol ya stained me blinkin teef yella for a fortnight.'

'Oh yeah that was the turmeric,' Trisha laughed. 'The lid come off.'
'Ar know!' Maizie raged. 'Ar faand it in me dinner, and what was that shit on the garlic bread, ay?'
'Yeah Trish,' Dee Dee asked, taking Maizie's side, 'what the fuck was that?'
'Well ar never ad no garlic for a start did I,' Trisha informed them, 'so I ad to make do wiv me erbal toofpaste.'
'TOOFPASTE!' Maizie cried, unsure if she'd heard her friend right. 'What the fuck?'
'Yeah,' Trisha explained, 'iss proper good it is, ar get it from the elf food place coz it aint got no chemicals and shit in it, iss basil and coriander flavor. I av it in me pitta pockets an'all sometimes when ar got no hoomus.'
'You really aint right d'you know that,' Dee Dee told her, her stomach churning. 'Ar fink ar'm gonna be sick to tell ya the troof.' She left her mother on the sofa and darted to the bathroom with her hand cupped over her mouth.
'Ohh Dee babe, you alright?' her mother said, following her.
'Is she ok?' Ramos asked.
'Not really mate,' Maizie told him, 'lark ar said, the chemo gear they've given er plays avoc wiv er guts summink chronic, the poor cow spends arf er life bent over the flippin karzi naah.'
Pearl stroked the back of Dee Dee's hair while she vomited into the pan. 'Mar poor baby,' she said with a quivering lip. 'Oh no,' she then said, looking at the strands of fallen hair in her hand.
'What?' Dee Dee asked, spitting. 'What is it?'
'Er oh nuffing,' her mother said, sparing her daughter the anguish.
'Muvva!' Dee Dee insisted, grabbing her hand from behind her back. 'What ya got?' She froze immediately on seeing the limp strands then tugged gently at her hair on her head removing a brittle clump with ease. 'Oh shit no!' she cried. 'Fuck no, no Mum not me air for gawd sake!' She scrunched the hair into her tightened fist and beat the edge of the

porcelain pan repeatedly, sobbing on her knees. 'NO NO NO FUUUUUCK NOT ME FUCKIN AIR!' Dee Dee had reacted sooner than most to the powerful Chemotherapy drugs.
Trisha and Maizie came dashing in to join them. 'What is it, woss up?' Maizie asked.
Dee Dee looked up from her mother's bosom and held out her shaking hand.
'Oh no Dee mate, no,' Maizie said, dropping beside them.
Trisha slumped back against the bathroom wall looking up and screaming in her head to the almighty to let her friend be cured that instant.
Ramos hung his head at the table, his own family like so many others had been touched by the deadly disease.
'Not me air Mum,' Dee Dee sobbed.
'Come ear babe,' Pearl said, rocking her distraught daughter as though she were still a babe in arms. 'Shhhhhhh, shhhhhhhhh, we're all ear for ya love and we're gonna get fru this togevva d'you ear me, togevva.'
'Too right we are,' Maizie added.
Trisha left the bathroom and slipped Rodney's lead onto his collar and disappeared out the door.
'Where's Trish goin?' Pearl asked, looking over her shoulder.
'She as to go aat when it gets too bad Misses D,' Maizie told her. 'You know ow sensitive she is, this shit tears er to bits sometimes.'
Trisha walked the surrounding streets pouring her heart out to Rodney who trotted obediently alongside her. 'Ar just want me old Dee back Rod,' she told him, pausing so that her companion could urinate against the wheel of a plumber's van. 'Ar just wish ar could wake up in the mawnin and fingsa be back to normal ar do mate, iss proper doin me ed in Rod.'
Rodney merely looked up at her and let out a solitary yap.

Pearl later put her daughter to bed and lay alongside her singing softly to sooth her to sleep as she had done when Dee was an infant. 'Nunight babe,' she whispered, kissing

Dee Dee's cheek before slipping from the room. 'Ohhhh Maize it breaks my art babe, seein er like that,' she said, sitting at the table and taking Ramos' hand.
'Ar know what ya mean Misses D,' Maizie agreed.
Rodney then came scurrying in after Trisha had slipped him from his lead. 'Ooooh ar tell ya what,' Trisha said, kicking off her shoes. 'Some people aint got no shame av they.'
'What you on abaat?' Maizie asked over her shoulder.
'Er at number forty two!' 'Trisha explained. 'Rodders stopped aatside er ouse to shit up er gate, so I ad a nose in the front winda and there she was bold as blinkin brass bollock naked wiv er maaf wrapped raand er old man's todger, while the lazy bastard was sprawled aat wiv a bottla beer watchin Top Gear. Anyway she see me lookin and told me to fuck off so ar left Rodney's package where it jolly well was, opefully the dirty bitch'll slip arse over tit in it in the mawnin.'
'Jesus Trish!' Pearl laughed. 'You don't change a bleedin bit do ya mate.'
'Tell me abaat it,' Maizie sighed. 'We av to live wiv the friggin fruit loop.'
Pearl later donned her coat and handed Ramos his own. 'We better be gettin off,' she told Maizie and Trisha. 'Keep an eye on mar baby for me won'tcha girls.'
'Yeah course Misses D,' Maizie said, rising from the table to see them to the door. 'Don't worry yaself too much will ya.'
'Goodnight ladies,' Ramos said, kissing both their hands.
'Night Rammy mate,' Trisha said, grabbing Rodney before he could scamper out the door.
'Ar be back raand tomorra,' Pearl told the girls. 'Ar get Dee some minestrone, she likes that.'
'Ooooh me an'all,' Trisha said eagerly. 'Ar'll get some ob nobs on the way ome, to dip in.'
Pearl tugged Ramos away with the image of Trisha dunking biscuits into her soup causing her stomach to turn.
'Ahhhh that was nice seein em wernit,' Trisha said, setting Rodney down after Maizie closed the door. 'Fancy a cuppa

me erbal tea?' she added, heading for the kitchen. 'Ar got lemon and ginger.'

'No ar bleedin don't!' Maizie replied abruptly. 'Poke it up yer arse, ar'm goin to bed.' Rodney then yapped at Maizie's feet for attention. 'Piss off ya little shit,' she said, before disappearing into her room as quietly as she could.

'Ahhhh what did she say to youuuuuuuu,' Trisha said, scooping Rodney from the floor. 'You tell your mum mum mum mum.' Ruffling Rodney's chin she let him lick her face once again. 'E'z mummy's little boy,' she said playfully. 'Yes e is, ohhhh yes e is.'

Maizie then opened her bedroom door and peered out half naked. 'Shut the fuck up will ya!' she barked.

'What?' Trisha asked, with Rodney still lapping at the side of her mouth. 'Iss only me and Rodders.'

'Ar'll give you Rodders in a minute!' Maizie said, looking over her shoulder at her sleeping friend. 'Ar'll draan the little bastard in the bleedin barf ar will.'

'Ohhhh don't say that Maaaize,' Trisha moaned, covering Rodney's ears. 'You'll urt iz feelins.'

'Well get to blinkin bed!' Maizie insisted. 'Or ar'll urt more than iz poxy feelins ar'm tellin ya!' she ducked back inside her room, checking on Dee Dee before slipping beneath her sheets.

'What did that nasty Maizie say to you?' Trisha asked Rodney, carrying him and her herbal tea.

During the night Dee Dee didn't need the washing bowl but instead she made five further trips to the bathroom, each time forcing herself to be sick, and each time Maizie woke and faithfully followed her friend, rubbing her back while Trisha lay awake with Rodney at her side and her hands clasped over her ears attempting to drive all thoughts of Dee Dee's sickness from her mind.

'What you doin up?' Trisha asked Dee Dee the following morning at the bathroom door. 'Ar know you said you was goin to work, but you bin up arf the night mate, I erd ya.'

'Look Trish,' Dee Dee said, pushing past her, 'ar'm goin to work wevva you like it or not, ok!' She stripped and climbed into the shower adjusting the temperature. 'Ar've already told all of ya, I aint givin up me job so don't try and stop me, alright!'

'Yeah alright Dee,' Trisha relented. 'Well take ya medicine won'tcha.'

'Anti-sickness my arse,' Dee Dee scoffed, 'them fings aint werf a wank ar'm tellin ya.'

'Ar know but the doctor said,' Trisha added, brushing her hair in the mirror, 'you gotta take em for the cider effects.'

'Side effects you doughnut,' Dee Dee replied, lathering her body. 'An ar reckon them poxy fings ar makin me worse.'

'Well like ar said,' Trisha told her friend, 'praps they aint kicked in yet so give em a chance ay.'

'Whateva!' Dee Dee scoffed, unimpressed with her prescription.

Maizie then emerged bleary eyed. 'Mawnin,' she yawned. 'You alright Dee?' she asked, pushing Trisha aside and squatting on the pan.

'Ar feel a bit better,' Dee Dee replied, switching off the shower and grabbing a towel from the back of the door. 'Ar be even better when ar get to work.'

Trisha donned her uniform, took a bite of her burnt toast, a slurp of her tea and made for the door. 'See ya later you'z two, ar gotta go!' she told her friends. 'You take it easy Dee yeah!'

'Shut up and sod off!' Dee Dee called back, growing increasingly tired of the constant fussing. 'And stay aata blinkin trouble!'

'Yeah, yeah alright!' 'Trisha laughed. 'MAIZE, DON'T FERGET TO TAKE RODDER'S AAT FOR A SHIT MATE!' she added at the door.

'IF I AV TO!' Maizie groaned raising her eyebrows.

'OH AND MAIZE!' Trisha called out, 'GIVE IM A CHEWEY STICK FING AN'ALL WILL YA, ISS GOOD FOR IZ TEEF, OH AN E PROBLY NEEDS WORMIN AN'ALL MATE SO WHEN E'Z AD A

DUMP SHOVE ONE OF IZ PILLS UP IZ ARSE. YA DON'T MIND DO YA? SEEYAAA!'
'Do what?' Maizie asked, flushing the lavatory. 'Now you are takin the piss, Trisha. TRISHAAAAA!'

Arriving at the Westmoreland centre Dee Dee and Maizie were greeted at the door by Richard. 'Morning,' he said, maintaining a professional relationship with Maizie despite their romance having well and truly blossomed. 'Dee, surely you should be at home shouldn't you?'
Dee Dee spun and glared at Maizie. 'You told im!' she snapped. 'Woja tell im for?'
'Dee I ad to,' Maizie replied, backing away ever so slightly. 'We love eachuvva so ar can't lie to im can I.'
'Ar told you to keep schtum did'n I,' Dee Dee snarled. 'I aint givin up me job!' she said, turning to Richard. 'You can't make me!'
'I won't ask you to, I promise,' Richard said, holding his hands in the air. 'But if you ever feel you need to take time out then I'll fully understand.'
'Yeah, well ar won't,' Dee Dee said, barging past him.
'She won't change er mind neeva,' Maizie told her lover, following behind. 'Babe ar dunno when ar can come over,' she told him. 'Dee ad a proper shit night last night, you wouldn't fink so to look at er would ya, ar know she's puttin on a brave face for this place.'
'Maizie darling I fully understand,' Richard said, lowering his voice as they passed several staff members. 'You know where I am if you need me, ok.'
'Thas just it Rich,' Maizie admitted, stopping abruptly. 'Ar do need ya, more than you'll ever know babe.'
'Oh right,' Richard said, pleased at her obvious commitment to him. 'Well I er, I hope you realize I feel the same way.' He stroked her arm and then snatched his hand away as a porter approached.
'Ohhhh come ear!' Maizie said, pulling him toward her and locking lips without a care.

'Mmmmm, Maizie please,' Richard squirmed. 'The staff!'
'Fuck em,' Maizie laughed. 'They're only gutted they aint gettin it.'
Dee Dee, although feeling decidedly under the weather, got the pick me up she much needed when Alice and Bonnie presented her with a crooked victoria sponge that chef had helped them make the previous day. 'For me!' Dee Dee shrieked. 'Oh mar gawd thas mar favrit, ow did ya know?' She spun the plate to observe the lop-sided sponge from all angles. 'If you'z two made this, you done a proper pukka job, ar'm well praada the paira ya.'
Alice clapped repeatedly while Bonnie hugged Dee Dee. 'Yeah ar mist'chu an'all,' Dee Dee said, cutting her cake. 'Mmmmmm thas gorgeous that is,' she said, taking a bite. 'Ar'm gonna take a bit ome for me mate Trish she loves a bitta cake, mind you she loves a bit of anyfing.'
Trisha in the meantime had not been her usual jubilant self that morning having been awake for much of the night herself, and this was more than evident in her work. After a call from head office reporting a young man in Victoria Park East London swinging a Staffordshire bull terrier puppy around by its lead she had stormed across the play area, skirting the swings and slide to where the bare chested youth stood with three of his jeering friends.
'OY YOU LITTLE SCROTE!' she barked. 'Gimme that fuckin dog!'
When the lad objected with several derogatory hand gestures Trisha lassoed his neck with her catch pole and swung him around until he crashed down onto the rubberized recreation matting. 'Now you know what it fuckin feels like you slag!' she snapped, scooping up the puppy and confiscating it in front of his submissive friends.
'Do you want to talk about it?' Adrian asked, after Trisha had secured the puppy in the back of the van.
'Naah ar'm alright,' Trisha said, buckling her belt. But nothing could be further from the truth, as the owner of six malnourished cats discovered when she kicked in his door

and ducked his head into his aquarium when he too objected to his cats being removed, one of which was later put to sleep as it was far too weak to fully recover from its ordeal.

'Are you sure you don't want to talk about it?' Adrian again asked when Trisha later removed seventeen house rats from a one bedroom flat on the ninth floor of a dilapidated tower block after three had escaped and terrorized local residents. The owner, who too had mistakenly refused to surrender his animals, had learned the hard way that Trisha when stressed was a force to be reckoned with. The verbal assault she unleashed upon him was merely the tip of the iceberg after he foolishly shoved her aside whilst Adrian ferried the rats to the van.

'What happened?' Adrian asked on his return, seeing the owner flat out cold on his living room carpet with a broken marijuana pipe at his side.

'Oh e fell on iz bong,' Trisha said dismissively, whilst retrieving the last of the rats. 'Five times.'

CHAPTER EIGHT

Despite a rigorous course of chemo and radiotherapy, and the unstinting will of her friends and family for her to get better, the growth and progress of Dee Dee's tumor did not abate and on March fifteenth of the following year it was decided by the medical staff at Saint Pancras that the only course of action left to Dee Dee was the complete removal of her right breast. The news came as the bitterest of blows after months of torment in which she fought tooth and manicured nail, having experienced a whole host of horrendous side effects from the very treatment designed to save her.

Throughout her harrowing ordeal Dee Dee maintained her obligations to Alice and Bonnie, coaxing the two of them on one occasion out and onto an open top sight-seeing bus around the capital, where she delighted in seeing the looks on their reclusive faces and hearing their ecstatic cries of, 'LOOK, LOOK!'

She now wore a pink beanie hat almost twenty four seven to disguise her rapidly thinning hair, but above all she maintained her dignity and never once let her head drop in public.

Not a word was spoken in the taxi on the morning of her operation. Dee Dee sat mortified with her mother and best friends sitting tightly at her side. Occasionally she glanced down at her breasts unable to fully comprehend the idea of one without the other.

'Ow's mar baby girl?' Pearl asked as they ascended the hospital steps.

'Ar'm alright Mum,' Dee Dee said shakily. 'That chemo shit aint done me no good, so less ope loppin off me tit does the job ay.'

'Ohhh Dee you're so brave mate,' Maizie told her friend with an arm around her.

'Ar've erd they can make you anuvva tit,' Trisha said, attempting to lighten the mood. 'Probly wiv wunna them jelly moulds in the Anne Summa's catalogue or summink, member when we made that big jelly nob for Jackie Lewin's hen do and she ad to lick the squirty cream off the end of it?'

'Trisha!' Maizie growled over her shoulder. 'They don't use a friggin jelly mould you idiot!'

Pearl and Dee Dee couldn't help but laugh at Trisha's preposterous suggestion, which eased the tension somewhat. 'Thas why ar love you Trish,' Dee Dee said, holding the door open for her friend, 'you're madder than a barrel loada monkeys aint'cha.'

'Woja mean?' Trisha asked, still mulling over the possibility of a jelly breast. 'Orange or blackcurrant?' she then asked Dee Dee, who looked blankly back at her.

'What'chu on abaat naah?' Dee Dee asked, pausing.

'Ya jelly tit!' Trisha replied, convinced of its plausibility. 'Ar wouldn't av lemon coz that tastes like shit.'

'Get in there you twat,' Maizie said, shoving Trisha inside. 'And shut the fuck up abaat jelly friggin tits will ya, this aint the time and it certainly aint the bloody place!'

Meeting with the nurse and surgeons Dee Dee was made aware of the forthcoming procedure. 'I see you have your friends and family with you today Dee, that's great,' one of the surgeons said, sitting opposite her. 'Ok, I fully understand how anxious you must be feeling right now,' he continued, pushing his spectacles along the bridge of his nose. 'But let me explain a thing or two, the operation itself will be performed under general anesthesia so effectively you'll be asleep throughout and won't feel a thing. The team and I intend to remove all of the breast tissue and possibly the nipple, but only if we really have to. The skin will then be stitched and a temporary line attached to drain off any excess fluid from the area. I'm sure the nurse here has mentioned our connections with several first class councillors should you feel the need to talk to someone after the procedure.'

'Ar don't want no councilors,' Dee Dee said adamantly. 'Ar got me muvva and me mates, thas all ar need.'

'Right you are,' the surgeon agreed. 'Now I also intend to remove a number of lymph nodes during surgery and send them to the lab for examination. Afterwards I must warn you that you will experience some soreness in the region, usually the chest, arm and shoulder which is purely temporary but the numbness in the arm may last a little longer I'm afraid. Oh and there is a slight chance of you contracting lymphedema. I'm just making you aware of all the facts you understand.'

'Lympha what?' Dee De asked, terrified of the near unpronounceable condition.

'Lymphedema,' the surgeon said. 'It's a medical term for fluid that hasn't been drained through the line that collects in the arm, hands, chest or back causing swelling.'

'Jesus fuckin Christ!' Dee Dee scoffed. 'So what you're tellin me is this is gonna be a proper baga shit ain it.'

The surgeons were each taken aback at Dee Dee's terminology. 'Well, well not exactly,' one of them smiled. 'And with regard to reconstruction you could have additional surgery here today, or opt to have it done later.'

'What, a jelly tit?' Trisha asked. 'See ar told ya Maize!'

'Shut up you idiot!' Maizie replied, listening intently to the surgeon.

'Ar'll av it later,' Dee Dee told them. 'Ar don't wanna be pissed araand wiv today more than I av to, just get on wiv it mate.'

'Ok,' the surgeon told her. 'Well the nurse will take you down and get you prepped for surgery and we'll be with you shortly. And er, try not to worry, my team and I carry out dozens of these operations each week.'

'Cheers,' Dee Dee replied. 'Oh and when can ar go ome, ar gotta be up for work in the mawnin?'

'I'm afraid you'll have to stay in overnight,' the surgeon said, conferring with his colleagues. 'Purely for observation you understand.'

'Oh you're avin a laugh aint'cha,' Dee Dee moaned. 'Ar'm takin Bonnie and Alice to the pictures tomorra ar can't be stoppin in ear all bleedin night.'

'I'm sorry,' the surgeon replied, heading out the door. 'But you won't be feeling at your best after surgery and will appreciate the rest, believe me.'

'Dee mate,' Maizie said, with a hand on her friend's knee. 'Ar'll explain to the girls don't worry, ar'll just say you aint feelin well and you'll take em anuvva day.'

'Ar don't wonem worryin,' Dee Dee replied. 'D'you ear me?'

'Like ar said Dee,' Maizie told her friend, 'don't worry abaat a fing ar'll see to em for ya.'

Dee Dee hugged her mother and friends. 'Ar love ya'z,' she told them apprehensively.

'Ar love you too babe,' Pearl told her daughter, weeping once again. 'You look after er won'tcha,' she told the departing surgeons who nodded in reply. 'Ohhh ar can't believe this is appnin,' she cried, 'not to mar baby girl, not to mar Dee.'

'Mum ar'm alright,' Dee Dee said, putting on the bravest of faces. 'You'z get yaselves off ome, it aint werf ya'z stoppin ear.'

'Do what?' Maizie said. 'We aint goin nowhere Dee, if you're stoppin so are we.'

'Yeah,' the others agreed.

'Ar got a baga toffees,' Trisha added, 'so we'll be alright Dee mate.'

'Fanks,' Dee Dee said, looking each of them in the eye one last time. 'Fanks all of ya.'

'Love ya babe!' Pearl said, watching her daughter disappear out the door, she then broke down in Maizie's arms. 'Ohhh Maize woss gonna appen to er,' she sobbed. 'Woss gonna appen to mar baby girl?'

'She'll be alright Misses D,' Maizie said, holding herself together for Pearl's sake. 'Gissa toffee Trish,' she said, in an attempt to make meaningless conversation and prevent herself from going completely to pieces. 'Trish!' she said, to her friend who was staring blankly at the door. 'Trish mate?'
'Ay, what?' Trisha said, snapping out of her delirious daze. 'Where they takin er Maize, where's me Dee goin?'
'To the operatin feater,' Maizie explained. 'She's in good ands Trish, try not to worry mate. Misses D, d'you wanna cuppa tea?'
Pearl nodded and followed the others to the cafeteria where each of them sat stirring their tea and losing themselves in the swirling beverage. Trisha this time made no attempt to seduce the pretty waitress having lost her lusty appetite.
A good three and a half hours later the nurse approached the solemn group. 'Hi, your friend is out of surgery now, the operation went very well but she's resting on the ward now.'
'Can ar see er?' Pearl asked, springing from her seat. 'Ar wanna see er. Where is she?'
'Like I said, she's resting at the moment,' the nurse reiterated. 'She'll be out for at least another hour or so I'd imagine.'
'What ward?' Maizie asked, standing shoulder to shoulder with Pearl. 'We just wanna see er, please Miss.'
'Yeah where's mar Dee!' Trisha said, adopting a more aggressive stance. 'What you done wiv er?'
'OK follow me,' the nurse said, relenting and leaving the cafeteria. 'But I must ask you to be quiet at all times, she needs her rest so please don't crowd her, and when she does wake she'll be groggy and tender from the operation, so minimal contact please.'
'Yeah, yeah course,' Pearl said, keeping step with the nurse.
'Shhhhh,' the nurse said, pushing open the door to Dee Dee's ward, but Pearl and the others pushed past her and scanned the beds for their loved one.

'There she is!' Trisha shrieked, before clasping a hand over her forgetful mouth. 'Sorry,' she whispered. 'Oh God look at er Maize,' she said at Dee Dee's side.

Dee Dee lay unconscious with a line in the back of her hand and another under her gown attached to her chest.

'Oh mar gawd,' Pearl gasped from the opposite side of the bed, bending to carefully caress her daughters face. 'Mar baby, mar poor baby look at er.'

Maizie gathered enough chairs and sat at the bedside keeping a watchful eye on her friend.

'D'ya fink they got it all?' Trisha asked, referring to the tumor. 'When they cut er tit off ar mean.'

'Ar bleedin ope so,' Maizie muttered. 'Ar really do Trish mate.'

'Oh please God,' Pearl said, clinging tightly to Dee Dee's hand. 'Please God let this be the end of it, please, please.'

'Right Trish!' Maizie told her friend. 'When Dee wakes up mate she's gonna need all the love we can give er d'you ear me, we gotta make er feel wanted.'

'She is wanted,' Trisha said, rocking ever so slightly. 'More than ever, ar bin prayin all night Maize, ar never got a winka sleep.'

'Me neeva,' Maizie admitted.

Dee Dee's pink beanie had been removed during surgery and replaced with a paper surgical cap. Pearl leant and kissed Dee Dee on the end of her nose. 'Love you baby girl,' she whispered.

Terry then arrived with Ramos. 'Ar come as soon as ar could,' he said, retrieving another chair. 'The old bill are all over the gaff for some reason, ow is she?'

'She's ad the op Tel,' Maizie said, returning his kiss. 'She's still drugged up to the eyeballs at the moment, we're waitin for er to wake up.'

Ramos sat at Pearl's side wrapping a manly arm around her waist and saying nothing.

The stone faced group sat willing their friend to wake, and more importantly, be cured when she did.

Eventually Dee Dee's eyelids fluttered. 'Misses D!' Trisha squealed. 'Look Dee's wakin up!'
'Ohhhhhh baby!' Pearl said, clasping her hands to her face. 'Babe iss ya mum, ar'm ear darlin.'
Dee Dee struggled to open her eyes and focus on her friends but when she eventually did a smile slowly crept across her weary face. 'Alright,' she said croakily, offering Trisha her hand. 'Ow's mar Trish?'
'Good Dee!' Trisha said, rummaging in her pocket. 'Ear mate ar saved you a toffee, they melted a bit so iss a bastard to get the wrapper off but they're proper nice.'
Maizie snatched the toffee from Trisha's hand. 'Thas the last bleedin fing she needs you idiot,' she snapped. 'You alright Dee mate, we bin sittin ear waitin for ya to come raand.'
'Dee babe ar bin so worried abaat cha,' Pearl said, pulling away from Ramos and nestling beside her daughter. 'Ow d'ya feel babe, does it urt, tell mummy.'
'Ar can't feel nuffing Mum,' Dee Dee told her. 'Ar'm numb from the bleedin neck daan,' she then caught sight of her chest line and traced the tube back to her gown peering cautiously inside, she then suddenly threw her head back and clenched her eyes tight shut as the grim reality sunk in.
'Ohhhh Dee babe,' Pearl said with a hand to her mouth.
Dee Dee held her breath for several seconds holding back the tears as best she could.
'Let it aat Dee,' Maizie told her friend, leaning to cuddle her. 'Let it aat mate, go on there aint no shame in it, you cry ya fuckin art aat if you av to, ar got'cha, ar got'cha mate.'
'Yeah,' the others said one by one.
Moments later Dee Dee could hold back the flood gates no longer and blurted out, 'FUUUUUUUCK!' sobbing uncontrollably, annoyed that she had let this thing get the better of her. 'Fuck, fuck, fuck, fuck!' she cursed.
Terry looked down at his feet the whole time to spare her feelings while Trisha repeatedly patted her friend's shoulder tenderly. 'Iss alright Dee,' she said, choking on the lump in her throat. 'Iss alright, iss alright.'

'Grrrrrrrr!' Dee Dee growled, wiping her eyes and pounding the bed sheets. 'Ar'm alright,' she then said, swatting Trisha's hand away. 'Onest ar'm alright just gimme a minute will ya.'

'Yeah, yeah course,' Trisha said, sitting back in her seat.

Moments later, to everyone's complete surprise, Dee Dee began to laugh covering her eyes with her hand.

'What?' Maizie asked, smiling too. 'What is it Dee?'

Dee Dee pointed to Trisha. 'Er!' she said, unable to contain herself. 'Silly bollocks there,' she added, 'I ad this proper fucked up dream while ar was drugged up, ar was bein chased raand the ospital by this dirty great jelly tit!'

'What?' Maizie chuckled. 'A jelly tit!'

'What flavour?' Trisha asked, deadly serious. 'Ar bet it was lime flavour wunnit, nobody likes lime.'

'I aint got a bleedin scooby,' Dee Dee said, composing herself. 'Ar was too busy leggin it raand the maternity ward chuckin babies behind me at the time.'

'Thas you that is!' Maizie said, shoving Trisha angrily. 'As if she aint got enough to worry abaat, your friggin jelly tits are scarin the crap aat of er.'

'Sorry,' Trisha said humbly. 'Ar'm sorry Dee mate.'

'Iss alright,' Dee Dee said, patting Trisha's knee. 'Iss proper funny now ar'm awake ar tell ya.'

The nurse returned shortly after. 'Ahh, I see you're awake,' she said, straightening Dee Dee's sheets. 'How are you feeling?'

'Ar dunno really,' Dee Dee replied. 'Ar can't feel a bleedin fing daan there but me arms startin to ache like fuck.'

'Ok,' the nurse said, taking a look at Dee Dee's notes at the foot of her bed. 'I'll discuss your medication with the doctors, oh and visiting time is almost up I'm afraid so your friends and family will have to leave.'

'Do what?' Maizie said abruptly. 'Not bleedin likely!'

'Hospital rules I'm afraid,' the nurse replied. 'I'm sorry there are no exceptions whatsoever.'

'Iss alright Maize,' Dee Dee told her friend. 'You lot get off ome ar be alright.'

'No you won't Dee,' Maizie insisted. 'You just ad a massive operation, yer ed's all over the place, so we aint leavin ya.'

'Ya gotta,' Dee Dee told her. 'Anyway ar need ya to go into work in the mawnin to check on Bonnie and Alice.'

'Yeah but Deeeee,' Maizie moaned.

'Go on, sling yer ook, ar see ya tomorra night,' Dee Dee said, dismissing her visitors. 'You will come get me tomorra wont ya Mum?'

'But Dee ar don't wanna leave ya neeva,' Pearl said, clinging to Ramos like a limpet. 'Ar just wanna get in bed wiv ya right naah an old ya tight all bleedin night ar do.'

'Well you aint gonna,' Dee Dee said adamantly. 'You're gonna go back to ya digs wiv Rammy there and get a good night's kip and leave me to do the same, alright.'

'She's right, come on,' Terry said, rising from his seat. 'Whateva ya need Dee, gimme a bell yeah,' he told Dee Dee, rubbing her leg through her sheet. 'Anyfing babe, ar mean that.'

'Fanks Tel,' Dee Dee smiled. 'Fanks for comin, all of ya.'

Maizie and Trisha kissed their friend and reluctantly followed Terry to the door, while Pearl had to be tugged sobbing from her daughter's bedside. 'Come my love,' Ramos told her, 'let her sleep.'

Left alone with a head full of mixed emotions Dee Dee began to drift off to sleep when one of the surgeons arrived clutching her pink beanie. 'Hi, we found this in theatre,' he said, setting it down on Dee Dee's bedside cabinet. 'I'd just like to say,' he added, 'as far as we're concerned your operation went very smoothly indeed. So after a visit from the doctor around lunchtime tomorrow I can't see any reason why you can't be allowed home.'

'Fank gawd for that,' Dee Dee sighed. 'These poxy places gimme the eebie jeebies they do, you can smell the deff in the air can't ya.'

'Yes, yes I know what you mean,' the surgeon agreed. 'I've been here for six and a half years and I still haven't gotten used to it, I doubt I ever will.'

'Did ya get it all?' Dee Dee asked. 'The cancer ar mean.'

'Well let's just say,' the surgeon said conservatively, 'we removed all we could but I will ask you to come back in a week or two as an outpatient for further tests, bloods and possibly an MRI.'

'Ohhh Jesus!' Dee Dee groaned, knowing now that the nightmare may be far from over. 'Can ar go back to work?' she asked. 'Ar really need to geez.'

'Yes if you wish,' the surgeon replied, a little shocked at her request. 'But you're not to do any heavy lifting, in fact no lifting at all for a few weeks and that includes a kettle of water I'm afraid. After that you'll be asked to do some light exercises, raising your arm above your head and such, to try to regain full movement.'

'Yeah ar carn even lift it,' Dee Dee replied, attempting to raise her right arm from the bed.

'That's quite normal in these circumstances,' the surgeon told her. 'We have an excellent physiotherapist on hand to help you as and when you require.'

'Fanks,' Dee Dee said, yawning. 'Ar'm gonna get some kip naah mate if thas alright,' she told him. 'Whatever you gimme as proper slaughtered me ar tell ya.'

'Yes ok,' the surgeon said, getting up to leave. 'Well, I'll pop along in the morning to see how you're getting on, sleep well.'

Dee Dee nodded and wriggled a little further down the bed, but despite her obvious fatigue she simply could not sleep in the unfamiliar surroundings with the sounds of moaning and snoring patients on either side of her.

Pearl was at the hospital at first light the following morning, waiting eagerly for visiting time to commence. 'I ope she's alright,' she told Ramos in the cafeteria. 'She don't like ospitals, she never as.'

Ramos stirred his black coffee having slept very little with his weeping partner at his side.
'There's mar bay girl,' Pearl eventually said, hurrying to Dee Dee's bed and kissing her yet again. 'Ahhhh, ow ya feelin, did ya sleep alright?'
'Yeah, yeah ar did actually,' Dee Dee said, sparing her mother the truth. 'When they weren't shovin drugs daan me neck. Mawnin Ramos mate, you ok?'
'Yes thank you, and good morning,' Ramos said, presenting Dee Dee with a beautiful bunch of gardenias.
'Ahhhh fanks,' Dee Dee said, burying her nose in the blooms. 'They're lovely they are.' She sat up to kiss Ramos's cheek, wincing in doing so.
'Dee lay daan!' her mother insisted. 'You'll do yaself a mischief.'
Trisha had slept in Dee Dee's bed that night, taking comfort in the subtle scent of her friend on her pillow, she and Maizie both staring at the ceiling until tiredness got the better of them. While Terry demolished a six pack of ciders on the sofa to cope in his own sweet way.
Maizie, as asked, attended the centre the following day receiving a much needed cuddle from Richard. 'Iss a flippin nightmare Rich,' she said, wrapped in his arms with her head on his chest. 'She's tryin so ard to cope wiv it, bless er, but ar know iss doin er nut in.'
'I'm so sorry,' Richard said, kissing her forehead. 'Look, she's getting the very best treatment at the moment isn't she, but she also needs everyone around her to be strong for her. If you fall apart then she will too.'
'Yeah ya right,' Maizie said, drying her eyes. 'Ar told er ar'd look in on Bonnie and Alice this mawnin, she gimme some bits for em, a new air brush for Alice and a levva book for Bonnie's poems.'
'OK darling,' Richard said, watching her leave his office. 'You know where I am right.'
'Yeah, yeah ar do babe,' Maizie replied. 'And fanks, ar mean it.'

After a circuit of the neighborhood with Rodney, Trisha left him with Terry and donned her uniform, making her way to the garden gate. 'Are you sure you want to do this?' Adrian asked, as she climbed in alongside him.

'Yeah, Dee said I ad to,' Trisha said, fastening her seat belt. 'Right, what we got?'

'We have to confiscate a lurcher from a family of travellers,' Adrian informed her. 'There are reports of cruelty and neglect.'

'Nice one!' Trisha said, rubbing her hands together. 'Ar'm just in the mood for them pikey slags.' And she was too, not even the sight of the fifteen strong family standing defiantly outside their caravan deterred her. 'Ar'm takin the mutt wevva you like it or not,' Trisha said, rolling up her sleeves. 'Which wunna you cocks are gonna try and stop me ay?'

After a brief stand-off and an exchange of pleasantries the travellers relented on the orders of their ma. 'You can't be hitting a girl Seamus,' she told the largest of her sons. 'Sure I won't allow it.'

'Taaaake the feckin dag!' Seamus said, kicking the emaciated hound in her direction. 'Ya craaazy bitch, d'you know that, comin in here like Calamity fecking Jane.'

'Yeah thas right,' Trisha warned, with Adrian locked inside his van. 'I am a crazy bitch an ar don't give a flyin fuck abaat any of you lot, d'you ear me, you're nuffin!'

The stunned travellers looked at one another bemused at the audacity of this slight girl, having seen of the burliest of bailiffs in their time. One of them, having heard enough, surged forward to tackle Trisha but was hoisted back and beaten about the head by his mother. 'Michael I told ya brother!' she barked. 'You'll not be hittin no girl, not while I'm still breathin, now get to feck before I take ya father's leather to ya!'

'Sorry Maaa,' the lad said, cowering. 'Sorry Maaa, sorry.'

'Dear God!' Adrian said, when Trisha loaded the lurcher in the back of the van and joined him in front. 'You have some balls Trisha, I'll give you that.'

'Iss only what Dee Dee taught me,' Trisha told him. 'Stand ya graaand and nine times aata ten the wankers'll bottle it.'
'And if they don't?' Adrian asked.
'Just go nuts,' Trisha said, taking a toffee from the glove box. 'Go for the biggest first and the rest'll shit a brick.'
'Riiiiight,' Adrian said, unconvinced and beating a hasty retreat.

Over the following six weeks Dee Dee attended the centre as she had promised, albeit on light duties, spending much of her time just sitting with Bonnie and Alice who had also become firm friends since meeting Dee Dee. She also regularly attended the hospital to be prodded, poked and scanned and have countless samples of her blood taken.
It was one evening when she and Maizie had returned home from work that she paused at the foot of the stairs wheezing and clutching her chest. 'Woss a matter Dee?' Maizie asked. 'Woss up?'
'Ang on a minute?' Dee Dee puffed, raising a hand. 'Lemmy catch me breff'
'Dee ar noticed you bin breevin evvy in ya sleep lately mate,' Maizie said, taking her friend's arm. 'We gotta get'chu looked at right naah.'
'Naah ar'm alright,' Dee Dee said, but she clearly wasn't. 'Ar just need to put me feet up thas all, ar probly overdone it in the garden wiv the girls thas all.'
'What is it?' Pearl asked, meeting them at the top of the stairs. 'Woss wrong, Dee babe what is it?'
'She can't get er breff Misses D,' Maizie told her. 'Iss bin appnin a lot lately.'
'Right, ar get me coat!' Pearl said, storming back into the flat.
'Mum what ya doin?' Dee Dee asked, wanting no fuss.
'Takin you up the ospital!' Pearl insisted. 'Ramos love, call us a taxi babe!'
'Mum ar'm alright,' Dee Dee said, unbuttoning her jacket.

'No you aint!' her mother replied, re-doing the buttons. 'We're gonna get'chu looked at and thas that. Don't argue wiv me Deborah.' When her mother called her Deborah she meant business and Dee Dee knew it.

'Alright, alright,' Dee Dee relented. 'Can I av a cuppa tea first ar'm garspin.'

'No we aint got time,' Pearl said, zipping her own coat. 'Ow long love?' she asked Ramos.

'Five minutes my darling,' Ramos said, donning his shoes.

'You'z ain all gotta come,' Dee Dee said, watching her friends and family readying themselves. 'Iss only a check-up for gawd sake.'

'Dee we're comin!' Trisha said defiantly.

While Pearl, Ramos and her friends waited patiently in the cafeteria, seated at the same table they had now become accustomed to, Dee Dee underwent further tests including a bone scan, chest X-ray , CT scan and an MRI. After an agonizing wait of well over an hour she was approached by the doctor and his nurse. 'Deborah, sorry I mean Dee,' the doctor said, seated close beside her. 'I'm afraid to say you have what we call a regional recurrence.'

'A what?' Dee Dee asked.

The doctor turned to his nurse. 'Would you ask Dee's friends and family to join us please,' he asked, which instantly filled Dee Dee with dread. 'Whyyyyyy,' Dee Dee asked sheepishly. 'Woss wrong?'

'Well your recent breathlessness is a condition called dyspnoea, usually associated with a serious lung infection.'

'Me lungs?' Dee Dee said, clutching her chest. 'Woss wrong wiv me lungs?'

'Let me explain,' the doctor said, setting his clipboard down. 'A cancerous or malignant tumor like the one you had on your breast is made up of millions of tiny cancer cells and sometimes cells can break away from the tumor and travel around the body via the lymph system or blood for instance, we call this type of spread a metastases or a secondary.'

'Secondary!' Dee Dee said, starting to get the gist of the conversation. 'What, anuvva cancer?'
'I'm afraid so,' the doctor said in a hushed tone.
'Dee!' Pearl said, bursting into the room. 'Dee what is it babe?'
'You better sit daan Mum,' Dee Dee told her mother.
'Why?' Pearl said, remaining standing. 'Woss wrong, doctor? What is it, woss wrong wiv mar girl?'
'Iss the cancer Mum,' Dee Dee told her. 'Iss come back.'
Pearl clutched her chest and staggered back against the wall. 'Oh gawd no!' she gasped. 'No, Dee no!'
Maizie and Trisha rushed to their friend's side while Terry stood rooted to the spot at the door, the colour draining from his face.
'No Dee it carn av,' Maizie said, hugging Dee Dee. 'It can't mate.'
'Fuck no, no, no,' Trisha mumbled under her breath.
'I'm so sorry,' the doctor said. 'I'll give you a minute with you family and friends, the nurse will be back to see you shortly.'
'We don't wanna minute!' Pearl sobbed. 'You gotta get it aat of er, naah!'
'I'm afraid it isn't that simple,' the doctor said, pausing at the door. 'Look I'll explain everything soon, but for now it's best you be with her.'
'Yeah, yeah course,' Pearl said, approaching her daughter. 'Ohhh mar poor baby,' she wept, afraid to touch her child for fear of hurting her. 'Mar poor Dee.'
'Ar dunno what to say Dee mate,' Terry said, stunned to say the least. 'Ar'm gutted for ya babe, ar really am.'
'Ar'll be alright Tel,' Dee Dee said, with a stiff upper lip, whilst screaming inside. 'Don'tchu worry abaat me mate.'
But as the doctor later explained to the group when breast cancer spreads to the lungs in such a way as hers had done, then it can be treated but not cured, any treatments given were purely to relieve the symptoms and slow down the

growth. Effectively she had been told her condition was terminal.
'No, no don'tchu say that!' Trisha said, grabbing the doctor by his lapels. 'Don't chu fuckin say that, you get that shit aat of er right naah, cut me open if you av to, take what ya need to make er better. Give er wunna mar livers or summink!'
'Miss you only have one liver,' the doctor reminded her, whilst edging away.
'Well let er av it!' Trisha barked. 'Just make er better, d'you ear me!' Trisha had to be physically restrained by Terry and Maizie. 'YOU MAKE ER BETTER!' she continued. 'ISS YOUR JOB AIN IT!'
'Trisha babe,' Dee Dee said, wincing at the raised voices. 'Caaaalm daan, it ain iz fault, come ear babe.'
Trisha rushed into her friend's arms. 'Ar just want you to be better mate thas all,' she cried. 'Please get better, please, please, please.'

In the weeks and months to come Dee Dee underwent chemo and hormone therapy in the form of Tamoxifen, but despite this and the inhaler and nebulizer she had been issued, her condition deteriorated.
Adamantly she rose at six fifteen every morning after countless sleepless nights to make her way with Maizie to the Westmoreland centre in her now unmistakable pink beanie. Once there she would sit with Alice and Bonnie, who by now knew something was seriously wrong with their closest companion.
'Mum,' Dee Dee said that evening as Pearl sat on her laptop researching alternative medicines, in the faint hope of stumbling across a cure on the worldwide web. 'Mum!'
'What love?' Pearl said, looking up. 'Woss wrong?'
'Nuffing's wrong?' Dee Dee told her. 'Ar wanna see me dad,' she added, having thought long and hard. 'Ar wanna see im before ar,' she hesitated. 'Ar just wanna see im thas all.'
Pearl took a moment to process Dee Dee's request, having not heard her daughter speak of her father in recent years.

'OK babe,' she finally said. 'Whateva ya want. D'ya want me to come wiv ya?'
'Naah,' Dee Dee replied, retrieving her coat. 'Ar gotta do this on me own.'
'You sure Dee?' Maizie asked. 'Me and Trish should go wiv ya, iss a long way ain it.'
'No you two wait ear,' Dee Dee insisted, 'keep an eye on me mum.'
'But Deee,' Trisha objected.
'Trisha!' Dee Dee said abruptly. 'Shut it will ya, ar'm goin on me own and thas that, ar'll get a cab there and back so there aint no need to worry. Ok!'
'Right well wrap up warm,' Maizie said, buttoning Dee Dee's coat to her chin and handing her her beanie. 'Put yer at on and don't ferget yer inhaler, you got ya phone?'
'Yeah, yeah, stop fussin will ya,' Dee Dee sighed.
'Dee mate,' Terry said from the sofa, where he sat sharing a pack of beers with Ramos. 'Ar don't mind nickin a mota and givin you a lift.'
'Thas nice of ya Tel,' Dee Dee said, heading for the door, 'but you stay ear and keep aata trouble. Pritcher's still pullin iz air aat lookin for ya.'
'That cock couldn't catch crabs,' Terry laughed. 'You go careful then yeah.'
Dee Dee left her concerned family and friends and walked the short distance to the main road pausing halfway to take a breath through her inhaler. 'Chadwell Eaf mate,' she told the taxi driver, stepping into his black cab. During the journey the cabbie eyed Dee Dee in his rear view mirror fantasizing in a world of his own which made her feel very uneasy, so to put a stop to his leering she slipped the pink beanie from her now bald head which startled him somewhat and caused him to look away and her to smile. 'Cheers,' she said, handing the driver his fare and stepping from the cab at the all too familiar Birchum Estate, where her bizarre journey had begun several years earlier. Pulling her beanie over her head and down to her ears, she crossed

the litter strewn car park where she and her friends had scrawled a hopscotch grid with chalk stolen from school many years before, and headed toward the main entrance looking up at the flat that she and her mother used to occupy. Whilst going over and over in her mind what she was going to say to her father when she saw him, she hadn't noticed him descending the concrete stairs in her direction.
'Dad!' she then said, catching sight of him.
'Dee,' her father replied, giving her a wide berth. 'Look ar don't want no trouble, ar'll leave you alone, ar won't say a word ar promise.' The last time the two had met Dee Dee had spat at the money he had offered her and spoke to him as though he meant nothing to her.
'No wait!' she said, as he rounded her to leave. 'Dad wait, please!'
'What?' her father said, stunned at her pleading tone. 'You aint called me dad in years. Woss up Dee?'
Dee Dee looked around. 'Can we go somewhere and talk?' she asked, blowing into her hands. 'Ar got summink to tell ya.'
'Yeah course,' her father said eagerly. 'What is it Dee?'
'Less go to the park,' Dee Dee said, taking his hand which again shocked him. 'You always used to take me there dint'cha.'
'Yeah ar did,' her father said, unable to fathom the change of heart. 'Dee woss this all abaat babe? Listen if you need some money just say so, ar got a coupla quid put by, tell me ow much ya need.'
'No ar don't want ya money Dad,' Dee Dee said, pushing open the park gates. 'You used to shove me on the swings, member?'
'Yeah course ar member,' her father replied. 'You used to make me push ya for hours ya did.'
'Sit daan Dad,' Dee Dee told him, choosing a bench opposite the playground. 'Come on sit yer arse daan.'
'Dee what is it?' her father asked yet again and choosing to stand. 'Is it ya muvva, woss appened to er?'

'It aint me muvva,' Dee Dee said, rubbing her knees. 'Iss me Dad.'

'What?' her father said, dropping onto the bench. 'Woja mean iss you? You ain up the duff ar ya, ar knew it, don't tell me ar'm gonna be a grandad after all these years. Oh Dee babe thas brilliant, me a grandad!'

'No ya doughnut!' Dee Dee said, cutting his elation short. 'I aint well.'

'Ay?' her father said, his face dropping. 'Dee woja mean you aint well, what you got? The flu or wunna them orrible bug fings thas always goin araand. This aint like you Dee, you aint never bin sick in ya life av ya. Well apart from the time ar done a barbecue on the balcony and give us all the shits from that rank chicken ar got daan the market, ar never did catch up wiv the arsewipe that sold me that shite.'

'No Dad!' Dee Dee insisted. 'It ain a bug, iss cancer.'

Her father froze immediately, his eyes drilling into hers. 'What?' he soon said, edging away and looking his daughter up and down. 'What did you say?'

'Ar said ar got cancer Dad,' Dee Dee said, tugging at her beanie revealing her hairless scalp.

'Oh mar gawd!' her father cried, covering his mouth. 'No, shut up Dee, shut up don't fuck araand, not wiv shit like that babe. This is some sick joke ain it, to get me back for leavin you and ya mum. Ohhh Dee ow could ya babe, thas well aat of order that is.'

'Dad I aint fuckin araand,' Dee Dee told him. 'Ar'm proper serious,' she took hold of his hand and pressed it to her chest where her right breast used to be. 'See,' she told him. 'They already cut wunna these off.'

Her father wrenched his hand away and sat in stunned silence. 'Babe,' he eventually said. 'Babe what, how, ar mean. No babe, no not chu, not chu Dee, no no ar'm not avin it babe, not chu,' shaking his head her father refused to accept the bitter truth. 'Naah this is some sick fuckin joke this is ar bet'cha.'

'DAD!' Dee Dee snapped. 'Ar've got it, I aint jokin and iss bad,' she added, slipping her beanie back on. 'I ad it in me tit but naah iss come back again.'

'Woja mean, come back?' her father asked, his head a knot of mixed emotions. 'Dee please babe tell me this is a wind up, please Dee.'

'No Dad,' Dee Dee replied solemnly. 'Ar got it in me lungs naah, look,' she produced her inhaler. 'Ar got wunna these to elp wiv me breevin,' pressing the end she took a deep breath.

'Oh fuck no!' her father cried. 'Fuck Dee no babe!' Grabbing his daughter he pulled her to him, holding her tight to his broad chest. 'No, not mar Dee, not mar little baby girl. No God no!'

Dee Dee said nothing, she merely slid her arms around his waist relishing every second with her estranged father. 'Ar mist'cha Dad,' she admitted. 'Ar know ar bin a right bitch but I av mist'cha.'

'Oh babe,' her father said, with puffing eyes. 'Ar've mist'chu an'all, every bleedin day I av, every bleedin day of mar life. Oh Dee not chu,' he said repeatedly, stroking her pink beanie and rocking his child in his arms. 'No for fuck sake not mar girl.'

After a period of several minutes Dee Dee broke away. 'Dad, can you do me a favour please?' she asked.

'What, yeah course babe what?' her father replied, wiping both eyes. 'Anyfing babe.'

'Push me on the swings,' Dee Dee said, stroking his hand.

Her father looked across at the self-same swings that still hung in the dilapidated playground.

Dee Dee got up and approached the centre swing gripping the rusting chains and slipping her bottom onto the faded yellow plastic seat.

Shaking from head to toe and feeling physically sick her father followed her. 'You sure Dee?' he asked. 'Ar mean shouldn't you be in ospital or summink, come on babe ar take you up there naah, get'chu sorted aat.'

'Dad they can't sort me aat,' Dee Dee explained. 'Ar got a secondary or summink so all they can do naah is slow it daan. Push me will ya Dad, please.'
Quivering, her father put his hands on his daughter's and gently pushed her from him, then again and again as he had done twenty years previous.
Dee Dee kicked her legs, threw back her head and closed her eyes, in an instant she was transported back to her childhood; the sound of Maizie and Trisha squabbling over a curly wurly on the roundabout brought a smile to her face. 'Thas it Dad, faster, faster,' she said, with the images of her youth crystalizing in her mind. She could almost smell the smouldering Ford Capri that her friend Mickey Spencer, AKA Black Mickey, had stolen and torched at the park gates. 'Flippin ell this takes me back Dad!' she cried. But the swing began to slow and Dee Dee opened her eyes and looked over her shoulder to see her father on his knees with his head in his hands. 'Dad!' she said, dragging her feet to slow the swing before hopping off, 'Dad!' Dropping beside him she draped an arm across his back. 'Dad iss alright, please Dad don't cry,' she said. To see her father a broken man somehow seemed worse than the disease eating away at her. 'Dad, Dad look at me,' she said, cupping his face in her hands. 'Look at me, iss alright onest. All ar want naah is me Dad back, can ya do that, can ya do that for me please.'
'Oh fuckin ell course Dee!' her father sobbed, kissing her again. 'Thas all ar've ever wanted, ar mean it babe.'
Helping her father to his feet Dee Dee ushered him to the park gates. 'Look ar gotta go, but ear's me number.' She pressed a piece of paper into his shaking hand. 'Ar'm livin in Norf London naah wiv Maizie and Trisha, yeah Norf London Dad, oh and Tel, e'z stoppin wiv us coz e'z still on the run, and muvva's over an'all.'
'Your mum?' her father said, having had no contact with Pearl for many years. 'Ow is she?'
'She's appy Dad,' Dee Dee told him. 'She's wiv a lovely fella who treats er right and worships the graand she walks on.'

'Good,' her father replied. 'Good ar'm glad.'
Hugging his daughter again, even tighter in an attempt to draw the disease from within her, Dee Dee's father refused to let her go. 'Dad,' Dee Dee said moments later. 'Dad ar really gotta go, gimme a ring tomorra yeah.'
'Dee babe,' he said, refusing to relinquish her hand. 'Ar'm so sorry for what ar done to ya, ar really am babe. If ar could turn back the ands of time ar would, ar would Dee an ar'd never let you go again, ar love ya so so much.'
'Ar know Dad,' Dee Dee said, 'ar love you an'all.' Kissing his cheek Dee Dee then broke free and left him slumped against the park gates. 'Seeya Dad,' she said in parting. 'See ya soon yeah.'
Watching his daughter to the very last, Dee Dee's distraught father's legs then buckled beneath him and he slid down the railings where he sat for some time cursing himself for the days, months and years he had been absent in his daughter's life. The grass may have been greener all those years previous when he began his illicit affair with Pearl's best friend in the flat below theirs, but the true cost of his betrayal was only now being brought to bear upon him. 'Shit, shit, shit no!' he cried.
'You alright mister?' a young lad on a scooter asked, skidding at his side. 'What ya cryin for?'
Grasping at the gates Dee Dee's father pulled himself to his feet and drew a sleeve across his face. 'Nuffing,' he said, staggering towards the stairwell of the tower block where he still resided, leaving the lad scrambling for the loose change that had fallen from his pocket.
Looking back at the estate from the end of the road Dee Dee managed a smile, reminiscing for a moment and harking back to the days when she and her two best friends ran riot, giving the local lads a run for their money and driving their neighbours to near breaking point, knocking on their doors in the dead of night and scurrying away in fits of hysterical laughter. She ran her hand along the pebble dash wall where Trisha had crashed a stolen bicycle sustaining

countless scratches to her face, for which she spent a night in the local hospital and received a caution the following day at the police station.

It was a tough but grounding upbringing, character building some would say. Turning up her collar she stood on the corner until a taxi's yellow light came into sight. 'Islington mate,' she said, climbing in the back and slamming the door. Dee Dee later handed the driver a generous tip and shoved open the garden gate pausing to use her inhaler.

'Are you alright?' Tatyana asked, arriving home at the same time.

'Yeah, yeah ar'm dandy,' Dee Dee nodded. Tatyana held the street door open for Dee Dee. 'Fanks,' Dee Dee smiled, clawing at the dado rail. 'Ar just over done it a bit thas all.'

'Are you sure?' Tatyana asked.

'Yeah yeah,' Dee Dee insisted, ushering the Romanian away. 'Go see to ya nippers, go on babe.'

Tatyana left Dee Dee at the foot of the stairs. 'Fuck,' Dee Dee said, looking up the steep flight struggling to catch her breath. Taking only three steps Dee Dee was forced to drop down onto her bottom, resting her head against the wall. 'Shit fuck,' she cursed, shaking her spent inhaler.

'DEE!' Maizie then called from the landing, having heard the street door close. 'DEEEE!' she rushed down the stairs. 'Dee woss up?' she asked, with a hand on Dee Dee's back.

'Ar'm alright,' Dee Dee wheezed, raising a hand. 'Me fingey's run aat thas all.' Tossing her inhaler over the banister she grasped her friend's hand. 'Elp us up will ya mate,' she said.

'Oh flippin ell Dee,' Maizie said, taking much of her friend's weight. 'Ar knew you shouldn't av gone aat.'

'Yeah ar should,' Dee Dee told her friend, dragging herself up alongside Maizie. 'Ar see me dad Maize, ar see im and it was brilliant.'

'Ahhhh ar'm glad Dee,' Maizie said. 'TRIIIIISH!' she then yelled, 'TRISHAAAA!'

Trisha and Pearl came rushing from the flat. 'DEEE!' Pearl cried, taking her daughter from Maizie at the top step. 'Dee love wossa matter?'

'She needs anuvva breeva fing Misses D,' Maizie said. 'Trish go get one from er bedroom will ya, go on urry up for fuck sake!'

'Shit yeah, course,' Trisha said, darting back inside retrieving another of Dee Dee's inhalers. 'Eeya mate,' she said, pressing it to Dee Dee's lips. 'Av a tote on that, go on.' Wrenching the inhaler from Trisha's hand, Dee Dee took three deep breaths.

'We need a bloomin stair lift don't we,' Trisha said, looking down. 'Me nanny Marge ad one when we was little, ar spilt me slush puppy on it an it burnt aat the lectric mota, fing is the poor cow was arfway up and got stuck on it on er way to the bog and shit erself.'

'Trisha!' Maizie said, helping Dee Dee over the threshold. 'Shut it will ya!'

'Shut it will ya,' Trisha said, mimicking her friend. 'Ar was only sayin.'

'Well don't!' Maizie barked. 'Put the kettle on will ya, make Dee a cuppa tea, and nunna that erbal shit neeva.'

'Ohhhh,' Trisha moaned, 'itta do er the worlda good, ar just got a new box this mawnin; sunflower, wheatgrass and stingin nettle. Iss meant to clense ya colon or summink.'

'God no fanks,' Dee Dee said, heading for the sofa. 'Me guts are bad enough as it is.'

'Just do er a bog standard cuppa will ya,' Maizie said, giving Trisha that all too familiar look that meant business.

'Alright, alright,' Trisha said, tutting as she stomped into the kitchen. 'Well ar'm avin one!' she called back, taking her organic tea from the cupboard. 'It says!' she added, reading from the box, 'drink your way to spiritual enlightenment, an a clean bum ole an'all. Ar made the last bit up meself in case you'z was wondrin!'

'WE WEREN'T!' Maizie yelled back. 'WHERE'S THAT BLOODY TEA?'

Fluffing Dee Dee's cushions, Pearl removed her daughter's shoes. 'You've proper overdone it aint'cha babe,' she said, massaging her feet.
'Yeah thas what ar told that bird daanstairs,' Dee Dee said. 'But it was werf it Mum, just to see me dad and make me peace wiv im, ar shoulda done it years ago.'
'Yeah well, you done it naah thas what matters babe,' Pearl replied, taking the tea from Trisha. 'Eeya av a sippa this,' she told Dee Dee.
Maizie removed her friend's beanie, her heart sinking at the woeful sight.
'Ar look like shit don't I,' Dee Dee said, cupping her mug.
'Don't be daft!' Maizie exclaimed. 'You look beautiful, you always av done, me and Trish never come close to ya babe.'
'Naah we never Dee,' Trisha said, sitting beside her. 'Thas why ar used to nick all ya make up, just so'z ar could look like ya.'
'Oh shut up the paira ya,' Dee Dee scoffed. 'Looka the stata me.'
'Dee we're ya bestest mates,' Maizie told her. 'You'll always be a beauty queen to us. Always.' Dee Dee hung her head and began to cry. 'Ay, ay, ayyyyyy,' Maizie said, taking her mug, setting it down on the coffee table and hugging her friend as did Trisha. 'Shhhhhh, come on babe iss alright. Dee we all love ya to bits, no matter what.'
Rodney, sensing the emotion, hopped up onto Dee Dee's lap and nuzzled his wet nose into Dee Dee's chest. 'Ello mate,' she sobbed, patting his head.
Pearl, the three girls and the bijon sat huddled together on the sofa until the teas had gone cold. 'Come on,' Maizie eventually said to Dee Dee. 'Less get'chu ready for bed Dee, you must be knackered mate.'

The next morning, despite a horrendous night of vomiting and stomach cramps, Dee Dee rose for work. 'Seeya later babe,' she said, kissing Trisha as her friend left the flat. 'Be good yeah.'

'Don't be daft,' Trisha smiled, grabbing her jacket from the hall stand. 'You take it easy Dee yeah.'

During the day Dee Dee in her uniform and beanie knocked on Richard's office door. 'Come in!' Richard said from behind his desk. 'Oh hello Dee,' he said, rising to his feet to offer Dee Dee a seat. 'Do sit down, is everything ok?'

'Oh yeah,' Dee Dee replied sitting. 'Bonnie's surfin the web on the tablet fing ar got er and Alice is asleep.'

'What can I do for you?' Richard said, retaking his seat with a concerned look on his face. 'Are you sure you're alright?'

'Yeah, yeah. Ar want Bonnie's notes,' Dee Dee replied. 'All of em.'

'Sorry,' Richard said, with a ruffled brow. 'Her notes, why?'

'Ar wanna read em,' Dee Dee told him. 'Ar wanna know why social services stuck er in ear.'

'Because no living relative could be found,' Richard explained.

'Yeah well that aint good enough,' Dee Dee said abruptly. 'Ar wanna see em meself. Please.'

'Well er, if you insist,' Richard said, heading for a locked filing cabinet.

'Yeah, yeah ar do,' Dee Dee told him. 'That poor cow shouldn't be in ear, she's still a young girl wiv er ole life ahead of er.'

'I know it's a tragedy,' Richard agreed, thumbing the files in the top drawer. 'Here we are,' he said, handing Dee Dee a sparse file. 'That's all we have on her I'm afraid. Do please return it when you are finished with it Dee, it isn't meant to leave this office.'

'Yeah yeah,' Dee Dee said dismissively. 'Ar bring it back when ar'm done yeah.' She left with the file tucked under her arm, leaving Richard slightly bemused.

That afternoon while Terry sank a few pints in the Three Squirrels with an old acquaintance, Trisha single handedly raided an illegal puppy farm rescuing seven weary Spaniels whose lives had been one long pregnancy for monetary gain. 'You touch me an ar'll snap ya fuckin arm off!' Trisha told a grossly overweight woman, whilst carrying the last of the dogs to the van, where Adrian again was waiting locked inside. 'And you better get used to prison food bitch!' Trisha added, looking over her shoulder. 'Coz ar'm reportin the lot of ya!'

After work Dee Dee and Maizie made their way to the station as usual but this time Dee Dee paused to cross to the opposite platform. 'Where ya goin Dee?' Maizie asked.
'Ar gotta go do summink,' Dee Dee replied, climbing the stairs steadily. 'You go ome, ar see ya later!'
'What?' Maizie asked bemused. 'What ya gotta do? DEE!'
'Summink!' Dee Dee called down. 'Don't worry!' she said, producing her inhaler from her pocket. 'Ar got me breeva, ar be back later!'
'You sure?' Maizie called back. 'D'you want me to come wiv ya?'
'NO!' Dee Dee barked. 'Look ar see ya later, alright!'
Maizie stood confused for a moment or two while Dee Dee disappeared out of sight.
Travelling on the metropolitan line Dee Dee eventually alighted and took the short walk to Paddington Green police station, the new home of her nemesis D I Pritcher. Looking up at the stark building with some trepidation, Dee Dee took a deep breath through her inhaler and climbed the steps. 'Ar'm ear to see Pritcher,' she told the WPC behind the front desk.
'Sorry, who?' the WPC replied, leaning forward.
'Pritcher!' Dee Dee said, raising her voice a little louder.
'You mean Detective Inspector Pritcher,' the WPC replied. 'Do you have an appointment?'
'No ar don't,' Dee Dee said, steadying herself against the counter. 'Ar just wanna see im, can ya get im for me?'
'I'll try,' the WPC told Dee Dee, picking up the phone beside her. 'But I doubt he'll see you, not without an appointment, what's your name?'

'Dee,' Dee Dee replied. 'Tell im it's Dawson, Deborah Dawson. E'll know me.'

The WPC hung on the line for a moment. 'Oh sorry to bother you sir,' she eventually said. 'I have a Miss Dawson here at the front desk to see you, she doesn't have an appointment but she says that you know her. Deborah Dawson sir.'

After a brief conversation the WPC put down the phone. 'I'm to take you through, please follow me,' she said, lifting a flap in the counter.

Dee Dee did so and after leaving her mobile phone in a tray at the desk as instructed and signing the visitors' book, she followed the WPC through the station's hallowed corridors.

'Here we are,' the WPC said, knocking on the D I's door. Opening it she leant inside, 'Miss Dawson to see you sir,' she said, ushering Dee Dee inside. 'Give me a call when you're done sir and I'll escort her out.'

Dee Dee was now standing in the lion's den face to face with the D I, both of them having absolutely no love for the other.

'Dawson,' the D I sneered, with an air of utter contempt. 'What the fuck do you want?'

'A favour,' Dee Dee said, approaching his desk.

'A favour!' the D I laughed. 'You got some bollocks Dawson, you and your slag mates caused me a shit loada grief and you waltz in ear askin me for a favour. Well ar tell ya what, you can do me a favour by turnin raand and pissin off aata my office.'

Dee Dee had to literally bite her lip to prevent herself from unleashing a verbal tirade upon him. 'Look, ar wouldn't be ear if it wern important,' she told him. 'You know that Pritcher, so just ear me aat will ya. Oh and as for the grief ar caused ya, ar won't be causin you anymore.'

'Ar doubt that,' the D I scoffed, 'once a feevin slag always a feevin slag thas what ar say.'

'Not anymore,' Dee Dee said, removing her beanie.

'Woss all this?' the D I asked, taken aback by her baldness. 'You gone dyke like ya mate?'

'Iss cancer you cock!' Dee Dee snapped. 'An iss terminal.'
'You crafty bitch!' the D I laughed. 'You fink ar'm fallin for that old chestnut do ya? Well I aint just got off the bleedin banana boat Dawson, if you fink you can shave ya ruddy ed and get me jumpin fru oops you're much mistaken. Naah, like ar said, piss off aat of ear before ar bang you up for wastin police time.'
Dee Dee unbuttoned her coat to reveal her flattened chest on one side. 'Ar spoze ar chopped me own tit off an'all did I?' she remarked, sucking on her inhaler.
Rocking back in his seat the D I sat speechless for a moment while the penny dropped. 'You mean you got,' he said awkwardly.
'Cancer,' Dee Dee said, preempting him. 'Yeah, yeah I av so you gonna elp me or not?'
'Elp ya!' the D I said bemused. 'Ow the bleedin ell am ar spozed to elp ya, do ar look like a bloody doctor?'
'No you look like a complete...,' Dee Dee again stopped herself from insulting the D I. 'Look,' she said sternly. 'This shit's gonna do me in so ar really need this favour. Please,' she said, almost choking on the p word.
'What favour?' the D I asked a little curious now.
Dee Dee produced Bonnie's file from her bag and slid it across the table. 'Er name's Bonnie,' she told him, 'she's in care.'
'And,' the D I said dismissively. 'What do you want me to do abaat it, I ain in the market for adoptin kids.'
'Look,' Dee Dee said, wheezing now. 'Er muvva died of an overdose a few years back, you probly got it on record somewhere. Anyway social services couldn't find any uvva relatives but ar know there must be someone aat there, ar know you got contacts Pritcher, you're a slimy bastard like that. Listen if you don't wanna do it for me, do it for er.'
'I aint got time for that shit,' the D I said, pushing the file back across his desk. 'Ar'm too busy catchin villains like you and your mates. Speakin of mates, are you ready to tell me where that prick Terry is?'

'Ar told ya I aint seen im,' Dee Dee said defiantly. 'I aint seen im for ages.'

'Bullshit!' the D I barked. 'You turn im in an ar'll fink abaat this girl of yours, there ya go, ar'm offerin you a deal.'

'You slag Pritcher!' Dee Dee cursed. 'You know ar could never do that even if ar did know where e was. Just look into Bonnie's case thas all ar'm askin, ar don't want nuffing for meself. Thas all the information we got, ar'll say it again if ya want... Please Mr Pritcher.'

The D I relished having Dee Dee groveling at his feet, but the smile soon dropped from his face when she began a coughing fit staggering to the wall. 'Dawson!' he said, not knowing quite what to do. 'What's the matter Dawson?' he asked, rising slowly from his seat.

Dee Dee shook her inhaler taking what little breaths she could through her severely weakened lungs.

The D I picked up his phone and dialed the desk. 'Fetch me some water!' he yelled, fearing a fatality right there in his office. 'NOW!'

'Fuck no not ear,' Dee Dee said to herself, fearing the worst.

The WPC came scurrying into the room a short while later carrying a bottle of water purchased from the vending machine. 'Oh dear!' she said, seeing Dee Dee slumped against the wall. 'Here take this,' she said, unscrewing the cap and pressing the bottle to Dee Dee's whitening lips. 'Are you ok, what's wrong?' she asked, as the D I looked on.

'Yeah, fanks,' Dee Dee said, catching her breath. 'Yeah, ar fink so, ar'm er, ar'm sick.'

'Well let's get you home,' the WPC said with an arm around her. 'You're in no fit state to be here.'

'No wait!' Dee Dee said, objecting and tugging her arm free and pointing to the file on the D I's desk. 'What abaat...'

'Come on,' the WPC insisted, helping Dee Dee from the D I's office.

'Please,' Dee Dee said croakily over her shoulder. 'Please Mr Pritcher!' She was then escorted back to the front desk.

The D I dropped back into his chair, pondering what had just happened and looking across at the tiny spots of blood on the wall, coughed from Dee Dee's lungs. He thought long and hard of the cat and mouse game that he and Dee Dee had played over the previous years. A game that was evidently being drawn to an untimely conclusion. He slowly dragged the file back toward him and turned the front cover.

Dee Dee was driven home in a police traffic vehicle at the request of the WPC. 'Flippin ell iss the old bill,' Maizie said, looking from their window seeing the squad car in the road outside.
'DO WHAT?' Terry cried, leaping from the sofa upsetting his can of lager. 'SHIT!'
'Quick Tel, ide!' Trisha told him, ducking behind the sofa herself.
'Trish what you doin?' Maizie asked her. 'We aint done nuffing wrong you idiot.'
'Oh,' Trisha said, emerging, 'oh yeah.'
Terry wrenched open the kitchen window, scrambled up onto the butcher's block worktop and climbed out onto the rear flat roof. 'Bollocks!' he said, seeing no way down. 'Shit, shit!' he then cursed, standing with his back to the flank wall fearing his extended run of freedom was about to come to an abrupt end.
'Flippin ell iss Dee!' Maizie said, when the police officers helped Dee Dee from the back of the vehicle, inhaler in hand.
'Did you say Dee?' Pearl asked, having closed the kitchen window behind Terry. 'Oh mar gawd,' she added, peering over Maizie's shoulder. 'It is er, woss she gone and done?'
Ramos was dozing in the armchair and woke suddenly when the girls dashed from the flat and down the stairs. 'DEEEE!' Pearl cried, throwing open the street door. 'Woss appened, what ya done, you aint bin nicked av ya?'

'No I aint Mum,' Dee Dee said at the gate. 'Cheers,' she told the two officers. 'You ain all bad ar ya.' The officers smiled and climbed back into their vehicle hearing a call on the radio.

'Dee mate what appened?' Maizie asked, rushing to her.

'Ang on,' Dee Dee said, clutching her chest, 'lemmy get me breff back.' Wheezing, she was then helped up to their flat.

'ISS ALRIGHT TEL!' Maizie called. 'THEY JUST BROUGH DEE OME!'

'What?' Terry said, peering back through the window having had an attack of vertigo out back. 'Av they gone?'

'Yeah iss alright mate,' Trisha told him from the kitchen sink. 'Ar bin finkin of puttin a winda box aat there so ar can grow me own erbs, woja reckon?'

'Whateva,' Terry said, scrambling back inside and dunking his foot into the sink that Trisha had just filled in the process. 'Fuck it Trish!' he cursed, shaking his market bought trainer and placing a hand on Trisha's shoulder to steady himself. 'Woss up?' he then asked, squelching through to the living room. 'Dee?'

'She's aata breff,' Maizie told him. 'The old bill brought er ome.'

'Dee babe,' Pearl said, helping her daughter to the sofa. 'Where ya bin love?'

'Ar just ad to do summink,' Dee Dee said, refusing to divulge the reason for her brief outing. 'Leave me alone will ya, all of ya, just gimme some space ar can't breev wiv you all crowdin raand me for gawd sake.'

Pearl and her friends backed away and sat at the table, watching her fight for her breath. 'D'ya want ya nebulizer Dee?' Maizie asked, knowing the piece of apparatus inside out at this point. Dee Dee nodded unable to speak.

Maizie retrieved the nebulizer from their bedroom and set it up beside the sofa. 'Eeyar mate,' she said, assisting her friend. 'Take deep breffs member.'

The following morning, Terry, Dee Dee and Trisha were all woken at 6:15 by the sound of Maizie shrieking in the bathroom. 'If thas anuvva fuckin spider,' Dee Dee said, rolling over in bed. 'Ar'll fuckin frottle er.'

'Yes, yes, oh fuckin yes!' Maizie cried, hopping on the spot. 'Yes you little beauty!'

'Jesus, what the?' Terry asked, jostling his testicles on the sofa.

'Maizie?' Trisha said, hunting her friend down. 'There you are, what ya bleedin doin?' she too asked.

Dee Dee joined the two of them looking decidedly unimpressed. 'Maizie d'you know what flippin time it is,' she cursed.

'Dee, ya never gonna believe it!' Maizie said, bobbing up and down. 'Ar'm pregnant Dee, ar'm gonna av a bloody baby. Me, Dee, ar'm proper up the duff mate look!' She produced a home pregnancy test. 'Ar just pissed all over it and look, it says ar'm bloody pregnant!'

'Do what?' Trisha asked, snatching the test from her and examining the blue lines. 'Bloody Nora!' she exclaimed. 'She is Dee av a look.'

'You're jokin,' Dee Dee said, looking over Trisha's shoulder.

'No, no I aint!' Maizie said excitedly. 'Iss for real Dee mate, ar'm gonna av a baby. Can ya believe it?'

'Flippin ell Maize,' Dee Dee said, shocked to say the least. 'A baby?'

'Yeah a baby Dee,' Maizie added. 'I ad a feelin ar was up the duff, but ar didn't wanna say nuffing. Me and Rich aint bin tryin for a baby but ar know e'z gonna be well chuffed when ar tell im.'

'What abaat chu?' Dee Dee asked. 'You always said you weren't bovva'd abaat avin kids.'

'Yeah ar know,' Maizie said, sitting on the edge of the bath staring at the test. 'But ar love Richard, an it just feels right wiv im.'

'You avin a chicken dipper Maize?' Terry asked.

'What?' Trisha said bemused. 'Ar was gonna av a bowla muesli Tel,' she replied.
'Nipper!' Terry explained. 'Chicken bloody dipper.'
'Oh,' Trisha said. 'Oh yeah course, ar knew that.'
'Thas brilliant babe,' Terry told Maizie, joining them all in the bathroom to kiss Maizie's cheek.
'Ar'm pleased for ya Maize,' Dee Dee said, retrieving a new inhaler from the bathroom cabinet. 'Ar really am.'
'Ahhh fanks Dee,' Maizie smiled. 'That means a lot to me, you all mean a lot to me. Ar'm gonna be a mum, can ya believe it?'
'You'll make a great muvva,' Dee Dee told her.
'Ar seen you wiv ya cousin Shelly's girls, you're a natral babe, ar just ope ar get to see you wiv yours thas all.'
'Ohhh shut up Deeee,' Maizie said, hugging her friend. 'Course ya will, you aint goin nowhere for a long bleedin time yet mate. Is she Trish?'
'No she bleedin aint!' Trisha insisted, whilst dropping her knickers to pee. 'D'you mind Tel?' she asked, seeing Terry leering at the door.
'Naah,' Terry smiled, 'ar don't mind at all, unless you're avin a tom tit that is.'

That day Maizie broke the glorious news to Richard and as expected he was delighted. 'That's wonderful darling!' he said, placing a hand on Maizie's stomach. 'How long, when?'
'Ar dunno,' Maizie told him, stroking his hand. 'Ar'm goin up the doctors tonight.'
Dee Dee sat with Bonnie for much of the day feeling as though she had failed her.
'For you,' Bonnie said, handing Dee Dee a neatly folded piece of paper.
'Me?' Dee Dee said. 'What is it?' Unfolding it on Bonnie's bed she smiled. 'Iss a poem, ahhh fanks love.' She then proceeded to read the crude offering out loud.

'Dee's my friend

Someday we'll be together

And I love her so
She picks me up when I am low
She holds my hand
And dries my tears
I'll love my Dee for a thousand years.

Dee you were my friend
When I had none
You are the moon and night and the morning sun
You were there
When no one came
You held my han, you said my name.

I love you Dee
Every day you come
I love you Dee

Dee Dee paused, her hand shaking and her heart breaking at the final two lines.

I love you Dee
Please be my mum.

She pressed the poem to her face and broke down in tears.
'Sorry Dee, sorry, sorry, sorry,' Bonnie said, hugging her. 'Sorry I didn't mean to make you sad.'
'You aint,' Dee Dee sobbed, throwing her arms around Bonnie. 'You aint babe, you made me the appiest girl in the ole world you av. No one's ever writ me anyfing like that in me life, iss beautiful, ar love ya Bonnie babe ar really do.'
Dee Dee read the poem to herself over and over, each time shedding another tear. 'Iss beautiful,' she said, caressing Bonnie's face. 'Really beautiful.'

Meanwhile word had spread throughout the illegal puppy farming trade that there was now a kick-arse animal welfare warden on the hunt for them, causing many of them to shut up shop and seek an alternative career path. Trisha had certainly made a difference in her short time at the society receiving no less than three commendations, the most ever awarded to a warden in the society's long and illustrious history.

Maizie and Richard learned that she was in fact three months gone and that their baby was due in late December. 'Ar don't wanna know what it is,' Maizie told her lover. 'Less just wait and see shall we?'

Richard agreed. 'Whatever you want,' he said, rubbing her stomach gently.

Dee Dee's daily ritual of tube trains and early mornings soon began to take its toll on her, and she found it increasingly difficult to cope despite her dogged determination and will to carry on. 'Maize,' she said, beckoning to her friend from her hospital bed during yet another visit and another course of treatment, 'ear.'

Maizie leant over and took her friend's hand. 'Woss up mate?' she asked. 'D'ya want me to do ya pillas?'

'Naah listen,' Dee Dee said, grabbing at Maizie's sleeve. 'Ar need ya to do summink for me, summink important.'

'Course Dee anyfing,' Maizie said, perched at her side. 'Anyfing, you know that.'

'Ar need you to take care of Alice and Bonnie when ar'm, you know.'

'Oh Dee don't say that, please,' Maizie begged, turning away.

Dee Dee wrenched her friend closer. 'Look!' she said, grimacing. 'We bofe know woss appnin to me an that don't scare me, but what does scare me shitless is that them girls ar gonna be left on their own again. Promise me Maizie, promise me you'll look aat for em, please.'

Maizie's heart sank at Dee Dee's pitiful plea. 'Course ar will Dee, you aint got nuffing to worry abaat babe. But lark ar keep tellin ya, you aint goin nowhere for a bleedin long time, not while ar got a breff in me body.'

'One uvva fing,' Dee Dee added, looking across at Trisha who was tampering with hospital equipment and struggling to replace a knob that had just broken off in her clumsy hand. 'Look after soppy nuts there.'

Maizie looked over her shoulder at their hapless friend, who was causing more damage in an attempt to mend the apparatus. 'Do I av to?' she joked.

'Yeah ya do,' Dee Dee urged. 'She's one of us Maize, it don't matter if she's fick as shit, she's still our mate. Promise me you two will stay close forever, promise please Maize, itta be a massive weight off me mind knowin you're there to get er aat of all the shit she's gonna get into. Look after er Maizie, ar love that soppy bitch so much, ar love ya bofe so much, you two ar me life, ar mean that, ar've bin so lucky avin such top mates as you two, we've ad some laughs aint we.'

'Yeah and we're gonna av a lot more Dee,' Maizie said, refusing to listen to Dee Dee's acceptance of her dire situation. 'Me, you and Trish, just like iss always bin. And you're right, we're stuck wiv the daft mare now aint we.'

'Ow's the baby comin on?' Dee Dee asked, touching Maizie's bump.

'Kickin the fuck aata me,' Maizie replied, moving Dee Dee's hand to where a tiny foot was prodding at her from the inside. 'Can ya feel it?' she asked.

'Bleedin 'ell yeah!' Dee Dee smiled. 'You can tell iss one of us can't ya.'

'Ar got free mumfs to go naah,' Maizie told her friend. 'Iss weird Dee, ar never fought ar'd say this but ar'm really lookin forward to bein a mum, doin all that mum shit, pushin me pram into the backsa peoples ankles and changin shitty arses.'

On this occasion Terry had attended the wake of an old family friend and was no doubt seven parts pissed and being his usual raucous self. Which was just as well, because while Trisha was single handedly destroyed a hugely expensive piece of hospital equipment and Dee Dee and Maizie were

having one of their girly chats, no one had noticed D I Pritcher looking in through the glazed door.
'Dawson,' the D I eventually said, pushing the door open.
'What the fuck do you want?' Trisha instinctively barked, standing between him and her friends. 'She aint done nuffing, she's sick for fuck sack can't you see that!'
'I aint come to nick er,' the D I said, clutching Bonnie's file.
'Ar spoze you come to gloat then av ya, you dirty slag!' Trisha said defensively. 'Well thas fuckin low, even for you Pritcher, so why don'tchu turn raand and piss off aat of ear or you'll be nickin me for assault.'
'Trisha!' Dee Dee snapped. 'Shut it will ya, ar know ya mean well but just leave it babe, it aint werf it.'
Trisha reluctantly stepped aside glaring at the D I in doing so and watching his every move as he approached Dee Dee's bed, where he received the cold shoulder from Maizie too.
'You left this,' he said, setting the file down at Dee Dee's side. 'There's summink in there you might wanna read.' He looked down at the clearly sick girl; the girl that had once lead him a merry dance and given him more than his fair share of sleepless nights. 'Ar'll er, ar'll be gettin off,' he said, turning with the slightest of lumps in his throat.
'Pritcher!' Dee Dee called, stopping him at the door. 'Fanks,' she added, picking up the file. The D I said nothing as he left.
'What was that all abaat?' Maizie asked.
'Yeah Dee,' Trisha added, joining her friends on the bed. 'Woss goin on?'
'Bonnie,' Dee Dee replied, 'iss abaat Bonnie.' Opening the file Dee Dee removed a piece of paper that had been added to the original document and scrutinized it carefully. 'Fuckin yes!' she said jubilantly. Swatting Trisha from the bed Dee Dee then threw back her sheets.
'What ya doin Dee?' Maizie asked. 'You aint finished ya meds mate.'
'Fuck em,' Dee Dee said, wrenching the line from her arm. 'Pass me me clothes will ya.'
'But Dee,' Trisha said at her side.

'I aint got time for your shit Trisha,' Dee Dee barked. 'Just pass me me gear for fuck sake.'
'Dee what is it?' Maizie asked, handing Dee Dee her clothes and helping her dress.
'Iss Bonnie,' Dee Dee smiled, pulling on her sweater. 'She's only got a nan and grandad!'
'Really!' Maizie exclaimed. 'Shit Dee, thas brilliant!'
'Too fuckin right it is,' Dee Dee replied, stepping into her trainers.
'Where are they then?' Trisha asked.
'Bloody Watford!' Dee Dee said, clutching the file. 'Can you bleedin believe it, that poor cow's bin on er own all these years, an er family's livin in Watford of all blinkin places.'
Rushing as best she could from the hospital with her friends at her side, Dee Dee hailed a taxi. 'Watford mate!' she said, sucking on her inhaler as she climbed in back. 'Benjamin Street, number six.'
During the twenty minute journey Dee Dee read the piece of paper over and over, her heart racing.
'Call it twenty five quid,' the cabbie told her on arrival.
'Ar get this Dee,' Maizie said, handing the driver thirty pounds. 'Keep the change geez,' she told him, stepping out behind Dee Dee.
'Right,' Dee Dee said, looking at the unassuming terraced house.
'You nervous Dee?' Trisha asked, climbing out beside them.
'Ar'm shittin a fuckin brick,' Dee Dee replied, pressing the doorbell.
The girls stepped back and waited on the crazy paved pathway as a shadowy figure appeared behind the stained glass door.
'Yes?' a middle aged woman with greying hair said, opening the door ever so slightly and peering out. 'What is it, what do you want?'
Dee Dee looked down at the piece of paper one again. 'Mrs Pearson?' she asked.

'Yes that's right,' the woman replied, opening the door a little wider. 'Do I know you, look if you're from the church my husband and I haven't any money so I suggest you try another door.'

'Wait!' Dee Dee said, as Mrs Pearson began to close the door. 'We aint from the church!'

'Well what is it then?' Mrs Pearson asked, growing ever impatient. 'What do you want?'

'Look, you don't know me,' Dee Dee told her, 'but iss abaat ya daughter.'

Mrs Pearson immediately froze. 'My daughter,' she said, opening the door fully. 'What about my daughter, do you know her, where is she?'

'Can we come in?' Dee Dee asked.

'Yes, yes please do,' Mrs Pearson said eagerly. 'Where is she, where's my Gemma?'

The girls were shown to the sitting room. 'This is David, my husband, Gemma's father,' Mrs Pearson said. 'Darling, they've come about Gemma, I think they're friends of hers.'

Mr Pearson sat bolt upright at the mention of his daughter's name. 'Gemma?' he said, dropping his remote control. 'Where is she, where's our daughter?'

'Was that er name?' Dee Dee asked.

'What do you mean was?' Mrs Pearson asked. 'Oh God, what's happened?' She dropped beside her husband grabbing at his hand. 'What's happened, where is she?'

Dee Dee looked at her two friends. 'Look ar dunno if ar'm the right person to be tellin you this,' she said apprehensively.

'Tell us what?' 'Mrs Pearson said, with a look of anguish. 'Please, please we have to know.'

'Can ar sit daan?' Dee Dee asked, hovering at an armchair.

'Yes, yes please do,' the Pearson's said, physically shaking.

Maizie and Trisha sat at a side table saying nothing.

'Ar dunno where to start wiv this,' Dee Dee told them, with the file on her knee. 'Gemma, your daughter…'

'That's right,' Mr Pearson said, 'we haven't seen or heard from her in over fifteen years. She ran away when she was just seventeen, with some lad we think, where is she?'
'Ar'm afraid ar got some bad news for ya,' Dee Dee said, shaking herself and puffing on her inhaler.
'Are you alright dear?' Mrs Pearson asked.
'Yeah,' Dee Dee said, pocketing the inhaler. 'This is really ard,' she told the Pearsons.
'Oh my God!' Mrs Pearson said, clasping a hand to her open mouth. 'Something's happened to her hasn't it? Oh David, please God no!'
'Is she...?' David asked, hesitating. 'Is she dead?'
Dee Dee too hesitated. 'Yeah,' she eventually said solemnly. 'Sorry, yeah she is.'
Maizie and Trisha hung their heads as a mark of respect.
'Oh no. NO!' Mrs Pearson cried, shaking her head in disbelief. 'God no, please no, no, not my Gemma.'
Dee Dee sat in silence for a few moments while the Pearson's clung to one another immersed in grief.
'I'm sorry,' Mrs Pearson then said, taking a tissue from her sleeve and blowing her nose.
'No, no,' Dee Dee replied, 'you aint got nuffing to be sorry for.'
'Would you girls like some tea?' Mr Pearson asked, rising from the sofa wanting an excuse to be alone.
'Yeah thatta be nice fanks,' Dee Dee replied.
'Yeah ta,' Maizie added.
'Four sugars mate,' Trisha piped up.
Mr Pearson trudged into the kitchen where he clung to the worktop and broke down in silence.
'Did you know her?' Mrs Pearson asked Dee Dee, tucking her tissue back inside her cardigan sleeve.
'No, no ar never,' Dee Dee replied.
'Then why are you here? Mrs Pearson asked bemused. 'I don't understand.'
Dee Dee took a deep breath and began to explain how Gemma died and that a baby was found at her side.

'A baby!' Mrs Pearson shrieked. 'My Gemma had a baby!'

'Yeah,' Dee Dee continued, explaining how social services had tried to no avail to track down Gemma's living relatives, and how Bonnie was eventually sent to the Westmoreland centre.

'Bonnie?' Mrs Pearson said, clutching her heart.

'Yeah Bonnie,' Dee Dee told her. 'Ar bin lookin after er, ar work there ya see.'

'David, David dear!' Mrs Pearson called, her husband returned with a tray of teas and reddened eyes, setting the teas down beside Dee Dee. 'What is it dear?' he asked, handing the girls their beverages.

'Fanks,' Dee Dee said, blowing hers.

'Gemma had a baby!' Mrs Pearson told her husband excitedly. 'Darling, our Gemma had a baby, her name's Bonnie. Do you remember she had a white rabbit called Bonnie when she was five years old?'

'Do you mean we're grandparents?' Mr Pearson asked Dee Dee, his spirits now lifted.

'Yeah, yeah you are,' Dee Dee explained. 'And she needs a family, desperately. Ar'm all she's got at the moment.'

'When can we see her?' Mrs Pearson asked eagerly. 'I wonder if she has her mother's looks.'

'Ar got a phota,' Dee Dee said, producing her purse.

Mr and Mrs Pearson sat in heightened anticipation as Dee Dee removed a folded photograph. 'Ar took this up London when we went aat for the day,' she said, handing the photograph of Bonnie standing arms raised in front of Nelson's column in Trafalgar square to her grandmother. 'She loved them pigeons,' Dee Dee smiled.

'Oh look dear!' Mrs Pearson gasped. 'Look isn't she beautiful, and look she has her mother's eyes, look dear!'

'Dear God yes!' Mr Pearson said, clutching the corner of the tiny photograph. 'Bonnie you say?'

'Yeah Bonnie,' Dee Dee replied. 'And she's proper clever an'all, she writes beautiful poems an everyfing.' Dee Dee

shared her experiences of Bonnie with her grandparents from the very first moment she entered her room.
'You have taken care of her haven't you,' Mrs Pearson eventually said. 'Thank you, thank you, and we don't even know your name my dear.'
'Ar'm Dee Dee, thas Maizie and the dopey lookin one is Trish,' Dee Dee explained.
'Oh fanks,' Trisha scoffed, but then a look from Maizie soon silenced her.
'So when can we see her?' Mr Pearson asked, sipping his tea. 'Sooner the better we hope, ay darling.'
'Yes of course dear,' his wife agreed. 'Much sooner please.'
'Tomorra,' Dee Dee replied, handing the couple a business card. 'Thas the address, me number's on the back.' Dee Dee coughed several times before continuing. 'Abaat arf eleven if thas alright wiv you'z, just gimme a bell when ya get there coz ar gotta talk to er first.'
'Yes of course, half eleven, that's wonderful!' Mr Pearson said, pocketing the card.
'Right we gotta be goin,' Dee Dee told the Pearsons.
'Wait!' Mrs Pearson said, clambering from the sofa. 'Before you go I want to show you something. All of you.' She lead the girls upstairs to her daughter's room. 'It's just as she left it,' she explained. 'As you can see she was a real girly girl, that's why we were so shocked when she ran off.'
'Corrrr, ar love it,' Trisha said, stepping into the almost entirely pink room which included matching drapes and bedspread. 'Who's that?' she asked, examining a poster of two teen pop idols from days gone by on Gemma's wall.
'I think they were called Bros or something,' Mrs Pearson replied, shrugging her shoulders. 'Gemma simply adored them, I remember she tied bottle tops to her laces just to be like them.'
'Iss lovely,' Dee Dee smiled, looking around.
'So how did you find us?' Mrs Pearson said, leading the girls back down the narrow stairs.

'Ar got a contact in the old bill,' Dee Dee informed her. 'E done it for me.'
'Well, we are truly glad that he did, aren't we dear?' Mrs Pearson said, addressing her husband before looking out of the window. 'How did you girls get here?' she asked, seeing no vehicle outside.
'We got a cab,' Dee Dee told her. 'Can we ring one from ear?'
'Nonsense!' Mr Pearson said, retrieving his keys from the mantle. 'I'll run you home myself. It's the least I can do.'
'You don't av to,' Maizie said, zipping her puffer jacket. 'We don't wanna put you aat.'
'Don't be ridiculous,' Mr Pearson smiled. 'You came with bad news but somehow in our hearts we knew that we would never see our Gemma again. But to hear she has a daughter, our granddaughter, is simply wonderful news. You don't know what this means to my wife and I, our lives have literally been a living hell from the moment she walked out of this house all those years ago. But now... now we have a reason to go on, a new beginning if you like.'
'Yes thank you so much,' Mrs Pearson said, taking Dee Dee's hand. 'Thank you, thank you dear.'
After a tearful goodbye with Mrs Pearson the girls were driven back to their North London flat in her husband's reliable Volvo estate. 'Thanks again,' he said, dropping them right outside. 'I mean that Dee Dee.'
'Thas alright,' Dee Dee replied. 'Just make sure you'z turn up tomorra, don'tchu let that girl daan.'
'Oh we won't I promise,' Mr Pearson smiled. 'Wild horses couldn't keep us away.'
'Good,' Dee Dee said, coughing and retching yet again, clinging to the garden wall this time.
'My God are you alright?' Mr Pearson asked, climbing from his car.
'Yeah yeah,' Dee Dee said, raising a hand to stop him. 'Just be there tomorra will ya,' she reiterated. 'Don't make me come lookin for ya.'

Maizie and Trisha helped their friend inside. 'Ar dunno ow you done it Dee,' Maizie told her friend. 'An ar don't wanna know, but what you done for that poor cow in that ome is bloody brilliant mate.'
'Ar just ope they turn up,' Dee Dee wheezed, struggling with the stairs.
'Dee babe, you aright,' Pearl said, seated with Terry and Ramos.
'Yeah muvva ar'm dandy,' Dee Dee replied, when she clearly was far from it. 'Listen ar'm gonna av a lie daan if ya don't mind, ar'm cream crackered Mum.'
'Yeah course love,' her mother said, leaving the table. 'D'ya want me to get ya summink, a drink or a samwich.'
'Naah, fanks Mum but I ain ungry,' Dee Dee confessed. 'All ar want is me pit.'
Trisha explained to Pearl, Terry and Ramos the events of the afternoon.
'Oh mar gawd!' Pearl gasped, welling up. 'Thas amazin, that poor girl livin all on er own all these years when er nan and grandad ar just up the bleedin road. Iss a cryin shame ain it.'
The following morning Dee Dee was up early shaking her friend in her bed. 'Maize!' she said, stepping out of her pajamas. 'Maizie come on, ar don't wanna be late.'
'Mmmmm yeah alright,' Maizie said, stretching beneath her duvet. 'What time is it?'
'Never mind that just get up!' Dee Dee insisted, keen to get to work to prepare Bonnie for her visit.
'You gonna be alright Dee?' Maizie asked, climbing out beside her friend.
'Yeah, don't worry abaat me,' Dee Dee said, pocketing two inhalers. 'Ar got me breevas.'
'You sure you wanna go in today?' Trisha also asked, helping button Dee Dee's jacket. 'I erd you up last night.'
'Ar'm goin and thas that,' Dee Dee spluttered, reaching for a tissue. 'Come on Maize urry up!'
'D'you want me to do anyfing Dee,' Terry asked, sitting up half naked on the sofa.

'No fanks Tel mate,' Dee Dee replied, beaming at the prospect of a good day ahead.
'Right then mate,' Terry said, reclining. 'You take it easy yeah babe, remember, gimme a bell if ya need me ok, ar mean that, and you Maize.'
'Yeah alright Tel,' Maizie said, leaning over the back of the sofa to kiss his cheek.
'You mind that baby an'all,' Terry told Maizie. 'Ar'm proper lookin forward to seein the little bleeda.'
Rodney came scurrying from Trisha's room hearing the door opening. 'Oh no ya don't ya little shit,' Trisha laughed, grabbing his diamanté collar. 'D'ya wanna bacon samwich Tel,' she then asked, heading for the kitchen with Rodney tucked under her arm.
'Do bears shit in the woods,' Terry replied eagerly, rubbing his stomach. 'Stick a fried egg in it an'all will ya babe.' Terry then rounded up his empty lager cans from the previous night and folded his duvet.

On arrival Dee Dee burst into Richard's office slamming Bonnie's file down on his desk. 'Ar faand em,' she said, puffing. 'Ar told ya social services aint werf a wank.'
'I beg your pardon,' Richard said, taken aback. 'What on earth do you mean Dee?'
'Bonnie's relatives!' Dee Dee said, getting herself worked up unnecessarily with Maizie at her side. 'She's got a nan and grandad an ar faand em.'
'Bonnie?' Richard said. 'My God, really?'
'Yeah babe iss true,' Maizie added. 'We went to see em yesterday.'
Dee Dee reached for an inhaler. 'They're comin ear today,' she said, struggling to catch her shortened breath. 'To see er.'
'Dee calm daan mate,' Maizie said, with an arm around her friend. 'Don't get'cha self worked up, member what the doctors said.'

'Fuck the doctors,' Dee Dee said defiantly. 'Ar'm so pissed off no one faand em years ago, the girl's lived in this place on er jack all this bleedin time, it breaks mar fuckin art it does.'

'Well we can't change that now,' Richard explained, 'but what matters is that you have found them. It's just fantastic news, I'll go tell her.'

'No!' Dee Dee said, baring his way. 'No ya don't, ar'm gonna tell er, they should be ear at arf eleven so ar'm gonna need to use the staffroom, can you let everyone know to keep aat.'

'Yes of course,' Richard replied. 'I understand.'

Bonnie was sat at the end of her bed brushing her flowing auburn hair when Dee Dee tapped at the door then entered.

'Deeeeee!' Bonnie shrieked, running into her arms. 'I missed you.'

'Ar mist'chu an'all,' Dee Dee told her. 'Listen sit daan Bonnie love,' she added, ushering Bonnie back to her bed. 'Ar got summink to tell ya.'

Bonnie sat holding onto Dee Dee's hand as she so often did.

'Ar dunno ow to say this,' Dee Dee first stuttered, 'but d'you know you ad a mum.'

'Mmmm,' Bonnie said, nodding.

'Well, your mum ad a mum an'all,' Dee Dee explained gingerly, 'and a dad.'

Bonnie hadn't flinched, not seeing the relevance at this point.

'Your mum's mum and dad are your nan and grandad,' Dee Dee continued.

'What's a nan?' Bonnie asked bemused. 'And a gr... grandad?'

'Famly,' Dee Dee said with a smile. 'Your famly Bonnie, d'you understand? You got famly babe, and they wanna meet ya, today.'

It took a moment of two for the information to filter through, but Bonnie's eyes slowly lit up. 'Family!' she cried, looking to the wall at the crude crayon drawings of a family outside a happy home with a rainbow above. 'My family?'

'Yeah,' Dee Dee said, rubbing Bonnie's arm. 'Your own famly babe.'

Bonnie ran to her wardrobe. 'Which one?' she cried, wrenching several frocks from their hangers and holding them in front of her.

'The pink one,' Dee Dee replied, 'and ya blue shoes.'

Bonnie was positively fizzing with excitement as Dee Dee helped with her hair and make-up. 'Sit still will ya,' Dee Dee laughed, attempting to apply a little lipstick. 'Bonnie babe, stop figitin!'

'My family!' Bonnie said, bobbing on her bed. 'My owwwwwn family.'

A short while later Dee Dee's phone rang in her pocket. 'Ello!' she said, stepping away from Bonnie. 'Are you ear?'

'Yes, yes we are,' Mr Pearson said, with his wife clutching his arm.

'OK wait there,' Dee Dee told him, pocketing her phone. 'Bonnie love, you gotta wait ear for a minute ok,' she told an excited Bonnie who was busily checking herself in the mirror. Bonnie nodded whilst choosing a hair grip.

Dee Dee met the Pearsons at the main entrance, while Maizie explained to the center's children that she was about to have a child of her own, answering all their awkward questions as best she could. 'Ar'm so glad you come,' Dee Dee told the couple. 'Bonnie's fulla beans abaat it she is.'

'Ahhhhhh,' Mrs Pearson said with a hand to her heart. 'Where is she?'

'This way,' Dee Dee said, leading Bonnie's grandparents to the staff room. 'Elp yaself to tea and coffee,' she told them. 'Ar just go get er.'

The Pearsons sat huddled together, overwhelmed that they would soon meet the daughter of their only child.

'You ready Bonnie?' Dee Dee asked, popping into Bonnie's room. 'Ohhh babe,' she then said, welling up seeing Bonnie

in all her finery. 'You look absolutely beautiful you really do, like a real angel.'
'Like an angel?' Bonnie asked twirling.
'Better than a ruddy angel,' Dee Dee told her. 'Come ear.' Dee Dee threw her arms around Bonnie, kissing her cheek. 'Ar'm praad a ya babe, proper praad, come on less go see ya nan and grandad.'
The pair walked hand in hand to the staff room but Bonnie stopped at the door. 'Woss wrong?' Dee Dee asked, reaching for the handle.
Bonnie grabbed Dee Dee's hand, preventing her from turning the handle. 'You're my family,' she told her, reluctant to enter.
'Ahhh fanks babe,' Dee Dee replied. 'Ar know that, but these people ar ya proper famly, ya mum's famly, ya blood babe.'
Bonnie soon relented and sheepishly followed Dee Dee into the staff room. The second that Mrs Pearson clapped eyes on Bonnie she broke down and wept uncontrollably. 'It's her!' she sobbed. 'It's our Gemma, darling look.'
Bonnie had indeed blossomed into an exact replica of her late mother. 'Oh darling it's her,' she added, blowing her nose on her tissue.
Mr Pearson rose from his seat helping his wife in the process. 'Bonnie,' he said apprehensively. 'Is that your name, Bonnie?'
Bonnie nodded, clinging tightly to Dee Dee's hand.
'That's a beautiful name,' Mr Pearson said, hugging his wife. 'Your mother, our daughter, had a rabbit called Bonnie when she was a little girl. I expect that's how you got your name.'
'Ohhhhh Bonnie love,' Mrs Pearson said, holding out a hand and mopping yet more tears. 'We're sorry, we're sorry baby. We never knew, we never knew.' The lost years were almost too much to bear for Mrs Pearson. 'We never knew,' she said trembling.

Bonnie wanted to approach her grandmother to console her but looked for Dee Dee's approval first. 'Go on,' Dee Dee urged her. 'Iss alright babe.'

Gingerly Bonnie stepped forward and held out her arms.

'Ohhhh baby,' Mrs Pearson said, embracing Bonnie for the first time. 'Baby, baby I'm sorry.'

Bonnie was positively tingling all over with mixed emotion. 'Shhhh shhh,' she said, rubbing her grandmother's back and smiling at her grandfather. Mr Pearson wrapped his arms around the pair of them, bringing a huge lump to Dee Dee's throat, she then turned to leave them in private.

'Dee,' Mr Pearson said softly, over his wife's shoulder. 'Thank you.'

Dee Dee smiled and pulled the door closed behind her, clenching her fist jubilantly. But her elation was short lived when she began a violent coughing fit, staggering away from the staff room so as not to disturb the Pearsons.

'You alright Dee?' Maizie asked a short while later, seeing her friend slumped against the corridor wall. 'DEEEE?'

Dee Dee's breathing had gotten progressively worse during the previous weeks, meaning that the smallest of daily chores soon became a mammoth undertaking. 'Dee mate what is it?' Maizie asked, now heavily pregnant herself with a matter of weeks until her due date. 'Dee talk to me!' she said, putting an arm around her wheezing friend. 'Oh Jesus Dee mate what ya doin to yaself?' she asked, grabbing a chair and seating Dee Dee.

'Don't,' Dee Dee said, unable to catch her breath. 'Don't say nuffing to Bonnie,' she added, pulling Maizie closer. 'Promise me Maizie, promise me.'

'Alright Dee!' Maizie nodded. 'Alright, but we gotta get'chu to the ospital right naah mate.'

This time Dee Dee did not object, knowing it was becoming increasingly difficult to cope. 'Yeah,' she said, thrusting her inhaler to her mouth. 'Yeah alright Maize, less go mate.'

'Maizie?' Richard said, appearing from his office. 'Maizie what's wrong?'

'Iss Dee, she's sick,' Maizie replied over her shoulder, with her head under Dee Dee's arm. 'Ar gotta get er up the ospital, elp me Rich, please elp me.'
'What do you want me to do?' Richard asked with a sense of urgency.
'Get me a cab!' Maizie barked. 'NAAH RICH, NAAH!'
'Never mind the cab,' Dee Dee said, clutching her chest, 'get a fuckin ambulance.' She then slumped in Maizie's arms unconscious.
'DEEEE!' Maizie cried, shaking her friend. 'DEEEEE MATE!'
'Dear God!' Richard said, sprinting back to his office and tearing his phone from the receiver. 'Ambulance, quickly,' he barked after dialing 999. 'The Westmoreland centre. Yes that's the one, do hurry please!'
Dee Dee came too momentarily grappling for her inhaler. 'Eeyar mate,' Maizie said, assisting her friend. 'Dee mate woss wrong?'
'Ar can't get me breff,' Dee Dee told her.
'RICH, WHERE'S THAT FUCKIN AMBULANCE!' Maizie then barked along the corridor.
Maizie sat beside Dee Dee, with her friend's head on her lap, waiting for the ambulance. 'Ar dunno what to do Dee,' she said, stroking Dee Dee's hair. 'Jesus mate, what do ar do?'
'Five minutes!' Richard said from his office.
'WHAT?' Maizie asked. 'WE AINT GOT FIVE MINUTES FOR GAWD SAKE!'
A passing porter handed Maizie a glass of water for Dee Dee. 'Try to keep her calm,' he told her, with some knowledge of her friend's condition. 'It'll slow her breathing putting less pressure on her lungs.'
'Fanks,' Maizie replied, rocking Dee Dee in her arms. 'Shhhhh, shhhh, shhh,' she said softly. 'Ar got ya mate, ar got'cha. The ambulance is on iss way.'
In less than three minutes two paramedics rushed into the centre carrying their crash equipment. 'She collapsed,' Maizie told them. 'Quick elp er will ya!'

Richard, being a little more level headed, explained Dee Dee's terminal condition to one of the paramedics while his colleague ventilated her and gave two rapid injections to her left arm to return her natural breathing rhythm. 'This'll help till we get her to the hospital,' he told Maizie.
'Then what?' Maizie asked. 'Ay?'
'She'll be examined by the oncologist no doubt,' the paramedic replied, zipping his holdall and readying a wheelchair to transport Dee Dee. 'What's her name?'
'Dee,' Maizie told him. 'Dee Dee.'
'Deeee,' the paramedic said, attempting to rouse her from her semi delirious state. 'Dee love I'm going to lift you into the wheelchair, is that alright?'
Dee Dee nodded with the oxygen mask fastened to her face.
'Good girl,' the paramedic said. Aided by his colleague, the two of them gently hoisted Dee Dee into the wheelchair and covered her legs with a crimson blanket.
'Can ar go wiv er?' Maizie asked, following as Dee Dee was wheeled from the centre. 'Phone Trish!' she told Richard. 'Tell er to get er arse up the ospital.'
'OK darling,' Richard said overseeing. 'I do hope she's alright.'
'Yeah so do I,' Maizie said, climbing into the rear of the ambulance.
Dee Dee was driven with blues and twos to the Saint Pancras with her friend close at her side.
'How long have you got to go?' one of the paramedics asked Maizie, observing her bump.
'Two an arf weeks,' Maizie informed him, thinking more of her friend at the time. 'Are we nearly there?'
'Another minute or two,' the driver piped up, mounting the kerb to pass a taxi.
'Nearly there mate,' Maizie told Dee Dee, clinging to her hand. 'We'll get'cha sorted don't worry.'
Dee Dee began to come round and attempted to climb from the ambulance trolley. 'Please stay where you are,' the

paramedic told her. 'You're in no fit state to be on your feet just yet, let's get you looked at first.'
With Maizie clinging to the chair Dee Dee was wheeled into the Saint Pancras and back to the ward that had become all too familiar to her.
'Dee, what have you been doing to yourself?' the doctor asked, once summoned.
'Tryna save the friggin planet as usual,' Maizie scoffed. 'She won't be told doc, she's stubborn as fuck she is.'
'Riiiight,' the doctor said, pressing his stethoscope to Dee Dee's heaving chest. 'You know the drill by now don't you Dee,' he told her.
Dee Dee nodded in reply, still wearing the oxygen mask.
'It's another scan I'm afraid,' the doctor added, asking the paramedics to wheel Dee Dee to another room.
Maizie sat waiting patiently at Dee Dee's empty bed while she was taken for a CT scan.
'Where is she?' Pearl asked, entering the ward somewhat out of breath herself with Trisha, Terry and Ramos at her heels. 'Where's mar Dee?'
'Gone for a scan,' Maizie told her.
'What appened, woss she done?' Trisha asked. 'Maizie what appened? Richy rang me so ar got Adrian to drop me ome.'
'She's proper overdone it this time,' Maizie told them all. 'She's bin knockin erself aat elpin Bonnie and Alice, and she aint spared a fought for erself.'
The group sat quietly watching the second hand of a clock on the wall slowly rotating over and over until eventually Dee Dee was wheeled back onto the ward.
'Dee love!' Pearl said, rushing to her.
'Let's just get her onto the bed shall we,' the doctor said, standing between mother and daughter. 'She needs rest, I've given her something to calm her so she'll be sleepy for a while.'
'Woss appnin?' Pearl asked frantically. 'Is she alright?'
The doctor said nothing, but it was his silence that in fact spoke volumes.

'Doc?' Pearl said, tugging at his coat sleeve.

'Can I av a word in private?' the doctor said, once Dee Dee was made comfortable.

'Stay wiv er Trish,' Maizie said, following Pearl and the doctor out into the corridor. 'What is it doctor, woss wrong?'

'I'm afraid it's not good,' the doctor told the pair of them. 'Dee's cancer has spread more quickly than we first predicted.'

'Oh no!' Pearl gasped, gripping Maizie's arm. 'Please God no!'

'What does that mean?' Maizie asked, her mouth drying as the words left her and a knot forming in her swollen stomach.

'It means,' the doctor replied, finding it difficult to explain, 'that we'd like to move Dee to a hospice where they can better care for her.'

'Me nan was in an ospice,' Maizie said shaking. 'She was only there for a mumf before she...,' Maizie paused, 'before she went.'

'No please doctor!' Pearl said, reaching for his arm again. 'There must be summink you can do for er, can't you operate, please she's mar baby girl.'

'I'm sorry,' the doctor replied, his heart going out to them. 'She'll receive the very best of care at the hospice, much more than we could offer her here.'

'Oh Maizie not mar Dee!' Pearl said, hugging Maizie.

'I'll er, I'll make the necessary arrangements,' the doctor said, patting Pearl's hand and walking slowly away.

'Woss appnin?' Trisha asked, having paced the room. 'Woss all this secret squirrel shit abaat?'

'Shut it will ya,' Maizie snapped, checking that Dee Dee was still asleep. 'They wanna move er to an ospice.'

'Why?' Trisha asked, without fully understanding the gravity.

'They just av to thas all,' Maizie said, in no mood for an explanation.

Pearl rounded Dee Dee's bed and sat stroking her daughter's cheek.

The following day while Mr and Mrs Pearson returned to the Westmoreland centre to complete a mountain of bureaucratic paperwork in preparation for Bonnie's release into their care, Dee Dee was taken by yet another ambulance to Saint Martin's hospice a short distance from the hospital and shown to her private room. Unlike the Saint Pancras with its stark clinical appearance the rooms at Saint Martin's were warm, inviting and homely. Dee Dee's in particular had a sumptuous pine bed with matching furniture, a deep pile rug at its side and beautiful scenic canvases on the walls.
'Hello Dee,' the staff nurse said, greeting her. 'This is your room now, I hope you like it. I must say it's my favorite, it has a lovely view of the river.'
'Iss nice,' Dee Dee replied, removing her mask. 'Really nice.'
'Dee look they got fish!' Trisha said, with her face pressed to the glass of an aquarium in the corner of the room. 'I ad a loada guppies and an angel fish fingy in a tank in me room back ome, member?' Trisha may as well have been speaking to the fish because nobody else was listening. 'Ar boiled the little bleeda's alive when ar stuck em next to the flippin radiator.'
'Ok,' the nurse told Dee Dee and the others, 'the rules here at Saint Martin's are, there are no rules.'
'Woja mean?' Dee Dee asked, ushering Maizie to her bed to take the weight off her feet.
'Well,' the nurse explained, 'we have no visiting hours here as such. Your friends and family can come and go whenever they choose, if they wish to stay overnight with you we will provide folding beds and bedding for them. Also Dee, on the odd days when you are feeling up to it, they can collect you and take you out as long as we have your contact details and that of your friends and family.'

'Blimey,' Dee Dee said, shocked at their apparent lackadaisical approach, 'it aint like a proper ospital then is it.'

'Oh heavens no,' the nurse smiled, removing a vase of wilted lilies from the side table. 'I'll just get rid of these while you get settled in. If you need anything there's a buzzer beside the bed and there's a sheet in the drawer explaining meal times and such. Oh and if for any reason you aren't keen on the food here you'll find a whole bunch of take away menu's in there as well. I can recommend the Great Wall if you like Cantonese, their crispy duck is simply mouthwatering, and they deliver to Saint Martin's, as do the others. Just order whatever you like, it's all free of charge and if your family would also like to eat please feel free.'

The nurse left with the lilies, which unbeknown to Dee Dee and the others belonged to the room's previous occupant who had recently passed away having bravely battled ovarian cancer.

'Flippin ell Dee,' Maizie said, looking round, 'this is pukka ain it mate.'

'Yeah never mind that though,' Dee Dee said, sitting beside her friend. 'Listen Maize ar'm gonna get up the centre as much as ar can, but ar want you to promise me summink.'

'Yeah anyfing Dee,' Maizie said, listening intently while Pearl hung her daughter's clothes in her new wardrobe, shedding more than a tear or two out of sight.

'Look in on Alice every day for me yeah,' Dee Dee continued. 'Promise me Maize, please iss important to me.'

'You know ar will Dee,' Maizie replied, hand on heart. 'Ar know ow much she means to ya.'

'Yeah,' Dee Dee agreed. 'She likes er tea sweet, four sugars, marmite on toast in the mawnin, oh and if ya get er a bag a bon bons ar be well grateful, she loves them.'

'Yeah mate, don't worry abaat a fing,' Maizie assured her friend.

Dee Dee placed a hand on Maizie's bulging stomach. 'You gotta look after yaself an'all Maize,' she insisted. 'Don't worry abaat me ar'll be alright, you fink abaat that baby in there d'you ear me.'

'Yeah but Dee,' Maizie moaned, clutching her friend's hand tighter; Dee Dee's illness had marred what would normally be the happiest of times for most women in Maizie's condition. 'Ar really want this baby an everyfing, but you're more important to me, ar know iss an orrible fing to say but iss true.'

'Naah you listen to me Maizie,' Dee Dee said sternly, while Trisha poured way too many fish flakes into the aquarium. 'That baby needs you to be strong and positive, you gotta eat proper an'all, ar noticed you bin skippin dinner ear and there. Well it aint good enough girl ar'm tellin ya, that littlun in there needs its grub an'all and you aint doin it no bleedin good starvin yaself and worryin yaself sick abaat me.'

'She's right Maize,' Pearl agreed, sitting beside them. 'You gotta keep ya strenf up babe, for the baby and for Dee.'

'Yeah ar know,' Maizie reluctantly agreed.

'Tell ya what!' Dee Dee said, reaching for the drawer in an attempt to raise the mood in the room. 'Shall we give the Great Wall gaff a bell and check aat the crispy duck, ar dunno abaat you'z lot but ar'm bleedin starving.'

'Oooh yeah,' Trisha said, leaving the aquarium fish gorging on their flakes. 'Can I av chicken balls?'

'Av what ya want babe,' Dee Dee smiled, 'we aint payin.'

While Terry and Ramos sat at the flat, sharing a bottle of fine brandy that Ramos' brother had sent over from Spain, the girls tucked into an oriental feast of butterfly king prawns, sesame toast and of course crispy duck.

Richard arrived at Saint Martin's a short while later with two bunches of yellow roses, handing one to Dee Dee and the other to Maizie, kissing her head in doing so. 'Ohhhh ain e lovely,' Maizie smiled.

'Yeah fanks Rich,' Dee Dee said, discarding her plate. 'Thas nice of ya mate. Mum this is Richard,' she said, making the necessary introductions, 'Maizie's geeza.'

'Pleased to meet you,' Richard said courteously, kissing Pearl's hand.

'Blimey you're right love,' Pearl agreed, 'e'z a proper charmer ain e.'

'Listen Maize,' Dee Dee told her friend, 'you get off wiv Richy if ya want, go on go put'cha feet up ar be alright.'

'No but Deeee,' Maizie objected, 'ar wanna stay wiv you.'

'Rich take er ome will ya,' Dee Dee insisted, 'and keep an eye on er make sure she eats proper.'

'She's right darling,' Richard told his love, rubbing her back. 'If you won't listen to me, listen to your friend.'

Trisha eyed the remains on Pearl's plate. 'You not eatin them balls Misses D?' she asked, hovering with her fork.

'Naah you can av em,' Pearl said, setting her plate down, 'ar'm stuffed love.'

Richard eventually persuaded Maizie to leave and took her back to his flat for a night of indulgent pampering, running her a foaming bath and popping rich Belgian chocolates into her mouth while she bathed; but no matter how luxurious her surroundings Dee Dee was never far from her thoughts.

Trisha later returned to the flat alone. 'Where is Pearl?' Ramos asked, stetting his mug of brandy down.

'Up the ospice,' Trisha replied, removing her coat and picking up her excited pooch. 'She wonnid to stay wiv Dee on er first night, Dee told er to come ome but she wern avin none of it.'

Pearl had insisted on staying with her daughter and asked for a put-you-up bed to be placed beside Dee Dee's, and while Trisha helped herself to Ramos' brandy, mother and daughter lay awake side by side into the small hours reminiscing, laughing together and at times weeping together. Dee Dee finally drifted off to sleep with her arm hanging from the side of her bed, her hand wrapped firmly in her mothers.

Over the following few days Maizie and the others visited Dee Dee constantly in between work commitments, with Pearl and Ramos spending the majority of their waking

hours at Saint Martin's making sure Dee Dee had all she needed to ease the transition from home to hospice.
'Muvva ar'm alright!' Dee Dee would often say when her mother straightened her bedding and fluffed her pillows.

That Friday evening Dee Dee beckoned to her two friends. 'Listen ar wanna go aat tomorra,' she told them, pressing the buzzer beside her bed.
'Ay?' Maizie asked. 'Woja mean aat?'
'Up the city,' Dee Dee explained, 'like we used to. Ar wanna go shoppin and piss araand on the buses. Will ya take me?'
'Yeah course Dee,' Trisha said without hesitation.
Maizie being Maizie was a little more level headed. 'But Dee, you sure you're up to it mate?' she asked, looking at the nest of tubes beside her bed gradually administering pain relief to her now frail friend.
'Ar will be,' Dee Dee told her as the nurse arrived. 'Member what we talked abaat Gina,' she said, taking the nurse's hand. 'Well ar wanna do it tomorra if thas alright wiv you.'
'Your day trip?' Gina replied knowingly, while checking Dee Dee's drug levels. 'Yes, yes of course it is Dee.'
'Ang on a minute,' Maizie intervened, 'she can't go aat mate look at er.'
'She'll be fine,' Gina said, topping Dee Dee glass with juice. 'As long as she remembers to take her tablets and refrains from anything too energetic.'
'Tablits!' Trisha exclaimed. 'Dee don't do tablits, do ya Dee, you never av.'
'Ar will this time,' Dee Dee said defiantly. 'Iss on me list.'
'List?' Maizie asked. 'What list?'
'Me fuck-it list,' Dee Dee told her.
'You mean ya bucket list,' Maizie said, correcting her friend and referring to the number of daring things many people chose to experience before the end of their days.
'No ar call it me fuck-it list,' Dee Dee explained. 'Coz what the fuck av ar gotta lose?'

'Oh don't say it like that Deeee,' Trisha begged. 'Ar don't even wanna fink abaat it, me and Rodders was up all night last night makin milky coffee coz we couldn't sleep, well ar made the coffee and e just sat there lickin iz bum ole.'

'Ar'll come wiv ya,' Pearl said, repositioning Dee Dee's pillows once again. 'That way ar can keep an eye on ya.'

'No Mum,' Dee Dee said resolutely. 'Just me and me mates, thas all.'

'Oh,' Pearl said, ceasing her fussing for a moment. 'Oh, alright, well take ya phone wiv ya won't ya, call me if ya need me, and you'z two,' she told Maizie and Trisha, 'you bell me if anyfing appens to er, d'you ear me!'

'Yeah course,' Maizie replied. 'Don't worry Misses D we'll take proper good care of er.'

Pearl rubbed Maizie's stomach. 'You take care of yaself an'all babe,' she told her. 'Not long naah is it.'

'Just over a week ar fink,' Maizie informed her, straightening her back. 'Ar can't bleedin wait to get it aata me.'

'Can ar baby sit for ya Maize?' Trisha asked, looking over Maizie's shoulder at her bump.

'No!' Maizie snapped instinctively. 'You aint teachin mar kid any of your shit!'

Trisha hung her head and then tapped Dee Dee's leg. 'Oh Dee ar fergot to tell ya!' she said excitedly. 'Ar got an order from M n S for me gastric pants!'

'Shut the fuck up!' Maizie said, finding this impossible to believe. 'You aint!'

'Yeah!' Trisha said beaming. 'Yeah I av. They want two faasand pairs of em, ar got a geezer in the Philipenes who's willin to knock em up for me for a paand a pair an ar can flog em for nine ninety nine, ar'm gonna be proper quids in!'

'Really!' Dee Dee asked, having doubted Trisha's absurd business venture from the off. 'M n S?'

'Yeah!' Trisha reiterated. 'M n bloody S. Me geezer wants me to fly aat there some time to look at some samples.'

'Bloody Nora!' Dee Dee said, patting Trisha's hand. 'Well done mate, well done I always knew you could do it.' This little white lie somehow seemed appropriate considering Trisha's elated mood.

The three girls and Pearl heard a commotion out in the hallway and an all too familiar face appeared at the door. 'Alright me bitches,' Bradley joked.

'Ello bruv!' Maizie said, getting up to greet her brother.

'Ow you doin sis,' Bradley said, embracing Maizie. 'Flippin ell girl!' he then said, stepping back and looking her bump up and down. 'You'z got yaself knocked up.'

'Yeah,' Maizie said proudly. 'Yeah ar did, ar got a new fella bruv, iz name's Richard an e'z proper lovely. Ain e Dee?' she asked over her shoulder.

'Yeah e'z a top bloke,' Dee Dee agreed.

'Flippin eck!' Bradley said again, before side stepping his sister and approaching the bed. 'Dee babe I only just erd,' he said, taking Dee Dee's hand. 'Terry told me, Dee ar dunno what to say mate.'

'Iss alright Brad,' Dee Dee told him, as a group of nurses gathered at the door eager to catch a glimpse of the rapping super star.

'Ello Misses D,' Bradley said, kissing Pearl on the cheek. 'Sorry. Ar come as soon as ar could.'

'Thas alright,' Pearl smiled, 'iss lovely to see ya darlin, ow's ya mum?'

'Sailin on de Med,' Bradley told her. 'She's already pranged me new yacht the dozy mare.' He then turned his attention back to Dee Dee. 'What av day said?' he asked. 'Can it be treated, ar mean you are gonna be alright aint'cha.'

'Ar wouldn't be in ear if ar was,' Dee Dee informed him. 'Iss bad mate, proper bad.' She reached for her inhaler, growing tired.

'Dere must be summink day can do for ya'z,' Bradley said, looking at his friend. 'Ar got money, shit loads of it, we can fly you anywhere in de world to the best doctors on de planit, ar don't care what it costs babe, come on less do it, pack up ya shit.'

'It ain as simple as that Brad,' Dee Dee told him, drawing a rasping breath. 'Ar'v ad the best treatment right ear but it wern enough, me lungs are riddled wiv it apparently.'

Four of Bradley's entourage then pushed past the nurses carrying armfuls of the finest lilies, roses and sweet scented freesias. 'Oh ar got'cha some flaa's,' Bradley told her, as her room was filled with blooms.

'Flippin ell!' Dee Dee smiled. 'Thas a shit loada flaa's mate, fanks, fanks a lot.'

Bradley paid little heed to his purchases. 'Dere must be summink we can do to cure ya'z Dee,' he insisted. 'Ar got dis Tibetan geeza dat elps me wiv me chi yeah, e'z proper good ar could ask im to av a look at'cha.'

'No fanks,' Dee Dee said, having been prodded, poked and pulled from pillar to post over the previous months. 'Seriously Brad ar'm alright wiv it, ar got all you'z lot raand me, thas enough for me.'

'Oh mar God Dee,' Pearl said, welling up, 'you're so brave.'

'You gotta be muvva,' Dee Dee told her. 'Issa case of avin to.'

Bradley signed several autographs to dispense with the onlookers and sat with his friends until Dee Dee once again drifted off to sleep.

'Ow ya bin bruv?' Maizie asked him.

'Yeah good sis,' Bradley whispered. 'Ar was in Santiago doin a gig when Terry rung me, ar cut it short and give em all dere money back and got me jet ome as quick as are could. Ar just don't believe it sis, ar really don't, not Dee.'

'Iss a fuckin nightmare bruv,' Maizie told him, looking lovingly at her dozing friend.

'So ar'm gonna be an uncle then ay sis,' Bradley smiled. 'Dass pukka!'

Trisha pulled Dee Dee's bed sheet up under her chin carefully so as not to wake her. 'Ar'm gonna babysit for ya ain I Maize,' she said, ignoring Maizie's earlier rejection.

'No you flippin aint!' Maizie remarked. 'Ar told you once, you aint goin nowhere near it.'

'Yeah ar know but,' Trisha said, pleading her case.
'Listen!' Maizie said interrupting. 'Mar baby aint growin up to be a bleedin basket case like you, d'you ear me. You can see it wiv me and Rich so ar can keep an eye on ya, ar don't want you fillin its little ed wiv a load of old shite.' Maizie was adamant that her new baby would be perfect in every way, and not tainted by Trisha's undeniable brand of lunacy.
Bradley was later informed by his PA that the paparazzi had gotten wind on his location and were on their way. 'Look girls ar better go yeah,' he told them, donning his cap. 'De last fing Dee needs is a buncha photo geezas wakin er up. Ar'm in taan for a bit so call me yeah, anytime sis you know dat, us four we go way back don't we.'
'Too right we do,' Trisha said, hugging Bradley. 'Ow's ya leg?' she asked, referring to the bullet wound she had inadvertently inflicted on him.
'It gives me some shit in de mawnins,' Bradley said, rubbing his leg. 'But ar got all ar got because of it so fanks again yeah Trish.' Bradley returned the kiss before leaving by the rear entrance, taking with him any unwanted attention.
The following day Maizie and Trisha arrived at Saint Martin's to find Dee Dee's bed empty and stripped of bedding. 'Where is she?' Maizie asked frantically, when a nurse arrived carrying fresh sheets. 'Where's me mate, where's Dee?'
Trisha covered her ears and turned away not wanting to hear the nurses reply.
'She's in the bathroom,' the nurse replied, making up the bed. 'She was sick this morning so we're changing her bed.'
'Oh, right,' Maizie said, feeling guilty at having feared the worst.
'Is she?' Trisha said, with her fingers still in her ears. 'Is she wiv the angels?'
'No you doughnut!' Maizie said, wrenching Trisha's hands from her face. 'She's in the barfroom!'
'Oh,' Trisha sighed. 'Fank fuck for that, ar fought she was...'
'Don't say it!' Maizie warned. 'Don't say it, please.'

Dee Dee returned shortly after, having dressed and put on her trademark beanie and looking altogether radiant. 'Alright girls!' she chirped. 'Shall we get goin then?'
'Jesus Dee!' Trisha remarked. 'You look great mate, av they cured ya?'
'Don't be daft!' Dee Dee scoffed. 'Ar bin pumped fulla so many drugs to get me fru the day that ar reckon ar could leave Usain Bolt and Mo flippin Farra standin in a race. Mind you ar know ar'm gonna pay for it later but who gives a fuck, iss all abaat today ain it, wiv me mates.'
'You sure abaat this Dee?' Maizie asked. 'We don't av to go aat ya know.'
'You try and stop me,' Dee Dee said defiantly. 'Ar bin lookin forward to this, one last bender, are you gonna be alright though Maize?' she asked, checking out her heavily pregnant friend. 'Wiv the baby bein so close ar mean.'
'Listen Dee,' Maizie explained, 'if you can make it aat ar'm damn sure ar can.'
'Well less go then,' Trisha said, taking her friends arm in arm.

Taking a taxi to London's West End the three girls cruised the cocktail bars sampling everything from a Singapore sling to a long island ice tea. 'Right who's ungry?' Dee Dee asked outside a swanky Park Lane brasserie; where only the rich and famous dined, and Ferraris, Lamborghinis and Bentleys lined the street and a well-tailored man, complete with top hat and white gloves, stood at the door to ward off undesirables.
'Ar'm bleedin starving,' Trisha said, looking along the street. 'Ar fink there's a KFC raand ear somewhere.'
'Fuck that!' Dee Dee scoffed. 'Ar wanna eat in ear, ar seen it on the telly.'
'Dee, we aint never gettin in there mate,' Maizie told her. 'What abaat Macky Ds?'

'Wait there,' Dee Dee said, approaching the doorman and having a word in his ear. 'Come on you'z two!' she then called, as the door was opened for them.

Trisha and Maizie both looked at one another then hurried after their friend. 'Fanks mate,' Trisha told the doorman in passing.

'Deeee,' Maizie whispered once inside. 'What did you say to get us in ear?'

Trisha stood in awe at the finery around them. 'Fuuuuck me,' she gasped.

'Oh nuffing much,' Dee Dee said, waiting to be seated. 'Just that you was avin Davey Becham's love child an e just paid you firty five mill to keep schtum, thas all.'

'Do what?' Maizie said, looking over her shoulder toward the door. 'Woja tell im that for?'

'Because,' Dee Dee replied, clicking her fingers to summon a waiter, 'you can only get in ear apparently if ya proper minted.'

'Table for three madam,' the waiter said politely.

'Yeah mate,' Dee Dee said, craning her neck. 'But don't put me next to that twat will ya.' Dee Dee was referring to the Prime Minister who was quietly dining with his wife. 'Me nan's ad er benefits cut by iz lot and then the tossers go and let anuvva undred faasand feevin foreigners in, ar mean where's the ruddy sense in that, ay?'

The waiter failed to get the gist of Dee Dee's rant but lead them to the opposite end of the restaurant anyway.

'Cheers,' Maizie said, lowering herself awkwardly into her seat.

'Ar'll av a Bacardi,' Trisha said without hesitation. 'And some poppadoms.'

Again the waiter looked puzzled. 'I'm sorry madam we don't do poppadoms,' he told her, taking out his pencil and pad. 'Would you like an appetizer?'

'Apple tizer!' Trisha said, screwing up her face. 'No ya nob, ar said ar wanna Bacardi din I.'

'Iss a starter you idiot,' Maizie reminded her friend.

'Well why did'n e say that?' Trisha asked, picking up the leather bound menu. 'What abaat cheesy nachos?' she asked. 'D'you do them?'

'No madam I'm afraid not,' the waiter again replied.

'No cheesy nachos!' Trisha exclaimed. 'What sorta gaff is this?'

'Trisha shut the fuck up will ya,' Dee Dee snapped, then turned to the waiter. 'We'll av the quails eggs, the Scottish salmon, the beluga caviar and the bestest bottla bubbly ya got, nunna that cheap shit mate ar want the good gear, nart ar mean, oh and make that a bottla Bacardi.'

'Dee av you seen the prices,' Maizie said, scrutinizing the menu once the waiter had disappeared. 'We aint got this sorta dough.'

'Iss on me fuck-it list,' Dee Dee told her. 'So ar'm avin it.'

Tray after tray of the finest cuisine was brought to the table of Dee Dee and her friends, and while Trisha tucked in greedily Maizie nibbled cautiously wondering how it would all be paid for. 'Ear mate!' Dee Dee called, having poured the last of the vintage champagne. 'Get us anuvva bottle geez.'

'One moment madam,' the waiter replied, 'I'll fetch one from the cellar.' Returning some five minutes later the waiter uncorked a second magnum of champagne.

'Deeee,' Maizie said, ducking behind a menu. 'Thas free undred paand a bottle, are you mad.'

'Ar don't give a fuck,' Dee Dee replied, having timed the waiters trip to the cellar and back. 'Ar told ya ar'm avin what ar want.'

After dinner and a desert of exquisite Belgian chocolate truffles and cognac ice cream the girls sat back bloated. 'That was bleedin aaansum,' Dee Dee smiled.

Trisha sat licking the remainder of the chocolate from her plate while Maizie totted up the exorbitant bill in her head with a look of genuine concern. 'Dee, d'you know ow much we've ad?' she asked.

'Shhhhh,' Dee Dee said, silencing her friend. 'EAR MATE!' she called again. 'ANUVVA BOTTLA SHAMPOO YEAH!'

The waiter nodded and disappeared through the gilt door once again that lead down the winding wrought iron staircase to the wine cellar.

'Right come on!' Dee Dee told her friends, rising from her seat. 'Shift yer arses.'

'What?' Maizie asked, remaining seated. 'What ya doin?'

'A runner,' Dee Dee told her, 'so get a ruddy move on.'

Tucking the remainder of the bottle of Bacardi beneath her coat Dee Dee made her way between the tables of celebs toward the front entrance, knocking one or two elbows and subsequently spilling their wine in the process. 'Get aat the bleedin way!' she said, shoving an X Factor judge in the back.

'Deeeee,' Maizie said, scurrying after her while Trisha pocketed Maizie's leftovers.

'Trisha!' Dee Dee barked. 'Shift your fuckin arse will ya!'

'Oh yeah, alright,' Trisha said, hurrying after them. 'You left a truffle Maize and arf a dozen muscles.'

'Cheers geez,' Dee Dee told the doorman when he politely opened the door. 'Come on urry up!' she told her friends.

'Laters,' Trisha said, leaving the brasserie.

The three girls shuffled along the street with Maizie still complaining. 'But Deeee.'

'Shut up iss on me list!' Dee Dee snapped in her defence.

'Wanna muscle?' Trisha said, offering Dee Dee a selection of seafood from her pocket.

'No ar don't ya doughnut,' Dee Dee laughed. 'Just urry the fuck up will ya.'

Maizie trailed behind. 'We coulda bin nicked and banged up for that Dee,' she whined.

'Yeah but we never did we,' Dee Dee said over her shoulder. 'Oh come on Maize lighten the fuck up will ya, we just ad a belly fulla posh nosh and the best bubbly all for fuck all, ow bad's that ay?'

'Ar fink iss brilliant!' Trisha said, gorging on table scraps.

The girls had rounded the corner out of sight of the brasserie by the time the waiter returned with the champagne, he stood puzzled momentarily, wondering if in fact all three girls had gone to the washroom together.
'They just left,' one half of a million selling pop duo said, pointing at the door.
'What?' the waiter said, setting down the bottle and making for the door with a modicum of dignity. 'Where'd they go?' he asked the doorman. 'Where are those damn girls, they left without paying their blasted bill!'
The doorman smiled a wry smile, having very little love for his employers who recently refused his holiday request. 'That way,' he said, pointing in the opposite direction. 'They went that way.'
'Blast!' the waiter cursed, looking along the empty street. 'Damn and blast!' He kicked at the iron railing outside, stubbing his toe before returning to the table to collect the champagne and curse again when seeing the twenty five pence tip Trisha had left tucked beneath her plate. 'DAMN AND BLAST!' he yelled, turning every head in the room.
'You're off your ed you are,' Maizie told Dee Dee, whilst stopping to rub her stomach.
'Ar'm just gettin started,' Dee Dee replied, sucking on her inhaler. 'Come on before me meds wear off.'
Walking the length of Regent Street amid the bustling, Dee Dee pinched a few pert bottoms that caught her eye until one particularly adorable Latino guy emerged from the crowd laden with designer shopping bags. 'Fuck it,' Dee Dee said. Seizing the moment, she stepped straight into his path causing him to stop abruptly. 'Ello ansum,' she said, clasping her hands either side of his face tugging him toward her to lock lips.
'Flippin ell Dee!' Maizie gasped, looking on as she mauled the startled student.
'Go on girl!' Trisha shrieked, goading Dee Dee whose tongue flitted in and out of the young man's mouth.

With his hands full of his recent purchases he was powerless to resist Dee Dee's advances. 'Cheers geez,' Dee Dee smiled, breaking away and cupping his manhood. 'Not bad,' she added, leaving him standing in stunned silence.

Seeing this Trisha was eager to follow suit and stopped a beautiful Brazilian siren in her tracks and moved in for a kiss, but instead of the tonsil tickling she'd imagined she received a short sharp slap across the face. 'Ooooh you're a feisty one aint'cha,' she said, rubbing her cheek. 'Ar love em wiv a bitta spirit.' The girl cursed her in her native tongue and side stepped her.

'Come on you!' Maizie said, dragging her friend away.

At various London landmarks the three girls paused and huddled together for a group selfie. 'Did ya get me in?' Trisha asked, outside the London Eye.

'Yeah,' Maizie replied, tongue in cheek. 'But ar can chop that bit off later.'

'Oh shut up Maize,' Trisha moaned. 'You won't will ya?'

'Naah ar'm only jokin,' Maizie admitted, getting in the swing of things by now and hugging her friend.

At one point Dee Dee eyed a particularly annoying bunch of city bankers sat at a table outside a riverside café, swilling bowls of brandy and ridiculing a homeless man crouched begging in a doorway beside them. 'Are you a hungry chappy?' one of them laughed, flinging a measly piece of lettuce in his direction.

'Wankers!' Dee Dee snarled, approaching their table.

'Dee what ya doin?' Maizie asked, keeping her distance.

'OY YOU COCKS!' Dee Dee yelled. 'You ain eatin that are ya?' she then asked, snatching the four rib eye steaks from their plates leaving them with just their salads. She then knelt beside the vagrant much to their horror. 'Eeyar mate get them daan ya,' she said, placing them in his grubby hands.

'I say what the devil d'you think you're doing?' one of the toffs mistakenly said.

'Kickin your fuckin arse!' Dee Dee growled over her shoulder. 'If you don't shut the fuck up!'

The four bankers hastily looked down at their plates, petrified to make eye contact with this lunatic, as they saw her.

'Thank you,' the vagrant said, taking Dee Dee's hand. 'Thank you so much.'

'Thas alright mate,' Dee Dee replied, taking her purse from her pocket and emptying every penny she had into his polystyrene cup. 'You need it more than me geez,' she told him. Maizie and Trisha also handed the man a twenty pound note which lit up his face. 'Thas mar girls,' Dee Dee said proudly.

During the afternoon Dee Dee became noticeably tired having taken the last of her tablets, which she begrudgingly washed down with a skinny latte in Covent Garden. 'D'you wanna go back Dee?' Maizie asked, watching her wheezing friend.

'Never!' Dee Dee said defiantly. 'Ar never wanna go back Maize, are wish ar could stay wiv you'z two forever, ar feel on top of the world right naah.'

Trisha turned her face away, quietly breaking down.

'Don'tchu cry for me Trisha!' Dee Dee snapped. 'Don'tchu dare. Ar've never been as appy in me entire life as I am right naah, ar love you'z two so much d'you know that.'

The three girls sat amongst the tourists and street performers embracing with tears of joy and sorrow flowing like sweet wine.

A Japanese tourist approached Dee Dee with his expensive camera in his hands. 'Please would you?' he asked, urging her to take a picture of him and his entire family of thirteen outside the historical market.

'Yeah no probs,' Dee Dee said, hoisting herself to her feet. The family crowded together and posed with their thumbs raised while Dee Dee adjusted the focus. 'SAY NOODLES!' she called to them, clicking the shutter several times.

'Ohhh that was nice of ya,' Maizie told her friend, after she handed back the camera.

'No it weren't,' Dee Dee laughed. 'Ar cut all their bleedin eds off.' The three girls burst out laughing as they strolled arm in arm around the cobbled square. Dee Dee paused at one of the many stalls selling toys and novelties. 'Woja want that for?' Maizie asked, seeing Dee Dee handling a child's replica pistol.

'Iss on me list,' Dee Dee replied, holding out her hand. 'Gissa fiver will ya.'

'Woss on ya list Dee?' Maizie asked, paying for the toy gun and following Dee Dee along the street.

'Ang on wait for me,' Trisha said, with a slinky tangled in her hands.

'One last blag,' Dee Dee replied, stopping outside a high street bank.

'Do what?' Maizie exclaimed. 'Don't be daft Dee.'

'You two wait ear,' Dee Dee told her friends. 'Ar don't want you'z to be any part of this, ar mean that, stay aat of it!'

'Yeah but Dee,' Trisha added.

'But nuffing!' Dee Dee barked. 'Ar'm doin this shit so don't try and stop me, alright!'

'Dee leave it mate,' Maizie urged her friend. 'Please Dee, this is stupid.'

'Stay aat of it, bofe of ya!' Dee Dee warned them.

'It aint werf it Dee,' Maizie persisted.

'It is to me!' Dee Dee said adamantly. 'Ar gotta do it Maize, for me.'

Dee Dee's two friends nodded reluctantly and took up their place on a bench on the opposite side of the street.

'She's mad,' Maizie said, shaking her head, 'stark ravin mad.'

'Naah,' Trisha smiled, 'she's appy Maize, be appy for er.'

Dee Dee joined the queue of customers filing toward a single window. 'Afternoon,' she said to the man in front, adjusting her pink beanie in the reflective surfaces. 'Nice day for robbin a bank ain it.'

The man smiled at her apparent humour. 'Yes it is, isn't it,' he agreed.

Some five minutes later Dee Dee approached the cashier but then immediately felt a hand on her shoulder which sent a chill the length of her spine. 'Fuck!' She spun around in readiness for a confrontation, but instead of an officer of the law or security staff a little old lady stood before her in a knee length woollen overcoat and matching hat.

'Excuse me young lady,' she said politely. 'Would you mind awfully if I took your place? Only I have to catch the bus in a few minutes, my Stan'll be waiting for his haddock and chips you see.'

'Course not darlin,' Dee Dee said, stepping aside. 'You fill ya boots love.'

'Oh thanks ever so much,' the lady said, patting Dee Dee's hand. 'You really are too kind.'

'Next!' the cashier called, tapping her biro on the bullet proof glass impatiently.

'Yeah, alright keep ya bleedin air on,' Dee Dee said, taking offence at her obvious lack of respect. 'Go on love,' she told the pensioner, ushering her to the counter.

'One moment deary,' the elderly customer told the cashier as she delved into her carpet bag. 'Now where did I put my purse?'

The cashier raised her eyebrows and muttered something completely unproffesional under her breath.

'Oh I am sorry,' the pensioner said, turning to Dee Dee. 'I know it's here somewhere.'

'No worries love,' Dee Dee smiled at her apparent frailty, 'you take all the time you want.'

'Errrr, Hello!' the insistant cashier remarked. 'We close at four thirty you know.'

'Listen!' Dee Dee said, over the pensioner's shoulder. 'You keep that shit up and believe me you aint gonna make it to free firty, let alone four firty!'

'Oh here it is,' the pensioner said, producing a black velvet purse and taking out her debit card. 'Can I please have twenty pounds,' she asked, sliding the card beneath the glass.

After close inspection the irritable cashier slid the card back. 'Not with that you can't,' she said smugly. 'It's expired.'
'I beg your pardon?' the pensioner said, cupping a hand to her ear.
'It's expired!' the cashier repeated, leaning toward the glass. 'Have you got another card?'
'No dear,' the bewildered pensioner replied, holding open her purse with her bus pass and a few paltry coins inside. 'I haven't, but my husband and I have been banking with you for over forty years. Can't I just have twenty pounds? My Stan's waiting for his fish supper you see.'
'Sorry, no can do,' the cashier told her in no uncertain terms. 'I'll have to issue you a new card, you should receive it between three to five working days.'
'Five days,' the pensioner said, steadying herself at the counter. 'Oh dear, oh dear dear dear.'
A red mist was gradually descending around Dee Dee. 'Just give er the bleedin money will ya!' she barked, with a hand on the pensioner's hunched back. 'You jumped up jobswerf.'
'Like I said,' the cashier replied unrepentant, 'no can do. Now are you waiting?' she added, dismissing the eighty three year old.
'Oh dear dear dear,' the distraught pensioner said, dropping her purse into her bag and turning to leave.
'Er can I help you?' the cashier asked, tapping her biro on the glass once again, which infuriated Dee Dee no end.
'Yeah you can fuckin elp me,' she growled, producing the pistol to the horror of the cashier. 'You can gimme all ya fuckin money,' she added, tapping the barrel of the gun on the bullet proof glass before poking it beneath and pointing it in her direction. 'Ar mean it you slag!' she added. 'Get a fuckin bag and fill it fulla fifties, or ar'll fill you fulla fuckin lead.' She then turned to the petrified customers behind her. 'Ar'va always wonnid to say that,' she told them, watching them flee the bank. 'Go on, piss off!' she laughed, brandishing the replica weapon.

'Bloody Nora!' Maizie gasped, seeing the frantic customers leaving in a hurry. 'She's only bloody doin it!'

'Go on girl!' Trisha squealed, wriggling on the bench. 'Make em av it!'

The cashier reached for an emergency panic button beside her but was spotted by Dee Dee's keen eye. 'Don't be a complete fuckin melt,' Dee Dee told her. 'Just fill the fuckin bag before ar get proper fuckin nasty, and believe me girl you don't want that.'

The girl nodded, sitting in a warm pool of her own urine and trembling, whilst cramming bundles of fifty pound notes into a cloth bag. 'Thas it, all of em,' Dee Dee said, craning her neck to check the drawer. When the girl had finished Dee Dee pulled the bag under the glass. 'Cheers big ears,' she said, turning to leave. 'Nice doin business wiv ya.' Waving sarcastically to the many security cameras Dee Dee pushed her way out of the revolving doors. 'OY OYYYY!' she yelled across the street to her friends, holding the bag of money above her head. 'AM I THE BOLLOCKS OR WHAT, AY?'

'Oh mar gawd!' Maizie gasped. 'She's only gone and done it Trish.'

'Fucking brilliant!' Trisha said, raising a fist to praise her friend.

Dee Dee then hailed a passing taxi on seeing the pensioner sat at the bus stop. 'Ang on a minute mate,' she told the driver. 'Eeeyar love,' she said, helping the old lady to her feet and ramming a fist full of cash into her bag. 'Get in this cab and go treat yer old fella to the biggest bit of addock they got, get im some mushy peas an'all.'

'But, but I...,' the lady stammered at this stranger's generosity.

'But nuffing,' Dee Dee smiled, 'go on, getcha self ome.' She then turned and disappeared back inside the bank.

'Woss she doin?' Trisha asked.

'Fuck knows,' Maizie replied, without a clue.

Dee Dee tossed the bag with the remainder of the cash back onto the counter toward the hysterical cashier. 'Ar don't want ya fuckin money,' she told her. 'Ar just wonnid the buzz. Cheers for that. Oh, and you mind your fuckin manners in future, d'you ear me.' Pocketing the pistol Dee Dee left once again, beckoning to her friends. 'Come on,' she told them, 'less get the fuck aat of ear.'

Beating a hasty retreat amid the twisting London back streets Dee Dee eventually handed the pistol to a young child standing beside his father. 'Eeyar boy,' she told him, 'go rob a bank.'

'Ar don't believe it Dee,' Maizie said, still struggling to come to terms with her friend's actions. 'Ar just don't believe you done that.'

'It was on er list wern it Dee,' Trisha reminded her friend. 'So she done it, good on ya Dee, good on ya.' Trisha turned to see Dee Dee sat on a stone step clutching her chest. 'Dee!' she said, sitting beside her. 'Dee what is it mate?'

'Oh no!' Maizie said, joining them. 'Dee you alright mate?' she too asked. 'Dee talk to me!'

Dee Dee looked to the heavens, her face pale and her chest heaving erratically.

'Oh no Dee, no mate,' Maizie said, holding her tight. 'Trish, get a fuckin taxi,' she told her friend. 'NAAH FOR FUCK SAKE!'

Trisha ran into the middle of the street looking this way and that in a complete flap. 'TAXIIIIIIIII!' she cried, seeing nothing. 'TAXIIIIIIIIIII!'

A black cab eventually rounded the corner and had to brake suddenly when Trisha darted in its path waving her arms. 'Saint Martin's mate!' she said, when he wound down his window. 'On the London Road yeah!'

The cabbie nodded and opened the rear door for Maizie to help her friend aboard. 'Is she alright?' he asked.

'Don't ask stupid fuckin questions and just drive!' Maizie barked at him, slamming the door closed.

During the journey Maizie cuddled Dee Dee whispering softly to her. 'Iss alright Dee, iss alright.'
Trisha, sitting opposite, rubbed Dee Dee's knee. 'Yeah iss alright mate, we're wiv ya,' she said, choking up. 'Me and Maizie ar wiv ya.'
'Phone er muvva,' Maizie told Trisha. 'Tell er to meet us up there.'
Trisha did so trying her damnedest not to alarm Pearl too much. 'Can you ask Terry to come an'all,' she added.
Pearl instinctively knew something was wrong and let her phone slip from her trembling hand. 'Ramos we gotta go!' she told her lover in a blind panic. 'We gotta go naah!'
Dee Dee could barely walk the short distance to the hospice entrance. 'Come ear,' Trisha said, hoisting her friend up into her arms puffing. 'Ar got'cha mate, ar got'cha,' she said, shoving open the doors with her bottom as Maizie waddled behind.
'GINAAAAA!' Maizie called out to Dee Dee's nurse once inside. 'GINAAAAAAA!'
Gina came rushing from a side room. 'Oh Christ!' she said, helping Trisha carry Dee Dee and checking her breathing in the process.
'What is it?' Maizie asked. 'Can you give er summink?'
Dee Dee was laid on her bed and the oxygen mask placed over her mouth. 'It's not good,' Gina said, after examining her further and taking Maizie to one side. 'I suggest you send for her mother and anyone else you can think of to be with her.'
'She's on er way,' Maizie told Gina. 'Scuze me ar gotta phone me fella, watch er Trish,' she told Trisha at Dee Dee's side. 'Don'tchu leave er.'
'Ar won't,' Trisha said, holding Dee Dee's hand. 'Ar won't Maize ar promise.'
Maizie telephoned Richard. 'Ar need you ear babe,' she told him. 'Ar need you to come right naah.'

Richard grabbed his jacket, still clutching the telephone. 'I'm on my way darling,' he told Maizie. 'Don't worry I'm leaving right now.'

A short while later Pearl, Ramos and Terry arrived simultaneously and huddled round Dee Dee's bed. 'Dee babe,' Pearl said, stroking her daughter's hand. 'Dee babe can you ear me?'

Dee Dee's cancer was in the final throes and she was now severely weakened by the strenuous but uplifting day with her lifelong friends.

'I've given her morphine,' Gina told her friends and family. 'She's in no pain.'

'Ow long?' Maizie asked, with the others listening in.

'An hour, two at the most,' Gina said solemnly. 'She knows you're here so just be with her.'

'Oh please no!' Pearl said, covering her mouth. 'God no!'

Trisha ran to the aquarium and buried her face in her hands sobbing, while Terry faced the window unable to stop the flood of tears.

'Oh shit no!' Maizie then cried, as Richard entered the room. 'No, no, no!'

'What is it darling?' Richard said, rushing to her side.

Maizie looked down at the water pouring from the bottom of her maternity dress. 'No, no, no not naah!' she sobbed. 'Not naah, please Rich no!'

'Jesus the baby's comin!' Pearl gasped, rushing to her also. 'Maizie ya baby's comin love!'

'No, no, no!' Maizie said, shaking her head. 'Not naaaah!'

Richard held her tightly. 'Darling we have to get you to the hospital,' he told her. 'We must Maizie.'

'No ar don't wonnit!' Maizie said, fighting against him. 'Ar don't wonnit ar want mar Dee, ar want mar Deeeee.'

'Shhhh,' Pearl said, in an effort to calm her. 'Dee wants you an'all, but she really wants you to av this baby love, so go an av it girl, av it for er.'

'Have your baby Maizie,' Ramos said softly at Pearls side. 'Have your child.'

Maizie was led in floods of tears from the room. 'Trisha you stay wiv er!' she yelled, clinging to the door frame. 'You stay wiv er d'you ear me, don'tchu fuckin leave er, not for one minute ar'm tellin ya. Ar love ya Dee, ar love yaaaaaa!'
Pearl lay beside her daughter talking quietly to her, while Terry and Ramos stood rooted to the spot. Trisha in the meantime tapped her head repeatedly on the glass tank cursing under her breath with a clenched fist.

Maizie was taken back to the Saint Pancras protesting all the way, and then wheeled to the delivery room. 'Get it aata me!' she told the team of nurses. 'Get it aata me quick, ar don't want nunna ya fuckin drugs just get it aata me right naah!' She was almost fully dilated with the baby's head now bearing down.
'It's going to be a quick one this,' a nurse said, spreading Maizie's legs. 'OK when you're ready I want you to push for me, do you think you can do that?' she asked.
'Course ar fuckin can!' Maizie barked, grabbing Richard's hand and squeezing it tight. 'Just urry up will ya!'
'OK take a deep breath,' the nurse told Maizie. 'Aaaand push. I can see the baby's head already.'
Maizie sat up, her reddened face contorted. 'Ooooooh!' she grimaced. 'Come on, come on!' she growled.
'That's it darling,' Richard said, offering words of encouragement. But Maizie only had one thing on her mind, getting back to Dee Dee.
'Keep pushing!' the nurse told her. 'That's it.'
'FUUUUUCK!' Maizie screamed, growing increasingly frustrated. 'COME ON, GET AAAAT!' she yelled at her unborn infant.
'I have the head,' the nurse said, gripping the baby's shoulders. 'One last push my dear, come on you can do it, that's it Maizie love.'
'ARRRRRRRRRGH!' Maizie cried, wrenching at Richard's hand. 'FUUUUUCK!'

'Excellent!' the nurse smiled as the baby slipped into her hands. 'Maizie you have a daughter, a beautiful baby girl.'

Maizie flopped back onto the bed exhausted. 'Is she alright?' she asked. 'Rich is she alright?'

'She's gorgeous,' Richard said, looking over the nurse's shoulder while she cut the umbilical cord. 'Absolutely gorgeous darling. Just like her mother.' He bent and kissed Maizie several times. 'We have a baby,' he whispered.

'Can ar go naah?' Maizie asked the nurse. 'Ar gotta go naah, right naah.'

'I beg your pardon,' the nurse said. 'Maizie your baby's fine, but you need rest and lots of it my dear.' She then placed the baby on Maizie's chest. 'Bond with your baby for a moment,' she added.

Richard tugged the nurse to one side while Maizie looked into her baby's eyes for the first time. 'Can I have a word,' he said, and proceeded to explain Dee Dee's situation.

'Yes, yes of course,' the nurse said eventually, with a hand on her heart. 'I'll do all I can to help.' Giving Maizie a mild pain killer, she then cleaned the baby and wrapped it in several layers. 'Keep her warm,' she told Richard. 'I've put some nappies and feed in a bag for you, she'll let you know when she's hungry.'

'Thank you,' Maizie said, climbing shakily down from the bed and dressing. 'Thanks a lot.'

'Good luck,' the nurse said, waving goodbye with a lump in her own throat.

Maizie gave the taxi driver the hardest of times on the way back to Saint Martin's, having been gone almost two hours. 'Urry up will ya!' she stormed, cradling her baby. 'What'cha waitin for!'

With her stomach still very much cramped Maizie handed their daughter to Richard, and climbed from the taxi. 'Urry up Rich!' she said, dashing as best she could into the hospice. 'DEEEEEE!' she called, making her way hastily along the hallway. 'DEEE AR'M COMIN!'

Dee Dee opened her eyes and turned her head on hearing Maizie's voice.

'Iss Maizie Dee,' Pearl told her at her side. 'Iss ya mate.'

Unable to raise her head Dee Dee held out her hand. 'Ohhhh Dee mate,' Maizie said, out of breath and weeping. 'Ar didn't wanna leave ya ar really didn't.'

Trisha joined them. 'Well?' she said expectantly. 'Where's the baby?'

Richard then entered the room carrying their daughter. 'Ear she is,' Maizie said, taking her from him. 'Iss a girl Dee, ar got a daughter.'

Dee Dee managed a broad smile. 'Woss er name?' she asked, in a rasping tone.

'Dee,' Maizie told her. 'Er names Dee after wunna me bestest mates.'

'Ahhhhhh,' Trisha blubbed, stroking the baby's cheek.

'D'you wanna old er?' Maizie asked Dee Dee.

Dee Dee nodded and smiled some more, while Maizie rounded the bed and lowered young Dee onto her chest lifting her friends arms to support her. 'There,' she said, stepping back. 'Dee, meet Dee Dee.'

Dee Dee looked deep into the child's eyes rocking her ever so gently, the baby lay still staring wide eyed back at her and for the briefest of moments there was a connection, a tiny spark instilled in the child from her namesake.

The evening sun shone through the venetian blinds illuminating Dee Dee's face as she slowly closed her eyes and lowered her arms. 'Oh God no!' Maizie gasped, retrieving her baby. 'Dee mate?'

Dee Dee, with the sweetest of smiles etched on her face, simply slipped away with her family and close friends at her bedside.

'Dee babe!' Pearl said, kissing her repeatedly.

Trisha leant and buried her face in Dee Dee's bed spread clenching it with whitened knuckles.

'Take er Rich,' Maizie said, handing Richard the baby and sitting beside Dee Dee. 'Take er ome please.'

Gina left Maizie and the others to be alone with Dee Dee, closing the door softly behind her.

Terry stood at the end of the bed gently rubbing Dee Dee's foot through her blanket. 'Love ya babe,' he said, dragging a hand across his eyes. 'Love ya.'

Ramos stood beside Pearl while she caressed her daughter and the reality of her passing gradually sank in. 'Don't she look beautiful,' she said, running the back of her hand across Dee Dee's cheek with tears flooding from her own.

'She always as,' Maizie agreed. 'The most beautiful girl in the ole world Misses D.'

'Wivaat a data,' Trisha said, lifting her head to stroke her friend's hand. 'Wivaat a daat Dee, you always av bin mate.'

Terry soon had to leave the room overcome by a wave of emotion. 'Sorry,' he said red faced, rushing to the nearest washroom. Once there he bolted the door behind him and ran the cold tap splashing his face, but no amount of cooling could dampen his tears. Shakily staring into the mirror with the tap running Terry began pounding at the wall until the plasterboard shattered. 'Fuuuuck!' he cursed, beside himself with grief. 'FUUUUUUCK!'

Several minutes later he rejoined the others, ashamed at having left. 'Ar'm sorry,' he said softly. 'Sorry.'

'Thas alright Tel,' Maizie said, taking his hand at the end of the bed. 'She's sleepin naah mate, she ain in no more pain.'

'Sleepin wiv the angels,' Trisha added, kissing her friend goodbye. 'Ar love ya Dee,' she said, planting another on her lips as only the closest of friends would. 'I always av, an I always will, forever. Me, you and Maizie, togevva forever thas what we always said dint we.'

Pearl took Trisha's hand. 'Fank you,' she said, nestling beside Dee Dee. 'And you Maizie, fank you for bein er mates, you'z free stuck togevva dint'cha, fru fick and fin.'

'Yeah we did,' 'Trisha said, her lip trembling, suddenly unable to cope a moment longer she backed away and ran to the door shaking her head.

'Trisha!' Maizie called after her. 'Trisha wait!'

'Leave er Maize,' Terry said, taking Maizie's arm. 'She needs to let it aat.'

Trisha ran sobbing down the hallway shoving open the double doors that lead to the communal garden where she raced to a central circular patio and dropped to her knees. 'WHYYYYYYY?' she screamed, rocking with her hands clasped to her face. 'WHY MY DEEEEEE, WHYYYYYYY?' She looked, to the heavens in a blind rage. 'WHYYYYYYYYYYY?' she bawled.

Trisha suddenly felt a hand on her shoulder. 'My dear would you like to talk?' the hospice chaplain asked, dressed in his robes. Trisha spun and sat on her bottom shaking a finger in his direction. 'NO WAY, NO FUCKIN WAY!' she said, wriggling away. 'There aint no God, there aint no God!' she cried, shaking her head. 'Don'tchu come near me coz ar'm tellin ya thas all bullshit, there aint no bloody God!'

The chaplain took a step toward her with his hand outstretched.

'STAY AWAY FROM ME!' Trisha barked. 'YOU STAY THE FUCK AWAY FROM ME D'YOU EAR!'

'My child I feel your pain,' the chaplain told her softly. 'So does the Lord.'

'THE LORD!' Trisha scoffed, wiping her running nose on her sleeve. 'E'z up there is e?'

'Yes, yes he is,' the chaplain replied. 'And he's all around us.'

'Well you ask im this,' Trisha insisted. 'You ask im why e took mar Dee, go on. ASK IM, ASK IM WHY E TOOK MAR DEE!' She fell to the floor pressing her face to the ground. 'Ask im!' she cried, pounding the concrete until her knuckles bled. 'Ask im, ask im!'

The chaplain knelt beside her saying nothing, but placing a hand on her head in prayer.

'Ask im please!' Trisha begged, burying her face into his robes. 'Ask im whyyyyyy!'

Gina eventually returned entering the room quietly. 'Can I get you anything?' she asked in a hushed tone. 'Tea, coffee?'

'No fanks,' Terry said, unable to avert his gaze from Dee Dee.
Maizie also shook her head.
'Miss Dawson?' Gina asked. 'Can I get you anything?'
'Ar'd love a cuppa please Gina.' Pearl admitted. 'Fanks love.'
'Ar'll av a coffee please,' Trisha said, returning red faced. 'Four sugars. Sorry,' she then said, taking Maizie's hand firmly into hers. 'Sorry Dee.'
'You aint got nuffing to be sorry for,' Maizie told her friend. 'Nuffing, d'you ear me, she's praada ya and so am I.'
'Are ya?' Trisha asked. 'Are ya Maize, really?'
'Yeah proper praad,' Maizie reiterated. 'Look ar know ar'm always givin ya shit an ar know ar don't say it often enough, but ar love ya Trish, you and Dee are me ole life. Ar know ar got Rich and the baby naah, but you and Dee will always be in mar heart, ar mean that mate.'
'Ahhhhh,' Trisha sighed, resting her head on Maizie's shoulder. 'Ar love you an'all, an ar'm proper praada you an'all Maize. You're a mum naah can you believe it?'
Gina returned with tea and coffee. 'Take as much time as you need,' she told the tiny gathering. 'But we will need to make some arrangements for Dee later today, if that's alright with you.'
'Yeah, yeah course,' Pearl said, taking her tea and sitting up. 'Fanks Gina, fanks for lookin after er,' she told the nurse.
'It was my pleasure,' Gina smiled. 'She's quite the character your friend.' Gina was careful not to mention Dee Dee in the past tense. 'We sat up many a night and she told me all about your exploits: the Arab Sheik, the ruby, the trip to Somalia to save the little girl, but most of all her love for her friends, and my God Trisha what she hasn't told me about you!' she laughed.
'Iss all true,' Maizie smiled, 'evry bleedin word of it.'
The group soon found themselves laughing as one by one, in the presence of Dee Dee, they recounted their favorite memories. 'Trisha came back to life after she got stabbed

up,' Maizie said, hugging her friend. 'She's unstoppable ar tell ya.'
'Dee was the nuts though,' Terry said, looking at her friend with fondness. 'Fearless. Ar don't know any geezer that'd stand up to er, she always done right by me an'all an, ar'll never forget er for that, never.'
'None of us will,' Maizie added.
'Well, you have some wonderful memories,' Gina told them. 'It sounds as though you accomplished so much together, it's quite remarkable really.'
Reluctantly the group soon had to leave, saying their heartfelt goodbyes to Dee Dee, each of them planting a kiss on her forehead and whispering a parting farewell.
'If you wish,' Gina told them to soften the blow, 'you'll each be able to visit her at the funeral home.'
'Yeah fanks Gina love,' Pearl said, hugging the nurse once again. 'You've bin brilliant you av, bloody brilliant.'
Gina herself wiped away a tear having gotten to know Dee Dee in depth during her short stay at Saint Martin's.

As expected the following few days were tough on Pearl and the others, she herself sleeping in her daughter's bed on occasion and sobbing into the early hours. Trisha hugged Rodney in her own bed also struggling to sleep, and although much of Maizie's time was taken up caring for her newborn baby, she would find herself staring into space recalling the good times and often mistakenly hearing her late friend's voice. She was also true to her word and visited the Westmoreland centre to introduce baby Dee to Alice and to explain to her, in a way that she would understand, why Dee Dee was no longer around.
Bonnie had finally left the centre where she had lived for as long as she could remember and moved into her mother's old room with her doting grandparents, taking with her her poems and drawings which she lovingly posted above her new bed.

Arrangements were made among rivers of tears and a date set for the funeral for the following Monday. Pearl and Maizie rang as many of their old friends and acquaintances as they could think of, many of them shocked to the core at the devastating news, including Mickey Spencer AKA Black Mickey and his sister Marcie, still residing in sunny Spain. Mickey himself broke down on the telephone wrenching his Rasta hat from his head to cover his face.

Trisha took compassionate leave from the society, being in no fit state to carry out her duties, and received a bouquet of flowers from Adrian and his wife offering their condolences. She sat at home screwing up pieces of paper, growing increasingly frustrated at her botched eulogies to her best friend. 'Ar can't do it Rod,' she sobbed, looking down at her four legged companion. 'It urts too much mate.'

The night before the funeral Maizie left her child with Richard to spend the night alone with Trisha, the two of them crammed into a single bed comforting one another.

'Ar don't fink ar can do it Maize,' Trisha wept. 'Ar don't fink ar can watch em put er in the graand.'

'You gotta do it for er,' Maizie told her. 'You gotta be there for me an'all, ar can't do it on me own Trish, ar need ya.'

The following morning after very little sleep the girls rose and stood at Dee Dee's empty bedside, hand in hand. 'What we gonna do Maize?' Trisha asked, trembling in her pajamas. 'What we gonna do wivaat er?'

'We're gonna be strong,' Maizie replied, hurting so much inside. 'Like she wonnid, and we're gonna be mates forever, aint we?'

'Course we are Maize,' Trisha agreed. 'Forever like we said when we was kids.'

Pearl and Ramos arrived, hugging the girls on arrival, as did Terry who had spent the night at a friend's house drowning his sorrows.

'You alright babe?' he asked, wrapping Maizie in his arms, he then beckoned to Trisha and the three clung to one another for a moment.

'She'll be ear soon,' Pearl said, stroking the girls' backs. 'The uvvers are meetin us up the church.'

Trisha fell into Pearl's arms and wept into her chest. 'Ar know love,' Pearl said, patting her back. 'Ar know.'

Shakily the group filed downstairs past Tatyana who stood with her head bowed at her door, she too rubbed Trisha's back in passing. 'Fanks Tat,' Trisha said, red faced.

Flowers, which each of them had lovingly chosen, had been laid in the front garden; a purple cushion from Terry, a beautiful bouquet from Ramos, a golden heart of chrysanthemums from Trisha and Maizie, and *Daughter* in white letters with crimson sprays from her mother.

Clinging together on the pavement, a bundle of raw emotion, they stood quietly waiting. 'She's ear,' Pearl eventually said, as a gleaming black hearse rounded the corner.

'Oh shit,' Trisha said, her knees buckling.

Maizie steadied her friend. 'Iss alright Trish,' she said, 'ar got'cha.'

The hearse drew alongside them with Dee Dee's coffin in full view through the window. Pearl buried her head into Ramos' chest as the flowers were loaded beside her daughter. 'Oh God, mar poor baby,' she sobbed.

'I'm sorry for your loss,' a funeral official said, taking Pearl's hand. 'Miss Dawson you'll be in the first car and her friends in the second, if that's alright with you.'

'Yeah fanks,' Pearl said, blowing her nose on a tissue.

With the neighbour's curtains twitching, and several of them stood at their garden gates as a mark of respect, Pearl and the others climbed into the funeral cars.

Terry sat beside Maizie and Trisha with a pounding head, having spoken of his friend throughout the night whilst downing a litre of vodka with an old acquaintance.

The cars moved slowly away with the official walking in front until the end of the road, where he climbed aboard himself before the procession skirted the busy London streets making its way toward Dee Dee's ancestral birth place and the church yard where many generations of Dawsons were laid to rest.

Sweeping through the cemetery gates Pearl and the others were immediately overwhelmed by the seventy strong gathering outside the chapel. 'Flippin eck,' Maizie gasped, stepping from the car. Such was Dee Dee's impact on the community and everyone who came in contact with her.

Dee Dee's father was first to approach Pearl, looking every bit a broken man. 'Ar'm sorry love,' he said. 'Ar'm sorry.'

Without hesitation Pearl embraced him. 'Yeah, yeah me an'all,' she sobbed. 'Oh er, this is Ramos,' she eventually said, breaking away. 'Me fella.'

'Pleased to meet'cha mate,' Dee Dee's father said, offering his hand. 'Really I am.'

'Oh mar gawd!' Trisha shrieked. 'Maizie is that?'

'Yeah ar rung im,' Maizie said, waving to Takashi Nakajima whom Dee Dee had befriended some years earlier. Takashi bowed respectfully holding a wreath of black roses and surrounded by his yakuza guard. The Hamilton's had also come to pay their respects with daughter Crystal at their side.

'Alright sis?' Bradley said, embracing his sister wearing black tinted Ray Bans with a smouldering blonde on his arm. 'Diss is Ashleigh, we're sorta doin it.'

'Ar bet'chu are,' Maizie smiled.

'Ello Mickey mate!' Trisha said, running into Mickey's arms, who lifted her feet from the ground. 'God ar narf mist'cha, an ar'm so glad you'z could come.'

'Are you kiddin!' Mickey asked, visibly shaken. 'We ad to be ear Trish, ar just don't believe it mate, ar really can't get me ed raand the fact that she's gone.'

'She aint,' Maizie said, hugging her friends. 'She'll always be ear, aint that right Trish?'

'Yeah,' Trisha sighed. 'Always.'

Trisha and Maizie were taken to one side by funeral officials while the others filed inside the seventeenth century chapel; at their request they had insisted on carrying the head of their friend's coffin between them.

'OK after three,' the official said, helping the coffin up onto their shoulders, Trisha's lip quivering taking her friend's weight.

'Iss alright mate,' Maizie told her, gripping the casket. 'Iss alright.'

While everyone was seated the first of Dee Dee's three favorite tunes faded in, Eva Cassidy's beautiful rendition of *Somewhere over the Rainbow* which brought a tear to every dry eye.

'OK right foot then left,' the official said, leading the way.

Pearl was beside herself, clinging to Ramos as the coffin filed by. 'Oh mar baby!' she cried out. 'Mar baby!' Her estranged husband buried his face in his hands, wracked with guilt.

No church officials were present that day, instead a life celebrant had been appointed to read Dee Dee's eulogy. 'Thank you everybody for coming, will you all please be seated,' the middle aged woman in spectacles said, standing at the pulpit. 'And thank you to Deborah's two friends for being so brave.'

Maizie and Trisha took up their places in the front row along from Pearl where they sat tightly arm in arm.

'Ok,' the celebrant said, smiling politely. 'I know Deborah's passing has come as a huge shock to many of you. I myself lost a close family friend and fully understand how you must be feeling. Now many of you know Deborah as Dee Dee so if you don't mind I am going to refer to her as Dee Dee from now on.

Born in Chadwell Heath in nineteen eighty seven to Pearl and Ronald Dawson, Dee Dee was an only child but soon found the sisters she never had meeting Maizie and Trisha in nursery school, and the three of them have remained firm friends ever since, inseparable some would say. As her mother and father would be the first to admit Dee Dee was no angel, getting into all sorts of scrapes as a young girl, standing her ground against the toughest of aggressors especially when her friends were threatened. Now we all know about her run-in with the law so I'm not going to dwell on that too much, only to say that Dee Dee didn't set out to do the things she did, it was merely a series of unfortunate circumstances that led to her eventually to a spell behind bars. But all the time she remained a true friend to Maizie and Trisha, treating them at times like they were her children, that was just her way. And speaking of Maizie and Trisha I'd like to invite them to say a few words and introduce the next piece of music.'

Maizie rose helping Trisha to her feet. 'Ar can't Maize,' Trisha sobbed, 'ar can't.'

'Yes you can,' Maizie whispered. 'Do it for Dee mate.'

The two made their way shakily to the pulpit and turned to face the solemn gathering. Maizie first removed a piece of paper from her pocket. 'I er, ar writ this for Dee and put me art and soul into it,' she said, trembling uncontrollably. 'But ya know what, ar don't need it,' she pocketed the paper and gripped the pulpit with Trisha, head bowed, at her side. 'Ar could stand ear for mumfs tellin you'z abaat Dee Dee,' she began. 'You all knew er, but me Trish and Dee we was so close, we knew what eachuvva was finkin. Yeah we done some fings but I aint makin no apologies for em, and neeva would Dee if she was ear. We were mates, proper mates wivaat exeption' A child let out a whimper at the back of the chapel. 'See that baby,' Maizie told everyone, 'thas little Dee. She means the world to me just like Dee Dee, an ar can see the likeness in er already, so ar know she's gonna be an andful.

Carryin me mate in ear today was the ardest fing ar've ever ad to do in me life but we done it for Dee dint we Trish?'

Trisha nodded. 'You've all got'cha memories,' Maizie continued, 'just like we got ours, cherish em, coz we sure as ell will, fank you.' Maizie stepped from the pulpit ushering Trisha forward.

'Maize ar can't mate,' Trisha said again, holding her stomach, 'it urts Maize.'

'Do it,' Maizie insisted. 'Do it for er Trish, please.'

Trisha stepped forward and unfolded her own piece of paper, the door then opened and the Pearsons walked in with Bonnie at their side. 'Sorry,' Mr Pearson mouthed, taking a seat beside Richard.

'I er,' Trisha stuttered, 'ar really struggled writin summink for Dee Dee.' She paused for a moment but a friendly pat from Maizie spurred her on. 'Coz there aint words to say what she meant to me, she still does to me, ar love er, not just any old love, real love, the kind that cuts ya to bits, proper love. Ar wouldn't change nuffing we done coz we done it all togevva, me Maizie and Dee Dee.'

Maizie wept at Trisha's side, tears of sadness and tears of pride.

'Yeah we got banged up,' Trisha told the gathering, 'but we didn't care coz we ad eachuvva. Dee Dee taught me so much, so much, but the biggest fing was to not be afraid of nuffing, and she weren't, even when er time was comin she eld er ed up an ar'm praad of er for that. Ar'll always be praad of er,' she turned to face Dee Dee's coffin. 'Ar love ya Dee,' she said, blowing a kiss. 'Love ya loads.' Turning back she tucked the paper into her pocket. 'Dee Dee had loadsa favrit songs,' she said, 'so we was spoilt for choice wiv this one, ar said it should be *Fridge over Troubled Water* by Simon and that Garfunkel geeza coz ar know she loved it.'

'Bridge you idiot!' Maizie whispered.

'What?' Trisha said, turning to her friend. 'What you on abaat?'

'It's bridge for gawd sake,' Maizie snapped.

'Oh right,' Trisha said, turning back. 'Sorry, *Fridge over a Bridge*, no ang on a minute that aint right,' she told Maizie. The two girls began bickering over the song title which raised more than a few smiles within the tiny chapel.

'This next one's Diana Ross and the Supremes,' Maizie said eventually, taking charge and shoving Trisha aside. 'She loved it an ar know iss definitely gonna appen.' The unmistakable classic *Someday we'll be Together* struck up and Maizie and Trisha stood beside Dee Dee's coffin with one hand on the polished mahogany and the other clasped together.

The tearful onlookers hugged their partners, leaving Dee Dee's father sitting alone with his thoughts, not even baby Dee stirred throughout the harmonious song. 'Love ya babe,' Maizie said as it faded out, kissing her hand and patting the coffin lid.

Trisha suddenly collapsed to her knees with her face against the casket in floods of tears. 'Deeeeee!' she cried. 'What mar gonna do, what mar gonna doooooo!'

Maizie held up a hand preventing anyone from intervening, dropping beside her friend. 'Shhhhhh,' she said, cradling Trisha. 'Ay Trish, shhhhh come on babe, you still got me and I aint never leavin ya, we'll always av eachuvva and Dee Dee won't never be far away from us, never.'

'Oh Maize!' Trisha sobbed. 'Don't ever leave me, please, please, please don't.'

'Ar won't ya doughnut,' Maizie smiled. 'We're stuck wiv eachuvva aint we, wherever you go ar'll be waitin for ya wiv a cuppa tea an a cuddle when ya get back, ar promise.'

'Promise?' Trisha said, looking up into her friend's eyes. 'Ya promise?'

'Yeah,' Maizie replied, helping Trisha back to her feet. 'Ar promise.'

'A beautiful tribute,' the celebrant said, taking to the pulpit once again when Maizie and Trisha were seated. 'Now I believe Terry would like to say a few words.'

Terry rose with dampened cheeks shaking Mickey's hand in passing, and approached the pulpit, clearing his throat he looked at the casket for a moment. 'What can ar say abaat Dee Dee,' he said with a smile. 'Flippin ell ar could go on all day abaat the times we've ad. But you all knew er, she was a force of nature, a one off, she was a praad woman who stood er graand right till the end, she never backed daan from nuffing in er life. She was the kindest most bravest person I ever met an ar was praad to call er me mate.' Terry paused again, faltering somewhat. 'Sorry this is ard for me,' he told the onlookers. 'She er, she taught me a lot abaat respect an ow to earn it, and what real mates are. Real mates that would die for eachuvva. When you got mates like that you don't need nuffing else, thas true love that is, an ar loved er, ar still do.' Unable to continue Terry rushed back to his seat receiving a hearty pat on the back from those around him.

'Nice one Tel,' Mickey said over his shoulder.

'Thank you Terry,' the celebrant said. 'I'd like to say a few words if I may, after speaking to Dee Dee's friends and family I drew a pretty clear picture in my mind of the sort of person she was; a strong independent woman with impeccable family values and an ever faithful friend. If you were lucky enough to have been close to her she would have undoubtedly fight your corner as well as her own. These admirable qualities are so rare in this day and age, and although she is no longer with us in body I am positive her spirit will stay with us forever.'

Baby Dee began to cry at that precise moment. 'There she is,' Maizie muttered, 'she's ear.'

'Right, this last song was chosen by her mother Pearl,' the celebrant continued. 'And I am told that Dee Dee particularly enjoyed her grandmother singing it to her as a child. Please would you all stand and make your way to the graveside.' The unforgettable sound of Nat King Cole's *Smile* began, as one by one Dee Dee's family and friends filed from the chapel and followed an official through the graveyard, to a picturesque plot beneath a damson tree beside her grandmother's grave. There the mountains of flowers had been laid, some from across the globe, with touching tributes attached.

Maizie, Pearl and Trisha walked slowly, dressed in black, and stood at the head of the grave as the coffin arrived. 'Don't let em put er in there,' Trisha begged, tugging Maizie's arm. 'Please Maize.'

'Shhhhhh is alright babe,' Maizie said softly. 'She's wiv er nanny.'

'Oh shit,' Terry then gasped, seeing D I Pritcher over his shoulder.

Maizie immediately flew into a rage launching herself at him. 'NO!' she barked. 'NOT EAR, NOT EAR!' She began beating on his chest. 'NOT EAR YOU BASTARD!'

'I'm sorry,' the D I said, 'I have a warrant.'

'NO!' Maizie continued to curse.

'Maizie!' Terry said, stepping forward. 'Iss alright mate, iss alright, onest. Ar don't wanna run no more.' Terry held out both hands while the D I cuffed him.

'Don't take im yet please!' Maizie begged. 'Please Mr Pritcher, don't take im yet!'

'Ok,' the D I said, gripping Terry's arm.

'LOVE YA TEL!' Trisha called out.

'LOVE YOU AN'ALL,' Terry replied, receiving a kiss from Maizie. 'Don't worry abaat me babe,' he told her. 'Ar'll do me bird standin on me ed an ar'll be aat in no time.'

Maizie retook her place at Trisha's side as their friend's coffin was slowly lowered into the ground. One by one everybody stooped to toss a handful of dirt into the hole muttering their own private farewells, and walking away many of them having to be comforted by loved ones.

Bonnie then squeezed between the mourners in tears, unfolding a hand crafted felt drawing of Dee Dee with a solitary word above it, *MUM*, she tossed it down onto the coffin and miraculously it landed face up with a beautifully crafted smile looking up at them.

Several umbrellas were then deployed as the heaven's opened. 'I'll meet you back at the pub,' Richard told Maizie, wheeling their child away.

'Alright love,' Maizie replied, standing firm with Trisha.

The Pearson's waved a fond farewell to the girls and lead Bonnie from the grave.
Pearl was too eventually led away by Ramos, shielding her from the rain with his jacket, as was Terry by the DI.
Maizie and Trisha remained hand in hand, their hair matted to their faces with tears and rain running as one down their flushed cheeks.
'Love you Dee,' Maizie said,
'Love ya mate,' Trisha blubbed.
Soaked to the skin the two friends embraced tightly alone at the graveside until there was a break in the clouds and the sun shone through creating the brightest of rainbows. 'There she is!' Trisha smiled over Maizie's shoulder. 'There's mar Dee!'
Maizie turned and the two of them looked up as the last drops of rain fell from the damson leaves. 'Yeah,' she smiled, squeezing Trisha's hand. 'Thas our Dee.'
A wake was held at the Wellington arms on the corner of the estate, attended by almost a hundred mourners, each chatting together sharing their own personal memories of the girl that had made a meteoric impact on so many lives in such a short space of time.

Terry was handed a five year sentence by magistrates, to whom he flicked a defiant finger, and when incarcerated received a hero's welcome from many of the inmates that knew of him.

Pearl eventually returned to Ramos' homeland, bidding the girls a fond farewell.
'You come see me won't cha,' she told them whilst climbing into the taxi.
'Will do Misses D,' Trisha said, leaning in the window to kiss her.
'Seeya,' Maizie said, waving with baby Dee in her arms.

The two friends visited Dee Dee's grave regularly to sit and talk to her. Maizie would inform Dee Dee of baby Dee's progress from crawling to walking, whilst Trisha filled her friend in on her chaotic society exploits with a randy ram and a pot bellied pig.
Eventually with Trisha's gastric pants business getting off the ground she was forced to leave the society, vowing to continue their work in any way she could, bidding Adrian a final farewell.
'I'm going to miss you Trisha,' Adrian admitted, having over time grown extremely fond of his partner. 'It's been an incredible journey and a privilege on my behalf, do keep in touch won't you.'
'Yeah course,' Trisha said, hugging Adrian. 'We're mates aint we.'
Trisha was finally about to embark on a trip to the Philippines to meet with suppliers and manufacturers and stood in the departure lounge entrance with Maizie, Richard and baby Dee.
'You sure you're gonna be alright?' Maizie asked. 'On yer own ar mean.'
'Yeah,' Trisha replied, 'ar can andle meself naah carn I.'
'It's everybody else I'm worried about,' Richard joked.
'Oy ya cheeky bleeda,' Trisha laughed.
Maizie looked deep into her friend's eyes. 'You phone me when ya get there alright,' she told her insistently. 'And come back to me won'tcha, promise me Trish coz it urts already and you ain even gone yet.'
'Yeah course ar will,' Trisha said, drying a tear.
'Promise me!' Maizie said, shaking her friend. 'Say it, say ya promise.'
'Alright ar promise,' Trisha smiled. 'Ar promise ya Maize, oh and fanks for lettin me be baby Dee's godmuvva, ar'm gonna teach er loads when she's bigger.'
'Oh gawd,' Maizie said, raising her eyebrows. 'What av ar gone and done?' She then rummaged in her pocket. 'Oh

look, ear,' she said, removing Dee Dee's pink beanie and popping it onto Trisha's head. 'Thissa keep ya warm.'
'Fanks,' Trisha said, checking her reflection in her mobile. 'Ar won't never take it off.'
After a tearful goodbye and many many hugs Trisha disappeared into the departure lounge. 'SEEYAAAAAA!' she called back, bumping into a leggy stewardess in the process. 'Oooh ello gorgeous,' she said, following the brunette closely.

Weeks later, having spoken to Trisha at great length every day, Maizie was sat in the flat she now shared with her fiancé with baby Dee bouncing on her knee watching her favorite soaps when there was a commercial break.
'RIIICH, RIIIIICH!' she called out, summoning her love from the kitchen. 'Iss Trisha's advert!'
Sure enough a team of top advertising executives had pieced together a glossy commercial for Trisha's gastric pants, which were flying off the high street shelves in their thousands. 'We know this don't we Dee,' Maizie told her daughter having sung the tune countless times when rocking her child to sleep. With Richard sitting at her side, Maizie again sang along looking at the selfie photograph of her and her two friends beside the London Eye.

'Iiiiiiiiiiiiiif yaaaaaaaaa
Stuff ya face wiv jelly
If ya stuff ya face wiv chips
Does it linger on ya belly
Does it linger on yer ips.

Do ya waddle when ya walk
Do ya rumble when ya run
Put daan ya knife and fork
Put daan ya bagel and ya bun.

Don'tcha worry don't despair

Someday we'll be together

Coz whateva ya circumstaaaaaaaance
Grab yaself a paira Trisha's gastric paaaaaaaaaants
Grab yaself a pair
Grab yaself a pair
Grab yaself a paira Trisha's gaaaaaaastriiiiiiiic paaaaaaaaaaaaaaaaaants!'

THE END

(Or is it?)

Someday we'll be together

This book is dedicated to my sister

Lillian Haughan

03,10,1956 – 10,05,2000

Who bravely battled breast and lung cancer,
and to those that fight a similar fight each and every day.

STAY STRONG!

A special thank you to
Lisa Gevaux
for her outstanding contribution.

Helpful info.

http://www.breakthrough.org.uk/about-breast-cancer/touch-look-check
http://www.breakthrough.org.uk/about-breast-cancer/touch-look-check
http://www.nhs.uk/chq/pages/1740.aspx?categoryid=60&subcategoryid=182

http://www.channel4embarrassingillnesses.com/video/how-to-check-yourself/how-to-check-your-breasts/

http://www.cancerresearchuk.org/about-us/contact-us

https://www.breastcancercare.org.uk/breast-cancer-information/breast-awareness/noticed-any-changes/family-history-assessment

http://www.nhs.uk/Conditions/Cancer-of-the-breast-female/Pages/Introduction.aspx

Men and women
Please check yourself!

34385702R00377

Made in the USA
Charleston, SC
08 October 2014